The PENDRAGON™ fiction line presents the best of modern Arthurian literature, from reprints of long-unavailable classics of the early twentieth century to new works by today's most exciting and inventive fantasists. The titles in the series are selected for their value to both the casual reader and the devoted scholar of the rich, varied story cycle known as the Matter of Britain.

Pendragon™ Fiction

THE MERRIEST KNIGHT

The Collected Arthurian Tales of
THEODORE GOODRIDGE ROBERTS

Edited by Mike Ashley

Interior Art by Shane A. Holloway

GREEN KNIGHT PUBLISHING

The Merriest Knight is published by Green Knight Publishing.

Please address questions and comments concerning this book, as well as requests for notices of new publications, by mail to Green Knight Publishing, 900 Murmansk Street, Suite 5, Oakland, CA 94607.

Green Knight Publishing
Publisher: Peter Corless
Executive Editor: James Lowder
Consulting Editor: Raymond H. Thompson
Cover Design: William W. Connors/Moonlight Studio

Visit our web page at: http://www.greenknight.com

FIRST PAPERBACK EDITION

10 9 8 7 6 5 4 3 2 1

Green Knight publication GK6210, October 2001.

ISBN 1-928999-18-2

Printed in the United States.

ACKNOWLEDGEMENTS

"Author's Introduction" © 2001, previously unpublished. Text courtesy University of New Brunswick, Harriet Irving Library, Archives and Special Collections.

"A Purfle for a King" © 1950, first published in *Blue Book*, July 1950.

"The Quest of the Saracen Beast" © 1950, first published in *Blue Book*, November 1950.

"A Fairy's Child" © 2001, previously unpublished. Text courtesy University of New Brunswick, Harriet Irving Library, Archives and Special Collections.

"The Madness of Sir Tristram" © 1950, first published in *Blue Book*, December 1950

"A Quarrel for a Lady" © 1950, first published in *Blue Book*, February 1950.

"Sir Dinadan and the Giant Taulurd" © 1951, first published in *Blue Book*, April 1951.

"The Goose Girl" © 1951, first published in *Blue Book*, August 1951.

"For to Achieve Your Adventure" © 1950, first published in *Blue Book*, October 1951.

"Mountain Miracle" © 1951, first published in *Blue Book*, December 1951.

"Quest's End" © 2001, previously unpublished. Text courtesy University of New Brunswick, Harriet Irving Library, Archives and Special Collections.

"Young Wings Unfurling" © 1947, first published in *Blue Book*, October 1947.

"Strike Hard! Bite Deep!" © 1947, first published in *Blue Book*, December 1947.

"The Merlin Touch" © 1948, first published in *Blue Book*, April 1948, as "A Quest Must End."

"Castle Cavanaugh" © 1948, first published in *Blue Book*, August 1948.

"Revolt in the Forest" © 1949, first published in *Blue Book*, September 1949.

CONTENTS

INTRODUCTION

It's a sad fact just how many writers are forgotten within a few years of their death, no matter how popular they were in their day. For every H. Rider Haggard or Arthur Conan Doyle there are hundreds and hundreds of authors like Jacland Marmur, Horace Annesley Vachell, Douglas Newton, Roy Norton, J. S. Fletcher, James Boyd, H. Bedford-Jones, Harold Lamb, Max Pemberton, Richard Marsh . . . oh, I could go on and on. True, some of these may be remembered by specialist collectors, and some of them may have their work resurrected and preserved by specialist small press publishers. But as a general rule I'd be very much surprised if anything like one-tenth of a percent of writers who were well known and popular in their day are still in print today or, if they are in print, remembered by anyone outside of a small circle of devotees.

This has nothing to do with the quality of their work. It's usually because there's no one left to push and promote their books. Over time memory of them fades and they sink into oblivion. It happened with Charles Dickens, believe it or not, whose works were overlooked within twenty years of his death, until G. K. Chesterton took up the cause. At different times it has happened with Rudyard Kipling and Thomas Hardy and Mary E. Braddon and, more recently, E. F. Benson. I tend to hope that quality will prevail in the end and at some time a good author will be remembered.

The same applies to Theodore Goodridge Roberts. In his day, he and his elder brother, Charles G. D. Roberts, were extremely popular. They contributed to most of the popular magazines and their books were regularly in print.

Although Theodore's work was often overshadowed by that of his more famous—and more prolific—brother, it was still much in demand. (Charles was even knighted in 1935.) Both had careers lasting for more than fifty years. Both produced books that were well received and highly collected. Charles' work tended to veer toward nature. Theodore also loved the wide open spaces and backwoods of Canada, and used them as the backdrop for his rousing historical romances and adventure novels, somewhat in the style of James Fenimore Cooper. Yet today Theodore's tales are scarcely known. The renowned Canadian editor and anthologist John Robert Colombo has said: "Roberts has yet to receive any serious consideration as a writer of novels, stories and poems in his native Canada."

Maybe his time is about to come. Just in the last couple of years a volume of Theodore's best poetry, *That Far River*, was compiled by Martin Ware and published by Canadian Poetry Press. Now, for the first time, his Arthurian stories are being collected together in one book.

Theodore was born in Fredericton, New Brunswick, on July 7th, 1877. His father, George Goodridge Roberts, was the rector of Christ Church Parish Church. Theodore was the youngest surviving child of six—a younger sister, Fanny, died in infancy. His eldest brother, Charles, was already seventeen and had entered the University of New Brunswick, where he would graduate with honors in 1879. Young Theodore reveled in the name of George Edward Theodore Goodridge Roberts, but he later abandoned the first two names and became known colloquially as "Thede" to his friends.

The literary talent in the family soon manifested itself in Theodore. He later told *Blue Book* that he was "rhyming industriously before he could write." *The Independent*, where his elder brother, William, was the literary editor, bought a set of his verses when he was fourteen. Together with works by his brothers, and his sister Elizabeth, some of Theodore's poems were assembled in *Northland Lyrics*, published in 1899. It was the first of what would be more than thirty books to carry his name.

Although he also attended the University of New Brunswick, he was too full of the joys of life. He abandoned study after just a few weeks and headed for New York in

November 1897. By April 1898 he was a war correspondent covering the revolution in Cuba for *The Independent.*

He founded his own *Newfoundland Magazine* in 1900, which he edited for three years, collecting together features and articles about local life and history, including his stories of the Beothuk Indians, some of which formed the basis for *Red Feathers* (1907). Norah Story in *The Oxford Companion to Canadian History and Literature* (1967) refers to Roberts' "gift for describing exotic scenes and his familiarity with the attitudes and speech patterns of the coast-dwellers of Newfoundland." Roberts' work dramatically reflects both the beauty and the savage intensity of the Newfoundland and Labrador territory.

In 1902, Roberts launched a new magazine, *Kit-Bag*. It saw only three issues, and Roberts' own serial, "The Red Haggard," appeared there, but remained unfinished. The serial was his first venture into Arthurian territory. It retold the adventures of Bertram de Sallas. Dinadan appears in the story as Bertram's companion and guide.

Roberts married in November 1903 and needed to boost his income. He had started to sell stories to the magazines, especially *Munsey's*, and his first solo book, *Hemming, the Adventurer* was published in 1904. It was followed by *Brothers of Peril* (1905), a stirring adventure story set in old Newfoundland. Then came *Red Feathers* (1907), one of his most lasting achievements. It is set long ago, in the early days of the Beothuk Indians, and draws upon their tales and legends. It had a considerable impact and has been reprinted several times, most recently in 1976. Roberts later brought together another collection of Indian tales as *Flying Plover, His Stories* (1909).

Books followed at the rate of one or two a year, even though Roberts and his wife were traveling extensively and raising four children. Roberts served in the Canadian army in France and England during the First World War and he used these experiences not only for future stories, but for *Thirty Canadian V.C.s* (1918). Roberts' most memorable books were those set in the Canadian backwoods, many of them written for young adults. These include *Tom Akerley* (1923) and *Red Pirogue* (1924). He also produced the rousing historical novel *The Golden Highlander* (1929), telling the adventures of Alastair MacIver.

Throughout these years he continued to contribute poetry to many magazines and later collected some as *The Leather Bottle* (1934). He also compiled a detailed study of the lives of United Empire loyalists and their descendants, *Loyalists* (1937). Roberts was awarded an honorary Doctor of Literature by the University of New Brunswick in 1931.

Now and again Roberts' thoughts would return to Arthur and the Knights of the Round Table. In 1928, he wrote a humorous story titled "Knight-Sweats," but it was rejected by all the major magazines, even when revised as "After Sir Thomas Mallory." Eventually he reworked parts of it into his regular "Under the Sun" column for the daily paper *The Telegraph Journal* during January 1930. These stories usually built upon a subject Roberts had been exploring in the column, starting with military glory. Roberts retold the traditional story of King Mark, Sir Palomides, and La Beale Isoud, and developed a new one featuring Sir Driant and Cullumbar. A third story would later be reworked as "A Quarrel for a Lady," the first of the Dinadan stories for *Blue Book* (February 1950).

Sir Dinadan may not be the first knight to spring to mind when thinking of the Round Table. He is not in the forefront, as are Sir Lancelot or Sir Gawain or Sir Percival, or even Dinadan's close friend, Sir Tristram. His main appearance in Malory's *Le Morte d'Arthur* is in Book X, where we find him teasing King Mark of Cornwall and Sir Lamorak, and generally causing mischief. His attitude later angered Sir Agravaine and Sir Mordred and he remained their enemy.

Dinadan was something of a troubadour, though apparently not a good one, as Malory describes Dinadan's ballad about King Mark as "the worst lay that ever harper sang." Generally Dinadan was good-natured and sensible, though his dislike of women meant he was never to win fair lady. He was cautious about entering into a fight until he was certain it was in the right cause, and that he had a good chance of winning. He wasn't one for heroics, but for a more reasoned approach. On more than one occasion he helped Tristram out of problems that Tristram's lack of tact had caused.

All this made Dinadan the ideal character for Roberts to choose to take a wry and satirical look at the Arthurian world. While there is plenty of action in Roberts' stories, these aren't blood-and-thunder adventure stories. They are clever and sophisticated explorations of the Arthurian world as seen through the eyes of a quick-witted, ingenious, and literary man. In them we see both the fun and the fear of these Dark Ages.

Roberts explained his fascination with Dinadan in his "Under the Sun" column:

> A cynic, Sir Dinadan! But that was not all. The charm of his character and wit has not received its just recognition. To my mind he was one of the best, and by far the most attractive, of all the knights of the Round Table. He was loved by all good knights, despite his somewhat acrid humor.

In 1930 Roberts started another short-lived, magazine, *Acadie*, published in Fredericton. Several Arthurian characters, including Dinadan, appeared in the magazine as filler paragraphs and Roberts even hid behind the name "Kay Pendragon" as one of the writers. At the same time, Roberts was reworking his "Under the Sun" columns for a book, revising the Arthurian stories, but in the end nothing came of this.

Roberts' work appealed to Donald Kennicott, the editor of *Blue Book*. Kennicott had edited the magazine since 1929 and worked as an assistant editor for many years previously. Although, like Roberts, he has become forgotten today, Kennicott was well respected in his day and was regarded as one of the great magazine editors. He made *Blue Book* the leading pulp adventure magazine of the 1930s and 1940s.

Roberts had sold occasionally to *Blue Book* over the years and more recently had appeared with several stories recreating the Arthurian world, starting with "Young Wings Unfurling" (October 1947) and including a sequence featuring the young knight Dennys ap Rhys and his adventures with King Torrice and the amnesiac knight dubbed Sir Lorn. All of these stories are included in this book.

Roberts must then have posed the idea of a further series. Kennicott could see the fun that could be had with the character of Sir Dinadan and encouraged Roberts to develop it. The result was a series of eight stories that appeared in *Blue Book* over the next two years. In fact,

Roberts submitted a ninth story, "Daggers in Her Garters," but by that time Kennicott was no longer editor of *Blue Book,* having stepped down in January 1952. The publishers changed *Blue Book* to a more action-oriented men's magazine. More sophisticated stories like Roberts' no longer fitted the format. "Daggers in her Garters" was not published and Roberts chose not to submit the final story, "Quest's End," to the magazine.

Instead, he reworked the stories to appear as a book and even started a new novel about Dinadan. Alas, time was catching up with Roberts. He died on February 24th, 1953 at Digby, Nova Scotia, aged seventy-five. He was buried in the family plot at Fredericton, New Brunswick.

Roberts was constantly re-drafting his stories, and not all versions survive. It is difficult, therefore, to be clear what was his preferred version of the Dinadan stories. In preparing the stories for publication I have used the *Blue Book* versions as the primary texts and set them out in accord with their internal sequence of events, which does not follow their published sequence. In revising these same stories for potential book publication, Roberts must have made significant changes as he introduced Dinadan in "A Fairy's Child," though that text conflicts with the opening of "A Purfle for a King" and the events at the start of "The Quest of the Saracen Beast." With minor revision, however, it is possible to fit "A Fairy's Child" into the sequence.

It is unfortunate that the text for "A Dagger in Her Garters" is lost. From the surviving text of "Quest's End" we know that "A Dagger in Her Garters" saw Dinadan best the knight Sir Breuse Sans Pité and win his wealth, thus enabling him to retire. In the absence of that episode, I have revised the beginning of "Quest's End" slightly for continuity.

In addition to the Dinadan stories, Roberts wrote several others with Arthurian settings. Three of these—"The Merlin Touch," "Castle Cavanaugh," and "Strike Hard! Bite Deep!"—were really episodes of a short novel, *Spur and the Prize.* I have added a fourth story, "Young Wings Unfurling," to fit under this generic title to form the main second part of this book.

Finally, in "Revolt in the Forest," Roberts produced a

finale to the Arthurian stories with an episode set at the time of the Norman Conquest, showing the residual power of the legend. This serves as a fitting conclusion to the current collection in the section titled "Legend's End."

This book could not have been finalized without the help of several people. I must thank John Robert Colombo and Raymond H. Thompson for their help and advice on this project; Mary Flagg, archivist at the University of New Brunswick, for unearthing long-buried documents; and Arthurian devotee Larry Mendelsburg for securing a readable copy of one of the stories. I must pay special thanks to Linda Hansen, Electronic Services Librarian at the University of New Brunswick. Linda has spent two years studying the Roberts papers and was extremely helpful in sharing with me the outcome of her researches and alerting me to the full extent of his Arthurian writings. Without her help, this book would not be as complete as it is.

—Mike Ashley
December 2000

Mike Ashley is now a full-time writer and researcher after having spent thirty-two years as a local government officer. He has produced more than sixty books and ten times as many articles. He has edited several Arthurian anthologies, including *The Pendragon Chronicles*, *The Camelot Chronicles*, *The Merlin Chronicles*, *Chronicles of the Holy Grail*, *Chronicles of the Round Table*, and *The Mammoth Book of Arthurian Legends*. He recently completed *Starlight Man*, a long-awaited biography of Algernon Blackwood, and is currently working on *The Mammoth Encyclopedia of King Arthur*.

THE
MERRIEST
KNIGHT

AUTHOR'S INTRODUCTION

The character and foibles of Sir Dinadan are familiar to all students of the Arthurian Legend as presented by Sir Thomas Malory.

A capable knight-at-arms, though somewhat cautious about engaging against odds except under especial pressure; a good comrade, loving and loved by all good knights; an acknowledged wit, though of a decidedly puckerish sense of humor; and a poet within the limitations of his wit—and yet, according to Malory, Sir Dinadan's chief claim to fame lay in the role of "jaber against love and lovers."

You may remember that it was this Sir Dinadan who, tête-à-tête one day with Queen Isoud, and ignorant of her identity, went on record for all time as follows: "'Madam,' said Sir Dinadan, 'I marvel of Sir Tristram and more other lovers, what aileth them to be so mad and so sotted upon women.' 'Why,' said La Beale Isoud, 'are ye a knight and be no lover? It is a shame to you: wherefore ye may not be called a good knight but if ye make a quarrel for a lady.' 'God defend me!' said Dinadan. 'For the joy of love is too short, and the sorrow thereof, and cometh thereof, dureth over long.'"

Here is proof, to my mind—though the historians and learned commentators make nothing of it—that the key to the character and foibles of the Dinadan we know lies hidden in some legends or songs overlooked by the good Sir Thomas Malory. The fact is, Malory did not know all about Sir Dinadan. To prove my statement, I shall now tell you some things that he did not know.

A PURFLE
FOR
A KING

Then came a messenger from King Rience of North Wales and Ireland, greeting King Arthur and saying that King Rience had overcome eleven kings and purfled a mantle with their beards, but there lacked one on the mantle; wherefore he demanded King Arthur's beard, or else he would enter into his lands and burn and slay.

"Well," said Arthur, "thy message is the most villainous and lewdest that ever was sent unto a king. Also thou mayest see that my beard is full young yet to be made a purfle of for a mantle."

—Sir Thomas Malory

King Arthur Pendragon was full young himself at this time, and possibly too young for the governance of the disputed realm of Britain, which he had inherited but recently, and under somewhat equivocal circumstances, from that old rip King Uther. Now he was all agog to set out for North Wales within the hour, at the head of such knights and footmen as might happen to be within trumpet-call at the moment, to teach Rience the Devastator that Arthur of Britain was not to be insulted with impunity. But the counsel of certain mature barons and knights prevailed, and the young king consented to recruit his military strength before attempting a punitive expedition into North Wales.

Now it happened that a young squire hight Dinadan was in the King's train at this time, in attendance upon the good old knight Sir Gyles of the Swamp. The mentality of this youth was somewhat in advance of his time, and his self-assurance was even farther in advance of his rank. King Rience's villainous message to King Arthur made a special appeal to his mind, and particularly to his peculiar sense of humor, and kept him awake till past midnight; and he sought audience with the King bright and early next morning, and soon talked himself into the chamber in which the puissant prince sat at breakfast with his foster-father Sir Ector and his foster-brother Sir Kay the Seneschal. He made his best bow three times.

"What can I do for you?" asked Arthur, graciously.

"Sir," replied Dinadan, "I ask your royal attention for a minute or two while I present a plan of action against villainous King Rience, which I am confident, Your Grace, will make him the fool of the world and the laughingstock of Christendom, and all without the cost of a man or a penny to Your Majesty."

"It sounds too good to be true," said the King. "Speak on."

The knights were silent; but Sir Kay, the younger one, smiled cynically.

"Sir, with your permission I shall go fetch King Rience's beard to you, and make so bold as to suggest its use as a purfle upon Your Grace's finest mantle—those unmistakable flaming whiskers and mustachios on a white field—for all the world to see and recognize."

"Hah!" cried Sir Ector. "Excellent! I can see it in me mind's eye. What a picture! But not so fast, young sir. How d'ye propose to get possession of those same savage facial appendages?"

"Quite," said the King.

Sir Kay maintained his silence, but his smile became even more cynical.

"Sirs, I have given the matter hours of thought," replied the squire confidently. "I propose, with Your Grace's permission, to hunt King Rience through his mountains and into his greatest castle in the guise of a troubadour, but equipped with Nick Barber's best razor and a beard-softening emulsion of my own concoction in addition to my lute, and there await my opportunity and then make the most of it. I may say that I am already something of a lutanist, and that I understand the theory of shaving at least, having watched Nick Barber flay Sir Gyles hundreds of times in the past year. In fact, sirs, it was for Sir Gyles' comfort that I gave thought and time to the invention of the emulsion of which I have spoken."

"Does it make the beard come away easier?" asked Sir Ector, wistfully.

"It does that, sir," Dinadan assured him. "And more than that, sir. The smell of it puts the patient to sleep for an hour at least. He's dead to the world at the first whiff. If you are contemplating a shave, Sir Ector, I'll be proud to mix you up a jar of it."

"Gramercy," said the old knight. "I feel that this beard does not become me."

"Sir Gyles has to be razored every morning, but now he thinks nothing of it," said Dinadan complacently.

"I've wondered about that," said the King. "Not a hair on his face except his eyebrows, and I've heard he wears a wig."

"Yes, sir, it's a wig. And his eyebrows are blackened every morning."

"Why?"

"The truth is, Your Grace—in the strictest confidence— the natural color of that worthy knight's hair is pea green."

The King and Sir Ector goggled. Sir Kay said to his royal foster-brother, "I must warn you, sir, that this young squire has a local reputation as a joker and jiber."

Arthur asked Dinadan, "Are you joking now?" in a low but formidable voice.

"God forbid!" cried Dinadan.

So he obtained the royal permission to essay the rape of King Rience's beard.

"But if you should think better of it, forget all about it," said the King kindly.

"Good luck, my boy! But to be quite frank with you, I'd liefer try to shave the dragon of Wantage," said good Sir Ector.

Even Sir Kay shook Dinadan's hand and said: "In case you don't change your mind, it's been nice meeting you."

King Rience was lord of many castles; and by the time he was located by Dinadan, that enterprising squire had lost count of nights and days and, along with his charger, his groom, and the groom's cob, a lot of weight. It was a grand castle situated at the upper end of a high but fertile and populous valley. Dinadan's beribboned lute attracted instant and favorable attention, for King Rience was partial to troubadours, harpers, and bards, and was himself something of a song-maker and musician, but in the Welsh manner rather than that of Provence. So Dinadan was welcomed at the front door, and Kedge and the horses into kitchen and stables.

This was indeed an impressive establishment, of a numerous and various household, and a yet more numerous mob of guests of all sorts and degrees. Big as the castle was, and thick though its walls, it buzzed and hummed like a hive in a blossoming orchard. Dinadan was lucky to get so much as a cot in a chamber shared with three bewhiskered native bards and their harps, and a tonsured friar.

"You look more like a cavalier to me," said the oldest harper.

"Than a what, venerable sir?" asked Dinadan.

"Musician," replied the ancient.

"Clearly an amateur," said another harper.

Before Dinadan could answer that, a fanfare of trumpets sounded from far below.

"Supper!" cried the friar, and was gone.

The bards grabbed up their harps and dashed after him. Dinadan followed composedly, with his long lute slung at his back by a wide ribbon.

The tables were set and already crowded in the great hall, under the wavering glare of torches. All the occupants of the high table, which spanned the dais at the upper end of the hall, faced the two lower tables, which stood at right angles to the dais and extended the full length of the hall; and Dinadan, for whom a seat had been found among the bards and some household officers near the top of one of the lower tables, had an excellent view of that exalted company. He regarded the King, whose great beard and mustaches flared as red as the flames of the torches, with lively interest; and the bejeweled and gorgeous dame on the King's immediate right with mild interest; and the damosel on the King's other hand—all white and gold save for the ruby-red of lips and emerald-green of eyes and necklace—with an incredulous stare.

"Who is that?" he gasped.

"The great, noble, and good King Rience, our sovereign lord and patron," replied the oldest bard.

"Nay, the lady!"

"Where d'ye come from, young man, that you don't know the most beautiful queen in Christendom when you see her? Queen Dian, our noble Rience's royal consort these twenty years and more."

"No, no! The damosel on the other side of him?"

"Hah! Just so! Their only daughter, Megan—the apple of the King's eye and the most beautiful princess in Christendom."

"Now I believe you. Gramercy."

There was much to eat and more to drink, and all of the best or near enough; but Dinadan practiced discretion with horn and cup; and preoccupied by the vision of gold, white, emerald, and ruby at the high table, he plied even his knife and spoon and fingers with less than his usual vigor. After the dozen serving-men at the low tables and the pages at the high table had been up and down and around a dozen times at least, King Rience wiped his beard and fingers on a fair napkin and bawled for order; whereupon there was order, save for the overturning of a benchful of fuddled grooms at the foot of one of the low tables. And then there was silence too, save for a few ill-suppressed belches from the surfeited commonalty and even fewer polite hiccups at the high table. Then the King called for his harp; and as it was right there at his elbow, he did not have to call twice. He heaved upright, overturning his thronelike chair in the act, tucked his magnificent beard into the neck of his vest of cloth-of-gold to keep it out of the way, and seized the harp.

"A small thing of me own composition," he announced.

Small? In artistic merit, yes, but in nothing else. Both vocally and instrumentally it was of large and tremendous action, and as big of matter as of manner. The voice combined the bellows of a bull and the howling of wolves; the tormented, outraged harp-strings twanged and clanged like the speeding of arrows and the strokes of sword and axe on iron and bone; and the words were all of victorious slaughterings of feebler peoples by the ancestors of King Rience and by Rience himself. It was a terrific performance.

Several ladies swooned dead away, each upon the contiguous masculine shoulder on her left or right as her heart inclined. Even the Queen shivered slightly.

But the Princess laughed. Her mirth was rendered inaudible by her father's bardic uproar; but it did not escape Dinadan, who happened to be looking at her. He saw it and was so thrilled and startled by the sight that he gaped like a zany. To him it was beautiful. Well, the lips were like rosebuds even in the grimace of laughter, and the little teeth were like pearls, devil a doubt of it! Then, while he was still atremble at that spectacle, the roses closed over the pearls and the emerald eyes opened wide and full upon his and all but blinded him. He blinked; and the green stars were veiled.

A string of the King's harp broke with a vicious whang. But what cared the King? Five strings yet remained to him, two of copper and three of brass; and not till only two of these were left did he sit down, amid loud applause. He pulled up and smoothed out his flaming beard and shouted: "Match that if ye can, Taffy ap Rhys!"

The whiskery bard who sat at Dinadan's right elbow grabbed his battered harp from between his knees and took the floor. But his performance fell far short of matching his sovereign lord's, though the subject matter was the same. But he had neither the voice nor the muscles for it. He did his best, however; and the King applauded, and then everyone who was still awake did the same. The third and fourth performers were harpers also, and their subject too was bloody violence. The Princess whispered to the King. He nodded.

"Now we shall be pleased to hear from a lutanist," he announced.

Princess Megan shot an emerald glance at Dinadan, then warmed and softened it with a rosy smile. Dazed though he was, he unslung his lute and took the floor. He bowed low to the King, lower to the Queen, then even lower and twice to the Princess, whose eyes were now as soft as fern-fringed pools of dew in a sylvan glade.

Then he fingered the strings of his instrument, which was a superior specimen of its kind and the gift of a doting godmother. They responded like sentient things, tinkling and twittering, whispering like a little breeze in ripe grasses and soughing like a wind in high treetops, sobbing like lost children, singing like thrushes, crying out like wild geese in weary flight under the stars. The lute pulsed like a living heart as its myriad voices rose and fell and rose again, leaping and sinking and flaring like a flame of fire in the wind. Soon the thrill in his fingers and against his breast gave Dinadan courage to add his own voice to those of string and wood.

> "*Time is long, and Life is brief.*
> *Youth and Spring are too soon over.*
> *At the binding of the sheaf—*
> *At the fading of the leaf—*
> *Pain and Age will have your lover.*

> "*Time is long and Life is brief.*
> *Every rose is Spring's undoing.*
> *Summer is a laughing thief*
> *Filching Beauty for gray Grief.*
> *Age and frost will chill my wooing.*

> "*Day is brief and Night is long.*
> *Joy and Youth are too soon over.*
> *Harken, Princess, to my song—*
> *Glad and young and brave and strong—*
> *Ere frosty Age possess your lover.*"

The ensuing silence was broken by the King.

"Hah!" he said, stroking his beard. "Ho and hum! Not bad—if you like that love-an'-dove sort of thing, which I don't. Very pretty, young man. Gramercy."

"I think it was sweet," said the Queen; whereupon three or four ladies at the high table clapped their bejeweled hands.

But the Princess said never a word. Instead, she raised a little gold cup to her lips, drained it and then threw it with strength and accuracy. It flew like a bright bird or a shooting star, but Dinadan snatched it from the air quick as thought; and thanks to the smoky and wavery light and the general fogginess of eyes and minds, only the two closest concerned knew what had become of it. The besotted poet filled it from the nearest flagon and drained it with an air of dedication and an appropriate gesture. He repeated the ritual—and again and again.

In short, that small cup of gold proved to be the undoing of his immediate plans. It had been his intention, at the beginning, to make the most of this opportune feast toward the daring purpose that had brought him here: to bide his time patiently and temperately till the ladies and weaklings retired, till the hardiest topers and King Rience himself were overcome and floored, then to make good his boast. He and Kedge would be leagues on their homeward way before the tyrant knew what had happened. But alas, Dinadan himself was overcome long before his host. He was lost to the world, with his face on the table, ere the ladies had been gone ten minutes.

Sunshine was slanting through the narrow windows when Dinadan raised his head and opened his eyes. Torches and tapers were burned out, but their smoke still crawled among the beams and rafters. The great hall looked like a fiercely disputed and finally deserted battlefield, but one upon which brown ale and yellow mead and red wine had been spilled in lieu of blood, and cups and horns, flagons and leather jacks cast away instead of broken swords. Motionless figures lay across tables; and more, including King Rience, doubtless lay under the tables, all as still as corpses, but all alive to drink another day. Dinadan got to his feet and staggered off with one hand pressed to his head; and though he knocked many times against stone and wood and stumbled often, it was upon soft greensward that he fell and lay at last.

He dreamed that his head and shoulders were under a waterfall. The water splashed and ran on head and neck so delightfully and realistically that he opened his eyes. His head dripped, and the grass was wet under his face. He turned onto his back and beheld a damosel standing over him, and a dripping wooden bucket in her hands. She was gazing down at him with emerald eyes; and though his own eyes were out of focus, he recognized her instantly—but before he could do anything about it, she upped and overturned the bucket again, splashing the last quart of its vivifying contents full in his face.

"Gramercy!" he spluttered.

She dropped the bucket and knelt beside him; and despite the water in his eyes, he saw that she was just as beautiful at short range in sunlight as at long range in torchlight.

"I began to fear I'd never find you—and here you are in my very own special nook in my own garden," she murmured softly, yet with animation.

"At your service," he mumbled, and sat upright, but sank flat again next moment.

"Your poor head," she murmured. "It needs more cooling."

"A thousand apologies," he mumbled, and closed his eyes.

He heard her commiserate, sighing at his ear: "I'll be back with more water in a minute, poor boy."

And so she was. He soon felt the cold water on his face again, but in gentle dribbles now instead of big splashes. When the bucket was empty, she threw it aside and fell to dabbing at his wet face with a small and lacy handkerchief.

"You are beautiful," he murmured.

"Your eyes are shut tight," she said.

He opened his eyes wide and repeated the statement in a better voice. She shook her golden head.

"You're just being polite," she whispered.

He sat up again and managed to stay up this time.

"Beautiful," he insisted. "The most beautiful I ever saw—and I have seen a lot."

"Poor boy, you've not yet fully recovered your sight," she murmured.

"Saw you last night and see you now," he assured her. "Gold an' white an' green and red. If I hadn't any eyes, I could still see you with my heart."

"Poor poet! What is your name?"

"My name? Dinadan. I'd all but forgotten it."

"Mine is Megan."

"Yes, I know. I asked."

"Do you like it?"

"I love it. Love Megan."

"And I love Dinadan."

"Have a care—or I'll forget I'm only a poor squire."

"A squire? Have you forgotten already you're a troubadour?"

"A troubadour, of course! A poor wandering poet with a lute."

"Dear Dinadan, you are making sport of me."

"Sport of you? God forbid! Why d'ye say so?"

"I'll tell you, dear Dinadan, for though I'm only an innocent and ignorant mountainy girl, I cannot abide a lie. I was looking from my window when you rode in on your great warhorse with a sturdy knave on a cob behind you, which is not the way with poor troubadours; so I think you are something else, despite your wonderful song. Do you want to know what I really and truly think you are, Dinadan?"

"You tell me," he whispered weakly.

"A knight on a quest. A noble knight of young King Arthur's court, come in disguise to rob my father of a precious possession."

He blinked in dismay and asked, "Of wot?" in a yet weaker whisper.

"Of me," she sighed, veiling her emerald eyes.

"Hah!" he gasped with relief; and then he was silent, unable to raise even a whisper. He clasped his wet head in both hands. She snuggled close to him and sighed: "In answer to my prayer."

Dinadan thought as hard and fast as his painful head and general queasiness permitted. He thought of the proud boast he had made to King Arthur and Sir Ector and Sir Kay, and of Sir Kay's parting words: "Just in case you don't change your mind." He thought of King Rience's flaming beard, and of the razor and phial of emulsion in his wallet, and shivered.

"There will be another feast tonight," she whispered, with her lips at his ear. "But you must be more careful of the usquebaugh than you were last night, my pet; and warn your groom to have the horses saddled and ready for a quick start; and I shall be ready too, with fast jennets and my trusty old Nurse Grundy. Then good-by forever to King Cadwallader!"

He unclasped his hands from his head and turned and looked at her. Their faces were not five inches apart.

"King Cadwallader?" he queried.

"A mighty prince," she sighed. "Next to Papa, the mightiest in Christendom. And quite mad for love of me. And if I marry him, he will help Papa put all King Arthur's realm to fire and sword. But you won't let me marry him! You will take me away tonight, won't you, my Dinadan?"

Then she kissed him.

"Tonight," she breathed against his lips. "When Mamma's in bed and Papa under the table. Don't forget to warn your groom."

And she kissed him again.

By the time Dinadan had recovered sufficiently from those kisses to see or think with any degree of clarity, Princess Megan was gone. He continued for many minutes to sit on the velvety sward of the secluded nook of the royal damosel's own garden, trying to control his emotions and marshal his thoughts. He pressed both hands to his thumping heart.

"I was never kissed before!" he exclaimed, in a half-choked voice. "Kissed at, maybe, but never kissed. Never, never before."

He got to his feet and left the nook and the garden, and soon found the stableyard and therein Kedge and others of his kind dozing in the straw. He roused Kedge and drew him aside.

"You know what brought me here," he said.

"Yes, sir—God save me!" muttered the groom, glancing aside and drooping his head.

"Cheer up, my good fellow!" laughed the squire, but guardedly. "Nothing to worry about now. The King of North Wales and Ireland can keep his ugly beard till it falls off, for all I care now, for I'm robbing him of the apple of his eye instead—and not by violence, mark you! And if that doesn't make a bigger laughingstock of him than the loss of a basketful of whiskers, I'll be vastly mistaken. And that's not all. In keeping a powerful king named Cadwallader from marrying her by carrying her off myself, I shall also, by that same act, keep the said Cadwallader from joining forces with King Rience against King Arthur. And without so much as a single razor-stroke. D'ye get it, good Kedge? All this—and herself too!"

The groom stammered, still without lifting his head, "D'ye mean that princess—with the green eyes?"

"That's the idea, stupid. The most wonderful eyes in the world, by my halidom!"

"Whose idea, sir?"

"Whose idea? Mine, of course! Well, maybe she thought of it first—and quite right, being a princess and me only a squire. But that's not the point. Pay attention to me now, good Kedge, and you'll be a squire yourself some day." And Dinadan laid hold of his groom by a shoulder and delivered strict instructions, shaking him gently the while.

Dinadan wandered about the purlieus of the castle till evening, hoping for another meeting with the Princess, and far too excited to sit still. He saw her only once again before supper, however, and this time at long range, where she was looking down from a high window; but she made him a conspiratorial signal with a jeweled hand and blew him a kiss.

King Cadwallader arrived shortly before sunset, with a considerable and heavily armed train, amid a wild braying of saluting horns and welcoming trumpets. King Rience was in the forecourt to receive him; and there the two savage monarchs embraced as if to each the other was the dearest thing in life; and at that sight Dinadan, standing modestly in the crowd, concealed with his hand a smile which was anything but modest.

The tables, including the high one, were packed almost to the point of overflow, owing to the influx of King Cadwallader and a few of his lords to the high table and of his followers of various lesser degrees, and none at all, to the lower boards. Dinadan was in the place which he had occupied the night before, but was now pressed so closely on the right and the left that he could hardly move an elbow. It still served his chief purpose, however, which was to look at his gold and emerald and ruby princess. Tonight, as last night, she sat on her sire's immediate left, but now she had King Cadwallader on her other side, and was fitted so snugly between the two that it was a wonder she could breathe. Her situation did not escape Dinadan's jealous eye.

"Move over, you big ox," he muttered.

"Wot's that?" demanded one of the two between whom he himself was pressed.

"I wasn't speaking to you," said Dinadan.

Guzzling and swigging soon became general throughout the great hall—despite the lack of elbowroom—from the grooms and stableboys at the bottom to the kings at the top, and quickly reached a high pitch at which it was maintained a long time. Dinadan ate and drank little, however, but sat with idle hands and glared at King Cadwallader, unconscious of the punishment he was taking from the busy elbows of his immediate neighbors. At last some of the weaker of the revelers began to slip and fall, some under the tables and some across them and some backward. Then King Rience hove himself onto his feet, again overturning his thronelike chair, and shouted for order; and after a few more scattered thumps and bangs, there was order of a sort. But Rience did not call for his harp this time; instead, he bawled: "Fetch my mantle."

A page appeared promptly with a great bundle in his arms.

"Hang it up and spread it wide."

The garment was fixed to the tapestry behind the dais, and spread and skewered wide and high, in jig-time. It was a voluminous mantle of sky-blue cloth, and curiously decorated. Instead of being edged with ermine, or with braid of gold or silver threads, it was purfled with human beards of a variety of colors and shades and shapes. Dinadan cursed at the sight, but not loud enough to attract attention.

"This is the mantle of Rience," shouted the King, swaying dangerously. "Of meself, greatest king in Christendom—present company excepted. Mighty King Cadwallader excepted. And look ye, 'tis purfled with eleven beards—beards flayed from chins an' cheeks of eleven kings—erstwhile kings—poor fools who dared to dispute my overlordship, ha-ha! But a place remains for one more purfle, mark ye—for the silky young beard of that saucy knave Arthur who calls himself a king—ha-ha! I'd tell ye wot he should be called, but for fear of shockin' the ladies—an' that's a bastard, ha-ha!"

Dinadan freed himself from the pressure on his right and left with difficulty, and he stood up and cried, "You're a liar!" and drew a dagger, ready to fight to a finish. But neither hand nor voice was raised against him, nor any eye turned upon him, for nobody had heard him. He saw that the ladies were gone, and that every reveler who remained in sight was rendered deaf and blind to his surroundings by the fumes of his potations. Even King Rience, though still on his feet and wide-eyed and open-mouthed, had ceased utterance and was obviously oblivious to all external natural phenomena. Dinadan turned to depart stableward, but in sheathing his dagger he touched the wallet at his belt and heard the clink of razor against glass; and at that moment, Rience sank and disappeared.

"Not so fast!" he exclaimed. "Adorable Megan and her sire's whiskers too! Full measure an' flowing over, that's my motto. And it won't take a minute."

He found King Rience prone and dead to the world behind the high table. He knelt and turned him over, rubbed emulsion generously into the flaming mustaches and whiskers, then wielded the razor with more vigor than skill. The mustaches, the beard, and the whiskers all came away, not to mention a few patches of tough hide; and Dinadan tucked all into the front of his jerkin, chuckling heartlessly.

"Full measure an' flowing over," he chuckled, and emptied the phial of its soporific contents upon the upturned face. "Sleep sound," he added, and hastened away to the rendezvous at the stables.

The long mountainous and twisty passage from the ravaged stronghold of King Rience to the pleasant court and town of Camelot was made by Princess Megan, Nurse Grundy, Dinadan, and Kedge with expedition and without accident. No sight or sound of pursuit threatened them, and the weather remained fine; and Dinadan's love waxed hourly, despite the fact that the lovely Megan's demonstrations of affection decreased in both ardor and frequency with the increasing of the distance between their horses' tails and the paternal fury.

"A simple mountainy girl cannot be too careful of appearances in a strange society, my sweet," she told him.

Upon the occasion of Dinadan's first audience with King Arthur, he'd had to talk his way past four doorkeepers, but now every door opened before him as if of its own free will at the mere mention of his name; and so he stood again before young King Arthur and Sir Ector and Sir Kay, but this time with the most decorative damosel in Christendom flashing and gleaming beside him. King and knights goggled, speechless.

"Your Grace," said Dinadan, "may I present Princess Megan, King Rience's only daughter, who is not only the apple of his eye but whose hand in wedlock was to have rewarded one Cadwallader, a savage and powerful prince, for strong military aid to Rience in a contemplated war against your realm and person. In brining this incomparable princess away at this time, I not only avenged an insult to Your Grace but reduce the force of the threat which accompanied it by half—to say nothing of the purely personal reasons which inspired my action."

"Quite," said King Arthur, in a dazed voice; and he stumbled to his feet and bowed to the Princess.

"God bless my soul!" exclaimed Sir Ector, rising and bowing too.

Sir Kay also rose and bowed, but in silence.

Princess Megan veiled her emerald eyes and smiled demurely, then raised golden lashes and snowy lids slowly and slid soft green rays from Arthur to Ector to Kay. The melting radiance lingered upon Sir Kay, who ogled back like a zany.

"It was my idea," she murmured. "When I learned this young man's mission, which struck me as childish and hopeless—I questioned his groom within an hour of their arrival—I took pity on the poor fellow; and as I was already pitying myself as the prospective bride of that horrible King Cadwallader, and grief-stricken at my father's cruel intentions toward Your Majesty and this fair realm, I thought of this plan of amending all, even at the price of separation forever from my beloved mother. But please do not think that I would belittle Master Dinadan's part in the adventure, for I believe him to be an admirable person in his place, though inclined to forget that place sometimes, and to mistake condescension for sentiment."

"Hah!" exclaimed Sir Kay; but the King and the old knight continued to regard the Princess and the squire in silence, with puzzled eyes.

Dinadan's face, which had gone white as milk, then red as blood, was white again, and his shoulders were sagging.

"I've learned my lesson," he mumbled, staring straight to his front.

"And saved your skin," commented Sir Kay.

At that, Dinadan straightened and turned upon the

knight such a deadly look that the other recoiled and fumbled at a dagger; but in a moment Dinadan turned back to
King Arthur and spoke in a controlled though metallic
voice.

"Sir, uncertain as to which King Rience valued most—
his daughter or his whiskers—I brought you both!" And he
pulled a mass of flaming red hair from the front of his
jerkin and placed it on the table.

THE QUEST OF THE SARACEN BEAST
(A Tale of Knights Errant Indeed)

. . . meanwhile came the knight following the Beast that had in shape a head like a serpent's, and a body like a leopard, and was footed like a hart; and in its body was such a noise as it had been thirty couples of hounds questing: and such a noise that beast made wheresoever it went.

—Sir Thomas Malory

Attracted by groans and fretful cries, Sir Dinadan turned aside into the greenwood shade and discovered an elderly knight recumbent among ferns and pillowed on moss, whereat he dismounted and made courteous inquiry concerning the cause of the stranger's position and lamentations.

"Cause enough, the Lord knows!" the stranger exclaimed, sitting up and clapping a mailed hand to his helmeted head. "Here was I within but spear's-length of the beast—within prodding distance for the first time in twenty years—when down on his knees went my horse with such violence that I departed the saddle by the way of his ears. Then he galloped away and left me grassed."

"What beast was that, sir?" asked Dinadan.

"The Saracen Beast, young sir," the other replied, speaking less excitedly now and fingering his gray mustache through his open vizor. "That monster famous in song and story, that has been the quest of good knights these hundred years and more. There was King Gort—then Sir Cockrum, a mighty champion—then Duke Ironsides,

who perished in it and was found a skeleton at the foot of
a cliff. Then Duke Peveral followed it till he contracted
rheumatics and bequeathed it to me, Sir Nigel of the Tower
and his favorite nephew, God help me, twenty weary years
ago. And now, alas, a mare's son fails me and I sit here
unhorsed!"

"Sir, I would horse you and speed you on your quest
right cheerily but for my lack of a second mount," Dinadan
assured him. "As it is, Sir Nigel—with my second horse
back at Camelot, and a somewhat pressing errand of my
own—I fear me I can offer Your Honor no more than a lift
to the nearest farmhouse or inn."

The elderly knight looked surprised and asked: "Why
did you leave it behind you?"

Dinadan looked embarrassed, and replied, somewhat
stumblingly: "He is not quite a warhorse, really—more of a
sturdy hackney, sir. And, to speak frankly, I left him at
Camelot in hock for my armorer's and my tailor's bills. And
my man Kedge along with him! Both of them in hock—to
be quite frank with you, sir."

"D'ye tell me so!" chuckled Sir Nigel. "As short of cash
as long of spur, what! How come, young sir?"

Dinadan admitted it with a smile at once whimsical
and rueful, and then explained his position briefly, thus: "I
am the third son of a northern baron whose mountainy
domain produces larch and heather and whortleberries in
abundance, but little else, and whose tenants pay their
rents with smoked venison and usquebaugh. Upon leaving
home I paged, and later squired, a stout and generous
knight, hight Sir Gyles; and a year since, King Arthur
dubbed me knight for a small deed connected with the
whiskers of treasonous King Rience of North Wales."

At that, Sir Nigel rose and embraced the younger
knight with a clanging of breastplates.

"I've heard of that doughty deed!" he cried. "It was well
done, by my halidom! It is an honor to meet the hero that
razored the villainous visage of that braggart."

"Nay, no hero!" protested Dinadan, in modest confusion. "Only a fumbling beginner, sir—but at your service."

"At my service, d'ye say? Then do I bequeath to you,
here and now, the high quest of the Saracen Beast, even as
my lamented uncle bequeathed it to me twenty weary years

ago. It is all yours, my worthy and trusty Sir Dinadan. So
mount now, and follow the Saracen Beast through thick
and thin, even as it has been followed by the mighty King
Gort, Sir Cockrum, Duke Ironsides, and Duke Peveral, not
to mention myself. Up and after it, noble youth!"

His embarrassment and confusion vastly increased by
the bequest and the old knight's rising vehemence, Sir
Dinadan was fairly flabbergasted.

"Gramercy, gramercy!" he stammered. "But who am I—
full young and untried—to follow those illustrious princes
and noble questers? And were I worthy even, I'd think
shame to leave Your Honor alone and unhorsed in this
forest."

"You are too modest, my boy," said Sir Nigel. "As for my
position at the moment, think nothing of it. It will mend. I
have a squire and grooms and spare horses somewhere
back along the way, who frequently lose touch but always
catch up to me sooner or later. So mount and spur now, I
pray you!"

"But, sir, I am in no manner prepared or provisioned
for this high adventure," poor Dinadan protested. "I was
but riding at random in the hope of meeting some knight-
errant less secure in the saddle than myself, and thereby
obtaining the means—his arms and harness and horse—of
recovering my chestnut hackney and my man Kedge. In
fact, sir, I am operating on a shoestring, and at the
moment, in greater need of quick money than of glory."

"You shall have both, my boy," said Sir Nigel. "I'll be in
Camelot tomorrow, and shall release your man and hackney, and make generous provision for them, without delay,
as I am a true knight. As for quick money, here are five silver crowns to enrich your pouch. And here is one of the
two flasks I always carry on my sword-belt. As for victuals
for today and tomorrow, my runaway charger carries two
saddlebags stuffed with the very best, to which you are
welcome. You have but to follow in his tracks to overtake
him, or more likely, to meet him on his way back; for it is
his habit, upon such occasions, to turn about and retrace
his steps when he realizes I am not still on his back. In
either case, snatch the saddlebags."

He pushed Dinadan gently yet strongly toward the latter's charger, and even boosted him into the saddle.

"Now I shall rest easy, my noble young friend, in the knowledge that I have relayed this high quest into such worthy and capable hands as your own," he added.

So, feeling that further protest would sound discourteous and ungrateful, Dinadan rode off on the quest of the Beast. He followed the trail of the runaway horse without difficulty, and had gone only a mile before sounds of movement in the leafy obscurity near him caused him to draw rein. The disturbance increased swiftly; and a large black horse, saddled and accoutered, burst suddenly into view and came galloping straight at him. A collision was narrowly avoided by quick footwork on the part of his dapple-gray; and in the moment of the black's passing, Dinadan made a long arm and snatched the coupled saddlebags. He went forward again, keeping to the double track of the runaway's going and coming with hardly a check, until he reached a patch of moist ground whereon Sir Nigel's horse had snubbed to a stop and reversed himself. It was all as easy to read as inked words on parchment.

"Now I shall have only the tracks of the Beast itself to guide me," Dinadan muttered.

Looking down from his high saddle, he saw nothing traceable leading onward from the gouges of iron-shod hooves. So he dismounted and peered closer, and still failed to find anything to his purpose.

"But what am I looking for?" he asked himself. "What do I know of this Saracen Beast and the kind of tracks it makes?"

He sat down on a convenient tussock of fern, and racked his brains. He had heard of the Saracen Beast before his meeting with Sir Nigel, but always incidentally and never with his full attention. Now he ransacked his memory for particulars concerning that high and exclusive quest and its exclusive object, neither of which had ever made a very strong appeal to the popular taste, evidently. He removed his helmet and gauntlets and clasped his bare head in bare hands. When and what had he first heard of it?

Hah, he had it! He was a mere toddler when a wandering bard had sung of it, and many more marvels, in his ancestral hall. The bard had called it the Saracen Beast. By his telling, it had been brought to Britain by a great traveler in a remote age, and had escaped from its cage and into impenetrable mountainy forests. He had clutched his nurse's skirts at the bard's description of that monster, and he shivered slightly even now at the memory. How had it gone?

"The head and neck of a great serpent, the body of an Afric leopard but twice as great and long, and the legs and hooves of a hart, and a noise in its belly as of thirty couples of hounds questing." That was it. But between the episode of the bard, and the meeting with good Sir Nigel, he had heard, or harkened to, only such talk of the Saracen Beast as had given him the impression that its pursuit offered little of knightly fame and even less of monetary reward. But now he, Dinadan, was pledged to it and embarked upon it, so there was nothing for him to do about it but his honest best.

Dinadan sighed, arose from the ferny tussock, hung his casque on the saddle and renewed his search afoot for the trail of the Saracen Beast. His tall dapple-gray Garry followed him with a polite show of interest.

He was rewarded sooner than he had expected.

"What's this!" he cried, staring at a cloven hoof-print in a patch of mud. "This is it—or the track of a royal hart of ten points, anyway."

He advanced again, scrutinizing the ground and finding further prints of cleft hooves in moist spots every here and there; and Garry followed close, snuffling inquiringly at his shoulder. So they soon came to a spring of clear water under a bank of flowering Maythorn and bramble; and by the depth of the hoof-prints in the soft margin thereof, Dinadan knew that his quarry had drunk its fill here. Now the sun was behind the westward forest and the leafy twilight was dimming; so Dinadan decided to pass the night beside the spring. He unbitted and unsaddled Garry, who straightway sank his muzzle to the water. He followed the horse's example, though the weight of his armor all but bogged him down. After extricating himself from the mud, he unarmed from neck to heels—a difficult task lacking squirish help. Then, after a swig at the flask which Sir Nigel had given him, he opened one of the saddlebags that he had snatched from the runaway's saddlebow. Here was superior fare, in truth! Here was a tart of jam and rich pastry which he shared, bite and bite about, with nuzzling

Garry. Here was a pigeon pie, of which the horse got only the pastry. They went fifty-fifty on the currant buns, but the knight had all of the roast chicken, and the charger all of a large barley loaf.

Dinadan slept soundly on fern and moss, but was early awake and astir. For breakfast, he and Garry shared what remained in the first saddlebag. Then (after a pull on the flask) he saddled and bitted Garry, but instead of rearming himself, he resumed the belt only, with his sword and a dagger convenient on his left hip and his wallet and Sir Nigel's flask to balance them. He placed all the rest— helmet, the back- and breastplates, shoulder pieces, thigh pieces, greaves, and the rest—upon and about the great saddle. But he slung his shield at his own back and shoul-dered his war-spear. So he resumed the quest of the strange Saracen Beast on his own feet, with the tall horse and all his protective harness clanking after. Though he went lightly now, he still went slowly, searching for big cloven hoof-prints. The ground became higher and dryer and the prints so few and so far between that he just about lost interest in them before the morning was half gone. He sat down on a mossy boulder to reflect and to moisten his throat.

"This is too bad," he told his horse. "In twenty-four hours I have lost that which Sir Nigel kept tag of for twenty years—unless the venerable knight was exaggerating. Or so it seems. But we'll take another scout around, of course: but I must confess that I don't see much of a future for you and me in this high quest of the Saracen Beast. It sounded impractical to me—a trifle too high and wide—when I first heard of it. But we'll do our best, of course—for another day, at least. We owe that much to generous Sir Nigel."

So the search for cloven hoof-prints was resumed.

"What's that?" exclaimed Dinadan. But he was not look-ing at the ground. His head was up, and so was Garry's.

"Hark! Hounds in full cry! The Beast with the noise as of questing hounds in its belly! Nay—it's real hounds—and they have brought the Beast to bay!"

He leaped forward and ran hard and straight toward

the clamor, with the gear-encumbered charger clanging after him. Now he heard the halloos of men mingled with the fierce outcry of hounds. He went through thick and thin, and soon burst from cover into a small glade and the scene of action. Here was the Beast. . . . Nay, this was no monster, but a noble stag of ten points doing battle for its dear life against hopeless odds; the center of a milling ring of fangs and steel. It still struck with horns and hooves, but with failing force. There was froth on its muzzle now, and blood on neck and breast and flanks, and the great eyes were dimming. Dinadan saw plainly enough that this was not the Saracen Beast, but only a great hart of ten points overmatched and about to die and therefore no concern of his; but a sudden furious madness of indignation and pity seized him, and he dashed into the mêlée with a defiant yell and buffeting hands and feet. Hounds and two fellows in wool and leather slunk or jumped out of reach of his arms and legs, but a third huntsman turned upon him and threatened him with a boar-spear.

But only for a moment. Before the fellow could deliver even a jab, Dinadan enveloped him like a whirlwind, snatched the short spear, and clipped him over the nob with its butt-end. Now a menacing but inarticulate roar caused our hero to look to his left; and he beheld a large person in a tunic of green silk coming at him on a tall horse. A personage, evidently, by the quality of his tunic, the curly feather and gold brooch in his green cap, and the arrogance of his voice.

Still roaring, this personage dismounted within a pace of Dinadan and threatened him with the butcher's knife with which he obviously intended to deliver the *coup de grâce* to the enfeebled stag. Dinadan, waggling the boar-spear in a calculating manner, warned him to make less noise and more sense, or he too would be laid flat with a broken head. At that, the other ceased his inarticulate bellowing suddenly and was silent for long enough to flap his mouth open and shut half a dozen times. Then in a controlled but dangerous voice Green Tunic demanded:

"Who are you, knave?"

To this Dinadan returned, in a voice that matched the questioner's: "Who wants to know, churl?"

At that, the two huntsmen who had jumped aside from

Dinadan's first onset struck at him from the rear, only to have their blows nullified by the long shield on his back. He turned upon them and struck with the clubbed spear, thus presenting the shield to a vicious slash of their master's knife. He turned again, quick as a trout, dropped the borrowed boar-spear, drew his sword, and sent Green Tunic stumbling back beyond the sweep of it.

"Fool, I am Sir Gregstone, lord of all this barony!" cried Green Tunic. "Put up that sword!"

Dinadan cried, "I am Sir Dinadan of the Quest of the Saracen Beast!" And he sent the two varlets leaping backward with a circular sweep of his long sword.

"The Saracen Beast, say you?" exclaimed Sir Gregstone, with a change for the better of both voice and countenance. "Just so. An exalted quest, truly, sir—ah—I didn't catch the name, sir."

"Dinadan."

"Dinadan. Quite. And what, then, of old Sir Nigel of the Tower?"

"He handed over to me, after twenty years of it, and went to Camelot."

"Just so. A fine old gentleman. But may I make so bold as to ask why you charged into this entirely private hunt of my own hart in my own forest, kicking my hounds and breaking the heads of my huntsmen?"

"I mistook your quarry for my own—your stag for the Beast—by the tracks of its cloven hooves," lied Dinadan.

"He's stole away an' got clean off, lord," grumbled one of the spearmen.

Of the other spearmen, one still lay supine with a cracked nob, and one nursed a broken shoulder.

"My mistake, Sir Gregstone," lied Dinadan, feigning regret.

"Let it pass," said Gregstone, but with a wry grimace. "A head of ten points, by my halidom! I've never seen a greater. But let it pass. And put up your sword, I pray you, Sir Dinadan, and come home to dinner."

"Gramercy," accepted our hero, who even at this stage of his career seldom refused an invitation to dine or sup.

The grumbling spearman knelt beside the fellow on the ground and tried to rouse him, but without success. Dinadan joined them, unhooked Sir Nigel's flask from his

belt and unstopped it, raised the unconscious churl's head
and shoulders, and tilted the flask to the parted lips. After
three swallows, the sturdy fellow was up on his feet and
staggering happily. Then Dinadan examined the other
casualty's shoulder, advised him to see a doctor and
administered two swigs from the flask. . . .

They came to Sir Gregstone's residence shortly after
high noon. It stood, or rather squatted, in a fair meadow,
and was girt by a wide moat like a paunchy champion by
his sword-belt. It consisted of structures of two or more
periods, some of hewn timber and some of masonry, with
a square tower in their midst. Its appearance was sub-
stantial and commodious rather than elegant.

Like its lord's, thought Dinadan, with a glance at Sir
Gregstone.

They were no more than across the drawbridge when
loud halloos in their rear caused Dinadan to halt and turn.
He saw a knight armed cap-à-pie riding hard toward them
on a red horse.

"Who is that?" he asked. "And what does he want?"

"Pay him no heed!" cried Gregstone. "He is but a crack-
pot. An' dinner is waiting," he added urgently.

"Nay, he bawls your name and dubs you coward,"
protested Dinadan. "He dares you to arm and come out to
him. Are you deaf?"

"I hear him, as I've heard him, almost daily, this past
month and more, the devil take him! Come in to dinner or
'twill be burnt to cinders."

"But he calls you coward an' knave and a disgrace to
your golden spurs. He calls you glutton and tyrant."

"He's mad. Heed him not. He'll come no nearer than the
bridge. Ignore him and come in to dinner, and he'll return
to his pitch in the forest."

"But all he asks is to run a tilt with you—but in villainous language, I admit. Why not arm yourself and oblige
him—and be done with his clamor? I'll be glad to squire
you."

"No, no! Not now, anyway. After dinner, maybe. I'll
explain it all after dinner."

Sir Gregstone pushed and pulled Sir Dinadan into the
great hall, and grooms followed with the horses; and while
Dinadan was being nudged and plucked toward a table set

beneath a canopy on a dais, the horses were led the whole length of the hall and out by a back door.

The two knights dined by themselves, but with service enough for a company of ten; and there was just as much too much of victuals and drink as of service. In truth, there was too much of everything except conversation, of which there was nothing for a long time. Dinadan was a good trencherman, but he could not hold a candle to his host in this respect, nor could he match him in the cup-and-can branch of gourmandry. At last, however, Sir Gregstone wiped his lips and fingers on a corner of the tablecloth of damask, sat back in his chair, hiccuped, and closed his eyes.

"Now what about the knight on the red horse?" asked our hero, prodding his host with an elbow.

Gregstone moved his fat lips, but nothing came of it. Dinadan prodded again and harder, and repeated the question louder. The fat lips this time emitted a thick whisper:

"It'll keep. Forty winks. No hurry."

Dinadan swore impatiently. Though he had plied knife and fingers and cup and horn with his customary heartiness, he was not sleepy, and his curiosity was as lively as ever. So he drew back his elbow for a third and yet sharper prod.

"Hold it!" someone exclaimed at his shoulder.

He held it, and turned his head and saw an elderly gentleman in a robe of black velvet standing behind him.

"I beg your pardon, young sir, but you'll gain nothing by nudging him," continued Black Robe, in a hurried and conciliatory voice. "His ribs are too well larded. He'll sleep for hours yet. But permit me to reply for him, sir. I know the answers as well as he does."

He introduced himself as Clark Andrew, one-time tutor to Sir Gregstone and for many years now seneschal of the great house and steward of the wide domain. At Dinadan's suggestion, he took a seat and helped himself to wine. He had already dined—"Before the sirloin was done too hard for my waggly tender teeth," he explained. He dismissed the servants with a gesture.

"And now, young sir, what would you know?"

"Why your Sir Gregstone ignores the challenge and insults of the knight on the red horse, venerable sir."

"Quite. I myself would ask that question if I did not know my bully lord and friend as I do. Should you repeat it to Sir Gregstone three hours from now, when he wakes from his postprandial nap, he will tell you that he ignores challenges and insults because he lacks suitable harness in which to accept the former and resent the latter. Mere sophistry, young sir—though 'tis true that of his two suits of armor, which were made for his father, one is now too small for him and the other still too large."

"D'ye tell me he lacks the price of a new suit of mail?"

"Not at all, young sir. God forbid! He could have a suit of the best Spanish made to his measure every sennight of his life, had he a mind to; but like his father before him, he is a better patron to cooks and tailors than to armorers. He is no jouster; nor was Sir Guff. He has neither the seat nor the spirit for exchanges of thrusts and cuts with equally armed cavaliers; nor had his sire. Harts and hinds are more to his taste as antagonists—but only after they have been properly winded and worried by hounds and huntsmen. And so it was with Sir Guff, who took his first and only tumble in a passage of arms as a young man and harnessed to match his slimness, and who had no further ado with body armor until, when as big around as a hogshead, he ordered a new suit of mail for a purely ceremonious occasion. And so it is that Sir Gregstone, a true son of his father, can excuse himself from combat on the plea that he has nothing to wear."

"Hah! So he is truly the lily-livered, chicken-hearted knave that the knight on the red horse names him."

"Near enough, young sir. And yet not altogether a knave. Not an out-an'-out villain for a ballad, so to speak. There's good as well as bad in him—as in most of us. He's not vengeful, for one thing. Take your own case, for instance, young sir. I have heard from the huntsmen how you came crashing in when he was about to dispatch that great hart of many tines—one of the greatest ever seen in these parts, so they say—and cuffed and kicked hounds and huntsmen and threatened Sir Gregstone with your sword, to the end that the stag escaped with his life. And yet you sit here as safe as if you were in your own house; and you might lie here just as safely, asleep as awake. If you come to any harm here, young sir, it will be from emulating your host's prowess at this table. In other words, all will be aboveboard. Ha-ha! Not bad, wot?"

"Very good, sir. You have a pretty wit. But I must tell you that I'd be in a poor state of health right now if his hunting-knife had not been turned by the shield on my back."

"D'ye tell me that he struck at you?"

"Yes—and it was when my back was turned."

"Even so, young sir, it was a surprising show of spirit on his part. But don't let it worry you. He must have quite forgotten his true nature in the chagrin and excitement of the moment. He lacks both spirit and energy, as well as inclination, to strike at you again from behind or before. Consider his behavior in the case of the froward knight on the red horse. All Sir Gregstone does in retaliation to that gentleman's challenges and insults, which have been of almost daily recurrence for the past month, is ignore them and him."

At that, Dinadan sneered: "Because he's afraid to fight!"

"There's no denying it, young sir," agreed the seneschal. "Sir Gregstone, like Sir Guff before him, is averse to combat—to the exchanging of blows, that's to say. In the matter of thrusts and cuts, he holds that it is more blessed to give than to receive. Yes, indeed. But his case is not as simple as you make it sound, my dear sir. If he were of a vengeful nature, or treacherously inclined, he would have rid himself of the pestiferous attentions of that knight weeks ago, by sending archers and pikemen out at him in broad day or a cutthroat after dark; for the vociferous challenger invites disaster every hour, open to arrows and mass attack daily, and lying asleep and unarmed every night in the same dell. And Sir Gregstone has only to say the word, and the murderous deed is done, for he is a generous master. But he has not said it; nor will he say it, for 'tis not in his nature, but turns deaf ears to the clamor and does not let it spoil his dinner."

"It sounds like madness to me," said Dinadan scornfully. "Madness and foolery! They both sound crazy, and worse, to me. Gregstone is an arrant coward, by your own telling, and a loathly glutton to boot, despite the one redeeming feature you claim for him. And his challenger must be utterly mad. Who is he? And what is he challenging about? What does he want of your guzzling coward?"

The seneschal scratched his bearded chin and a hairy ear, and drained and refilled his cup, before answering.

"He calls himself Sir Kelter," he said, and paused for a sip. "But what he wants," he continued slowly, as if weighing every word, "I am not prepared to say, as I have not the honor—questionable, maybe—of his confidence. I fully agree with you, however, that he must be mad: but there are so many varieties of madness in the knightage—in its junior circles especially—that I'll not venture an opinion on the exact nature and degree of his affliction."

"Maybe he is just spoiling for a fight?" suggested our hero hopefully.

"He is in a pugnacious mood, unquestionably," the other agreed.

"Maybe he would like a go at me?" Dinadan resumed. "Just a friendly bicker—or whatever he wants. Blunt spears or sharp ones, I'd leave him the choice."

The seneschal wagged his venerable pow and said, "I don't think he would like it, young sir."

"Not like it! Why not? I am a knight of King Arthur's own dubbing—hight Sir Dinadan—and good enough for my years. Not as good as many and yet better than some—both ahorse and afoot!"

"I don't question your quality, Sir Dinadan. Nor your prowess, sir. On the contrary. To be frank with you, bully knight, I have observed you closely; and not only that, I have visited your great charger and examined your fine harness; and I doubt if Sir Kelter would welcome Your Worship as a substitute for Sir Gregstone. And after all, his ire appears to be very particularly aroused by the person of Sir Gregstone."

"That may be; but if he is half as fierce as he sounds, he'll not refuse a fight simply for lack of a quarrel."

After a long minute of deep thought and another cup of mead, the old man said: "In my opinion, it is a bang at Sir Gregstone that he wants, rather than a fight. But if you, sir, are serious in your suggestion of meeting him in combat, you have only to go forth on Gregstone's charger and with Gregstone's green shield dressed before you."

Dinadan didn't half like the idea of doing battle on a

strange horse and sporting his craven host's shield, but he felt such an urge for action that he accepted it. So he and the seneschal retired to the stables, leaving Sir Gregstone snoring in his chair.

With his companion's help, Dinadan was soon in his suit of superior and tested mail, the price of which had been several times more than he could afford. Then, after a brief visit to Garry's stall, for the purpose of embracing and apologizing to his puzzled dapple-gray, he went forth on a strange horse and behind a strange shield with the intention of amending the manners of a strange knight.

When Dinadan issued upon the meadow beyond the drawbridge, Sir Kelter was hovering at the forest's edge some two hundred yards away. At a blast on a horn blown by the venerable seneschal, Kelter wheeled, gave vent to a long-drawn whoop beginning on a note of incredulity and rising swiftly to a hoot of derision and an exultant shout, then laid his spear and launched to the attack. Whereupon our hero laid his spear and dressed the green shield and knocked spurred heels on the bulging flanks of his mount.

"Get going!" he urged. "Action front!"

But the horse only tossed his great head in protest and sank his great hooves deeper in the sod.

"What sort of warhorse are you?" Dinadan inquired, with appropriate epithets.

But breath and heels alike were wasted, for the animal was no sort of warhorse at all, but the biggest and laziest plowhorse within five leagues in every direction. In the meantime, Sir Kelter and the red charger came on, hard and straight.

"So be it, fool!" muttered Sir Dinadan. "Let them do the running—the devil take you! What happens when an irresistible force meets with an immovable object? We'll soon know!"

A number of things happened practically all at once. Sir Kelter's wavering point—he was only a third-rater after all, despite his noise—went wide in the last critical split second; but Sir Dinadan's held true. So Kelter sailed backward from his saddle on the point of our hero's bending lance—but with his breastplate no more than dented behind the pierced shield—and came to earth violently on the back of his neck. Then the collision! The forces of motion and immobility involved were so great that both horses fell down; and though the plowhorse dropped where he stood, without giving back an inch, the vibrations of the shock flung Dinadan from the saddle to the ground, where a hoof of one or the other of the stunned steeds clipped him on his helmeted head.

Upon regaining consciousness, Dinadan did not open his eyes at once, but tried to collect his wits; and while so stilly yet laboriously and painfully employed (for his head felt terrible), he heard a voice close at hand. It was the voice of Sir Gregstone; and though it was reduced to a wheezy whisper, he recognized it.

"But use your brains, I beg you!" wheezed Sir Gregstone with urgency. "This is the better match on every count, as I've explained a dozen times already. Must I go all over it again? So be it! He is by far the better jouster—since you set such store by the silly arts and mad antics of chivalry. Though handicapped by a mount that refused to budge, he hit your vociferous Kelter straight and hard and grassed him like a carp. That he was unhorsed by the collision, and so got his head trod on, was no fault of his. It might have happened to King Arthur, or to that master of romantic tomfoolery Sir Launcelot du Lake, under like circumstances.

"Kelter can take no credit for it, that's certain, for the spill was due entirely to his mount's stupidity, and the knockout was purely accidental, no matter which horse stepped on him. Instead of pouting, you should be thanking your stars for the quality of his helmet. Use your wits, child! With such a helmet as that, and every other item of his harness of matching quality—and consider that dapple-gray charger too—this Dinadan is as well turned out as any earl. So quit your sulking and make the most of this opportunity."

A peevish feminine voice protested: "But you yourself named him for a fool, Papa, when you said that only the feeble-minded or utterly mad ever undertook that quest."

"True for you," wheezed Sir Gregstone. "I said that, and I repeat it. King Gort, Sir Cockrum, Duke Ironsides, Duke Peveral, and Sir Nigel—each and every one of those

questers of the Saracen Beast was either as mad as a
March hare dancing in the moonshine, or as simple as the
village idiot: for if such a beast ever existed—which I
doubt—it was dispatched even before old King Gort's time,
or it would have fallen since to one of those eager questers,
who were all good men of their hands, whatever can't be
said for their heads. Nay, the Questing or Saracen Beast is
not, and never was, anything more than an obsession bred
of an old wives' tale or a poet's fable. It exists and survives
only in the imaginations of its succeeding pursuers, each
of whom must needs be mad, or at least chuckleheaded, or
he would have nothing to pursue. And so the fabulous
quest has been passed on from madman to madman—but
whether by accident or design I don't know.

"But this I do know, child. It has always moved on an
exalted plane. From King Gort to Sir Nigel, every quester of
the Beast has been of high blood and exalted possessions.
And do you think for a moment that old Sir Nigel of the
Tower would pass it on just to any come-by-chance hedge-
running knight-errant? Don't be silly. I promise you that
this young knight is a rich earl's son and heir at the very
least, and more likely a duke's. So bestir yourself now that
you have him at your mercy, while he is doubly a crack-
pot, so to speak; for you'll never have another chance—not
with that nasty temper you got from your poor lamented
mother—to make so fine a marriage. And if this fine young
knight lacks something of intelligence, he will make the
happier husband—the happier for himself as for you. I am
sure that my own marriage would have been happier for
all concerned had I been less generously endowed with
intelligence and sensibility."

"Not to mention gluttony and cowardice, dear Papa,"
jeered the lady.

Breathing in angry snorts, Sir Gregstone exclaimed,
"Your mother's own daughter! But harky to me, hussy! If
you let this Godsend slip through your fingers and continue to encourage that insolent pesky knave who calls
himself Sir Kelter but is more likely a runaway scullion
than a born cavalier, I shall lose my well-known sense of
Christian forbearance entirely, and Black Tim or Sticker
Mike will slit his villainous gullet."

Then there was silence; and after minutes of it, Sir

Dinadan ventured to lift one eyelid just far enough for a peek. He was in a small chamber dimly lit by a smoky candle. So I have been out for hours, he thought. He saw that which twitched his venturesome eye wide open. It was a lady. She stood just beyond the candle, looking down at the smoking wick. He regained control of his eyelid. She snuffed the candle, waited till it burned clearly, then took it up and moved toward him. She stood close beside the narrow bed he was on, and gazed down at him with eyes as green and hard as emeralds. God help me! he thought, watching through screening lashes and trying to breathe like an innocent sleeper. She continued to gaze down at him, stooping a little. Her hair was like spun gold; her cheeks and brow were like eglantines and Easter lilies, and her small mouth was like a ruby. And now her green gaze took on a considering, musing softness.

"Maybe he really means it," she murmured. "And he may be right, for once. And to spare dear Kelt a slit gullet—why not? With a noble simpleton for a husband and my darling still alive and kissing—why not? A respectable son-in-law for Papa, and freedom for me. I'll do it!"

She stooped lower and touched her lips to his. He twitched sharply. She straightened up slowly, with a gratified smile on her ruby mouth (having mistaken his twitch for a reaction to her kiss instead of to a drip of hot tallow on his ear), murmured, "Till tomorrow, my poor fool," replaced the candle on the table, and left the room.

Dinadan opened both eyes, then sat up cautiously and held his sore head in his hands, trying to steady it. After a little while, he recovered a piece of his armor from the floor and tried to put it on, but with such excess of anxious haste and lack of strength and direction that he accomplished nothing in ten minutes of frantic effort; and he was still fumbling futilely when discovered by the seneschal.

"What now, young sir?" asked the seneschal.

"Not so loud!" begged Dinadan. "Shut that door—for God's sake! An' lend a hand, I pray you, good Master Andrew. This cursed breastplate!"

"Nay, that's the backplate! What gives?"

"I'm leaving. No place for me. Must be gone before morning."

"What's your hurry?"

"That lady. I—she—God save me from such a fate!"

"Hah! I get it. Permit me to squire you, young sir."

The old seneschal had Dinadan ready for the road before the candle needed a second snuffing, then led him down and out to the stables by backstairs and passages, saddled Garry for him and gave him a leg up, then led horse and rider away by a muddy lane and over the moat by the rear drawbridge. After thanking the seneschal warmly and promising to send a handsome acknowledgment as soon as he was in the money again, Dinadan expressed sportsmanly regret at thus condemning young Sir Kelter to a slit gullet.

"Though I'd personally prefer a slit gullet to marriage with that lady," he added.

"Tastes differ," chuckled the other. "But don't worry. Sir Gregstone's bark is worse than his bite."

So Dinadan rode back to Camelot: and that was the end of the illusionary quest of the fabulous Saracen Beast. Years later, he heard that Sir Kelter, who had lived to marry that lady and to cut his own throat, had been the secret and ambitious son of that crafty and ambitious seneschal.

A
FAIRY'S
CHILD

After the Quest for the Saracen Beast, Dinadan left on a secretive expedition, lest others might follow, and was not seen for many a moon.

—The Book of Maelor

Sir Hew of the Two Mountains rode in a waste place in the fall of the year, on an errand of strayed beeves, attended only by a cowherd, a huntsman, half a dozen wild mountainy men, and two couples of staghounds. He was a two-days' march from his castle and already wearying of the expedition. He wore leather and was mounted on a shaggy pony. His quality was to be distinguished from that of the huntsman, who also wore leather and was mounted on a shaggy pony, only by the golden brooch and heron feather in the front of his leather cap. He cursed the lost beeves in the very lingo of the wild mountaineers. He drew rein and swigged from a leather bottle unhitched from his saddlebow, then sent the bottle around. And yet he was a great lord of lands, and had been a polished man of the world, and a brilliant figure at the court of King Uther Pendragon, in his earlier years, far away and long ago. The fact is, he had been sinking into rustic ways of behavior and thought ever since his retirement from the world of chivalry and fashion, which retirement had followed closely upon the general breakdown and scramble of his erstwhile aristocratic physiognomy in the course of a knightly passage at arms with one Sir Mash du Marsh. He had taken to wife the daughter of a wild chief of the wild mountainy men soon after his retirement to his ancestral uplands.

And now Sir Hew drew rein a second time, whereupon his wild and rustic attendants halted hopefully and turned expectant glances toward his saddlebow, where hung the great bottle of "mountain dew." But the thought of another treat was not in the knight's mind at the moment. He raised and extended an arm and pointed a finger.

"What the devil is that?" he asked. "And if it is what it looks like to me—and that's a dapple-gray warhorse—what is it doing in this forsaken wilderness?"

The huntsman, the cowherd, and the hairy mountaineers all shifted the angles of their vision from the knight's saddlebow to the direction indicated by the knightly finger. What they saw was a horse, and it twice the size of any horse any of them save the huntsman had ever seen before. The mountainy men emitted uncouth sounds of astonishment and dismay through their whiskers.

"A proper warhorse, as ever was!" exclaimed the huntsman.

"Ay, a knight's charger, such as I myself was wont to fork in braver days!" exclaimed Sir Hew, in rising excitement. "Where, then, is the knight? It will be some young fool of a knight-errant riding on some harebrained quest, depend upon it—but devilish welcome to me nevertheless. 'Tis fifteen years since I last set eyes on a man of civilized breeding, unhorse me else!"

The big horse grazed among the frost-nipped fern and outcrops of gray granite on a hillside beyond a long and narrow lake. On the nigh side of the lake the ground rose also, as fernily and rockily as beyond the gray water but less abruptly.

It was on the nigh side of the mere that Sir Hew and his fellows encountered the errant knight. The stranger walked unarmed, in stained linen and leather, slowly and with an aimless air. He seemed not to see the approaching company. He was young and tall and lean and in need of a shave. Sir Hew drew rein at about twenty paces and hailed him courteously.

"Young sir, how fares your knightly quest?"

The other halted and looked blankly at the mountain lord and the shaggy pony. He pressed a hand to his brow.

"What quest?" he asked.

Sir Hew was nettled, and spoke accordingly.

"If you are not a knight-errant on a quest, why are you in this wilderness at this desolate season of the year? What ails you that you loiter here, pale and unshaven and unarmed?—and a likelihood of snow any day now! The songbirds are flown, and even the woodcock have winged away. The squirrel has made his harvest of beechnuts for the winter. If you ride on no crazy, chivalrous quest, then what the devil brings you here at this time of year?"

"A quest?" repeated the stranger, vaguely. "Yes, I rode on a quest, I do believe—but I have forgotten what it was."

Sir Hew dismounted and looked keenly into the stranger's face—keenly but not unkindly.

"Where are your arms and armor? Did wild mountainy men—fellows like these, in wolf-skins and sheep-skins—set upon you and bump your poor head and rob you? Or did something worse befall you? Are you bewitched, poor lad?"

The stranger's dark eyes gazed vacantly into space as he murmured, "She found me roots of relish sweet, and honey wild and manna dew, and sure in language strange she said, 'I love thee true.' I set her on my pacing steed, and nothing else saw all day long, for sideways would she lean and sing a fairy's song."

"God help you!" exclaimed Sir Hew.

But the stranger would not be interrupted. He intoned his sad, wild, amazing story to the end.

"I saw pale kings and princes too, pale warriors—death-pale were they all—who cried, 'La Belle Dame Sans Merci hath thee in thrall.'"

Sir Hew laid big hands on the man's shoulders and shook him, then called for the leather bottle and forced an ounce or so of its contents between the bewitched knight-errant's teeth. Then they all went in search of the young man's arms and armor. The stranger walked beside the elder knight like a sleepwalker, and muttered wild words to himself. The mountaineers quartered the hillside like dogs; and presently one of them checked and gave a shout and pointed a finger. The others hurried up; and there, in a ferny hollow, lay the knightly armor, all complete, but with the shine of its plates and chain-pieces darkened and dimmed by dews and frosts. The casque, with its bedraggled plume, lay a little to one side; and a spider had spun its web under the raised vizor. The shield lay face down. Sir Hew stooped and turned the shield over. Its face was as plain as its back, and the iron plates were dark and dim.

Later, at some distance, they found the saddle and trappings of the horse, a two-handed sword, and a long spear of ash with an iron head. The huntsman rode around the lake and fetched the charger. The cowherd saddled the great horse, and the young knight mounted without protest but equally without enthusiasm. And so all heads were turned homeward, southward, for the castle of the Two Mountains. Sir Hew talked and questioned; and his servants and wild mountainy men crowded close for fear of missing a word; but the bemazed knight paid no heed and replied to no question. But Sir Hew was not discouraged. He was pleased with the sound of his own voice and the consuming interest of his humble followers; and so he told wonderful stories of his own chivalrous past, naming many great names.

The sun sank and the frost struck. Sir Hew called a halt in a glade, beside a deserted hut of stones and wild thatch. The men in wolf-skins gathered fuel, lit a fire, and gathered dry fern and heather for beds. The huntsman and the cowherd saw to the big horse and the shaggy ponies. A side of young mutton was put to the fire. Sparks flew aloft in swarms like golden bees and leaping red flames painted the wavering walls of the night. The mountainy men skipped in and out of the heat and glare, feeding the fire and twirling the blistering mutton and looking like hairy devils. The knights sat just clear of roasting range, hunched in their cloaks; and Sir Hew still talked and questioned, but the stranger gazed into the heart of the fire without a word. The hounds sprawled at their master's feet. The side of mutton fell from its improvised spit into the flames; and the skipping devil who rescued it caught a-fire and lost all the hair off his wolf-skin shirt. The laughter of his companions, including His Lordship of the Two Mountains, went up higher than the soaring sparks into the frosty air; and just as that gust of mirth began to thin and subside, the bewitched young knight of the forgotten quest fell to laughing loud and high. At the first sound of that outburst, Sir Hew turned upon the stranger in astonishment.

Astonishment gave way to boisterous approval, and he smote the other so heartily on a shoulder with an open hand as to overset him and roll him on the sod.

"So you are a man of flesh and blood after all!" cried Sir Hew; whereupon the other righted himself in utter silence and fell to staring into the fire again with haunted eyes and desolated visage.

The huntsman produced loaves of barley bread and passed them round. Then he served the scorched sheep, giving his master and the defaded knight-errant the first hack at it. The older knight chopped with a heavy hand, saying that mountain mutton was almost as much to his taste as mountain venison, but the bemused gentleman would have none of it. Sir Hew unstoppered his great leather bottle and pressed it upon his bedazed companion and himself; and the huntsman, cowherd, and wild hillsmen washed their mutton and barley bread down with mountainy mead. The hounds grabbed discarded ribs and shanks, and the cracking of bones between pointed fangs sounded louder than the cracking and snapping of the flames and faggots.

At last Sir Hew licked his fingers, wiped them on the lining of his cloak, and burst into song. It was a mountain song, all about hunting and feasting and frolicking; and the hounds and the mountainy men howled heartily in the chorus. At the end of the twenty-first stanza, he raised the leather bottle and tilted it against his lips—and he was surprised to find that no more of its mellow contents remained than what he could dispose of easily in two gulps.

And now the young knight of the forgotten quest piped up a lugubrious air in a voice to match.

> "I met a lady in the meads,
> Full beautiful—a fairy's child!
> Her hair was long, her foot was light,
> And her eyes were wild."

The great hounds sat down on their tails and pointed their snouts to the stars and howled right dismally. But the young knight wailed right on.

> "I set her on my pacing steed,
> And nothing else saw all day long;

For sideways would she lean and sing
A fairy's song.

"I made a garland for her head,
And bracelets too, and fragrant zone.
She looked at me as she did love,
And made sweet moan."

Sir Hew sighed profoundly and prompted one of the howling hounds to silence with a well-gnawed rib of sheep. The bewitched knight wailed on.

"She took me to her elfin grot,
And there she gazed and sighed deep;
And there I shut her wild, sad eyes—
So kissed to sleep."

The wild mountaineers shivered and flung more brush on the roaring fire, and the huntsman dipped again into the crock of mead. The strange knight piped on like a wintry wind in a large knothole.

"And there we slumbered on the moss,
And there I dreamed, ah, woe betide!
The latest dream I ever dreamed
On the cold hillside.

"I saw pale kings and princes too,
Pale warriors—death-pale were they all—
Who cried, 'La Belle Dame Sans Merci
Hath thee in thrall!'

"I saw their starved lips in the gloom,
With horrid warning gaped wide;
And I awoke and found me here
On the cold hillside."

"God defend us!" cried Sir Hew, laying hold of the daft knight's shoulder. "What devil's rigmarole is this?—worse than the pipings of goat-hoofed Pan in the old heathenish days of my great-great-grandfather!"

The young knight was silent. He had finished. The hounds ceased their starward howling. The mountainy men muttered prayers to their wild, cruel, outlawed mountainy gods.

"Is that a shadow?" asked Sir Hew, in a cracked voice.

He pointed a finger. Everyone looked. The big hounds looked and lifted their hackles and shrank their bellies close against the sod, shivering and silent. It was not a shadow. It was an old man in a russet gown and a snow-white beard, with a shepherd's crook in his right hand.

"Long life to you, my good lord of the Two Mountains, valorous and generous Sir Hew," said the ancient.

The knight thanked him in an uneasy voice, and begged him to sit down and refresh himself with mutton and mead, wondering fearfully the while who the mischief he might be, for there was no blinking the strangeness of his sudden appearance at the edge of the fire. The new-comer dismissed the suggestion of food and drink with a wave of the left hand, moved around the fire, and stared keenly at the younger knight.

"I heard your dolorous ditty, young sir," said he. "It is an ancient song, of ancient inspiration, but not widely known. I should be interested to learn where you picked it up."

The befuddled one gave him a blank, wild-eyed look, then returned his gaze to the glowing heart of the fire.

"Dinadan, harky to me," resumed the old man, in an impressive tone of voice. "A stranger and a mystery you may be to good Sir Hew, but you are neither to me. Young Dinadan of the Little Wood, third son of a poor knight of the North, and yourself knighted but a year ago by King Arthur Pendragon, at Westminster, in recognition of your service over the matter of King Rience."

The knight-errant pressed a hand to his brow.

"You may be right," he replied. "I seem to recatch a glimmer of something of the kind. And as you know so much, Reverend Sir, name me the high quest on which I rode away from King Arthur's court."

"It is for you to answer questions, not to ask them. Have you seen this Fairy's Child?"

"Why do you think so? And why not?"

"When did you meet her, and where?"

"Who wants to know, and why?"

The old man made a gesture of impatience and ordered one of the wild mountainy men to fetch him the young knight's shield. The shield was laid at the ancient's feet, face up. He knelt and fell to rubbing the dim iron plates with the tail of his russet gown. Sir Hew and Sir Dinadan approached and stood over him, peering curiously to see what he was about. The huntsman, the herdsman, and the mountaineers crowded around. The old man rubbed and rubbed, hissing the while through his teeth like a varlet grooming a horse. He rubbed the entire surface of the shield over and over, now with a circular motion, now across, now up and down. At last he withdrew his hand and squatted back on his heels.

"Your worthy sire's badge is a goshawk, and the rallying cry of your family is 'Strike hard.' But what have we here? Do you see it? Look!—shaping and brightening as if through thinning fog."

"I see it!" exclaimed Sir Hew. "A white charger. A mounted knight, fully armed, with his spear sloped. Horse and rider gleam and glow, and seem to move yet remain in the center of the shield. And here letters appear—words— shining like fire!"

"Read them," said the old man, with an ironical note in his voice.

"Latin," said Sir Dinadan.

"Ay, to be sure—Latin," echoed Sir Hew.

"Have you two noble knights forgotten your Latin?" sneered the old man.

"I have—if I ever had any," admitted Dinadan.

"*Expectans . . . equito,*" read Sir Hew, slowly. "Dear me! It sounds simple. Something about a horse, unhorse me else! I am expecting a horse. If not that exactly, something very like it. Or, I am waiting for my horse. How's that, Reverend Sir?"

"Rotten!" exclaimed the old man, rising to his feet and uttering a harsh laugh. "*Expectans equito*—Waiting, I ride. Consider that, young Dinadan. 'Waiting, I ride.' It is written. Long shall be the waiting, I promise you, and long and rough the riding. And at the far end of it—what? That will depend upon yourself, young sir; for you will find nothing at the end of that long way that you have not carried with you in your heart."

He turned, stepped one pace, and vanished.

The knights gaped at nothing and the mountainy men shivered. The big hounds cowered against the knightly legs. Sir Hew was the first to recover his wits and power of speech.

"Merlin!" he said. "That mighty warlock, older than antiquity. He hasn't been seen in these parts since I was a lad. My worthy father held him to be the master wizard of the world."

"Never heard of him," said Sir Dinadan, staring dolorously down at his shield. "But, wizard or no wizard, I defy his mumbo jumbo! *Expectans equito*, is it? We shall see about that! I ride my own gait, and travel or tarry at my own pleasure, wizards and warlocks notwithstanding."

"And witches?" queried Sir Hew. "Were you traveling or tarrying when I met you beside the lake? And was it of your own free will, poor lad?"

The young knight hunched his cloak about his face and turned away.

THE MADNESS OF SIR TRISTRAM

Dame Bragwaine rode to the court and told the queen, La Beale Isoud, that Sir Tristram was nigh in that country. For joy Isoud swooned; and when she might speak she said: "Help that I may speak with him, outher my heart will brast." Then Dame Bragwaine brought Sir Tristram and Sir Kehydius privily unto the court and into a chamber; and to tell the joys that were betwixt that queen and Sir Tristram no pen can write it. And when Sir Kehydius saw La Beale Isoud, he was so enamoured upon her . . . privily he wrote unto her letters and ballads. . . . And when she understood his letters, she had pity of his complaint, and unadvised she wrote another letter to comfort him withal. . . . And as it mishapped, Tristram found the letter that Kehydius had sent unto La Beale Isoud and also the letter she wrote unto Kehydius. . . . Then upon a night Sir Tristram put his horse from him and unlaced his armour, and so he went into the wilderness and brast down trees and boughs. Then was he naked; and he waxed lean and poor of flesh. . . . And he fell among swineherds; and when he did any shrewd deed, they beat him with rods.

—Sir Thomas Malory

Sir Dinadan drew rein and addressed his squire. "'Tis twenty days since we rode forth from Camelot."

"Twenty-three," the squire amended, in a patient voice.

"And in that time I have encountered and bested four knights-errant."

"Five, sir."

"Four or five, our pouches are still empty."

"You are too soft, sir."

"But each and every one of them swore by his halidom that his arms and horse were the whole of his worldly possessions; and all pleaded hungry wives and children at home."

"If you had kept your vizor shut—"

"Just so! With my vizor shut, they'd not have seen my foolish face. I get your meaning, my friend."

"Nay, sir—the kindness in it."

"Nay, good Kedge, don't spare me. I'm a fool, and I admit it—but only to you. I distrust my own judgment. What would you do now, in my place?"

"Well, sir—since you ask me: if I were you, we'd turn right around an' head back for Camelot at a gallop."

"But we left there of necessity—this time as upon former occasions—because our money was spent and our credit exhausted. Why return now, with our pouches still empty?"

"To refill them, sir—your pouch, that's to say—and boxes an' strong rooms to boot—the easiest way."

"Ah, my poor Kedge, are you still harping on that frayed string?"

"You asked my advice, sir. With a rich wife, you could live at court the year around, and give every day to the inventing of songs and *bons mots*, and every night to the reciting of them in the highest and merriest companies, with never a thought of the cost, and no risk to life or limb."

"But you know my opinion of women!"

"I've heard it often enough, sir—the gibes and the raillery; but knowing that it's all because some designing or frivolous chit has made a monkey of you upon occasion, and having frequently witnessed the pleasure you take in female society and the pleasure women of every condition and age appear to derive from your company, I cannot accept it as final, sir."

"Made a monkey of, d'ye say? Ah, my dear Kedge, my heart has been nigh broken more than once and twice by their trickeries and faithlessness. As for my apparent partiality for their society, it is because of their intelligence. They are capable—save in exceptional instances—of appreciating my best efforts both as a poet and a wit. Their attraction for me, as mine for them, is solely of the mind."

"Very good, sir. Then why not a marriage of minds? But with a gold ring, of course, and a bishop to perform the ceremony. I could name half a dozen ladies of superior intelligence—three widows and three spinsters—two of them duchesses—and all rich enough, who would jump at your offer, sir."

"I could name them too. Forget them!"

"Yes, sir. But I could name others just as intelligent and—"

"Forget *them* too! I've learned my lesson. I've no further use for the so-called fair sex—hah, but most unfair!—save only as audiences and hostesses. If I sing of love, 'tis with tongue in cheek; and the while the fat ones all but brast their stays, and the thin ones scream like peahens at my quips and quirks, my bitter heart gives their merriment the lie. They have made a cynic of me at twenty-eight—a disillusioned cynic, which is a thing no poet can afford to be— the devil take them! But for their gleaming false eyes and soft lying lips, I'd be the greatest poet in Christendom now, instead of just one of two or three, and also the knight-at-arms of most prowess and honor in the world, instead of just one of half a dozen. And all in ten years. Ah, me!"

"I mind the first one like yesterday, sir. You were but a squire then, and I but a groom. A designing chit, I grant you, sir—but it was for that affair of that princess and her sire's beard the King made a knight of you, and you promoted me to squiredom and gentility. She played you false, and wed Sir Kay the Seneschal, and broke your heart. But may I suggest, sir, that Sir Kay now looks like an even bitterer cynic than yourself? After all, she was, and still is, a redhead."

"A redhead? She was beautiful—externally—as a summer dawn and a night of stars."

"A redhead nonetheless, sir. And with green eyes. And so was the next one who broke your heart a redhead, sir. And the third was a towhead, and the fourth kind of betwixt and between. And so on. And you stuck your neck out for the chopper every time, sir, till I've blushed for you. Hell, sir, I'd be a gibing cynic too if—well, in your boots, sir. Why don't you fall for a brown-haired or black-haired damosel for a change, sir, for your peace of mind? Their hearts may be of truer stuff. I know of one such who is beautiful enough to inspire any poet and—ah—well enough heeled, in her own right, to support him."

Dinadan cried out: "Have done! I trust none of them between the ages of eight and eighty. I'd as lief jump into a river with a millstone 'round my neck, or pull an oar in a Turkish galley, as take on the gyves of wedlock. I'll starve first—by the knuckle-bones of the twenty-seven lost virgins of Mount Gomery!"

Kedge heaved a sigh and said: "In that case, sir, shall we go straight forward, or turn to the right or the left, in search of a quiet spot in which to starve peacefully?"

The horses lifted their heads and pricked their ears; and Dinadan raised a cautioning hand and whispered: "Hark! A harp."

Kedge nodded and murmured: "Ay, sir, a harp. And a right heartbreaking tune."

Knight and squire dismounted and went forward softly, and the curious chargers went after them almost as softly. So they won through the leafy underbrush to the edge of a little glade, and beheld a ferny well in the glade, and a damosel seated beside the well with a small harp of silver on her knee. They checked at the sight. The harpist's tresses, which were long and luxuriant and dark as seaweed, veiled her face.

"Her attitude matches her music," whispered Dinadan. "Both are eloquent of bereavement and grief—and both are false, probably,"

Kedge protested: "You'd not say so if she was a redhead or a towhead!"

"I trust none of them!" Dinadan retorted, louder than he had intended.

The damosel ceased her harping, raised her head and swept the veiling tresses back from her face. For the passage of six heartbeats she regarded the knight, who was slightly in front of the squire, with eyes which Dinadan himself would have hesitated about attempting to describe, then veiled their mysteries with white lids and curling lashes. Dinadan, staring like a zany, opened and shut his mouth several times without uttering. But Kedge did better.

"Lady—at your service!" he gasped.

The white eyelids and their appendant dusky lashes fluttered up and instantly down again. Then Dinadan found his voice, or a sliver of it.

"Not so fast!" he whispered aside to Kedge, but with his eyes still upon the damosel. "I can speak for myself."

Kedge muttered an apology. Then Sir Dinadan spoke up.

"Damosel, I am a knight-errant, hight Dinadan, of King Arthur's court when not abroad in search of chivalrous adventures, and am always ready to bring spear and sword to the succor of any overmatched cavalier or lady in need of a champion."

Kedge muttered: "A redhead or towhead, for choice."

Dinadan ignored him. The damosel looked again. Her eyelids and lashes fluttered like the waving wings of white-and-black butterflies.

"I am not in need of a champion," she said softly and uncertainly, yet clearly enough. "Or am I? I thought I had a champion—a slightly mad one, but brave and strong. But he is gone. He is lost. He wandered away—he often wandered in the wilderness; and that time he did not return; and I fear some evil thing has befallen him. My poor heart is broken."

Kedge said: "Lady, Sir Dinadan here is an authority on broken hearts. His own has been broken so often that he has become a cynic. But I doubt that he knows how to mend them—with the exception of his own, of course. He mends that by being a cynic and reviling all women as false and unworthy of love."

Dinadan didn't so much as glance aside at his trusted squire. For why? He didn't hear him. In truth, he heard nothing save the damosel, and he saw nothing else.

"But that is not fair!" cried the damosel. She stood up; and she lost nothing in the standing. And her eyes were wide upon Dinadan's stricken optics. "It's not fair or true! And I wonder at you, sir—a generous knight like you—I can see your kind heart in your handsome face—speaking so knavishly of women."

Dinadan, having heard only her contributions to the conversation, felt confused and embarrassed, and looked the parts. But he was even more conscious of a great urge to champion her, whether or no her case called for championing. He moved forward dazedly yet determinedly and halted within a pace of her; and the squire and the horses advanced and halted with him.

"Mad indeed—to wander away from you!" he exclaimed. "But if you want him found, I'll find him for you. If you want him back, I'll fetch him back, mauger my head! And his too! Who is he? What's his name?"

"I don't know his name. He never said it. I think he did not know it himself—had forgot it, or he would have told me."

"A nitwit!"

"Nay, no nitwit! Slightly mad, but no fool! And fie upon you for defaming him behind his back. You'd not dare do so to his face, I trow, for I judge him a knight of more prowess than yourself. And he loved me dearly—and I him again."

Dinadan shook with conflicting emotions, but only for a count of seven. Then, to his attentive squire's not unmixed relief, he answered meekly:

"Ah—love. Beware it, lady. Stuff for songs! Forget it, even as I have forgot it. Broken hearts? Broken bubbles! But about your strayed lover, now? How am I to know him when I find him for you? What is the device on his shield?"

"I don't know. He had no shield when he came to us. I think he had cast it aside. And no horse, neither. I think it had run away, hours and miles before—for he was foul with mud to the knees, and his golden spurs were tangled with weeds. I was playing on my harp by candlelight when he came suddenly out of the dark like a—like a shining angel."

"Hah! A shining angel! Just so. He was still fully armed, I take it."

"He had lost his lance, but only a few bits of his harness. And his casque. But he still had his sword."

"And you say you were playing on your harp."

"Yes, it was my music that brought him from stumbling about in the apple-yard. I looked up, and there he was looking in at me. And when our eyes met, he came in through the window. But it is a long story."

"I must hear it all, however, or how am I to know him when I find him?"

Then Kedge, who had for minutes maintained a considering silence, spoke up respectfully but to the point.

"Lady, may I presume to suggest that Sir Dinadan might keep his attention more closely upon the story of your lost lover—pay more heed to your words than to the play of your lips and eyes, that's to say—if he were seated; and I don't mean on the greensward. And if he had horn and trencher within easy reach. For we have come a long, dry, and hungry way since our last bite and sup."

At that, the damosel blushed from the V of her bodice up to her sable tresses; and she apologized in pretty confusion for her thoughtlessness and begged them to follow her.

They had not far to go. The fields and hedges were weedy and ill-kept. The moat was extensive, but choked with bushes and reeds; and for water it had nothing to show but mud puddles. The main drawbridge was down permanently, and its ponderous hoisting gear rusted and broken. The manor house—or castle, rather—was as extensive as the useless moat and in as sorry a plight. Outer and inner walls were breached and gnawed by time and weather; half the roofs were fallen; a half of the battlements of a tower had tumbled into the moat; stables, byres, middens, and unpruned orchards crowded in on the flanks and rear; and the massive flagstones of the court-yards were upheaved and cracked by wild roots and fringed with weeds.

"God save us! Rack an' ruin! Is everyone dead here?" Kedge growled.

At a call from the damosel, a lout in leather appeared and made to take the horses: Kedge would have none of him, however, but unbitted and unsaddled and stabled the chargers himself, and saw to their baiting in a masterful manner, then left them in the lout's care with a promise of slashed skin and broken bones should they come by any mishap; and he cuffed the fellow, to show that he meant what he said. . . .

Later the damosel and the knight and the squire sat at a table in a high hall. From the rafters depended spiders' webs as heavy as curtains with dust and the wings and shells of flies. The board was dressed with platters and trenchers, horns and jacks and leather bottles, but the meats were salty and ill-cooked, the loaves and scones soggy or scorched, and the ale was thin and the wine sour.

Sharp and dry though the cavaliers were, they ate and drank in strict moderation. The damosel took neither bite nor sup, but told her sad story as follows, though more wordily.

The unnamed knight had come in at her window, drawn to her from the darkness by the music of her harp, like a moth to a candle. Without a word of greeting, but with an enchanting smile, he had knelt at her knee, taken the harp gently from her hands and played upon it himself with such matchless skill that her heart throbbed and sang and wept with the music as if the harpstrings and her heartstrings were one. And he had given her back the little harp, and she had played for him as well as she could—ah, better than she had ever played before. Then he had taken the harp again, and played again, and handed it back again; and so, turn and turn about, they had exchanged wordless songs of love and yearning until the flame of the candle had fallen and drowned in the hot grease. Then he had kissed her. And so love had enveloped them; and for sennights or maybe months—she had lost all count of time—her life had been all loving and musicking and this ruinous demesne a heaven on earth.

Kedge muttered: "More like a fools' paradise!"

But that crack passed unheeded; and the damosel told how, whenever he was out of her sight more than a few minutes, she had only to call him back on her silver harp. One of the melodies they had wrought together, and some-times but a fragment of one, always brought him to her through brush and brier. Always—till the last time he had wandered. That had been nine desolate days and nights since. She had played the harp all about the inner courts and the purlieus of the place, and even around the outside of the moat and as far abroad as the sylvan well beside which they had found her—but never farther, for fear of gypsies and unicorns. All to no purpose, alas!

"I will find him," Dinadan assured her softly. "And fetch him to you," he added after a moment's pause, and not so softly.

"Alive or dead," said the squire cryptically.

"Not dead!" she cried.

"Nay, do you not worry," Dinadan soothed her. "He will come willingly enough, I doubt not."

"Or more the fool he," said Kedge; and he looked at the damosel and added: "On two counts, lady. First, a man would be indeed a fool to resist being brought back to you; and second, Sir Dinadan shows a stubborn nature in his dealings with men, no matter how often he is made a monkey of by—But let it pass!"

The three agreed that the likeliest method of gaining touch with the lost lover would be to lure him with harp music; and as the damosel could not desert her aged grandparents to carry that music afar in the wilderness in person, that she should teach Sir Dinadan the mysteries of that instrument.

"And that should not take long, for he is musically gifted and one of the world's best lutanists," Kedge assured the lady; and Dinadan admitted as much with a modest smirk.

Thus it came about that Sir Dinadan added harping to his many other accomplishments. But it was not done in a day, nor five even, though he received instruction every morning, every afternoon, and then again after supper by star-shine or candle-shine. School was kept mostly in the cobwebby high hall, and sometimes in a runaway rose garden or a natural bower in the wild orchard, and more rarely in the dusty chamber where old Sir Gyfyl and old Dame Ingrid dozed time away in cushioned chairs. The little harp passed back and forth a thousand times between teacher and pupil, twanging high and low, fast and slow.

As for Kedge, he felt out of the picture and busied himself with other matters. By example, and then with well-judged cuffs, he taught the louts around the stable the proper care of horses. He invaded the kitchens, and there he distributed instructions and cuffs among the loafers of both sexes so effectively that next day's broths and roasts and puddings came hot to the table. He mustered a force armed with brooms and hayrakes and hoppoles and ousted the fat gray spiders and their curtainy lairs from the high hall. He set complaining fellows to work with bushhooks and spades.

"This place might be saved from rack and ruin even yet," he told the Damosel Alyne one morning, where she and Dinadan sat in a bower with the little harp idle between them.

"Nay, the place is well enough," she said.

Then he asked: "Has Sir Dinadan proved an apt pupil?"

She averted her face and murmured: "No, his poor fingers are all thumbs, I fear."

So he looked at Dinadan; and the knight avoided the glance and muttered: "I haven't got the hang of it yet, my friend."

At that, the squire exclaimed "Hah!" with a wry grimace. "Just so. Lady, I was mistaken in him. I see it now, on second thought. For twiddling on a lute and crooning of love-ditties, at which Sir Dinadan is as good as any wandering troubadour, is mere child's play to the mastery of the harp. I had better myself undertake to learn to lure your strayed lover home to you, though I have no more gift that way than yonder moldy haystack."

Dinadan sat upright with a jerk and cried: "Say you so? Twiddling on a lute is child's play, is it? And twanging on a harp calls for more skill than I am capable of, does it? Saint Swithin's whiskers! I'll show you!"

He snatched the little harp to his knee, plucked a string or two, then went at it like a cat sharpening her claws on a table leg. There was tinkling, then a singing, then a sobbing. (Kedge smiled behind his hand and the damosel arched her pretty brows.) There was a buzzing as of bees, then a rushing as of a plunging eagle's wings, then a high and thin crying as of angelic voices and the horns of Elfland and the harps of Heaven. (The damosel sighed and veiled her eyes and the squire's square face took on a dreamy look.) Then Dinadan's voice joined the singing of the strings.

When the music ceased, Alyne was in tears and Kedge was sighing like the bellows of a forge. Dinadan himself looked none too happy, and his voice was grim when he addressed the lady.

"Could your own harping crack-brained lover harp better than that?"

Her only answer was more tears.

"And you, my friend?" he asked of Kedge.

"Sir, I gibed but to bring you to your senses," Kedge whispered. "I knew you had mastered the thing, however you may have hoodwinked the damosel—but I feared you were losing the mastery of yourself."

"What then, good Kedge?"

"What then, sir! Do you ask? Your pledged knightly word, sir—to seek the lost knight, the lost lover—and fetch him back to her, by your halidom and mauger your head!"

The knight gnawed his lip and bunched his brows.

"You are right. It is time we were gone. Trust you to keep your feet on the ground! But this time—ah, 'twill truly break."

"Sir, better a broken heart, or a broken neck even, than your knightly word broken."

"Yes, yes, honest Kedge, I quite agree with you. But it hurts! We shall go tomorrow then, bright and early—and no matter what gets broken, my knightly word will remain inviolate."

But Sir Dinadan departed alone next morning, and not very bright and early either; for Kedge, while setting a gang of hedgers to work at break of day, when he had better have been seeing to the horses, had fallen into a ditch and sprained an ankle. So, after binding the ankle, Dinadan had left his squire in the damosel's care and gone forth alone on the quest of the strayed nameless lover. He took both horses, using Kedge's for a beast of burden, for the search might prove long and victuals and drink hard to come by in the wilderness. But he carried the damosel's little silver harp in his hand.

Dinadan's heart was not in the quest ahead, but behind him in the tumble-down castle. He would liefer fail in it than win it, for his private opinion of its object was that he was not only a fool but a dishonorable knave and faithless deserter too—wickedly designing rather than honestly mad—a dirty, cowardly, despicable scoundrel, in short. His heart was not in the search, but his hatred was, hot and waxing hotter with the passage of every mile.

"If I find him—and I'll do that, by Saint Peter's key!—I'll take him back to her willy-nilly, and show her who's the better man and the true knight—if he dies of it!" he swore.

Never before had his susceptibilities been so mortally stricken as by Damosel Alyne: and he really believed it, God help him! So he rode in a daze as well as a maze, letting his horse take what forest track he would—of deer, wild swine, unicorn, or half-wild human. So he chanced upon a shaggy hut shortly before the sun went down. A shaggy woman and some shaggy children were before the hut, but the children vanished like young partridges at the sudden appearance of the armored knight and the two tall horses. But the woman stood her ground, with an axe in her hand, and glared suspiciously.

"Fear me not, good woman," said Dinadan. "I come in peace—sword in scabbard, see!—and harp in hand. I seek a wandering cavalier who is slightly—ah, you know." And he cocked an eyebrow at her and tapped on his forehead with a forefinger.

"Hah, that poor gentleman!" she exclaimed, with obvious relief and amusement. "He was here, lord, and ate like a wolf an' drank all our brown ale. But he was mad without the drink—shouting and climbing trees. But harmless, lord. Wouldn't hurt a fly. Why d'ye seek him, lord? Is he Yer Honor's brother?"

"God forbid! No, that's to say—no kin to me. I seek him for a lady."

The woman laughed and asked: "Wot would a lady want with that poor soul? He passed the night he was here high up in yonder oak."

Dinadan shook his head and asked: "Where is your man?"

She came closer and spoke confidentially.

"We found a dagger he cast away—a rich tool with gems like white and blue fire in the hilt of it; so Gart followed in his tracks to give it back to him, poor soul."

Dinadan said nothing to that, whatever he thought. He gave the woman a roasted fowl, a great scone, and a cake stuffed with plums from one of his hampers, then resumed his journey, though twilight was thickening to dusk in the forest. And he went faster than he had gone before, despite the obscurity. Soon he dismounted and went afoot, with both good horses following close. So they stumbled through thick and thin till close upon midnight. Then Dinadan unsaddled, unbitted, and watered and grained the horses; supped well; and, after partially disarming himself, took a hint from the reported behavior of the lost lover and climbed into a convenient tree, taking his sword with him. He was down and about at the lift of dawn, after an uneasy night. They rested at noon, beside a brook; and there he found a pair of knightly greaves in the reeds, still undimmed.

"If he be more knave than fool, he turned to his left here and went downstream, for easy going: but if he be more fool than knave he held straight across and through bush and tangle," he reasoned.

After an hour of such reasoning, during which he and the horses dined and rested, he tossed one of his three remaining pennies for a decision: heads, the knave's way, tails the fool's.

Tails won, so he forded the brook and plunged again into the tangled ups and downs of the wilderness. A few hours later, he stumbled upon a great sword in a scabbard studded with bright stones, and the great belt too; and these he hung to the saddle of Kedge's charger. Next day, he found a fine breastplate and a backplate to match it in a thicket of hollies.

"The madman must be all unarmed and unharnessed by now," he said, marveling; and there he tarried and played the silver harp a long hour, on the chance that the object of his quest might be lurking close at hand. But nothing came of it.

Three days later, within an hour of high noon, Dinadan's ears were startled and offended suddenly by an outburst of rude shouts and jeers and hooting laughter. He dismounted, drew his sword, and moved cautiously toward the sounds through the intervening underbrush; and the horses followed as cautiously. Soon he looked out at an extraordinary scene. Here was a forest glade hedged with crude huts and smoking potfires along its farther side and alive with people between himself and the huts; and in the midst, a naked man skipping, leaping, and turning this way and that the while men and women and children lashed at him with green rods and dry sticks and whooped at his antics. But the naked man was silent.

"Hold!" bawled Dinadan. "Stay your hands, churls!"

All eyes, save only the naked man's, turned and fixed. All hands were stayed. All sound, and all motion save the skipping of the naked man, ceased as instantly as if struck by a deathly frost. Only the naked man paid no heed.

Dinadan shouted again, "By God's wounds!" and stepped

forth fully from the covert with the long sword in one hand, the silver harp in the other, and all his armor flaming white from crest to toe. And the tall chargers came after, tossing their heads and pricking their ears.

"You there!" he cried. "You, sir! If you're a man, stop that capering and come to me!"

But the naked fool—for a fool he looked, and a piteous one at that—continued to skip and twist to right and left and forth and back without so much as a glance at the fierce intruder. Then Dinadan tucked the sword under his left arm and took the harp in both hands and struck the strings. He struck again and set them all ringing and singing. At that, the naked man stumbled and fell, staggered upright and stood for a minute as still as stone, then gripped his head in his two hands. Looking at Dinadan, he uttered a piteous cry and started staggeringly toward him, shouldering the petrified beaters from his path. Dinadan harped on, and even more inspiringly than before. Still crying out piteously, the naked man stumbled to a stop and looked back, and his outcry changed in volume and tone to a furious roar; and, turning again, he hurled himself forward, wrenched the sword from its scabbard under Dinadan's left arm and, still roaring like an avenging lion, leaped and turned in the air and rushed upon his late tormentors. Then the people came to life and scattered like partridges—all save a big man who held a stout oaken staff instead of a green sapling in his hands. He was not quick enough. In the very act of jumping aside, he was caught by the whistling arc of steel.

The naked man stood gazing down at the thing before him on the reddening greensward. Dinadan went forward and stood beside him.

"In two pieces!" Dinadan exclaimed, shaken. "But doubtless he deserved it. A shrewd stroke, by my halidom! But come away now. They'll be swarming upon us with spears and axes in a minute, and arrows will be flying. Come away. I have a spare horse."

But the naked man paid no heed to the words but continued to gaze down grimly upon the dead man.

"Come away—or we'll both die like wild boars," Dinadan urged. "If you're a knight—for that was a knightly stroke— you'll get no honor here, nor come by any reward, though you carve and split a score of these savages, but only a

messy and ignoble death. Come away now, good knight—or
poor fool, whatever you are!"

So saying, Dinadan laid hold of the other with a heavy
hand and made to turn him and draw him away; whereupon the naked man struck and staggered him with a
naked left fist to his helmeted head and started to raise the
wet sword against him. This was too much for Sir
Dinadan's sore-tried temper. Quick as a flash, he retaliated
with a shrewd bang of the little harp on the other's unprotected head. Down crumpled the naked one—fool, knave,
mad knight, and lost lover or whatever he was—and lay
still. Shaken then with remorse, Dinadan flung the broken
harp away and lifted the pathetic figure—thin and bramble-
scratched and welted and bruised, yet formidable withal—
in both arms and turned back to the horses.

An iron-headed arrow knocked on his armor somewhere
and fell harmless. He urged the good horses backward into
the coppice, laid his senseless burden on the ground for the
half-minute it took him to rearrange the arms and gear on
the spare horse, then lifted it to Kedge's saddle. He bolted
from cover then, snatched up his sword, which the madman
had dropped when bashed with the harp, and bolted back
quicker than the telling. But quick as he had been, he could
hardly believe what he saw upon his return: the limp figure
upright in the saddle, with the left hand on the reins and
the right pulling the castaway sword from its gem-studded
scabbard. And even while Dinadan gaped, the four-foot
blade came clear and whirled in air, shearing saplings like
grass. The tall horse reared, spun on its hind hoofs, and
would have dashed into the open if Dinadan had not
jumped to its head and dragged it down.

The naked man roared: "Unhold him—or you die!" And
the great sword showered leaves and twigs on him.

But he held on and roared back:

"Fool! Spears and arrows await you out there—and you
naked as a trout! Fool, mind that sword! But for the
horse's sake I'd let you go, whoever you are, the devil take
you! Stay your jerking on the bit, and that swordplay, or I'll
forget your nakedness and stick you through the middle
like a bag pudding!"

The menacing sword-arm sagged limply and the jerking
bridle-hand came to rest; and the naked man stared down

from the high saddle at the full harnessed knight, and Dinadan stared up at him.

"Naked, d'ye say?" he asked, in a dazed voice. "Am I mad, then? Or bewitched or bedeviled?"

Dinadan exclaimed, "Hah! I know you now!" and let go his hold. "But we must win clear of this, or feed the foxes! Here's my shield. It will cover your front—or better still, sling it to cover your back."

He mounted.

"Follow me!" he cried, launching his tall charger through thick and thin.

The other followed. But by now they were surrounded; and vengeful rogues armed with boar spears and axes sprang up before them from the underbrush. The long swords flashed to the right and the left, and the battlewise horses dodged and charged as nimbly as terriers. The long swords ran red to their hilts. The shouts and screams fell and faded away to rearward; and still the tall horses crashed through thick and thin.

Dinadan drew rein and dismounted and turned.

"How fared you, sir?" he asked.

The naked man dismounted too. The long shield hung down his back. He drew it around to his front and smiled grimly at the hatchet embedded in it.

"That would have done it," he said, quietly. "A good shield. Gramercy, sir."

Dinadan nodded and fell to examining the horses. Neither of them had taken so much as a nick.

"Lucky," he said, with a sigh of relief, and loosed the girths of both and lowered the saddles and gear to the ground.

"What now?" the other asked.

"We'll rest a little, then return to Sir Gyfyl, Dame Ingrid, and their granddaughter the Damosel Alyne," said Dinadan, regarding him searchingly. "*Alyne.* Don't tell me you've forgotten *her*—or are you quite mad?"

The naked man heaved a sigh and moaned, "I've forgot everything, God help me!"

"Don't you know who you are?"

"Nay, nothing. If you know who I am, and what I was— I can see what I am: a poor naked fool—be merciful and tell me."

"Don't you know that sword in your hand?"

"I know it. It is my sword."

"And the shield that but now saved your naked back from the hatchet there?"

"A good shield—but not mine."

"Your name is Tristram. Sir Tristram, a Cornish knight, young, but of prowess both horsed and afoot."

"Hah! Tristram."

"Now you remember?"

"Nay, I remember nothing. But now that you have said it, Tristram—I know it in my marrow."

So they ate and drank; and they conversed pleasantly, for Sir Tristram was knowledgeable despite the fact that his conscious memory was a blank. Then Dinadan bathed Tristram's welted back, treated the worst hurts with a healing ointment, and gave him his only other shirt, which was of fine linen, and an old buckskin tunic. Then Dinadan brought the greaves which he had found beside a brook, and the breast- and backplates he had found in a thicket of hollies, and the gem-studded belt and scabbard he had stumbled upon in a tangle of eglantine. Tristram knew them all as well as he knew the sword, but rack his brains as he would, he could not remember when or why he had discarded any one of them.

"Even before you won to that ruinous castle, you had lost your horse and shield and helmet," Dinadan told him. "You came to the damosel's harping afoot and muddied to the knees and bareheaded. You came in to her through the window, from the outer dark."

Tristram sighed and said, "I know nothing of it."

"And you kissed her," Dinadan persisted. "D'ye tell me you know nothing of that?"

"Even so, my friend. Nothing."

Then Dinadan told him all he knew of that affair, as he had heard it from Alyne's own lips.

"All news to me," said Tristram. "Damosel, kisses, old ruins—I remember none of it. It's all lost to me—it and all else of my past. I was the sport of savages—an abject clown beaten with rods—when you saved me. Before that, nothing. I might as well have been dead, or unborn."

Dinadan believed him.

They rode on, good companions. On the second day after their dramatic meeting, they came upon a dismal swamp.

"I never saw this before," said Dinadan. "I must have made a wrong turn somewhere."

So they made a turn which he hoped was a right one. Next day they came upon another landmark that was strange to Dinadan—a ruined and deserted hermitage and chapel.

"I never saw this before," said Dinadan.

So he changed direction again: and so they were lost completely in that vast wilderness.

A sennight later, the wanderers drained the last of the leather bottles and ate the last stale scone and rasher of rancid bacon. As for the horses, they had been for so long reduced to a diet of thin grasses and other bitter herbs of the wilderness that they had all but forgotten the taste of oats and beans. Then, for three days, the cavaliers browsed with their steeds and grew thin on wild berries.

"This is all my fault," Sir Dinadan complained, as the two stumbled aimlessly through brush and brier with the horses stumbling after. "A blind guide would have served you full as well."

"Nay, Din, 'tis my fault," said Sir Tristram. "Had I not lost my wits, you would not have come in search of me and so lost both of us; in which case, I should still be as you found me, or dead of their rods and staves, and you still enjoying the hospitality and harping of that damosel Alyne. But this will be a more honorable death than the one you saved me from. But, even so, I'm in a fair way to die in ignorance of the cause of my stark madness."

Dinadan stood and turned and said gently, "Nay, Tris, I can enlighten you. If it will be of any comfort to you, my dear friend—and since you may not live to learn it from another—I will tell you what I heard of you before I left Camelot."

At the word *Camelot*, Sir Tristram struck a hand to his head.

"That love had smitted you suddenly to madness and driven you raving into the woods," Dinadan continued; and Tristram continued to stand like one stunned; and Dinadan went on, "Love, my poor friend! A bitter brew at the best—but hell's drink, in your case, and it scalded you to madness. For you loved a queen—Queen Isoud of Cornwall."

At that name, Sir Tristram uttered a stricken cry, then shouted: "To Camelot! To Camelot! To horse! To horse!" and he looked 'round about him wildly.

But the horses were not there, for they had gone on while the knights stood: but they were soon discovered, drinking at a well. At sight of that well, Dinadan gaped.

"This is it!" he cried. "'Twas here I first saw Alyne!"

Tristram cared nothing for that piece of information, but was for mounting and spurring blindly in quest of the fount of his madness. Dinadan was hard put to it to hold him and bring him to reason. They did not come to blows, but it was touch and go. Tristram came to his senses at last, thanks to the queasy prompting of his berry-lined stomach.

"You're right!" he gasped, clinging to Dinadan for support. "Your damosel must provision us. I see it now—for now I'm as sane as you are. Lead on now—to the buttery-hatch."

They had not far to go. A banner flapped on the only remaining tower of the ruinous castle.

"That's something new," said Dinadan.

The drawbridge was still down and its outer end still embedded in the bank, but the moat showed almost as much water as mud now and only fringes of the bushes and rank rushes that had clogged it. Wondering, Dinadan led across the bridge, and there saw yet more to wonder at: trimmed hedges, cleaned ditches, and mended walls.

"Kedge has been hard at work," he muttered.

Now Kedge himself appeared from behind a newly thatched byre, went back on his heels at the sight of them as if at a blow in the face, bestirred himself to a few heavy steps, halted again, and stood gaping like a zany.

"What the devil!" cried Sir Dinadan. "What ails you? Don't you know me?"

The squire moved his lips, but nothing came of it. Dinadan advanced, grabbed a handful of the front of the squire's tunic, and shook.

"It's me, dolt! What kind of knavish welcome is this? Speak up, friend Kedge—explain yourself—or I may lose my temper!"

Kedge managed a whisper then, though a cracked one.

"Not so loud, sir, I beg you! Very sudden, sir—an' unexpected. The damosel—the Dame Alyne—had a vision in a dream."

And there he stuck, looking the very picture of confusion and distress. But Dinadan's temper was up, so he spoke again without lowering his voice.

"What gibberish is this?—damosel, dame, Alyne? Does something ail her?—and the good dame too? 'Not so loud!' quoth you. Is someone dead? Or everyone, perchance? And yourself gone mad? Speak out, or I'll shake you out of your shirt—weak with starvation though I be!"

"Nay, sir, but hear me—for old sake's sake! She saw you dead in a vision—stark an' cold. And her other harping lover too. The one you went after to fetch back to her, mauger your head. Both stark an' bloody on the ground. She went mad."

"So she is mad," said Dinadan, in a flat voice; and he dropped his hand nervelessly from Kedge's chest.

"Nay, not now, sir," Kedge stammered. "I—ah!—that's to say, she—a good abbot happened along and—married her."

"An abbot married her? Are *you* mad too?"

"Nay, sir—to me."

Dinadan was silent, blinking at nothing in particular.

Then Sir Tristram, who had endured the conversation with obvious impatience, spoke for the first time since leaving the sylvan well.

"The devil take all that! To the buttery!"

The hungry knights did not visit the buttery, however. Instead, Kedge and two scullions brought victuals and drink of the best to them behind a haystack; and the chargers were well served too, and also out of view of any window of the castle.

Kedge apologized: "It is wiser, sirs, not to destroy her faith in her tragical vision, I think. That's to say, better let sleeping dogs lie."

"Dead dogs," amended Dinadan, with a cynical grimace.

The knights departed between sunset and moonrise, accompanied by a tinker who swore that he knew the shortest way to Camelot as well as he knew the shortest way to his mouth with a bottle, and a strong forest pony hung about with victuals and drink. They went a mile, in silence save for the prattle of their guide and the snorts of their refreshed and rebeaned chargers. Then Dinadan railed out upon women, and particularly against damosels and never mind the tinges of their tresses: red, yellow, brown, and black, they were all unworthy of trust; and as for loving one of them—never again!

"You know nothing about it, good Din," said Sir Tristram, loftily. "Only the lover of Queen Isoud knows the meaning of the word *love*."

"God defend me from that knowledge then, good Tris, since capering naked in the wilderness is the fruit of it," gibed Dinadan.

Tristram sighed and said, "Nay, a misunderstanding of some sort. It has slipped my mind: but when I see her again, it will be exclaimed and forgotten again."

Then the tinker exclaimed, "Lords, when I hear Your Lordships, I thank God that I'm but a poor tinker, with a wife in every hedge an' no worries save the leaks in other folks' pots an' cans!"

A Quarrel for a Lady

"Madam," said Sir Dinadan, "I marvel at Sir Tristram and more other lovers, what aileth them to be so mad and so sotted upon women."

"Why," said La Belle Isoud, "be ye a knight and no lover? It is shame to you! Wherefore ye may not be called a good knight but if ye make a quarrel for a lady."

"God defend me!" said Dinadan. "For the joy of love is short, and the sorrow thereof, and what cometh thereafter, dureth over long."

—Sir Thomas Malory

Sir Dinadan rode abroad on a sweet summer morn in a sour state of mind, accompanied only by young Bendybus.

"Sir," said the squire, after they had gone a league or more in a dreary silence.

"Sir to you?" returned the knight politely but without the slightest enthusiasm.

"May I speak my mind, sir?" asked the squire.

"That's as may be. Tell me first, how much do I owe you in back pay and in lost wagers all together to date?"

"Twenty gold sequins and seven silver crowns, sir, to a penny."

"So much? The devil! In that case, you may speak your mind, my lad."

"Gramercy. What I want to tell you, sir, is that you have no head for business."

"Quite! What would I do with it, if I had it—having no business either."

"You're wrong, sir. What's all this jousting and questing

and dragon-slaying but a business, if rightly considered? Other knights make a business of it, even if they don't advertise the fact. I know a dozen such, and most of them your inferiors in prowess, who had retired to live in idle luxury. And the top-notchers—Launcelot, Tristram, Lamorak de Galis, and so on—though too energetic to retire, have accumulated fortunes too vast to compute. But here *you* are, sir, without a second shirt—unless you count the one I am wearing—and only seven pennies in your pouch. Explain me that, sir."

Sir Dinadan shook his head, murmuring: "You tell me, Bendybus."

"Lack of business acumen," said the youth sternly.

"Go on, I'm listening," sighed the knight.

"Very good, sir. To begin with, you don't sell yourself to the ladies."

"Sell myself to the ladies! Fie on you!"

"Figuratively speaking, sir. You don't take them seriously enough."

"Never mind how I take them, my lad; they laugh at my jokes," retorted the knight, with a show of offended vanity.

"Not always," said the squire. "But often, I'll admit. But even so, what do they get you? Your jokes, I mean. A dinner."

"Do you suggest my charging a penny or so for every joke I crack at the festal board when dining or supping out?"

"I'll not put a price on your quips and jibes, sir, but I'll venture to point out that they sometimes cost you far more than they could possibly be worth to anyone as pearls of wit or wisdom. For instance, take the case of the widow whom you freed from the greed of a tyrannous brother-in-law about six weeks ago."

"I'll always remember it!" exclaimed the knight, brightening. "I'll never forget her nose."

"That's the point I'm coming to," said the squire.

"God defend you!" jibed Dinadan.

"Cut the comedy and listen to me, sir," begged Mr. Bendybus earnestly. "That was a neat job you did that day, and I was proud of you—until your cursed sense of so-called humor came into play. The lady was fairly melted and aquiver with honest gratitude: but it wasn't till the middle of dinner that I learned of her intention to reward you with the title-deeds of two of her seven fat manors, or I'd have warned you somehow. The damosel on my left told me all about it. The evening's festivities were to be crowned with the presentation. But what happened?"

"Nothing," muttered the knight, avoiding the other's reproachful glance. "No presentation of title-deeds, certainly."

"I know that. I'm asking what happened when that plum pudding was brought in. Everything was lovely till then. What did you whisper in her ear when she began to serve that pudding?"

"Nothing. A mild whimsicality suggested by—but forget it! Not one of my best, certainly. But you must admit that the pudding and the dame's nose appeared to have much in common. However, I'm not defending it. A small joke, at best."

"Small but expensive," retorted the squire. "The cost was exactly two manors of seven farms each. You need a muzzle!"

They rode a mile in silence. It was broken by the knight.

"I have considered your suggestion of a muzzle, my dear fellow, and it doesn't appeal to me. Surely you can think up something that would be becoming?"

"Yes, sir, I can—and more practical too," replied the squire, with animation. "A business manager! A true friend with your best interests at heart and possessed with keen business acumen, to advise and guide you in all your chivalrous exploits and subsequent dealings. With me as your manager, you would soon be lolling in the lap of luxury, sir."

"And you, my dear Bendy?"

"I'll do all right on my commission of fifty percent of gross receipts, sir. Or shall I say twenty-five percent, sir?"

"Say what you like, my boy. Don't bother me with your own problems: or what's a business manager for?"

"Quite right, Sir Dinadan. We'll say twenty-five percent. I trust that the advantages of employing a manager possessed of keen business acumen are now becoming apparent to you, sir."

"Yes indeed," agreed the knight. "Gramercy."

They soon rode in a leafy park, and traversed it and came to the edge of a fair meadow wherein humped a respectable castle; and there they drew rein and sat contemplating the peaceful scene. But not for long. A slight sound, half sob and half sniffle, caused them to turn their heads and bend their glances nearer to hand; and so they became aware of a young lady who stood in the sun-flecked shade of a nearby golden birch and regarded them with teary eyes. They saluted gracefully.

"You have been weeping," said Dinadan, commiserat-ingly. "What's your trouble, little one? A broken doll, per-chance?"

Mr. Bendybus whispered warningly from a corner of his mouth, "Don't try to be funny! She's as big as I am."

He exaggerated, though she was certainly too big to play with dolls. But she looked pleased and, after one more sniffle, dabbed her eyes and nose with a scrap of lace. She smiled luminously at the knight and murmured, "It is worse than that, gentle sir."

"D'ye tell me so?" he exclaimed. "I am but a poor knight of King Arthur's court, yclept Dinadan, but entirely at your service, sweet child, in any trouble from broken toys to broken vows and even to broken necks."

Bendybus cautioned again in an off-stage whisper: "Don't overdo that kid stuff!"

"You are sweet, Sir Dinadan—and I've heard wonderful things about you," murmured the lady. "And now I shall tell you why I wept." And straightway she told a tale of oppression, and with commendable brevity.

She was an earl's daughter and an orphan. This castle and these lands were hers by inheritance, but she was not yet in control of them nor even of herself, for she suffered the guardianship of a cruel old-fashioned uncle and would continue to suffer it until she married; but little good would a husband do her, for he was to be selected by her guardian. Her dearest wish was to go to King Arthur's court and there do what she could in the matrimonial line without regard to her uncle's wishes or prejudices—but this the cruel, stupid monster would not permit. And so she had wept and wept till she was a sight.

"A sight indeed—to gladden sad eyes," murmured Sir Dinadan.

Bendybus shot him a suspicious and apprehensive glance, but might have saved himself the trouble, for the knight added, in a matter-of-fact voice: "I shall discuss the matter with your uncle."

"You are wonderful!" cried the lady. "But not with that shield, I beg you, Sir Dinadan! Big as Sir Bash is, he is a coward; and should he recognize your shield—that of one of the seven best knights of the world—he would avoid the discussion. I will fetch you a less terrifying shield."

She started for the castle, moving swiftly but gracefully across the meadow. Her gown and the meadow were alike all green and gold. Knight and squire watched her all the way to the castle in silence, but with very different expressions on their faces. The latter's look was calculating, but the former's was dazed, or at least mazed.

"She's got me guessing," said Bendybus.

"Me too," said Dinadan.

"She's up to some game," opined the squire.

"Game?" protested the knight. "That dear innocent babe?"

Bendybus gave him a puzzled glance and said, "You don't seem quite your usual jibing self, sir—or are you trying to be funny?"

"I'm not aware of cause for fun in that charming damosel's distressful situation," reproved the knight.

Then he dismounted and loosed the girths of his saddle to ease his horse, and Bendybus followed his example. Anon the lady came back to them, drawing a shield after her lightly across the buttercups and golden-eyed daisies. It was a plain white shield unadorned by any blazoning and scatheless of bruise or scratch of combat. A virgin shield, devil a doubt of it!

The lady lifted it and gave it into Dinadan's hands; and simultaneously she gave into his eyes a smile so shy and yet a-gleam and a-flash that even the calculating young Bendybus experienced an unwonted twinge of heat in his veins.

Bendybus was first to speak. He asked where and when Sir Dinadan was to meet and deal with her uncle, and to what extent exactly—allowing for accidents, of course—the tyrannous guardian was to be dealt with. She made reply directly to the knight, without so much as the flick of an eye at the officious squire.

"I don't want him slain, or even sorely hurt. But he is

too sure of himself—of his importance in the scheme of things. He needs a taking down a peg or two. Given a hard tumble and a stark fright, he will be more amenable to reason in the future, I am sure. I shall go home now, if you will promise to follow as soon as you are ready."

"Your wish is my law," the knight assured her.

"Dear, dear Sir Dinny!" she cried softly. "Here is one of my best pair of gloves, to wear on your helmet." She handed him a glove of perfumed green leather. "And don't forget—just a tumble and a scare will serve my purpose. I'll be watching from a window, dear Dinny."

With that, she turned and glided away across the verdant grass and the golden buttercups and golden-eyed daisies.

"Did you hear that?" oozed the knight. "She called me Dinny."

"Snap out of it!" snapped the squire.

Half an hour later, Sir Dinadan and his clever but now somewhat puzzled Mr. Bendybus rode from the dappled shade of the park onto the shining meadow, and softly over the grass and buttercups to the moat bright with swans and waterlilies, and across the drawbridge to the shaven lawn which lay in front of the forecourt and the keep as smoothly as a carpet.

"Close your vizor, sir," cautioned Bendybus. "Should he espy your grand mustachios he might reasonably doubt the virginity of your shield and so refuse combat."

Dinadan shut his vizor.

"I hope that he may prove as easy as she made him sound," the squire added, dubiously.

Then a robustious bellow issued from a narrow window.

"Get out, you saucy knave! Go home—before you have to be carried on a stretcher!"

"Hah!" whispered Bendybus, and he signaled to Dinadan for silence.

Another bellow: "If I come down to you again, you pup, I'll split more than your shield!"

"Hah! I get it," whispered the squire. "So that's the game? A sly minx—as I might have guessed."

"What are you muttering about? And who's a sly minx?" asked Sir Dinadan.

Bendybus replied that, quite obviously, the lady was using one of the best knights of Christendom—Number Twenty-three by official rating, to be exact—to further an affair with a local lover who had evidently suffered a split shield already at Sir Bash's hands. Dinadan denied this, but with more vehemence than conviction.

"She isn't that kind of girl," he concluded.

Bendybus laughed cynically. For long minutes after that they sat their horses in a sulky silence. Anon Sir Bash issued from the courtyard. He was a formidable figure, tall enough and rather too wide—and much too thick—for either his own or his charger's comfort.

"Look!" whispered Bendybus. "No squire—he's that sure of the outcome."

He rode softly to Sir Bash, dismounted and saluted and asked politely if His Worship contemplated mortal combat.

"Tell the pup I'll spare his life again, but warn him he'll not get off as easily as he did before," sneered the knight of the castle.

Whereupon Mr. Bendybus saluted again, remounted, and returned to Dinadan.

"I advise you to watch your step, sir, for I suspect there's more to this than meets the eye," he said.

"Quite enough of it meets the eye to serve my purpose," Sir Dinadan replied, with a touch of his old imperious manner.

It was with more than a touch of his very best manner— a seemingly effortless and elegant precision—that he poked Sir Bash backward out of his saddle and over his horse's tail. The thick knight came to earth in a half-sitting posture, with such force as to sink his point of contact— "point" purely by courtesy—to a depth of several inches in the tender sward. And there he remained like a monument, bereft at once of both wind and wit, until a dozen dumbfounded varlets lugged and dragged him away and into the castle.

"How was that?" asked Dinadan, a little proudly but a little anxiously too.

"Perfect!" exclaimed Bendybus. "If he didn't get a fright, I'll eat a boot, and if he took a serious injury, I'll eat the other one. That's what she asked for, and now she has it. In short, sir, we delivered the goods."

"I trust so," murmured the knight. "I hope she is as pleased with the result as you are."

"Why wouldn't she be?" returned the squire. "It's what she ordered." And after a minute of considering silence he added with a peculiar smile, "She had better be."

Sir Dinadan raised his vizor to its full extent, thus uncovering his eyes and nose and mustachios, and asked, "What d'ye mean by that?"

"I mean, sir—speaking as your business manager— that if she fails to express her pleasure at your admirable performance in coin of the realm or other negotiable form within the hour, or by sunset at latest, I shall render our bill to her guardian uncle—with full particulars," replied Bendybus, coolly.

"No, no!" protested the knight. "That would never do! Don't you realize that whatever good my slight service may do the poor girl would be utterly undone should Sir Bash learn of the trick—that's to say, the innocent deception— we have played on him?"

"*We?*" jeered Bendybus. "Be yourself, sir! We were on the receiving end of that innocent deception too. She made just as much of a monkey of you and your knighthood as of Sir Bash and his, to be quite frank about it. But I'm not seriously concerned with the ethical aspect of your share in the trick, being but a humble squire myself, though I will say that for a knight of the Round Table to impersonate some—But let it pass! My point is, I mean to see that you are not double-crossed on top of being made a monkey of."

Before the bewildered, righteously indignant, conscience-stricken, reproachful, and besotted knight could even begin to express any of his confused and conflicting emotions, he was astonished out of them by a sudden and terrific change in the appearance and behavior of his companion. The plump face of Bendybus went ash-gray, then fire-red; the pale eyes popped and fixed in a stricken stare; lips thinned and stretched in a horrid grimace; wild words rasped forth; and a trembling fist was thrust under the knightly nose.

"Fool! Your vizor—wide open—your cursed mustachios in full view! The jig's up! Blast you for a moonstruck goat!"

Sir Dinadan was paralyzed with astonishment—but for no longer than ten or twelve seconds.

"Calm yourself," he said, clouting the other on the left side of the helmet with a mailed hand at the same moment.

Bendybus rocked in his saddle, blinking, and spat a little blood.

"See that!" he complained. "You made me bite my tongue."

"That may teach you to control it, and your temper too," returned the knight, not unkindly.

"Gramercy," mumbled the squire, but not as though he meant it; and after a final bitter glance at the front of the castle, and a silent curse on every narrow watchful window there, he turned his horse and rode slowly off.

Sir Dinadan followed. They returned to the place at the edge of the grove where they had first met the damosel in green but an hour ago. There they dismounted; and Bendybus gathered up the saddlebags, spare lances, and other gear that had been shed when they cleared for action, and Sir Dinadan's battle-marked true shield. These articles he distributed between the horses, doing all this in a sulky silence; the while Sir Dinadan moped upon a near-by mossy stump with both hands clasped to his head.

"Where to now?" asked Bendybus, grumpily. "We've still the price of a dinner of beer and bacon—unless your seven pennies are gone with your five wits," he added, in a much lower voice.

"Bide awhile," said the knight. "She is sure to send me a message of thanks."

"Thanks for what?" sneered the squire. "For letting the cat out of the bag by letting your mustachios out of your helmet in plain view of the windows? I'll wager she feels otherwise than grateful to you now, sir; for if her uncle hasn't already spanked her and sent her dinnerless to bed for tricking him into risking death from the spear of a professional jouster, he's not the person I think him."

"What are you saying?" cried the knight, rising from his mossy seat in perturbation. "Spank her? I'm going back— and if he has so much as laid a finger on her, I'll cut him to bits!"

He ran to his charger and mounted between the untidy bulks of luggage and equipment at saddlebow and cantle, drew his two-handed sword, and, flourishing it high in one hand, headed fast for the castle.

"Stop, stop!" implored Bendybus: "Would you stick your addled head into the lion's mouth?"

"Ay, and knock out his teeth!" shouted the besotted knight, without a backward glance.

There was nothing for Bendybus to do, in either the capacity of squire or of business manager, but to mount and follow. He rode hard but not far, for an urgent figure issued from the castle and came running across the draw-bridge with upflung arms and flying white whiskers and inarticulate cries, causing the knight to pull up just this side of the bridge to avoid a collision and himself to draw rein to spare the knight a rear-end bump. The old man louted low at Dinadan's right stirrup, and even clung to it while gasping for breath.

"Worshipful Sir Knight—Sir Bash's compliments—and will Your Honor condescend to attend him in his chamber—with his humble apologies—as he does not feel quite equal—nothing serious—to the effort of coming out and—paying his respects to Your Worship on Your Honor's own ground—so to speak," he gasped.

"Take your time, my friend," said Dinadan kindly. "If you mean that Sir Bash requests a word with me, right-o! I was on my way to a word with him anyhow."

"Not so fast!" exclaimed Bendybus, urging his horse forward and glaring down suspiciously at the old man. Then, leveling his glare at the knight, he rasped, "Would you be made a monkey of—and a dead monkey this time!—twice in the same day? Are you so utterly sotted and bewitched that you can't see the foul truth of this request—the cloak over your head and the daggers in your back the moment you cross that threshold? If so, God defend you for the sorriest fool in Christendom!—and the deadest, Sir Dinadan of the Round Table—when they throw your corpse to the eels in the moat!"

"Sir Dinadan?" cried the messenger. "D'ye mean *the* Sir Dinadan, young sir?"

"There's but the one, to the best of my knowledge and belief—and thank God for that!" replied the squire, return-ing his glare to the ancient major-domo, or whatever he was. "But what's to caper and smirk about, you old loon?"

The messenger told them. Believing that he had been unhorsed by the same insolent local clodhopper whose

shield he had split and whose life he had so contemptuously spared only a week before, Sir Bash's emotions had
hurt him a thousand times more than had his bruised but-
tocks. He had wept with shame, then all but strangled with
anger; and in the madness of his rage and humiliation he
had cursed the Damosel Clara and sworn, by his halidom
and God's wounds, to destroy her heritage and then
himself. But his ravings had ceased when a watcher at a
window had come running with the word that the cavalier
of the virgin shield had opened his vizor and disclosed the
beetling brows and eagle nose and great mustachios of a
veteran professional battler. That word had healed Sir
Bash's lacerated vanity like magic; and so he had sent his
oldest and trustiest servant to beg the honor of the knight's
and his squire's company to dinner.

"And if the knowledge that his opponent was an adult
and experienced jouster rather than a rustic hobbledehoy
means so much to him, imagine the added salve to his feelings to learn that he was unseated by the spear of the
incomparable Sir Dinadan," concluded the old man.

"You flatter me, good friend," murmured the knight.
"But I warn you that all my concern is still for the young
lady's situation, despite the somewhat invidious position
in which her lack of frankness—quite unintentional, I'm
sure—has placed me as an advocate and observer of the
nicest shades of chivalrous behavior."

The major-domo looked apologetic and bewildered.

"Permit me, sir, or we're like to starve to death in our
saddles," said Bendybus to the knight. Then, addressing
the ancient, he said, "In other words, Sir Dinadan is still
so sotted on your Damosel Clara, despite the scurvy trick
she played on him, that he is as indifferent to Sir Bash's
state of mind as to his own material interests."

"Trick?" queried the major-domo, still bewildered.
"What trick, young sir?"

"The same trick that brought her uncle's curses upon
her, old dolt! She didn't mention her lover to us. Oh, no,
she is far too sly for that! For though the use of a bare
shield to bring a bully to book may be excused, for a knight
of the Round Table to impersonate a particular and known
duffer, for whatever purpose, is quite something else
again."

"Hah, I see it now! Lady Clara is a clever puss. How Sir Bash will laugh when I tell him!"

"Laugh! Then why did he curse and threaten her?"

"Oh, young sir, that was while he still believed he had been grounded by the local lout. It wasn't the trick that frenzied him, it was the humiliation."

And now Bendybus was nonplused.

"I give it up, sir," he said to the knight. "Simpletons, evidently—with the exception of that Clara. I doubt that Sir Bash has the wit for treachery even if he has the will. I think we had better risk it, sir. I am decidedly peckish."

"Lead on, friend," said Dinadan to the major-domo; and he sheathed his great sword.

It was a notable dinner. Sir Bash insisted on sitting up to it, with a swan's-down pillow in the seat of his chair and another at his back. Sir Dinadan was on his right and the damosel and Bendybus were on his left. Sir Bash proved himself a simple soul in truth, and a jovial one to boot.

"A great day for me!" he cried, over and over. "To run a course with a knight of the Round Table—to be grassed by Sir Dinadan—a memorable day indeed!"

For a time, the guest of honor contented himself with murmured modest disclaimers in reply, but after a second horn of mead and a second helping of pigeon pie, his eyes brightened and his funny-bone tickled.

"A red-letter day for me too," he said. "And a lucky day. For look you, Sir Bash, what is the difference between grassing a knightly opponent and being grassed by him but a matter of luck? A trick of chance! A mere matter of inches and seconds. Had your spear been straighter by six inches, or ten at most, and a few seconds faster, then it would have been as straight and soon as mine. And in that case, which of us would have taken to the air, think you? The lighter man, depend upon it! To wit, yours truly; and right now the pillow of swan's-down would be under me instead of you."

Sir Bash goggled. He shook his head and scratched it.

"D'ye say so?" he cried. "You amaze me! As close as that? I can't—if you'll forgive my presumption—quite believe it."

"But a matter of inches and seconds, dear Bash, I assure you," returned Dinadan, gravely.

Bendybus, who had been fairly stretching his ears so as not to miss a word, now smiled complacently and murmured, "He is on the road to recovery, I do believe."

The damosel glanced at Bendybus obliquely—but dear heaven, with what eyes!—and whispered: "He suffered nothing that a little arnica won't cure."

"I referred to Sir Dinadan," mumbled the squire, trying to avoid that glance.

"But what has *he* to recover from?"

"Never mind that. But I wish your uncle had a window in him, or was transparent."

"How absurd! But why?"

"That I might see Sir Dinadan—if his left eyebrow is cocked an inch higher than the right."

"I'll look," she said; and she leaned far forward—halfway across the table, in fact—and peered around Sir Bash's bulk.

Upon recovering her seat and conventional pose, she whispered, "It's cocked, but not that high."

"Gramercy," returned Bendybus. "At this rate he'll soon be his old self again with the possessor of every requirement for success except business acumen."

"What is business acumen?" she asked; but while he told her at considerable length and with appropriate gestures, she made better use of her eyes than of her ears.

Sir Dinadan, in the meantime, had talked Sir Bash into two minds, or maybe three, concerning the identity of the victor in their recent tilt; and now the fat knight all but ignored trencher and horn, at one moment congratulating his guest and at the next himself and so on, around and around. The hours wore on, and dinner-time wore thin and extended to supper-time without either knight leaving his seat; but when the first course of supper was served, Sir Bash was sound asleep and gloriously adream. Ever and anon a snort, a puff, or a grunt issued from his nose or lips or chest. Ah, what dreams! At unhorsing Sir Guy, he snorted; upon pushing Sir Palomides overboard, he puffed—and no wonder!; and the splintering of a spear on Sir Launcelot's shield fetched up a grunt from the very depths of his being. And so, face down on table and stern on swan's-down, he astonished King Arthur and was elected to a seat at the Round Table: the while Sir Dinadan continued to ply fingers and spoon and horn, for in truth he had been on a low diet of late. . . .

On three mornings in succession, Sir Dinadan bid his squire see to the saddling of their horses, but without any apparent result. On the fourth morning, he said, "We really must be off today, my boy."

"I don't agree with you, sir," replied Bendybus. "As your business manager, I advise against it strongly. I have to consider your fee, sir—not to mention my commission. Had you not spilled Sir Bash under false pretenses, it would be easy enough to collect the price of a cart-horse and an outsized and outmoded suit of armor. But, under the circumstances, the sum involved is for services rendered, and therefore debatable; and I have the niece, not the uncle, to deal with. It can't be done hastily, but I'm already working on it; and if we are smart, sir, we'll collect what we can by the way of our teeth and gullets in the interim, just in case."

A few hours later, Sir Dinadan and his host played at chess together. It was soon apparent that Sir Bash had something besides the game on his mind, for his moves were even stupider than usual.

"What ails you?" asked Dinadan.

"I'm worried," said the fat knight, leaning back in his chair and emitting a windy sigh terminating in a hiccup.

"Indigestion," suggested the thin knight.

Sir Bash shook his great head and mumbled, "No, no, it's Clara."

Dinadan cocked an eyebrow, narrowed the other eye, and twitched both ears, but said nothing.

Bash added, "I'll have no peace till she's married."

Again Dinadan said nothing. Bash leaned forward, overturning chessmen with his bulges, whereupon the knight of the Round Table sat back, fearing another sigh.

"Happily married—safely and suitably, that's to say," continued Bash, earnestly if a trifle gustily. "To a husband of my choice, in short. And now I have chosen. And you are it. Speak up, my friend—my worshipful Round Tabler—and bring me peace."

"But—but—my dear Bash—what about her—the lady's—ah!—peace and happiness?" stammered Dinadan, with a red face.

"She'll jump at you, my dear Din—and has done so already, or I miss my guess."

"But I'm in no position to make such a proposal—to so much as dream of such bliss. Ah, Bashy, I'm as poor as a miser's mouse—all due to my lack of business acumen and my too-sensitive funnybone, so Bendybus tells me."

"Bah and faugh to your poverty!" cried Sir Bash. "Clara has enough for both of you, my dear Din—ay, and for a dozen of you, if it comes to that—or will have when she marries you. And the sooner the better, for my peace of mind. Tell her today and we can have the wedding next week."

Sir Dinadan the Jiber rose slowly from his chair and moved about the chamber like a sleepwalker. And soon he talked like a sleeptalker.

"Tomorrow—the natal day of my patron saint. Tomorrow I will lay my heart at her feet. Nay, it is already there! Tomorrow I shall pick it up and give it into her hands. . . ."

The two knights were halfway through breakfast next morning, and Sir Bash was just beginning to wonder what was detaining Clara and young Bendybus—Sir Dinadan was still in too much of a daze and maze to be aware of even his lady's absence—when the ancient major-domo handed a sealed letter to his master, and Sir Bash broke the seals. Ten minutes later—for he had to spell the words over and over, being as slow of wit as of eye—he uttered a spluttered bellow and thrust the parchment under, and all but against, Sir Dinadan's high nose. The sotted knight could not choose but to read.

"Revered Uncle I herewith inform You that My Bendy and Self are now One thanks to ye Venerable Hermit of Creepy Hollow and now well upon the Road to Camelot. I brought away my Dear departed Mama's trinkets in 3 saddlebags and a pouch including Dymonds and Emeralds and Grandmama's Stummicker of Rubies and as My Bendy has a wonderful Head for Business You need not worry on My behalf. Tell Dear Dinny with a kiss I'm sure he will soon be quite his Old Self again.

Ever y'r Loving Obedient
—Clara."

Sir Dinadan blinked. For a minute, nothing but his eyes showed any sign of life. Then he stood up, but only to sit down again and continue to blink. The he laid hold suddenly of a great horn of ale on the board before him, raised it to his lips, drained it, and set it down lightly.

"Quite," he said; and his left eyebrow went up a full inch. "Gramercy, little one."

SIR DINADAN AND THE GIANT TAULURD

So this earl made his complaint that there was a giant hight Taulurd by him that destroyed all his lands, and how he durst nowhere ride nor go for him. "Sir," said the knight, "Whether useth he to fight, on horseback or on foot?" "Nay," said the earl, "there be no horse able to carry him." "Then will I fight him on foot," said the knight.

—Sir Thomas Malory

After supper, the hostess demanded of Sir Dinadan a song of love, and all the other ladies supported her; and so Sir Dinadan being the only gentleman present, the demand was unanimous.

"Fie upon Your Grace!" he cried, knitting his brows and flashing his eyes in mock distress. "A song of love, quoth-a! Nay, God forgive you—and defend *me*! For well you know my opinions on that subject. Ask me for a song of hate—of murder or battle—or of the hunting of wolves, wild pigs, dragons, or giants—of anything betwixt heaven and hell, except love!"

The hostess, who was an elderly dowager duchess, laughed unrestrainedly, as did the other ladies, with the sole exception of the only young one present.

"Hah, madam, you are cruel!" Dinadan railed on. "You bid me to sup, and now you command me to sing of love—to sing for my supper, like poor little Dan Tucker. And of love, of all things! Nay, Duchess, your hospitality deserves a better return than any song I could make on that obnoxious subject."

At this, even the youngest guest laughed, though

uncertainly; and the hostess, with tears of mirth hopping on her fat cheeks, cried: "Sing what you will, naughty boy—only sing!"

The knight's air, attitude, and facial expression changed as quick as winking, and all for the better, and he said, "Gramercy, ma'am" to the Duchess as if he really meant it. He shifted his chair a little away from the table and brought his lute, which was slung behind him by a broad ribbon about his neck, around to his front; and he said mildly: "Nay, Duchess, of what *you* will!" And, with a poetical, faraway and yet introspective look in his eyes, he touched his fingers to the strings. And so he played, now slow, now fast, now high, now low—but soon a melody took shape.

"Of love," he said, and twitched and peaked a cynical eyebrow.

Then he sang. He sang of love and lovers, in general and in particular. He sang of famous love affairs of the past, naming the great lovers by name. It was beautiful and heart-melting; and faded lips trembled, and faded eyes shone and misted, and tears ran on cheeks both fat and thin. Even the bright lips and eyes of the youngest lady trembled and misted slightly. Then he sang of notable, and even notorious, affairs of the day, but without naming the lovers concerned therein; and this too—the words and the music alike—enchanted ears and hearts. The applause was generous. When it subsided, Dinadan stood up and bowed to right and left.

"I am honored by your approval of my pretty song," he said. "I could sing more, but to a less honeyed tune—of the bitter and salty fruits of love—lovers mad and naked in the wilderness, thirsty in the desert, crippled in hidden places, and dead and bloody on the ground; maddened, exiled, crippled, and slain in the name of love, to feed the vanity of women. But you would not like it."

Now his face was grim. He turned to the hostess, at whose right hand he had sat, and said: "I thank you for the noble cheer and graciousness, ma'am. And now I must beg to be excused, for I must be up and about full early tomorrow."

He did not explain that if he failed to raise the wind, to the tune of five hundred silver crowns, by noon of the next day, his best suit of armor, and his spare horse, and the best of his wardrobe even to the gorgeous garments in which he stood, would be seized by a certain flinty infidel who held a chattle-mortgage on the lot: but the good Duchess more than suspected the truth, for young Sir Dinadan's haphazard economy was a subject of comment in the best and even the not-so-good circles of society. Now the dowager hostess extended a plump hand, which the cavalier took lightly in his lean and hard sword-and-lute hand, and bowing low, saluted with his lips. He straightened his back then, but instead of retiring, he stood and widened his eyes at something in the palm of his hand.

"Nay, madam, you know better," he murmured, with a sigh that was almost a moan.

"A trifle!" she protested. "A mere nothing between good friends."

He said, with a sad smile: "Ay, a mere nothing worth a king's ransom. Nay, dear lady, it cannot be. Had I saved your life or honor with spear and sword, shed and lost blood for you, it would be another matter. For that sort of thing—knight-errantry—is my profession. But all this play of wit and this raillery against love to make you laugh, and then these songs of love and lovers to wring your heart, are as purely social and noncommercial as Your Grace's delightful suppers. For deeds of arms I take my fees—when I can get them, that's to say—like any honest laborer his wages, but I guard my amateur standing as a poet right jealously."

So saying, he gave the great diamond back to the Duchess, bowed again, and retired from the hall.

"The dratted young fool!" muttered the Duchess, returning the ring to a plump finger.

The young damosel who sat at the hostess's left hand, asked gravely: "What ails the poor man?" And she added, before the other could speak again: "Not modesty, that's obvious."

The Duchess dabbed at her wet eyes with tips of bejeweled fingers and sighed. "Nothing ails the poor boy that a wise and witty wife—and rich, of course—couldn't cure."

"Then why isn't he married? He seems personable enough, despite his self-conceit and his scurvy condemnation of the fruits of love. Can't he find a personable damosel or she him—witty and wise and rich enough to marry and mend him?"

"A damosel! Pah an' bah! That's the poor foolish young man's trouble: damosels. A murrain on them!—present company excepted, of course. They are what ails him—the hussies! As faithless as witless, the chits have befuddled and befooled him till he—well, my dear, you have heard with your own ears what he thinks of the fruits of romantic love. They lack the brains and experience for wit and wisdom and understanding sympathy with a poet's mind and heart. So, in their feckless, shallow, selfish vanity they have made a railing cynic of him. Yet he can still—at my request—sing gloriously of love and lovers, as you but now heard him do. At my request, ah me! And if he spoke villainously of lovers mad and athirst and crippled and dead, it was not his true self speaking. Properly handled—fondly guided and guarded and appreciated by someone of equal wit and superior worldly experience—he would soon be cured of his cynicism."

So that's it—you fat old goose! thought the girl, veiling her eyes. And she murmured: "I see what you mean, Duchess."

Now back to Sir Dinadan: because he was too proud, or too shy, to make the embarrassed state of his exchequer known to any of his knightly friends, and (as we have seen) too proud—or maybe too cautious—to accept gifts from ladies, the chattle-mortgage on his best suit of armor and spare charger and the pick of his wardrobe was foreclosed at high noon.

"Always at Your Worship's service," said the money-lender, rubbing his hands together at the conclusion of the business. "Always ready to accommodate you, Sir Dinadan, and at the same infinitesimal charge in the future as in the past, though I starve and my children go in rags. Good fortune to Your Worship now, and power to your elbow. Call again soon."

"God forbid!" muttered Dinadan.

He dined dismally at his inn; then, with the assistance of the kindly taverner, got himself buckled and latched and laced into such articles of plate and chain body-armor as remained to him. The ensemble was complete, although some of the items were dented, and all were tarnished. Now he had only one horse, but it was the best he had ever owned and as good as any knight's best—the great Garry. And his arms were of the best, and so were the big charger's accouterments. But he and Garry were so hung about with gear, which included two spare lances, that they cut a conspicuous figure. So he rode forth by a back way and sought the hills behind the town by mean alleys and obscure lanes. Even so, he did not win through unobserved. Dogs barked and a donkey brayed; raggedy folk of various ages disappeared before him into low doorways of hovels and peered after him from windows that were no more than holes. A lad in green finery appeared suddenly from behind a hedge, stood staring for a moment, then turned and darted back out of sight.

"Hah, a page!" said Dinadan. "Silks and velvet, and a gemmy gold brooch in his cap! What devilment is he up to here?"

He soon won clear of the last poor hovel and was within the toss of a pint pot of the shade of a hanging wood.

"A little faster now, good Garry," he urged; and the burdened charger lurched into a trot that set all their gear to jouncing and clanging.

They were within a spear's-length of the wood when the dappled shade directly in front stirred softly and emitted a lady all in white and silver atop a white jennet; and that was not all, for a lad in green finery and with a gemmy brooch in his cap was at the lady's stirrup. Dinadan pulled Garry to a jolty stop.

"The same page!" he muttered. "Premeditated! What's the meaning of it? Who's spying on me?"

A suspicion of the hospitable dowager duchess flickered in his mind but was instantly dismissed, for the lady on the jennet bore not the slightest resemblance in either shape or carriage to that generous and sprightly grandmamma. Now she rode forward and stopped close and brushed aside the little veil which fluttered from the front of her high, pointed cap. And she smiled and frowned with the one look—a thing he had never seen done before.

"At your service, damosel," he said, but uncertainly, and glanced aside.

"Gramercy, sir! But do you mean it?"

"If you are threatened in person, honor, or estate—in dire peril of any kind, my sword and spear are at your service."

"You would say the same to any damosel."

"Damosel or dame—or wench or poor woman in need of protection—or any overmatched knight, or churl too, for that matter—according to the vows of knighthood."

"But you don't know me."

"Nay, you sat at our hostess's left last night at supper."

"Ah!" she sighed; and now she smiled without frowning.

She veiled her eyes with fluttering lashes and murmured: "I am but an ignorant country girl, and the ways of royal courts, and of mighty champions as well as of great poets, are all new to me, but I must venture now to beg a perilous service of you."

"Name it," he cried impulsively.

She said: "I would not do so if you had not spoken last night of hunting giants and dragons."

He interrupted: "Nay, I spoke only of singing of hunting them. In truth, I've never so much as set eyes on either a dragon or a giant. Nay, I do not claim to rival Saint George or Jack the giant-killer: but I will undertake anything once, and mayhap twice at a pinch, within the rules of chivalry— and the pinch is upon me now."

The damosel gazed upward from her low jennet at the knight on his tall horse, inclining toward him and making play with her eyes; and he met that play as well as he could, but with more of a goggle than a gaze.

"It is a giant," she whispered.

He continued to goggle in silence, stricken with the realization that her eyes were the most disrupting and altogether wonderful of his experience, and that—God defend him!—the rest of her was a match for them. Now those eyes filled with tears, and she bowed her head.

"But never mind," she sighed.

He made a sudden partial recovery of his wits and cried: "What's that?"

"I said it's a giant," she murmured.

"Hah, a giant!"

"Eight feet high—and wide and thick. But never mind him. He devastates my father's lands—oh, the cruel monster!

But it is too much to ask of any young knight. Forget it—
and my thoughtlessness—and go your way in peace."

She made as if to turn her jennet aside, but was stayed
by his cry of protest.

"Not so fast! Where is he? I'll have a good go at him,
mauger my head!"

At that, she put a hand to her eyes and wept.

"What now?" he asked, his voice thick and soft.

"Nay—I'm afraid—for you," she sobbed.

Then Sir Dinadan swore by his halidom that he would
chop that giant down even if he stood as high and thick as
a watchtower.

At that, the damosel's tears ceased as suddenly as an
April shower, and she cried "Gramercy!" brightly, and
turned her head and spoke to the page in green.

The page skipped back into the wood, to reappear in a
minute mounted on a country cob and followed by a stout
woman on another cob, and a groom leading a large horse
loaded with bags and bundles and hampers. Then the page
went ahead, with the groom and pack-horse next, and then
the woman. The damosel and the knight brought up the
rear. Thus they skirted the edge of the hanging forest for a
short distance, and then turned up into it.

"You were all ready for the journey, Damosel,"
remarked Dinadan.

"Please call me Agnes," she said, with a shoot of an eye.
"My mother eloped with my father on Saint Agnes' Eve, and
so I was named for that saint."

"Agnes," he murmured. "A lovely name. And you call
me Dinadan."

"Nay, not that mouthful!" she protested. "I'll call you
Din—or, better still, Dinny."

He shuddered; for the very first girl who had made a
monkey of him had called him that. Dinny! He shuddered
again, and was about to suggested "Danny," when he realized that it too had humiliating and therefore unhappy
associations. So he smiled as well as he could and said
nothing. But he thought: I must be careful now. No one of
them is to be trusted with a man's heart—not even the
most beautiful in Christendom, as Agnes surely is. Ah,
Agnes—as good as beautiful, I'll swear! But I must be
thrice careful now, for to take a wound from her would be

mortal. But his only utterance was a profound sigh; and at that she shot him with both eyes.

"What ails you, Dinny Boy?" she asked softly.

That was better, for it was what his kind parents had called him in the carefree days of childhood; so he answered cheerfully: "Nothing." And she, thinking of the old Duchess's words to the effect that nothing ailed him that a wise and witty wife could not cure, smiled innocently with her lips and enigmatically with her eyes, but tenderly withal. They spoke little after that in the next hour, but all the while kept as closely side-by-side as the trees and bushes and the hazards underfoot permitted. So, perforce, they went slowly and joltily.

At last Dinadan exclaimed: "You would have come away without me!"

(A sharper stumble on Garry's part than usual had jolted the thought into words.)

"Why do you say that?" she asked, with a quick look.

"You were all ready for the road," he said.

She laughed: "D'ye call this a road, Dinny Boy?"

"Nay, nor even a track for wild swine," he answered. "And since you mention it, I'll make so bold as to say that I doubt that gay springal's ability to lead the way. But road or track, you were all ready to take it without me."

She glanced aside and said: "Don't worry, Dinny Boy. Victor is very clever in the woods, and out of them too; and he has a map of the way home, which we made together last night."

"Victor? Do you mean that jackanapes in green?"

She averted her face and smiled; and eyes and lips were in agreement this time; and neither was enigmatic or innocent, but both were complacent. But that smile meant nothing to Dinadan, for he couldn't see it; and when she looked at him again, it was with an expression of childish hurt. Her lower lip trembled, and her eyes were dim.

"Why do you miscall him so? He is an honorable page—and will be a squire when he's old enough—and maybe as good as knight as you, some day."

"That's not much to ask of him," sneered Dinadan.

"I don't ask more of him—of my dear little brother," she sighed. "Unless it be a kinder heart than yours," she added, even more faintly.

Dinadan's lips uncurled, and he actually gaped; and he blushed from scalp to chin and ear to ear, angered and confused for his unwarranted jealousy, and even more so for his uncouth display of it: for was he not a man of the world and a cynic to boot? So he hung his head and muttered: "Nay, I'm the fool of the world!" And now the damosel smiled complacently again, and this time without averting her face.

Before sunset they halted beside a brook and there Dinadan, Victor, the groom, and the woman made camp while Agnes, seated on a moss-cushioned stump, looked on. They unloaded, unsaddled, unbitted and baited the horses; and then young Victor helped the knight get out of his armor, and the woman and the groom pitched a little tent of silk. Dinadan noticed that the servants had to shift the tent here and there several times before it was to the damosel's liking.

"Agnes is hard to suit," said Victor.

"Hah," said Dinadan noncommittally.

"And she has her own way in everything."

"D'ye tell me so?"

"And she always thinks she knows best. Take yourself, for instance, sir."

"Myself? For instance of what?"

"Of her conceit of her own opinion, and her self-will. This giant business could have been handled without her butting into it. There was no need of coming to Camelot to find a knight to give battle to that giant. I could name at least three nearer home by twenty leagues who would be fools enough—no offense intended, sir!—to take him on if she asked them to. But not Sis! Not for Agnes! She must travel thirty leagues and more, and then back again, to fetch a champion."

"Just so. But not so fast, if you please. You spoke but now of *fools* who would do battle with that giant. What d'ye mean by that?"

"Just that, sir. Nobody but a fool would meet him in single combat. He can cut clean through a ten-ton haystack with one stroke."

"A stark stroke indeed," said the knight thoughtfully. "But why single combat? Since he is a cruel monster who devastates your father's lands, why has he not been attacked in force and destroyed like any other mad beast?"

"Nay, sir, this grisly Taulurd is no fool. Not fool enough to stand against odds or be ambushed by archers, at least. He retreats to the highest mountains, where only goats could find him, at the first sign of a gathering against him, and then comes down at night—but never twice in the same place in the one month—and knocks over a few farmsteads and carries off cheeses and hams and new-baked loaves and kegs of mead and ale. But he must be slightly mad too, for he leaves letters behind him in which he challenges the knightage of Christendom to meet him in fair single combat under the rules of chivalry and fight him to the death. But the challenge is for gentlemen only, for he claims to be one himself."

"What, a giant a gentleman? I never heard of such a thing!"

"Well, sir, if his claim be true, you shall not be dishonored by being cut in two by a churl."

"Gramercy!" said Dinadan dryly.

Then the damosel called them to supper. All supped well, though Sir Dinadan could not put the giant Taulurd from his thoughts until after his third horn of ale. Then he felt so much easier in his mind—to say nothing of his stomach—that at the damosel's request he played and sang three old songs and a new one; and the last one was the best of the four, and of love.

The Damosel Agnes and her nurse occupied the tent, and Dinadan, Victor, and the groom slept in their cloaks on moss and fern. They were early astir next morning, and Victor helped the knight into his hardware even as he had helped him out of it the night before, without being asked to. And while he latched and tied and buckled, he talked; and most of his talk consisted of questions, for he possessed an active and curious mind, and was just fourteen years of age.

"D'ye know Sir Launcelot du Lake, sir?"

"I have that honor."

"Did you ever fight him?"

"Nay, God forbid!"

"Why, could he beat you?"

"Ay, horsed or afoot—me or any other knight in the world."

"How big is he, then?"

"How big? Why, no bigger than myself."

"Did he ever kill a giant?"

"There's a song that says he killed the giant Brian Kelly in Ireland years ago, in an all-day combat, and all but died himself of the wounds he took in it."

"How big was that giant?"

"The song calls him as big as Goliath of Gath."

"And 'twas almost more than the world's champion could do to master *him* in a day-long fight! And yet *you*—not one of the world's best, by your own saying—would give battle single-handed to giant Taulurd. You're mad, sir!"

"Ah—not at all."

"Sir, harky to me! I say this because I like you. If you are not mad, or at least bewitched, you're a fool! I say this for your own good, sir. Agnes went to Camelot to find a champion able enough to rid us of Taulurd in single combat, regardless of expense up to a half of all our father's earthly possessions, which are considerable. And what happened? Did she get Sir Launcelot? No, nor even asked him. Or Sir Lamorak, Sir Ector de Maris, Sir Bors, Sir Percival, Sir Tristram of Liones, or Sir Palamides the Saracen? No, nor addressed herself to any one of those champions, but came away with you, willy-nilly. You both must be mad! But it's you who'll die of it, sir."

"But why?" Dinadan murmured uncertainly.

"Because Taulurd's too big for you."

"Nay, why did she pick on me?"

"For no reason. For a whim. She's full of whims, and has always been allowed to indulge them. If I were you, I'd turn aside and go my way right now, while she's still in the tent. I say this for your own sake, sir, because I like you."

"Gramercy. But she has my knightly word for it. I swore by my halidom to have ado with that giant."

"God defend you! But never say I didn't warn you."

At that moment, the damosel emerged from the tent. She was all in green and silver this morning, and her cheeks were roses, her brows a lily and her eyes beyond any poet's power of description; and she smiled and waved a hand.

"I'm not dead yet!" muttered Dinadan; and he smiled and waved in return.

But the lad Victor swore hotly, though not loudly.

So, after breakfast, they rode again, with Victor leading, and Agnes and the knight bringing up the rear, all as before. The way was still rough and tangled; and Dinadan felt an uneasy suspicion that Victor might be up to some trickery. But not for long. He encountered Agnes' upward gaze a few times, holding it longer each successive time, and soon forgot all else. So they stumbled through thick and thin till close upon noon. Then Victor called a halt and came bursting back to Dinadan.

"There's a big knight on a big horse hovering in a glade just ahead!" he cried.

"Hah!" exclaimed Dinadan, straightening in his saddle. "Does he want to fight?"

"What else would he want, sir?—pacing up and down, spear in hand."

"Good! I'll be ready in a minute. Does he want it with sharp spears or blunted? I have one of each."

Then the damosel laughed like tinkling bells.

"Oh, no, Dinny Boy," she said. "You are on your way to slay a giant for me."

"One thing at a time," he said, beginning to clear for action by casting off the bulkiest item—a great sack of oats—of the goods and gear which cumbered his saddle before and behind and on both sides.

Victor told him that the hovering knight carried a blunted spear and a covered shield, and straightway fell to helping him clear for action. The damosel crowded in on her jennet.

"Dinny Boy, this stranger is no concern of yours now, for you have given me your knightly oath to rid me of that giant!" she protested, shooting both eyes.

"True, dear Agnes," he replied. "But by my vows of knighthood, I am pledged to meet every challenger to chivalrous combat."

So he rode forth into the forest glade, and the boy rode at his left stirrup; and the groom with the great packhorse, and the nurse on her cob, and the damosel on her palfrey still protesting and upon the brink of tears, all followed.

At sight of them, the strange knight bawled: "You can't pass here! I keep this way against all comers."

"That's to be demonstrated," replied Dinadan, and he laid his blunted spear and dressed his shield before him.

"Defend yourself!" roared the other, and came at him at full speed.

"Don't hurt him!" screamed Agnes.

Now the great Garry was under way and running hard and straight; and now a clanging thud shook the air, and the damosel covered her eyes with a trembling hand.

"Ho-ho!" exulted the groom.

The damosel ventured to peep between her fingers, then cried, "Glory be to God!" For the knight flat on the greensward was not Dinadan, nor was the charger seated on its tail like a dog her champion's.

Dinadan helped the unhorsed knight to his feet, and Victor did the same for the unknighted horse.

"'Tis ever thus," said the knight. "This is my fiftieth tumble on this same ground. I always depart the saddle at the moment of contact, though with the firmest intention— but no longer a faintest hope—of remaining fixed. The fact is, the knack of keeping my seat is a phase of the art of chivalrous combat that I have never mastered."

"I wonder, sir, that you persist in this adventure," said Dinadan politely.

"Nay, to challenge and dispute the passage of this glade is a family tradition, and I swore to my father on his deathbed to maintain it."

"Then I wonder, sir, that you don't dispute it afoot, and with swords instead of spears."

"That may not be, alas! Because my sire, and his, and his too, were all superior jousters, but not so good on their feet, the sacred tradition demands horses and lances. But never mind that now: it is time for relaxation and refreshment."

So this good though frustrated traditionalist, hight Sir Joram, entertained the travelers with the best of victuals and drink in a fair pavilion, and then bought his forfeited horse and arms back from Sir Dinadan at a generous price of his own naming. So the travelers departed and went their way in the same order as they had come, save for young Victor's frequent halts and backward casts to goggle and smile admiringly at Sir Dinadan. And Agnes too regarded the knight with a new look as well as the old ones.

"You are wonderful, Dinny Boy," she told him.

"How so?" he asked, modestly.

"A wonderful poet, of course—I knew that. But the way you knocked that big Sir Joram off his horse was simply too wonderful!"

"Were you surprised?"

"Yes, I was. I was shaking with fear for you, and hid my eyes; and then I looked and saw him flat on his back. Oh, yes, I was almost as surprised as thankful to see that great big Sir Joram on the ground and you still jinking in the saddle, Dinny Boy."

"Nay, not so big," he protested; and he would have continued and asked why she looked to him to rid her of a giant if she had doubted his ability to deal with a chance-come knight-errant, had not the question faded from his mind before the impact of her glances.

So they traveled till sunset without further adventure; and throughout the next day too; and so on, day after day, till a few hours past nightfall of the seventh day, when they arrived at the edge of a black moat.

"Here we are, and didn't lose so much as a horseshoe!" young Victor exclaimed proudly.

"True for you, dear lad!" cried Dinadan. "Not even a horseshoe! Congratulations!"

And yet he knew, exultantly though confusedly, that his heart was lost—again—this time beyond recovery.

Victor blew three blasts on his horn, then two blasts, then three again; and then the red of torches flared high and low from a vast bulk of blackness beyond the black moat, and answering horns brayed, and the clanks of a great winch and the creaks of great hinges sounded, and at last the great drawbridge came down with a thump.

The father of Agnes and Victor was the Earl Fergus, and their mother was the Lady Fay; and when Sir Dinadan was presented to them, it was plain to see that they had never heard of him and were puzzled and disappointed at their daughter's choice of a giant-killer. But they were too kind and polite to show their feelings by worse than blinks and arched brows; and they plied him with courteous attentions and the best of meats and drinks at supper. After the removal of platters and trenchers, the lady said kindly: "Sir, observing a fine lute at your back, I venture to hope that you will oblige us with a little music."

"Your servant to command, madam," answered Dinadan, who had quenched his thirst with a horn of mead and several cups of Spanish wine; and he drew the instrument around to his front and set his fingers to the strings. Then he flashed his eyes at Agnes and sang and played better than ever before.

"Isn't he wonderful?" cried the damosel. "He's the best poet and lutanist in Christendom."

The Lady Fay bowed her head, for she was too deeply moved for words. The Earl was vastly impressed too, but he drained a cup and found his tongue. He addressed his daughter.

"I believe you, dear child. Yes, indeed; but I thought it was understood that our need was for a knight-at-arms— the best, or at least the second-best—but surely not for a poet, my dear, no matter how good, as such."

Agnes replied: "But you don't know Sir Dinadan, Papa! If you had seen him lay that great big Sir Joram flat on his back, you would not speak so."

"That's right, Papa!" the lad Victor exclaimed. "I saw it. I was right there. And why wouldn't I be? For I'm his squire."

"That was nothing, sir and madam," Dinadan protested modestly. "Good Sir Joram is the unhandiest knight, and the most tottery in his saddle, I ever laid lance against. But don't think too badly of me, I pray you, for I have toppled many a better jouster than him, with sharp spears as well as blunted, and held my own on foot too, sword to sword, on occasion. There was big and vile Baron Uffel for one, who had ten ladies starving in a tower."

"Uffel?" queried the Earl. "We are out of the world in this place and don't hear everything. What of him, young sir?"

"It was two years ago, sir. After unhorsing him, I got down and fought him afoot. He was bigger on his feet than horsed, but I was faster. So we slashed and hacked half a day, and he split my shield in two. But he himself was in two pieces when I was done with him; and so I let the poor ladies out of the tower."

Agnes and her mother were shaken beyond the power of utterance, and young Victor was speechless with admiration, but not so the Earl.

"How big was this Uffel?" he asked.

"Why, sir, he was bigger than Sir Lamorak—but not as good, or I'd not be here now."

"Well and honestly said, my friend, and I'll speak you as honestly. This giant is bigger than a windmill, and can cut through a haystack with one stroke of his sword."

"So I have heard, sir. But size isn't everything. Tell me, does he fight best on horseback or on foot?"

"Not on horseback, that's certain, for there's no horse big enough to carry him."

"Then will I fight him on foot," said Sir Dinadan.

At that, the lord and lady and Victor all cried out in horrified protest, but the damosel veiled her eyes and was silent.

"To go against him on a big horse and run him through with a war-spear—that would be your only chance!" cried the Earl.

"Nay, sir, no true knight keeps his saddle against an opponent on foot. 'Twould be a dastardly act, sir—a breach of the laws of chivalry."

"Are you a fool—mad, that's to say—or bewitched?"

"Maybe all three, sir; but I have sworn by my halidom to essay this giant, so that I'll do; and since he must fight on foot, so must I."

The Earl swore in his beard. Then he and the Countess and the lad all looked searchingly at the damosel, who continued to sit with veiled eyes and an enigmatic smile. Then the three exchanged questioning glances, with much arching of eyebrows: but Dinadan, gazing languishingly at Agnes, missed all the byplay.

Earl Fergus sighed as if with relief, then addressed the young knight again, but in a changed voice and manner.

"You're probably right, dear Sir Dinadan. Drink up and fill again."

❖   ❖   ❖

Our hero was for setting out to seek the giant first thing in the morning, but his host explained to him that a rendezvous must be decided upon, and Taulurd notified of it, and the exact hour—all of which could not be done in a day, or maybe two or even three, as no raid had been reported of late, and the monster might be high in the mountains. So Dinadan penned a proper challenge, at the Earl's directing, as follows:

> "I, Sir Dinadan, a knight of that mighty prince Arthur Pendragon his dubbing, do challenge ye giant Taulurd to single and mortal combat according to the sacred rules of High Chivalry in Dragon Valley under St. Elmo Mount at nigh noon of the feast day of St. Michael—to which I swear by my halidom and do herewith set my unicorn seal and my name
>
> —DINADAN."

This document was given to a trusty fellow, who returned at nightfall with word that he had passed it on, according to the Earl's instructions, to a certain trusty mountaineer who knew the giant's whereabouts.

Now Dinadan was faced by four days of inaction, a fact which he regretted in a sense; for despite his brave talk, he was beginning to wonder if he had not overstrained the obligations of knighthood in the matter of undertaking to dismount for the encounter. In another sense, he was glad of the delay, for it gave him four more sure days of life—of life with Agnes, the most enchanting of all the damosels of his hectic and disastrous experiences. He loved her. And she loved him, and told him so on the second day. He made a beautiful song of it, for which she kissed him tenderly; but soon after that, instead of making another song or singing the same one again, he became silent and sad, and sat with drooping head.

"What ails my Dinny Boy?" she murmured at his ear.

His only answer was a sigh.

She murmured closer: "I shall love and cherish you all your life long."

"Which may not be long at all," he mumbled.

"If you mean that giant, cheer up!" she cried. "You'll take no harm from him, I know, or I'd sense it in my heart; and the Raven of Fergus—sure precursor of sorrow to this house—would be flapping at my window every night. But instead of that dismal fowl, a robin—the Cadwallader bird of happiness—has sung to me every midnight since our return. My mother was a Cadwallader."

So he cheered up, being a respecter of family traditions and a firm believer in all omens and supernatural warnings, good and bad.

Sir Dinadan set out at dawn of Michaelmas Day for his rendezvous with Taulurd the giant, accompanied by Victor to show him the way. He was in good spirits, though fuddled by the damosel's parting caresses; and when the sun came up, disclosing Saint Michael's daisies like drifts of fairy smoke under every hanging wood, he broke into song; and mighty Garry, well rested and full of oats, pranced like a colt. Victor's hackney pranced and whickered too, but the lad himself was silent, and still in his saddle save for frequent furtive turnings of his head to right and left and over a shoulder.

They came to the Dragon Valley under the chapel of Saint Elmo, but the giant was not there. They waited till past high noon, and still he did not come. So they rode onward into a higher valley, and from that into a yet higher, with Victor leading the way; and still the lad spoke little and sang not at all, and continued to shoot covert glances at the thickets and dark shaws to right and left.

"D'ye look for the giant to leap out upon us from a holly bush, dear lad?" asked Dinadan brightly, toying with the thought that maybe his challenge had frightened Taulurd clear over the mountains and out of the country.

"Nay, sir, if he comes at you, 'twill be from straight in front," Victor answered gravely.

"Why so glum, then? D'ye doubt the issue? And all the omens on my side!"

"Omens? God mend your simplicity!"

At that moment the giant himself appeared before them from behind a knoll of huge boulders and crooked thorn-trees, resembling—so was Dinadan's first thought—a great rock rather than a creature of flesh and blood. He was almost square in shape, and moved like a mass of stone and wood. He was encased in hairy hides as stiff as iron plates, and carried a round shield of leather embossed with horn on his left arm. His sword, which he flourished in his right hand without apparent effort, was half as long again as Dinadan's standard two-handed weapon. Victor's horse tried to bolt, and even the courageous Garry shied at that appalling apparition.

"Charge!" screamed Victor. "Let him have it! It's now or never!"

"Tut-tut!" said the knight, dismounting. "Hold Garry. Keep him out of this. He might get hurt."

He advanced up the gentle slope with his long shield dressed before him.

"Giant Taulurd, I presume?" he called out politely.

"The same," squawked the other, in a voice more suitable for a small varlet than a bulky ravaging giant. "Are you alone?"

"Quite, save for my honorable squire here," returned the knight. "Didn't you get my letter?"

"I don't believe all I read," Taulurd squawked. "But you look honest, and I'll treasure your name as a true and honorable knight. So say your prayers, Sir Dinadan!" And with that he swung his great sword in a semicircular sweep which swished short of its objective by half-ell if an inch.

"Gramercy," said Dinadan. "You're a poor judge of distance."

He stood his ground. Taulurd recovered his equilibrium with a stagger, advanced one ponderous pace, and set himself for another swing and let it fly with a grunt. That second stroke was even more terrific than the first; but Dinadan avoided it with a skip backward.

"I'm not a haystack," jeered Dinadan; and then, while the giant stumbled to get his big feet under his point of balance again, Dinadan cast away his shield, grasped the hilt of his sword in both hands, sprang in lightly, and as lightly was out again.

Victor uttered a cry of astonishment, and the giant a squawk of consternation—and with cause, for the shapeless rolls and folds of hides in which the massive torso had so lately been encased and draped were now fallen about his legs and feet.

"Bah!" cried Dinadan, addressing his squire, but still watching his discomfited antagonist. "I but cut a thong or two; and look at him, fat and hobbled and undone! He was too heavy for his legs, anyhow, and too slow to fight anything but a haystack. So this is your horrible giant?—and

my high adventure?—the devil take him! I'll have no more
to do with him. I'm a knight, not a butcher." Then he
jabbed at the quaking giant. "I won't foul my sword with
your blubber. I spare your gluttonous life. You will be dead
of your own fat within the year, anyhow."

Taulurd, cowed and abashed and using his monstrous
sword as a staff to steady him on his cluttered-up legs,
sobbed and squawked his gratitude and relief in so shame-
lessly abject a manner that both the squire and the knight
blushed for him.

"Gramercy, gramercy, noble sir! The saints will reward
you, merciful knight. I'm old and harmless—and will
mend my ways—turn holy hermit and deafen heaven with
my praise of merciful Sir Dinadan. I'll fast on roots and
wild honey—no more beef and beer—never another ravaged farmstead—by the knuckle-bones of blessed Saint
Elmo!"

"Have done!" cried Dinadan, in disgust; and he would
have turned away then, but stood nerveless and still as
stone instead: *for a long arrow quivered in Taulurd's fat
throat, sunk halfway to its feathers.* And even while he
stared, horrified yet incredulous, another arrow struck and
sank there, and four or five more pierced the unprotected
gross breast and belly; and the giant, spouting blood,
opened his dimming eyes wide upon Dinadan, and cried
"*Treachery!*" and crashed to earth and lay still.

Then Dinadan moved, but woodenly. He looked to his
right, and over his right shoulder, then to his left; but the
rugged coverts of bushes and boulders showed nothing of
life. Then he turned and looked at Victor.

"So?" he whispered hoarsely. "You fixed an ambush—
and have made a false knight of me—and a liar and a
dastard—and a murderer."

The lad's face was white as chalk, and he answered
with a cry as harsh as the knight's whisper.

"Nay, not me! 'Twas *her* doing. She would keep you
from harm—by fair means or foul!"

"Agnes?"

"Who else? She always has her way!"

"But the omens?"

"There were no omens, good or bad. But she feared for
your life; and so an ambush of archers was set in the

Dragon Valley, and when he did not meet you there, the archers followed us here."

Dinadan moaned: "God's wounds!"

Now an old man all in wolf-skins and white whiskers came suddenly from behind a rock and knelt beside the dead giant and cried out that his kind master had been murdered.

Dinadan went to him and said: "Old man, harky to me! If you know a way out of here—over the mountains and clear out of this vile land of lies and dishonor—show it to me."

The mountaineer rose and pointed to the entrance of a narrow, climbing glen on their right.

"Lead on, then, poor fellow. Lead truly, and you have a new master: no giant now, but the fool of the world—and a forsworn dastard, to boot!"

"Me too!" blurted young Victor. "I go with you, sir—for you're the best knight I know, never mind your simplicity— through thick and thin, mauger my head!"

So they mounted and moved into and up that narrow glen, leaving the abashed and frightened archers still hiding in their coverts; but death was in Sir Dinadan's heart as surely as in the gigantic corpse on the ground behind him.

THE GOOSE GIRL

They emptied a pot or two in sweet accord; and when the good ale got to their hearts the talk turned upon women; and when it got to their heads, they fell to gross bragging. At last one cried out villainously how the meanest goose girl of his country outshone the very pick of high dames and damosels and even dukes' daughters of less favoured regions; whereupon the other broke the braggart's head with a pewter pot.

—The Book of Maelor

Sir Dinadan and his youthful squire Victor were twelve days out from Camelot on a line which the knight had never before explored beyond a league, when the squire was assailed suddenly by fever and stomach cramps. But the heroic youth kept his saddle till they came upon a rustic hermitage, though with heavy sweating inside his harness and great discomfort in his vitals. The hermit claimed to be a skilled physician, and Dinadan believed him because of his honest and kindly face. Between them they soon disarmed Victor and got him to bed, where the hermit went to work on him with brews of wild herbs, applications of cold wet moss to the head and hot wet moss to the stomach, and a lancet. He slept all night, with Dinadan and the hermit keeping watch turn and turn about, and in the morning drank a bowl of thin barley gruel, with one of them supporting him and the other holding the bowl. Then he slept again.

"I must move on today, good Brother Ambrose, or

tomorrow at the latest, for our need of a profitable adventure is acute," said Dinadan.

"Then you will go without your squire, good sir," replied the hermit, kindly but firmly. "He will not be strong enough for the saddle within the sennight or maybe ten days, for in ridding him of the noxious humors which threatened his life I had, perforce, to all but drain his veins. But what blood I left in him is as pure as morning dew; and by the time Mother Nature and I have replenished the reservoir of his heart, he will be in better health than ever before."

"Gramercy," said Dinadan.

"I shall graduate his stomach from gruel to porridge with thin milk, then with cream (I have an excellent cow)— and anon to broiled troutlets from the brook, and so on, by way of the white meat of a spring chicken, to boiled bacon and peas," said Brother Ambrose. "So go on your way, good knight, with an easy mind, and make your adventure with a stout heart, for both your squire and his charger shall receive the best of care and provisioning while you are gone."

So Sir Dinadan went on with his great horse Garry, leaving Victor and Victor's horse and four of his last five silver crowns with the good hermit. He had been fooled by the pretty faces of damosels oftener than he could count on the fingers of both hands, but he was a shrewd reader of character in the faces of men.

He moved in a wilderness where every track was of the cloven hoofs of wild cows and wild swine and deer. So dense were the thickets and so rough the way in places that he dismounted and led his heavy-burdened charger. Progress was slow. On the third day out from the hermitage, he decided that he had chosen a hopeless line of country for his purpose, and promised himself that if he failed to find a man-made road by sunset, he would change direction, for on this line a mad wild bull was far more likely to be encountered than any chivalrous adventure. But Fate, in the shapes of a gaggle of geese and their attendant, caused him to change direction in the first hour of the afternoon. The geese hissed and flopped about in the underbrush when he and Garry came heavy-footed and unexpected amongst them; and he knew them for domesticated birds, because they didn't take wing.

"Tame geese in the wilderness!" he exclaimed. "A sure sign of a homestead close at hand. Good! But which way did they come?"

He glanced about him and beheld the goose girl. She was a tall girl in coarse wool only, and not a great deal of that. Her face was weather-stained and hung about with tangled strands of yellow hair. She stood almost in arm's-reach of his left stirrup, and regarded him with questioning eyes and a half-smile.

"God bless us!" he exclaimed.

"Gramercy," she murmured, and fluttered her eyelashes.

"You startled me, my good girl," he said. "First your geese, then yourself. All most unexpected in this dreary wilderness. Did you come from a farm?"

After a moment's hesitation, she nodded.

"Will you lead me to it?" he asked.

Again she hesitated, then nodded again and murmured: "I can try, anyhow."

"Try? What d'ye mean by that? Don't you know the way?"

"I am thinking of you, sir. It is not only a farm, sir. There is a castle, too."

"Hah! A castle. So much the better. Lead on, I pray you, my good girl: and in due course, and with reasonable luck, I shall reward you handsomely."

"Gramercy," she murmured, and moved to Garry's head.

Now in pure courtesy, Dinadan got down from his saddle and joined her there; for despite his frequent railings upon the inconstancy of the female heart, it was not in his nature nor breeding to go horsed in the company of any woman—damosel or wench, high dame or poor crone—trudging afoot. So they went side by side, and the big horse followed close.

"What of your fat geese?" he asked her.

She shot him a measuring look and said: "If you knew what awaits you, sir, you would have no concern to spare for my gaggle of geese."

"Why not?"

"All your concern would be for yourself."

"Hah! What awaits me?"

"The keeper of the castle."

"Is it an ogre's castle, then? Fie, fie, girl! I lost my faith in fairy tales years ago."

"The keeper of that castle is nothing out of a fairy tale, nor lord of the castle neither, but a great bully of a man who keeps it from this side of the moat, letting only hinds and swineherds and the like in and out; and so he has done these ten months past."

"D'ye tell me so?"

"Yes, for your own good. There is no knight-at-arms within to match him, and the lord took such a hurt at jousting years ago that he may sit nothing harder than a cushion now, and passes the days in monkish studies and the play of chess."

"Poor fellow! But has no knight from without essayed to get in the castle?"

"Two. That's to say one, in very truth."

"One or two, my good girl?"

"One made the essay and died of it. The other took but a look and ran away."

"God save us! The rogue must wear a right villainous look. But I promise you I'll not run from him, no matter how terrible his aspect."

"And his action is more terrible yet. He is the deadliest knight in the world."

"Is he, now? How does he call himself?"

"Sir Grudwyn."

"Never heard of him. But what of his arms? Are they rich?"

"The helmet and breastplate are damascened with gold, and the hilt and scabbard of the sword studded with rubies."

"Hah, gold and rubies!" exclaimed Dinadan. "Just what I need. Lead me to them, good wench."

The goose girl frowned at him and asked coldly, "Are you Sir Launcelot himself then—or a fool?"

"Nay, not Sir Launcelot," he replied cheerfully. "Lead on."

"A fool, then," she said, but in a kinder voice. "So be it, Sir Fool. But I have warned you."

A few minutes later Dinadan bethought to ask: "To what end does this Grudwyn keep the castle?"

"In wicked spite," she answered, with averted eyes. "Because he may not enter himself, no other shall enter. If the damosel be not for him, then she's for no one."

Dinadan checked so suddenly that his charger bumped into him.

"Damosel, d'ye say?" But I might have known it! Is there no end to them? Must there be a damosel mixed up with every adventure I undertake, to bedevil it or me?"

She gave him an unpleasant look, disillusioned and scornful.

"Take heart, noble sir," she said. "You have nothing to fear. I will take you around and set you upon a safe road beyond, without letting that merciless Grudwyn catch so much as a glimpse of you."

"Not so fast!" he exclaimed. "He keeps the castle from this side the moat, you say. Then I may do what I can with him, and come afterward with his arms and horse, and all the while keep the ditch betwixt the damosel and myself. Lead on."

"You are very sure of yourself," she murmured, sighing.

"I need the money," he said cheerfully.

She sighed again and led onward, now moving three full paces before him; and after a little she gestured to him for caution, knelt and peered ahead, then beckoned to him with a finger. He advanced softly and knelt beside her; and together they peered out from the underbrush.

"There he is," she whispered. "To the left."

But Dinadan did not shift his gaze instantly, so vastly impressed was he by the view directly in front of him. He saw greensward as smooth as tapestry, and beyond it a willow-fringed moat with white swans and lilies on its still surface, and beyond the water the barbican and walls and bulging towers of a great castle, and the drawbridge cocked high in air like a gigantic arm of iron and oak raised in threat and defiance. It was big enough for a king; and yet he saw no stir of life save the deliberate movements of the swans. After gazing his fill at that marvel, he looked to his left.

The goose girl whispered at his ear: "Under the great oak there."

He saw a knight in a robe of red silk sprawled at ease in the shade.

"A sluggard, asleep and unready at this hour," he jeered.

"Ride forth, then, and you'll find him awake and ready enough, I trow," she answered tartly.

He sneered and said: "Nay, I'll walk over and slap him awake, the hulking slug-abed!"

And he rose from his knees and made a forward step—but only one step. Then she sprang and gripped him by the sword-belt and gave so shrewd a yank that he staggered back, and was all but brought to earth by her violence and the tangling of his spurs.

"Fool!" she cried in his astonished face—for now she was in front of him, and with both hands pushing instead of pulling. "If you *will* die, die fighting! He is not asleep—nor unarmed; and his horse is close at hand! Would you go to him like a silly calf to the butcher? Give him a fight at least. He might suffer a mishap."

He steadied himself against a shoulder of his equally astonished charger.

"What the devil!" he muttered. "He will suffer a mishap, I warrant you—unless you disable me before I get at him."

At that, she let her hands fall and stood still, with bowed head; whereupon Dinadan turned his back on her and readied Garry and himself for action. He loosed a sack and a hamper from the saddle and dropped them to the ground, took the greater of his two spears in hand and cast the other down, then drew his long shield around from back to shoulder and mounted.

"God defend you!" cried the girl.

"Gramercy," returned the knight, but coldly, for he did not enjoy being pushed and pulled about and called a fool.

So he rode forth from the screen of the forest, drew rein when fairly in the open, fewtered his spear, and shouted: "Run, rogue, run!"

Then the sleepy scene came awake and alive in the blink of an eye, as if by magic. Another shout rang hard upon Dinadan's like an echo, and the shouter appeared, running and leading a great black horse all saddled and armed; the knight beneath the tree came quickly but heavily to his feet and cast off his robe and showed himself armored from neck to heels; and heads appeared along the battlements of the castle, and white faces at narrow windows.

"The wench was right," muttered Dinadan.

Now the shouting squire reached Grudwyn, helped him up onto the black charger and gave him his shield, and a spear like a tree.

"The good girl was right," murmured Dinadan.

And to the dapple-gray Garry he said: "Action front, dear lad, and may God defend us."

So Garry tossed his head and flexed his legs and went a few paces with more posturing than progress, like a dancer who would attune his feet to the music before stepping out.

"Here they come," warned Dinadan.

Then Garry changed his gait and launched himself to the attack as straight and hard as arrow from string; and Dinadan leveled his spear and held it true. The two iron spearheads struck like one, each upon the very center of the opposite iron-plated shield; and the hurtling onslaught checked while the two stout poles of sinewy ash-wood arched, quivering, between the stricken, stubborn shields—only to splinter and break at last, and release the arrested weights of horses and men and metal to stumble and crash together and stagger apart. Garry got his four feet under him smartly and wheeled wide and lightly. Grudwyn's charger was heavier and slower. Dinadan readjusted himself in his saddle—from which he had come within an inch and an ounce of being pushed—and cast away the butt of his shattered spear. He saw Grudwyn do the same, and Grudwyn's squire coming running with a new spear.

"If it's to be spear against sword, I'll do better afoot," he muttered, speaking from experience; and he was about to dismount, but was stayed by the appearance of the goose girl at his knee, bearing his other spear.

"Gramercy," he said, and took the weapon from her, stooping sidewise. "You're a good girl—and you were right when you warned me of his trickery. But run away now, or you might get hurt in the scuffle."

She looked up at him and fluttered her eyelashes, which were darker than her tangled tresses.

"Don't do that!" he exclaimed. "That's a damosel's ploy, and not for an honest goose girl, no matter how pretty you are." And with that he swung away from her, straightened spear and horse and went at Grudwyn like a thunderbolt.

Grudwyn and the black charger were the heavier, but Sir Dinadan and his dapple-gray were the quicker and faster; and so it was that the murderous keeper of the castle was no more than headed aright, and his new spear was still shaking like a reed in the wind, when that thunderbolt struck him and jarred him from his saddle and heaved him back and down over his horse's tail. Thereupon Dinadan cast his spear aside, dismounted quickly and drew his long sword.

"Would you butcher him flat on the ground?" cried the squire, shrill with dismay and astonishment.

"God forbid!" said Dinadan. "Set him upon his feet and put his sword in his hand."

So the other ran to Grudwyn and strove hard but vainly to set him upright. And now the goose girl came running to Dinadan.

"Have at him now!" she begged. "He would not spare you if he had you down. Slay him for the merciless brute he is."

"Nay, I'm no butcher, but a true knight," he protested. "The wind's knocked out of him, that's all that ails him at the moment. Once he's up and sword in hand, I'll slay him, I promise you."

She cried at him: "This is no time for courtesy and the rules of chivalry! Take your advantage now. He is deadlier afoot than horsed."

"So am I," he said. "Don't worry. I'll feed him to the foxes all in good time."

By now Grudwyn was on his feet, but unsteady and still supported by his squire; and his great sword was naked in his right hand, but held limply and point on ground, more like a staff than a weapon.

"Don't trust him," the girl whispered. "He is as whole and ready as you are. Trust not his base squire, neither."

Dinadan replied, "Leave them to me, my little friend," and put her gently aside and went forward cautiously behind his shield and sword.

"He's big, but I've had ado with and undone bigger," he told himself. "And he took such a shock he's fit to fall flat again even now, of his own weight and dizziness."

The squire moved away, leaving Grudwyn swaying alone and apparently held upright only by the support of his sword: but Dinadan, who was a fool only in his encounters with damosels, observed and took note of the fact that the point of the great sword was sunk no deeper than an inch or so into the tender sward; whereupon he uttered a hoot of scornful and hateful derision, and advanced yet more cautiously. He went a slow pace to the right, then a few jigging steps to the left, then three skips straight ahead and one backward, and more sidewise hops and deliberate paces, but ever closing in upon Grudwyn with a fixed and baleful scrutiny. Then, of a sudden, Grudwyn dressed his shield, whirled up his sword, bellowed, and charged like a bull.

Dinadan avoided that onslaught lightly, and Grudwyn carved nothing but air. Grudwyn snubbed to a stop and turned heavily but with surprising quickness. Dinadan faced about to meet him, and saw that which startled his attention from the business in hand—the squire (who was in less than half-armor) rolling on the grass with his arms up and locked to shield his head, and the goose girl belaboring him furiously with her stout oaken staff. He gaped with astonishment, but was recalled to the menace of Grudwyn by a swish of steel so close to his head that it clipped his crest and set his helmet ringing.

Now Grudwyn was upon him, pressing him back and hammering on his head, over the tops of the grinding shields with the pommel of his sword. He wrenched and staggered clear and made a backhanded stroke even while staggering. It was a lucky stroke, for though it only rattled at the bars of Grudwyn's vizor, it won him a moment in which to steady himself and strike again. And this was a shrewd stroke in very sooth, forehanded and swung full from the shoulders. It set Grudwyn back on his heels with a split shield and a left arm benumbed to the neck. The wrecked shield fell to the ground, and Grudwyn cursed.

"Now's your chance!" screamed the goose girl. "Chop him down!"

Dinadan glanced aside and saw her standing a little way off, and Grudwyn's squire lying as still as death at her feet.

"Why did you do that?" he asked.

She cried: "He would have stabbed you from behind, else!"

Then he saw the foot-long dagger on the ground.

"You saved my life, good girl," he said wonderingly. "The base knave would have found the chink beneath my left arm, devil a doubt. I owe you my life. I never thought to owe it to a goose girl—nor to any other female neither for that matter, God wot! Gramercy!"

She screamed: "Fool! Look to Grudwyn!"

He leaped aside even before he looked, but even so was sent reeling and staggering with a dent in his helmet—a dent that would have been a cut through steel and skull but for her warning. He saw comets with fiery tails, and heard bells clanging in tottering minster spires, but all the while he kept his feet under his point of balance and in motion. He thrust blindly and heard a grunt; and then rushing comets and spinning darkness passed and disclosed Grudwyn swaying, stooping, on fumbling feet. His first impulse was to leap forward, but thought was quicker. He had pricked his enemy, but surely not deep enough for a mortal, or even a disabling hurt. So instead he loosed his shield from his left arm and flung it at drooping Grudwyn's feet—an act which required a mighty fling, for it was a shield of extraordinary size and weight.

"Fool!" cried the wench. "Now you've cast away your chance of life—and passed your only advantage to him— oh, pitiful fool!"

Sure enough, Grudwyn had raised the shield and dressed it before him quicker than it can be told. But Dinadan only smiled and murmured to himself: "We'll soon know who is the fool."

Now Grudwyn charged again behind shield and whirling sword, and Dinadan avoided him lightly and banged the back of Grudwyn's helmet as he plunged past; and as he ploughed to a stop, and again as he came heavily about, Dinadan banged him shrewdly on neckpiece and backplate.

"Stand and fight!" roared Grudwyn.

"Nay, would you have me split my own shield?" Dinadan jeered.

So Grudwyn continued to charge and slash, check and turn, still slashing, all the while carving nothing but air; and the massy shield on his left arm sank an inch lower every minute.

"A heavy shield, in sooth, but a mere plaything on the powerful arm of the mighty Sir Grudwyn," jeered Dinadan.

"Stand still—but ten seconds—and I'll cut you in two," gasped Grudwyn.

"All in good time," said Dinadan, skipping lightly.

So Grudwyn continued to scar the greensward with his mad and weighty plunges and turns, while Dinadan circled just out of reach of the whistling sword, and the heavy shield sank lower every minute. But at last, and as suddenly as a flash of lightning, Dinadan stood firm and struck full-strength once, twice, and again, forehanded, backhanded, and forehanded again through steel links and bone. Grudwyn toppled and crashed; and Dinadan made to step away lightly to avoid the gushing blood, but fouled his spurs in something behind him and went over backward.

Sir Dinadan opened his eyes, beheld a slanted sunbeam, and closed them. When he opened them again he saw candlelight. He blinked, looked again, and saw the face of an old man in a black hood.

"Brother Ambrose?" he queried.

His voice was so feeble a voice that he hardly knew it for his own.

"Nay, Doctor Mendax," said the old man.

"Candles," Dinadan murmured. "Where am I?"

"In bed, young sir."

"Why?"

"Why? You may well ask. But for me, you'd be in a grave."

"In a grave? Gramercy! But why?"

"You would be dead, that's why. But compose yourself. Relax, and drink this."

The doctor raised Dinadan's head a little with his left arm and held a cup to his lips. Dinadan drank, and instantly slept again. When he opened his eyes the third time, it was still upon the feeble shine of two candles, and the doctor was still there.

"It has come back to me," he said. "I was fighting afoot with a false knight—it all comes clear to me now—and cut him down with three mortal strokes. Then my heels tripped on something. What happened then?"

"You were stabbed from behind," said the doctor in a soothing yet relishing tone of voice. "A deadly stab, young man. A mortal thrust. But thanks to the knowledge and skill of poor old Doctor Mendax, you still live and will soon be sound."

"Gramercy, learned sir. But who stabbed me?"

"Grudwyn's squire."

"Nay, that tricky knave was dead. I saw him dead on the ground, where the goose girl had whacked the life out of him with her oaken staff."

"That's what she thought too; but when you stumbled backward over him and he arose and sank a poniard in you, she had to whack him again—which she did with a vengeance. And now he and Grudwyn occupy the same ignoble grave."

"A deadly wench and overprone to cry 'Fool!' at her betters. But a good girl at heart, and a good friend to me, for it seems that I owe her my life twice or maybe thrice."

Doctor Mendax chuckled and said: "Ay, you can say that, young man—a deadly wench indeed, but certainly a good friend to you, for you'd have bled white if she hadn't come and pulled me out of bed and out to you by main strength, willy-nilly. Had she been a minute slower, even my skill could not have saved you."

"So I'm within the castle, I presume," sighed Dinadan.

"Ay, and in the very best bed."

"And what of my horse Garry?"

"He is in the best stall in the best stable."

"And the big black?"

"In the next stall in the same stable."

"And Grudwyn's sword and armor? It's all mine now, you know—horse and arms—by the rules of combat."

"All safe and at your disposal."

"Gramercy, venerable sir. And will you tell me how soon I can be up and away?"

"You have faith in me, young sir?"

"Yes."

"Good. No other physician in Christendom could answer your question truly, just as no other could have stopped the outflow of your life-blood as I did, but I can and will. Follow my instructions to the letter, young sir, and you will be on your feet on the tenth day from now, and on your horse on the twenty-fifth. No other honest doctor, nor even that old warlock Merlin with all his deviltry, could do as well by you."

"I believe you," said Dinadan. "And I have, seemingly, even greater faith than yourself in your professional abilities. The diamonds and rubies which stud the scabbard and the hilt of Grudwyn's sword are worth a king's ransom: and they are all yours—less the trifling price of a croft and a cow for the goose girl—if you have me healed and horsed in half the time you mention."

"You flatter me," smirked the doctor. "Not that I couldn't do it," he went on, staring into the flame of the nearer candle. "It's a temptation, I confess. With such wealth as that, I could extend my scientific researches even to the uttermost ends of the earth and take a fling at the night life of Camelot into the bargain. Ah, me! But my inborn honest nature protests; and so I must ask, in fairness to yourself, what's your hurry to be gone from here?"

"Fear of the damosel," Dinadan mumbled, in a shamed voice. "Laugh if you will, but it's the truth. Damosels are my undoing. And there's one in this castle. The goose girl told me so. And she must be the most beautiful in the world—most of them are, God help me, and as false as beautiful—or Grudwyn would not have striven so madly and long to keep all other cavaliers out simply because he could not get in himself. But it was not to get in that I fought him and cut him down. It was for his arms and horse. But for my empty purse and pressing debts, I would have avoided the castle entirely upon learning that a damosel was involved in the adventure. But I was stabbed from behind, and here I am."

The old man scratched his cheek thoughtfully and asked: "Don't you know the reward for delivering the castle from the murderous great rogue's tyranny?"

"I've not been told it, but I can guess it," Dinadan sneered cynically. "The fair hand of the beautiful damosel—not to mention the false heart—in the holy bonds of matrimony."

"Nay, your guess is wide and high, young sir. The reward is a fair manor of six farms and a tubful of silver crowns. The damosel's hand, and the five manors and castle that go with it, are for her own giving or keeping. And

you are wrong about her heart too; and as for her beauty—
in my opinion, her nose is a trifle too short for classical per-
fection. And perhaps the same can be said also of her upper
lip."

"That may well be—but, knowing my weakness, I fear
she would appear perfect to me just the same. And now
that I am in funds again, I care nothing for the six farms
and tubful of crowns. So all my concern is to win clear of
this castle with my horse and arms, and base Grudwyn's
horse and body-armor, at the earliest possible moment,
before worse befalls me."

"Extraordinary! I'll do my best to expedite your recovery from a wound which would have proved fatal but for
me. Drink this now and relax."

Dinadan slept again. When he opened his eyes, it was
upon a beam of brightest sunshine which lanced through
a narrow window and straight and level across the chamber to the arras on the opposite wall. He felt hungry and
thought of broth, and even of hot pease-porridge flavored
with a knuckle of ham; and even of a jack of ale. He looked
as far to his right and left as he could without turning or
lifting his head on his stiffly bandaged neck and shoulders.
But that was not far, and he did not see anyone.

"Are you there, venerable sir?" he asked.

"No, it's only me," said someone beyond his range of
vision.

"Hah!" he exclaimed. "The goose girl. What brings you
here?"

"You, sir," she murmured, and stepped into view, but
not into the bright beam of sunshine. "The doctor sleeps,
and I have been on watch since dawn."

She was dressed—if you call it that—just as he had
first and last seen her, and her yellow hair still hung in
tangles.

"Gramercy," he said. "But what of your geese?"

"I don't know, sir. I work in the scullery now."

"A scullery wench! But cheer up, my good girl, for with
the diamonds and rubies from the scabbard and hilt of
Grudwyn's sword I am now in a position to reward you for
saving my life from the dastardly tricks of that knave and
of his equally base squire. I shall establish you in a snug
cottage with a fair meadow before it, an orchard of apples

and cherries behind it, a cow in the meadow, chickens and beehives in the orchard, and geese too if you want them, and a servant to milk your cow and cut your honeycombs. All this shall be yours—and a modest fund in coin of the realm besides—forever and a day."

"Gramercy, sir."

"Nay, you have been a good friend to me. And you must have a garden, so that I may think of you sitting on a cushion, sewing a fine seam, and eating strawberries and honey and cream."

"Gramercy. And what of yourself, sir? Shall you settle down in the manor which my lord will bestow upon you for freeing him of Grudwyn?"

"Nay, God forbid! I have heard of that reward, from the doctor—six fat farms and a tubful of crowns to boot. But I'll have nought to do with it. I did not fight Grudwyn to free the castle to the admittance of your damosel's cowardly suitors, but to possess myself of his arms and horse. I am a free knight-errant, and I intend to remain such, mauger my head! And the sooner I get out of here, the better I'll like it."

"Are you afraid of something? You, the strongest knight in the world?"

"Gramercy, child. But I'm afraid, nevertheless. I'd liefer have ado with Sir Launcelot himself than so much as exchange glances with any damosel. So I'm afraid of meeting the damosel of this castle, even if she isn't a raving beauty."

After a moment of hesitation, the goose girl whispered: "Why do you say that? Have you ever seen her?"

"Nay, but I've heard that both her nose and upper lip are too short."

"Too short for what?"

"For beauty."

"Who says so?"

"Doctor Mendax."

"That old fool!" she exclaimed, turning her head as if at a sound; and before he could utter a word of protest, she was gone from his restricted line of view.

"Overprone to cry 'Fool!' at her betters, but a good girl at heart," he murmured.

The physician appeared beside the bed half a minute

later and inspected his tongue, counted his pulse, and felt his brow for fever.

"How am I doing?" he asked.

"Marvelously well, young sir. How do you feel?"

"Hungry."

"Excellent! Just what I had expected to hear from you, so I came prepared. This way with broth, Jynkyn."

A fellow appeared bearing a steaming bowl with a horn spoon in it.

"Hah!" exclaimed Dinadan, and he sat bolt upright.

"Have a care!" cried the doctor, pressing him back on the pillow. "Would you reopen the wound and so undo all I have done? I'll feed you. But I'll risk the raising of your head and shoulders a trifle."

He stuffed a second pillow beneath his patient's head and commenced feeding him generous spoonfuls.

"Too thin for my taste," complained Dinadan.

"Perhaps it will be thicker for supper; and maybe you can have a rasher tomorrow or the next day, so marvellously have I doctored you," soothed the ancient.

When the bowl was empty, Dinadan asked for a horn of ale.

"You shall have a full jack of the best with your supper tonight, young sir. Drink this now and relax."

And Doctor Mendax pressed a cup to his patient's lips.

Dinadan was roused from his drugged sleep by hands on his shoulders, shaking him. He opened his eyes and saw the goose girl stooping over him.

"What now?" he gasped. "Have a care! The wound! Where's the doctor?"

"Gone—and all your diamonds and rubies with him!" she cried, still shaking him. "As for your grievous wound—fiddlesticks!"

He gaped up at her, speechless with astonishment and confusion.

"Are you quite a fool—except in mortal combat?" she went on in an angry and desperate voice. "That was not a stab, but only one more bang on your silly head. When you went backward over the squire, and he—I thought I had finished him—squirmed up with a knife in his hand, I swung my staff again, but missed him and hit you instead.

But I got him with the next swing, the tricky knave! And you were brought into the castle, where Mendax bandaged your neck and shoulders, and that lie was invented. And here you are."

"Why?"

"To give him time to pry all the rubies and diamonds from the scabbard and hilt of Grudwyn's sword, it seems. So up and after him!"

"Hasn't anyone gone after him?"

"Nay, 'tis your business."

"Nay, for I meant to divide them between you and him. What now of the croft and cow I promised you? Now I must reward you out of the price of Grudwyn's horse and armor, God help me! And what of them? Have I been robbed of them too?"

"They are safe enough," she said, and released his shoulders and straightened her back and made as if to turn away, but changed her mind. "As safe as yourself," she continued in a queer, shaking voice. "I'll send Jynkyn to help you arm and take you to your horse. As for Grudwyn's horse and armor, here's their price in gold and silver." She flung a heavy purse down on the bed. "As for that croft and cow—and strawberries an' cream—the devil take them!"

With that, she turned and ran to the door, but checked there for a moment and turned again and cried strangely, "Good luck to you—and thanks for nothing—you fool!" and disappeared.

"God defend me!" exclaimed Dinadan. "What ails the wench? And where did she get this purse of money?"

He sat up and tore and uncoiled ten yards of bandages from his neck and shoulders. "Fiddlesticks" was correct—there was no wound. At this discovery, he cursed Doctor Mendax for a rogue and himself for the fool of the world and leaped from the bed with such violence as to almost knock over the fellow Jynkyn, who had entered at that moment with an armful of garments of linen, leather, chain, and mail.

"Is everyone in this place mad?" he asked, when Jynkyn was busy latching and buckling the iron plates.

"I be a poor knave an' knows nothing, Yer Honor," said Jynkyn.

Dinadan gave him a coin from the great purse and asked: "Why did Doctor Mendax rob me and run away?"

"It was only for lack of full pockets he didn't cut an' run years ago, in my humble opinion. But me lord was too smart for him, an' kep' all the cash an' jewelry under lock an' key."

"Why did your lord detain him? Of what use to him was that old fraud and thief?"

"For to play at the game of chess, Yer Honor, that's wot. My lord bests everyone else without hardly puttin' his mind to it, but the doctor has given him many a shrewd tussle, especially since His Lordship promised him a prize of a pension and a palfrey if he ever checkmated him. That was seven year agone, come Candlemas; and the poor old gent never come nearer it than a stalemate."

"So he turned thief," sneered Dinadan. "Anything to escape from this madhouse! I feel the same way myself."

The chamber was in darkness by now, but Dinadan was fully harnessed and in such haste to be gone before worse than robbery might befall him that even his hunger and thirst were forgotten. He followed Jynkyn's stumbling guidance down twisting stairs and along crooked passages, and at last out and into the stableyard. Garry nickered at his approach. The tall charger was soon bitted and saddled, and the knight mounted; and then Jynkyn led them, by dim and circuitous ways, to the front courtyard and thence across the drawbridge. Dinadan gave him another coin.

"Good fortune, an' safe roads to Yer Honor!" exclaimed Jynkyn, louting low.

Dinadan returned the purse to his wallet and was about to move off, but a sudden thought struck him and checked him.

"Where did that goose girl get the money to pay me for the horse and arms I won from Grudwyn?"

"God fend yer innocence, sir," chuckled the fellow. "She be no more a goose girl nor the Queen of Sheby! She took to tanglin' her tresses an' paintin' her pretty face—an' everything else wot wasn't covered by that skimpy kirtle—with juices of yarbs an' berries, so's to win past Sir Grudwyn an' spy about for a champion."

"D'ye mean she's a damosel?"

"Ay, the Damosel Isbel herself."

At that, Dinadan shivered from his shorn crest to his spurs, then cried out in wordless and bewildered consternation; and Garry thrust forward so suddenly as to almost overturn Jynkyn.

"Who's mad now!" cried the staggered varlet disgustedly, for he had expected yet a third coin.

But he received no answer, for horse and knight were already crashing and stumbling in the dark forest.

Later, when Dinadan discovered a great wallet of meat, a leather bottle of ale, and even a bag of beans for Garry tied to his saddle, he sat on the moss a long time with his bewildered head clasped in both hands, and conflict and confusion in his heart.

"So she provisioned me for the road," he concluded bitterly. "She made sure that hunger would not drive me back. Now I can trust no female under eighty years, not even goose girls, any more!"

FOR TO ACHIEVE YOUR ADVENTURE

> When he overtook the damosel, anon she said, *"What doest thou here? Thou stinkest all of the kitchen. Thy clothes be bawdy of the grease and tallow that thou gainest in King Arthur's kitchen. Therefore turn again, bawdy kitchen page, for I know thee well. . . . What art thou but a luske and a turner of broches and a ladle-washer?"*
>
> *"Damosel,"* said Beaumains, *"say to me what ye will. I will not go from you whatsoever ye say, for I have undertaken to King Arthur for to achieve your adventure; and so shall I finish it to the end, else die thereof."*
>
> —Sir Thomas Malory

One of King Arthur's amiable if eccentric customs was, upon certain feast days, to delay his dinner until he had witnessed or received word of some fresh marvel or curious new adventure. Now it was on a Whit Sunday, and the hour of noon (which was dinner-time), that a hungry gentleman of the court looked from a window and beheld the approach of three men on big horses and a little dwarf on foot. He saw the riders dismount at the front door and observed that one of them topped the others by a head and a half, although all were taller than ordinary.

"This promises well!" he exclaimed; and so he hastened to the King and said with assurance, "Sir, you may sit down to dinner with an easy conscience, for an extraordinary adventure is nigh to hand or I have lost my erstwhile keen sense of such matters."

"I'll take your word for it, my friend," said the King, who

was peckish himself, having breakfasted early; and with that he led the company to the Hall of the Round Table, this being one of the days especially ordained for the assembly of the knights of that high fellowship.

Of the one hundred and fifty chairs at the table, all but a third were quickly occupied. Of the fifty absentees, some were questing private adventures which brooked no respite, some skirmishing with the King's enemies far afield, some in prison, some abed of wounds or fevers; and probably some occupied new graves or lay dead at the mercy of foxes and crows.

Now the three strange horsemen and the yet stranger dwarf entered the hall. Two supported the third between them and the dwarf strutted behind. The supporters were in silk and fine half-armor, but the one between them was garbed all in country wool and leather, as a herd- or ploughman. But in his garments alone did his appearance suggest a low fellow. In the words of an ancient chronicler, "He was large and long and broad at the shoulders, and nobly visaged, and the fairest and largest-handed ever was seen." Yet he leaned and hung upon the squires as if his length and weight were too much for his own strength. But when he halted with only the table between himself and the King, he straightened his back and knees to his full height, bowed low, and then stood upright again.

"What will you?" said Arthur, with a gracious gesture of the right hand. "Speak up and fear nought."

"God bless Your Majesty and all your noble fellowship," said the stranger.

"Gramercy," said the King. "Say on."

"I am come, puissant prince, to ask three favors," said the stranger.

Arthur nodded.

"But I promise there shall be no shrewd nor unreasonable asking," the other continued, "but only of such favors as may be granted easily in royal charity and knightly honor."

"Fair enough," said the King. "Name them."

"First, Your Grace, I humbly crave of your bounty sufficient meat and drink daily for my needs throughout the coming year."

"Granted. Any lost dog is welcome to as much. What

next, young man? Speak up now and ask for something worthy a Christian prince's bestowal."

The stranger thanked the King warmly, then humbly begged to be excused for making further requests until another Whit Sunday a year hence.

"So be it," said Arthur kindly. "And in the meantime you shall have meat and drink enough, no matter how great your appetite. Now tell me your name."

"Ah, gracious and puissant prince, that I may not honorably do at this time!" cried the other apologetically.

"Quite," said the King; but he looked disappointed. Then he turned to Sir Kay, who was High Seneschal of all his castles and strongholds, and bade him supply the young man generously with all he might require daily throughout the next twelvemonth. Whereupon the stranger followed Sir Kay from the hall; and those who had come with him, including the little dwarf, retired to their horses and galloped off.

This Sir Kay was a lord of great authority, but of no popularity with either his peers or his inferiors. His temper and manners were such as did not endear him to any honest person, gentle or simple. Now he mocked and insulted the young stranger.

"The King is as romantic and gullible as any old wife or sky-raking knight-errant, but I am of different stuff," he sneered. "He may think you of worshipful blood, but I can see that you are a low fellow by birth, even as you have proved yourself a lout in spirit. Any gentleman would have asked for a horse and arms and a perilous adventure: but such as a beggar is, so he begs. So, since marrowbones, dumplings, and ale aplenty are the height of your ambition, you shall have your fill of them till you bulge with fat like the pig you are. And since you lack a name, I give you one now—'Beaumains'—in derision of your monstrous uncouth hands. Ha-ha!"

The youth listened to all this in silence, but with a balanced face and a strained look about his beardless lips; and still he made no protest even when he was set down at meat with potscrapers and turnspits and the like in the greasy scullery. But Sir Kay's behavior toward the uncomplaining stranger displeased, and was protested by, certain good knights who chanced to get wind of it; and one day the great Sir Launcelot himself rebuked Sir Kay for it.

"If the youth is in truth what you say, then you are taking an ungentle advantage of his lowly station," quoth the peerless knight, but in his habitual mild voice. "And should he prove himself, or accident prove him, a person of high merit in himself or of high blood then you will have a red face for your bullying and bad manners. You call him Beaumains, and with cause—but you bestow the name in petty derision, like a jealous scullion. Have done, I pray you, for the credit of the order of knighthood."

Hard words, though softly spoken: but Sir Kay made to smile them off, though with nothing of mirth in his grimace, for he would sooner have jumped into the moat in full armor than come to blows with Sir Launcelot.

"Just so," said Sir Dinadan, who happened to be of the company, in a cheerful tone of voice. "And your memory is equally at fault with your manners, Sir Seneschal, if you have forgotten that other young man upon whom you once exercised your spleen in the bestowal of a name. You dubbed that one 'La Cote Mal Taile,' because he was rustically attired and you believed him to be poor and friendless. And who did he turn out to be but an honest gentleman's seventh son, who is now Sir Brewnor of the Round Table, and would as lief demean his quality by tilting at the chief cook in a contest of skewers as by breaking a spear on the chief seneschal."

That was a nasty dose for the important foster-brother of King Arthur to swallow, but he downed it in two wryfaced gulps, for Sir Dinadan, although young and even a better poet than a knight-at-arms, was no pushover.

So Sir Kay went about his business of stewardship, which was safer than disputing a question of chivalrous behavior with such forthright and heavy-handed arguers as Sir Launcelot and Sir Dinadan.

Now these two knights and several others would have welcomed Beaumains to their own tables and society, like a young kinsman or friend, but he refused their courtesy with the same meekness as he accepted the discourtesies of Sir Kay. And thus he served out that humiliating apprenticeship a full twelvemonth.

So the Feast of Whitsuntide came again, and with it as many of the Knights of the Round Table as could keep their rendezvous, and again King Arthur refused to go into the dining hall without a promise, or at least a hint, of some imminent marvel or adventure. But the delay was short, for the word came soon of the arrival of a damosel urgently demanding audience with the King. So Arthur and all the knightly company entered the Hall of the Round Table and took their appointed seats; and then the damosel was brought before the King with due ceremony, and a little gilt chair was brought to her, upon which she sat with a high air.

"Now what is your petition, young lady?" the King asked kindly.

"I am here in behalf of a noble dame who is so besieged by a vile tyrant that she cannot win forth from her castle but in peril of her life or her honor; and because it is known that many of the best knights in the world are with you, I have come a long and hazardous way to pray Your Grace to deliver this noble lady from this ignoble duress," said the damosel, but with a voice and an air more suggestive of a demand than a petition.

But she was as comely a damosel, and as richly bedight, as any at any court in Christendom; so Arthur, being only human, refrained from telling her to mind her manners. Instead he requested the noble lady's name and that of her besieger, but in a somewhat constrained tone of voice.

"My lady's name you shall not know at this time, but as for her tormentor, he is called the Red Boar," replied the damosel.

"Just so," said Arthur, glancing to his right and left. "The Red Boar? Never heard of him. But he sounds a common scurvy fellow to me. And to say sooth, this whole affair rings shrewdly and uncouthly in my ears, and saucily too; and I tell you honestly, young lady, that were I a private knight instead of a responsible king, I'd liefer seek honor championing the League of Swineherds against the Guild of Charcoal-Burners than in this ambiguous knightly adventure of yours."

"Do I hear aright?" cried the damosel, in a high voice and with a red face. "Is this the vaunted chivalry of King Arthur and his fellowship of the Round Table?"

And she shot a defiant and scornful glance at the King, who avoided it, then around at the knights who, taking their cue from their liege lord, followed his example of detachment. Even Sir Dinadan, though again in need of a profitable adventure, sat mum.

"Fie upon you, one and all!" she cried. "And you call this table of yours the seat and center of chivalry! Bah and pah to you! I've seen your equals in valor and courtesy—and belike your betters—chomping bacon and guzzling cider round the buttery-hatches of beggar-beset monasteries!"

The shocked stillness and silence which followed upon the tirade was broken by a disturbance at the door which drew all eyes, including the King's; and he saw the youth nicknamed Beaumains pushing to enter the hall and two porters pushing and whacking to keep him out.

"What now?" cried Arthur, grateful for a diversion. "It is our petitioner of a year ago. Admit him, varlets!"

But Beaumains was already in, having cracked the porters' heads together, and was kneeling, cap in hand.

"Sir, grant me speech now!" he cried eagerly.

"Right civilly asked," said Arthur. "Speak, young man."

"Gramercy, lord! 'Tis the full year now since Your Grace granted me one request and permission to make two more."

"I remember it well. What would you now?"

"Sir, I would essay this adventure of the distressed lady and the Red Boar."

At this, some smiled and a few frowned, and Sir Kay whispered "Good riddance!" and the damosel cried in sneering derision that the poor oaf must be as mad as insolent, for the Red Boar was a match for fifty such base-born louts.

"Peace!" said Arthur to the damosel; and to Beaumains he said, in a different voice, "Think again, young man. Would you have me grant you certain death?"

Beaumains stood up then and said, earnestly yet humbly, "Sir, I have received nought but gracious favor at your hands, and so now pray your further kindness in all good faith. . . . Sir, that with God's help and your permission I shall prove a match for the ruffian Red Boar, I do not doubt."

Now Sir Kay leaned to the King and whispered, "The lout may be right, at that, for he has shown monstrous strength in the handling of cauldrons in the kitchen, and he has been fed like a prize porker."

Arthur scratched an ear reflectively.

"Be it on your own head then," he said. "The adventure is yours, my young friend. And so I must find you arms and a horse."

"Gramercy, generous prince!" cried Beaumains joyously. "But as to arms and horse, these are in the forecourt even now—my humble thanks to Your Grace just the same. I saw them from a window."

At that moment a squire came in and announced a dwarf on a horse much too big for him, and another great charger hung all about with arms and armor, at the front door. At that, Arthur and most of the knights present quit their seats and hastened from the Hall of the Round Table to see this marvel at first hand; and in the consequent jostle Sir Launcelot and Sir Kay were jammed cheek by jowl.

"What of your baseborn scullion now?" asked Launcelot, in a soft voice but with a hard elbow at the seneschal's ribs.

"That was my little joke," gasped Sir Kay. "I knew it all the whole—or why did I recommend him for this adventure? If you doubt it ask the King."

Every champion present was eager to take part in the buckling and latching of Beaumains into his bright harness, which was of as fine plate and chain as any they had ever seen; but in this case, what with arguments and the snatching back and forth of this piece and that, many hands made hard work. But Beaumains was all rightly and tightly harnessed at last, and up in his high saddle, and with a great shield before him and a great spear in his right hand. And so he and his dwarf rode forth and over the drawbridge.

In the meantime, the damosel had ridden off on her jennet. But the dwarf had observed her going and what way she went; and so he followed, and Beaumains with him. And Arthur and his noble company returned to their dinner; and on the way between courtyard and hall, the King exclaimed, "But what of his third request? He must have forgotten it in the excitement."

"Yes, sire," said Dinadan, who happened to be at the royal elbow. "And by your leave I will follow him and learn of him."

"Well thought on," said Arthur. "And I should like to

hear also how he fares with the saucy damosel and the outcome of his encounter with the Red Boar."

So Dinadan withdrew on an empty stomach and, as soon as might be, he took the road in pursuit of Beaumains and the dwarf, even as they pursued the damosel.

The damosel went a league swiftly, then another at a softer pace, and thereafter let her jennet amble or even stop now and then to pluck a tidbit of tender herbage. "He will overtake me at his peril," she said. "I'll put him in his place, the forward varlet!"

It was midafternoon when Beaumains and all his weight of horses and iron came heavily abreast of the jennet, with a thumping of great hoofs and a clanking of arms, and saluted the damosel with a toss of his spear.

"Who is this?" she cried in mock surprise.

"Your appointed champion, fair damosel, at your service—to the death even," replied Beaumains, stammering in his eagerness.

"Champion?" she jeered. "Fie upon you, fellow! D'ye think I have no eyes and cannot see your greasy kitchen rags behind that false show of steel? And to the death, d'ye say? You may die in the service you were born to, at the hands of a master cook or mayhap of tumbling into a cauldron of soup, but never will you die like a gentleman nor in my service; and were I bigger, I'd whip you for your insolence."

He said nothing to that, but only showed abashed eyes and a red face in his open helmet.

"Champion, quotha!" she railed on. "Back to your pots an' pans, rogue!—before some errant knight happens by and drubs you with the flat of his sword, at my bidding."

"Nay, that I may not do, for I was given this adventure, and charged with it, by my liege lord King Arthur!" he protested.

"Is it his adventure or mine then?" cried the damosel. "A fig for your liege lord! But since I must suffer your company until some happy chance rids me of it (I'm praying that you'll tumble from your unaccustomed seat and break your neck), ride at my other side, I beg you, for I've a nose as well as eyes and would as lief have a kitchen midden as you 'twixt it and the wind."

So he drew rein till she had passed ahead, then rode up on her other side, and the dwarf with him.

"Fall back, scullion!" she cried. "Your place is twice the length of your spavined ploughhorse behind me—but you'd be all the way back to where you started from if I had my wish, heaven knows!"

Again Beaumains and his attendant checked their chargers and let the damosel pass ahead.

"Sir," said the dwarf, "I beg you to take the flat of your hand to her, for she is the veriest shrew I ever had the misfortune to meet, and but for fear of your displeasure, I'd tell her so myself."

"Peace, good Gligger," said Beaumains.

"Peace? Dear sir, that's something we'll know little of in this company!"

"We must bear it, however, in the way of duty," sighed Beaumains.

So they went forward another league without haste, and in silence save for the mutterings of the dwarf Gligger.

Anon, a shout in their rear caused all three to look back; and there was a full-armed knight on a tall dapple-gray approaching at a gallop that shook the ground; and he came to a jouncing stop only when he was fairly knee-to-knee with Beaumains.

"Well met, my young friend!" he cried. "The King sent me after you with a question."

Now Beaumains knew him by voice and shield for Sir Dinadan, and so replied warmly, "I am His Majesty's beholden humble servant, sir, and Your Honor's too. What is the question?"

"Why, my friend, you told the King you would ask three favors of him, one at that time a year ago and the others today. The first was for a year's board and bed, which was granted and has been honestly discharged; and the second was asked and granted this very day; but what of the third request? You rode off without naming it. Name it now, I pray you, that His Majesty's curiosity may be set at rest."

"The third request? It clean slipped my mind. . . . It is important too, by my halidom! But in the excitement of arming and spurring on this adventure my wits flew away in every direction like a covey of partridges."

"I can understand that, my friend," said Dinadan kindly, with a shoot of an eye at the damosel, who had urged her jennet close to the warhorses and was listening with a glint in her fine eyes and a curl of soft lips that was more a sneer than a pout. "But name it even now, I beg you."

"Why, sir, it was to have been for the company of a good knight to witness my behavior in this adventure, and possibly to dub me knight at the end of it, should I prove myself worthy of that high honor by overcoming all obstacles in the achievement of it."

"Fair enough! King Arthur would grant you that reasonable request blithely, I doubt not. What knight had you in mind to observe and pass judgment on you?"

"Why, sir, any one of the first fifteen would have contented me; but now, alas, 'tis too late to obtain the King's consent," sighed Beaumains.

"Not so fast!" exclaimed Dinadan. "Of this first fifteen, d'ye say? Why not seventeen? For the heralds have raised me from the nineteenth to the seventeenth place on their list in the past month."

"Seventeenth? They be fools then, or knaves; for, of all the champions in this realm, there be only ten too able for you with horse and spear, and no more than fifteen to match you afoot and slashing, mauger my head!" Beaumains protested, with spirit.

"D'ye tell me so?" cried Dinadan. "Gramercy! Gramercy! I fear you overrate my powers; but I'll not dispute your rating, for by it I qualify to serve you: and as I am as sure of the King's approval as if I had heard him grant your third request, and in the mood for a change of scene and occupation, I pray you to press forward to your adventure."

Beaumains was delighted, but not so the damosel.

"Do you call yourself a knight, yet pray to serve a scullion?" she sneered.

"Even so," said Dinadan.

"Fie upon you then!" she railed. "You are a disgrace to your goldy spurs, else you would take this adventure of mine upon yourself and order this greasy lout back to the scouring of his skillets."

"Which God forbid!" cried the knight. "I have risked limits and life for many damosels, only to be made a fool of in every case for my pains."

She looked him up and down and up again at that, and then straight in the eyes, and said coldly and with a horrid curl of her red lips, "That I can well believe."

"Even so," replied Dinadan, outwardly calm but sadly pricked in his vanity, "let me tell you, young lady, that never have I met with a damosel, nor any dame either, of so shrewish a tongue and such villainous manners as yourself."

At that the damosel stared at him with round eyes and a round mouth while the color drained from her cheeks and brow; then her eyes filled with tears and she set whip to her jennet and rode off at a gallop. Gligger, the dwarf, chuckled gleefully and doffed his cap to the knight, but Beaumains looked distressed.

"A dose of her own medicine," said Dinadan, but with a note of uncertainty in his voice and a flicker of it in his eyes. "But 'twill do her no harm, and mayhap some good even. Let us hope so, anyway."

Beaumains sighed and murmured, "It hurt her, I fear."

"God shield your tender heart!" laughed Gligger. "Hurt her, d'ye say? Ay, in her vanity, maybe. But the medicine *I'd* give her, were I bigger, and a cavalier instead of a humble servant, would hurt her more—and not in her vanity only!"

"Peace, good Gligger! And God defend us all from such humility as yours!" chided Beaumains.

So they pressed on after the damosel. The hoof-prints of the jennet were plain enough on the soft earth and tender herbage of the forest track. And they soon came upon a wider track, and by sunset upon a wayside tavern; and there they drew rein and the taverner came out to them.

"Has a damosel passed this way?" asked Dinadan.

"Nay, she has not passed," said the taverner, in a low yet desperate voice. "She is here, sir—here again, even as she was last night. Then she was for Camelot, to get Sir Launcelot or maybe even King Arthur himself for a champion—and now she's back in a higher temper than before, and bids me look out for two rogues in stolen arms and an ugly jackanapes with a feather in his cap, and all upon stolen horses—craving Your Nobility's pardon! And she bids me refuse Your Honors the front door an' keep

Your Lordships to the stables an' the scullery. God help me—for I can discern Your Worship's high stations at a glance, and the small master's gentility too—but so high and hot is her temper, I'd liefer cross King Arthur himself than her, as I hope for salvation!"

"I believe you, my good fellow," said Dinadan, and thereupon dismounted.

"Think nothing of it, good taverner," said Beaumains. "It is the damosel's humor. She plays a part, on a wager, that's all."

And he too got down from his high saddle.

"Then 'tis a pity her humor doesn't match her person," gibed the dwarf.

So they went to the stables, where they found the jennet in the best stall; but, with the help of a man in a sheepskin jerkin, they housed the three chargers well enough and watered and fed all four beasts, but without any help from the taverner, who had excused himself apologetically and hurried back to his post within easy earshot of the unpredictable demands of the damosel. Then Sir Dinadan and Beaumains got out of their harness. A wench brought them a great jack of ale, from which the knight drank first, Beaumains next, then Gligger, and, last, the man in the sheepskin all that remained. Then the taverner reappeared, carrying a lanthorn, and led them across the yard to the scullery, walking softly and with finger on lip.

"She supped right yeomanly and now sleeps," he whispered.

So they entered the scullery and from there stole on tiptoe to the kitchen, where the mistress and the wench went about the business of the hearth furtively and three or four children sat mum and motionless, as if in terror of their lives. With whispers and guiding shoves, the three travelers were set at a narrow table and served each with a bowl of rich broth and a horn spoon.

"Not so loud, dear lords!" beseeched the taverner fearfully. "Quieter splashing an' sucking, I humbly beg ye!"

The dwarf cast aside his spoon, lifted the bowl to his lips with both hands, and gulped down the contents to the last drop; and all the others could hear of the process was the convulsive laboring of his gullet. Dinadan and Beaumains made to follow his example—but the knight's esophagus proved unequal to it and he choked on a gobbet of fat and might have strangled of it but for the mighty back-thumps dealt him by Beaumains. So Dinadan was saved, but at the price of peace; for the offending morsel was ejected with an explosion like the snort of a wild bull, and the great bowl was knocked from his hands to shatter on the stone-flagged floor. The stunned silence which followed was almost instantly broken by indignant shrill screams from an inner room, ordering the taverner to clear his house of rogues and scullions on pain of having it pulled down about his ears.

"Now who would do that pulling for her?" jeered Gligger.

"Her father's archers," gibbered the taverner. "She's a duke's daughter. She told me so. Back to the stable, dear lords, or I'm utterly undone."

The three travelers returned to the stable and, in a little while, they were served there with bread and bacon and more ale. And there they slept in their cloaks, on clean straw. They slept soundly. Dinadan was the first to wake; he sat up instantly and looked about him sharply, like the good campaigner he was. He saw Beaumains and Gligger in the straw beside him, and his Garry and the other two chargers in their stalls. Then at the sight of an empty stall, he leaped to his feet with a shout. His companions sprang up, dazed but with knives in their hands.

"The jennet's gone—saddle and all!" Dinadan cried.

Beaumains uttered a stricken moan, but Gligger grinned and sheathed his knife. Now the taverner came cringing in at the open door.

"Lords, dear lords, be merciful!" he whined. "The lady would have it so, and I be a poor man with but the one life—not a noble knight an' adventurous—an' a poor wife an' five poor children. And she left a script for Your Nobilities."

He extended a scrap of parchment, which Dinadan snatched and from which he read aloud, but haltingly, for it was unclerkly penned, as follows:

"Fools dont ye know when ye be not wanted. I dont need yer company nor like it God wot. Go seek sum damosel in sorer stress than Me an of stronger

*stummick. If ye be good knights or only honest simple
men let be I pray ye in Christ Hys name for I crave a
Champion no more than a beard. Follow me not."*

Dinadan repeated it, then asked, "What d'ye make of
it?"

The taverner wagged his head and knocked on it with
knuckle. Beaumains sighed. Only Gligger found his tongue.

"She'd liefer our room than our company, seemingly,"
he said, and took the script from the knight's hand and
bent his brows upon it. "Here she says we're not wanted
nor loved—which I've suspected from the first. She charges
us to let be for she desires a champion no more than a
beard on her chin. Is she mad then? Nay, like a fox! If she
has no need of a champion, why did she come bawling to
King Arthur demanding the best knight in the world to rid
a castle of a red boar?"

Beaumains shook his head and sighed. "Nay, methinks
she plays a part."

"Hah—a part?" exclaimed Dinadan. "Maybe you have
something there. A part, quotha! Play-acting! She requests
a champion, but belike against her will, so she asks in so
villainous a voice and manner that Arthur and all his
knights are offended and only you, my friend—a youth
unknown and unarmed—accepts her adventure; and she
flees away even from you. She does not desire a champion,
that's certain!"

"Nay, sir, she prayed you do drive me off and take the
adventure upon yourself," Beaumains protested.

"Hah, so she did! But come to think of it, that's no
proof she truly craves a champion. She was for choosing
the less of two inconveniences then—the would-be
champion she could most easily rid herself of at pleasure—
and so she chose me."

"But why, sir? She knows you for a proven knight."

"The terrible intuition of her kind. She had but to look
in my eyes to know me for fair game, even as every other
damosel I've ever had ado with has known and proved me
to be. But this one will find herself mistaken, mauger my
head! We shall follow her and solve the mystery, but softly
and secretly."

So they baited their horses, broke their fast hastily with
cold victuals and drink, armed and saddled, and then went

after the damosel as fast as they could follow the jennet's tracks, which were plain enough in the soft ground. After riding an hour and more at a round pace, they issued from the forest into the valley of a little river; and here were meadows level though narrow, and a stone bridge of two arches, and a big knight on a big horse at the hither end of the bridge. So they rode his way softly, but were no nearer than five lengths of a horse of him when he laid his spear in rest and bade them halt; whereupon they drew rein.

"Sir, did you see a damosel on a white jennet pass this way?" inquired Dinadan politely.

"I did, and spoke with her too," answered the stranger in a jeering voice. And then he asked, and even more jarringly, "Which one of you is the scullion?"

"I am the one she dubs scullion," said Beaumains. "Why do you ask, sir?"

"That you will be glad to hear, for she bade me spare the poor pot-walloper."

"That you may not do, sir, if you be an honest cavalier, for this adventure is mine, of King Arthur's granting."

"Fiddle-de-dee, knave! Not for your Arthur nor any other prince does Sir Brun of the Bridge have ado with low fellows, save with stick or whip or the toe of his boot."

At that Dinadan whispered aside to Beaumains: "Are you a match for him, lad—on your word of honor?"

"Ay, sir, horse or afoot, by my halidom!" Beaumains whispered back.

"So be it," said Dinadan; and he turned back to Sir Brun and said, "This gentleman is of high blood and great prowess at arms, and he has passed a year in King Arthur's scullery on a wager, and has taken on that damosel's adventure on a wager also, and is now impatient to deal with you and get forward to something nearer his match than a blubbery rustic bridgekeeper."

"What's that?" screamed Sir Brun. "*Blubbery?* You lie! You fear to meet me yourself!"

Dinadan sighed and said to Beaumains, "You see how it is, lad. I have no choice in the matter. But the next shall be yours, I promise."

And he laid his spear and dressed his shield and rode at Sir Brun, who was already in motion to meet him: but the ride was so short that there was not enough force in the clash to break either spear or jounce either knight from his saddle. Then Dinadan loosed his spear and let it go and so came pushing knee-to-knee with his antagonist; he leaned and gripped him by the top of the casque with his right hand and spoke a quick word, whereupon his dapple-gray Garry swung and backed with a skip and a twist, and Sir Brun came out of his saddle like a hooked carp out of a pond and thudded to earth. Dinadan followed and set a mailed foot on Sir Brun's breastplate quicker than the telling.

The bridgekeeper begged for mercy with what breath was left in him after that thump. "Take my arms and horse, but spare my life!"

So Dinadan and Gligger disarmed him from top to toe, and hung all the pieces, along with his sword and spear and shield, to the saddle of his big horse; then the three went their way, leaving Sir Brun in a low state of mind and little else.

"Sir, that was something I have never seen done before," said Beaumains, in an awed voice.

"What was that?" asked Dinadan.

"Your method of unhorsing that big knight, sir."

"Oh, that! Effective, I grant you, but not quite the sort of feat of arms for commemoration in song and story. A trick, in fact; and to succeed in it your horse must be as tricky as you. But it has saved both Garry and me from a lot of unnecessary effort and bumps and slashes."

At noon they caught up with the damosel, where she sat on a mossy stone with a plum tart in her hand and a little basket of more such kickshaws on her knee. At sight of them, she sprang to her feet with an inarticulate cry, overturning the basket.

"Sorry to upset you," said Dinadan smoothly, with a glance at the spilled pastries. "We received your penned admonitions and charges, but ventured to follow our line of duty nevertheless."

She cried, "God defend me!" And then, "How did you cross the river?"

"Even by the bridge," said Dinadan; and with a gesture he called her attention to the fourth charger and its burden of arms and harness, which she had overlooked in her excitement.

She looked and understood.

"Oh! The rogue!" she gasped. "The big vile braggart! He swore that Launcelot nor Tristram was no match for him; and he would stop you for a month or forever if you pressed him; and as for the scullion and the manikin, he would chase them halfway back to Camelot. So I gave him a purse of gold—the villainous fat liar!"

"So?" queried the knight, slanting an eye at the dwarf.

"Bless my soul!" exclaimed Gligger. "I slipped it into my wallet for safekeeping, sir, and it clean slipped my mind."

"You should have mentioned it," reproved Dinadan mildly. "Had I known of a full purse, I'd have left the rogue his horse and arms. But no, on second thoughts you did well, my boy! Now, return the purse to the damosel; and let us hope this will show her the unwisdom of paying in advance for that sort of service."

The dwarf got down from his high horse, pulled the fat purse from his wallet, and, louting and smirking innocently, proffered it to the damosel.

"Nay, not that!" she cried and struck it from his fingers, then clapped both hands to her face and wept and sobbed.

So Dinadan and Beaumains dismounted, the knight muttering the while, but Beaumains hardly breathing; and when Dinadan stopped to pick up and pouch the purse, Beaumains went near to the weeping damosel and down on one iron knee before her.

"I'll act as Your Ladyship's treasurer," said Dinadan.

She heeded him not, though her sobs subsided, but turned a disdainful glance upon Beaumains.

"Why kneel you there?" she cried. "D'ye think I'll dub you a knight? Out upon you for a fool!"

"I kneel to beg a boon of you," he answered humbly. "I pray you to charge your hirelings to set upon me instead of upon Sir Dinadan in future, for how else am I to perform a feat of arms for his judgment?"

"To horse! Here's treachery!" screamed Gligger, climbing to his own high saddle even as he screamed.

"An ambush!" bawled Dinadan; and he was no more than up and spear in hand when three knights came hurtling from cover and at him, and two more close on their heels.

First, he picked the nearest of the leading three out of

the saddle like a winkle out of its shell; then, discarding his spear, he crowded in between the remaining two of the van and knocked on their helmets with a short war-hammer that was his favorite weapon for mounted in-fighting. He drew his sword then, ready to apply other tactics to his next opponent or opponents. But now there were none; the other two lay sodded.

"Sir, you left but two for me," complained Beaumains, who stood nearby on his own feet, leaning lightly on his sword.

"Your own fault, my dear lad," said Dinadan, in a voice of mild reproof. "If you hadn't been down on your knees you'd been the sooner mounted and spurring."

"I admit that, Sir Dinadan. The fact is, I hadn't time to mount, let alone to spur."

"Not mounted, d'ye say? And yet you brought 'em both to earth! How did you do it? For no proved champion could do better, by my halidom!"

"Why, sir, I slashed an' grabbed an' pulled an' slashed again to right an' left, for all I was able."

"Able enough!" cried Dinadan, dropping his sword and dismounting, and embracing Beaumains with a clanging of breastplates. "I'll bestow the accolade even now, and right gladly; then back to Camelot to show your goldy spurs and change our winnings—four horses and sets of arms are mine and two are yours, but I'll call it fifty-fifty—for coin of the realm, before that deadly damosel leads us into another and fatal trap."

"Gramercy, sir," said Beaumains; and he sank to one knee and bowed his plumed head.

Then Sir Dinadan took Beaumains' own sword and struck him on the left shoulder and the right and the left again with the flat of it, and chanted in a reverent voice, "In the names of the Holy Trinity I do hereby dub you knight. Arise Sir—, Sir—"

"Gareth," murmured Beaumains.

"Gareth, d'ye say?"

"Gareth of Orkney, sir."

"Arise, Sir Gareth!"

And the new knight obeyed, and thanked Dinadan again, and glanced about him.

"I know the King of Orkney," said Dinadan. "That's to

say I've met him three times, in the very best company—at royal joustings, in fact—for two tumbles and one draw. Truly a doughty jouster."

Gareth murmured modestly, "My own father, sir."

"Hah!" cried Dinadan. "Will Kay have a red face when he hears that!"

"Where is the damosel?" asked Gareth.

"Sir, at the first clash she went headfirst into that thicket, like a fox to earth," said Gligger, pointing a finger. "But here she comes out."

The damosel issued from the tangled hawthorns on her hands and knees. Her tall headdress now was crooked, her tear-smudged face was scratched, and her fine gown was ripped and bedraggled. Still on all fours she stared blankly at the two knights and then at the motionless figures on the greensward.

"All sped," said Dinadan harshly.

"Dead?" she gasped incredulously.

The knights exchanged significant glances.

"It was not an occasion for chivalrous courtesies," said Dinadan sternly.

She stood up then and pointed a trembling finger at the most richly armed of the corpses.

"That was my father," she said; and though her voice was low and clear it chilled her hearers to the marrow. "A false knight, forsworn and outlawed—leader of robbers and murderers. He sent me to bring some great and rich knight of King Arthur's court to him—Arthur himself even, or else Launcelot or Tristram or Lamorak or another of great fame and wealth—to be held for ransom. He forced me to swear on my dead mother's rosary to make my plea to Arthur, and to bring the victim to the trysting place, mauger my immortal soul! I made my plea, but in so unmannerly a fashion that no great champion, but only this youth, would undertake my adventure. And then you came, and would not stop or be driven off—neither of you. So I gave all my gold to the braggart at the bridge to stop you both: for without any champion I'd be free of my vow to keep that tryst. He didn't stop you. But I would have turned you somehow—even warned you at the price of eternal damnation—but they shifted the ambush two full leagues this side of the trysting place."

And then she laughed; and the two knights stared at her in amazement, and even Gligger looked dazed. And her laughter grew higher and wilder, and she pointed again and screamed exultantly, "And look at them now!" Then she swayed and fell and lay twitching.

The knights brought her out of that fit, or swoon, or whatever it was, with splashes of cold water from a near-by spring and sips of liquor from a leather bottle. She sat up at last, a pitiful figure, and hid her face with her hands.

"An astounding tale, if true," said Dinadan. "I am inclined to believe it, and doubtless Sir Gareth is too, but we must take you back to King Arthur, that he may hear it from your own lips."

She bowed her head yet lower in meek acquiescence. Then Dinadan took the purse of gold from his wallet and gave it to Sir Gareth.

"It is your adventure," he said. "I'm but an onlooker."

So Gareth helped the bedraggled damosel to her feet, and to where her jennet stood patiently, and up into the saddle. She looked down at him and whispered, "Will the King punish me?"

"Nay, for what?" Gareth answered. "He is a just but merciful prince. At the very worst he may place you in a convent, for the good of your immortal soul."

"Shall I need money in a convent?" she whispered.

"Nay, you would lack nothing. But you have money. Here, take back your purse now, for fear I might lose it on the way."

Dinadan then called Gareth for help in rounding up the newly acquired horses from the surrounding thickets. The knights and Gligger worked afoot, and the knights right heavily and hotly in their suits of mail; but the task was accomplished at last.

"We'll leave the five dead rogues as they are," said Dinadan. "We have enough hardware now without adding that junk to it. But the damosel! Where is she?"

She wasn't there: neither she, nor the jennet. They shouted, but got no answer. They shouted again and yet again, but all to no purpose.

"Stolen away," said Dinadan. "A guilty conscience, I fear. Ay, guilty indeed, to go without her purse!"

"She—had her purse," stammered Gareth. "I—she—I didn't think she'd run away."

Dinadan smiled cynically, but his hand on the new knight's shoulder was kind.

"Live and learn, dear lad," he said. "Even I am still learning!"

MOUNTAIN MIRACLE

When Sir Dinadan and Sir Gareth won back to Camelot from the adventure of the perfidious damosel, and King Arthur knew the young knight of Dinadan's making for a son of his beloved sister Queen Elizabeth of Orkney, great was the rejoicing, many were the feasts and flings of celebration. But these did not satisfy Arthur, so he conceived a tournament and games that would make a mere poppy show of anything of the sort ever seen before in this realm. And to give all lovers of hard knocks and high jinks plenty of time in which to assemble, he ordained it to begin on St. Michael's Feast and to continue a sennight and a day; and to this end he sent trusty heralds in every direction throughout his realm and beyond it, and beyond Cornwall into Wales and even to Ultima Thule, and by ships to Ireland and Brittany.

—The Book of Maelor

Now Sir Dinadan was in clover again, and even deeper than ever before, having received a fat purse from King Arthur in addition to an honest price for the spoils of his spear and sword. And now he had no other mouth or back dependent upon him save those of his loved charger Garry (unless you count the dozen and more cripples and blind beggars who clustered about his lodgings whenever he was in town), for he had not employed a squire since homesick young Victor had left him and returned to Castle Fergus. Now he engaged the two best rooms at his inn, and the best of the stabling there for Garry, and a groom for each. He gave doles daily to his clamorous almsfolk, and bonuses every Sunday. He had a hairdresser in every morning to comb and curl his ringlets, and a barber to razor his cheeks and chin. He called a skilled limner in to repaint the rampant unicorn on his shield. He got his lutes out of pawn and had them restrung, and looked to the refurbishing of his wardrobe.

Now Dinadan lived in the manner he would liefest of all others in this world. On fine days he rode Garry abroad for an hour or two after breakfast, and again after dinner, but lightly, and both horse and man lightly housened in silk and velvet instead of leather and iron. Sometimes he played at pall-mall, or skittles, or shuttlecock, with other agile gentlemen of the court, and with noble dames and damosels and maybe a few queens looking on and applauding. But he sat at home in his lodgings a few hours every day, and many hours in foul weather, making new songs, both the words and the tunes, and writing the words on parchments and trying the tunes with voice and lute. And almost every evening he supped at some high table, and as often as not treated the company to music after meat; but not always, for his moods were not as constant as was his appetite for good victuals and drink.

So Dinadan supped one muggy July night, after a day of rain and song-making, with a witty dowager duchess who was one of his oldest and merriest friends. Feeling in a low mood and spent after his day-long battle of rhymes, he was somewhat set aback to find a full score of company, and strangers amongst them, instead of a dozen, and all familiars. But at the thought that the hostess had the best cook and the best cellar in Camelot, as well as the liveliest wit, and that his sure friend young Sir Gareth sat just across the board from him, he took heart.

When the sounds of spooning and supping and all sorts of bowl and trencher action were past, and even the clattering and gurgling of cups and cans and bottles a little reduced, a large stranger—strange to Dinadan, at least—called loudly and right assuredly for a song.

"Now for a song, Duchess—a ditty of love to a merry tune!" he bellowed like a bull. "Now for this tame poet I have heard about! Bid him sing for us now, fair hostess!"

He was a big man around as well as up and down, and richly dressed and bearded, and he sat at the dowager Duchess's right hand. The lady cried "O fie!" and plucked him by a sleeve and whispered in his ear.

"Ho!" he exploded. "Ho-ho! Temperamental, hey?"

She plucked and whispered again in obvious agitation, whereupon he laughed indulgently and patted her plucking hand with a paw as big and hairy as a bear's.

"Leave him to me, dear lady. Dinkydan's the name, wot?"

"Dinadan," the poet corrected mildly.

Now all eyes were turned upon Dinadan, who sat loosely and cup in hand, with his gaze among the bannered and cobwebby rafters. His friends regarded him expectantly, some of them even apprehensively, and the strangers curiously.

"Hah, just so!" exclaimed the large stranger. "You are Dinadan."

"Sir, to you," replied Dinadan softly, but loudly enough, at the same time shifting his position slightly and lowering his dreamy gaze from the rafters to the wine in his cup.

The other gaped in angry astonishment and would have protested with oaths against this belittling of his ducal dignity (for a duke he was, though of a remote and savage duchy), had not their hostess plucked and whispered again. So he swallowed his monstrous oaths, but with difficulty and wry grimaces.

"Sing for the Duchess!" he cried instead, in a voice half-choked with fury.

Dinadan smiled thinly into his cup and murmured as thinly: "The lady is quite capable of asking for herself."

"Please, Dinny," pleaded the dowager Duchess. "Duke Boreas intends no scathe. Please sing for us."

"Hah! Boreas!" Dinadan exclaimed, but consideringly, like one thinking aloud. "A wind from the north. Very appropriate."

Now he stood up and looked kindly at his hostess, yet far from happily, with a crooked smile and one eyebrow cocked and the lid of the other optic slightly drooped, and so addressed her gently.

"Madam, I have sung at your bidding twenty times if one, and hope, with luck and God's mercy and your kindness, to do so as often again at least, and shall do so even now, but this time on a condition."

"A condition?" she wailed. "Oh, this is not like you!"

And all his friends present had the same thought, and they surmised that some shrewd play was afoot.

"You say sooth, lady," he sighed. "Erstwhiles I have ever sung for you from a full heart, no matter how sorely I railed at love and lovers, but tonight I have only a full stomach, and it somewhat queasy. However, I shall obey you to the extent of my ability and with my newest numbers—but only on condition that the vociferous person on your right first sings for his supper too."

"Person?" roared Duke Boreas. "Eh? D'ye mean me? D'ye call *me* a person?"

The hostess clapped her plump little hands to her ears. Some of Dinadan's friends chuckled, and others of them giggled. The six strangers, who had evidently come to the feast with Boreas, glared and scowled and plucked at their beards.

"I could think of other names for you," said Dinadan softly, "but would be sorry to offend the ears of the ladies."

Duke Boreas opened his mouth to roar again, but the fury of his indignation paralyzed his vocal cords and he only gaped.

"If you can't sing, how about a dance?" Dinadan went on smoothly and with a reasonable air. "What, you can't dance? That's too bad. And yet I have seen very good dancers of very much your shape and size, usually performing to the beating of a drum; but in my childhood I once saw an old bear who had learned to dance to any music. Can't my lord duke do anything to entertain the company and repay our fair hostess—in part, at least—for the trenchers you have cleared and the cups and cans you have drained?"

This was shrewder than his intimates even had expected, and they gasped apprehensively; and all the strangers from the northern wilds gnashed their carnivorous teeth; and Duke Boreas himself lurched and lunged to his feet, fumbling at his side the while for the hilt of the sword, which fortunately had been left in the antechamber. But he found his voice, and so he straightway vented his wrath in a bloodcurdling declamation of what he could and would do to Dinadan's liver and lights and other vital organs at the first opportunity. The hospitable Duchess popped up and slapped the visiting Duke's whiskers with gem-encrusted hands.

"Gramercy," said Dinadan politely, but whether in thanks to his hostess for her gesture in his behalf or to Boreas for his bloody intentions, who knows? "But now is hardly the time for it, nor this the place," he continued. "But if my lord duke has come all the way from his mountainy fastnesses to play a part in King Arthur's great joustings and junketings at Michaelmas, at the Castle of Maidens, why not keep it till then, and so contribute to the success of the royal tournament instead of upsetting our gracious hostess's digestion here and now—not to mention my own?"

Boreas snarled: "So be it! Then I'll—I'll—" But he had already disposed horribly of every organ, limb, and feature in the knight's possession, so he let it go at that.

"Agreed," said Dinadan pleasantly. "The time, the Feast of Saint Michael; the place, the Castle of Maidens. With sharp points and edges, I presume. Quite. And as the appointment is for over two months from now, may I suggest that Your Grace make a note of it?"

"I'll remember," promised Boreas.

"Gramercy," said Dinadan; and he turned to the duchess with a curved instead of a crooked smile and a flutter of an eyelid.

"Madam, I apologize humbly. But now that your illustrious ducal guest has so politely excused himself from making the initial acknowledgment of your hospitality on the good and sufficient plea that he can neither sing nor dance—but I suspect that only his innate modesty deters his grace from excelling in both arts—I shall try to make amends by singing for both our suppers."

"You and your jabes an' jokes will be the death of me yet!" cried the Duchess, with tears of relief in eyes and voice; and Dinadan's other friends present looked vastly relieved and surprised too, and Boreas and his six bewildered to the point of stupefaction.

"God defend you, madam, and from any worser death too!" replied Dinadan unctuously, and added matter-of-factly: "May I trouble you for the loan of a lute now?"

A page with a lute was at his elbow in a jiffy.

Now he twanged, now high, now low, and tauted one

string and eased another. Now he strummed, and the sound was as aimless and tuneless as the babble of a brook, and inquiring eyebrows were raised by a few who did not know him very well, and supercilious eyebrows by the seven who did not know him at all, and Boreas gurgled deep in his throat: "I could do as well meself!" And the brook babbled on, lisping and tinkling, till even the Duchess began to fear that the lutanist was dozing, overcome by his potations or the monotony of his strumming. But hark! The brook runs faster—faster and deeper and louder. Here's no lisping now, but sibilant complaining; no tinkling, but splashy clashing. Now the aimless brook runs full and strong between its banks and over its boulders. No babbling now, but a deep and increasing roar topped by splashy shouts: no brook now, but a mountain torrent in spate.

The seven strangers stare, each to his front, and breathe thickly. They see the old gray kelpie washed from his familiar pool and floundering furiously in the twisting, sloshing turmoil of waters black and green and brown, all sinewed and fanged with white. They see it as surely as they hear it. And now, of a sudden, Dinadan's fingers are still; and in the silence the bursting flood and quaking rocks are gone from before their entranced eyes, leaving only this scene of candleshine agleam on cups and silver flagons and spilled wine, on bejeweled throats and breasts, on faces as fixed as masks and eyeballs like polished agates.

Boreas cried in a strange voice: "I heard the eagles screaming!"

"I took it for Old Kelpie," muttered another mountaineer.

"You were both right, I hope," said Dinadan. "Gramercy." He was pleased with himself and them.

"And now something littler and lighter, and words to match," he said; and straightway he tinkled and sang a rustic sweet ditty to do with a shepherd and a dairymaid and kisses behind a haystack.

The Duchess and other ladies laughed and clapped their hands, but none of the cavaliers, and Boreas and his fellows least of all, appeared much impressed.

"Wot d'ye know of dragons?" mumbled Duke Boreas. "Hah, a fight with a dragon! My sire fought a dragon—the biggest fire-spitter ever seen—single-handed, to the death. *There* be something to sing about!"

"Just so," murmured Dinadan consideringly. "I've never fought a dragon myself, nor seen one. Born too late. A fire-spitter, did you say?"

"Ay, with a belly hot as a forge, and fire from his nose like sparks from an anvil."

"Just so," agreed the poet, and fell to plucking at his lute, but only for a moment. "Nay, I need a harp for this!" he cried. "Madam, a harp, I pray you!"

And a harp was at his elbow in a count of seconds, for Sir Tristram, who was a skilled harper, was also a frequent guest at this table. It was a short harp, but strong and of nine strings, and after a few plunks and twangs, Dinadan had it humming like a swarm of bees and clanging like swords on helmets. And now the clangor outrang the humming, and the ladies held their ears.

"A dragon! A dragon!" shouted Dinadan, through and above the tumult of the brazen strings.

Thus and then "The Slaying of the Dragon" was made and uttered for the first time, for that hour and forever. By one old chronicler it is recorded as "Dragon-song of Dinadan" and by another as "Dragon-death," but by that name or this, fearsome fragments and wild vibrations of it have clanged down the centuries even to this day.

At last the dragon was slain and reborn to immortality; and Dinadan sat down, limp and spent. All eyes were upon him, some fearful, some fierce, and some simply dazed. Duke Boreas' were fierce and dazed both, and at once flaming and glazed; and in appearance as in behavior he was like one bedeviled to madness, grabbing at the air before and above him with strangling fingers, swelling and flexing the muscles of his heavy shoulders and thick neck and snorting like a bull; and all the other mountaineers were flexing their muscles too, and clawing the air and their whiskers and snorting. It was an awesome scene.

"That was horrid," wailed the Duchess. "Oh, my poor nerves!"

"I quite agree with you," sighed Dinadan: and he filled and drained a large cup and sighed again; whereupon the seven strangers filled and drained cups and cans, and heaved great sighs, in imitation: and the poet moaned on: "I got carried away. Couldn't feel tireder if I'd slain him with my own hands, the poor creature. And look at your harp!"

He set it on the table, so all could see that only five strings of the nine remained unbroken—only the strings of brass. Then he turned from the table and went hurriedly yet stumblingly from the chamber and the house, and so home to his inn, and so to bed. And all night he dreamed, and always he was battling for his life with sword or axe or teeth or claws, for now he was a mountainy duke, and next he was himself, and now he was even the doomed and desperate dragon. But he was sleeping peacefully enough—the peace of exhaustion—when aroused by the good taverner with his good breakfast. He felt much better after the bacon and ale.

"But that performance was a mistake," he told himself. "Not only did I offend the Duchess and wreck her harp, and bedevil those wild mountaineers, but I wrecked and bedeviled my own dreams too. I'll stick to 'love' an' 'dove' hereafter—tongue in cheek for laughs and straight for tender tears—and not let the divine afflatus run away with me again."

It was a fine morning, so he rode abroad on Garry. But before they had gone an easy mile, he heard shouts and the thumping of galloping big hoofs behind him. Turning his head, he beheld Duke Boreas and his six pelting after him on great horses as shaggy as themselves; and he would have ridden for dear life then, had not a second glance shown him that all were in silk and velvet like himself, and every head was uncovered, and every feathered cap held high in a big right hand. So he turned about and waited. When Boreas came nigh and drew rein, the six did the same; and when the Duke dismounted to stand, with cap in hand, all followed his example: so, in courtesy, Dinadan dismounted and uncovered too; whereupon Boreas advanced with open arms and a countenance to suit, and clasped Dinadan to his breast.

"Well met!" he cried, and loosed his arms and clamped both hands on the knight's shoulders. "Me cap's off to you, sir!"

In truth, his fine headgear, with its feathers and great brooch studded with diamonds, lay unheeded in the dust.

"Gramercy, sir," murmured Dinadan, wondering what next. "And mine to you, Duke."

"Hah, but that was a song!" cried Boreas. "Never and nowhere was ever so grand a song as that made before, mauger me head! I've heard bards aplenty—the best in the North an' so the best in the whole world—but never a song to match your dragon-song. I fought that grumly monster the long night through, hacking an' hewing like a woodman, till the bed broke down with the violence of our struggle an' woke me up; but the reek of his breath blasting up from his burning vitals stuck in my nose till after breakfast. Sir, no warlock could conjure me up a nightmare to match your dragon!"

Dinadan was at once pleased and apprehensive.

"I am glad that you think well of the song, Sir Duke, and pray you to forgive me the nightmare—which, indeed, I had the honor of sharing with you," he said hopefully.

"Say ye so?" cried Boreas. "Sir, the honor is mine! And wot I think of the song is that if my lamented sire could hear it, he would burst forth from his tomb with pride an' heroic ardor. But come, Sir Dinadan, and honor me by breaking bread at my poor table."

So they all remounted and rode back to town at a soft pace, and to a castle which King Arthur had placed at the disposal of very important guests. And so they dined; and after hours of chomping and gulping, Duke Boreas dismissed his six gentlemen and told Dinadan a pitiful story and made a strange request.

He whispered it between gusty hiccups. He had a daughter. (At that Dinadan shivered, despite the buzzing and glow of usquebaugh in head and stomach.) She was his only child and the apple of his eye. (Again the knight shivered.) But she was frail of body and listless of spirit. (Dinadan felt better.) She moped and drooped all day long, and no doctor's physic nor charm nor cure of old wives and witches touched her. She continued to fade away before his eyes. So he had come to Camelot to take King Arthur's own physician back with him to save her dear life; but that learned man was sick abed himself and refused to budge. Then he had all but given up hope of saving her, but upon hearing Dinadan the lutanist, and Dinadan the harper on top of that, hope had been rekindled in his breast. Now he gripped Dinadan's nigh shoulder and prayed him to come to that castle of gloom and sing his dragon-song to the poor child.

Replete with victuals and drink though Dinadan was, and moved with pity for daughter and father alike, he quaffed another cup and protested that such treatment would more likely kill than cure. The Duke, after due consideration and the filling and emptying of a cup himself, rejected the objection.

"Nay, not so, for all she needs is rousing, having been born melancholy of a melancholy mother, poor soul! For years now have I striven, to rouse her to take an interest in life by gentle means and not so gentle, and all to no avail. But that song of yours, Sir Poet—'The Slaying of the Dragon'—if that didn't bring her to life, she'd be happier dead."

Dinadan felt highly flattered but sorely confused too, and he protested again.

"But if it killed her? Even if she were happier so—which sounds unlikely to me—what of your feelings to find her so?"

"Me too. The castle is like a tomb from tower to keep. That's why I came away. But I have no fear. Nay, only the fear that we may be too late to save her."

They set out for the North at the first gleam of morning. Dinadan, on Garry, rode knee to knee with the mountain Duke, and the six mountain Barons came after in couples; and Dinadan's grooms on hackneys, a dozen mountain grooms on shaggy ponies, and wild footmen pulling and pushing on beasts of burden, came streaming after. It was an impressive cavalcade, for Boreas believed himself to be the greatest duke in the world, and paternal anxiety had not dulled his appetite for meat and drink. They traveled till noon, dined prodigiously, and marched again till sunset. They supped deep and long and slept in a portable pavilion. They breakfasted right ducally at dawn, and rode again at sunrise; and the second day was like the first. But the third day differed slightly; and with every succeeding period of twenty-four hours the difference grew, the marches lengthening daily—in time even if not always in leagues—and recesses for eating and sleeping ever shortening proportionately. It was as if the Duke's anxiety for his daughter increased ever with the decreasing of the distance between them.

The change of tempo relieved Dinadan's mind of nagging

though confused suspicions of Boreas' sincerity and his own acumen. This was surely proof that the Duke had not lured him into a wilderness on a wild-goose chase, or worse, with a cock-and-bull story.

"We'll be back in time for the tournament, I suppose," he said one morning, between a bite and a swig of a hasty breakfast before sunrise.

"Oh, that," grunted Boreas with his mouth full. "Why not?"

"'Twill be a queer thing then, for you and me to have ado with sharp spears," said Dinadan.

"With sharp spears?" the Duke spluttered. "Ho, d'ye still bear that madness in mind? Nay, never you an' me, Dinadan—with sharp spears nor blunt neither!"

"Gramercy! But should my dragon-song fail to rouse the poor damosel—or maybe rouse her to her mortal undoing—what then?"

"Then will I found a great monastery an' meself turn monk; and you, me friend, will fare home unscathed to the joys an' junketings of Camelot."

"Not so!" cried Dinadan, moved to the very roots of his generous and impulsive being. "Nay, dear Boreas, I'll turn monk too!"

At that, the Duke sprang to his feet and pulled the knight upright and embraced him.

"Fie upon such dismal talk!" he cried. "You and me with tonsured heads? Nay, we'll dance at her wedding. To horse! To horse!"

Daily the way grew rougher and the wilderness more rugged. They toiled up and down hills, and in the gloom of hanging black woods, and so into the ultimate mountains by steep glens and crooked gorges, climbing to the croak of ravens and scream of eagles, and so came at last to the Castle of Winds.

The young Damosel Wanda was still alive, but in bed and deeper sunk than ever before in that curse of melancholia inherited from her mother, who had died of it. Her tresses were gold, but paler than daffodils; her face was small, and as pale and still as a mask of alabaster; the color of her eyes Dinadan could not tell when he was first brought to her, for they were closed; and the narrow hands crossed on her breast were as still and white as if she were the marble effigy of a lady on a tomb.

"Daughter, the valorous knight Sir Dinadan—the greatest poet of this age—has come all the way from Camelot to sing to you," said Boreas.

The pale lips stirred with a murmured "Gramercy" too faint to hear, but the eyelids stirred not at all.

The ancient nurse whispered to the Duke: "The poor lamb's past heeding any earthly music. Nought but the Trump o' Doom can rouse her now, I'm feared."

But Boreas placed a chair for Dinadan and put the harp of the knight's own selection into his hands. Dinadan fingered the strings reluctantly, fearful of breaking that tenuous thread of life with a shrewd or discordant sound.

"Fear not," Boreas assured him. "Play now."

So his fingers ceased their fumbling, and the harp breathed a melody as of bees and hummingbird moths in blooming lilacs.

"Louder," urged the Duke.

So the melody swelled and lifted and quickened, though still of gauzy wings and honeyed blossoms.

"The dragon now!" urged Boreas in a desperate voice.

Dinadan looked up then from his flying fingers to the heedless blind mask as pale as alabaster on the pillow as white as marble, and he thought: She is past hearing or caring, so 'twill harm her no more than if she were carved of stone in her own tomb, poor heart. And he looked down again at his fingers and shifted them to the strings of brass and copper; and the air was rent by a brazen clang, then filled and shaken with awful clangor. He stood up then and gave tongue, outshouting the wild tumult of the harp with wilder words; and so he fought and slew that dragon again, but this time with his eyes fixed upon the savage plucking and tearing of his fingers among the maddened harp-strings.

Then silence, save for the Duke's gusty gasps and snorts. Dinadan glanced aside fearfully and saw the old nurse crouched on the floor with both hands to her ears. Then, and yet more apprehensively, he looked at the bed. He uttered an inarticulate cry, brief but charged with more emotions than relief only, and staggered backward a pace and sat down hard. *For the damosel's eyes were wide open*

and regarding him—and they were as green as emeralds.
And he maintained and returned her look as fixedly, but as
a doomed bird the paralyzing stare of a snake.

God save me! he thought—if it could be called thinking.
Green. The greenest I ever saw—God help me!

And he tried to blink, but could not so much as twitch
a lid. He tried to glance aside, but his eyeballs stuck like
frost-bound pebbles. Then Boreas grasped both his
shoulders with mighty paws, raised him and turned him
about, and embraced him.

"It roused her!" cried the Duke. "Like I knew it would.
You've saved her, dear lad! But enough for now. Come away
now, for I can see it was a sore strain on your vitality as well
as on your fingers an' larynx."

❖   ❖   ❖

For the moment at least, the spell was broken; and
Dinadan departed from that chamber right willingly,
though with shaking knees and his host's support and
guidance. Together they descended to the buttery, where
more than butter was dispensed, and there each of them
disposed of two long horns of the very best. Now the four
household bards appeared, each with his harp, and louted
low to their lord and just as low to Dinadan.

"Did you hear it?" asked Boreas.

"Ay, in the antechamber, according to orders," replied
the leader of the four, who had a wreath of wilted foliage on
his bald pate and a beard of such length and profusion
that he wore it tucked into his girdle. "It nigh brasted me
heart an' ears alike," he added.

"A great song," said the Duke, with a challenging note
in his voice.

"Ay, lord, a masterpiece."

"Repeat it then, Bard Gomery."

"Nay, lord, I'm an old man. If I were able, the effort
would prove me undoing; and unable, I'd be the ruination
of the most terrible grand song ever heard even in these
mountains."

"Fair enough," said Boreas.

He glanced inquiringly at the other harpers, but each
shook his head. So he signaled to the cellarer, who straightway brought two long horns of mountain dew and two great
jacks of ale to the bards, knowing their individual tastes in

such matters; and he signaled again within the minute, and for refills for Dinadan and himself too. After a short silence disturbed only by gulps and heavy breaths, the youngest of the household bards—but even he was middle-aged and more than fully grown—drew a hairy wrist across his mouth and spoke.

"Lord, I'll essay it."

At that, Boreas cried: "Right manfully said, good Jard ap Rhys! But first another sip to limber larynx an' fingers. Ho, Master Cellarer, more sips all around!"

Horns and jacks were filled again. After another liquid silence, Jard ap Rhys wiped his mouth again, then set his jack on the floor and applied both hands to his harp. Well, he had powerful hands, God wot! The clangor was terrific.

"Hold! You went wrong there!" cried Dinadan, grabbing the nearest instrument and clawing like mad. "This is how it goes!"

So Jard clawed like mad in imitation, and so the volume of clanging clamor was doubled. Old Gomery quivered and reared like an old warhorse to the braying of trumpets, saying, "I'll take it now, young feller, me lad!" and pushed himself in, harp and all, between Jard and Sir Dinadan, facing the knight. But Jard refused to give over, and so now there were three harps in uproar together. The air shook; the motes in the sunray from the little window danced; and the curtainy cobwebs among the rafters stirred and shook down dust and the bright shells of sucked-dry wasps and bluebottle flies.

"The words now!" bellowed Boreas, waving his right arm, horn and all, and spattering the company with mountain dew.

"The dragon!" shouted Dinadan: and Gomery and Jard ap Rhys shouted it like a close echo.

Now Dinadan sang, and the mountain bards bawled and chanted word for word with him and no more than a breath behind him. It was tremendous, devastating, exhausting.

"Never again!" gasped the poet, dropping the borrowed harp and flopping across the buttery-hatch.

He rested for an hour in a little garden of roses. After dinner, he and Boreas rode softly in a crooked valley for a few hours. Then he idled in the garden till supper; and after supper he retired early to bed and slept fitfully, dragon-ridden. He breakfasted in bed. Refreshed and elegantly dressed, he accompanied Boreas to Wanda's chamber. They found the damosel sitting high against the pillows, with wide-open eyes and slightly parted lips; and now her lips were like the petals of a wild rose, and there was even a faint suggestion of pink in her thin cheeks.

"My darling, this is Sir Dinadan, in case you don't remember him from yesterday," said the fond father.

"I remember him," she murmured, smiling faintly.

Dinadan bowed low.

"He saved your life, darling," the Duke told her.

"Gramercy," she murmured. "It was wonderful."

"She took her broth like a good girl this morning, an' a duck egg too," said the old nurse.

The Duke exclaimed, "God be praised—an' this knight too—for the miracle of the age!" And he asked softly: "D'ye crave more music now, me darling? Maybe something soft an' low this time, or merry an' jinxing like young lovers dancing? If so, just ask Sir Dinadan prettily, and you'll get it."

The damosel did not look at her father, but continued to gaze greenly at Dinadan; and Dinadan continued to gaze back eye to eye, for he could not help himself, and maintained a polite and serene countenance despite internal tremors of foreboding.

"Please," she sighed.

Now Boreas set a chair close beside the bed and prayed his guest to sit: so the bodeful poet sat. Now Boreas produced a lute and presented it.

"Soft and low now, dear friend," he whispered.

So, with a shrewd effort, Dinadan lowered his gaze from the green eyes to the lute on his knee and played soft and low. He played a weeping willow tree and a little weeping wind to sob in it. Now the Duke drew up another chair and seated himself; and the willow wept and the little wind sobbed, on and on and on. Soon the old nurse came to Dinadan's shoulder and whispered: "Ye've played 'em both to sleep, sir."

Dinadan ventured to lift his gaze from the lute-strings to the face on the pillow. Sure enough, her eyes were shut. But even while he toyed with the thought of slipping out and away to the refuge of the garden, they opened wide, and full upon him.

"Nay, I am not asleep, though dreaming a magic dream," she murmured. "And I tried to put words to the dream bred of your magic music," she murmured on. "But I am not a poet, and am in no wise magical, but you are the greatest poet in Christendom. So I pray you, of your gentleness, to double the magic with your voice."

She smiled. And he essayed a smile in return, but achieved only a desperate grimace.

"At your service," he mumbled, for lack of an honest excuse; for how could he, who had come here for the sole purpose, and of his own free will, to minister to this damosel with song, now refuse her request for more? "What will you?"

"A song of love," she sighed.

Now God defend me! he thought wildly; and again he tried to detach his gaze from hers, but again in vain. Keep your head now, and sing her the bitter truth of it, he told himself. Cure her of that blind folly. Kill it now while still blind and feeble and harmless in her ignorant heart. Crush it like the viper it is—the very serpent of the Fool's Paradise!

"So be it," he muttered. "A song of love. A song of lies."

And he strummed a string, and straightway began to sing a song so harsh and bitter that experienced gallant dames, including broad-minded queens and tough old duchesses even, had blanched at it and stopped their ears against it before now. But when he saw the light fade in her green eyes, the red fade in her lips, and the dawn-pink of eglantine flee her thin cheeks, pity filled and melted him, and resolution and voice failed him. Remorse smote him, and panic lest he had roused her to life yesterday with the fiercest song he had ever made, only to break her innocent heart now with the deadliest song any man had ever made.

"God forgive me!" he muttered. "My mistake. Forget it. A joke—an' a foul one. But I'll amend it—with God's help—or I'm no poet nor a merciful man even! Hark now to the truth about love."

He strummed again, but with soft fingers now. He sang again, but now voice and words alike were as sweet and smooth as honey and dew. And so he made one of the most memorable love songs ever, and one of the longest,

though he felt nothing of the grand sentiment for this particular damosel, but only pity and anxiety for her, and the
tender memories of lost love over all. Oh, he was a poet all
right. And as he saw the green eyes brighten again, and
the pale lips and cheeks bloom once more, relief, and
pride in his song, carried him high and far beyond that
chamber and above the world, where he soared like an
eagle and looked down at forest and mountain, castle and
croft and people, like a god surveying and approving his
own creations: and feeling godlike, he sang like a god; and
such was the potency of his performance that he himself
soon succumbed to it, and slumped motionless and silent
in a trance of enchantment and of sheer exhaustion.

Dinadan was roused from that trance by heavy paws
on his shoulders and a gusty whispering in his face. It was
Duke Boreas.

"Look ye! Another miracle!"

Dinadan looked at the bed, and sat straight and gaped
at what he saw there. The damosel's eyes were closed, but
lids and lashes lay as lightly as a moth's wings. Her lips
were smiling sweetly and as bright as rose petals dew-
washed. Her cheeks were pink too, and childily round now
instead of thin; and now there was a rosy glow on the
alabaster brow as if a fairy lamp burned behind it.

"She's beautiful!" he gasped, astonished.

"So she is! And I'm as surprised as you! She wasn't ever
before, save to meself and her poor mother an' Nurse
Bolster maybe, but now she's a spanking beauty—or ye've
bedeviled me eyesight."

"Nay, nothing like that, Duke. I'm no warlock nor
enchanter. She's a beauty all right! I have seen only one
more beautiful—but she was false as fair, ah me!—or two,
if I count Queen Isoud of Cornwall."

"Another miracle then, like I said before. First you
rouse her to life with the fierce Dragon-song; an' that was
only yesterday. An' now you turn her into a ravishing
beauty—me poor little sick melancholy lamb—with a song
of love. Hah, love! Come to me arms, me dear lad!"

And he pulled the knight upright from the chair and
hugged him hard, exclaiming "Gramercy, gramercy!" the
while, over and over.

Dinadan disengaged himself as gently as possible and said: "Glad to have been of service. Think nothing of it."

"Think nothing of it, d'ye say? Ho-ho! One of my mountains is yours already, and a high castle to match it—I'll make a record of it this very day; an' I wouldn't wonder if all my mountains an' castles will be yours when I am done with them, by the look of things. Ha-ha!"

And he slid an arch glance from Dinadan to the sleeping beauty and back again. The knight, still staggering from the embrace and dismayed at the prospect, gasped and stammered.

"Nay, nay, God forbid! That's to say—gramercy, gramercy—but may you live a hundred years! I—ah!—pray you to excuse me now. Utterly exhausted! Worse than slaying the dragon."

"Just so, dear lad. You an' me for the buttery now—I be all atremble meself—an' leave our beauty to her beautiful dreaming."

So they departed Wanda's bedchamber together and descended to the buttery: and there, after draining one horn himself while Boreas drained three, Dinadan stole away to the little garden, leaving the Duke spellbinding head butler and master-cellarer with a fuddled account of the second miracle, and the sudden ravishing beauty of the Damosel Wanda. And there he sat down in the shade of a little tree full of pink bloom and golden bees and clasped his head with both hands. And so he sat and thought desperately, but to no purpose, of the coil into which he had sung himself. But not for long.

"Noble Sir Dinadan, pray forgive this intrusion," said an anxious voice.

At that, he looked up and saw a tall youth standing before him, and smiling down at him, but with a troubled countenance.

He sighed: "Don't mention it. What would you, young sir?"

"I heard the miracle song—but it wrought no miracle to me, sir, for my eyes have seen her beauty ever," replied the youth, speaking so hurriedly that he all but gabbled. "I was behind the arras when you sang it, and when you were gone, I went to the bedside and looked at her. Ay, she's beautiful! But to me she was always so, though never so rosy as now since she sickened four dreary years ago."

"D'ye say so?" cried Dinadan eagerly; and he got to his feet as eagerly. "D'ye say she was always beautiful to you—this Damosel Wanda—as beautiful before my song as after?"

"Ay, sir, by my halidom! White or red, thin or round, she is beautiful to me."

"Hah! A real lover then, true and constant an' blind! And quite mad, God help you! Who are you, young sir? And what would you of me?"

"Sir, I am Lyon ap Denys, bred from little boyhood as a page in this great house and kindly nourished, and now I am captain of the castle guard. And Wanda and I were playmates daily, and she loved me even as I love her, until that melancholy sickness from which you roused her befell her. And of you, noble an' generous Sir Dinadan, I ask only that you return to Camelot and your amorous queens an' merry dames an' leave my dear love to me."

"I would leave her to you blithely, my friend—but what if she sank again into that melancholy trance?"

"Nay, sir, then would I rouse her out of it even as you did, for I have your wonderful dragon-song in my ears an' fingers to the last immortal word an' clang."

"Hah! So you are a skilled harper then?"

"Ay, sir, as any in these mountains."

"Good! But what if her sudden beauty should pass as suddenly as my song of love brought it into being?"

"Why, sir, she would still be beautiful to me."

"Just so—and still loved by the Duke, but not still beautiful to his proud eyes. Then her father would come seeking me; and not only for her beauty's sake but for her health's sake too."

Lyon admitted this ruefully.

"Now harky to me," said Dinadan. "I am as eager to be gone as you are to have me go; and when you show me your ability to keep the zest for life afire in your damosel's heart an' veins an' pretty lips, then I'll be off, and with an easy conscience."

"But I am a fumbler at the lute," sighed Lyon. "We are all harpers an' bawlers in these mountains, God help me!"

"God help you indeed! But you have a voice and ears

and fingers, and you're a lover, so I'll essay to amend your incapacity." And stepping closer, Dinadan spoke on for a full minute in an earnest whisper.

After the midday feast, Dinadan excused himself from cup and horn on the plea of an aching head, but instead of retiring to his couch he went secretly from the castle and its purlieus and into a high glen, taking the borrowed lute with him; and there he was soon joined by Lyon ap Denys. There the two remained till the westing sun was wheeling on the mountain-top, passing the lute back and forth between them, and fingering the strings turn and turn about, and singing soft and low in turn and sometimes together.

Soon after sunrise next day, Duke Boreas roused his guest to accompany him to Wanda's bedside.

"But mayhap she still sleeps," protested Dinadan.

"An' wot if she does?" chuckled the Duke. "Thanks to you, me darling chick is now as easy to look at asleep as awake."

So the knight dressed hastily and went reluctantly. They were halted in the antechamber by unexpected sounds from within.

"Wot goes on?" gasped Boreas.

Dinadan shushed him and whispered, "Quiet now! 'Tis music—save the mark!—of lute an' voice. Now what the devil?"

"Music?" snarled the Duke, but into his beard. "I never before heard such villainous discordant twiddlin' an' cat-erwaulin'! Enough to undo all your miracle-making!" And he would have charged across the antechamber and into the bedroom beyond but for Dinadan's restraining hand and voice.

"Easy does it now," the knight cautioned. "We'll take a look first." And his grip on the Duke's arm was like iron.

So they went softly to the curtains which hung across the doorway and parted them a finger's breadth and peeked within: and what they saw there dumbfounded them both.

The damosel sat high and leaned forward and sidewise, with wide eyes green and bright as emeralds yet mistily soft, and lips and cheeks and brow all roses and roseate snow; and a youth knelt on both knees beside the bed, fumbling unhandily at complaining lute-strings and croaking like a raven; and a little way off, the old nurse dozed in her chair.

Dinadan loosed the curtains from his left hand but tightened the grip of his right on the Duke's arm. And he moved backward and turned around, removing and turning the stupefied Duke with him. And so they withdrew from the antechamber; and it was not till they were in the hall below that either spoke.

"It was that springal Lyon ap Denys!" gasped Boreas.

"Ay, and making a travesty of the song I taught him yesterday, bedeviling words an' music both!" exclaimed Dinadan. "And I warned him he hadn't mastered it yet. But he thought differently, it seems. Ay, and he was right! You saw her—eyes an' lips an' all!—twice as beautiful as I made her yesterday with the sweetest love song in the world rendered as only I am capable of? And the way she bent toward him? Hah, there's a lesson for me! A lover is a greater miracle-man than a poet!"

"Then why the devil didn't the young jackanapes rouse her from her trance long ago?" cried the Duke.

"He didn't know his power," said Dinadan thoughtfully. "Ay, that's the answer: it took a loveless poet to teach a lover the power of love. Hah, that's a thought! And now, dear Boreas, since you have no further need of me here, I'll be getting along home."

The Duke sighed and scratched a hairy cheek. Then he brightened suddenly and clapped a paw on the knight's shoulder.

"Fair enough, dear Dinadan! Nor much further need of me here neither. So if you'll just stop for the wedding, I'll go along back to Camelot with you."

QUEST'S END

*Though a Lord has wealth, estates, and power,
does this satisfy all yearnings?*

—The Book of Maelor

With the wealth and lands bestowed upon him by Duke Boreas, Sir Dinadan was at a loss for further reasons for denying King Arthur's request that he forsake professional knight-errantry and settle down to a life of lordly respectability. For his loyalty and service, the King handed Dinadan a wondrous purse. There was now no gainsaying his wealth, nor any reasonable prospect of dissipating it in a month, in a year, even in a lifetime. Yet this life of comfort did not prove as agreeable to Dinadan as he once had thought it would.

"Why so dour?" King Arthur asked Dinadan heartily from farther down the banquet table. "You can make songs all day long with an easy mind and a full stomach, and try them out every night on any company you choose, including Queen Gwynever an' me, without a care for the cost of lute strings."

"Gramercy," said Dinadan, without enthusiasm.

"And the next thing we know," the King continued archly, "there'll be a grand wedding in the royal chapel itself, and then you'll be making up lullabies an' nursery rhymes."

The King chuckled in his beard.

Dinadan forced a wry smile, and excused himself and went home. The King's facetiousness did not amuse him.

The truth was that, after a year of lordly landed respectability, he was not easily amused. Now that he had every day and night of all the year 'round for songmaking and feasting, divine afflatus and merry carnal appetite alike languished and failed in him. Now he sat, pen or lute in hand, for unhappy hours without inking a single word or twanging a single note. He sat silent and glum in the midst of the very same companies whose risibilities he had tickled with quips and jibes, whose tears he had sprung with ditties of desolated young lovers, and whose very souls he had shaken with his battle pieces in other days.

"What am I now? Neither poet nor man!" he cried, and cast his pen to the floor and kicked his nearest lute. "My head has become a dried bladder lacking even a fool's dried peas to rattle in it; my heart is a dry clod, yet moldy; and life is savorless on my parched tongue and like ashes in my throat!"

Then Dinadan would have spent the whole of his evil and enervating wealth in the building and endowment of a great monastery and himself have turned monk, so desperate was his discontent: but King Arthur soon dissuaded him from that pious intention, speaking at first with laughter and quips and quirks, but at last laying down the law right Pendragonly with fist-thumps on the table.

So Sir Dinadan became as morose and churlish as he had been lively and companionable when a necessitous knight-errant, and seemed neither to find nor give pleasure in any company save that of his gray charger, Garry. Day after day he passed more and more of his time with that great horse, in stall and paddock and idly riding in field and forest.

One morning, his honest servant Dunderkyn said to him, "Master, I hear ye talk with Garry like he was a gentleman and yer boon friend."

"What of it, good fellow?" returned the knight. "How else would I talk with him? He is my dear an' trusty friend and the longest proven such in the world, and as true a gentleman—ay, and of as noble blood, by my halidom!—as any knight or baron or king astrut on two legs in Camelot."

"But ye converse like he was answerin' word for word with the tongue of a Christian."

"Quite, good Dunderkyn. We recall happier, if leaner, days, when every morning promised something brave and new of song or adventure; and nights of frost when we shared the one cloak, and days when we shared the last barley loaf; and parlous moments of combat when I turned cut or thrust from him with sword or shield or very breastplate, and he saved me from disaster with tricky side step or mighty leap, and many a time with hoofs and teeth. Ah yes, my Garry and I have brave things and kind to recall and talk over."

So Dunderkyn went back to his currycombs and brushes fully convinced that his master was mad or bewitched. Otherwise, why had he, horse-loving Groom Dunderkyn, never heard a human word from Garry or any other horse noble or simple, but only neighs, whinnies, snuffles, and snorts?

At an early hour of the very next night, honest Dunderkyn received sure proof of his master's madness or bewitchment or whatever ailed him. He was no more than abed when roused by Sir Dinadan and taken covertly to the knight's private quarters; and there his lord and master displayed a parchment bearing a seal of red wax, and pronounced its contents to him, as follows—for Dunderkyn was no clerk.

> "*To All Men, noble, gentle, and simple, greeting. Know ye by this Instrument, I, Dinadan, a knight of King Arthur hys Court and Fellowship, do ordain my trusty servant hight Dunderkyn to keep and gouvern in my Name and Authority all my lands and habitations of this my Barony yclept Dragonford and all other my lawful possessions, goods, gear, rights, and privileges; and to this I set for All Men to know, and for any man to deny at risk of my displeasure and correction, my Unicorn seal and my hand and style thus*
>
> —DINADAN OF DRAGONFORD."

Dunderkyn was dumbfounded; and when the knight bade him help to arm him he obeyed in silence; and it was not until they were in the stable, and Garry too was panoplied as if for war, that he found his voice and raised it in protest.

"This be madness! Wot would ye, all armed an' caparisoned, man an' horse, i' the dark o' the night? This be grammarye!"

"Nay, friend, not madness but sanity," returned Dinadan kindly. "As to grammarye, 'tis but the enchantment of our lost free ways; and we would break its spell with indulgence—one more last adventure of youth—and so have done with it."

But Dunderkyn was skeptical and shook his heavy head.

"See you not?" the knight continued. "We rode on a quest, however nameless, and left it unachieved. It awaits us somewhere—my questing Garry and me—to be fulfilled. After that fulfillment, and the quest ended, we shall know peace."

"Death," said the groom, heavily. "For lord an' churl, death be the last adventure, abroad or abed."

Dinadan let that pass and mounted into the high saddle.

"Not so fast, Master!" cried the groom. "However mad, would ye go on a fool's chase without provision for man or beast? Would ye have noble Garry starve on thorns an' bitter lichens in some bedeviled desert?"

"God forbid!" said Dinadan, and straightway dismounted.

Now Dunderkyn fetched the big plowhorse which had followed Garry so stoutly throughout the entire length and breadth of Britain, and saddled him and fixed bags of oats and beans before and behind. Next, he fetched a leather bottle, and a smoked ham, and other victuals in two baskets, and hung and tied these on as well as he could. Then he made to get up himself, but Dinadan pulled him down again.

"Nay, honest friend, this madness is not for you," said the knight.

"Who will save ye from murderous wenches with knives in their garters then?" cried the fellow.

"Without you, trusty friend, to deliver me, I shall eschew all such ambushed perils. Once skewered by one such, or nigh enough, twice shy!"

"Even so, Master—which same I venture to doubt—who will play groom to Garry an' Punch an' squire to yerself?"

"I can ply as brisk a currycomb as any varlet."

"But yerself, Master? The unbucklin' an' unlatchin' at day's end, and the bucklin' and' latchin' every mornin'? There be two buckles at the back ye'd need an arm six foot long an' double-jointed to handle aright on yerself."

"True!—or near enough. But now my need of a trusty seneschal overweighs my need of a squire. So you, steadfast and hard-tried friend and servant, trustiest of all men either noble or simple, must hold and keep Dragonford even against the world, till my return. You have my written warrant, which King Arthur and all just lords will honor and no court of law will deny. And here is my ring."

Then Dinadan withdrew a great ring from a finger and gave it to Dunderkyn, who by now had lost all power of protest. The ring was set with a great stone of carnelian into which a rampant unicorn was cut deep. Then Dinadan mounted Garry again, who pawed the ground.

"Look for us back in a sennight," he said. "Or a month. Or by Christmas, at longest. God keep ye, dear Coz."

And in the turn of a hand, he and Garry, and the big plowhorse at the charger's tail, were gone and enveloped in darkness; and Dunderkyn stood staring and silent, dazed and dumbfounded by conflicting emotions.

Sir Dinadan rode till dawn, leaving the course and the pace to Garry; and heavy-footed Punch followed close. Owing to natural obstructions and darkness, the pace was slow and the course twisty. By first dawn light, he recognized the surrounding shaws and moors as a waste area of his own lordship which he and Garry had seen before in idle excursions; so he turned right, for that way lay his northern and nearest boundary. He rode at a better pace until the sun won clear of the crags and hanging woods of Dragonridge in the East, then dismounted at a spring in the edge of a great forest of oaks.

He threw down his cumbersome lance and mailed gauntlets and then, still helmeted and sworded, freed both horses of bits, saddles, and all burdens, let them drink their fill, and measured out beans and oats to them. Not till then did he unhelm and slake his own thirst. Then he cast off his massive belt and its weight of long sword, short sword, and dagger, and breakfasted hurriedly. He was uncomfortable in his heavy harness, but as he intended to up and ride again soon, he dared not risk any major unbucklings: so, when the horses had emptied their nose-bags and rolled in the ferns to their hearts' content, he mounted and marched again.

The country was of heathered moor broken by wooded knolls and projections of the vast forest to the westward. Not so much of human habitation as a feather of hearth-smoke showed in any direction; but, the season pressing upon the feast-day of Saint Michael, the bloom of the archangel's azure daisies curled low about the edges of shaw and forest like fairy smoke. The air was bright and clear and the cloudless sky as high as heaven itself. Dinadan's heart lifted; and, for all their burdens of man, arms, saddles, and provender, the big horses pranced. Grouse whirred up and away, and a wild russet sow and her half-grown pigs plunged and scattered from their path. Red harts and hinds, and smaller fallow deer, leaped aside or turned and regarded them with gentle eyes.

At noon, Dinadan got down and again unburdened and unbitted Garry and Punch beside a spring in a shady glade. Now he was happier than he had been at breakfast time. After tending the horses, he unlatched his helm and cast it down atop the discarded lance and sworded belt.

"That's better!" he exclaimed and set to work at loosing his body-armor.

This was no easy task, for some of the joinder-points were behind and at least one of these was quite out of his reach. But he was in no mood to be denied and was soon entirely free of his hardware, though at the cost of a twisted latch and a broken buckle. But he was too well pleased with himself to allow mere trifles to bother him. Now he dined, and that far more generously and comfortably than he had breakfasted. He ate all of a medium-sized squab pie save the pastry, which he shared fairly between the horses. He took a drag at the two-gallon leather bottle, which was full of strong ale. He ate a plum tart, and a strawberry tart, again giving the pastry to his attentive companions.

"The first time in a year that I've truly enjoyed victuals and drink!" he exclaimed, and took another drag at the bottle.

He lay on his back in soft fern and sighed, "If I had brought along a lute I could make a song now—the first song in many dreary dumb months." But having no lute, he slept.

He awoke at sunset, but remained awake only enough to bait the horses and dispose of another pie and a few more tarts. His next awaking was at dawn; and within the hour he had Garry and Punch ready to march. But readying himself proved more difficult, and when it came to fastening the backplate, which depended upon the twisted latch and broken buckle, quite impossible. So he mounted and rode with his upper back protected by linen and leather only.

After half a league, he changed his course slightly to the right and so entered the heavy forest slantwise. It was an ancient forest, yet vigorous; and as he moved beneath the wide boughs he thought of nymphs and hamadryads and the like, and wished again that he had brought a lute. But so strong were his visions of luring faces and flitting limbs and the urge to catch them in song that, despite his lack of instrument, he was soon singing happily, now low, now high. This was delightful. Now that he was an errant knight again he was a poet again.

Several hours later, Garry came to a sudden halt and stood with ears pricked forward, whereupon Sir Dinadan as suddenly shut his mouth on his song and gave ear too.

"Just beyond those hollies, I make it," said the knight. "Sobs or hiccups. It sounds like someone in distress. Let's go see."

Garry advanced and Punch followed close; and so they went to and behind the clump of hollies, and the charger halted again. A human figure lay prostrate there with hands to face and shoulders quaking. It was a small man, or a mere boy, and a churl by its uncouth attire. Sir Dinadan got down, let fall his lance and went close.

"What ails you?" he asked, loudly but kindly.

The distressful quaking of the shoulders stopped instantly and for seconds the whole body lay still and flat as death. Then head and breast lifted slowly on slowly stiffening arms and a tear-stained face turned upward and backward in fearful enquiry. Then, quicker than the telling, the fellow came to his feet and stood with his back squarely to the knight.

"Tut, tut, friend," chided Dinadan mildly. "You be too big a lad to lie blubbering. What's your trouble?"

The answer, choked and broken, was quite unintelligible.

"Calm yourself and speak up like an honest man," Dinadan urged gently. "I'll not eat you nor even baste you, being neither dragon nor ogre but a Christian knight. Out with your coil now, and I'll amend it if I can."

"My swine! All have escaped me!" cried the other.

"A swineherd, hah? And your master will whip you cruelly? Just so! Well, having no love for cruelty of any sort, nor for whippers of man or beast, I'll look into this matter. Now lead me to your master, my poor fellow."

"Nay, not that!"

"Why not?"

"He is a mighty baron."

"Hah! A mighty baron, say you? So much the better. I've had ado with such rustic tyrants—mighty only in their own opinions—aplenty before now, and learned them the error of their ways. Lead on, lad."

"Nay, not that!" cried the swineherd; and he turned and sprang, quick as a fox, to Dinadan's side, and stood close but with averted face and added hoarsely, "Take me away!"

After shifting his ground slightly in an attempt to obtain a full view of the other's face, which was frustrated by a quick shift of foot to counter it, Dinadan protested that a swineherd was the very last thing he could find any use for in his present circumstances.

At that, the youth cried urgently, in an uneven voice, "But you could use a squire or page!—else why ride defenseless behind, and the backplate on your saddlebow?"

"You have sharp eyes, friend," said Dinadan. "And a quick wit. But your voice? What ails it? It be just at the cracking point between boy's and man's maybe, so let that question pass. Yes, I could use squire or page, or groom even—but what could I do with a swineherd now, and all my grunters long leagues behind me, rooting in my own forests?"

"Only take me away now—safe away from here—and I will squire you and e'en groom the great horses—if you be truly the merciful Christian knight you say!" cried the other in a voice even more desperate and broken than before, yet still with drooping head and averted face.

After a few moments of thought and a sigh of resignation, Dinadan replied, "Since I said it, I'll abide by it, come what may; and I thank God there be no damosel nor wench involved in it. So get you up on the Suffolk Punch, if you can find a place to sit or hang on."

The lad was at Punch's side before the last word was spoken, then mounted among the bags and baskets in a trice. So Dinadan remounted and Garry advanced again with Punch close on his heels.

"Faster, faster, if you love me!" cried Punch's rider.

Dinadan looked back at him and laughed.

"If our pace depended upon my love of you, lad—the more love, the more speed—we'd stand stock-still," he said, and laughed again, but not unkindly.

At that, the other uttered an inarticulate sound, but surely of anger and distress, and with hand and heel shook Punch from walk to trot, and so past knight and charger and away over moss and fern at a gallop. Then, without waiting for word or signal from his rider, Garry mended his pace too, but smoothly, and was soon alongside the gallopers; whereupon Punch snubbed himself to his customary pace.

"So you'd play me false!" barked Dinadan, reaching across and clamping an iron hand on the swineherd's shoulder. "So that's your game, rogue?—you'd run off with my horse and gear!"

The lad flinched and cried out briefly but piteously at the pain of that grip, then went all limp and hid his face and wept.

"God's wounds!" swore the knight, withdrawing his hand from the quivering, thin shoulder. "Tears at a touch! What the devil? Would you have me commend and reward you for trying to rob me? Nay, rogue, but for the soft heart an' head I was born with, I would strip off your tunic and lay on with a stirrup-leather. 'Twould be no more than my duty, knave. But to the devil with it! Get down now onto your own feet and go back to whence you came and the rogues you serve."

But the fellow made no motion to obey. Now he had both hands to his face and spoke in a desperate voice between them.

"Nay, no rogue, by my mother's soul! I rode hard for my safety, and yours—God send you wit to see it! Hark!"

Now he lowered one hand from his face and raised and turned his head this way and that.

"Hark! D'ye hear it? They be after me already!"

Dinadan too turned his head this way and that, straining his ears within his open helmet.

"A hound," he said. "Ay, a couple of hounds. They chase a stag."

"Nay, they chase me. And so you too. But never a stag nor any beast, for they be man-hunters only—trackers and tracers of escaped serfs and other poor souls in flight. But themselves be gentle an' no killers, so leave the bloodshed to the cruel men who follow them and perforce hold them on leash or lose hounds and quarry alike. Away now as you love life—whilst there is still time to win to running water and so break the scent!"

"Not me, by my halidom!" swore Dinadan. "No couple of hounds, nor yet a pack, can start me like a hare or a fox. But get you down, poor crybaby, and run if you will, and where you will, but I ride or bide at my own pleasure."

"God mend your wits!" cried the other in a bitter and frantic voice; and then, with a leap from Punch's back and a swift dash, he disappeared in the underbrush, leaving the knight gaping: for he had not fled forward nor to either flank, but rearward.

"Just so!" muttered Dinadan. "The scurvy false rogue—the vile tear-spouter—mistrusts the hounds' noses and so goes back to guide the hunt himself straightly and surely to me. Hah, the black heart of him! But why all his pother about flight to running water? Why lay he prostrate and woeful when I first came upon him, and stiffened as with the palsy of death at my voice? Ay, he was not pretending then!—or don't I, even yet, know the face of fear when I see it? The poor mad loon, crazed with terror, runs straight to his punishment—God harden his dirty hide! Hah, harky to that now!"

Now the baying of hounds was all but drowned by a louder, though farther off yet faster approaching, harsh braying of horns. Dinadan turned his head, twisting in the saddle the better to listen and look; and so did both horses, with pricking ears and rolling eyes but no shifting of hoofs. Dinadan looked for a great hart or stag to break cover in desperate flight from that pursuit, with antlers of many tines laid back on foam-flecked neck. But nothing appeared save a few hares, and a fox padding slyly and without haste. Yet the sounds of the chase neared and increased, and urgent shouts of men were added to the baying and braying. Dinadan was puzzled.

"What do they hunt then?" he asked himself. "Did the poor lad tell the truth then?—and he is their quarry, afoot or horsed?"

And now he became aware of a startling change in the clamor of the chase. Though the braying of horns and the shouting continued, the baying of the hounds had ceased. Now there fell a silence as brief as sudden, which was shattered by louder and fiercer shouts than before and a wilder blowing of horns—but still no baying of hounds.

"They've got him!—the poor fool!" cried Dinadan. "But I'll save his dirty back, mauger my head! To the rescue now!"

Garry turned end for end at the word, without touch of bit, and Punch turned with him; and while they kept their ground on impatient hoofs, Dinadan readied himself for action. He threw down his great lance and drew his great sword.

"No call for jousting," he muttered. "'Twill be all slash an' slash again."

He brought his shield around from where it hung behind, then remembered his unarmed back and replaced it.

"But stay!" he exclaimed, checking Garry's first eager stride. "Harky to them now. They still come on, but wider spread now—and blow their horns an' bawl louder than before, but with a note of confusion now. And still the hounds run mute. Maybe they've missed their quarry. Hah! See what comes!"

It was the swineherd, running hard and wobbly, and beside him a couple of great black-and-liver hounds loping on a leash. And he came to them—and the hounds with him—gasping but speechless, and got up heavily onto Punch's back and turned him about and rode off, and the hounds with him; whereupon the gray charger turned again and followed at the same pace, neither pressing nor lagging, without "yea" or "nay" from his rider, who was struck dumb by astonishment. So they all went across fern and moss and mast, winding among great oaks and tough thickets, now at a trot and now a hand-gallop; and not till they came to a little river did the swineherd glance backward or the knight give utterance.

"Follow me close and we'll diddle 'em yet!" cried the lad; and, after no more than a split second's hesitation and an instant's flash of bloodless face and desperate eyes over a shoulder, he rode Punch into the water, wheeled him and went splashing upstream, knee-deep, with the hounds leaping and splashing at his stirrup.

"What the devil now?" protested Dinadan; but he knew the answer—that water holds no hoof-prints—and so let Garry follow without further protest.

After a mile or more of that splashing, the swineherd wheeled Punch to the right at a place where the stream was overhung with hazel and alder and plunged ashore there straight through the bushes, the mute hounds with him; and Garry followed eagerly, without leave or protest from his rider, who held as dumb as the hounds. Now the swineherd rode hard over moss and fern again, and kept on walloping through thick and thin till Sir Dinadan swore and even Garry lost patience. Then Garry increased his pace and was soon in the lead and snubbing to a stop; whereupon heaving Punch snubbed to a stop too; and Dinadan cried angrily, "Enough of this! I'd leifer stand an' fight twenty devils than risk the breaking of a good horse's leg. An' to what end? The horns are silent now and the chase is outrun and lost."

Without replying by word or look, the other swayed and drooped where he sat, toppled sideways, slipped, fell to earth, and lay motionless on his face. The hounds sniffed him and wagged their tails. Punch, still heaving like a bellows from his recent unwonted exercise, looked around and down in anxious concern. Dinadan dismounted hastily and knelt beside the prone figure.

"What now, poor lad?" he asked. "Are you hurt? Did you take a wound?"

He received neither word nor sign in answer, as if he had questioned deaf ears.

"A wound, poor soul!" he muttered. "And maybe mortal. But not on back or sides. Nay, no blood here. On his front then."

He shook off his mailed gloves and, with both bare

hands, made gently to turn the swineherd over. But the fellow did not turn; so he tried again, and with a little more force though still gently, but again without success.

"Not dead anyhow, for I felt life in him," he muttered. "But he will die of a certainty if I don't find his wound an' dress it. Not swooned neither, for I felt resistance between my hands. But to turn him onto his back willy-nilly might do him mortal hurt. So what the devil?"

He got to his feet and stood perplexed. He turned his head this way and that, listening for sounds of pursuit, but caught no faintest whisper of horn or voice. He noticed then that the sun was low in the West, and the thought came suddenly that it might be only hunger and fatigue, and no wound at all, that ailed the lad. He took the leather bottle and a basket from Punch's back and turned with them to where he had left the swineherd prone on the moss: but the fellow was not there, but a pace or two away and on his feet, and leaning against Garry as if for support.

"I was afraid you had taken a wound, poor lad," said the knight. "But no blood, praise the saints! Eat and drink now whilst I unsaddle, for we have run far enough."

"Gramercy," murmured the other.

So Dinadan placed bottle and basket on the ground and set to work on the horses. When both were stripped to their sweated hides, they went to a nearby trickling spring and drank their fill; and the hounds went with them and drank too.

"Hah! Here's a mystery had slipped my mind!" exclaimed Dinadan, staring at the hounds.

He turned to the swineherd, who was kneeling now and eating ravenously.

"How came you by the hounds, lad? I'd have asked sooner, but astonishment and the shrewd pace you set jolted it out of my head."

The other did not look up, but answered low and thick, through a full mouth, "I took 'em."

"Took 'em? But 'tis to marvel at! Pray rede me that riddle."

The lad swallowed hard and, still with bowed head, made answer mumblingly.

"From the fellow who held them. He held the leash with one hand an' a horn to his lips with t'other. They broke from cover—the hounds pulled hard forward and he pulled hard back, blowing hard on his horn for the hunt to come up with them. So they broke from cover whilst horsemen and footmen yet floundered in the thickets. So I took the leash an' ran with the hounds—fast and unseen—and so won back to you."

"Just so!" exclaimed Dinadan, but without conviction in voice or manner, for he was worse bewildered than before. "You took the leash and came away with the hounds. And what of their keeper? What did he do?"

"Nothing."

"Nothing? Nay, good lad, I cannot believe that he did not cry out and pursue."

"Nay, he—he cried not—nor pursued. He—he didn't know."

At that, Dinadan gaped incredulously and cried, "He didn't know! Be ye mazed, poor lad?—or stark mad?"

The youth hung his head yet lower, and whispered shakily, "He didn't see me. I struck him down—with a great stone—before he saw me—and so came away unseen—with the hounds, so none could follow."

Now he put both hands to his face, went all limp, toppled forward from his knees and lay flat.

"How now?" muttered Dinadan, more perplexed and emotionally disturbed than ever. "Slew a huntsman with a stone?—this poor sniveler? Nay, I'll not believe it. Yet here be the hounds and spent the hunt."

He went close to the forlorn figure on the ground and spoke kindly.

"'Twas well done, good lad, however contrived. Ay, bravely done, by my halidom! So cheer up now and show me a brave face."

The only response was a slight quivering of shoulders.

"Tears and swoons—more like a wench than a man," Sir Dinadan sighed.

Though still sorely perturbed, he became conscious suddenly of the fact that he had gone since breakfast without bite or sup. He took up the big leather bottle and drank heartily of the strong ale. Then he would have investigated the basket from which the swineherd had eaten, but remembered the horses. So he measured out oats and beans to Garry and Punch; and then he became aware of the interest of the two hounds in his every movement. Their sad eyes followed his steps and turns, and sought his face at every stop, beseeching and reproachful.

"You too?" he exclaimed. "Now God defend the larder!"

So the knight searched his store of provender till he discovered a roasted leg of mutton, whereupon he set-to with a knife and cut off chunks for the hounds and a slice for himself. Being hungry, he chewed and swallowed fast; but, being hungrier, the hounds gulped without any pretense of mastication. He cut again, and again, and so on— all the while boggling slices in his efforts to keep pace with his gulping guests—till nothing of the mutton remained but the bone. By now the sun was down and the forest all dusky.

Dinadan left the bone to the gnawing hounds and moved off heavily, as full of sleep as of mutton. He stumbled to the horses and embraced Garry and mumbled kindly to Punch. He found the swineherd where he had last seen him, but curled on his side now and apparently sound asleep. He returned to the jumbled heap of gear and fumbled there till he found a cloak which Dunderkyn had strapped to his saddle; and this he now loosed and carried back and spread lightly over the sleeping swineherd.

"Ay, 'twas a brave deed," he exclaimed, but mumblingly. "There be the making of a man in you, for all your tears and vapors. You can count me your friend now, so sleep well."

He returned again to the pile of gear and there got out of his harness unhandily and flung it down piece by piece. Now he sought and found his great belt with its weight of side arms, drew the long sword and a dagger and, gripping the first in his right hand and the other in his left, lay down right there and slept.

Thanks to fatigue and a full stomach, Sir Dinadan's slumber was deep and long; for during the past year and more he had lived too softly and unexcitingly to sharpen his appetite for victuals and drink. It was bright morning when he opened his eyes. He lay still for a little, gazing straight up into the leafy forest roof and trying to tag a flitting dream. The dream dissolved like a tatter of mist, leaving nothing of it but a sense of loss. Now he sat up and came back to earth.

"What's this?" he asked.

It was the cloak which he had spread over the swineherd the night before, as he recalled clearly—but now it lay on himself.

So he brought it back to me while I slept, he thought kindly, and looked about him.

He saw the lad and the horses and the black-and-tan hounds, and all the rattling incidents of yesterday flashed bright as blazonry on his mind. The lad was grooming Punch, and Garry and the hounds looked on. Garry had already been groomed, to judge by the gleam of his dapple-gray coat.

A good lad, and the making of a right trusty man, thought Dinadan; and he got lightly to his feet and called out benignly, "Well done, friend."

Swineherd, horses, and hounds turned attentive faces his way; and in that pause, while they regarded him and he them, all motionless and silent, he heard the twang of a bowstring and the quick whisper of a speeding shaft, and quivered to the impact and pang of an arrow on the front of his left shoulder.

"'Ware rogues! Take cover!" the knight bawled; and even while he snatched up his sword, four hairy fellows burst from the underbrush. Three held boar-spears, and one a bow ready bent with arrow on string. The spearmen came straight at him; and even as he leaped to meet them with whirling sword, he saw the fourth rogue's raised and full-bent bow jump crookedly from his grasp and fall to earth, arrow and all.

"Now what struck him?" he wondered even in the act of decapitating the leading spearman and avoiding fierce jabs from the irons of the remaining two.

But they did not remain much longer. Dinadan slashed and sidestepped till sweat blinded him and nothing was left for his sword to bite on. Then he wiped his eyes and beheld the swineherd and his dear horse Garry close in front and regarding him anxiously, and behind them the plowhorse and the sad-avisaged hounds, and to right and left four hairy corpses sprawled or crumpled on wet moss and blood-spattered fern.

"Just so," he said. "Poor souls! But up and away now before the whole savage tribe swarms on us like hornets!"

With that he ran to the jumble of gear and goods on the ground; and all save the dead men ran with him. There he dropped his bloody sword and set about the saddling of Garry, but unhandily because of the stiffness and pain in his left shoulder.

"Give over!" wailed the swineherd. "That arrow must be pulled out and the wound dressed, or worse may befall."

"Nay, 'tis nothing," said Dinadan. "'Twill keep till we have time to spare. Lend a hand now."

They soon had the horses saddled and bitted and hung about with arms and gear. Dinadan gave no time to rearming, but stowed each piece of armor wherever he found a possible place for it on either Garry or Punch; but he sheathed his sticky sword and buckled on the great belt. So both mounted and rode, and the hounds followed mutely.

Dinadan led the way, and that with no other thought than of leaving the general direction from which the clamorous hunt had come, and the vicinity of the onset by masterless rogues, as speedily as possible. But he left the pace to Garry, for the footing was rough. So they went a difficult league, and then another without pause, at a walk often in thickets and among rocks, and sometimes at a stumbling trot, and now and then even at a hand-gallop across an open glade. And so on till past high noon, when the gray charger halted suddenly at a mossy spring, and the plowhorse pressed forward and stood beside him, and both plunged their muzzles into the cool water.

"Far enough for the nonce," said Dinadan, dismounting heavily. "We'll unbit an' bait 'em," he continued in a slurred voice. "Ay, an' ease the girths—but not unload nor unsaddle."

Now the swineherd dismounted and moved fast, and in a minute had both horses unbridled and the girths of both saddles loosed. That done, he went close to Dinadan (who stood like one bemused) and gave the feathered shaft protruding from the knight's shoulder a stricken look, and averted his face and uttered a pitiful cry.

"Hah, the arrow," muttered Dinadan. "Still there. But a mere trifle an' soon mended."

He fumbled one-handed in the jumble on Garry's back, found and searched a saddlebag and drew forth a handful of crumpled linen, which he passed to the swineherd.

"A clean shirt," he said. "'Twill serve for bandages."

Again Dinadan explored the same saddlebag, and this time he pulled out a stone flask of about a pint's capacity.

"Trust good Dunderkyn not to forget the usquebaugh!" he exclaimed, but still in a thick voice. "It too will serve—to cleanse the wound withal."

He looked about him strangely and muttered, "Did we bait this morning? It has slipped me mind."

The youth, standing near with drooping head, whispered, "Nay, the attack was too sudden—and we came away too fast."

Nodding, Dinadan pulled down a bag of oats from Punch's mixed load, set his left foot on it and tore it open with his right hand. Now the swineherd came to his assistance, measured out a double feed of the grain before each hungry horse, and retied the bag.

"Good lad," said Dinadan.

He moved off a few slow paces and sat down with his back against a convenient tree.

"Come here, good lad, an' pull me out this pesky arrow," he called.

The youth came on reluctant feet and stood and trembled before him with averted face, but made no motion to touch the arrow.

"How now?" the knight complained. "One sharp pull will do it, for that was a feeble an' crooked shoot. If the rogue had shot again when he stood within a spear's length of me, then 'twould call for a shrewd tug indeed and my vital spark quenched at the end of it. But no, all was sprung and undone and fallen to earth of a sudden as if hit by a thunderbolt."

"Nay, 'twas nought but the great mutton bone the hounds had left," whispered the other, still with bowed head and averted face. "I saw your peril an' snatched it up an' flung it hard an' true."

Now Dinadan stared, with the dullness gone from his eyes, and spoke in a clear voice.

"D'ye tell me so? Ay, hard an' true, by my halidom!—as a very bolt from heaven. Gramercy, friend! Ay, friend indeed, for you saved my life surely! And it may be you saved all our lives before, when you struck down that huntsman an' brought away these hounds. Here be food for thought—cause again for thanks to God for a humble friend in need. . . . There was Dunderkyn, for one—but he is a man full-grown and a bull for strength. And another was a goose girl. Nay, in truth she was no honest poor wench, but an artful damosel dissembling for her own ends. Ah, that goose girl! I've lost count of the times she saved my life that day by cunning an' courage, and at last by batter-ing an armed rogue to death with her oaken staff. . . . And now yourself, dear friend. No minder of geese you, but a herder of swine. And yet ye be proner to tears an' swoons than any wench or damosel or petted queen even that ever I've seen—but as brave an' trusty a comrade withal as ever I've fared with—save only my horse Garry."

He paused and pressed his right hand to his head, but only for a moment, then resumed his talk, though not the thread of it, and now without animation. "So this world goes ever—feasting an' fasting—song an' sorrow—'round and 'round. 'Death in Life' preach holy clerics, but a good knight will ever chance Death in one more fight—one more bout with Evil. So be it. This arrow in my shoulder now—an evil thing, of a surety, an' with me too long. So what? I pluck it forth!"

He reached across his breast and made to grasp the shaft, but his fumbling fingers missed it; and before he could grab again, a defter hand struck his aside, and pain stabbed and as swiftly passed, leaving him limp but at peace. Ay, at blessed peace—but not for long. Now, blink-ing, he was aware of the swineherd standing over him with the bloodied arrow in a bloodied hand, and horror and pity in stricken eyes and on blanched face.

"Well done," he mumbled. "A shrewd pull. Gramercy."

For answer, the swineherd tottered and sank and lay still.

"Again?" complained the mazed knight. "I be the one should swoon, God wot!"

Heedless of his wound, he got to his feet, stooped, laid hold of the unconscious swineherd with his right hand and dragged him—but gently withal—to the spring. He splashed cold water in the youth's face, but without effect. Now, in a strange frenzy of anxiety, he tore open the front of scarred leather and raggedy wool and resumed the splashing yet more frantically, even using both hands despite stabs of agony through his left shoulder, blinded the while with pain and water. Exhausted all of a sudden, Dinadan sank to his knees and wiped his eyes clear with a trembling hand. He gasped, staring.

"God's wounds!" he whispered, still as stone.

Now the drenched and disarrayed swineherd twitched and sat up and met Dinadan's stricken gaze with a blinking of wet and bemused eyes.

"A wench!" whispered the knight, like one distraught.

The other glanced down, gave a little cry, clutched the torn front of the tunic and went red as fire.

"It was villainously done," sighed Dinadan. "But I didn't know, poor wench."

"Ay, a poor wench in very truth!" she cried piteously, and sprang to her feet and ran and fetched the stone flask and clean shirt. And now she had a little knife in her hand, and knelt before Dinadan and fell to cutting blood-sodden leather away from the wound; and all the while her eyes were fixed upon her task in fearful scrutiny, his stare of half-recognition and utter disbelief was upon her face.

She let fall the reeking knife at last, snatched up and unstoppered the flask, and, with a grimace of pity and a gesture of desperate resolve, splashed the wound with the strong liquor. Dinadan twitched at the sting of it, but recovered instantly as she began to sway again, took the flask from her trembling hands and forced some of the potent stuff between her lips. She swallowed and gasped.

"Look at me," he said.

Her eyes met his for a moment.

"Bewitched—or mad!" he sighed, and glanced down at his torn red shoulder. "The fever of it touches my brain. Cleanse it again and bind it, I pray you, whoever you are."

She obeyed without question, and swiftly and deftly, though all the while her tears welled and ran.

"Gramercy," Dinadan said. "But it cannot be. She never wept nor swooned, but threw me a purse and sent me forth into the night. But it will pass."

"Nay, you ran away," she whispered.

"It will pass," he muttered, and got heavily to his feet and stood unsteady.

Now she stood too, and close to him, and cried, "She

shed tears enough when you were gone!—and learned swooning too since then, in grief and dread!"

"Heed it not!" he muttered. "A fantasy. Fever or worse. A runaway swineherd: an' my enfevered brain, or bewitched eyes, make for me a wench of him—and that goose girl of far away—and now that fair proud damosel of long ago."

"Nay, 'twas but two bitter long years ago," she cried; and with that she moved yet closer and put up both arms and pressed a hand tenderly to either side of his neck.

Now, gazing upward, she whispered, "Look down, Dinadan. Look down into my eyes, an' through them into my heart, an' see the truth, and no fantasy."

So he looked down into her eyes and heart and knew that she was no fantasy of fever or bewitchment, nor himself the victim of any madness save true love's own enchantment. And as she told him of her father's death and the seizure of her birthright by a hated uncle and a yet more hated cousin, and her escape from the cousin, his right arm went around her; and by the time she had told brokenly of her long travail after, ever in terror and hunger and disguise, his left arm was around her too.

So they stood embraced, while the big horses looked on benevolently and the sad-faced hounds lay waiting patiently with their heavy dewlaps on their paws.

And so I leave them, as sure as themselves of their winning home and living happy ever after.

SPUR
AND THE
PRIZE

YOUNG WINGS UNFURLING

Chapter One
THE FLUTE AND THE FIRE

Sap is the blood of a tree. Blood is the sap of a man. A man is not a tree, thank God! A tree cannot pull up its roots, but a man can lift his feet.

It was early morning of a day in spring. Hawthorns were in bloom, and fiddleheads of fern uncurled and sloughed thin brown skins. A butterfly split its cocoon and unfurled and spread its crumpled wings to dry in the sun. A lark went singing up and up and out of sight. A vixen barked among the dew-wet rocks.

Good Brother Ambrose lay on his back and snored. His was a long back, and wide at the shoulders. His large mouth was open, disclosing strong teeth somewhat blunted by grinding on dried peas and such. The mastication and digestion of flinty beans and peas and parched barleycorns reduce the natural choler of the human blood and thereby promote virtue. Dear Brother Ambrose! It was now more than fifteen years since he had fled the World and the Flesh and the Devil. But as I stood and gazed down at his open and shut countenance, I suspected that he had had his fun, and called many a tune and paid many a piper, before retreating to this mountainy wilderness.

"But what about me?" I asked.

The new-hatched butterfly raised and lowered its drying wings of mulberry and azure; and receiving no other answer, I turned and stepped out and off, leaving Brother Ambrose flat on his back and snoring. . . .

I was a man. I had lived a score of years, almost—a score lacking but twenty-four months, to be exact. I had outgrown Brother Ambrose's homilies and instructions and restricted library of the Early Fathers. My head was stuffed with churchly Latin, but my nose was full of smells of May-blossom and leaf-bud and greening moss and uncurling fern. My eyes were full of new sunshine, of painted wings, and of blue and flashing distances crowded with receding tors and crags and hanging woods. My heart was full of skylark song. I had a silver penny, a sharp knife of thrice-forged and thrice-tempered iron, and a staff of seasoned holly shod with iron. I had a wallet of doeskin, and therein four barley scones of my good friend's baking. I had a feather from a golden eagle's wing in my cap, fastened with a golden brooch. I had a mountainy man's strength and health.

I saw a wolf, glimpsed and gone like the shadow of a sky-raking falcon. I saw a cock bustard running, a hare crouched in her form, and a raven on a thunder-blasted snag of oak. I saw a white forest cow in a dell, with horns as long and sharp as boar-spears, and a white calf suckling. She snorted and tossed her horns and chopped the sod; and I went up and around that dell by sheep-paths among rocks.

I halted six hours later, at high noon, and drank from a bubbling spring and ate a scone. After a little rest, I traveled again. I wondered if good Brother Ambrose had by now spied out the tracks of my flight on moss and sward. I saw a dog otter on a rock in the burn; he was mustached (Brother Ambrose is my authority) like old King Uther Pendragon. I saw where a wild bull, or maybe a unicorn, had polished a horn on the rind of a young oak. I heard a snort and crash in a thicket of hollies, and ran half a mile.

My spirits flagged in the lonely empty afternoon. Only the Old Gods and their kind keep awake all abroad in this hollow sunlight all stilled and dusked by lengthening shadows of crag and tor. I sheltered and waited in a glade between oaks and beeches, and thought sadly of Brother Ambrose. Was he still casting about for my tracks—peering down anxiously at the new grass and wet moss and the little places of mud? Or was he kneeling at the door of our hut, in prayer and lamentation? I saw him with my heart, kneeling, bowed, his long face sunk in his thin square hands. I had seen the strength of those hands on the throats of wolves and the horns of a wild bull, and had felt their gentleness a hundred times when I was little and weak.

I arose from a mossy hummock, ready to turn about and retrace my ungrateful steps to the deserted hut and my only friend. But I did not turn, for I caught a scent of fire on the still air. It was not the reek of smoke, but a finer, cleaner thing—the thin fragrance of clear flames of bone-dry white cedar. Head up and feet astumble, I traced it on the windless air. I passed through a tangled coppice and into another glade, and stopped and stood stock-still at the sound of a flute.

I beheld a small fire burning with flame as clear and pale as glass in the level sun-tide washing between slanted shadows of rock and tree. I saw four people about the fire, and their gear scattered on the greensward. By their garments of dyed woolens and linen, I knew them for intruders from the great world of towns and fairs and farms. Mountainy folk go in fur and leather. One of them was a tall, large woman, long and thick of bone and flesh. She wore a shapeless garment which trailed on the ground; but her arms—as bulged with muscles as Dear Brother Ambrose's—were bare to the shoulders. Her black hair was in long beribboned braids. I had never seen or imagined such a sight, for the females of the wild mountains wear scant garments of fur and hide and sheepskin, like their males; and never had I been closer to one of those even than half-bowshot. But Brother Ambrose, pressed for information, had once warned me that women were to be known and avoided by their trailing garments and beribboned hair. Why the warning, I wondered now; for I disliked her looks strongly. I was disappointed.

Another of the company was a short, round man. He was round of head, of neck, of face and of belly, and his shoulders were rounded. He sat on the moss beside a black leather bottle, cup in hand. His face was red and cleanly shaven. A younger and taller man stood nearby on straddled legs, and blew into a flute of yellow wood. The fourth member of the company was a slender boy of thirteen years or thereabouts, in a short green tunic with a scarlet belt and with golden curls on his shoulders.

The woman screamed at the boy to fetch water and wood. Her voice was harsher than a raven's. She flung a leather bucket at him. He snatched up the bucket and turned directly toward me and moved swiftly. I crouched in the blossoming greenery. I retreated, still crouching, backward into the hawthorns and through tangles of black juniper and alders; and suddenly my feet were in water. They slipped on wet clay, and I sprawled forward on hands and knees. I lurched upright and stood knee-deep in the ice-cold spring, and shook to the hammering of my heart.

The boy appeared, and saw me instantly. He stopped as if hit on the head. He opened his mouth, then closed it without sound. The bucket dropped from his hand, and he stood and stared, wide-eyed. His smooth cheeks were bloodless beneath their tan. But my face was red, for I felt like a fool, standing there in the icy water. I stepped up onto dry ground.

"I don't bite," I mumbled.

I tried to look both friendly and brave, but I was in terror of that big, beribboned woman.

The lad placed a warning finger on his lips. He moved toward me slowly. He came close to me; and I saw a long red scratch on one cheek. I glanced down and saw bruises on his slender legs, which were bare from the crumpled tops of the patched buskins he wore, right up to his thighs.

"Who are you?" he whispered.

"Mark," I told him.

But he paid no attention to my answer. He had not listened to it. He snatched my left hand with his right hand and pulled at it.

"Come away from here! Quick! Don't stand gawking!"

He yanked me off my balance and moved away, pulling me with him. He ran; and I ran with him, dumbfounded. He quickened his pace. He kicked off the old buskins, which were far too large for him; and we ran faster. Now we ran side by side, and still hand in hand. The grip of his slender fingers was hard as wood. He did not look at me now, but straight ahead and to his footing. But he stumbled once, and I saved him from falling by turning inward quickly and catching him around the middle with my left arm. Then he gave me a swift glance, but did not speak. We ran on, side by side as before, but no longer hand in hand. When his pace slowed and faltered, I slowed mine to match it. He stumbled again, and this time fell flat and lay gasping. I still had breath enough, but flopped down beside him, for his pride's sake. And for his company, in which I was already beginning to find pleasure.

Chapter Two
I Had Heard of These Things

He lay face down, with quaking shoulders. I touched the nearer shoulder with a light hand, and it became still. The slender body and limbs became stone-still from head to heel, as if his breath and heart had died in him at my touch. Was he afraid of me? Then why had he come close to me and seized my hand and dragged me with him in his flight? I was confused. I withdrew my hand and sat up and looked down at his golden curls, the narrow back, and the straight slim legs discolored by welts and bruises; and my heart hurt with pity.

"You did well, boy," I said. "You have brought me fast and far, in a masterly manner—so masterly that I came without question and am here without knowledge."

He raised his face a little from the moss and turned his head slightly, as if to hear better, but did not speak.

"You are strong and fleet, for a little lad," I said.

And still he did not speak.

"Is the woman your mother?" I asked.

At that, he came up on his knees and faced me. His cheeks flushed and his eyes flashed, and he cried out at me.

"My mother? That filthy common bitch?"

I was startled and embarrassed. Again I felt like a fool, and even more so now than when he had discovered me standing knee-deep in the spring. I felt as if I had somehow lost the advantages of my riper age and greater size.

"I crave your pardon! But how should I know?" I stammered. "She is the first I ever set eyes on—for all I know to the contrary."

The flame of anger cooled on his cheeks and in his eyes. He regarded me curiously.

"The first *what* you ever set eyes on?" he asked.

"Woman," I said; and my glance wavered.

"God's wounds!" he cried, staring.

I was shocked and confused yet further by that blasphemy; but before I could reprove him, he said:

"Are you a nitwit? You do not speak like a swineherd, nor look quite the fool you act. Who are you?"

"I am Mark, as I have already told you."

"Mark? Mark what? Of where?"

I thought of the little mountain tarn behind our hut.

"Of the Lake," I said, in better voice and manner, regaining something of my natural self-assurance. He is but a foul-mouthed, ignorant, runaway jongleur's apprentice, after all, I thought. "And who are you?" I asked, with condescension.

By now the sun was down behind the tops of the wild mountains.

"You would be no wiser if I told you," he replied, in a weary and disdainful voice. "What could you know of a person like me?" he added, yet more disdainfully.

I did not like that—neither the matter nor manner of it.

"Of a person like you, little boy?" I said. "Only what I have seen and heard since you attached yourself to me. I have read of people, of saints and sinners, but nothing like you for which I thank God and Brother Ambrose. Do I care who you are? I am not in your company of my choice, but of your dragging. Do I talk and behave like a fool? Yes—in suffering your impudence. And do I not speak like a swineherd? So be it. I am not a swineherd. The swine are all wild in these wild mountains. The boars have tushes a yard long. I killed one single-handed, over a year ago. My spear broke, and I finished him with this knife. I carry scars of that fight. And yet I allowed a puny, saucy brat like you to drag me away willy-nilly from a clear fire and a leather bottle. My heart mastered my head. I pitied you, for I saw terror in your eyes. But now I am a fool, a clod, a nitwit. Have a care, little boy, or you may feel the weight of my hand."

I spoke bitterly, as I felt. I had taken a sharper hurt than I could understand.

He covered his face with his small, hard hands. His thin shoulders and narrow back quivered and quaked with his sobs.

Rising, I looked down at him. I was at a loss. I knew

nothing of children, and had known no other childhood than my own. I could not remember any human playmate save poor Brother Ambrose, whom I had deserted. My other playmates had been fox cubs, a wildcat kitten, a badger tamed by Brother Ambrose, a gyrfalcon with a broken wing, and young ravens and crows. I possessed but one memory that must have been of an earlier experience than anything I had known with Brother Ambrose in these wild mountains. It was of a great white horse standing in rich grass beneath a tree full of white and pink blossoms. Brother Ambrose had never explained that bright picture.

I gazed down at that pitiful kneeling shape. It looked very small and forlorn in the gloom of early night in that high glade.

"Be a man!" I begged.

The sobbing checked for a moment, as if he held his breath, then racked on again.

"Be a man," I repeated. "What are you afraid of? You need have no fear of my hand. I have never raised it against the weak and defenseless of beast or human, and never shall. Brother Ambrose and his books—and my own heart too—have taught me better. I am no lousy jongleur. I am kind and merciful, according to my strength. Were you a man like me—as large and strong, or larger and stronger—I would not be so soft and reasonable with you. But as it is, child, you have nothing to fear from me."

I knelt beside him and spoke in simple terms of good Brother Ambrose, of our studies, of our adventures, and of the hut of stones and thatch under the high crags beside the dark tarn.

"I remember no father or mother," I told him, "and no other guardian or friend or human playmate than that good hermit from whom I ran away this morning, God forgive me!"

The boy became quiet and withdrew his hands from his eyes. His face was no more than a pale blur in the gloom.

"I learned nothing but good from him," I said. "Latin and the wisdom of the Early Christian Fathers, kindness and hardihood, skills of arms and the chase, manners and fair play, and the noble game of chess."

"If he was so kind and good—your wonderful Ambrose—then why did you run away from him?" asked the boy.

"To see the world," I said. "He had seen it, and would not come away to see it again, though I plagued him day after day. To see Camelot, of which my friend had spoken sometimes with tears and wild gestures, and once had babbled about in his sleep. Royal Camelot, of crowding towers and gables, where armorers and swordsmiths beat sparks from iron day in and day out, and knights and squires and troubadours and foreign princes and sooth-sayers fill the humming streets and clanging courtyards, and banners fly, and shields and tavern signboards swing in the wind, and ladies and damosels walk in walled gardens and along the green terraces, and look down from high windows. Bright Camelot, where torchlight and music flood from open doors and casements, and noble and merry folk laugh and feast within, and wine and mead are quaffed from cups and bowls of gold and silver, and strong ale from great horns and leather jacks; and where the King and Queen give praise and bestow prizes for the past day's knightly deeds."

"It is a long way to Camelot," sighed the boy. "A long and crooked way from this horrid wilderness wherein we are lost and benighted, without food or shelter, and in deadly peril."

And he fell to weeping again, with both hands to his wet face.

"And you—poor, nameless, boastful hobbledehoy—are my only hope!" he sobbed.

I could hardly believe my ears. But what else could I do? He had spoken loudly enough, though thickly. I mastered my first impulse to clout his ear. I mastered my outraged heart.

"It is well for you—you should thank God for it—that gentle Brother Ambrose had the schooling of me," I said in a half-choked voice. "Poor, am I? And what of yourself, runaway brat? Runaway jongleur! A hobbledehoy, am I? And nameless? And boastful? Holy Mother of Grief! I've had my fill of you, sniveler! I shall take you back where you belong—to your flea-pocked jongleurs—and you may watch me beat the fleas out of their dirty tunics. I will show you who I am, and what I am, by the knuckle-bones of Saint Wiggin! Come! I've had my fill of you."

He leaped to his feet and flung himself against me, with thin arms tight around my neck.

"No—no—*no*!" he cried in my face. "They would beat me—with whips and sticks. They would kill you with knives. Let me perish first in the wilderness, good boy! Good Mark! Brave Mark! I will not go back. They are cruel and vile. Let us run again, dear Mark!"

I did not move. I scarcely breathed. He held me tight. And a strange suspicion possessed me. What was it that I had read of one Queen Gwyn, in a book which Brother Ambrose had tried to conceal from me with mumbled excuses? What had I read of that gay young queen's breast that I had not understood? Of her breasts. Breasts, that was it. My heart shook me from heels to head.

"What—who—what are you?" I stammered.

The slender arms clung tighter. The slender body pressed closer. I tried desperately to order my poor wits and to still my leaping pulses.

"I spoke in anger," I said. "Yet in jest. I did not mean it. You are safe from those rogues, for all of me. I am neither churl nor knave, though I know not my father's name. Here is food. A barley cake! I shall make a shelter for you. Fear nothing. I am strong enough to protect you from lousy jongleurs or hungry wolves."

The arms relaxed about my neck and were withdrawn. The quivering body withdrew. A hard little hand found my right hand and gripped my fingers. Then we moved forward in the dark, handfast and dumbfounded. We stumbled and supported one another. We fumbled among bushes and boulders. Thus for a mile or more of crooked distance without a moment's letting go of hands or a word spoken. But when I felt dry bracken and dry heather of last year against my legs, I told my companion to sit down and rest, and I would construct a shelter of some sort against the chill of the night. Stumbling to the right and left, I felt out little cedars and firs, which I uprooted; and with my knife I hacked matted boughs from large pines and larches. Of all this I made a crooked, bushy little hut, which I carpeted deep with dry fern and heather.

I found my companion.

"Here is a barley scone, and here is your house," I said.

Nothing was heard for a little while save the crunching of crusts between our teeth. I was the first to finish my cake.

"What am I to call you?" I asked.

The sound of my companion's slower munching ceased.

"I shall be honest with you," I went on, without waiting for an answer, and with my wits and heart laboring. "You have called me a fool and worse; and I have called you a saucy boy and worse; and I think that we may both have been wrong. I admit my ignorance of the great world and of many worldly things. I confess ignorance—and innocence—on many counts. But among Brother Ambrose's books is one called 'The Song of Queen Gwyn'—not a devotional work—which he strove to keep out of my hands, but in vain. My curiosity was aroused. I read that book. But for that book—that sprightly 'Song of Queen Gwyn'—I would perhaps still believe you to be a boy. But as matters stand—and it is but fair that I tell you this—I have a suspicion that I may have been wrong."

And there I stuck, at a loss for words.

After a silence which increased my confusion, my companion spoke in a strange small voice—a muffled voice.

"Do you mean that now—now you suspect me of—not being a boy?"

"That is so," I mumbled.

"But why? What have I to do with your old Queen Gywn?"

"She was not old—not in the book—and she was—"

There I stuck again, and wished that I had kept my mouth shut. After a dozen of my heartbeats, my companion spoke again, and in better voice—in a kinder voice.

"You are right, good Mark. I am not a boy. I never said I was a boy. It was you who said it, good Mark. As for calling you a fool, dear Mark—and a hobbledehoy—I am sorry and ashamed. I mistook ignorance and innocence for stupidity. But now I know you to be brave and strong and noble. And clever! And I never thought you were a swineherd. Not really, dear Mark!"

"You must be a girl," I mumbled.

"A girl? I am fifteen—almost as old as you—and as much a woman as you are a man."

A woman! Brother Ambrose had not warned me against such a woman as this. I had thought female children were called girls. And this was surely a child. And yet Queen

Gwyn, of the book, had not been called a girl, though as described by the writer, she must have resembled my companion in some particulars, at least. There must (I reasoned, confusedly) be large thick women, and others like that sprightly queen of the song and this one. This girl, this companion of mine, must be the same kind of woman, more or less, that Queen Gwyn had been. And yet she had been beaten by baseborn rogues! My blood boiled at that thought.

"Call me Sylvia," she murmured.

"Sylvia," I said, liking its sound.

"My father was Gyles de Montclair," she said.

"Is he dead?" I asked.

"How do I know?" she returned. "In six years he may have died in bed or been killed in battle. I was left motherless at five, and my father took a Spanish woman to wife, a wandering dancer. The noble Montclair! He had brought her home from a fair. When she grew too fat with high living to dance, her sport was to beat me and make faces at me. So I ran away when I was nine. Some gypsies, who knew me, found me and took me back; and that woman met them at the gate and paid them a bag of silver pieces to take me far and far away. The gypsies treated me very well, but were afraid that I might be discovered with them, so they sold me to the jongleurs two years ago. And now I am here. You will not sell me, dear Mark?"

I swore a resounding oath at that. I clapped a hand to my knife.

"When you quit my care, it will be only at your own wish," I cried. "And I will take you to your father, if that be your pleasure; and I will show him the rights of the matter. I do not fear the Spanish woman. Where is your home, Sylvia?"

She did not know. It was six bitter years, and hundreds of weary journeys away. It was a wide house of stone and great timbers, with a high tower of stone, and a deep moat. Her father's village lay within bowshot, with a little river winding through it. But if the river had a name, she had never heard it, or had forgotten it.

"It may be on the way to Camelot," I said hopefully.

She crept into the shelter I had built for her, and I lay down near the entrance to it on an armful of old heather.

My thoughts were racing—but to what goal? My situation might well have caused even a man of the world a measure of bewilderment and anxiety. Here I was but a day's flight from Brother Ambrose, and already I had a damosel on my hands! A frightened child-damosel. I could protect her from wild beasts and wild people, of that I felt confident—but how was I to feed her? Why had I not thought to bring away a whole back-load of scones and smoke-cured venison?

I was disturbed by a rustling within the shelter, and next by a hand on my face. It was the girl.

"Methinks there is a viper in my bed," she whispered.

I crept within and made chaff of the fern and heather of her couch with a stout stick. I backed out, and she crawled in. I lay down again, but not for long. Again the rustling, and again the fumbling of the light but hard little hand. And again the whisper.

"Dear Mark, there's a spider in that horrid den!"

In hunting for the spider, I all but knocked the place to pieces. Then I crawled back to my own nest and fell asleep in the blink of an eye. But it was not restful sleep. I fought with a masked robber, and discovered the face of Brother Ambrose behind the mask; I fled from a unicorn, with the girl Sylvia in my arms.

Chapter Three
I KILL A JONGLEUR

I awoke in the chill dawn. Shadows and mists of night clung black and white in the glens and gullies, but sunlight washed and overspilled the mountains. I glimpsed gold on my breast, but not of the rising sun. I looked, twisting my neck—and remembered yesterday. The damosel lay close beside me, with her bright head nested in the hollow of my left shoulder. She was asleep. She breathed without sound, but I could feel the gentle stir of her breathing against my heart. My heart raced, but its galloping did not seem to disturb her. I shifted my position a little, softly, softly. At last I got to my feet without awaking her.

We broke our fast on scones and cold water.

"I was afraid, last night," said the damosel, giving me a fleeting but clear-eyed glance. "But not of vipers and spiders, dear Mark. I am not afraid of such small things, nor even mice. My fear was that you might escape me if I let you out of my sight; and as I could not watch you in the dark, nor with my eyes closed in sleep, I had to touch you. I had to keep in touch with you, asleep and awake. You sleep like a log, good Mark."

"I gave you my word—but let it pass!" I muttered.

I was embarrassed; and to change the subject, I asked what had brought those jongleurs so far from their world of towns and fairs. Then I heard a tale of crimes, robberies and murders, which those three had committed against men and women and children, and of desperate flights from avengers.

"David stabbed an old man and a little boy to death ten days since, who had come upon him killing a sheep and made shrill outcry," she concluded.

"David? Is he the loon who plays the flute?" I asked.

"And throws knives," she said. "And whips me. He beat me yesterday. No, it was the day before."

"Why did he beat you?" I asked in a thick voice.

"I would not be his wife," she whispered.

Heat and cold went through me. I burned with the black flame and black frost of loathing and hate. I turned my eyes from her bright bowed head—and only in the nick of time. I came to my feet quicker than thought, staff in hand.

He stood not ten paces off—the loathly jongleur. He had a short sword in his right hand, and a terrible grin on his face. I felt nothing of fear. I had killed a wild boar, a wolf, a wild bull. I felt nothing but hate. He moved suddenly and fast, but I moved faster. I struck first, and leaped aside, turning, and struck again. He staggered, and I flailed him again, and he lost his sword. Now he snarled and spat blood and curses. A long knife appeared in his hand. The bones of his upflung hand cracked like dry twigs to the stroke of my iron-shod staff. I hurled him down and struck downward, but he twisted aside on the ground, and now there was a knife in his left hand. It flashed upward— but even as it ripped my right cheek, I struck again with all my strength and loathing.

I stood and stared, breathing hard. Blood ran down my face and neck, unheeded. I heard nothing of the girl Sylvia, and did not turn my head to look for her. My eyes and thoughts were upon the dead jongleur. Wolf and boar and bull I had killed in honest fury of combat, for my dear life's preservation; but I had killed this man in hate, and without thought of my own life. I had killed him against odds of weapons. So fierce and deadly and calculating was my hate that I could have killed him with my empty fingers.

I went to a little spring, and knelt and bathed my shallow wound until the bleeding stopped. The clear water was all red by then, and I felt weak and weary. I moved aside and hunched on a tussock of fern; and then I saw Sylvia for the first time since my sudden awareness of the jongleur. Now she was kneeling at the little spring, as I had knelt there, but instead of laving her face, she was washing something between her hands—washing, wringing, dipping and wringing again. Squinting, I saw that it was a strip from her tunic—from that short tunic which could ill spare even an inch of its stuff. A moment later, she stumbled up and came to me at a wavering run and tied the cold, moist bandage around my face with fumbling fingers. Then she crouched beside me, but did not look at me.

"He—that dirty rogue—will never touch you again," I said.

She did not speak; but, and still without meeting my glance, she pulled up on a thin cord at her neck and brought into view a little knife in a doeskin sheath. She drew it from the sheath and turned it about in her hand, regarding it fixedly and curiously. Suddenly she turned a little and set the point of the knife quickly and lightly to my arm. I winced at the prick of it. She uttered a strange, short, mirthless note of laughter. She spoke then, but still without bringing her glance to mine.

"If you had not killed him, I would have killed him. It is sharp enough, isn't it? He felt the point of it yesterday. Nay, the day before yesterday. I was ready—but could I have kept awake always? And then you came. I was ready; and had he killed you, I would have killed him—dead throughout eternity—had it taken a thousand stabs."

She sheathed the little knife.

"I do not need it now," she said, still with averted eyes. "You may have it, good Mark."

"Nay, keep it," I said. "There may be more fights, and I may be killed yet."

She dropped the little knife back into its hiding-place.

"He was a knife-thrower," she ran on in a low voice. "He was very skillful. I stood against a door, and he stuck knives in the wood all around me. Sometimes he cut me a little, so that my blood ran on the door, just for sport. It made the people laugh, to see me wince and bleed, and to hear my cries."

I sprang to my feet.

"God rot him! And may every fool who laughed at that sport roast in hell!" I cried.

At that, she flung herself against me in an outburst of sobs and tears, and clung to me, pressing her face to my breast: but before my astonished arms could enfold her, she had sprung away. She stood with her back to me, stifling her sobs.

I let it go at that. I too was shaken. In silence, I gathered up the short sword and the longest knife. Then we went from that dread place. We traveled rough ways for hours, moving and stumbling close together and sometimes touching hands, but without exchange of word or look. I began to feel remorse at having cursed the dead jongleur's immortal soul. I was glad and proud of the killing, but misdoubted the rightness of the cursing. Dear Brother Ambrose would have killed him, under the circumstances, but would have left him uncursed. I had given him his earthly deserts, but who was I to damn his dirty soul? Brother Ambrose was the better Christian of the two of us.

I sat down on a mossy rock and pressed a hand to my bandaged cheek. The damosel turned and came back to me and laid an anxious hand on my shoulder.

"Does it hurt, poor Mark?"" she asked.

"Nay, it is my conscience that hurts me," I said.

She withdrew her hand.

"For slaying that—that jongleur?"

"Nay, I suffer no remorse for the slaying! Had there been six of him, I would have slain all, with God's help— and so perish all who have ever caused you pain or fear! But to curse his lousy soul was unchristian."

The hand returned to my shoulder.

"It was already cursed," she murmured. "One more curse will damn him no further; one less would not save him. Forget him, dear Mark. It is your poor face I worry

about. Come to this little well and let me dress your wound
again."

I could have laughed at that, but she was serious. We
went, hand in hand, to where ice-cold water trickled from
the ferny base of a great rock. She was a long time, but
gentle beyond describing, about the task of removing, wet-
ting, and returning the bandage to its place. When it was
done, we stood and smiled uncertainly.

"It is time to eat," I said.

But my wallet was empty; we had eaten all the scones.
I had nothing to offer her. I was filled with shame, though
empty otherwise. I cut two short cudgels of thorn, and
hunted to the right and the left. I spied a big jack hare on
his haunches, and I knocked him over with the first throw.
I was proud, but Sylvia covered her eyes with a hand. I
went aside and skinned and dressed the thin, sinewy carcass. With a flint and a knife, dust of dry fern and twigs of
old heather, I made fire. When the roasting was done, the
damosel came and sat beside me, and I carved her the best
pieces. It proved tough, dry, and tasteless, but we were
thankful for it.

Chapter Four
"THAT WAS A KISS"

"And now will you kill me a wolf, dear Mark?" she
asked, licking her fingers daintily.

She held them in air, glancing around, then wiped
them dry on the breast of my leather tunic. The act did not
offend me. I saw nothing unmannerly in it.

"But you would not eat a wolf?" I protested.

She laughed at that, and so I laughed too.

"Nay, 'tis the skin I want, stupid Mark. I need a cloak,
or something of the kind. This tunic is too short and scant,
I think. Or are my legs too long?"

She looked at me anxiously and inquiringly. Her eyes
were not like any other I had ever seen, unless I had forgotten them since babyhood. They were not like Brother
Ambrose's, though his were brave and clear and kind, nor
like any beast's or bird's. I cannot say what they were like,
save only that they were beautiful and that I felt a desire
to look at them more often than I dared to; though why it

was a question of daring I did not then know, in my ignorance and innocence of life and the great world.

"My poor legs are too thin," she said. "And they are bruised and welted. Look at this welt. But he is dead now, that grinning devil—dead at your hands."

I nodded my head and stared at my hands, opening and closing them. They were strong and square. I did not look at my companion's legs, nor at any part of her. A voice within me warned that the less I looked at her, the better my chances of enjoying peace of mind and calm of spirit.

"You don't like my looks," she murmured.

I kept silent.

"Nor anything about me," she added.

I retorted angrily: "Then why did I slay the jongleur?"

"He would have killed you, else," she said.

"Nay, 'twas for you—little fool!" I shouted at her, red of face, and hurt of heart and vanity.

Then I bowed my head for shame. She came and knelt beside me, and laid an arm across my shoulders.

"Then you do not hate me, dear Mark?" she murmured.

I shook my hanging head.

"It may even be that you like me?"

I nodded.

"And you will not desert me?"

"God strike me dead first!" I cried.

I felt a hard little hand under my chin, raising my head. I did not resist. Her eyes were close to mine. They were all I could see, as if the whole spring world of sunshine and blossom and crag and leaf had been drowned in their bright and shadowy depths. I was drowning too, and closed my eyes. I felt her lips on mine; and my heart wrenched and labored in my side as if it were breaking. Lips and arm were withdrawn. I opened my eyes like a diver returning to the surface from the depths of a mountain tarn.

Sylvia was standing a pace or two away, with her back to me.

"That was a kiss," she said, without turning.

I said nothing. I knew nothing of kisses.

She continued: "Hereafter, though queens love you, never will you receive or give a kiss, but that first kiss of mine will slip between her lips and yours."

"So be it!" I muttered; and then I cried "Queens?" and laughed like a fool.

My heart and brains were alike shaken and jumbled in wild and sweet confusion. Verses from "The Song of Queen Gwyn" came to me with meanings never guessed before. The damosel turned and looked at me, with arched and anxious brows for a moment, then with a strange smile. I mastered my extraordinary emotions, and stood up and went and collected my sword and staff and knives. I did not look at Sylvia, though I felt her enigmatic gaze and smile upon me. I flourished the sword.

"And now for the wolf!" I cried, with feigned enthusiasm.

Chapter Five

MAN OR WARLOCK?

I went ahead by crooked ways, and Sylvia followed close. We walked a long time, in silence. Not once did I look behind me, but my ears did not miss a step of her light feet on moss or sod or stone. We had come three leagues or more from the ashes of our fire and the bones of the roasted hare, when my companion screamed. I turned, and beheld a shape out of a nightmare. The blood chilled in my veins and my scalp crawled—but I drew the sword and flung myself between it and Sylvia.

The monster's head was encased in rusted iron, which I knew for a helmet with a closed vizard, by Brother Ambrose's talk of such things. There was a glint of pale, crazed eyes behind the bars of the vizard. On the broad breast bulged a curved plate of rusty iron, from beneath which hung wolf- and wildcat-skins. The long arms and legs were half uncovered, save for their own hair like long gray moss. They were gnarled and kinked like wind-clawing roots of an ancient oak uptorn by flood and storm. They were like the legs of a hunter-spider. One knotted hand gripped the cross-hilt of a long straight sword. The other held aloft a human skull as white as chalk in the sunshine.

Sylvia trembled against my back.

"'Tis a warlock!" she whispered.

That was my thought too, but I strove against it.

"Uncover to Sir Bevan, whose quest was the Questing Beast," said the monster.

The voice was like a winter wind in the smoke-hole. The language was not of the wild mountaineers. It was one of the two which Brother Ambrose had taught me—not the monkish, bookish Latin, but the speech of Royal Camelot, and the world of ladies and knights and troubadours. My blood warmed a little; for it must be human, after all, however mad; some ancient knight lost and gone mad in the wilderness. And I had heard tales of the Questing Beast from Brother Ambrose.

"Nay, fool, I am not Sir Bevan," he cried, as if he had read my thought. "This is Sir Bevan, the noble and forsaken knight of the Sweating Skull. Uncover to him, rogue!"

I heard Sylvia gabbling desperate prayers with her face between my shoulderblades. I doffed my cap to the grinning skull.

"I am Young Roland," said the old madman. "I am that faithless squire. Sir Bevan, this peerless knight, and my unworthy self, pursued the Questing Beast through days and nights and weary weeks, and at last into the accursed mountains and to the Mere of Herons. There, bewitched, I turned aside. There I failed him. For mad nights and days I was bedeviled and bedamned by a hell-spawned water-sprite—a girl as white and smooth as Easter lilies and red-lipped like roses—fairer than any Christian damosel—but green of eyes and hair, and soulless, and with a flame of hellfire in her white breast instead of a heart.

"And when she fled my arms, with mocking laughter, I sought Sir Bevan and my Christian duty again. I found him—but dead and dismembered, his head here, his heart there, his limbs hacked and scattered. His great horse had suffered a like fate. But a score of savages were dead too, some speared through, some cut in halves, one rib-crushed as if by arms of iron, for Sir Bevan was a mighty man of his hands. Remaining mountaineers set upon me in swarms, but I still had my horse, and was armed and ready. I spitted the savages like larks—three on my spear at a time—before my horse was hamstrung and brought down. Then a dozen fell to my sword. And now, horseless and with Sir Bevan's death on my conscience, I bide here and hereabouts, and hunt and slay unchristened savages in loving memory of this betrayed knight, and to the glory of God. But of late years, I have found but few to slay, and now I can find none at all, though I search high and low. But if you are of these foul and unshaved heathens, I must deal with you."

"Nay, I am Mark, a Christian!" I cried. "Does not my speech tell you so, good sir? But if you want Latin, I'm your man! *Expectans equito. Dum spiro spero.* And this poor youth is my companion in adversity."

He glanced from me to the damosel and back again, and then aside, his eyes glinting as cold as flakes of ice behind the bars of his vizard.

"So be it," he croaked.

He jabbed the great sword a hand's-breadth into the turf and let it stand so, swaying, while he fished a folded square of linen, yellow with age, from behind his breast-plate. He unfolded and spread the linen on the ground and placed the skull upon it, with reverent care. He knelt, mumbled a prayer, wrapped the skull in the cloth and tucked it under his left arm, and got stiffly to his feet. He raised his rusty vizard—and but for the palely glinting eyes and beaklike nose, his whole face looked to be a tangle of white whiskers. He freed, flourished, and shouldered the long sword.

"Come to the Mere of Herons," he commanded.

I followed old Young Roland at a cautious distance, but Sylvia pressed upon me toe-to-heel, even with a grip on the back of my belt at times. I could feel her shivers. Now and then we passed uninhabited, broken huts with fallen roof-trees, singly and in desolate clusters.

"The handiwork of Young Roland," croaked our guide, with a terrible gesture of arm and sword.

He set a hard pace, possessed by the energy of mad-ness, and the endurance and agility of a goat; and I put from my mind all thought of breaking away while he held that sword. I was thankful when we came at last to a mar-gin of the mere, and two rough but undamaged huts, and our guide halted.

"Await me here, while I prepare food and drink for you," he said, with a glittering backward glance.

Then he stooped double and entered one of the hovels, still with the sword in his right hand and the linen-wrapped skull under his left arm. Sylvia came to my side and clung to me. There we stood as if spellbound, with daunting smells of rank smoke, live embers, cold ashes, old bones, and rotting hides in our noses. Her tremors shook me.

She whispered: "Are you still—afraid of him—dear Mark?"

"I never was—of that old loon!" I whispered back. "But I don't like him—nor trust him. And now is our chance to escape," I added.

"Look! He is making up the fire for supper! And we shall have more strength for escaping after we have eaten," she said.

A puff of dark smoke spangled with red sparks belched up from a hole in the sagging roof.

"Now! Come away now!" I urged.

"But I am hungry," she protested, though she continued to quiver and quake with fear.

I was about to drag her away, but just then the terrible creature reappeared, brushing sparks from his whiskers.

He had left his helmet and breastplate and the skull within, but the sword was still long and naked in his right hand. Now he was all hide and hair and fur—of wolf and fox and wildcat and of his hideous self.

"Await me there—and you shall eat and drink your fill," he said; but to me it sounded more like a threat than an invitation to supper.

He stalked to the edge of the mere, where a small raft was moored among greening rushes and osiers. He stood his sword upright in the mud and made a great step onto the raft. There he crouched and pulled a squirming net up and inward. He flung six fat carp ashore, one by one. They jumped on the grass like tumblers at a fair. (I had no memories of tumblers or fairs, but Brother Ambrose had told me of them.) Sylvia laughed, though she still shivered.

"I can do better than those fat fishes," she cried.

She released my arm, took a few mincing steps, then sprang high, turned heels-over-head in air, and came lightly to earth on her feet. She sprang again, but turned over backward that time. She was taut for a third skyward leap, but I jumped and clutched her and held her tight.

"Would you break your neck?" I protested.

She changed from hard to soft in my embrace. I might have thought she possessed neither sinew or bone, had I not known better.

"What is my neck to you?" she whispered.

I gazed down at her neck, while cudgeling my brain for a seemly answer to her question. But I could think of nothing that would not have sounded foolish. I was about to loosen my arms, though without haste, when Roland passed close to us, with the six fish in a willow basket, and glanced at us in passing with eyes like flakes of mica in a rock. So I did not loosen my hold upon Sylvia. He stooped and reentered the hut. We remained motionless and silent. He reappeared in a minute, and stood and eyed us bleakly.

"The skull of Sir Bevan has ceased to sweat," he said.

My companion shivered against me. I had nothing to say: but an icy, twitching tingle went up my spine and crept on my scalp. My arms twitched and tightened.

"Which means, I take it, that the good knight is satisfied at last with my poor efforts to avenge his ignominious death at the hands of unregenerate savages," resumed the madman. "So now my task in this benighted wilderness is accomplished, and I can return to the world and resume my interrupted career of chivalry with an easy conscience."

He paused, and his tongue-tip, startling red, flickered for an instant between his hidden lips.

"Go a day's march to the north, a two days' march to the east and south and west, and you will find no man nor woman nor child," he continued. "They stayed and were killed, or they fled to securer retreats. Neither will you find that water-sprite. I killed her. I slew that nymph, that witch, whose sea-green eyes and hair like sunlight spun through young beech leaves, and round breasts whiter and softer than sea-foam, lured me from my duty. She had no soul. There are many and various witches—beautiful and forever young—unchanged by the years, being soulless—yet reduced to nothing by a sword-stroke. The blessed Bishop Hew of Ludsgate wrote a book about all such, for a warning—about water-sprites, wood-nymphs, marsh-maids, and mermaids of rocky coasts and sandy places, and the White Sisters and Queen Blanche—all lovely to sight and touch, all deadly to knightly souls."

He drew breath and lowered his baleful glance.

"He takes me for a witch," sighed Sylvia.

He lifted his gaze to my face.

"Beware the White Maid of Tintagel!" he croaked.

Then he turned and stooped and went into the hut again.

Sylvia shivered in my arms, and I shook with her shivering and my own.

"Now's our time!" she shrilled against my breast. "Let us go—let me go now—come away, you dolt!—or he will kill me as he did the beautiful water-sprite—the mad and wicked old fool!"

She squirmed in my arms.

"But your hunger?" I protested.

Smoke and the smell of scorching fish came out to us. But the damosel's hunger was forgotten, evidently; for she thrust and twisted so violently—all the softness of her slender body turned suddenly to sinew and bone again—as to escape from my embrace. She ran swiftly toward a rocky knoll. I remained stock-still for a moment, in two minds. Would I run too, or stop and fight? How could I serve her best? What chance had I, with a short sword, against that mad but war-wise old squire and his long sword? I shook off my hesitancy and ran too. Sylvia went flashing and turning upward among boulders and bushes, and I followed at my best pace. She checked, turned and crouched in a clump of stunted thorns, and I stumbled to my knees beside her.

"Look!" she gasped.

I peered out and down through the screen of little leaves.

The hairy old avenger issued from the hut bent double, and straightened his long back slowly. He carried a smoking trencher in his hands. He weaved his shaggy head from side to side, and I saw the pale glimmer of his eyes as they turned in their bony sockets. The searching glance checked at last at the base of our knoll, then slid upward slowly, over bushes and boulders, to the very thicket from which we gazed down at him. Again it checked for a moment, gleamed fixedly and yet more balefully, then flickered aside.

"He saw us!" cried Sylvia against my shoulder, in a voice as thin as the pipe of a grasshopper, yet vibrant with horror.

He set the trencher down on the grass, then moved to the smaller hut with grotesque action, as if he walked on sticks, but with frightful speed. There he plucked open a small door and was enveloped by belching smoke. But he did not flinch; and when the smoke thinned, we saw that he held a long, wide and flat object in his hands. He stood the thing against the wall of the hut.

"It's bacon," sighed my companion.

"A smoke-cured side of a wild pig," I whispered back. "I know it well—sliced and grilled. Brother Ambrose and I had a bigger smokehouse than that. The swine of our mountains fed on beechnuts and acorns and truffles and all manner of sweet roots, and their flesh was exceedingly sweet, and not too fat."

I said that to take Sylvia's mind off her terror of the madman, who by then had carried the great side of smoke-cured meat into the larger hut.

"This may be just as good," whispered Sylvia. "It looked good from here. And maybe he did not see us, after all. I think he would have run after us if he had seen us. I think that maybe he is so mad he has forgotten all about us."

I knew she was aware of her hunger again, and more keenly than before.

"I don't know about that, but I mean to make a raid on his smokehouse as soon as he sleeps," I said.

"Some mad people never sleep," she replied, in a desperate voice. "And if he is truly a warlock, he never needs to sleep."

"That old loon is no warlock," I told her firmly. "He's nothing but a bad old man with an addled brain. Him and his sweating skull! I'm not afraid of him—not while I have an eye on him. Strong as he is, he is all bones and bristle. He is not as strong as that loathly jongleur I killed. If I had his great sword, or even if he had only a short sword like mine, I would take all the bacon we need, willy-nilly, from right under his whiskers."

The sight and talk of bacon had revived my courage even as it had sharpened Sylvia's hunger. The mad old squire emerged from the gloom of the larger hut again, and placed a second trencher beside the first. Sylvia pinched my arm.

"Sliced and broiled," she whispered.

Old Young Roland fetched a brown loaf and a black leather bottle from the hut, then squatted close to the feast, with his front toward our knoll, and fell to. He clutched at the provender with both hands. Never had I seen or read of such unmannerly behavior. The sight would have shocked and infuriated dear Brother Ambrose. He fed his champing maw with both hands, stuffing it with bread and baked fish and bacon all at once, and washing the gluttonous mouthfuls down, at risk of strangulation, with mighty swigs at the leather bottle.

"May he choke to death on a great fish-bone!" prayed Sylvia, staring in horrid fascination. "But don't look at him, dear Mark," she went on, still looking herself. "He does it to tease our hunger and thirst—to tempt us down—the old devil!"

I was of her opinion, but I did not close my eyes or avert my gaze. We both continued to gaze at the sickening sight as if bewitched.

"Look!" she gasped, pinching me again.

He had drained that great bottle. He shook it, then flung it from him. Then he heaved and hoisted himself until his stiff knees were straight under him. His face was raised to the thicket in which we crouched. Despite the fading daylight, we could see the pale glimmer of his eyes.

"He is coming for us!" gasped Sylvia, pulling and plucking at me and trembling against me. "Come away! He's a devil! A warlock! Not a man to fight like a man!"

"Wait," I said.

The monster moved grotesquely, more than ever as if his legs were sticks—as if they were crooked sticks. He stepped over the trenchers and came three paces toward our knoll, still staring up at our thicket. Sylvia trembled against me but made no sound. He halted and stood swaying. He turned, stepped back across the trenchers, and leaped to the open door of his den and disappeared within, quick as a fox.

"You see," whispered Sylvia. "The drink has not slowed him. If he were human, he could not move so fast. He'd be drunk."

"He's human," I muttered.

But I was beginning to doubt it.

"Look!" gasped Sylvia.

He was back at the point from which he had leaped. Now he had a boar-spear in his left hand, and a second leather bottle in his right. He let the spear fall at his feet and raised the bottle with both hands. He lifted it high above his head and toward our hiding-place, as if in salute, and uttered a cry of hate and derision and diabolical mirth which still rings in my ears in nightmares. It chilled the marrow of my bones; but at the same time, it filled my heart with a red fury of hate—for Sylvia's sake. For she was clinging to me now in a passion of terror, all but strangling me with her slender arms. Her face was pressed hard against my neck.

"There, there!" I croaked. "He'll not harm you—man or devil!"

And I kept my eyes on him. I saw him tip the vessel to his upturned mouth and hold it there while my hot heart thumped ten times. He lowered it and uttered that hellish cry again.

"I'll kill him for that!" I swore.

He drank again. I loosened Sylvia's arms a little, the better to breathe.

"He knows we are here," I said. "Let me stand straight and uncramp my muscles. He is still swigging at the second bottle."

Sylvia loosed her arms and withdrew her face from my neck, but stood up when I did, and continued to shiver against me. I continued to watch the madman, straining my eyes against the dusk. I saw him fling the second bottle from him even as he had flung the first. I saw him stoop and recover the short spear, though he stumbled in the act.

"Good!" I cried, grasping my iron-shod staff. "He is coming—and with only a boar-spear. He has forgotten his great sword. Hah—he stumbles again! The drink has gone to his head—the mead or usquebaugh or strong ale. He is no more a warlock than was that accursed jongleur, and will as surely die."

"No, no!" she begged, gripping me by an arm and pulling at me. "He is old and crafty—even if he's not a warlock. Come away now! He only pretends to be drunk—the easier to catch us. He would burn me for a witch! Run, you fool!"

That did it. My courage had begun to waver and the urge of my hateful rage to weaken, but both flamed up again, hotter and higher, and yet cold and steady with bitterness at that word from her dear lips. *Fool!*

"Not so!" I cried. "I've run far enough from that wicked knave! You run, if you must—but this fool stays and fights!"

I wrenched free of her and pushed my way through and clear of the screening thicket, staff in hand. Staff against short spear. It would be a fair fight. Brother Ambrose had always preached the virtue of fair fighting.

He was halfway up the slope, leaping and stumbling. The ground was steep, and rough with knuckles of rock and great boulders. I moved down to meet him, but not as fast as he moved up toward me. Nor as crookedly; for he sprang from side to side in his ascent, and even his stumbles were out of line. Once he came down on all fours and remained so for seconds, swaying his dropped head from side to side as if utterly befuddled and exhausted, as harmless and as defenseless as a toad, and completely at my mercy for the moment.

"Now!" cried Sylvia, behind me. "Strike now!"

But I was not in striking distance; and how was I to slay one that made no effort to attack or escape or defend himself, though he were Satan himself? Two strides would have placed me in my staff's length of his unprotected, befuddled head: one stroke would have cracked that hoary skull like a nut—but my feet stuck to the ground. Good Brother Ambrose had instilled the spirit of knightly chivalry into my very muscles and nerves.

Sylvia screamed—and he was upon me. I twisted aside, fending with my unready staff. The head of the jabbing spear missed my neck, but the shaft and the hand gripped on it hit hard. But even as I staggered from that blow, I struck with my left hand. My knife was in my left hand. I felt it pierce tough leather, and the jar of hand and hilt on bone; and a scream so terrible and bestial and despairing rang out that I loosed the grip of my tingling fingers. The writhing body fell away from me. It fell to the ground, still screaming like a damned soul. It rolled on the steep slope, still screaming.

Now Sylvia was upon me.

"Well struck—by God's grace!" she cried. "He will kill no more babes and women and water-sprites. To the bacon now! And the long sword!"

"My knife," I said, dazedly. "It is a good knife."

But when she pulled at my empty left hand, I followed her down from the knoll, still in a daze.

"The saints and angels were on your side, or you would be dead now and I—would be dying," she said, dropping my hand and facing me with a long look that was half of fond reproach and half anger. "A child could have speared you to the heart while you stood gawking—but for the unseen hand that turned the point aside."

"But it is the madman who is dead—and of my knife," I said.

"An accident—by God's grace," she answered. "You ignored my cry. You had him at your mercy, but stood like a fool—with no thought of me."

"He lay helpless and defenseless—so I believed. And it was my duty as a Christian and a gentleman to wait till he could regain his feet," I protested.

"And he regained them—and struck to slay you!" she cried, with bitter scorn. "Must all the saints and angels always be on hand to save you from your stubborn folly? And what of a Christian gentleman's duty to me?"

"I have already slain two men in your service, and the death of the jongleur was no accident," I said. "And I have fed and sheltered you to the best of my ability; and now I shall go to his hut and bring out that side of bacon and what bread I can find there, so that the Damosel of Montclair may eat her fill tonight and tomorrow, and even until she find a more satisfactory provider and companion."

With that, I turned sharply and ran toward the larger of the two hovels, but checked at the entrance, my hot indignation dispelled by a cold stab of thought—and most of my vainglorious courage with it. The skull! It lay within, in the heavy dark. The sweating skull! But old bones do not sweat, I told myself. 'Tis a madman's raving. But the place is evil: damned and bedeviled. The old avenger's bloodlust has bewitched it. It is accursed. Natural laws do not rule in this cruel and unholy darkness. But I stooped and bunched my muscles and twitching nerves for the plunge. I would fetch out that bacon if I died for it—to shame the ungrateful girl. I began a defiant oath, changed it to a desperate prayer, shut my eyes and—staggered backward, yanked violently by my belt. I twisted around—

and Sylvia's arms were about me. Her face was a pale mask, and her eyes were black holes in it. She cried out in a broken voice:

"Not there! If you enter there—that place of evil and sorcery—and perish, body and soul, if you are already bit by that madness—what of me? Oh, dear Lord Christ, if Mark is mad, let the same madness bite me too—that I may perish with him!"

Her arms fell from me. She pressed her hands to her face, and sobbed wildly. I pressed my hands to her shoulders and tried to still her shaking and trembling. Now all my fear was for her, and it mounted to a terror deeper than my fear of sorcery.

"Be still, dear heart! Nay, I am not mad! What have we to do with madness—you and I, who have never shed innocent blood? I'll not enter there, I swear it! I was a fool to think of it instead of the smokehouse!"

I lowered my hands to her waist, lifted her and held her against my breast. Her sobs quieted, and her arms slipped up and about my neck, but she did not speak. . . . And then I remembered the mad old avenger; and I set her on her feet and loosed our embraces suddenly.

"My knife!" I cried. "It was Brother Ambrose's gift!"

I ran back to the base of the knoll and to the side of the corpse. Or was it a corpse? Now I was full of caution, and I hesitated about stooping and looking closer for the knife. I would have prodded the crumpled thing with my staff, but for the fact that I had dropped it somewhere. But now Sylvia was beside me; and she had my staff. No spoken word passed between us: but she stooped forward and poked at the figure on the ground with the iron-shod end of my staff. She thrust hardily five times.

"Dead," she whispered.

Then I went close and stooped low, and soon found the haft of my knife and laid hold of it; and all the while I was aware of the staff being pressed against the thing on the ground, for my protection against trickery, by all of my companion's strength. I withdrew the short blade.

"Is it bloody?" Sylvia asked in a fearful whisper.

I held it close to my eyes.

"Yes," I said; and I thrust it into the turf, and again and again, as if to clean it.

But it was a lie. The blade was as dry as if I had stabbed a skeleton.

"God be praised!" cried Sylvia. "He was no warlock, but only a cruel old human devil after all. Glory be to the saints!"

I said nothing to that, but returned the knife to its sheath with fumbling fingers. She was right, but she would not think so if I told her the truth. He had been nothing but a cruel old madman. I had thought so myself, for I did not believe in warlocks and their kind. Dear Brother Ambrose had schooled me well. *But there had been no blood or any moisture on the blade that had pierced his evil heart and sped his hateful life!*

And so I went back to the huts in silence, for the lie to Sylvia irked my conscience, even though I had told it for her own comfort. I went to the smokehouse and opened the door; and when the smoke had thinned, I found by touch and lifted out a great ham and threw it on the ground. Sylvia was beside me again, silent but watchful, and still armed with the iron-shod staff.

"The loaves are in there where he slept and cooked—if any are left," I said.

She shook her head, vastly to my relief; for I did not relish the thought of entering there.

"I could not stomach bread of his kneading," she said, and shivered in distaste.

I stepped to where the long sword still stood upright in the sod and laid my right hand on the hilt.

"This is a knightly weapon and may serve us well," I said, making to pluck it to me.

But it did not come away, though it was sunk by only a hand's-breadth in the ground. I tried to work it clear, but without avail. Then I tried to draw the great cross-hilt toward me. It stood stiffer than a tree. I set both hands to the hilt and pulled hard and harder, but without effect—till it came away so suddenly that I staggered back and all but fell. But I held tight to the great sword, which was now free and responsive to my hands.

"What was it?" cried Sylvia.

"Nothing," I said, steadying heart and lungs. "Stuck in an old root or something. But now—see, it is like a wand in my hands! Now we are free again—even as this knightly sword is free again—to go on our way to Camelot."

She came close and murmured: "Take me in your arms again, dear Mark, for I am still faint with fear."

I laid the sword down gently, then took her in my arms and held her tenderly.

"Now kiss me," she murmured, with her face against my breast.

I thought of Brother Ambrose. He had taught me that all sin is not of cruelty and hate and violence and treachery. He had told me that sin may be sweeter than honey.

"That I may not do—not here and now," I stammered. "Not that I do not want to! That would be different. To kiss you against my wish and desire would be no sin. But as it is—my heart and my very soul craving your kisses—it would be a grievous and parlous sin."

"Did your old Brother Ambrose tell you that?" she murmured, still with her face in the hollow of my left shoulder.

"Yes, he did—but at the time I did not know what he meant, exactly," I answered, still stammering. "Then I did not understand," I added.

"Nor you don't know now!" she cried. "Nor understand. Nor did that foolish hermit understand. And you are a man now—and he is still a hermit—and a coward. Only a coward would be afraid of kisses. Only a coward—or worse than a coward—would run away from kissing and jousting and feasting and adventure to these miserable wild mountains. Or what else did he fear? Had he committed murders and robberies, like vile jongleurs and lawless gypsies? Ah, that is it! Your saintly old Ambrose fled and hid from worse than kisses, methinks! He was more concerned about his mortal neck than for his immortal soul, I trow!"

I cried out that it was not so, with a rough oath. And I pushed her from me with rough hands. Who was she—this ignorant girl I had saved from the jongleurs at risk of my life—to revile and defame my dear, gentle, honorable friend and guardian? She was beautiful; but how would her beauty have served her if I had not been at hand? And would I have been so eager to defend her, and so able to strike and kill for her, had I not learned Christian charity and knightly chivalry and battle courage from Brother Ambrose?

I felt a hot, base impulse to slap her face. Instead—and red of face for my shame of that knavish impulse—I clapped a harsh hand to each of her shoulders. God, how frail and tender they felt! But they did not flinch away from my fingers. And still I wanted to hurt her. I drew her to me roughly and crushed her soft lips with my lips. . . . She made no struggle or attempt at outcry; and suddenly and shamefully the burning anger and passion turned to pity in my heart. I freed her from my brutal embrace, and stepped back and staggered blindly onto the lumpy sward, dazed with shame.

"God forgive me!" I moaned. "Christ pity me!"

Sylvia came to me and steadied and held me with hands and arms and all her slender body.

She whispered, "For what, dear Mark?"

It was a tremulous sound, quivering on the verge of tears.

"For hurting you!" I cried. "For defiling you! I'm no better than the loathly knife-thrower—or the beastly madman!"

I sank to my knees and begged her forgiveness. I fumbled for and found her small hard hands and pressed them to my face, that she might feel my tears. She stooped low and spoke tenderly against my abject head.

"I am not hurt, dear Mark. You should have whipped me for speaking so of your good friend. But I meant no word of it, my dear. I am your friend too. I will never imperil your soul, which is more precious to me than my own. And you did not hurt or frighten me—or in any way offend me. But now you are breaking my heart, dear Mark—with your tears on my hands."

I blundered to my feet.

"Will you ever trust me again?"

"I have never distrusted you, poor boy."

She drew my face down to hers and brushed the tears from my eyes with tremulous lips.

Chapter Six
THE CUTTHROAT PACKMAN

We went away from the Mere of Herons, burdened with weapons and smoked wild meats. A few stars showed, among them a few known to me by name and position, thanks to Brother Ambrose; and so we held to the southward, in the general direction of Camelot. But the way was tough and obscure and our progress slow and stumbling. I went in front, fumbling; and Sylvia kept so close to my heels that she bumped against me frequently. After hours of it—two or three—we both were tottering from hunger and fatigue.

Then I found a deep cleft between leaning rocks. It was roofed with sprawling ground-hemlock and with juniper and floored with dry moss. I made fire and soon built up a comforting and illuminating blaze; and by its wavering shine we discovered enough large gnawed bones of deer to tell us that wildcats or wolves had denned there in the past. I gathered and threw out the old bones while the damosel sliced smoked venison and bacon with my keenest knife. I gathered dry fern and heather and laid Sylvia's bed at the back of our retreat, and my own at the mouth of it, with the fire between.

We ate many slices of the broiled meat, and wiped our fingers carefully on heather.

"See what I have!" said Sylvia.

She held it up. I recognized it as one of the leather bottles which the mad old squire had set out at his solitary feast.

"It's not the one he guzzled from," she said.

She pressed it into my hands.

"After you, damosel," I said, politely.

"Nay, you drink first, dear Mark," she returned. "Your thirst is the greater—and I don't know what it is. It may be poison."

We laughed at that. We were very gay. I withdrew the wooden stopper and sniffed. I sipped. Old, strong mead. Honeydew. There was no mistaking it. Brother Ambrose was an expert at just such brewing. I sipped with more confidence, and passed the bottle back to Sylvia. Turn and turn about, we sipped and sipped. Sylvia's eyes sparkled. Our tongues wagged with wit and laughter. Now and then I placed fuel on the fire. Back and forth between us passed the leather bottle, losing weight slowly but surely. Sylvia sang a song about daffydowndillies, but I had to deny an urge to reply in kind, owing to the lack of appropriate words and a fitting air. Brother Ambrose had overlooked the lighter branches of my education.

But the thought came to me, like an inspiration, that I might dance for her in return for her merry ditty. Dancing, it seems, is a form of self-expression which comes naturally to the young; and I had often skipped and hopped for my own satisfaction, without instruction or encouragement even from Brother Ambrose, like the young of goats and mountain sheep. I was about to get to my feet and commence the artless performance, when my companion, bottle in hand, leaned forward suddenly above our failing fire and stared past me with terrified round eyes.

"Look! Quick! A great wolf!"

Her voice was shrill with horror.

I flung myself about-face and onto my feet in one violent, scrambling motion. I snatched up the handiest weapon—the dead jongleur's short sword—and plunged blindly forward to dispute the beast's passage at the mouth of our retreat. I did not see him. But what of that? The light was bad; and my own shadow, cast by the low fire behind me, was black before my eyes. I plunged through the narrow way, and out of its rocky jaws, stabbing and slashing fiercely at my own retreating shadow. Just outside, I lurched to an unsteady stop; and although the wolf was still invisible to my blinking eyes, I continued to hack and thrust and shout defiance. Then laughter rang in my ears, high and shrill and merry. I backed into the mouth of our shelter. With my left shoulder against one of the leaning rocks, I turned my head and looked within.

Sylvia was laughing. Seated there beyond the little fire, she shook and swayed with laughter, and waved the leather bottle. I stood gaping, bewildered.

"O funny Mark!" she cried. "O dear silly brave Mark! There wasn't any wolf. Wolf—wolf—wolf! And there isn't any wolf!"

It seemed funny to me too; and I laughed. The more I laughed, the funnier it seemed to me. What, no wolf? My mirth almost overthrew me. And when the bottle fell from Sylvia's hands onto the red embers and the spilling liquor caught afire and set up a high blue flame, I was utterly overcome with the humor of it. My shoulder slipped, my knees folded, and I tumbled to the ground. I straightened my knees, rolled onto my back and closed my eyes. . . .

I was stiff with cold and damp with dew when I opened my eyes. Dawn was in the sky. I raised my head from the sod, only to drop it again, heavy as iron. Heavy and hot and painful. I felt all over for bumps and cuts, but found neither. I wondered dully and painfully what could have happened to my poor head. There seemed to be something wrong with my stomach too. . . .

The sky was brighter when I turned over onto my hands and knees and crawled back into the rock-walled shelter. The fire was a little mat of gray ashes with a twisted scrap of charred leather on it. I remembered the both of them. I looked across the ashes and saw Sylvia sleeping on her couch of heather and fern. Then I remembered how merry we had been, and wondered innocently if the unaccustomed food or the more unaccustomed drink had been the cause of it.

"Time we were on the road to Camelot," I muttered.

I subsided upon my own unruffled couch and slept once more.

It was past noon by the time we were afoot and moving again. We moved slowly, placing our feet cautiously so as not to jolt our heads. Sylvia said that she was to be more pitied than me, for she had drunk more than I did.

"And so did Brother Ambrose whenever he fermented wild honey," I said. "He never let me have more than one cup."

Sylvia began to laugh, but stopped because it hurt her head. She pressed her hands to her temples and eyes.

"That old Ambrose took better care of you than I do, dear Mark," she said, stumbling over tussocks.

She sat down on a mossy rock, still clasping her head.

"But I shall try to be a better guardian from now on, poor boy," she cried through her hands.

"I shall never leave more than one cup for you, in future—just like good Brother Ambrose."

She laughed a little and wept a little.

"What ails you?" I asked.

"You looked so funny—made such a terrible jump—when I cried 'Wolf!'" she gasped.

Our progress was slow that afternoon. At dark, we slept where we fell. When I woke at dawn, I found Sylvia beside me with her bright head on my breast. I slid out from under gently, and pulled and bunched an armful of bracken and placed it beneath her unconscious head. She smiled sweetly in her sleep. I knelt to kiss her, but thought better of it.

"At this rate, we would never get clear of this wilderness," I muttered.

I sprang to my feet again. My head and eyes were painless and clear once more, and my heart was singing. The still air was chill; so I pulled heather and fern and covered my companion beneath a deep drift of the stuff, leaving only her head exposed. I bathed my face and eyes at a tinkling ice-cold brook. The shallow wound on my cheek was cleanly healed. I made fire, heated flat stones, and fried bacon and smoked venison. I had eaten half a dozen slices, and was still slicing and frying, when Sylvia flew out of her nest with a joyous cry, scattering heather and fern, and came skipping to breakfast.

We traveled fast and far and gayly that day. The highest of the mountains were behind us now. We saw a score of long-fleeced, white-faced sheep in a green glen, which looked larger and fatter to me than the wild mountainy sheep I was accustomed to.

"They are tame sheep; and soon we shall see a shepherd and his dogs," said Sylvia.

I had heard of shepherds and dogs from Brother Ambrose, and had read of both, but had never seen any of either.

"There is a dog," she said, pointing a hand. "Come away before he scents us or sees us. They are very fierce in guarding their flocks. They are stronger and fiercer than wolves."

The beast stood at the far edge of the glen. He was as tall and long as any wolf I had ever seen. We slipped aside into a grove of firs without attracting his attention and continued on our way. Later we saw more tame sheep, and another dog, and a man in a sheepskin shirt and kilt. We held on our way, furtively. Sylvia whispered that the shepherds were as savage as their dogs. That night, our fire was only large enough to cook at; and we let it fail and fade out after we had eaten. Sylvia had a terror of these half-wild shepherds. We passed the night in a copse of holly and flowering may, with last year's fern and heather to keep us warm.

The two following days were without adventure; and then things began to happen to us:

"Hark!" whispered Sylvia, halting me with a hand on my arm.

I could hear nothing but the rattle and slobber of a small, swift stream beyond a bank on our left.

"Moaning and cursing," whispered Sylvia. "Somebody's hurt. Come cautiously, for it may be a beggar's trick."

We advanced by a narrow path; it twisted among rocks and bushes and dipped down to the stream. At this point the stream was very shallow, and dotted from shore to shore with stepping-stones. At the near end of the ford, at the edge of the quick water and within a few paces of where we halted and crouched, sat a man with his left leg stretched out before him and both his hands gripped about the knee of it. He moaned and groaned in agonized tones. He rocked his large body back and forth in time with his lamentable utterances. He was a big man, and the black hair of his head and face was long and streaked with gray. He wore woolen cloth and tanned leather. A wide-brimmed hat and an iron-shod staff lay beside him on the pebbles, and a large, bulging leather sack slumped lumpishly against a boulder near at hand.

"A packman," whispered Sylvia at my shoulder. "And a thieving rogue, for certain. I know the breed. As wicked and tricky as jongleurs, and worse than gypsies. I don't like the look of him. Let us steal away, dear Mark, and cross the stream at another ford."

"But he is hurt," I protested. "Slipped on a wet rock and broke a leg, it seems. He is in great pain. And if we don't help him, what help will he find in this unpeopled region?"

"Then why is he here in this unpeopled region?" she retorted. "He is a packman—a peddler. Does an honest packman look for business where there are no people? I think he is in flight, and hiding from the scene of his crimes, like those murdering jongleurs."

"But we don't know that. And he is hurt."

"That's as may be."

"I shall help him."

"In that case, dear Mark, lend me one of your knives. Nay, your great staff will suit me better."

She took my staff from me.

"What do you fear?" I asked.

"Live and learn, dear Mark," she replied, speaking and smiling gently. "Had you seen as much of the wicked world as I have, you would not ask, dear innocent; and if I did not love you like a little brother or my very own baby, I would let you learn the hard way, my pet."

I smiled, unruffled. This surprised me—and Sylvia too, I think. A few days before, I would have flared up with even less cause. Now I felt doting amusement only. I descended the short banks to where the bagman sat groaning and gripping on his outstretched leg. Sylvia lagged five or six paces behind, limping and leaning on my staff as if about to drop with fatigue, although she had been as spry as a cricket only a minute before.

The stranger looked up at me. His dark eyes flickered a glance past me at my companion, then back to me. He twisted his bearded lips, as if in acute pain, and groaned miserably.

"Well met," he moaned. "Well come, brother."

His quick glance flickered over me, from my feet to the golden brooch in my cap.

"I have broken my leg at the knee, young sir, God help me!" he moaned on. "And I'm a poor man—with my living to make—and far from friends and home."

"Let me examine it," I said. "It may be a strain of the muscles only. I learned something of anatomy in my youth, from one of great experience."

He withdrew his gripping hands, which were remarkably large and sinewy and hairy, and exposed a puffed knee. I fingered the kneecap and the joint. I had suffered just such an injury six or seven years before, and Brother Ambrose had cured it in a week with bandages of woolen cloth and packs of moss all kept damp and cold with spring water.

"Nothing worse than a sprain," I said importantly; and still stooped above the knee, I told the sufferer how to treat it for a quick and complete recovery.

He listened attentively.

"God bless you, young sir," he said heartily.

And then, just as I was about to straighten my back, his hands flashed to my throat, and fingers like an eagle's talons gripped and crushed my windpipe. I struggled feebly, in a strangled silence, and sank to my knees. I would have sunk lower but for the agonizing support of his hands. I saw his eyes like black flames, as through a mist of smoke and streaming stars. I heard a cry, as from a great distance, and then the crashing and bursting of mighty waters on grinding rocks.

I came gasping back to air and life with the splashing of cold water in my face. I opened wet eyes and saw Sylvia's face staring down at me. After a few dazed moments I sat up, supported by her tender arms and tender breast. I looked at the treacherous packman. He lay sprawled face down on smooth rock and wet sand, with his feet in the singing stream. His shaggy head was within arm's-length of me. I gave it one glance and shut my eyes.

"Who did it?" I whispered.

I felt Sylvia's lips on my forehead.

"Not Brother Ambrose," she answered softly.

I knew who had done it, and what with—my iron-shod staff. I knew that my corpse, instead of the devilish bagman's, would be sprawling here now, but for this girl's wisdom and strength and courage.

"You have only poor Sylvia to guide and protect you now, dear Mark," she added, with a tremor between tears and laughter in her voice.

My throat still ached from the bagman's fingers.

"I owe you my life," I croaked. "I'm a fool! I'm a clod! But it is yours. I would die a hundred deaths for you."

She pressed her face to my shoulder and wept. I put an arm around her and pressed my lips to the top of her golden head; and there beside the dead rogue and the singing water we clung together.

"Never let me go, dear Mark!"

"Never. So help me God!"

"Spoken like a Christian gentleman," said a slow voice with a note of delicate mockery.

Chapter Seven
DAME CARMEL

I looked up, and beheld a woman on a small white horse halted within a spear's-length of us. But this was neither a creature of the kind I had seen at the jongleurs' campfire nor a girl like Sylvia. This (I thought) may be one of those ladies of which Brother Ambrose had spoken sometimes, but always with a reserve that had fretted me, in his instructive talks of courts and castles; and the small horse, which is certainly not a wild pony, must be a jennet.

The lady wore a flowing skirt, and a high, pointed headdress, and a band of flashing stones around her neck.

"Don't be afraid," I whispered to Sylvia. "Look, it is nothing to fear. It is only a lady, I think."

Sylvia turned her head sharply to look. Then she let go of me and I let go of her, and we got to our feet. Now the lady was looking at the sprawled corpse, leaning forward and narrowing her eyes; and the jennet was staring at it with podded eyes and distended nostrils.

"Who is it?" asked the lady.

Sylvia answered her before I could utter a word.

"A knave. And a dead one. A rogue of a bagman. He begged for help, and then grabbed Mark by the throat."

The lady shifted her eyes to Sylvia, and opened them wide.

"Good riddance," she said, but her voice was still low and smooth. "These cutthroat packmen are like a plague of dirty flies. But who killed him, may I ask?"

I meant to take the blame for that deed, if any blame were attached to it, but Sylvia was too quick for me again.

"I killed him," she cried, clearly and defiantly. "I killed him to save Mark's life, even as Mark slew the jongleur for my sake."

The other regarded her curiously, and smiled slowly.

"You speak like a lady," she said.

"I am a lady," said Sylvia.

And then I found my tongue.

"As I am ready to prove to any varlet or gentleman who questions it, with staff or sword!" I cried; and I glanced around at my scattered weapons, and for an armed man of some kind, any kind, to use them on.

The lady looked at me and laughed.

"And you speak like a learned clerk," she said.

"Which he is!" cried Sylvia. "And a gentleman too!"

"God's wounds!" exclaimed the lady. And then she said "Gramercy!" and laughed again.

Sylvia moved one step toward the small white horse. Her slender shoulders were straight, and her bright head was high.

"Montclair is my name, and Gyles of Montclair is my father's name," she said.

The lady, still smiling, looked us both over again, from head to foot.

"And stolen by wicked gypsies?" she suggested softly.

"Yes," said Sylvia.

The lady's laughter tinkled again.

"'Tis God's truth!" I cried; and had she been a man, I would have unhorsed her with my empty hands and slapped her face.

"And you too?" she asked, arching her brows and curving her lips at me. "Are you too a victim of the wicked gypsies?"

"I have never set eyes on one of that people," I told her, none too courteously. "I was carried to the mountains when I was so young that my memory holds nothing of the event, by my noble and long-suffering guardian, good Brother Ambrose."

She interrupted me.

"What Ambrose?"

I answered that I knew of no other, save only the saint.

"Tell me the whole story, boy!" she exclaimed impatiently, her voice gone thin and hard.

I was about to reply that only Brother Ambrose and Sylvia could speak to me like that, and my dear guardian had but rarely done so, when Sylvia turned her head and smiled at me.

"Please tell her all you know about both of us, dear Mark," she whispered.

So I told what I have already set down on these sheets of parchment, but with fewer words and poetical embellishments. The lady listened attentively; and though she often twitched her eyebrows and gloved hands as if with impatience, she interrupted my narrative only twice.

"How big was that bull?" she asked; and I had to tell

again that the wild white bull which Brother Ambrose had seized by the horns and overthrown was the biggest and fiercest I had ever seen.

Later, she cried out, "Your friend Ambrose could have taught you better than that!" and laughed with a bitter shaping of her lips.

Her eyes, still fixed upon my face, took on a faraway look.

"And he might have been better employed than in wrestling wild bulls—but more perilously, be assured of that," she added.

I concluded my story with the episode of the treacherous bagman. The lady glanced at the corpse with a grimace of distaste and away again with a quick shudder. She gazed searchingly at my companion, who gave her look for look. She returned her scrutiny to me.

"You both have honest faces, so why should I doubt your words," she said. "I have heard the name Montclair, but know nothing of the family. And I have read of just such fools as your poor Ambrose, boy. Now pick up your swords and follow me. And you too, girl. I'll send a fellow to bury that carrion."

She was about to wheel the jennet—she had its head up and pulled halfway around—when Sylvia cried: "Who are you to tell us to follow you, good dame? Or to command us in any matter?"

They regarded one another a long time in silence; and I looked to and fro between the richly robed lady on her high saddle, and Sylvia afoot, bare-legged and tattered, with wonder and a flicker of apprehension. The stranger was the first to break that silence; and her glance wavered for an instant as she spoke.

"You may call me Dame Carmel."

"That does not answer my question," said Sylvia.

The lady's glance wavered again, and all her face became as red as her bright red lips and the bright red spot high on each cheek, which had caught my attention and pricked my curiosity at first sight.

"Insolent!" she cried; and her silky smooth voice was shrill with anger.

She raised her slender whip as if to strike Sylvia, but I was too quick for her. With one leap I was beside her, and had her gloved wrist in my right hand. She did not struggle to get it free, but glared at me with white flames of fury in her eyes. I met that hateful fire without blinking. It cooled and clouded, and her eyes took on a baffled look. Then the blood ebbed from her face, leaving pallor everywhere save for the small splashes of red high on either cheek and on the carmine lips; and suddenly those lips quivered, and I saw the glint of tears. I loosed her wrist and stepped back. She brushed the back of her hand across her eyes. Then she spoke brokenly, with her face averted.

"I do not command you—but beg you, of your kindness, to come with me—and partake of my hospitality."

She completed the turning of the jennet, and moved off slowly. I gave Sylvia a questioning glance.

"That was fairly spoken, methinks," I said hopefully.

Nodding her agreement, Sylvia smiled, took up my iron-shod staff and gave the deadly end of it a few cleansing dips in the quick stream. I recovered my swords: the short one that had belonged to the jongleur, and the knightly two-handed weapon with which the late Sir Bevan had pursued the Questing Beast.

"And I know you are hungry, dear Mark," said Sylvia.

We set out briskly on the track of the slow-pacing jennet. Dame Carmel looked back at us with nods and smiles.

"If she thought us ragtag and bobtail vagabonds, she saw her mistake when you grabbed her arm," said Sylvia with relish.

I let that pass, feeling somewhat ashamed of it.

Sylvia asked: "Do you think she is pretty, dear Mark?"

I shook my head, but doubtless without assurance, for I did not know just what I thought of that lady's appearance.

"But prettier than me," said Sylvia.

I denied that with some heat.

"But that might be her diamond collar and silken gown and painted lips," said Sylvia.

"Painted?" I cried in astonishment.

My companion laughed and called me a poor innocent, and was about to embrace me when Dame Carmel looked back again with more nods and smiles.

"Save your astonishment till we reach Camelot," said Sylvia, knowingly.

Dame Carmel drew rein; and in a minute we were beside her. She pointed ahead with the little whip.

"That is my house," she said.

Sylvia regarded it with polite but calm interest, but I cried out with wonder at it. It was a great house of stone and hewn timbers and purple slates. It had two round towers, high and battlemented for watch and ward, such as I had heard of from Brother Ambrose and read about in several of his books.

"And all this is my demesne, all around and farther than you can see," added Dame Carmel, with a circular motion of hand and whip.

We were met by a score of people of the place before we reached the base of the hill and the outer wall of tree-trunks and boulders. The foremost of these was an elderly man in leather; but by the gold inlay of the haft of his dagger, the plume in his cap, and marks on the front of his jerkin where a breastplate had rubbed it, I knew him for a gentleman, and guessed him for the lady's squire and captain. She called him Jorrill.

"Good Jorrill, there is a dead knave beside the Kelpie Ford who will please me better half a league back among the knolls and under a ton of rocks," she told him.

He bowed and spoke a few words to one of the fellows at his shoulder; whereupon three of them withdrew. His leathery face was expressionless.

"Friend Jorrill, this young lady is the Damosel Sylvia of Montclair, who was given to gypsies by a wicked step-mother, sold by the gypsies to wicked jongleurs, and rescued from the jongleurs by this learned young clerk who is called Mark of the Lake," she said gravely.

The squire bowed to Sylvia, without any word or look of surprise or extraordinary curiosity. His face suggested nothing more than polite interest. Then he looked at me; and for a fraction of a second, that still face was all alive. It was blank again in the blink of an eye.

Chapter Eight
A KING COMES HOME

I was alone in a fair chamber. I sat on the edge of a princely bed, with my swords on the velvet coverlet beside

me, and my iron-shod staff on the floor at my feet. My head
was in a whirl. The door opened, and the young page who
had led me here but a few minutes since entered again. His
name was Gervase. He had a silver cup in one hand, and
various garments draped over the other arm.

"With the Queen's compliments," he said, giving me the
cup.

"Queen?" I cried.

"That's nothing," he jeered. "Kings and queens are
common as brambleberries in this realm of Britain. It's
easy seeing you've lived with mountainy sheep an' unicorns ever since you were a baby. But drink the wine,
Mark. We could give none better to our overlord Arthur
Pendragon himself, for it is from the best butt in the
crypt."

I drained the cup to the last drop.

"I have known her to deny it to knights and earls," said
Gervase, eyeing me curiously.

"About this queen? Do you mean Dame Carmel?" I
asked, feeling the benefit of the wine.

He nodded and said: "Queen Carmel of the Marches."

He tossed his burden of garments on the bed.

"Help yourself," he said. "Some are mine; some are old
Jorrill's; and some belonged to the late King. Nothing is too
good for you, it seems."

I examined the things, and confessed that I knew nothing of fine clothes. At that, Gervase's manner became more
friendly.

"Try the shirts first," he advised. "Strip to the waist.
Here is something of mine that could not be matched this
side of Camelot."

He held up a garment of silk for my inspection and
looked at me. I was naked down to my bullskin belt. He
started and stared, and cried out an oath unbecoming his
tender years and his delicate appearance.

"What ails you?" I asked.

He advanced a pace, but with an air of wariness,
extended an arm and a stiff forefinger and prodded my left
shoulder, but cautiously.

"What ails it?" I asked.

He muttered, "No offense, good Mark," and prodded my
other shoulder and the muscles of my chest.

"Remarkable!" he exclaimed. "Astonishing!"

"If I start prodding you in return, Master Popinjay, you'll be truly astonished," I said.

He skipped backward two paces.

"No offense!" he cried. "But pardonable and admiring amazement. You were but a well-grown youth in your jerkin, but out of it you are a full-grown man."

"Give me that shirt!" I cried.

"Too small," he said. "Calm yourself, good Mark. We must find something else."

We tried all the garments Gervase had brought before I was fully attired in linen and silk and buskins of soft red leather; and even then I was punched and constrained here and there. Only the grand boots were big enough, and they were too big.

"Can this be that mountainy young Mark of the Lake?" cried Gervase, turning me around and around. "Now you cut a royal figure, my clerkly friend. And rightly so. Save for worthy Squire Jorrill's trunk-hose, you are garbed from heels to head from the royal, even if somewhat outmoded, wardrobe of the late lamented King Ban of the Marches. Nothing of mine had the honor of being big enough for Your Majesty."

"I feel like a fool, and doubtless look it," I said. "A gentleman I am, with Brother Ambrose's word for it—but why all this? Why does your Queen Carmel treat me with this high consideration? Me, poor Mark, knowing neither father nor mother nor any friend save Brother Ambrose, until I found Sylvia. I don't understand it. What manner of person is this Queen of the Marches?"

"All honey or fury or melancholy," said the page. "She keeps less court than some of the lords and knights who hold their lands at her pleasure, and yet Lucifer could not show more pride upon occasion. They tell me she was a great beauty in her day."

"Is she not a beauty now?" I asked.

Gervase stared at me as if he doubted his ears.

"But she's old!" he protested. "Dame Rosamond says she has been a widow fifteen years, and that she was a grown woman with a big baby before the King was killed."

The door opened again; Jorrill entered, this time. Now he was dressed in silk and velvet. He stood and gazed at me; and all the life of his still, dark face seemed to be in his yet darker eyes.

"The Queen wants you," he said; and though he did not turn his head or even shift his glance, the page picked up the empty cup and the garments which had failed to meet my dimensions, and sauntered from the chamber.

The elderly squire came closer to me. "Who are you?" he asked.

"If you expect an answer, you will have to put the question more courteously, my good sir," I said.

"Hah—my mistake!" he exclaimed. His gaze wavered but came back.

"You are right, young sir," he went on, but in milder tones, "and I beg you to forgive my bluntness, which I come by honestly, and to tell me who you are."

"When a man has never heard the name of his father or his mother, how is he to know who he is, Sir Squire?" I said.

He considered that gravely for a moment and shook his head.

"But surely you told the Queen something," he objected.

I told him what I had told the lady on the jennet, but in fewer words. He twitched with excitement, and finally grasped me by both shoulders.

"I see it!" he exclaimed, but his voice was no louder than a whisper. "You remember nothing before that mountainy life. You were too young. Fifteen years—nay, more than that by two, by three months. You were but an infant, fifteen years and three months ago. That's it! Hah!"

"What?" I asked; and as his fingers were pinching into my shoulders like iron hooks, I put my hands up and removed them.

Nothing daunted, he laid hold of the breast of my royal borrowed jerkin.

"Your guardian—this Ambrose—what shape and size of a man is he?"

Suspicion flashed in me and then burned clearly and steadily. My good and gentle friend had fled from the world. He had been in peril. But he had taken me, a squalling infant, into exile and hiding with him. Had the peril been to me? Or to both of us? And what manner of peril could it have been—could it be—to keep that good and brave and mighty man in hiding all these years? And did this hired captain think to frighten and confuse me into discovering him? And why? What did this Jorrill know or suspect, to excite all this questioning and conjecturing? I felt an enveloping anger.

"Who are you to question me?" I whispered back at him, lowering and advancing my face toward his. "What is your concern with my friend's size and shape, or with my own age? If the Queen wants to know these things she—"

He let go his hold on me as if the fine stuff of the dead King's jerkin had suddenly caught afire.

"Nay, not that!" he cried. "Say nothing to her of this— my idle questioning—I beg you! I charge you! It is nothing. Forget that I asked. Come with me now, good boy—and keep your mouth shut!"

I sneered at him.

"Queen Carmel could have told you Brother Ambrose's size and shape, for she had heard it from me on our way from the ford. And as for keeping my mouth shut, good Jorrill—mind your own mouth, lest you find it choked with a churchyard sod!"

He stepped back and dropped his right hand to the jeweled haft of his dagger. I shifted my weight a little for a jump in any direction, and fisted my low-hanging right hand, but did not shift my eyes from his eyes. And there I saw the red intent to kill cool to uncertainty and dim to fear.

He whispered, "Not a word of this to the Queen, I beg of you, good Master Mark."

"A quick change of tune!" I sneered. "And all for fear of your own royal mistress. But to me she seems a kind and right generous dame."

He lowered his eyes and bunched his brows and stood there scowling as if in deep and difficult thought.

"You misjudge me," he muttered. "I was not myself; I am distraught."

He looked behind him at the half-open door by which he had come in, hesitated for a few twitching seconds, then turned and ran to it, paused for a moment to look out past and around the edge of it, set a hand to the great latch of iron and stepped back, shutting oak and iron tightly in place, but without sound. He faced the room again.

"Hah!" he cried.

For I was not where or as he had last seen me. Now I stood within a pace of the bed, and held the short sword of the dead jongleur in my hand.

"You misjudge me," he muttered.

With quick fingers he loosed his belt of fine Turkic leather, and with a quick swing of the arm he tossed it, sheathed dagger and all, to the floor at my feet. I was agreeably surprised, but still suspicious. I did not throw my sword away.

"It is your fault if I misjudge you," I said grimly. "And what hocus-pocus is this?" I asked. "I learn the world's ways fast. What of the hidden knife in your breast?"

At that, he cried out in a voice of hurt reproach, and fell to beating his front and sides with open hands to show that no weapon was concealed there.

"So be it," I said unpleasantly. "Have done with the mummery now, and say your say."

He advanced halfway to me and stood there.

"You charge me with being afraid of Queen Carmel," he said. "It is the truth, young sir—but my fear of her is not for myself. I have served her long and faithfully without fear. But it is my Christian duty to warn you, young sir, even at the cost of my word of honor and oaths of fealty. You are in hourly deadly peril here from that queen. Remain till tomorrow's dawn, and you will not see tomorrow's sun."

I was dazed and daunted; because of the creeping chill at my heart, my anger flared again, and I warned him to have done with his unseemly joking.

"Joking?" he sighed. "Look at me, poor lad. Nay, 'tis no joke."

I looked; the flurry of vain anger died in me, and terror gripped me.

"And Sylvia? Is she in peril too?" I cried. "What of her? Where is she now?"

"Not so loud!" he protested.

He came nearer.

I know nothing of that damosel," he whispered, fierce and fast. "The Queen pets her now—but that may mean no more than her petting of you. I don't know who she is—she's nothing to me—but you I know. Harken to me now! Take heed of every word!"

He came yet nearer; and I listened like one spellbound.

"She had a lover when she was a damosel. He was a knight, but poor—a seventh son. She married King Ban of the Marches; and within the year, that knight came from the court at Camelot and swore fealty to King Ban. The Queen gave birth to a son. When that child was in its third year, the King—he was in his cups and had been listening to a jealous lady of the household—suddenly accused his queen and that young knight of adultery, and disowned the infant. The knight struck him with a bare fist and fled with the infant. The King died of that blow—of a broken neck—but not before he had retracted that charge. For fifteen years and some months nothing was seen or heard of that knight or that child."

Jorrill paused, regarding me with narrowed eyes.

"What is this to me?" I whispered.

"And she is Queen," he went on. "She had ruled the Marches all these years. She has had other lovers, and other babes, 'tis rumored; but now she plans to marry again."

"What is this to me?" I asked again.

"Ambrose was that knight's name," he answered, and flicked his tongue along thin lips. "Sir Ambrose. Brother Ambrose. A man of might, and yet a learned clerk."

"I am his son?"

"Nay, the King retracted that."

"But I am her son?"

He nodded.

"Then why does she wish me harm?"

"You are the King. She plans to wed her latest lover, with King Arthur's sanction—unless she takes a fancy to yet another before the Overlord's permission comes from Camelot. In either case she is still the Queen of the Marches—unless the true King should come and claim his heritage.

"I don't understand this, but I think you lie!"

I slapped his face with my left hand, seized him by the throat with my right and flung him to the floor. I was about to stoop and raise him for another fling when—

The Queen stood on the threshold of the open door. She came toward me, smiling. She did not so much as glance at Jorrill, where he crawled along the floor. I did not move. When she was nearer, I saw tears in her eyes and sliding down the white and red of her cheeks. She came close and put her arms around my neck and drew my face down to her lips. Her tears wet my cheeks, and her lips moved against it.

"Well spoke—and well struck, my son."

I had nothing but confusion in my head; and having nothing to do with my arms, and being somewhat off balance, I put them around her. So we stood embraced for minutes; but when the cramp in my bowed neck became unbearable, I had to straighten it; and then I saw that Jorrill was gone from the room, and his belt and dagger with him.

"That squire has gone!" I exclaimed.

She removed her face from my breast and looked around.

"He will not return," she whispered. "He can do you no deadly mischief now: nor me, with his lies!"

I remembered the murder in his half-shut eyes.

"Why does he hate me, who never saw him before today?" I asked.

"It is your father's son he hates. It was he, poor fool, who told the King—"

She looked up at me through welling tears, her carmine lips parted and trembling, and all her face and brow and throat as red as the painted spots on her cheeks. My heart warmed and softened to her; and I knew the emotion for love, though it did not flame and sing, like my love for Sylvia.

"His tongue was foul with lies, so I struck him," I said.

She whispered: "That I am your mother is no lie."

"Then what of me? God's wounds! Who am I?"

"You are the King."

"Did Brother Ambrose kill my father?"

"Nay, he killed the King. But murder was not in his heart. He struck bare-handed—for pity and love of me. The sin was mine: but be merciful in your judgment, for I have loved only him and our little son all these weary years—though I thought you both lost to me forever."

She clung to me again; and again I kissed her painted lips.

"And what of sin and kisses now, Saint Mark?" cried a

strange-sounding voice from the threshold of the open door.

I raised my head and looked; and for a heartbeat I did not know the vision flaming there in gold and ermine and ice-green fire for my raggedy companion of the mountains.

"This lady—this queen—is my mother," I stammered.

Queen Carmel turned her face toward Sylvia without removing her head from the hollow of my left shoulder.

"Come here, sweet fool," she said. "There is room here for both of us—sweetheart and poor old mother."

She made a pitiful sound of sobbing laughter.

"Brother Ambrose is my father," I said to Sylvia. "Which makes me a bastard," I added.

"But King Ban withdrew that charge—and now you are the King," sobbed Queen Carmel.

Then Sylvia cried: "What do I care what he is—king or knight or poor clerk—anything but a jongleur!—so long as he is mine?"

She ran to me; and so it was that I had both of them in my arms when Gervase the page appeared on the scene. He halted and gawked.

"What now?" asked the Queen.

"Old Jorrill—he's dead, ma'am," stammered Gervase. "Of a broken neck. Captain Jorrill, ma'am. It was a big bearded rogue in wild skins. He asked to be brought to you, ma'am—at the buttery-hatch. And Jorrill was there and cried an oath and drew a knife on him. And he hit the squire with a bare fist—just once—and threw four archers into the yard. Now he battles against a dozen and shouts a war-cry. Hark! 'Strike straight! Strike hard!'"

The Queen twisted away from me, knocked Gervase out of her way and was gone. Her screams of mingled endearments and threats rang back to us.

"'Tis Brother Ambrose!" I cried. "I've heard him shout it at boar and bull—'Strike straight! Strike hard!' Come!"

But the battle was over and my father had my mother in his arms when Sylvia and I got there.

STRIKE HARD! BITE DEEP!

Chapter One
THE MAZED KNIGHT

The King and his court were but newly come to Carleon with a tail of captainless men-at-arms and bowmen, of itinerant armorers and smiths, farriers and horse-leeches, magicians in reduced circumstances and prophets without honor in their own countries, quacks and fortune-tellers and self-proclaimed discoverers of the Philosophers' Stone and the Fountain of Youth, conjurers and jongleurs and tumblers, troubadours of inferior talent or in hard luck, blind harpers, preaching friars, packmen and piemen, cutthroats, cutpurses, mendicants, gamecocks, dancing bears, and gypsies.

The dust of this invasion and envelopment lay like a sea fog on the landscape, and was thickened by the smoke of multitudinous fires. But by the time of the arrival of the Lost Knight, or Sir Lorn le Perdu, and his party, which was past midnight, the dust had settled and most of the smoke had dissolved in starshine. The young knight, a still younger gentleman named Dennys ap Rhys, and the swineherds Oggle and Maggon who served them as grooms, found accommodation at a crowded inn, after showings of teeth and iron and even a few buffets.

Might was right that night, in and around Carleon. Sir Lorn bestrode as high and heavy a charger as any of the King's stable, and as ponderous of tread as if he were shod with anvils; and the knight cleared his own mailed feet from the stirrups and kicked forward and outward ever and anon, now to the right and now to the left, when the riffraff massed about them and were slow to give way. And Dennys, on a strong mountain half-breed, wheeled and curveted, to clear a passage for the beasts of burden, which were hung about with spears and armor and provisions and gear. These were mountain ponies, small but of surprising hardihood. The grooms, flourishing boar-spears and bristling with back knives and spiked hammers, brought up the rear on two more ponies. The innkeeper protested at the door, but retreated when the warhorse splintered the threshold with a hoof. Horse and knight entered after him, bringing the frame of the door with them, both lintel and jambs. Sleepers on the floor rolled aside and staggered up in every direction, and their howls of fright and fury outrang the rending and splintering of timber. The ashed embers on the hearth were kicked to flame and torches were fired: but by the time the dark was dispelled, so were many of the original occupants of the room, and the Lost Knight's party was in full possession, ponies and all.

A door opened at the foot of a staircase, and a gentleman draped about in a robe of red silk was disclosed, holding above his head a candle of beeswax in a silver stick. The top of his skull was polished and pink, but his face was whiskered and mustached and bearded magnificently in pure white.

"What's this?" he asked.

"No doin' of mine, Yer Lordship!" cried the taverner. "This fellow—this knight—and his varlets and beasts, forced their entrance against my hand and voice, and have all but wrecked my house."

"What knight are you?" the old lord asked of Sir Lorn.

The knight, still in his saddle and stooped forward sharply for lack of headroom, did not reply. Dennys, who had dismounted, advanced and bowed and spoke respectfully.

"Sir, you put a hard question, to which neither my master nor I know the answer; but he is called the Lost Knight, or Sir Lorn le Perdu, and with reason; and now we are come a long and crooked road to Carleon for the joustings. That we entered here against this honest fellow's protests I admit freely, but I assure Your Honor it was done without thought of evil on this good knight's part. In truth, it was done likely without thought of anything, in a mental abstraction."

"Ah, so that's it," said the old lord, "a mazed knight. I have read of many such, and have even known a few in my adventurous years. Gentlemen given to mental abstractions, that's to say. They are ill people to have ado with, as I learned to my cost when I jousted with one who called himself Sir Devilbane, and was pleased to mistake me for an imp out of hell. I was but one of a dozen he laid in the dust on that occasion; and it was for that day's work he received knighthood from King Uther Pendragon."

He shifted his glance and addressed the innkeeper.

"Look you to me for the damages, good Gyles. I am taking these gentlemen to my own chambers for refreshment and couching. Look you to the varlets and beasts and gear—and well, if you value your life!"

He shifted his glance again, and addressed the silent young man doubled up there atop the tall white warhorse.

"Sir, I beg you to step down and break bread with me. I have rare French vintages in my private vault here, and a lark-and-pigeon pie in my private larder."

Sir Lorn dismounted and said, in a flat voice and without facial expression: "Gramercy, noble lord."

And so he and Dennys left their horses and grooms and followed the old man in the red robe up the staircase and into a fine apartment lit by a score of candles in branched silver sticks. The walls were hung with arras upon which scenes and figures were wrought in glowing colors and lively attitudes: the chase of a unicorn in a forest glade by black hounds and a white bracket; a cavalier in half-armor on a red horse; a lady in azure and gold on a white jennet and fellows in leather toiling afoot with short spears in their hands; the meeting of two knights in full force at the moment when the lesser departs his saddle backward over his horse's tail; a troubadour twanging a lyre and singing to ladies and damosels in a garden of roses; knights at wine and meat in a hall hung with shields, and great hounds cracking bones among the rushes on the stone floor; the slaying of a fen-dragon by a young knight in a place of green reeds and waterlilies; and last a long cavalcade of chivalry crested with plumes and banners and uptossed spear-points, with the castellated towers of Camelot for background.

Sir Lorn le Perdu went around the room slowly, gazing at the tapestries without comment. The old lord looked at Dennys with a lifting of eyebrows as big as mustaches. Dennys nodded.

"Sir, he seeks something to touch his memory to life," Dennys whispered.

"Is it dead?" the other whispered back.

"It sleeps," Dennys told him. "But only in his brain. He remembers with his heart and hands."

"How do you know him for a knight, then, if he has lost his memory?"

"Sir, his golden spurs were on his heels when he was discovered in the wilderness, and the great white horse at his shoulder, and his arms and harness and shield no great way off."

"His shield? What is the device?"

"None, sir. A shield of unpainted iron scales backed with hide and wood. The only marks on it are dents from spear-points and scars of sword-strokes."

The old lord nodded, and was about to question further, but an exclamation from the knight stopped him; and even as he turned toward the sudden sound, even more arresting sounds assailed his ears, and he held action to match them. A panel of the arras tore away and crumpled down, and men rolled on the floor like fighting dogs—the knight and two others: but the two did the rolling, in vain efforts to get out from under the clutching and pounding hands and knees of the knight. Dennys leaped to his master's help, but by then the strangers lay limp and still. Sir Lorn got to his feet lightly and with a hint of animation on his melancholy face.

"They stirred behind the picture I was looking at, so I plucked them forth," he said simply.

He glanced down at the motionless figures in leather and added, just as simply: "I banged their heads, for fear they meant mischief with their knives, but I don't think I killed them."

"Shrewd bangs!" exclaimed the old lord. "They meant mischief, rest assured of that—to my goods and my life too! Gramercy, young man!"

Now three oldsters came in by way of two doors, tottering and stumbling in anxious haste, one clutching a fine gown about him and shuffling in slippers of Spanish leather, and two barefooted and tying their points with fumbling fingers.

"Have we disturbed your just slumbers?" asked the old lord softly. Then he cried out shrilly: "God's wounds—d'ye stuff your ears with pillows?"

The gentleman in the dressing gown and the fellows in wool made deprecating gestures, but spoke no word.

"But for this alert and powerful young knight, we might all be murdered in our beds before dawn," continued His Lordship, but now softly again, in tones more of resignation than of wrath. "These two cutthroats were behind the arras. Bind them and carry them to the cellar, and fetch two flagons of wine and a crock of meat back with you. Give them the keys, Sir James, and tell Luke to lay the board with trenchers and four of the silver-gilt cups, and the new pie."

Within a short while, the four were at table and being served by an ancient called Luke. Sir Lorn was on their host's right hand, and Dennys was on his left, and old Sir James sat at the young squire's other side. Luke tottered around with a flagon, then with the great pie of larks and pigeons, then with the flagon again. The old knight moaned that to eat and drink at this barbaric hour would be the death of him, owing to a weakness of the stomach that was the result of a shipwreck on the coasts of Ireland and the consequent enforced diet of shellfish.

"But for these gentlemen, good James, you'd be dead by dawn of more than a bellyache," jeered the old lord. "And as for your shipwreck—I dare say I have been wrecked on every coast of Christendom, but do you hear me complain?"

He looked to his right, at his guest of honor, with an engaging smile, and said: "I'll wager ten hides of good land against a cast horseshoe he was older than you are now, though still but a gawky squire, at that time."

Sir Lorn's only reply was a puzzled and apologetic smile.

"Gawky I never was," the old knight protested, with a flicker in his faded eyes, but in the same voice of self-pity and whining complaint. "A squire, yes. Knighthood was hard come by in those days. Golden spurs did not hang on every bush."

Then Dennys ap Rhys, who had drained his cup twice, spoke up hardily.

"Worshipful sir, permit me to inform Your Honor that if that shaft is intended for my master, you are shooting wide of the mark. Young my master may be, but he did not pluck his golden spurs from a bush!"

Sir James made no answer, but hunched his shoulders and wagged his beard skeptically, and eyed the succulent bits of lark and pigeons and pastry on his trencher distastefully.

"You speak with assurance, good youth," said the old lord to Dennys kindly. "And may I ask—since your friend will not speak for himself—if your high opinion of him is based upon hearsay or observation?"

"Noble sir, I have heard nothing," Dennys replied; "but I can tell Your Lordship that this knight's reason for not speaking for himself is that he knows nothing of his past, as I have said. He knows no more of himself than I have learned of him in the nine months since our first meeting."

"It should be a short story," said the host, smiling back and forth between his young guests. "But short or long, I am curious to hear it."

Dennys turned an inquiring look upon Sir Lorn le Perdu, who met it with a faint smile and a slight nod.

Chapter Two
DENNYS TELLS WHAT HE KNOWS

Dennys told it simply: in the fall of last year, he and his father and six of their people went into the wilderness in search of strays from their flocks. They reached the high valley of that dark water called the Kelpie's Pond just before sunset of their third day out, and the serfs made a little shelter of fir boughs and a great fire of deadwood from a grove of wind-twisted hawthorn and mountain oak. It was an ancient and desolate land. Soon after sunset a white frost fell from the frozen stars. The herdsmen drew closer to the fire. Even after their supper of mutton collops and barley bread and ale, they continued to press upon the fire, but as much for its singing light as its heat; for this was reputed an unholy place, still frequented by more dangerous beings than its wild human and beasty denizens—than its heathen men and great wolves and the scaly things that bred in the crevices of its highest rocks. Even Dennys and his father were glad of the dancing shine and bright sparks, as well as of the heat.

One of the tethered ponies whinnied in the outer darkness behind the fire and the hut of boughs, and was answered by a louder whinny from the darkness beyond the opposite margin of firelight. Every eye moved; but no man there, gentle or free or in a serf's iron collar, moved more than his eyes: and the breath caught in every windpipe and the blood slowed in every vein. A tall man stepped into the circle of light and stood there, silent and motionless. The head of a great white horse appeared at his shoulder.

Dennys thought, Kelpies don't ride horses! and his breath and blood moved again. The same thought must have struck the father too, for he got to his feet and cried: "God be with you!"

The stranger inclined his head but said no word. Dennys got up then and passed around the fire, but shaking in his shoes the while. He stood close to the stranger, who was in leather save for his legs, which were armored from the knees down. But he knew enough of the polite world to recognize this leather, by stains and marks of bruises and abrasions which could come only from friction with plates and chains of iron, as the fighting underwear of a knight. "Sir, you have lost your harness," he said. And then he looked down at the spurs on the iron heels, and stooped and saw that they were of gold.

So they called him the Lost Knight, though he looked too young for knighthood. While he ate and drank beside Rhys ap Tudor, draped in that worthy gentleman's cloak of castor skins, Dennys tended the great white horse. He removed saddle and bridle and the plates of bronze from face and chest. The high saddle had been rolled upon and somewhat damaged, and the bit of the bridle was tangled with coarse herbage. Dennys rubbed him down, fed him a loaf of barley bread, and tethered him on a patch of fine grasses and mountain clover that was close by.

❖ ❖ ❖

In the morning Dennys and his father and the herds-men wandered about the margins of the lake, but now more in search of the Lost Knight's equipment than of lost sheep. The knight himself kept to the encampment, some-times sitting with a hand to his brow and sometimes standing and gazing vacantly around at plain and lake and rocky tor and looming mountain.

Dennys came upon the knightly sword—sword and scabbard and belt studded with gold and bright stones, all together. One of the herds discovered a mighty spear with a bent point, and yet another serf stumbled upon the great shield. It was Dennys' father who found the helmet in a ferny hollow, its plume bedraggled with frost and dew, and the open vizard crisscrossed with a spider's web. The breast- and backplates and thigh-pieces, and numerous parts of fine-linked, supple chain mail, and the knightly secondary armament—after spear and long sword—of short sword, Spanish dagger, and the spike-headed mace, were found by noon.

The party returned to camp then, and to a surprising scene. The Lost Knight sat hunched on an outcrop of gran-ite, elbow on knee and head on hand in an attitude of deep thought, and scattered about the sward in various final attitudes were four dead men with crushed skulls. They were heathens of the wildest and most savage of the mountain tribes. They had crept close, without using their short bows, and sprung upon the unarmed knight with boar-spears and knives. But he had leaped aside and snatched up a half-burned trunk of a young oak from the dead coals of the fire; and when he had smitten down four, three survivors had turned to escape back to their rocky fastnesses; and then the warhorse had broken free of the peg he was tethered to, pursued, and overtaken one of the fugitives and killed him as a dog kills a rat. The knight had taken but little hurt—a shallow stab in the left shoulder and a shallow cut along a rib—and the great horse none at all.

They went home from the wilderness in less time than the out-trip had taken them by half a day, with a score of strayed sheep that had not fallen to savages or wolves trot-ting before them, and the Lost Knight riding between father and son on his white warhorse. It was Dennys' pleasure to act as the stranger's squire, bearing shield and spear, and with his half-breed mountain horse hung all about with pieces of armor. But when they came to the northern edge of the manor, which lay in a wide vale of groves and fields and walled yards of apple trees and plum trees, the knight dismounted, at Dennys' request, and allowed himself to be harnessed and armed cap-à-pie. So they issued from the hanging wood of fir and were espied with wonder by a variety of people. Plowmen stopped their slow oxen and gaped and hallooed; children left off their games, and gammers and gaffers their gossip; herds and wards sounded their horns; and heads appeared above walls and at the windows of the manor house.

The family and all the household made much of the mysterious stranger. The ladies of the family devoted most of their waking hours to him. From Dennys' grandmother, Dame Gwyn, down to his sisters Edyth and Mary, by way of his mother and two aunts, one and all seemed to have lost all their former interests in life. They would learn his past, though he knew it not himself—mauger their heads! And they would teach him the present and even shape the future for him. His paucity of speech did not discourage them. His forlorn condition, his knightly state, youth, melancholy mien, gentle smile, and good though dimmed facial features, won all hearts. And his two wounds.

But Dame Gwyn healed those in as many days with a salve of herbs of Druidical origin. And it was Dame Gwyn who found the name for him. She fixed his gaze and attention with her bright black eyes, and recited names to him, pausing briefly after each for his reaction. She opened with *Matthew, Mark, Luke,* and *John,* but without effect. The names of the other Apostles, and of the Prophets and a score of Christian martyrs, were spoken to no more avail, as were those of hundreds of old kings and heroes; for the dame was deeply read in books, both sacred and profane. After that she went on haphazardly, offering anything that came into her head. And at last her persistence was rewarded; for at her utterance of the word *Lorn,* the distraught youth started in his seat and widened his eyes and gasped, "Yes!" So Dame Gwyn pronounced his name and style to be Sir Lorn le Perdu, and hung a small charm from his neck that contained a splinter of the True Cross, and prophesied great things of him.

Winter came early with storms of wind and snow; in the heart of the storm came a horde of savages and outlaws from the northern wastes, and mayhap even from the craggy fastnesses of No-man's-land beyond the Wall and just this side of Ultima Thule. Many warders and herds and foresters perished in their isolated huts, even in their sleep, stabbed and bludgeoned in the dark or by tossing torch-shine. Fire was put to hovels and houses and ricks; and confusion and terror invaded the great valley and was spread by cotters and farmers fleeing in clouds of snow and smoke.

The alarum reached the manor house; and it was not long before Rhys ap Tudor and his son Dennys ap Rhys led two score armed men through the outer wall of timbers and sharpened stakes, both horsed and afoot.

They had armed with as little disturbance as might be, for the ladies said that the knightly guest needed his sleep and was in no condition for mortal combat. But they were no farther than a bowshot from the gate when the warhorse overtook them, screaming and galloping, with the knight shouting in the high saddle. And horse and rider passed through their toiling ranks; and Dennys shouted too, and galloped after.

"A Lorn—a Lorn!" shouted the melancholy knight in a voice that outrang the gale. "Strike hard! Bite deep!" And Dennys riding furiously, cried: "A Lorn, a Lorn!"

They came upon the main body of the raiders in a farmyard, massed in the awful light of flaming hayricks and a flaming house under a billowing, shaking canopy of smoke and driven snow shot through with sparks. Then the white horse and the Lost Knight fell on with teeth and hooves and sword; and Dennys on his half-breed gelding followed close and did what he could with an ancient sword that once was wielded by Dame Gwyn's father, who had been the Black King Owen of the old ballads. Screams of terror mingled with the battle scream of the white horse and the shouts of knight and squire. Round targes of hide and the fur-clad savages behind them were cut clean through by Lorn's sword, and cracked and staggered by

Dennys' antique blade of bronze; and limbs were torn and bodies crushed by chopping teeth and hammering hooves, for the mountain-bred gelding was soon biting and striking and kicking as viciously as the white stallion. When Rhys ap Tudor arrived, there was no fighting left for him and his men, but only pursuit into the white storm, and blind slaughter beyond the red glare of the fires. . . .

The rest of the winter passed peacefully in that remote manorial valley. The melancholy knight learned to smile when spoken to prettily by a lady or damosel, and even to laugh upon occasion, and once said six words in one breath to old Dame Gwyn, with whom he was on especially friendly terms. He and Dennys exercised at arms every day, using old swords of soft metal and blunted edges, and daggers of fir which broke on their leather jerkins like thin ice. Sometimes they donned their armor and mounted their horses bareback and tilted with blunted spears roughly made for them by Howell the wheelwright. Those mock spears of inferior wood broke at a touch; but a touch was usually enough to send either saddleless champion backward over his horse's tail.

At that game, the knight took almost as many falls as the squire. But afoot it was quite another matter. With any manner of sword, or with wooden staves or cudgels even, Sir Lorn could sweep Dennys away with a half-dozen strokes. It was a notable thing that at all this play in rickyard or snowy meadow, the great white horse comported himself more like a lamb than a killer, without so much as a show of teeth or hoof, or a snort of his battle cry, at Dennys or the brown gelding.

In early spring, a wandering company consisting of a troubadour who claimed to be from Brittany, three jongleurs, a packman, and an Irish scrivener came to the manor house and were received with good cheer. They were as hungry as wolves and as thirsty as the Questing Beast; and they supped so well on the evening of their arrival that they slept till the following noon. They would have returned to their slumbers after dinner but for the protests of the household, and especially of the ladies. The jongleurs were the first to respond to the demand for entertainment. Their leader, a plump man in his fifties with the face of a wrinkled boy and round, faded blue eyes, took a russet apple from a dish and presented it to Dennys, with a mocking bow and a sly smile.

"Gramercy!" said Dennys; but he felt the apple move in his hand, whereupon he dropped it quickly; and behold, it was a warty brown toad hopping on the flagstones, and between two hops it was gone, as if dissolved in air. Then, still smiling, the jongleur took Dame Gwyn's shawl of silk from her shoulders; and what he would have made of that, had she not snatched it right back from him, the devil only knows. And she cried out at him, naming him a saucy rogue. Unabashed, he stepped away and took a boar-spear from a rack of sylvan weapons on the nearest wall. This he held close to his face for seconds, muttering the while in a strange tongue, then gave a sudden, fierce shout and flung it upward at the gloom beyond the rafters. All eyes turned upward, in expectation of its fall.

"It is already fallen down into its place," said the fellow; and there it was in its rack on the wall, sure enough!

Many gasped in wonder, but not old Dame Gwyn. "Hocus-pocus!" she scoffed. "It never left the rogue's hand!" Whereat she cackled with laughter, and he laughed with her, as if all others present were their inferiors in wit and wisdom; and she gave him a silver three-penny piece, for which he thanked her humbly and sincerely. The second jongleur, a thin man who looked more like a learned clerk than a vagabond, gave an indifferent exhibition with four daggers, of which he appeared to be afraid. The third and youngest of that team, a mere lad, turned handsprings and air-springs. When the troubadour's turn came, he said, "This is a piece I learned of an old bard in Brittany, but out of Ireland, who told how he had sung it before all the kings and queens and courts of Christendom and won fame thereby, which he could not understand, for it was a common old nursery rhyme where he came from." And he twanged the strings and sang in a disconsolate voice:

"*Bright Lady, I had ridden far,*
With a dream for guide, and a shooting star,
A milk-white doe and a golden bee.
I found you under the wishing-tree.

"Long we wandered, hand-a-hand,
From Dublin e'en to Fairyland,
By hill and vale, by tarn and mere,
By leafy glade and silver strand.

"Oft did we dally by the way,
At dark of night and heat of day;
Lip to lip and breast to breast,
Whilst moons and suns went East and West.

"For war-horns brayed—but not for me.
A fig for vaunting chivalry!
Let fools who will, and knaves who must,
Spatter their blood and eat their dust!

"Bright Lady, pity me who ride
With only Will-o'-the-wisp for guide—
Forsook by thee—lost and alone—
By rocky track and grieving tide.

"Ah, Christ, that I had labored then
In that red field of beasts and men!
Pity me now, O pitiful Lord,
Who did not perish by the sword,

"But wander, desolate and alone,
Bruising my feet on stock and stone,
Crying upon a lost white hand
To lead me back to Fairyland."

The troubadour had no more than drawn breath after his last pathetic note, than he uttered a cry of dismay—for the young knight had him gripped by the front of his doublet. The lost one's face was convulsed as if with anguish, and his eyes flashed madly, but he made no sound. For a minute—while the company stared at him spellbound—he shook the terrified minstrel like a thing of rags and sticks; then he flung him aside and dashed from the hall. Every man there, save the unnerved troubadour, gave chase. But it was a short chase; for the knight soon stopped of his own accord, and turned and came back to his pursuers, blank of face and heavy of foot. The troubadour and his fellows departed next day; but the words of that sad song remained, for curious old Dame Gwyn had paid the scrivener to write them down from the minstrel's dictation.

That was the end of the story as told by Dennys ap Rhys at the old lord's supper table; and at its conclusion it was observed that Sir Lorn, who had sat silent throughout the telling, was sound asleep.

"Very interesting," said the old lord reflectively. "I have heard other versions of the same piece. Its theme is of no mortal lady, needless to say; and she goes by various names. Nothing is more likely than that our friend is one of her victims. I have known others—and some who recovered completely from the experience, which this young knight will do in time, doubt it not. In fact, I am not at all certain that I did not once come within a hand's-turn of encountering her myself, and have never ceased to regret whatever it was that came between us; for I have never been one to cry 'fie' or 'avaunt' at any aspect of romantic beauty, mortal or supernatural."

At that, old Sir James grumbled that it was time for bed.

Chapter Three
DENNYS HAS AN ADVENTURE BEFORE BREAKFAST

Late as it was when Dennys got to sleep, he was awake again soon after sunrise. He saw the rich tapestries on all sides, flagons and cups empty and deserted on the board, and the Lost Knight sprawled in slumber on a couch of silks and soft furs; and so, in the blink of an eye, he recalled the incidents of their arrival at the inn, and the hospitality of the old nobleman, and he knew where he was. Sounds of the waking of inn and town and the encompassing camp came to him through walls and floors and windows, and stirred his blood and spirit. He dressed lightly and went down the winding stairs to the room which he had seen by torchlight and in wild confusion the night before.

Confusion and hubbub still reigned in level sunshine, but now only of impatient fellows demanding their morning bacon and ale, that they might be about their diverse and devious affairs and diversions. Servants of the inn struggled among them with jacks and tankards, being snatched at for their wares and then pushed aside, while they in turn snatched for farthings due them or for recovery of the mead or ale. Dennys tried to pass without

attracting attention, through to the jagged aperture that
had been the doorway before last night's entrance of Sir
Lorn on his warhorse, for he was eager for a glimpse of
Carleon and the royal court. But a big fellow with eyes but
half open and his points still untied laid hold of him by the
shoulders before he was clear of the press, and demanded
the jack of ale he had paid for.

"I know nothing of it," said Dennys.

"Ye lie!" bellowed the other.

"Unhand me, knave!" said Dennys; and he moved both
his arms at the same moment, sinking his right fist in the
bulging belly, and his left in the bulging jowl.

The rude fellow subsided slowly, his eyes wide open
now, but blank with surprise, and his mouth open but
speechless. The pressure and shouting on every side was
so witless and violent that the incident passed unheeded;
and Dennys was clear of the mêlée a moment later. He
went around back to the inn yard, and discovered his
groom Oggle working the winch over the well with one arm
while embracing a kitchen wench with the other.

"One thing at a time, good Oggle," he advised.

The groom released both his holds simultaneously and
sprang away, and the rope whirred out; the bucket
splashed in the depths, and the girl fell down.

"You see what I mean," said Dennys pleasantly: and he
helped the wench to her feet and gave her a kiss and a
black penny.

He was in high fettle. The day and the world were
young; the sun was bright; and promises of new scenes
and sensations buzzed and lilted and glinted all around
him. This was Carleon, an open gateway to the world of
chivalry.

This was the threshold of Life. But he kept his feet on
the ground and made an inspection of the stable to which
Oggle had led him at a word. It was a strong place of mor-
tised stone, and reserved for the use of customers of con-
sequence. Here he found Sir Lorn's great horse Bahram (so
named by Dame Gwyn from the depths of her knowledge),
his own brown gelding Hero, and his ponies, and two high
but aged chargers and several hackneys which, so a stout
fellow in a chain shirt and armed with a short sword and
a half-pike told him, were the property of the King.

"The King!" Dennys exclaimed. "King Arthur?"

"There are other kings than Arthur Pendragon, young sir," the armed groom replied disdainfully. "And some of certainer parentage. There is Your Honor's host and my liege lord for one—King Torrice of Har."

"I might have guessed it," said Dennys. "That old lord with the vast whiskers and pink scalp! He looks a proper knight, sure enough!"

"I have heard such tales of His Majesty's youthful prowess from my grandsire, and of the mighty deeds of his prime from my sire, as would dumbfound you, young sir," said the other. "And even I," he went on, "have seen him unhorse tolerably good knights, and hold his own on foot against gentlemen of one-fifth his years."

At that, Dennys cried out: "God's wounds! How old is he?"

"Older than the wizard Merlin," said the stout groom, with solemnity. "And he is lord of twenty baronies, and fourteen castles, and manor houses beyond reckoning. And yet he lives here at the inn, like a landless private old gentleman, while his vassals despoil him in the land of Har, and others rob him in this place."

"Is he mad?" asked Dennys. "But no! His eyes are sane," he added.

"That is truth," said the groom. "But he is a poet. He has made more and better poems, I wager, than all the beggarly troubadours afoot today in this island of Britain; and in Ireland too, where even swineherds and shepherds practice the art while the wolves carry off their charges. And he is a knight with a quest; and being a poet, the object of his quest is a thing, or a being, beyond the ordinary imagination. And after riding on that quest longer than the lifespans of three ordinary mortals, and all over Christendom, he settled down at this inn five winters since, because a gypsy who called herself the Queen of Egypt told him that his quest would be achieved here in Carleon if he would but stay still and abide his time; which irks His Majesty but suits that old fox Sir James very well, and poor old Luke and the other ancient knaves, but is hard on an active, adventurous man like me."

"What name does he give his quest?" Dennys asked; but before the groom could begin the answer, Sir James tottered into the stable with his feet in slippers, and a dressing gown clutched about him, and his voice raised in snarling complaint.

"Horses before high noon! What itch bites him now? Hi, stir your sticks! Where are you snoring now, fellow? Is this what you're paid for, think ye—to guzzle an' wench all night and sleep all day?"

"I am here and awake, Your Worship," cried out the armed groom, with a sneer and a bite in his voice. "I have stood on guard here all night; and now I have the honor to report that every beast in this stable has been fed an' groomed an' watered—not only our liege lord's, but his guests' as well."

"Don't bawl at me, you rogue!" bawled the knight, with a vehemence which all but ejected his few remaining long front teeth. "Or you'll be sent packing, along with that sham knight and his cowherd squire and cutthroat grooms!"

Dennys was about to speak up, but checked himself at a warning glance from the armed groom and turned and slipped out of the stable instead. He walked haphazardly, shaken with hot anger against that malignant old knight.

"Were he two score years younger, I'd feed his crooked tongue to the crows," he fumed. "A sham and a cowherd, are we? A pox to him!"

He wondered that King Torrice, though himself older than Merlin, could put up with the snarling, doddering old carper. . . . Screams tore him out of his abstraction. He found himself in a lane between huts and hovels and crooked palings. Here he glimpsed both dust and muck, and a variety of filth and a dead yellow cat. He did not pause for a second glance, however, but flattened the crazy fence on his left with a thrust of a foot and sprang into the narrow yard behind it. The screams, which were of childish terror and pain, and as pitiful as the death-cry of a rabbit, came from a hut at the back of the yard. Without a check, he leaped to the hut, flattened the shut door as he had flattened the fence, and leaped within. There was light enough to see by, from a small windows and the doorway. He saw a woman holding a squirming naked child face down across her lap, and a man stooped over them with a cobbler's awl in his hand. The awl had a red tip. Dennys smelled scorched flesh. (All this in a single second of time!) The man and woman had their faces turned to him, open-mouthed but silent. The child's cries still rang and sobbed.

Snatching up an oaken stool by a leg, Dennys hurled it with all his might—and all this so swiftly that the stool found its mark while the man's mouth was still open. The fellow went over backward onto the red coals on the hearth. The woman stood up, and the child rolled from her lap to the floor; but before she could move again, Dennys had her by the throat. It was a smooth round throat, but he gripped it without pity. Her bright black eyes were wide with terror; but he cursed them while he glared into them. He flung her furiously atop the senseless body on the hearth, then took the naked child in his arms and fled from there.

Dennys saw people clustering on his left, so he ran to the right. He saw a group in front, so he turned aside and leaped a fence and ran among scattering children and fowls, cats and pigs. A lean dog confronted him, but with more of inquiry than hostility in its air and attitude, and slunk aside just before he reached it. He crossed another fence and came to another vile and narrow lane and turned to his right along it. He heard shouts behind him, so kept up his hot pace. Now he noticed that the child in his arms had ceased its outcry, though sobs still shook it. He glanced down. It was gazing up at him with a look in its teary eyes which he could never describe or forget.

He glanced up again within the second, yet only in the nick of time, for here was a rogue with a knife coming at him and not ten paces distant. But the approach was war-ily zigzag and therefore slow. Dennys checked and glanced quickly around and behind him. He saw the same lean dog within a yard of his heels, trotting with lifted head and one sharp ear cocked forward, but quietly withal. He thought fast: No foe and perchance a friend. He turned, but kept his feet shifting and sliding, and extended the child toward the dog. The dog wagged his tail. Still shift-ing and turning, Dennys set the child on the ground, and still stooped double, charged the man with the knife, and drew a poniard with each hand at the same moment. The fellow stood, and after a fatal instant of indecision, made to throw his knife. But Dennys threw first.

Short one of his best daggers—for the ruffian crawled off with it imbedded in his middle—Dennys recovered the child, after freeing its arms gently from the dog's neck, and resumed his confused flight. Now a dozen pursuers were in sight, and a few stones were thrown, and ragged shouts of "Stop thief!" went up. The dog turned, with bared fangs and bristling hackles, but turned again and came on at Dennys' whistle. Dennys saw the glow of a forge, and red and white flakes of fire flying from hammered hot iron, close ahead and on his right; and his heart rose, for here was a smith of some sort. And if the smiths of Carleon were of the same kidney as the smiths of home, here was sure succor.

"A hand, a hand!" he cried. "Up, smith! To the rescue!"

The anvil stopped ringing and the sparks flying, and a man in an apron made of an ox-hide issued from the smithy. He was of heroic dimensions; and he swung a sledgehammer in his right hand and held before him with his left a great bar of iron with a point which pulsed from white to pink to red and threw off a thin haze of smoke.

"Good smith!" cried Dennys. "I'm no thief nor kidnaper! I took this small child from torturers who burned it with red iron, so hear me God—Jesu!"

"Take it inside," said the smith, with scarcely a glance.

Dennys sprang past him into the smithy, with the dog at his heels. It was a place of gloom lanced by a shaft of sunshine and pricked by the filming red eye of the forge; and even as he peered around him, he heard the smith shouting in the lane.

"A smith, a smith!" shouted the smith. "To me, smiths all! To me, Brothers of the Iron!"

Dennys heard the yells and hoots of the crowd. He set the child down on the clay floor and left it to the dog. He took an iron bar from beside the anvil-block and returned to the lane. There the crowd was thickening and the smith was advancing upon it with slow and ponderous tread and still bellowing: "To me, smiths all!" The crowd was edging in on right and left. Dennys darted to the left and jabbed fast, using the bar like a half-pike with one hand, and a long dagger with the other. Staves and spike-headed clubs were swung at him, but never in time, for short jabs and stabs are faster than swinging blows. Three louts fell, and others retired upon the main body, one of them crawling on all fours.

But the mob continued to grow and to close in, and the air was thick with stones and sticks. Dennys took such a knock on his left shoulder that he dropped his dagger, and while stooping to recover it, he took one on his leather cap that staggered him; the leather of that cap was from the hide of a wild mountain bull, however, so his skull remained uncracked. But for a minute he reeled as though blinded, and went berserk and swung the iron bar with both hands, spinning the while like a top against the front rank of the mob and into it, crushing bones and weapons and driving the leaders back against the pressure from the rear until there was no room for an arm to be raised in attack or defense. Menacing shouts and whoops changed to yells of terror and yelps and grunts of pain; and now the smith was in action with hammer and hot iron; and of a sudden, more smoky men in cowhide aprons appeared at the rear of the mob and fell on with a variety of implements and weapons peculiar to their craft: whereupon utter panic possessed the crowd, and tore it, and scattered it.

Dennys came out of his berserk rage and crumpled to his knees, and would have slumped forward on his face if a pair of horn-hard hands had not clamped his ribs and lifted him and held him upright. It was well meant by the smith, but it was a sorry service to the squire; for at that moment the final missile of the fray—a large cobble flung haphazardly—came whizzing to a violent stop against an unprotected side of Dennys' head.

Chapter Four
DENNYS HAS A BROKEN HEAD

Dennys heard a voice he did not like.

"Vagabonds! I warned you. Frauds! Murderers—else how did they come by the armor and horses and gear? He had proved himself no knight—he tumbled at a touch! And this rogue here? He is a proven kidnaper!"

"You lie!" shouted Dennys.

It was conceived as a shout, but it came forth a rasping whisper. He opened his eyes, and saw the sagging jowls and mean mouth and shallow optics of Sir James. He essayed another shout of defiance, and this time achieved a louder and clearer whisper:

"You lie!"

The thin lips and pale eyes above him snarled and glinted.

Another voice spoke.

"There's your answer, my bold James. He gives you the lie."

Dennys shifted his glance without turning his head, for his neck was as stiff as a board, and saw on his other side that hospitable old gentleman whom he knew now to be King Torrice of Har, and older than Merlin. The King smiled at him and Dennys whispered again, though his jaws were as stiff as his neck, and his tongue felt too large for his mouth:

"Where is the child?"

"In safe hands," said the King.

"I took it from torturers," said Dennys.

"It?" sneered Sir James.

"You did well, my lad," said the King.

"And the dog?" asked Dennys.

"The dog too," the King replied gravely. "Both are safe under this roof."

"You have not asked after your precious Sir Lorn le Perdu," sneered the old knight.

"What of him?" cried Dennys, starting up, but falling flat again instantly with a yelp of pain.

"Perdu," Sir James replied; and he chuckled meanly and said it again: "Perdu!"

Again Dennys started from his pillow, but only to subside again.

"He lies again," said King Torrice calmly. "In fact, I am beginning to wonder if he ever speaks the truth.

"Our young friend took a few tumbles yesterday, and may take a few more today, for experienced horsemen and spearmen have ever the advantage of very young cavaliers. Even I—but let it pass! I warrant you that, in a few years time, our Lost Knight will be as firm in his saddle as I was at his present age."

"My wits are confused," mumbled Dennys. "You spoke of yesterday—of my knight taking tumbles then, but by my reckoning we were on the road yesterday and encountered only bagmen and like riffraff. Yesterday? Lord, we met neither with tumbles nor occasions for tumbles yesterday—by my reckoning."

The carping old knight uttered a derisive hoot, but the old King of Har spoke gravely and kindly.

"Your reckoning took a buffet and a tumble, good Dennys; and while you lay here, with a leech from young Arthur Pendragon's train at work on your damaged skull—which the learned man pronounced the thickest he ever saw, glory be to God!—Sir Lorn rode for a few honorable falls in the lists only two longbow-shots away. In truth, it is a full twenty-four hours since the honest smiths brought in you and the child, with the honest dog at their heels. I rewarded them, in your name, and have seen to the comfort and safety of child and dog."

"Gramercy!" Dennys acknowledged. "Gramercy, Sir King!" He pressed his right hand to his bandaged head, but instantly flinched and dropped it. "But with me laid useless here, who squired my master? Who harnessed him and served him with new spears?"

"You would be surprised," the King murmured, smiling.

"Even you wouldn't believe it!" snarled Sir James.

"He was well tended," King Torrice went on, and now with a chuckle in his voice and a merry twinkling of his eyes. "He was well buckled indeed and latched and armed, fear not! No knight there, whatever his name or prowess or degree, was better squired—nor half as well, by the knuckle-bones of Judas!—than young Lorn le Perdu."

Dennys was silent with grief, believing that his friend had forsaken and forgotten him for a more experienced comrade and attendant, or a more powerful and fashionable: for some earl's son in search of adventure, perchance. But he was soon enlightened.

"In other words, King Torrice of Har hid his royal head in a squire's casque and played the varlet to that nameless vagabond's shameless pretensions," sneered Sir James. He paused, veering his shallow glance this way and that, but always avoiding the others' eyes. "And his reward was dust in his nose," he concluded, fairly snarling.

The King ceased smiling now and turned a bleak and considering look upon the carping knight.

"Mind your speech and your manners, James," he

warned in a low voice. "Ay, and your thoughts too. They have all worsened fast, of late: not that they were ever good. Have a care that you don't force me to forget that you owe your miserable life to me—for it is a responsibility that irks me increasingly, the longer I know you."

The knight's jaw sagged, and his barbered face went white—even the sharp nose, save for a purple tip. He blinked his eyes, which were no more human now than scales of mica, and breathed noisily in short gasps through open mouth and long sparse teeth. Then he got to his feet and stalked from the room. King Torrice met Dennys' bewildered gaze with a smile and a nod.

"A most unpleasant old man," he said lightly. "But more fool than knave: at least I still hope so. Now I must see to our champion, and off with him to the lists. I shall tell him of your improved condition; and if he should feel in better spirits tonight than he does this morning—which I wager he will—I'll bring him in after supper. Now I shall send the leech to you—a renowned chirurgeon."

The great doctor arrived, moving fast, with one of King Torrice's ancient servitors tottering far after him, burdened with an ewer and a basin and a roll of bandages.

"Conscious, clear-eyed, and sane!" the visitor gabbled, stooping and peering. "Exactly as I predicted, and to the minute. You are fortunate, young sir. If there had been an hour's delay in fetching me, or if any other chirurgeon in this realm had been summoned instead, you'd be dead now. And 'twas only by chance that I was disengaged at the time of the arrival of King Torrice's urgent messenger, for practically all the best vital organs and bones of King Arthur's court are in my care, including his own; and my written certificate that your head has been mended by me will serve you as an introduction to society as well as any warrant of knighthood or even a patent of nobility, I dare say."

While gabbling and bragging, the doctor's hands and eyes were as busy as his tongue. He unrolled yards of bandage from Dennys' tender head, examined and washed the wound, salved it, and swathed all in clean linen.

"Most satisfactory!" he exclaimed. "Chicken broth for breakfast, and this pill directly after it. You, my good man, attend to what I say to this young gentleman, and look well to this pill, for Doctor Watkyn's words cost a silver penny apiece, and the very least of my pills the price of a firkin of butter. See to it that he swallows this pill with his last sup of broth; and that he remains recumbent till noon, at which time he will be so far recovered—thanks to my skill and God's mercy and a thick skull—as to permit the elevation of his head and shoulders on three pillows, and the consumption of another bowl of chicken broth."

"Gramercy!" said Dennys.

Dr. Watkyn bustled off. Dennys addressed the old servant.

"What of my broth?"

"'Tis in the kettle, sir."

"And what of the child I took away from the two torturers?"

"She does bravely, sir. She is in Eliza's care, and the dog too. King Torrice charged Eliza, who is my daughter, to tend her like a princess, and the thin dog like a queen's pet."

"She? Is it a girl, then?"

"Devil a doubt of it, sir! And no common one, by my guess: or why were the two Yer Honor rescued her from— the man was found roasted on his own hearth, but the woman got away—trying to burn a brand on her? But Master Watkyn's salve will heal it in a day, so he says himself. And she be safe with Eliza, sir, never fear! For there's a wench that would have made a man-at-arms to match any knight alive. And now she wears knives in her garters, and keeps half-pikes and long-hafted maces standing in every corner of her room."

"I want to see her."

"She's a grand sight, sir, though no beauty from a young gentleman's point of view; and no chicken, neither; and I warn you, sir, she'll knock a man down with no more provocation nor a look."

"Are you mad? That pitiful child?"

"God forgive me! I thought you spoke of Eliza! I'll have her fetch her, sir—my daughter fetch Yer Honor's little damosel—when I fetch the broth."

"So be it, good fellow," murmured Dennys, closing his eyes.

❖   ❖   ❖

He dozed into confused dreams. A weight on his sore left shoulder wakened him, and he opened his eyes and looked sidewise at a broad black muzzle and yellow mask and amber eyes. A lip lifted and disclosed formidable fangs: but it was not a hostile grimace; and the eyes showed warmth of trust and affection through their amber shining. It was the dog of yesterday. The heavy head withdrew from his shoulder. He shifted his glance upward, and met the fixed regard of yet another pair of eyes.

These were neither amber nor trustful, but gray and black like the depths of a mountain tarn, and searching and cold in their regard. It was a woman who stood beside his couch and looked down at him. He guessed her sex by the two long and thick braids of hair which hung before her shoulders and down past her waist. This hair was coarse and black and strong, like the tails of mountain ponies. But for the hair, the head and neck and shoulders might well have belonged to a full-grown—nay, an overgrown—porter or swineherd or forester. Likewise the face; for the jaws looked to be as strong, and the nose as broad and depressed, as a bull-baiting mastiff's. He met that stare for as long as he could. He held it till his sore brain began to spin and his eyes to dim. He blinked and cried out suddenly and fretfully:

"God's wounds! What ails you, woman? What's your errand here? Speak up—or go away!"

She veiled her eyes and bowed her head, and spoke with voice and air of mock submission.

"I beg Your Honor's pardon. I am here at your bidding, with our little damosel. I am Eliza."

He looked lower and saw the child, and knew her only by her eyes; for only in them did she resemble the pitiful naked creature of yesterday's adventure. She stood close beside his cot. But this was not the infant of that mad rescue and chase. This was, in very truth, a little damosel. She wore a bonnet of fine lace, which hid her short and jaggedly snipped pale hair. The face framed by the bonnet was like a white flower blushing to rose. Her parted lips were rose petals. She wore pearls at her throat, and a narrow gown of white samite threaded with gold. But her eyes, still misted with tears though her lips smiled now, looked into Dennys' eyes just as he remembered from yesterday.

Embarrassment was added to his bewilderment. It replaced the spasm of childish anger and fear which the woman's stare had inspired. He tried to think of something to say. He belabored his sore brain for appropriate words of greeting to an agonized, terrorized small child that had become, overnight, a smiling damosel in white samite. A small damosel, in truth—but just that, nevertheless. But the only result of the effort was a stammered question.

"What is your name?"

"The gypsies called me Cynara," she whispered. "But Eliza says that is a pagan name—a wicked gypsy name."

"The gypsies? But your skin—your eyes—your eyes are not like theirs!"

The woman said: "She's not one of those people, as any fool can see. But she cannot remember her own people."

"Those two fiends of hell were not gypsies," he said.

"True—but she had been in their hands only a sennight," said the woman.

Now the little girl's mouth began to tremble and change from smiles to the pitiful grimace of terror; and she shivered against Dennys and crouched forward and slipped thin arms around his neck and pressed her face against his breast. As her arms tightened, stabs of pain shot through his head. It was all he could do not to cry out. Instead, he gritted his teeth and shut his eyes and drew the small body closer and held it so. Despite the pain he was in, he spoke with calm assurance.

"You have nothing to fear. You are safe now. I'll not let anything hurt you, little one."

The clasp of her arms loosened slightly, but vastly to the relief of his anguished head, and her trembles lessened perceptibly. It seemed to him that she listened for more, though she did not raise her face from his breast.

"Be happy," he went on. "Rest easy. There is no evil here to harm you, little Cynara. You are in my keeping for now. You have Dennys to fend for you now—and from this time forth."

He felt the woman's disturbing gaze upon him, and looked up and met it again; and he was relieved to find less of hostility and black suspicion in it now.

"And who will fend for brave Squire Dennys?" she asked derisively.

But there was anxiety as well as derision in her voice and eyes. She stooped over him, and continued in an urgent whisper:

"Are you blind, poor lad—or demented, like your lost master? For lost indeed is that poor young knight—utterly, heart and soul! And you are in peril of your own soul and body, in this place. It was the curse on your master—for he is accursed, in very truth!—that brought you to this house. What do you know of this king? Even Peter the groom does not know his true age. He too is accursed or bewitched, this King Torrice, for all his learning and prowess—and a fool to boot; or how else would he suffer that old rogue Sir James? Beware of that hoary knight. He hates and fears your witless master, and you too, and will get rid of you, if he can. He is as crafty as wicked; and if he cannot trick you to your deaths, he will kill you himself."

"Why?" asked Dennys.

She lifted her head and veered it, then stooped lower and whispered:

"I hear him. Take this. Under the sheet with it! Accept nothing from his hands—and threaten to strike if he crowds you."

She stood upright quickly, only to stoop again as quickly and lift the little girl in her arms; and Dennys was alone three seconds later. Even the dog with amber eyes was gone. But he could not think he had dreamed that visit, for his right hand grasped the haft of a dagger beneath the sheet. Is she mad too? he wondered. Is everyone mad here but me? And Cynara? And even she must be bewitched, to grow so fast.

He glanced up and saw Sir James on the threshold, bearing an earthen bowl in his two hands. The ancient knight approached with greater speed than Dennys had credited him with the strength for. He drew a stool to the right side of the cot, and on it set the bowl. He straightened his back and smiled and spoke smoothly.

"Your broth, my young friend. Your chicken broth, just as prescribed by the great Doctor Watkyn. If King Torrice of Har sees fit to serve Sir Lorn le Perdu as squire, why should not I, poor old Sir James of Redrock, play butler to Squire Dennys? Think nothing of it, my lad. Drink it down. 'Tis at just the right heat. The good Watkyn made such a point of this matter of temperature that I told him I would see to it myself. Here, let me raise your head and hold the bowl to your lips."

"I have no appetite for chicken broth, honored sir," lied Dennys. "Nor for any kind of broth, at this moment. The steam of it even raises my gorge. Stand away, Sir James— I warn you!—for my stomach heaves and quakes."

"Nonsense!" exclaimed Sir James, gone sharp and jerky of a sudden in both voice and manner. "Quaff it off! Doctor's orders!"

He took up the bowl in his right hand. He was close now. With his left hand he reached for the pillow beneath Dennys' head. And then a strange thing happened. The bowl fell to the floor and broke, and the broth spattered and splashed abroad. With an oath, Sir James jerked straight and stood staring down at his empty hand and past it at the ruin on the floor.

"Something struck me!" he cried, his voice gone thin as a gnat's. "My wrist! Something hard!" His pale glance flickered the length of the couch and all around. "What goes on here? There's deviltry here!"

"I doubt it not, worshipful sir," Dennys murmured; and he smiled among his bandages, lying straight and still between sheets of linen, beneath a silken quilt.

To look at him, one would never guess that his right knee had been so out and active.

"But here comes another bowl, so why worry over spilt broth?" he added.

Sure enough, here was that old fellow Eliza's father, bearing an earthen bowl on a pewter tray. This was just such a bowl as the other had been, but a horn spoon stood up in it. The fellow moved circumspectly and with downcast eyes and a suggestion of humble benevolence about the droop of his whiskers; but when the wreckage on the floor came within his range of view, he stopped and recoiled as if at a buffet in the face, and all but dropped his burden.

"Have a care!" cautioned Dennys. "Good Sir James had an accident with his offering, and I'm in no mood to be cheated of my breakfast entirely, for I feel hungry now."

He looked where the old knight had stood but a few seconds before, just in time to glimpse the stooped and narrow back as Sir James glided from the room.

"This is beyond me," muttered the servant, beginning to shiver. "Sir James fetched broth to you, d'ye say? Then he stole it from under Luke's nose. Did you sup of it?"

"Not a sup, old man," Dennys assured him. "Your daughter Eliza told me to take nothing from him. Set it down here before you spill it, and calm yourself. Eliza is a grand wench, and I'd liefer call her friend than foe. Tell me your name, old friend; and help me with the broth."

Eliza's father's name was Matthew, and he was known as Matt. He was a timid soul; and it was hard for Dennys to believe that he had sired masterful and intrepid Eliza. But he was an excellent serving-man, for his years. He raised Dennys' head and shoulders on extra pillows and helped him to his broth as well as any nurse. He had a fund of information and a lively tongue, but a quavering utterance. He was a natural gossip and artless scandal-monger. Born in a swineherd's hut in one of the great forests of Har, he had herded swine till he came to his full growth, but as that growth had fallen short of require-ments for warding against wolves and thieves, he had gone down to the nearest castle and been hired there for a scullion.

The wandering King Torrice had visited that one of his many castles between foreign adventures, and tossed pen-nies about so freely that Matt had stolen off in his train. There had been gray in the King's whiskers even then, but he was still a mighty man of his hands. And as for his adventures—a young gentleman would not believe them. Sometimes, in trying to recall them to mind, Matt doubted them himself. They were all undertaken, or encountered by chance, in furtherance of a quest which His Majesty had followed since his early manhood—but of the name and nature of that quest, Matt was as ignorant now as he had been when a scullion in his first scullery. But there was something queer about it. Many things about it seemed queer to honest Matt. The ladies concerned, among them. Nay, the ladies most of all. For there were ladies and damosels—ay, and queens even—in every adventure of that quest of King Torrice of Har, that strange and seem-ingly endless quest.

It was believed by some people, said Matt, that the King's quest had been for the Fountain of Youth, and that he had succeeded over a hundred years ago; but he did not share this belief. Whether or not King Torrice had ever drunk of the Fountain of Youth or of any other spring or well of a like character, or maybe of a magical elixir in a bottle, he didn't know; but in his humble opinion the royal quest was of a far more mysterious and perilous nature than that implied by those people, despite the fact that there had been a lady—one, at least—in every adventure of it.

Take the adventures in Spain, for example. Once the questing king had won his way, by wit and physical prowess, into the Queen of Spain's boudoir, only to excuse himself and back out, after a few questions. Matt had been told this the following day, by a gentleman then serving Torrice as senior squire. Yet she was a straight round queen with starry eyes—or had been, for she would be a grandmother by now, if still anything. But the King of Har had done the right thing by her pride. He had sent her, the very next day—before she could have him dispatched by poisoner, strangler, or stabber—a grand song of unrequited love and a necklace of rubies to match it. Always the perfect gentleman: that was King Torrice!

It had been the same with the Abbess of the White Abbey of Salamanca. After the toils and perils of winning to her, he had lost interest within the minute. That episode too had cost him a poem and a necklace, though both were shorter than in case of the Queen. And it was always so, said Matt. It was always as if the questing King expected to find something different, each time, from anything he had yet found. He was after something more than human beauty, so it seemed to Matt: but when Dennys suggested that the royal search was for heavenly beauty, or for the Holy Grail perhaps, the old gossip shook his head with a skeptical air.

"There be witchery in it, as sure as God gave me two eyes and a nose," he said. "And maybe deviltry—for the one runs parlous close to t'other, as any hedge magician will tell you for a horn of ale. Which God forbid, for King Torrice is a good and generous lord."

While Matt rambled on, Dennys' glance wandered idly and was arrested by a black cat. The animal came into his field of vision from the outer chamber, walking slowly but with assurance, and its tail straight up. It had eyes of topaz and a sleek coat. It marched straight to the wreckage on the floor and went to work on it, beginning with the fragments of white and brown meat, then licking up every vestige of broth, but Dennys was so intent on old Matt's jabber that he did not give the cat's behavior a thought.

"Has Sir James a quest too?" Dennys asked.

Matt looked all around before answering.

"Ay," he whispered. "All the lands and goods of the King are his quest. 'Tis his doing that we bide here, year in and year out. He is the devil, that old knight!"

"Then why does the King befriend him?" asked Dennys.

"For pity. We saved him from robbers in a wood, in his shirt. They had him tied to a tree, and he was crying like a baby, and a knife was at his throat. It was a sight to melt any heart. But at King Torrice's first shout, the knife was dropped, and all the rogues fled and got clean away. But I have thought since that the fellow with the knife could have stabbed or slit before he fled, if he had a mind to, and still got away. There wasn't a mark on that knight—and him squealing like a stuck porker; and when his bonds were cut, he wriggled on the ground like a worm—the loathly old snake!"

"What ailed him?" asked Dennys.

"Nought ailed him. It was all a play for the King's pity. It was a sight to twist the heart worse than a hurt baby— that old knight crying an' squirming at King Torrice's feet for mercy an' deliverance, an' clawing at his knees—and his skinny shanks sticking out of his shirt. Ay, a pitiful sight—but it was all scurvy trickery. The robbers, the knives, the squalls an' tears—all a play! The rogues were in his service. I see it now. And the King, all bemused with his mad quest an' his rhymes, clothed him and armed him from the skin out, and horsed him an' put money in his poke an' took him into his care.

"And what now? Why do we bide at this inn? A fortune-teller—as black an old gypsy queen as ever you saw—told the King his quest would be achieved here, to his eternal glory an' joy, if he would but wait it. Ay, she read it in the stars, and the palms of his hands, and her crystal ball— an' well she was paid for that telling by Sir James—with a bracelet of rubies from the King's strongbox. And now I see it like the nose on your face, young sir. The old viper fears you and the mad young knight; for King Torrice has shown a returning of his old spirit since your arrival at this inn. So look to yourself, Sir Squire. And look to your befuddled knight. Beware Sir James!"

"Gramercy!" said Dennys. "Your daughter Eliza has already warned me, and given me a dagger from her garter."

He produced the dagger. Matt goggled at it.

"The wench never showed a favor before to any man," the old fellow mumbled.

Chapter Five
DEVILTRY, WITCHERY, AND A BATTLE

Sir Lorn le Perdu took three more tumbles on the second day of the joustings; but with his fourth spear he had better luck, unseating his opponent without coming to earth himself. His score for the two days was one win against six falls—nothing to brag about. The Lost Knight took it philosophically, however, and King Torrice, his acting squire, made the best of it.

"There was a time—but a very short time and a very long while ago—when even I dented the sod with my rump-plates almost as often as I stopped in the saddle," said the venerable King.

"This doesn't signify," said Lorn, with a faraway look in his eyes. "This child's-play means no more than did our exercises in the stableyard at Dennys' home. Sharp spears and swords are what we like, Bahram and I. When it's an affair of sharp iron, then we both fight."

"Tell me, my boy," prompted the King, with gentle urgency.

Lorn pressed a hand to his brow and thought hard, but could not recall any other mortal combat than the battle with savages in a storm of snow.

"But there were others, I assure Your Lordship," he said earnestly. "I have worsted—ay, and slain—strong knights as well as mountainy savages. They are here, but they sleep." And again he pressed a hand to his head.

The main event of that sennight of jousting was to be a battle unto death or surrender of thirty knights of King

Arthur's train against thirty knights collected, for the occasion, under the banner of a Welsh chieftain or prince named Llewellyn. It was to begin in the morning, and if need be, last all day. It was not till after supper on the second day, and when King Torrice and Sir Lorn sat with Dennys, that the young knight's intention to take part in the morrow's conflict became known to his friends. The King had given an amusing account of his squelching of the rumbumptious grandson of the late Sir Rustard of Ruswick; and Dennys had laughed at the picture of those royal and venerable whiskers emerging from that humble squirish helmet, pressing both hands to his own tender head in the act. Lorn had sat throughout the recital with his wonted faraway look and air of melancholy abstraction, and never a word; so when he spoke at last, the effect was startling, though his voice was mild.

"It will be different with me tomorrow. Sharp spears and swords."

After half a minute of startled silence, King Torrice said: "We'll take a good rest tomorrow, lad, while those zanies bash and slash like unicorns and wild boars; and so you'll be ready for the knightly combats of the next day. Mob fighting is for them that like to grovel and roll like mad dogs, and butt and slash like rams and wolves, without art or honor."

"I like it," murmured the other. "And so does my horse."

"But 'tis to the death or surrender!" cried the King.

"I'll not surrender, worshipful sir," murmured Lorn.

The King protested with a dozen arguments, and Dennys protested too.

"Would you have Bahram killed?" asked Dennys, on the verge of tears. "You promised him to me if ever you had no more need of him."

"Ay, consider that noble horse!" urged the King, glad of another argument. "They'll hamstring him! Then they'll slaughter him! I know what I'm talking about, dear lad. It's the riffraff of chivalry that engages in mêlées. They fight for ransoms and harness and horses. A knaves' business!"

"Not a suitable form of exercise for a green knight, certainly," said a voice from the shadows; and Sir James advanced into the candlelight.

"What the devil?" cried King Torrice.

"Nay, puissant lord, 'tis but your poor servant James of Redrock," whined the old knight. "I nodded at the supper table. I dozed. Weight of years and my enfeebled stomach and head. That grilled marrowbone. And that second cup of sack. But permit me, young sir, to add my voice to my royal benefactor's sage counsel. The rough-an'-tumble of sixty murderous, greedy battlers armed sharp of point and edge is not for untried and delicate young gentlemen like yourself. I beg you to heed the advice of King Torrice, my young friend."

Then Lorn le Perdu stood up and swore by the knuckle-bones of all the Apostles that he would have to-do in the morrow's tournament, and show friend and foe alike the stuff he was made of. Sir James sighed profoundly, and turned and went away, bowed as if with sorrowful resignation.

When Dennys awoke, the sun shone level through the window, and Lorn le Perdu was gone. His heart was like a cobble in the very pit of his being—as hard and heavy as the great stone that had laid him low in that foul lane. He sat up. His head did not stab or spin. Good! He would arm and join that battle and save his knight, mauger his head. He was on the edge of his couch when Matt arrived with a bowl of broth. The old fellow cried out at him to lie down.

"Have no fear for your master," the old fellow cried on. "The King will fetch him out alive, mauger his head!"

Dennys would have argued the point, but for Matt's threat to fetch Eliza from the nursery.

"I don't object to your daughter," he said. "We're good friends." But his mind was distracted from one loyalty to another. "I want to see her. And her little charge Cynara. How does she fare?"

"Like a princess," Matt assured him.

Dennys spooned up half the bowl of broth, greedily but with his thoughts shifting and flickering.

"What of Sir James this morning?" he asked.

"Faugh!" cried Matt. "That viper! He mopes in his chamber—but there's a gloating glimmer in his snaky flat eyes."

"Your daughter warned me," Dennys mumbled, as if

talking to himself. "Gave me a dagger. Charged me to take nothing from him. So I knocked the bowl of broth from his hand with a knee, quick as winking. But it wasn't wasted. The little black cat lapped it up."

"Hah!" exploded Matt: and he stooped and gripped the front of the squire's nightshirt with jerky fingers. "Black cat, d'ye say? How d'ye know that? Speak up, young man!"

"Not so loud from you, old man," Dennys reproved the fellow, with squirish dignity. "And spare my shirt. You might have seen if for yourself, but for your babbling about King Torrice and the Queen of Spain. A small black cat came in and ate the gobbets of chicken, and licked the floor clean and went away. What of it?"

Matt released the shirt and straightened up. He cried "Hah!" again, rocked on his heels and finally folded up on a stool.

"They found her this morning," he whispered. "That little mouser—stiff an' stark under the King's bed."

"Stiff an' stark?" queried Dennys, with a stiff tongue, as if a sudden frost had struck its root.

"Dead," Matt whispered. "As dead as you would be if ye'd drunk it." He got nimbly to his feet and came close to Dennys again, and continued to whisper, but now with a note of relish: "We've got him. I'll tell the King. You'll tell him. This will open his eyes. We've got 'im now, the snake! This will pull his fangs! Now we'll be rid of 'em—as soon as the King gets back from the tourney."

Dennys was vastly shaken by the thought of his narrow escape from death. And such a death! A cat's death! So deeply was he shaken that he set the half-empty bowl aside and averted his glance from it, with a shudder. He got between the sheets again at Matt's bidding, but refused to finish the broth. Matt went away with the bowl, after charging him to lie still and at the same time watch out for treachery, and promising to be back in a few minutes.

There were two doors to the room. With his head high on the pillows, Dennys could keep both doors under surveillance without moving anything but his eyes. He had not been alone more than two minutes before his vigilance was rewarded. An edge of one door stirred, then remained so still for the count of ten that he began to doubt his eyes. But it stirred again. It came away an inch from the jamb—

another inch, three inches—moving softly and slowly. Dennys narrowed his eyes and watched through the lashes. A head came into view around the edge of oak, and the flat, shallow, mica-pale optics of Sir James appeared, sliding and glinting. That horrid scrutiny remained upon Dennys' face for seconds, then slid aside. Now the scrawny neck appeared, weaving and twisting. A thin shoulder followed. Then all became still, as if struck to bone; and a moment later head and neck and shoulder withdrew, and the door closed as smoothly as it had opened.

Dennys got out of bed and into his clothes at top speed, without a thought for his damaged head; and he was tying the last of his points when a door opened—not the one around which Sir James had looked in—and old Matt's Eliza entered hurriedly, with the little girl in her arms and the tall dog at her heels. The dog sprang past her and fawned on Dennys. Eliza came close to Dennys and stood staring at him, and Cynara turned in the woman's arms and smiled and put out her hands to him. He took the little hands in his, and smiled back through his bandages. But the stalwart woman Eliza wore a grim visage.

"I heard of the cat," she said, in a voice to match her face.

"I owe you my life," said Dennys. "But for your warning, I'd have drunk the stuff instead of knocking it from his hand. Gramercy, good Eliza! Look to me for protection, from now on. I'm not a king, nor yet a knight, and I have a broken head—but Dennys ap Rhys ap Tudor is at your service, good wench. Look you to our little damosel, and I will fend for both, mauger my head!"

For seconds she continued to regard him with hard, inscrutable eyes, and then eyes and mouth softened suddenly, and she said, "I believe you," and pressed the child into his arms.

Cynara clasped him about the neck, and he held her tenderly. He was deeply moved by the woman's belief in him as a protector, and yet more deeply by the pressure of the little girl's arm and face, which seemed to him expressions of something more and sweeter than mere faith. He tightened his hold slightly on the small soft body, and stood in a daze until Eliza spoke again.

"Our good king is mad, for all his kind heart," she said.

"Mad an' bewitched. And your young knight is mad. . . . Mad, and bewitched too, as any fool can see. I can smell madness and bewitchment in both of them, for all the King's learning an' twenty baronies, and your master's gentle an' melancholy visage. But you are whole in mind an' heart, for all your broken head. Skulls mend. So I beg you to take our little lass away from here before further evil befalls her."

"She is safe here, in our care," Dennys protested. "The only menace in this house is Sir James, and the King will deal with him soon enough. No peril from outside can touch her."

"You speak like a numskull!" flared Eliza. "What of the rogues your master caught behind the arras? Were they from inside—of the King's people or the taverner's even? They were from outside, where hundreds more like them slink and watch, ready to slit a throat for a tuppenny bit, and where that woman is. You were the death of the man, but the woman got clean away. D'ye think she will not try to recover what you robbed her of—what she paid silver to the gypsies for—and you hold now in your arms? Why did they burn the child's flesh? For love, think you?"

"God knows!" Dennys exclaimed. "I don't, that's sure: but I do know that hellcat will never wrest her back from me. Do you know the answers to your own questions, woman?"

Eliza glanced fearfully around, then came even closer to him and lowered her voice to a whisper.

"It is the mark."

"What mark?" he said. "I saw but a red burn."

"There's no burn now," she told him. "The chirurgeon's salve cured it like magic, and now there's only the sign God or Satan or the fairies marked her with before she was born."

"What is it?

"Do you want to see it?"

"Why not? Who has a better right to see it? 'Twas I brought her away from the torturers. God's wounds—I am her savior and guardian!"

"Swear then by those same holy wounds you will never fail her or desert her in her need, while you have life!"

Dennys swore as bidden; whereupon Eliza took Cynara

from his arms and undid the gown of samite and gold, and bared the narrow back to his view. And he saw the mark half a span below the left shoulderblade, blushing on the milk-white skin like a wild rose, like rose petals in tint and texture, but in shape a little hand, as though the right hand of a newborn babe had been laid there and had left its imprint there by some trick of alchemy. Looking closer and blinking a quick mist from his eyes, Dennys swore again by the wounds of spikes and thorns and spear; and he stooped yet lower and touched his lips to the mark quickly, and then stood straight as quickly; and at that the child twisted around in the woman's arms, quick as a kitten, and laid hold of him with both hands and drew him down to her till their faces were pressed together. To straighten himself, he had to take her from Eliza, for the grip of the small soft arms was like the strangle-hold of a wrestler. Eliza, who had released Cynara without protest, uttered a strange note of laughter.

"Are we all mad?" she cried. "All of us bewitched and bedeviled?" She laughed again, but the sound was of consternation and bewilderment and at once an acceptance and a defiance of Fate. "Ye've swore a mighty oath, young sir, and a parlous, like than not, God have mercy on us!"

Dennys, trying gently to ease the pressure of the small damosel's arms and face with his left hand, and at the same time holding her body closer, all unwittingly, with his right arm, paid no attention to Eliza. It was not until Cynara was wrenched from him—the embraces of both broken suddenly and violently by that powerful woman—that he became aware of Matt's advent. The old man came on with upflung arms and waving whiskers, tottering in his haste.

"All's well!" he cried; and he tottered against Dennys and clung to him for support. "Word from the tourney," he gabbled, gasping and clinging. "By a trusty messenger. The King is safe. An' your witless knight too."

Eliza told him to sit down and recover his breath and then tell all he knew; and he obeyed her; and this is the gist of his tale:

Sir Lorn le Perdu was of the Welsh Prince's party. When the signal to join battle was given, Lorn's white charger, the mighty Bahram, refused to move; and so it was that twenty-nine knights of the Prince's banner rushed in thunderous line to meet King Arthur's onrushing thirty, leaving Sir Lorn like a statue at the starting-point, to the surprise of all beholders. Then Sir Lorn cast away his spear and drew his sword and dismounted and ran afoot toward the battle; and the great horse lay down. Sir James had drugged the horse's corn, swore Matt. But to no avail, praise be to God, for Sir Lorn soon found an unhorsed knight of King Arthur's party and cut him down with the third stroke. And he cried, "Strike hard! Bite deep!" and pulled a large knight from his saddle to the ground, and helped him courteously to his feet, and then mastered him with five strokes.

Then a horsed knight—but a knave at heart—rode at Lorn with his spear, but to his own undoing, for the Lost Knight avoided the point, and cut it off, and smote the man through the middle in passing. And when King Torrice saw that foul attack from his place among the squires, he mounted and dressed a spear and hurtled into the battle. Seeing that, the squire of one of Arthur's knights hurtled after him. And then all the squires of both parties took to horse and spear; and so it became a double and mixed tournament of knights and squires all together and in equal numbers, the like of which may not happen twice in a century.

The heralds ran and bawled to the unruly squires to desist, withdraw—only to be knocked and rolled like skittle-pins by squires and knights alike, until King Arthur signaled from his high seat to carry on. Then there was the strangest to-do, and the most jumbled and least decorous and yet, I dare say, the most diverting, that was ever seen on the great field of Carleon. Many a haughty knight was tumbled from his high saddle that day by an ambitious squire; and many a squire was rolled end-over-end by an indignant knight or another squire; and even the great Sir Kay, High Seneschal of Camelot, received such a thrust on his vizor from a froward fellow on a hackney, that he all but went over his warhorse's tail for pure chagrin.

There was a squire on a tall horse—an aging and crafty horse—who unseated three knights with his first spear, then got a new spear into his hand as if by conjury, and tumbled another of Arthur's champions, then rode clear of

the mêlée and the dust of it to breathe himself and his
horse. But by and large, the knights had the mastery
mounted and the squires proved themselves the better
men afoot, save in the case of Sir Lorn le Perdu, who had
joined the battle on his own legs (thanks to Bahram's
strange indisposition) and continued to cut down knights
and squires indifferently, as they came at him or he sought
them out.

So that battle raged back and forth, and this way and
that in swirling eddies, with some losses of life but more
losses of arms and harness and horses; and no onlooker
dared say if the victory would be with the chivalry under
King Arthur's banner or with the followers of the Welsh
Prince, Llewellyn by name, who was still in the saddle, but
groggy from loss of blood. (King Arthur, be it understood,
did not lead his party in person—not for lack of courage or
hardihood, God forbid! but for reasons of state—and sat in
judgment over both sides.)

The battlers had lessened greatly in both numbers and
fury when the most extraordinary thing of all the wonders
of that morning happened for all to see: Bahram, that great
white warhorse, raised his armored head from the sod and
sniffed and snorted. He got his hooves under him and
heaved himself up. So he stood for a half-minute, glaring
and snorting at the strugglers in the field; then he shook
himself till all his war-gear creaked and clanked; and then
he bared his teeth, vented a bloodcurdling scream and
charged at and into the thickest of the battle. He overthrew
horses and their riders with the impact of his weight and
fury. Many horses, riderless and otherwise, wheeled and
fled at his approach. He dragged a stout knight from a high
saddle with his teeth, and would have crushed him in his
armor like a clam in its shell but for a shout from his master. Then he wheeled to the Lost Knight, who mounted him
straightway, still with his sword in his hand and all but a
mere cupful of his blood still in his veins; and at the
moment when Bahram carried Sir Lorn into the fight
again, the squire and tall horse who had withdrawn to
recover their breaths returned to it with renewed gusto.

It was not long afterward that King Arthur signaled for
hostilities to cease, and the heralds repeated and multi-
plied the order with voice and trumpet. The victory was

given to Llewellyn and his party; and that prince summoned Sir Lorn le Perdu and the squire on the tall warhorse to him; and so the three rode slowly to a space of greensward before the galleries full of ladies and great lords and Arthur in their midst, and there dismounted. The Welsh Prince leaned against his horse, and the squire leaned against his, though lightly; but Sir Lorn stood as straight as a tree. Now, at a sign from King Arthur, Prince Llewellyn's helmet, from which the red dragon crest had been shorn away, was unlaced and removed by a gentleman of the court; whereupon Arthur descended swiftly from his place and embraced the Prince, amid the applause of the multitude, and passed him tenderly into the hands of Doctor Watkyn, that matchless chirurgeon, who led him away with care.

And now, at a word, Sir Lorn le Perdu sank lightly to one knee; and when his helmet came off and that pale and bemused and romantic countenance was seen, the shrill applause of the ladies rose above the wondering acclaim of the men, and a shower of roses fell. Arthur gaped, forgetting his kingly manners for a moment, then raised him and embraced him.

"Have I seen you before?" the King asked, in a bewildered voice and a bewildered yet searching look.

The knight replied: "Not to my knowledge, sir."

"How are you called? asked the King.

"Lorn le Perdu, sir," replied the knight.

The King muttered, "More of this anon," and stepped to where the formidable squire stood at a shoulder of his tall horse. The squire would have knelt then, but Arthur checked him.

"Do you know that young knight?" he whispered.

"I am his squire," said the other.

"More of this anon, young man—at dinner and supper," said Arthur; and at his nod, the squire stooped to the unlatching and unlacing hands of the courtier.

At the appearance of the bald pate and the magnificent snowy whiskers of King Torrice of Har from a squire's casque, Arthur gasped and recoiled a pace, and uttered an astonished oath, and the startled courtier vented a yelp and dropped the helmet to earth, as if he had scorched his fingers.

All of this was hearsay to old Matt, but from the mouth of the head groom Peter, who had beheld every stroke and then crept forward at the tail of King Torrice's horse to hear every word.

Chapter Six
MORE OF CYNARA

Dennys sat alone for hours. His first exultation for his friend's mighty deeds and their royal recognition soon began to sour within him. He did not begrudge the Lost Knight his success, nor was he surprised at it, but he envied the old King—older than Merlin!—his part in that tournament and his share of that glory. He, Dennys ap Rhys, had been cheated by Fate of his rightful place and opportunity. But for a cobblestone flung by a base knave in a disreputable slum, he, not King Torrice, would have squired Sir Lorn this morning and joined the fray at the first excuse and acquired merit and renown. He did not doubt, at the moment, that his deeds of arms would have matched the old King's. He told himself that even if his mounted performance had not matched the King's, he would, like Lorn, have wrought such prodigious havoc afoot, after and if he had been unhorsed, that King Arthur would have knighted him on the spot. *Arise, Sir Dennys!* How would that have sounded? But no, by a scurvy trick of Fate, his great opportunity had fallen to the lot of one who had no need of it—to a puissant lord rich in baronies and manors, and a knight who had been a known champion long before the birth of any other contender in that tournament. And he cursed the injustice of it. Tears of self-pity and unreasoning anger misted his eyes.

"And now my head feels almost as good as ever it did!" he cried. "By tomorrow I could have given and taken hard knocks with the best of them. If the battle had been called for tomorrow instead of today, I'd have been there, mauger my head! Or if that accursed cobble had hit me a day sooner. But that could not have been, for we were still on the road then. If it had never hit me—that would be better still. That would be best—if I'd never got my head broke in a brawl with lousy rascals—if I'd but stopped in my bed that morning."

And then he heard himself. The meaning of his wild words struck into his heart, and his jealous anger and self-pity were consumed in a hot flare of shame.

"God forgive me!" he cried.

He sprang to his feet and paced the floor, cursing himself for a knave. All he felt for himself now was loathing. Again he heard the screams of a terrified tormented child. Again he saw the small quivering body, and the red-tipped awl in the man's hand, and the faces of the tormentors turned to him like gaping masks.

"I killed him," Dennys muttered. "Good! It was well done. And I brought the child away—little Cynara." Again he felt those thin soft arms about his neck, and that soft face against his lips. "It was well done. No knightly deed at joustings and tournaments was ever better done! Lord Jesus, I thank you! I fought on Your side then, and You on mine!"

Now he felt in better conceit of himself, and his rage against Fate was forgotten. Now he sat down and thought with a degree of composure; and though the sense of gratitude to the Divine Mercy was still with him, all the pictures in his mind were of the child Cynara, as he had first seen her and held her in his arm and run with her for dear life, and as he had last seen and held her this very day.

Old Matt entered on the tottering run, with more news. Sir James was nowhere to be found. Matt himself, and several others, had searched the inn from cellars to garrets. And the strongest of King Torrice's strongboxes had been broken into and emptied. The King had always kept his most valuable jewels and a few full purses in that box. Well, it was empty now.

"He's well rid of the old snake, even if he took the worth of five thousand crowns with him," said Matt. "For his plan was to beggar us all to the bone. But when he saw that the King was beginning to distrust him an' to weary of him—which was the very night you an' yer worshipful master came to this place—he lost his cunning. He tried to poison you, but only killed a cat. He poisoned the great warhorse, but not to kill him. I see his snaky plan. He would have had that horse on his legs for just long enough to carry the knight into the battle, but sluggishly, and then to fail him suddenly in the first fierce clash. But it did not happen so, and your master joined the battle afoot, unscathed and vigorous and in a destructive temper of concern for his horse. When that viper heard the truth, he saw the failure of all his cunning and the end of his wicked play. And so he robbed the strongbox and stole away."

"Did he take a horse?" asked Dennys.

"Nay, nor yet a mountain pony. He left his knightly arms and harness too. An old cloak and hat of Luke's are missing. He has not gone in a guise to catch the eye, but like a poor whining mendicant, or maybe a sufferer in a lost cause or for a new philosophy, mark my words. No longer a snake with a snake's fangs and cunning, he is a worm now with wormy cunning—an' with a prince's ransom hid next his skin!"

"You talk like a philosopher or a clark yourself," said Dennys admiringly.

"You are a young gentleman of uncommon discernment, sir; and I'll not deny that my mind and soul are far above my worldly station, sir," the old fellow replied, with a mock-modest smirk.

"If ever I come by a castle of my own, I'll make you my seneschal," Dennys promised him.

The old man moved closer to the young one; and now he had a new look in his eyes that was at once considering and anxious and hopeful; and he spoke in a lower voice:

"And in the meantime ye'll maybe say a word to the King on my behalf, sir—just in case he should think that I had neglected my duty in the matter of the ravished strongbox?"

"I'll do that," Dennys promised.

"And now," he went on, "I must ask you to fetch victuals and drink to me; and I don't mean chicken broth. I am hungry and thirsty as a hunter. Let it be red meat, and pudding, and a horn of ale. Nay, a jack of strong ale. And bring word of my little lass. See that your daughter wards her safe and sure."

Matt departed; and Dennys took to pacing the floor again, but calmly now. His head felt as good as new, save to the touch, and as clear as glass. And his limbs were vigorous. Nothing was amiss with him now, physically, save an empty stomach and a dry gullet; and his spirit matched his head and limbs. He was at peace with his soul. He had lost an opportunity to shine on the field of glory, but now he felt nothing of regret for it, nor of his first jealous envy of the old King. And there would be other opportunities. Once he had Cynara in the great valley of home, where every hand would befriend and protect her, and even the ghosts of his ancestors would stand watch and ward, he and his enchanted knight would put forth again on the quest of glory. He was still Sir Lorn's squire and oldest known friend. King Torrice was older, true enough—older than Merlin!—but had known him for less than a sennight: whereas he, Dennys ap Rhys ap Tudor, had known and cherished the lost knight these nine months past. And if Lorn and the King held to each other's company, well and good! As they were both bewitched, what could be more natural? In that case he, Dennys, would squire them both.

His train of thought was broken by the entrance of Eliza, Cynara, and the tall dog. Once within the room, the little damosel released the woman's hand and came running to him and laid hold of him as high as she could reach. Eliza and the dog advanced much more soberly. Cynara clutched the breast of his jerkin and pulled on it.

"I would buss you, Denny," she piped. "But you are too high. Come down. Or take me up."

Dennys was about to stoop to her, when Eliza's voice checked him.

"Leave be!"

Dennys glared at the woman, then stooped and kissed the child's upturned face lightly, then stood straight and glared again. And she glared back at him. But his eyes did not waver, and he bent his brows fiercely. He was no longer helpless in bed. He saw her black gaze change and waver, vastly to his relief. But he gave no sign of relief or uncertainty.

"Mind your manners, wench!" he said, in a voice so harsh and menacing that he scarcely knew it for his own. "Have a care lest I look for another nurse for my little ward."

At that, the rugged cheeks went as gray as a dishcloth, the mastiff-jaws quivered, the formidable head drooped, and the shoulders, as wide as a wrestler's, sagged and trembled. Then, moving swiftly but heavily, she sank to her knees and clasped him about his knees before he could check or avoid her. Dennys would have wrenched himself clear with violence, but for the little girl; for she too had been caught in that embrace, and was now pressed between the woman and himself.

"What the devil?" he cried in sudden panic. "D'ye mean to crush the child? Ease your hold, or I'll twist your neck!"

Cynara, pressed tight though she was, managed to look up at him with a smile and to speak, though somewhat breathlessly.

"Don't hurt 'Liza. She's crying. Poor 'Liza."

It was true. That masterful being of bone and muscle and arrogance was sobbing and blubbering and quaking in a pitiful manner; and as her convulsions of grief increased, the clasp of her arms loosed. Dennys swore in consternation and again in pity. His anger fell away with the slackening of the pressure of those terrible arms.

"Give over!" he begged. "I didn't mean it. You're a grand, trusty wench—and if Cynara wants you, so be it! Now unhold me—let the little lass clear, and get up on your feet."

She obeyed, moving with an appearance of slow heaviness, but swiftly, as bears move. She turned in the act of rising from her knees, and withdrew a few paces and stood with her back to him and Cynara. Her massive shoulders, still stooped, continued to quake with half-stifled sobs, and her head remained bowed. Cynara, still close against Dennys but pressing now instead of pressed, laughed softly and spoke softly.

"Don't cry, 'Liza. Dennys will be good to us. He won't ever send you away. But if you ever again try to stop me when I want to buss him, maybe I will send you away."

Dennys stared down in astonishment at the childish upturned face, which smiled instantly back at him. He was amazed. He was confused.

"No, no, my little Cynara, you would not do that!" he protested. "Not to brave good Eliza—who loves you so dearly, and will guard you like a dragon."

The child laughed up at him again and said: "You love me dearly too."

"Yes. Certainly I love you. Haven't I proved it—with a broken head? And you love Eliza, who takes such good care of you, and doubtless thinks she does everything for the best."

"I love 'Liza, but I love Dennys more."

At that moment Matt entered with a horn in one hand and a trencher in the other, and a fellow from the kitchen bearing a great covered dish.

"A horn?" exclaimed Dennys. "Are you deaf, good Matt? I told you a jack; and now I am even thirstier than I was then."

"Ay, sir, a jack of strong ale it was," Matt agreed. "But Eliza said no, 'twould be too much for Yer Honor's poor head an' like to rouse a fever. So 'tis but a horn, young sir, and of small beer, at that."

After a moment of hesitation, Dennys took the horn. He saw the woman raise her head and look at him over a shoulder.

"Eliza was right," he said. "I'd be a fool and a knave to question it. She saved me from a cat's death—a fact I forgot a few minutes ago, God forgive me!—so why wouldn't she save me from a fever? Gramercy, Eliza!"

He drank then, and by the time the long horn was drained, the woman and the child and the dog were gone, and also the scullion who had fetched the great dish, and only Matt remained. The old man stood goggling at Dennys with round eyes, and wagging his whiskers and muttering.

"I never saw the like of it. Tears in the eyes of that masterful wench. Tears of humility an' devotion, by Judas! She has brought tears to others' eyes many a time, by the slapping of faces an' banging of heads on floors an' walls—of herds an' foresters an' saucy scullions. But her own eyes! Bewitchment, mark my words, young sir! The little damosel has bewitched her."

"You talk like a fool, old man," Dennys replied, but good-humoredly. "She's fond of the child—an' why not? She has a soft, motherly heart behind her iron ribs."

He uncovered the dish and set to work, with fingers and a small dagger and a horn spoon, on a stew of beef and dumplings. Matt looked on in silence until fully half of that mighty stew had passed from the dish to the squire's interior. Then he spoke again.

"I say she's bewitched!"

Dennys replied without looking up from the stew, and indistinctly because his mouth was full of dumpling.

"You're mad. Go to!"

"An' have a care for yourself, young sir," warned Matt.

Dennys swallowed the dumpling and looked up at Matt's solemn face. He frowned, then laughed lightly.

"If I be in peril of witchery too, don't tell me Eliza's the witch!" he jeered.

"Nay, not that great wench," said the ancient slowly, and still as solemn as an owl. He stooped lower and went on in an anxious whisper: "Harky to me, young sir! These eyes have seen things of fair fame an' foul, of this poor human life mostly, but of hell an' heaven too: of all manners of witcheries an' sorceries, an' sleights of magic both black an' white, an' evil in many an innocent guise. Day an' night, the imps of Satan beset our paths in fair an' cunning shapes—of lost an' bereaved damosels an' ladies and—"

"Have a care!" Dennys interrupted, his voice low but dangerous. "One wrong word now, old fool, and I'll feed your clapper to the crows!"

"Ye mistake me!" protested Matt, shaking with fright but standing his ground. "'Tis the mark I warn ye of. I glimpsed it by chance but an hour ago. The birthmark."

"What of it?" Dennys asked, his voice still low and deadly, but now curious too.

Matt's whisper thinned almost to nothing.

"I saw it once before—on a dead king's back—in Ireland, long ago. And I heard of others who carried it—princes an' queens—for good an' evil, but mostly for evil, so I heard in that perilous country. 'Tis the mark of a high royal race—the highest in all that land—branded on them before birth by angels, or maybe devils."

"What of it?" Dennys asked again, but with a quaver of apprehension in his voice now.

"She was stolen from a king's house. Gypsies stole her an' carried her off for a ransom—an' dared not take her back. Sooner or later, they brought her into this country; an' the best they could do was sell her to a pair of jongleurs; an' they too feared the mark, an' so tried to burn it off. Or it may be the gypsies stole her in revenge for cruel acts. However that may be, young sir, a child with that kingly birth-badge on her should be in stronger hands than in a poor squire's."

"What do you suggest?" asked Dennys.

"Give her into King Torrice's keeping."

"Nay, that old King is mad. He cannot guard his own property from knaves and thieves. And he is bewitched, by your own telling."

"To King Arthur Pendragon, then. Ay, to that high over-lord himself! Go to him and tell him all, young sir; and he will send men-at-arms to this unsafe inn to fetch her to his castle; and he will take Eliza too, for her nurse."

Dennys stood up slowly; and Matt backed away from him.

"Your years and infirmities save you," he said quietly. "But have a care, old man. Should King Arthur hear of the little damosel, I'll know whose neck to wring. I took her from her tormentors. I shall take her to safety. And I have sworn, by God's wounds, never to fail her or desert her. A poor squire, am I? So be it. And bewitched? So be it. But the word of Dennys ap Rhys ap Tudor is as good as any king's. Go away now—get out—before I lose my temper."

Chapter Seven
THE RETURN OF THE CHAMPIONS

King Torrice sent for enough fine articles of raiment from his wardrobes to furnish forth both himself and Sir Lorn to match even King Arthur, and a warning to all concerned not to expect him until they saw him.

The afternoon passed slowly for Dennys ap Rhys ap Tudor. His temper took on an edge. He thought with increasing irritation and contempt of Matt's homily on witches and evil enchantresses. He thought of the object of the old fool's wicked, ridiculous, cruel suggestion. Cynara, tortured and helpless—that pitiful baby! Cynara, clinging and trusting, that innocent child! He clapped both hands to his head in the stress of thought, and did not notice that he felt no pain from the pressure. Cynara, that small damosel. Cynara, laughing, into his eyes with misty stars and pressing against his lips with dewy petals of roses. He sat down, still clasping his bandaged head. Old Matt entered, with apprehensive looks and conciliatory gestures. Dennys leaped to his feet and shouted:

"What now, fellow?"

"Nothing!" yelped Matt, ready to turn and run for his life—or for his tongue, at least.

Dennys calmed himself with an effort. He blinked at the old man, then spoke quietly, but with a sneer.

"I feared that Sir James had come back and pried open another of King Torrice's strongboxes."

"Nay, Yer Worship. Master Gyles has doubled the guard. Eliza sent me, sir. I asked her, sir. If you have no fever, sir—her own words—another horn of small beer will do Yer Honor no harm."

What with the beer, and a visit from Gyles the taverner, who feared that King Torrice would hold him in part responsible for the loss of the jewelry and money and who begged Dennys humbly to say a good word for him, the squire's mind was distracted from a distressful train of thought. His temper returned almost to normal and his manner with Matt to its usual friendliness.

After a supper of roast duckling with green peas followed by a strawberry tart, he told Matt to fetch a cup of French wine without reference to Eliza. The old fellow obeyed, for now he stood more in awe of Dennys than of his masterful daughter. After the wine, Dennys insisted upon a game of chess. They both played very badly, what with sleepiness on the young gentleman's part and nervousness on the old servant's. Both their kings were in check, but without their awareness, when Eliza came into the room. She entered and approached the chess players with a strange air of timidity; and when they looked up at her, she spoke in a voice as timid as her demeanor, and with her gaze on the chessman between them.

"I have brought her from that chamber at the back, and the dog too—all three of us—to one beside this, which I think will be safer," she said.

Dennys came wide awake.

"You did right," he said. "I was about to suggest it. Something of the kind, anyhow. 'Twas well thought of, Eliza. Beside this, d'ye say? Which side?"

She pointed to a wall and said; "You enter it by that door," and pointed to a door, "and then by the door on the left."

"One bang on that wall, good wench, and I'll be with you with sword an' dagger!" cried Dennys.

"Gramercy, young sir," murmured the woman, but with her eyes still lowered to the ivory pieces.

But her father uttered a little muttering cry of protest.

"But I sleep there—an' Luke an' Dick along with me—at the King's beck an' call! It won't do. He won't like it."

"Fiddlesticks!" exclaimed Dennys, who felt splendid after his pint-sized cup of wine. His heart felt invincible, and his brain vigorous and nimble.

"You and your Lukes an' Dicks can move your cots out back," he said, with a generous gesture of the right hand which overturned half the chessmen. "And if they bandy words about it, or so much as hem and haw, send the rascals to me," he added, with a threatening gesture which overturned the remaining chessmen.

"The beds are already rearranged, kind sir," Eliza murmured, with a quick glance and smile at Dennys.

She turned and went away as she had come, but now with her perturbed sire scurrying after. Left to himself, Dennys nodded and slumped until he slept at last with his face on the chessboard.

Sudden clatter of iron on stone and a hubbub of voices brought Dennys straight up on his chair. His first thought was of a threat to Cynara—that Eliza's fear of attack was confirmed—and he leaped to his sword. But he realized his mistake before the blade was clear of the scabbard, for there was no suggestion of stealth in the disturbance, to which sounds of banging on wood and the voice of the taverner pleading for patience, and a rattling of bolts and bars were added from within the house. He heard the front door slam open against a wall, a voice raised raggedly in song, and stumbles and bumps in the narrow staircase; and he knew the champions were home, and discarded his sword.

A door of that chamber flew open, and King Torrice, still singing, barged in, with Sir Lorn moving less energetically in his wake. That indestructible cavalier and perpetual quester, bearded like Saint Peter and older than Merlin, flung himself upon Dennys and embraced him. Dennys returned the embrace in self-defense, and they swayed and staggered together; but the young knight sat down on the nearest chair, with a pleasant but vacuous smile on his face. Three old servitors, Matt and Luke and Dick, entered the room. At sight of them, the King released

Dennys and advanced upon them and laid hold of Matt and Luke, each by a beard.

"Sir James?" he demanded. "Where is Sir James?"

"Stole away—run off—with all Yer Majesty's jewelry!" cried old Matt, the note of distress in his voice heightened by the painful pull on his whiskers.

"Hah!" exclaimed the King. "Stole away, d'ye say? Run off with jewelry? So I'm rid of him at last, praise be to God! Fetch wine! Cups and flagons of the best!"

He released his hold on the two beards; whereupon all three servants dashed away to do his bidding.

The wine came, in flasks and flagons accompanied by cups; and the King, the knight, and the squire drank to themselves and one another and the confusion of their enemies. The King was toastmaster. Some of the toasts he proposed, and all three honored, were beyond Dennys' comprehension. "To the joint quest!" was one of these. "To the soul of beauty in seven shapes!" was another. But Dennys was not in an inquiring or analytical state of mind. His heart glowed with affection and admiration for his companions. Was there ever before such a good comrade and glorious champion as Lorn le Perdu, or so friendly and generous a king as Torrice of Har? He sat on his cot and applied himself gallantly to the task of acknowledging every toast by draining a full cup. Old Matt saw to the replenishing. And the Lost Knight sat on the other cot and drained his cup—a smaller one than the squire's—every time old Dick filled it; and Dennys noticed that the vacant look had taken on a simper of complacency.

But the King did not sit, nor even stand still. He could not have stood still if he had tried to, for his body was in constant danger of toppling and crashing like an axe-smitten tree; and so, to avoid the fall, he had to keep his legs under him by quick footwork in spurts of speed now to the right, now to the left, now in a circle. This did not interfere with his vocal cords or his swallowing muscles, however; but it was hard on poor old Luke, whose duty it was to keep the royal cup replenished.

Dennys reclined on his cot, then lay flat. His right hand sank to the floor, his limp fingers relaxed their grip, and he heard the empty cup clatter and roll. He smiled and closed his eyes; and his cot became a cloud, a floating and gently swaying and slowly revolving cloud, upon which he was lifted like a cherub, up and around and through the ceiling to heaven.

Chapter Eight
THE AWAKENING OF DENNYS

Dennys became conscious of a wet face, and of more drops and dribbles of moisture descending upon it, and he supposed himself to be out in the rain. Asleep on the mountainside, that was it. Nothing new in that. Nothing important enough to wake up for and inquire about, certainly. So he sank back to unconsciousness without having so much as attempted to open his eyes. . . . Again he became conscious of a wet face, but now it was not a mere drip and dribble, like a rain from the south on the hills of home, that caused the awareness. This was a blow, as if from a wild surf—as if a wave had struck and broken against his face and deluged his head and breast.

Suffocating, half-drowned, choking and gasping for air, he sat up and opened his eyes. Eliza! She stood over him, with a dripping but empty bucket still bottom-up in her hands. Her face was haggard, and her eyes were tragic; but they changed for the better instantly, as if despair had changed to hope quicker than thought. He got his breath, closed his eyes, and would have fallen back to his wet pillows and disrupted slumber, but she was too quick for him. She set the bucket aside and grabbed and held his wet shoulders.

"No, no, ye've slept long enough!" she cried.

He brushed a hand across his eyes; and now he saw the taverner and Matt where they stood a few paces off, regarding him.

"What now?" he mumbled. "I was asleep. Unhand me, good wench. I was late to bed last night."

"Nay, not last night," she told him, in a shaken voice and with fear in her eyes. "You slept like the dead all last night—and all the day before too. Rouse ye now, for Christ's sake!"

"D'ye say so? What ails me, then? Did some rogue break my head again?"

"Nay, 'twas the wine you drank with the King and Sir Lorn."

Wine? Ah, he remembered it now—that wine in flasks and flagons and cups; and that old king staggering this way and that, and ranting of quests and adventures and the seven shapes of the soul of beauty; and the Lost Knight sitting on his couch with a faraway but kindling look on his face, lifting and lowering his cup of silver-gilt in silence.

"And what of them? Do they still sleep?"

"Nay, they awoke betimes, and bestirred themselves, young sir—but that was yesterday."

"Yesterday? Do they joust again, those two champions? And me still skulking with a sore head!"

"They went away, horsed and harnessed—but not for the joustings here in Carleon. They're gone on a high quest—to the world's end, like as not—or into Fairyland."

"Nay, Lorn would not leave me thus—just for the want of waking!"

"'Tis God's truth, young sir!"

"The devil's truth!" cried old Matt. "Both mad! The King as mad as yer bedeviled young knight! Bewitched, the both of them, to forsake us here!"

Dennys, dumbfounded, regarded the old man with stricken eyes. Eliza, still stooped over him, though she had released his shoulders, spoke again, and yet more gently.

"It is better so, good sir. Those two fey-struck champions would prove mad company for a sane gentleman and—" she lowered her voice to a sigh "—unsure, untrusty guardians for a little, imperiled lass."

The taverner advanced and spoke for the first time.

"Enough of this!" he exclaimed. "Heed her not, Sir Squire—nor old Matt, neither. The King will return soon, and yer noble friend with him. He told me so. They but ride on some chance small adventure of chivalry to pass the time till Yer Honor's full recovery. His Kingship told me so, in them very words. An' he left his great horse Rex in his stall, saddle an' rich trappings complete, and a mort of arms an' gear an' knightly harness. You an' yours can rest easy in my strong house an' my trusty care, Sir Squire."

"Gramercy, good Gyles," muttered Dennys. "Let me sleep now, good friends, for my eyes are hot and heavy."

So the three left him; and despite the weight of his eyes and the ache in his brain, he saw, and wondered at, the taverner's care in herding Matt and Eliza from the room before him and in closing the door. But he was in no condition to wonder long. He closed his eyes, and drifted into black oblivion. . . .

Dennys sneezed once and again and sat up and grabbed with both hands even before he got his eyes open. He stared at finding old Matt in his clutches.

"Hush-hush!" shushed Matt. "Quiet now. I but tickled yer nose with a feather, to wake ye. Lay back now, an' if that rogue taverner comes back, shut yer eyes. For rogue he is. Eliza's right. Lay back now—he's maybe spying on us—an' harky to me, if ye love yer life."

Bewildered but impressed, Dennys lay flat again.

"Eliza's right. The little damosel's not safe here. Nobody nor nothing worth a groat's safe now the King's not here. An' I've a bag of silver crowns he gave me for the road; and the horse Rex is for you, with all else he left behind. We got to clear out before another dawn, or the rogue taverner will have all, an' the little lass, an' our dear lives. Eliza spied on him last night, an' saw him hiding lordly jewels in cracks in the wall, like a magpie. Maybe he was hand an' glove with Sir James. If that false knight is ever found, 'twill be down a well. An' the King an' Sir Lorn will never return for ye, young sir, mark my words."

"Why not?" whispered Dennys.

"Quiet now! The King has got the notion into his poor head yer bewitched knight is his grandson, or maybe great-grandson. I heard him telling it to Sir Lorn. And it could be, even if he cannot name the grandmother offhand. So they've gone in quest of her."

Matt stopped short; and Dennys beheld such an acute grimace of warning on the old man's face that he checked a stream of questions on the very tip of his tongue. He saw Matt straighten up and step back a pace; and then he heard the voice of Gyles the taverner, smooth and unctuous, from a few yards off.

"How fares our poor young gentleman now?"

"Fever," sighed Matt. "The wine fuming inside the cracked skull—God forgive us! He mutters an' raves, poor lad!"

At this Dennys began to mutter, for he could think fast at need. The innkeeper entered his field of view; and he narrowed his eyes and continued to mutter. Gyles came close and stooped, with a smile on his wide ruddy face. Dear Lord Christ, what a smile; it bared the greedy teeth, and all but hid the gloating eyes. Dennys felt a grip on his heart as of icy fingers, but he kept on with his crazy mutter; and he widened his eyes into what he hoped was a crazy stare.

And now he glimpsed, beyond the taverner's stooping shoulders, that which all but silenced his muttering and deflected his stare. Old Matt, standing straight in rear of the taverner, raised his right arm high—and in his hand was a short-shafted, spike-headed mace: but it was not until the mace began its swift descent that Dennys shut his eyes and lost his voice entirely. He heard the impact of mace on skull—the crack and crush of bone—and simultaneous grunts from striker and stricken. The sudden corpse, still quivering, fell across him, and rolled and thudded to the floor; and while in the act of quitting the cot himself, he heard old Matt gasp proudly: "As stark a stroke, by Judas, as ever I struck!"

Chapter Nine
DENNYS HEADS FOR THE HILLS OF HOME

They rode softly, as the saying is. Once mounted, and until they were clear of town and camp, they showed no evidence of haste or the need of it. No one would guess, by their movements or appearance, that they had left behind them one man dead and two men bound and gagged. The leader was up on a tall, pale, gaunt warhorse which trod with impressive deliberation rather than vigor. He was in full armor even to the plumed helm, but the vizor was open. The armor was of the best quality, but an outmoded style. The great shield, which hung on his left shoulder, was dented, and displayed an imposing though somewhat dimmed device; but any herald could have read it—gules, a unicorn rampant and armed, argent and or.

But within those knightly plates and that great casque was a mere squire, and a none too self-assured squire, at that—Dennys ap Rhys ap Tudor. At his charger's heels came two mountain ponies with a curtained litter slung between them. Close behind the litter came a formidable figure in a squire's harness and casque, astride Dennys' good brown gelding Hero. Bundles and baskets and a leather bottle dangled from the saddle, along with a mace and a battle-axe, but from the rider's big right fist stood up a two-edged sword of extraordinary length and weight. Then came old Matt and the herdsmen Oggle and Maggon astride mountain ponies, all in leather and iron, and armed to the teeth and hung about with goods and knightly gear; and through and around all trotted a tall dog.

Clear of the cobblestones of the town and the rank dust of the camp, the little cavalcade broke into a trot; and when they drew rein at the first lift of dawn, the curtains of the litter parted, and a little, frightened face looked out. A soft cry issued from the squire's casque, the sword fell from the great fist and the formidable figure flung itself from the brown hackney's back and dashed to the litter, still crying endearments. There it lifted the occupant up and out and held her close, but tenderly, to a breast of iron; and the child clasped the iron-clad neck with both small arms, crying "'Liza, my 'Liza!" between tears and laughter.

"A mad world!" muttered Dennys, still up on his high saddle. "And a perilous. An' a haphazard, God wot! My lost friend finds himself a mad king for a grandfather: and both of them witch-ridden. And I find a king's daughter—may all the angles shield her an' guide my hands an' wits!—to carry to safety, mauger my head!—and to her royal home over the sea even, when she is big enough to travel so far."

He dismounted with deliberation befitting his lordly shield and harness and the height and dignity of the ancient warhorse. His responsibilities weighed on him heavier than his armor; but when he saw Cynara smiling at him across one of Eliza's mailed shoulders, his heart and brain felt like blowing thistledown, and his helmet like a velvet cap, and his footgear of cunningly wrought links of brass like slippers of morocco leather.

After a few hours' rest, Dennys and his party resumed their northern way, but not on the open road. Fearful of pursuit from Carleon, Dennys led his little company through copses and forest fringes. They went by easy stages and at a snail's-pace all day, but when the stars glinted again they returned to the trodden track and made better time. Thus they progressed, at varying speeds and generally northward, and without human interference, until noon of their third day out of Carleon, when Dennys called a halt in a forest glade.

"Water and grass," he said; and he was about to dismount, when a short spear came flying and glanced and pitched from his gorget.

The attackers were upon them from all sides—a score of rogues in leather and rusty iron for the most part, but a few in tags and rags of stolen finery, but all armed with knives and boar-spears. Dennys wheeled into action on his tall horse, stooping and striking to his right and left; but Eliza, on the brown gelding, was quicker. Eliza roared defiance and damnation while she slashed and thrust; and the hackney kicked and struck and bit and screamed, even as he had been taught to fight by the mighty Bahram, in the distant valley of home.

But the attackers were not easy marks for long swords; as all they wanted was horses and goods and gear, they changed their tactics after seven or eight of the more reckless of them had been cut in two by just so many strokes. Now they tried to avoid the knight and squire—little did they suspect that the "knight" was but an apprentice squire and the furious "squire" but a nursemaid!—and at the same time, dispatch the grooms and panic and stampede the beasts of burden. Once in the surrounding tangles of timber and brushwood, where a reserve of their gang watched and waited, the ponies and all they carried would vanish like smoke.

They were as agile as weasels; but Oggle and Maggon were agile too, and old Matt was crafty. The grooms and Matt were afoot and the five ponies in a tight little herd, with the litter in the middle of it, within two minutes of the first rush of the attack. The dog sprang here and there, gashing leather and flesh to right and left. Dennys was about to dismount, the better to come to grips with the elusive foe, when the old warhorse spared him the effort by stumbling to its knees and pitching him clear of the saddle and everything. He landed on all fours, but was on his feet and running before any advantage could be taken of him. He chased a dozen of the enemy twice around the snorting ponies, shouting a battle cry—"A Lorn, a Lorn! Strike hard! Bite deep!"—the slogan of the friend who had forsaken him.

He came up with them and struck, and struck again, and at the screams of the victims, the others turned on him, and yet others joined them, and in a twinkling, they were all upon him like a pack of wolves. They went over him like a wave. He came up, still hacking and jabbing and giving far worse than he got. He went under again, still struggling, but without hope; he awaited the vital stab, the last mortal agony—but instead, and too suddenly to be realized instantly, the weight of battering feet and knees and groping hands was withdrawn. He staggered up, staring in amazement at what he saw.

No living enemy remained in the glade. A great white horse—Bahram, or was he dreaming!—stood within ten paces of him; and there was Lorn, in half-armor, running toward the ponies, which had finally panicked and broken away in every direction; and there were the grooms and Matt and the tall dog dodging this way and that, and Eliza on the brown hackney wheeling and shouting—one and all bent upon reherding the pack-train. The curtained litter was wrenched from its lashings, and the little damosel Cynara was spilled to the ground, screaming. Lorn snatched her up. In the same tick of time, Eliza hurled herself from the saddle and snatched the squirming child from the knight's hands. Between them, the frail gown and the frailer shift beneath it were torn from neck to waist.

"God's wounds!" cried the knight. "The Fairy Hand! Little Brigid! I've found her at last!"

Now Dennys bestirred himself. He staggered to them. Bleeding from several shallow cuts, and bruised and dazed, he steadied himself against stalwart Eliza, who by now had the little girl clasped to her iron bosom.

"I found her," he said, with a thick tongue.

And now old King Torrice emerged from the forest on a winded old horse, with mounted grooms and pack-horses following.

Now they had nothing to fear from attack. Reinforced by the King and the knight and their four attendants, the party was too strong for any wandering company of outlaws. But King Torrice, after hearing the extraordinary thing Sir Lorn had to tell, was impatient to be up and away again.

"I knew it the instant I saw it," said the Lost Knight; and his tongue was so stiff from disuse that it could hardly shape the words. "I remembered it then—and everything. Nay, not everything. I sought her for years—little Brigid—by that mark—till I forgot her and it—and my sacred vows."

"One thing at a time, dear lad," said the King. "Are you telling us that you know this child?"

"Yes, by the Fairy Hand. I set out to find her—long ago. A small infant then—not a year old. I would know her by the mark she was born with. They are not all marked so. One now and then, from remotest times—always of that race. Some call it Queen Mab's Hand. She was a queen of Elfland in ancient times."

"Never mind Queen Mab now, dear lad," said King Torrice. "It's yourself and this little girl we want to hear about, and how and where you met her before and all that. You said 'little Brigid' just now. What's the rest of it? Brigid who?"

"Cavanaugh," said the knight. "That's the name. Her mother is Queen Brigid. Her father is King Malachi. She was stolen out of the castle. Gypsies couldn't do that. It was Prince Seumas. He denied it. But he confessed at last to giving her to a gypsy, and said he would get her back— but that could never be, for in his rage Malachi killed him then without stopping to think."

"Just a moment, dear lad! This Prince Seumas? Who was he?"

"Why, King Malachi's half-brother. Younger by thirty years. They promised him the crown, Malachi and Queen Brigid both—that he would be The Cavanaugh some day, if they never had a son—and it was not likely, at the King's age, there'd be any more babies after this one. But when he heard that the Fairy Hand was on her, he knew they'd not keep that promise—for fear of offending the fairies. So he did what he did—and died for it. I made a vow, on a splinter of the True Cross, to seek the infant, and find her and take her home, or perish in the quest. Five others made the same vow. Three were kin to Malachi and three to the Queen. Four were knights, so the King knighted two of us. Then a bishop shrived and blessed us, and we rode our six separate ways. Bahram was a young horse then, not come to his full growth. But Bahram was not his name then—and if he had one then, I cannot recall it. He is a gift from Queen Brigid, and of a noble race. Dame Gwyn named him. That was but last winter."

"Never mind the horse now. Tell us of yourself, dear lad, and your quest. For how long did you follow it? Why did you forsake it, and where and when? And when did you cross the sea from Ireland?"

"Three summers and three winters I searched over Ireland. I don't know when I crossed the sea. I know nothing about that. I was in the mountains of Killarney. A voice called to me from a tower, at the fall of night. There was singing and music sounding from the windows of that tower. A door opened and showed red torchlight. I rode to that door—and came, afoot, to Dennys' campfire in the mountain of Eidyn."

Pressing a hand to his head, the knight sighed.

"You came a long way without knowing it, poor lad," said King Torrice, stroking his beard thoughtfully. "But that was by necromancy, to say the least of it. Killarney, hey? But we haven't time to investigate that now. One thing at a time—or only two, at the most: that is my rule. Our immediate task is to return the child to her parents' arms and you to your kith and kin. To which of those two are you sib, by the way? The King or the Queen?"

"The Queen, who was a Kelly," said Sir Lorn—but you could see he was thinking of something else, or trying to, anyhow.

"Har! A Kelly!" exclaimed Torrice. "But never mind that now. We'll see what we see when we get there. We're practically on the way. A bite of dinner and we're jinking."

Then Eliza spoke up. The great wench had laid aside her armor and all her weapons save a dagger, and now she did her best to look and sound meek and maidenly.

"Your Grace, Master Dennys took wounds and hard knocks and lost a deal of blood. He will be fitter for the road tomorrow than he is today, Your Grace."

King Torrice looked from her to Dennys, who reclined nearby on the sward and looked at the green leaves overhead.

"Forgive me, good lad!" he exclaimed. "So many things on my mind—and so sudden! I've been remiss." He got to his feet stiffly. "I shall now search and dress your wounds, good Dennys."

"Nay, they've already been searched and dressed, Your Grace," said Eliza—but now there was a shade less of meekness in her voice and likewise in the carriage of her broad shoulders.

"Quite so, good wench," returned the King hastily. "In that case, good Eliza, we shall press on—and you with us, of course, to mind the child—for we must not delay that sacred reunion a moment longer than need be; and Squire Dennys can follow after at his convenience."

She was about to reply to that, but Dennys sat up and checked her with a glance. Then Dennys got his legs under him and eyed the old King, and spoke levelly.

"Sir, I doubt that one day more or less now will make or mar that reunion: but I have no doubt that it had better be a day late than never. And so I shall not let you and Sir Lorn take her from me—nay, not even in true Eliza's care! She is my charge, and I am her guardian, under heaven and despite hell! Cynara or Brigid—tortured waif or princess—I will hold her and bring her to safety, by my halidom! I found her and took her from her tormentors. I have never forgot her nor forsook her. But what of you, Sir King? For all your wisdom and great heart and open hands! Another adventure, a new quest, and you are up and away! And what of this young knight? He forgot his quest and the vows he took on a splinter of the True Cross. I am his proven friend and tested squire, yet he rode off while I slept. I tell you—both of you—with all due respect for your rank and your golden spurs—you are bewitched and not to be trusted. I will die before you take her from me—and not with an unblooded sword neither, by Christ's wounds!"

The old King stared at him, struck speechless by conflicting emotions. Even Eliza was shocked at the squire's frankness and audacity and the deadliness of his tone and look. Then Sir Lorn rose quickly and close to Dennys and gazed at him earnestly.

"God's truth!" he exclaimed. "I forsook my quest," he went on mournfully. "And I deserted a friend while he slept. Forgive me, my friend. 'Twas the head that failed you, not the heart. Bewitched? Ay, devil a doubt of it. Or how else did I forget my vows?"

He turned from Dennys to King Torrice, who was still breathing gustily through his high nose and plucking at his beard.

"Dennys speaks truth, Your Grace," he said. "I am bewitched and so untrustworthy. And you too, sir—or something like it. Forgetful, anyhow. Two of a kind, sir. But Dennys is different. As for me, sir—well, I'll take my time from Dennys; and I pray you humbly to do the same, dear sir."

After a brief silence, during which his breathing became quieter, the old King smiled and said, with a sigh, "So be it, dear lad!" And he smiled at Dennys too, and then at Eliza, and added, "But don't keep me kicking my heels here any longer than need be, I beg you!"

Chapter Ten
CAVANAUGH CASTLE

Though it was five years since the loss of their infant daughter and only child, King Malachi Cavanaugh and his young queen were still as doleful a couple as you would find in Ireland. It was close upon five years since the six knights, three of Cavanaugh blood and three sib to Queen Brigid, had ridden away so bravely to recover their little kinswoman or perish in the attempt; and as nothing had been heard of any one of them, it was only natural to believe the worst. Malachi, though neither young nor physically fit (he had been dragged, more dead than alive, out of many an intertribal battle in the years of his long, lean bachelorhood and hard apprenticeship to the crown and lands of Cavanaugh), continued to lead local search parties whenever he was able to fork a horse, from which he was always brought home in a litter, cursing.

At sunset of the winter solstice, he returned from the last expedition of the kind he would ever make and was carried straightway from the litter to his bed, as usual; and, as usual, Queen Brigid knelt beside the bed and tried to comfort him. But it was cold comfort, for she wept. They were thus employed—the man cursing his helplessness

and the woman sobbing with grief and pity—when the bray
of a horn caught the Queen's attention. She raised her
head and stilled her sobs.

"Hark," she whispered.

"What now?" he complained.

"A horn on the hill. There—again—and shouting below.
And the inner gate!" She sprang to her feet and turned
from the bed to the door. "They are opening the gate—and
everyone shouts—in the yard and on the walls—everywhere—all shouting like mad!" She took up the candle and
ran from the room.

Now the hall was full of people and clamor and the
tossing red and black of a dozen torches. A great wench,
unhelmeted but armored to the chin, placed the little girl
in the arms of the dazed Queen. And three knights knelt
before her, looking up at her. She knew one for her young
kinsman Lorn, who had ridden away so assuredly so long
ago. Now he muttered, "Better late than never, Brigie," with
a shamefaced smile. And the old one, whose gold-inlaid
breastplate was half-hidden by a snowy beard, smiled at
her too, but roguishly. But the third, who was no more
than a youth, looked at her gravely, even critically. She
whispered down to him, stooping above the child in her
arms: "Is she—I'm afraid to look—truly my baby?"

"The mark is there, as it was when I found her," said
Dennys; whereupon the Queen uttered a glad cry and
turned and ran up the winding stairs.

The three cavaliers rose from their knees and were
instantly jostled and clasped and pulled from hand to
hand by ladies and damosels of every age and favor and
courtiers of every rank and condition. Lorn was kissed by
Kellys and Connells, Cavanaughs and MacMurraughs,
Bryans and Ryans and Flynns and Geraldines, for the hero
he was; and King Torrice and Dennys, though strangers,
fared very well too. Cups of wine and horns of mead and
ale were thrust into their hands, or splashed on them,
from every direction. Two fiddlers struck up the far-famed
Jig of Cavan; and every heart and foot started prancing to
that tune, including those of King Torrice and Sir Lorn,
armor and spurs and all; but Dennys went out to see how
old Matt and the grooms and horses were faring.

King Torrice was looking for a quiet corner to sit down

in and catch his breath and maybe another cup of wine, when something flew against him and grabbed his beard and screamed a name that stood him stock still in his tracks. It was a little old lady in brocade and gemmy gold chains and bangles, with eyes like green fireflies and a tiara of emeralds askew on her white curls.

"Guy, ye rascal, ye can't deny it!" she screamed. "And I'll not deny it, wotever it makes of me who's passed for a decent widow these last nine years!"

He took hold of her thin wrists to ease the drag on his whiskers.

"You're mistaken, madam—for I haven't the honor—my name being Torrice," he gabbled.

At that she fell to laughing and to twisting his beard gently instead of pulling it; and then she whispered: "Don't lie to me, me grand Guy Harper—me poetical husband—for I'd know ye any time, anywhere, by the roving gleam in yer eyes and the flyaway twitching of yer high nose."

"But madam, I am King Torrice of Har!"

"I'm not talking about who ye are, me darling, but who ye were when I married ye."

"But you mentioned nine years of widowhood, madam; and I assure you, and can prove it, it's over three score years since I was last in Ireland and this is my first visit to Cavanaugh Castle."

"But wot about Castle Kelly, ye rascal? And the sweet little Molly O'Kelly who married Guy the troubadour despite her fond parents' prayers an' sneers. I was first widowed by yerself, ye tyke, the night ye stole away from me bed an' board and the daughter ye'd never seen—and all that was over sixty years ago, sure enough! Don't try to tell me ye've forgot all that now!"

He did not try to tell her anything, but only scuffled his feet and tried feebly to disengage his beard from her fingers. She took him by a wrist with both her hands and led him to a bench against a wall, and there she set him down and herself close beside him, still with the grip on his wrist.

"Now harky to me," she said. "After the birth of our little girl, a man came to the castle and told how Guy the Harper had been slain by robbers and he had seen the corpse with his own eyes. It was a grand story, even if me

proud father did invent it and pay the poor man ten silver
crowns to tell it—which he confessed on his deathbed, but
into nobody's ear but me own, like the grand gentleman
he was. Now wot have ye to say to that, me fine flitting
troubadour?"

King Torrice said nothing, nor did he so much as
glance at her, but she could see he was listening hard and
thinking hard too.

"It wasn't long before I married again," she went on,
"but this time an Irishman and a gentleman for a change,
and was a good wife to him till he went to glory nine years
ago; and I've been a good mother to all my children. Me
second girl, Kate Connell, married before her half-sister
Mary Harper did—she was all Irish—a forty-second Kelly
cousin; and their daughter, me own granddaughter, is
Queen Brigid O'Cavanaugh herself. Now wot d'ye say to
that?"

"What of your oldest child—Mary, I think you called
her—by your first marriage?" he mumbled, slanting a
quick look at her.

"Our own little Mary—is it herself ye're curious about
after sixty years?" she cackled. "Well, I'll tell ye, Guy
Harper or King Torrice or wotever ye call yerself: she married a Geraldine, and I gave her a grand wedding. She's not
here, being at Mount Gerald; but her son's here, as ye
know without me telling it, ye fox!"

"Your daughter Mary's son, madam?"

"Ay, and yer own grandson!—and if ye don't know it
without me telling ye, how come the two of ye to turn up
here together as thick as thieves?"

"Madam, if you are referring to my young friend Lorn le
Perdu, I assure you that we met quite by chance last June
at Carleon, when neither of us knew anything about the
other—that's to say he didn't know me to be King Torrice
of Har until he was told—and he, poor lad, didn't know
anything about himself either, at that time. It's a long
story—about bewitchment and the baby he was searching
for and everything—and I'll be delighted to give you all the
particulars tomorrow, madam, but you really must excuse
me now."

That old quester was out of her clutches and vanished
into the confusion of dancers and drinkers and torchlight

and queer shadows, as quick and limber as an eel, before she realized what was happening; and she didn't set eye or hand on him again that night. There were hideouts aplenty in that castle; and nobody interfered with anybody that night unless it was to urge another cup of wine of usquebaugh on him. It was a great and joyous occasion: but the grandest celebrations of the return of the little Princess were yet to come.

The castle was late astir, though it was a glorious day of sunshine and white frost. It was one hour past noon when the head of the parade issued from the gate in the outer wall. Four heralds in tabards of green and silver and gold rode abreast, blowing silver trumpets. Next came King Malachi and Queen Brigid, stirrup to stirrup. Malachi, on a black charger, sat straight as a young knight; and you could see his laughter, though it was drowned by the trumpeting and shouting. The Queen, all in white samite and ermine, rode a white palfrey and blew kisses right and left from rosy fingers. Three cavaliers in rich armor rode in line, with their shields on their shoulders and their vizors raised. On the right was an ancient with snowy whiskers and an eagle-beak and the plume on his casque sprouting from a crown of gemmy gold. In the middle, on a great white stallion whose hooves shook the frozen earth, rode young Lorn Geraldine, who had fulfilled his vow of five years ago by bringing home the stolen princess. On the left, on a horse of remarkable height and dignity, rode the youth whom rumor already named as the greatest champion of the three, though but a Welsh squire called Dennys ap something or other. And the crowds bawled "A Har, a Har!" "A Geraldine, a Geraldine!" "A Dennys, a Dennys!"

Next, high on the shoulders of eight cadets of the best families in the land, came a litter with parted curtains and the recovered heiress of the Cavanaughs, in white fur, laughing out of it to right and left. "A Brigie, a Brigie!" bawled the crowd. Beneath the litter stalked a tall brown dog with amber eyes, and close behind it rode a great wench, fully armored and with a naked sword in her right hand, but unhelmeted. Then came the local chivalry, harnessed and armed, their horses neighing and curveting, followed by archers and pikemen in shirts of mail and steel caps. The grand procession passed through the town and clear around it and back through it again.

There was a kingly feast in the castle that day. It began in sunlight and went on in candlelight, torchlight, and fireshine. At the start, Malachi made a knight of Dennys ap Rhys and rich gifts to Sir Lorn and King Torrice; and Queen Brigid gave each of them a kiss—but she took the fun out of it for Torrice by whispering in his beard, "I've been told all about you by Granny O'Connell."

The feast went on. The Queen and all the ladies retired, but the feast went on and on. King Malachi and young Sir Dennys fell asleep in their chairs. Other gentlemen were overcome by slumber, some on chairs and benches and some on the floor. But King Torrice kept both himself and Sir Lorn wide awake, with whispering and nudging.

Sunrise found King Torrice and Sir Lorn well on their way somewhere.

"That's no life for us, my boy," said the King. "We were born to rove. But should you ever want to settle down, just say so, for you will find me reliable and trustworthy and reasonable, no matter what your grandmother told you about me. Yes, no matter what my failings as a husband, I'll never fail you as a grandfather or a fellow-quester, mauger my head!"

"Gramercy, Grandfather," replied Sir Lorn, almost cheerfully.

THE MERLIN TOUCH

Chapter One
THE FORGE IN THE WILDERNESS

Quests ridden on, and sweated and bled for, and per-adventure perished in, are as multitudinous as the stars. They have been of dreams, vanities, love, ambition, hate, whiffs of temper and idle whimsy; for the Fountain of Youth, the Phoenix's nest, unicorns with golden horns, dryads and nymphs and yet more elusive beauties, the Questing Beast which ran with a noise in its belly as of a pack of baying hounds, and was chased by King Pellinore and others of renown; and latterly the Holy Grail, which was sought by many and achieved—quite obviously with the assistance of celestial hierarchy—by exemplary Sir Galahad.

Almost all questers rode singly, and won their places in song and story as solitary champions, but a few shared their quests and went in couples, and of these were old King Torrice of Har and his young Irish grandson Sir Lorn Geraldine. Once met (as already recorded), only death could break that fellowship or divide its mad adventure.

For more than a sennight they had followed tracks which had come to nothing, day after day, save narrower and rougher tracks. It was fifteen days since their last dealings with a farrier or any other kind of smith; and now, what with broken shoes or no hoof-iron at all, every horse was lame; and every man, whatever his degree, was on his own two feet. King Torrice was in a fretful humor, for pedestrianism was as foreign to his spirit as it was to his feet, and irked his soul equally with his corns. But young Sir Lorn maintained his habitual air and appearance of baffled thought and pensive abstraction, walking equably and unconcernedly. In truth, it was only when violently employed with spear or sword that he seemed to know or care how many legs were under him and at his service. Ah, but he knew then, never fear, and made the most of whatever number it happened to be!

"We'll be carrying them on our backs before we can win clear of this cursed wilderness," complained the King.

Next moment, one of the squires cried out and pointed a hand.

"A smithy! Look there under the great oak. Forge and anvil complete, by Judas!"

All came to a dead stop and looked, like one man and one horse: and there it was, sure enough—a rustic hut with an open front disclosing forge and bellows and anvil.

"But no smith, of course," said the King. "He's gone off in despair—and small blame to him! A fool he must be to look for trade where there's no population—unless he counted on the patronage of unicorns and wild cattle."

"Nay, sire, look again!" cried the same squire. "At the forge. Stirring the fire. But I'll swear there was no blink of fire a moment ago!"

All except Sir Lorn gasped and gaped in astonishment, and even he looked interested; for there, for all to see, was a human figure where naught but wood and iron and the leather bellows had been visible a moment before. A lively figure, at that, with the right hand busy at the red glow in the blackness of the forge, and the left raised high to the upper beam of the bellows; and while the travelers still stared as if at a warlock, the bellows creaked and exhaled gustily, and the fiery heart amid the black coals pulsed and expanded. A piece of white-hot metal was withdrawn in the grip of long pincers and laid on the anvil and smitten with a hammer, and sparks spurted and flew.

Then King Torrice bestirred himself; with a mutter in which irritability was somewhat tempered by awe, he turned left into the ferns and brambles, and advanced upon the smithy stiffly but resolutely, with his hoof-sore charger stumbling after, and did not halt until his whiskers were threatened by the sparks. Then he spoke in a loud voice, but the tone was constrainedly affable.

"Greetings, good Master Smith! Well met, my fine fellow!"

After six more hammer-clangs of cold iron on hot, the smith looked up from the anvil. He too was of venerable appearance and whiskery, but most of his snowy beard was tucked out of view and danger into the top of his leather apron, whereas Torrice's luxuriant appendage flowed broadly down his breastplate even to his belt.

"So here you are!" said the smith. "Well and good! One score and three completed, and this one will fit the tally." He nodded toward clusters of horseshoes of various sizes dangling from spikes in a wall, then thrust the cooling iron in his pincers back into the heart of fire.

"What d'ye say?" the old King-errant gasped. "Irons ready for six horses? Even so—and I don't believe it!— they'll not fit my six!"

"I'll attend to you in a minute," mumbled the smith.

The bellows creaked and snored, and the fire glowed; and soon that piece of iron, again white as noonday sun, was back on the ringing anvil, and the sparks were flying again like golden bees. King Torrice stood silent, gawking like a boy, until the iron was beaten exactly to the smith's fancy, and pierced for nails, and finally plunged into a tub of water with a hiss and jet of steam. Now the smith was at his horse, and old nails and fragments of old shoes and hoof parings fell simultaneously.

"He must have six hands!" muttered the King.

Now a little hammer went tapping as fast as the sedate charger could lift and lower his feet.

"Next!" cried the smith.

Sir Lorn's great white horse came next, then the squires' hackneys, and last the two pack-horses led by grooms, but all so fast—for every ready shoe fitted—that the King and the squires began a suspicious inspection. The smith straightened his back, tossed his apron aside and uttered a cackle of laughter.

"You are wasting your time," he said, and fell to combing his whiskers with a golden comb that appeared in his hand as if by magic. "All is at is seems, if not more so," he added, and cackled again.

"In all my life I never saw anything like it," said the King.

"You could forget a few things in that length of time," said the smith.

Torrice stiffened and asked loftily: "What do I owe you, my good fellow?"

"I'll name you a special fee, a mere token price, having taken a fancy to Your Worship," replied the smith. "What d'ye say to paying for the nails only, and never mind the shoes and the labor? One farthing for the first nail, a ha'penny for the second, a penny for the third, and so on?"

"I can afford to pay what I owe," said Torrice, with a royal air, "and am accustomed to paying more, so you will oblige me by stating your charge and having done with it."

"Not so fast!" cried the squire who had spotted the forge. "What d'ye mean 'and so on,' old man? Tuppence for the fourth nail and fourpence for the fifth, is that it?"

The King exclaimed fretfully: "Enough of this vulgar talk of farthings and pennies! Pay him what he asks, good Peter."

"Nay, sir, mauger my head!" cried the squire. "I learned that manner of computation from a farrier at Saint Audrey's Fair, in my youth, an' would still be in his debt— and I had but one beast, mark ye!—if I hadn't settled the score with my stout cudgel, there an' then."

The smith laughed heartily, patted Squire Peter's shoulder and chuckled: "Spare the cudgel, friend, and I'll be content with a horn of ale."

"I don't get it," muttered Torrice. "All this jabber about nails. But let it pass." His voice and brow cleared. "But ale you shall have, worthy smith, and a share of our supper, and three silver crowns for your pouch."

"Gramercy," said the smith.

The horses, all firm of foot now, were soon unsaddled, unloaded, and hobbled in a nearby glade of sweet grasses to which the smith had led the way. But now the sun was behind the westward treetops. A small pavilion was pitched; a small keg was broached; and a fire was made of deadwood from thickets of underbrush. By the time the black pots were boiling, the smith's horn had been replenished twice, and a white star was glinting in the East.

It was a simple supper of boiled corned beef and bacon and wheaten dumplings, barley scones, and cheese and honey; and for drink there was malt ale for all, and mead and usquebaugh too for the knights and squires and thirsty guests. The smith ate and drank more than anyone else, and at the same time, did most of the talking. The King, who had been taught never to drink with food in his mouth, and never to speak with his mouth full, was horrified at the simultaneous flaunting of both rules of behavior: and at last he cried out a protest:

"There's plenty of time, friend! Have a care, or you'll choke!"

The smith laughed, and said: "I apologize for offending your quality, of which I cannot pretend ignorance, for this is not our first meeting. I would know you anywhere and at any time for what you are, no matter how small your retinue and how restricted your commissariat at the moment. But don't misunderstand me. Your present company makes up in character and promise what it lacks in strength. This young knight is suffering from a misadventure, but the fact that he survived it with nothing more serious than a gap in his memory and a grievous void in his heart is proof that he is destined for great things."

"What do you know of that?" Torrice interrupted, loudly and with a violent gesture.

"What I see," replied the smith coolly.

"And what's that? There's nothing to see!"

"Nothing for dull eyes, you mean. But as I was saying, this is the first time I have known the munificent Torrice of Har to lack a few flasks, at least, of French or Spanish wine."

"So you know me?" the King cried. "But I was never in this forest before!"

"Nor was I," the smith chuckled; and while all save Sir Lorn gaped in wonder, he added: "Are you so old, my friend, that you no longer recognize the master touch?"

The King clapped a hand to his head, and sighed and muttered.

"Merlin! I should have known it at the forge. But you were not so helpful at our last meeting—on the contrary. But that was long ago." He stood up and did the correct thing, though still dazedly. "Duke Merlin, this is my grandson Lorn Geraldine—an Irish grandson. And these two gentlemen are our squires Peter and Gervis."

Sir Lorn stood up and louted low, cap in hand, but no

slightest flicker of eye or twitch of lip paid the tribute of recognition to that potent name. But the squires' reaction was entirely flattering. Standing bareheaded and bowed double, Peter and Gervis regarded with awestruck eyes and blanched faces the person who had so lately shod their horses; and the uncouth fellows at the far side of the fire sat with podding eyes and hanging jaws, powerless to stir a muscle. The great magician looked around with a gratified smirk.

"Gramercy, friend," he said. "You have heard of me, it seems—and only good, I'm sure. But sit down, gentlemen, I pray you. Let us be at ease together again."

King Torrice said to his squire: "Peter, be so good as to fetch that flask of green glass you wot of."

"Good Master Peter, by fetching all four flasks you wot of, two green and two brown, you will spare yourself a deal of footing to and fro," said Merlin dryly.

"Quite," said the King resignedly; whereupon Peter moved off hastily toward the stacked baggage.

Those treasured flasks contained potent foreign cordials, and not wine at all. The squires took their shares of the first one, then slept where they lay. The young knight went onto his share of the second flask, then retired to the pavilion on wavering legs but with unabated dignity. This left the two ancients tête-à-tête; and the talk, which had been anecdotal, changed in its character.

"A fine young man, your grandson, despite what happened to him," said Merlin. "Bewitched, of course! His case suggested the fine and merciless art of—but why name her? She goes by more names than Satan, and has done so since before Stonehenge was set up, like as not: *Lilith, Circe, Queen Mab, la Belle Dame sans Merci, the Maid of Tintagel, the Lost Lady of Caer Loyw, Fair Fiona, Dark Essylit, Weeping Rosamund, the Damosel of the Tower,* and as many more as I have fingers and toes, but all one and the same perilous and indestructible witch, in my opinion. There are other and lesser enchantresses abroad; and as one can never be quite sure of one's ground in such matters, a man is well advised—ay, even such a man as myself—to avoid them all. I have taken chances, naturally— but as you see, without serious consequences.

"But my case is beside the point, considering the fact

that my power of wisdom—call it magic, if you like—is greater than that of any known or recorded wizard or witch, and I doubt that I would have suffered more than a slight and temporary emotional disturbance even if I had ever fallen into the clutches of Lilith herself, under whatever guise or name. But your case, friend Torrice, is different; and I must confess that your respectable mentality—I say *respectable* for want of a more precise term—surprises me somewhat, after all your years of errantry. I am sure it has been by good fortune rather than by good management that you have escaped the attentions of one or more of those mischievous ladies."

"I'm not so sure of that," said the King, unstoppering the third flask and replenishing both cups. "In my quest of Beauty, which I have followed devotedly, save for occasional domestic interludes, ever since winning my spurs, I have had many contacts with ladies, many of whom were mischievous; and I am not at all sure that some of them were not witches. I have never consciously avoided that sort of thing, but in the interests of my high quest have sought it, and even now I would not avoid the most disastrous of them all."

"Stout fellow!" exclaimed Merlin merrily, but on a note of derision.

He laughed, but briefly. He leaned toward his companion in sudden gravity and wagged a finger at him.

"Have a care, my friend," he cautioned. "Don't be too cock-a-hoop about your powers of resistance and survival. You've been lucky, that's all. I admit that your luck has held a long time, but I warn you that it will not last forever. That you have encountered many enchantresses in your long and comprehensive quest I'll not deny, but I tell you— and I'll stake my reputation on it—that every one of them has been entirely human. There wasn't a witch in the lot. Just daughters of Eve, all of them; and even they have caused numerous deviations from your quest, and not a few considerable delays.

"Don't think I don't know what I am talking about, old friend, for I have followed your extraordinary course with interest ever since chance first brought you to my attention, though you have been blissfully ignorant of my surveillance most of the time. And I'll tell you now when that

was. It was a great day with you, poor Torrice—young
Torrice, then—the day an old woman in a red cloak gave
you a little crystal vial containing two ounces of what she
claimed to be the Elixir of Life. You have not forgotten it, I
see."

"Certainly not!" cried the King. "Why should I forget it?"
he demanded, with a defiant gesture in the course of which
he drained and refilled his cup. "I drank it, didn't I? And it
was a long, long time ago, wasn't it? And here I am!"

"True, my friend, here you are, and a marvel of spirit
and physical fitness for a man of your age. Ay, or for one
of a quarter your age. But what you swallowed that day
was not the real thing—not the magical liquor you believed
it to be. It was but an experimental step in the develop-
ment of the true, the pure, the perfected elixir. But even so,
it was not without merit, as you have proved. It has served
you well so far, my friend: but it is my duty to warn you
that the virtue of the stuff you drank on that May morning
of the first year of your—ah, if you'll forgive the expression,
your delightfully latitudinous quest—cannot be depended
upon indefinitely."

"It was the Elixir of Life! And I am as good as I ever
was!"

"Nay, not quite."

"Not quite? What do you mean by that?"

"Calm yourself, old friend. I speak for your own comfort
and guidance. I mean that the old woman in the red cloak
gave you a liquor that was not the perfected article, and
that you are showing signs of—"

"Not so! I'll prove it on your person with spear or sword,
horsed or afoot, if you promise to keep your unholy magic
out of it! And what the devil do you know of my traffic with
that old hag?"

"I abstain from all armed encounters, for the very reason
that I could not keep my advantage of magic out of them
even if I would: and my answer to your question is: *I was
that old woman.*"

Sobered as if by a bucketful of cold water, Torrice hung
his head in silence. Merlin was also in no mood for further
speech at the moment, but refilled his cup and sipped with
a contemplative and compassionate air.

The King was the first to resume the conversation.

"But what of you? You have drunk of it."

"Yes, when I had perfected it, I drank it," said Merlin.

"Then I may still drink of it," said Torrice hopefully.

"Nay, old friend, or you would live forever," Merlin replied gently.

"Why not? You will live forever. Then why not both of us?"

"I have my wisdom to support me—magic, to you, but the greatest in the world, by any name—to strengthen and console me. You have none of it."

"I could learn it."

"Nay, good Torrice of Har, not in a century. Nor in a millennium, for that matter. You lack the necessary—ah!— you are not the type for that sort of thing, dear old friend."

"Never mind the magic, then, but give me the elixir."

"No, I don't want to be the object of your curses throughout the ages. You have discovered a grandson and companion-at-arms. Do you want to outlive him? Consider that prospect, my friend."

The King considered it, sighed deeply, and shook his head. He stared and sat blinking at the red embers of the fire.

"How long have I left to go?" he whispered.

"Long enough," said Merlin cheerfully. "I can't be more exact than that," he added; and the lie was cheerful too.

"And the end?" whispered the King anxiously.

Before replying to that, the magician pressed a hand to his brow as if in an extraordinary effort of foresight.

"I see it. Hah! Well done! Nobly done! . . . Ah, old friend, I envy you."

"Gramercy! And the lad? What of his—How fares he— at the last?"

"Nay, I cannot see so far."

Chapter Two
THE SMITH IS GONE BUT THEY HEAR OF A PILGRIM

The squire named Peter was the first of that company to awake to the new day. The sun was still behind the east-ward wall of the forest when he opened his eyes. Having lain out all night, he was damp with dew from head to foot. He sat up and blinked at slumbering Gervis, at four overturned flasks of rare outlandish glass on the dew-gemmed sward, and at the black and gray of the fallen fire. The events of the previous evening flashed in his mind, confusedly yet vividly, and painfully, for his brain felt tender and his eyes too big and hot for their sockets.

"Honest ale will be good enough for me from now on," he muttered.

He made his stumbling way to a brook which skirted the glade, knelt there, and immersed arms and head in the cool water. Vastly refreshed, he went back and stirred Gervis and the grooms to action; and all four, without a word but as if by spoken agreement, began rounding up the horses and examining their hooves.

"So it wasn't a dream!" cried Gervis; and he called all the saints whose names he could remember to bear witness that the episode of the forge had been sober fact. "I never thought to have that old warlock shoe a horse for me," he added.

"When you have served good old Torrice as long as I have, nothing will surprise you," Peter answered with a superior air.

"A search of the smithy now might be worth our while," suggested Gervis. "The secret of that trick would be useful, and it might even win a battle under certain circumstances."

So the two squires left the glade by the way they had come into it less than twelve hours before, in the hope of wresting a hint at least of Merlin's formula for horseshoeing from the deserted smithy while the magician continued to sleep off his potations in the pavilion. They had not far to go; and the backtracking of the passage of six horses and seven men over fat moss and through lush fern was a simple matter. And there they were. There was the great oak, anyway—the identical old forest patriarch bearing scars of thunderbolts, a heron's nest and three bushes of mistletoe, and doubtless, a hamadryad in its wide and soaring world of greenery. The squires stood and stared. They moved their lips but no sound came forth. Gervis' tongue was the first to thaw.

"Not here," he whispered. "Not the same tree. This isn't the place."

But he knew better. This was a unique tree. And here were the two ancient thorns that had crowded one end of the smithy, and the hollies that had crowded the other end of it. This was the place, certainly. A fool would recognize it. Everything was here, just as it had been—except the smithy.

Peter shivered and found his tongue and said: "We'll go back and take another look at the horses' feet."

They returned to the glade and inspected all twenty-four hooves again. The new shoes were still in their places.

"I feared they had flown away after the smithy, forge, anvil, and bellows," muttered Gervis.

"They may yet," said Peter grimly.

"But he seems to be a merry old gentleman and a true friend to King Torrice," said Gervis.

"There's more to that old warlock than meets the eye," Peter answered. "As for his friendship—well, from all I've heard, I'd liefer have him with me than against me, but it would suit me best to be entirely free of his attentions. He has a queer sense of humor, and a devilish odd idea of a joke, by old wives' tales I've heard here and there. Take King Arthur Pendragon's birth, for instance: you know about that, of course! Well, was that a decent trick to play on a lady? For all his high blood—he was born a duke, no doubt of that—the mighty wizard Merlin is no gentleman. He doesn't think like one—not like our Torrice, nor like our Lorn, nor like you who can boast an honorable knight for a father, nor even like me, stable-born and stable-bred. Ay, though my gentility be scarce a year old, I'm a better gentleman than Duke Merlin, by my halidom!"

"I agree with you, my Peter—but not so loud, for here they come from the pavilion," warned Gervis.

King Torrice, in a kingly long robe of red silk, issued from the pavilion and looked to his front and right and left with an inquiring air. Sir Lorn, in an equally fine robe, appeared and stood beside his grandfather, yawning and blinking. And that was all. The guest, the great Merlin, did not come forth. The squires ran and halted and uncapped before their knights.

"How are the horses' feet?" asked the King.

"We have inspected them twice this morning, sir, and found all in order and every shoe in its place," Peter replied, and after a moment's hesitation, added: "But the smithy is gone, sir."

King Torrice nodded. He looked thoughtful, but not surprised.

"So is the smith," he said. "Let us hope and pray that his handiwork does not follow him."

"Every iron is tight and true, sir," Gervis assured him.

Peter spoke hesitantly.

"Sir, may I suggest that it might happen? His handiwork might follow him—the twenty-four iron shoes—even on the hooves of Your Honor's horses—if all I've heard of that old warlock's magic be true."

The venerable quester blinked and asked: "How so, lad? D'ye suggest that their potency could, and might, pull the hoofs off the horses? And why not, come to think of it? It smacks of the Merlin touch, by Judas!"

"Yes, sir—but I did not mean it just in that way. I meant to suggest that he might, if in a tricky mood, bid the twenty-four shoes to follow him—horses and all."

"Hah!" the King exclaimed; and he swore by half a dozen saints. "That's his game, depend upon it! And I was simple enough to think he had done us a good turn out of pure good will! The master touch, indeed! But what does he want of us? What devilment is he up to now? 'A horn of ale will settle my score,' said he. And he leaves an empty cask, empty bottles, and four empty flasks of Araby. But he is welcome to all that, and would be welcome to a hundred silver crowns besides if I knew that the score was settled. But forewarned is forearmed; and we'll see to it that our horses go our way, not to Wizard Merlin's, even if we have to unshoe them and lead them afoot again."

Breakfast was eaten; pack-horses were loaded; the squires harnessed the knights and then each the other; and all four mounted into their high saddles. It was in all their minds that the march would be resumed in the same direction from which it had been diverted by the discovery of the smithy; so when all the horses wheeled to the right and plunged from the track as if by a common and irresistible impulse, King Torrice cried "Halt!" and pulled mightily on his reins. The squires pulled too, and the grooms pushed manfully against the thrusting heads of the pack-horses; but Sir Lorn, up on mighty Bahram and with his thoughts elsewhere—probably in Fairyland—

neither drew rein nor cried halt, but crashed onward through fern and underbrush. The pulling and pushing and protesting of the others was of no avail. Where Lorn's great white warhorse led, the King's old charger, the squires' hackneys, and the stubborn beasts of burden would follow.

"Sir, this is what I meant!" cried Peter, coming up on the King's left.

"Gramercy!" gasped Torrice, who seldom forgot his manners, especially to his inferiors in rank.

Now they were beneath great oaks, with fallow deer bounding before them through netted sunshine and shadow, and tawny wild swine scattering right and left. Now charger and hackneys and ponies took their own heads for it, and ran as if possessed by devils. At the same moment Lorn drew rein and turned his head and waved a hand. The King and squires were soon up with him. He pointed through a screen of saplings.

"A good track," he said. "A wide and beaten track."

They all looked. There below them lay a better track than they had seen in a sennight, sure enough.

"It must go to some fine town, sir!" Gervis cried.

"I don't like it," said the King. "'Tis not of our own choosing."

"'Twill lead us out of the wilderness, sir, wherever to," Peter said; and in his eagerness to see a market and a tavern again, and houses with ladies and damosels looking down from windows, his distrust of Merlin was almost forgotten.

"Still, I don't like it!" Torrice muttered. "Nor what brought us to it against our wills. I have gone my own way since first donning gold spurs. I'm a knight-errant, and a baron and king. I acknowledge no human overlord save Arthur Pendragon—and I might defy even him at a pinch, as I have defied his father King Uther upon occasion. And now am I to jink this way and that at the whim of a tricky old magic-monger and the itch of bedeviled horses? Nay, by my halidom!"

Just then the white stallion and Sir Lorn went through the saplings and down the short bank, turned left on the track and trotted purposefully; and the King's charger and the King followed, willy-nilly; and the hackneys and the squires; and the grooms and their charges, clanking and running and eating dust.

"Hold! Hold!" King Torrice bawled, worked up by now to a fury of defiance that was foreign to his naturally placid though restless spirit—but all he got for it was a bitten tongue.

But that flurry of advance took the little cavalcade no father than around the next curve in the track. There Lorn pulled up, and all the others at his stirrups and his tail. Then all saw that which he had seen first. It was a dwarf standing fairly in the middle of the way and louting low.

"What now, my good manikin?" asked Torrice suspiciously: and he looked searchingly at the little fellow, looking for Merlin in yet another disguise.

Clearly and briefly the dwarf revealed his business. His mistress, Dame Clara, a defenseless widow, begged their lordships' protection from a cruel oppressor who had confined her within her manor house, beaten her stewards, driven off a full half of her flocks and herds, and was even now collecting her rents into his own pouch and demanding her hand in marriage.

"A widow," said the King reflectively, stroking his beard and wagging his head. "A beautiful widow, I presume—and as virtuous as beautiful, of course."

"The most beautiful lady in the land, Sir King!" cried the dwarf.

"Sir King?" queried Torrice. "Hah! So you know me, my friend! We have met before, is that it?"

"Nay, Your Kingship, but a poor old palmer home from a pilgrimage to Jerusalem visited us but a few hours since, and informed my mistress of the approach of the great King Torrice of Har and his noble Irish grandson Sir Lorn, and assured her that now her troubles were ended," replied the manikin.

Torrice looked at Lorn in consternation. He placed a shaking hand on the other's mailed thigh.

"You hear that, dear lad? Merlin—just as I expected! But he'll not make monkeys of us—to pluck his chestnuts out of fires. I'll wrench off those cursed shoes with my bare hands first! We'll turn now, and ride hard the other way."

The young knight said, "Yes sir," but immediately acted contrarily. Instead of wheeling Bahram, he stooped from his saddle and extended a hand downward to the dwarf, who seized it and was up behind him quick as a wink; and next moment all six horses were trotting forward again, with the great white stallion leading, with the King's tall gray—despite the King's protests—pressing him close.

The forest fell back on either hand, and they rode between ditches and hedges, green meadows and fields of young wheat and barley.

"Not so fast, young lord," cautioned the messenger. "Your great horse may need all his wind in a little while."

Lorn slowed the stallion's pace to a walk, and the rest slowed as well.

"I fear we'll pay dearly yet for our new shoes," said the King.

"But this is in the true spirit of our quest, sir—to succor distressed ladies and damosels," Lorn answered, with unusual animation in voice and eye. "How better can we discover what we are questing for, dear sir—whatever that is?"

"The Soul of Beauty," said his grandfather. "In her true and imperishable shape! But at that time I believed myself to be imperishable too. But never mind that now. You are right, dear lad—the quest is the thing; and the higher and harder it is, the more honor to the quester, win or lose. But I'd feel happier about this if Merlin hadn't a finger in it."

They came to the brow of a hill and looked down upon a wide and verdant vale. There was a little river with a red mill, a great water wheel, and a pond lively with fat ducks. There were cornlands and grasslands; orchards of apple, pear, and plum; hop gardens which foretold brown ale; little gardens of sage and thyme and savory foretelling well-stuffed ducks and capons and Michaelmas geese spitted and roasting to a turn; thatched roofs of farmsteads; and in the midst of all, the slated roofs, timber walls, and stone tower of a great manor house. They drew rein and gazed at the fair prospect.

"What is it called?" asked King Torrice.

"Joyous Vale," the dwarf replied in a pathetic voice. "It was named in a happier time than now, Your Kingship," he added with a sigh.

"And where is your grievous tyrant?" asked the King.

"His pavilion is behind that screen of willows beyond

the ford there; but he will show himself at the sound of a horn," said the dwarf.

Torrice stroked his beard and said: "As we have come thus far at Merlin's whim, we may as well see this thing through of our own will and in our own way. Peter, you have a horn. But just a moment, if you please. Lorn, the fellow is yours. If there is another, I'll attend to him. If there are more—" he smiled kindly at each of the squires in turn "—we'll have a proper ding-dong set-to, all for one and one for all. And now the horn, friend Peter."

It was already at Peter's lips; and he blew as if he would split it and his cheeks too. The echoes were still flying when a tall and wide figure in a blue robe appeared from behind the willows, stared, shook a fist, and retreated from view.

"That is Sir Drecker, the false knight," said the dwarf. "He has a comrade as knavish as himself, but not so large, called Sir Barl, and four stout fellows who are readier with knives than swords. If they are all in camp now, Sir Drecker will soon reappear in full force; but if his rogues are tax-collecting and looting cupboards around about, Your Kingship will not have to do with him yet awhile, for he will avoid contact until he has a sure advantage."

"D'ye say so, Master Manikin!" cried the King, snapping his eyes and bristling his whiskers. "Then you don't know me and my grandson, nor these two gentlemen our squires, nor, for that matter, these two grooms neither! We'll hunt him like a red pig! We'll exterminate him and his dirty marauders like rats in a granary!"

The dwarf smiled slyly, well pleased with the old King's temper. Sir Lorn, gazing fixedly at the willows beyond the little river, did not speak, but his nostrils quivered and his lips were parted expectantly. The horses stood with tossing heads and pricking ears.

"Here they come!" cried the dwarf.

Two knights on great black horses came slowly into view from the screen of willows. Their vizors were closed and their shields dressed before them, but their spears were still at the carry, cocked straight up. They wheeled and drew rein above the ford.

"They have chosen their ground," said the dwarf.

"And very prettily—if they think we are fools enough to

go charging down and through and up at them like mad bulls," jeered the King. "But where are the others?" he asked.

"Hiding under the bank, sir, among the osiers, depend upon it, Sir King—just in case their knives are needed," said the little man in green.

Torrice jeered again.

"In silk and fur-lined slippers I am one of the world's most artless fools, but in leather and iron I am quite another person," he told them. "Just as I have acquired all the skills of knightly combat, even so have I learned all the answers to the cowardly tricks of such scoundrels as these: by the hard way. Now give me your attention."

Chapter Three
FIVE DIE, BUT ONE RIDES AWAY

Torrice and Lorn rode down to the ford at a hand-gallop, with closed vizors, dressed shields, and leveled spears; and the oppressors of the lady of the manor laughed derisively within their helmets, for now they would have nothing to do but push the witless intruders back into the river, men and horses together, as they scrambled, blown and off balance, to the top of the bank. But it did not happen just so. The false knights moved forward easily to the sounds of splashing and the clanging of iron on stones down there below their line of vision; but when nothing appeared at the top of the bank—no head of horse, no plume-topped casque, no wobbling spear-point—they drew rein. Now all was silent down there. And now the two squires of the intrusive knights came on at a hand-gallop, and clattered down to the ford and so from view; and silence reigned again.

Sir Drecker felt a chill of misgiving. He cursed, but uncertainly, and ordered his companion to advance until he could see what was going on under the bank. Instead of obeying, Sir Barl uttered a warning cry and pointed a hand. Drecker looked and saw a dismounted knight straightening himself at the top of the bank some ten spear-lengths to his left. Drecker laughed, for the advantage of horse and spear and shield was all his. He wheeled his great charger; but not even a good horse can be jumped to full gallop from a standing start, however deep the spurring. In this case, the spurring was too deep. The horse came on crookedly, with rebellious plunges. Sir Lorn moved suddenly in every muscle, and his sword whirled and bit the shaft of the spear clean through. Lorn dropped his sword then, and laid hold of the tyrant with both hands and dragged him from the lurching saddle. He knelt to unlatch the tyrant's helmet.

"Mercy!" screamed Drecker; and he straightway made a prayer pitiful enough to soften a heart of stone.

Lorn stayed his hand, but the weakening of his purpose was due to disgust, not pity.

"Faugh!" he cried; and he rose from his knees and booted Drecker's iron-clad ribs with an iron toe.

He stood straight and looked around him. He saw King Torrice come up from the ford on his venerable gray, moving slowly but with leveled lance, and ride at Sir Barl, who was ready and riding hard. Lorn's heart misgave him for a moment, but recovered as quickly when Barl's horse went clean out from under its master and galloped away, leaving that unhandy rogue grassed beneath a split shield and a punctured breastplate. Now he remembered the rogue Drecker, but only to see him up and running and already ten yards off. And now his white stallion Bahram topped the bank within a few paces of him, swung his great head and glowing eyes to survey the field, snorted like a dragon, and went in thunderous pursuit of Sir Drecker.

After one backward glance, the tyrant went faster than any knight in full harness had ever before gone on his own unaided legs. He fled toward his own horse, which stood at no great distance. He would make it, even though the white stallion should continue to gain a yard on him at every earth-jarring bound. He would just make it, with nothing to spare—but once in his saddle, he would beat the devil off with his mace. He saw the mace, short-hafted and spike-headed, where it awaited his hand on the saddlebow; and it held his agonized gaze, and spurred him to the utmost cruel fury of effort, like a bright star of salvation. Now! One more wrench of muscles, nerves, and heart, and he would be safe! He flung himself at the saddle, touched it with outflung hands—*and the black horse swerved.* Screaming like a snared rabbit, he fell flat on his vizored face.

Sir Lorn, who had stood staring like one entranced, shook off a mailed glove, thrust two fingers into his mouth, and whistled like a kelpie. The great stallion clamped all four hooves to earth, tearing and uprolling the sod before him, and stayed his course a hand's-breadth short of his quarry. He stood uncertain, tossing and swinging his head and clashing bared teeth; but at a second shrill blast, he wheeled and trotted back to his master. Lorn patted his neck and was about to mount, but was checked by King Torrice.

"Too late," said Torrice, pointing.

Sir Lorn looked and saw the scoundrel whom he had spared twice up on his strong horse and in full flight, across meadow and cornland, toward the nearest edge of forest.

"Why did you let him go, dear lad?"

Lorn looked apologetically at his grandfather, who was afoot only a pace away, with the old gray's reins in his hand.

"A false knight," continued Torrice mildly. "Murderer, torturer, infanticide, seducer, traducer, and common thief, according to the manikin Joseph. He would be better dead."

"I'm sorry," Lorn muttered with a red face. "Had he cursed me, or had he turned on Bahram—but no, he squealed for mercy. Mice have more manhood. I stayed my hand, and Bahram's hooves, for very shame—shame of all creatures made by Almighty God in His own image."

The old man was startled, distressed, and confused. For all his ding-dong years of unconventional, even crazy questing, and his competence in the making of romaunts and rondels, he was still, at heart and head, a gentleman of the old school rather than a philosopher.

"Never mind it, dear lad!" he cried hurriedly. "There's no great harm done, I dare say. But your squire could have used that big horse very well. We have five remounts, however; and the least of them is bigger than a hackney. All proper warhorses. I shall shift my saddle to the late Sir Barl's big courser, and so let faithful old Clarence here travel light from now on. We have done very well. Five dead rogues and five quick horses, and not a scratch taken."

"And the blackest rogue and the biggest horse gone

clean away!" moaned Sir Lorn. "But never again—no matter how so he may squeal and pray like a soul in torment!" he cried.

They crossed the little river and went behind the willows and took possession of the pavilions and everything else that they found there. The false knight who had fallen to King Torrice's spear, and the four knaves who had fallen to the swords and knives of squires Peter and Gervis and grooms Goggin and Billikin, were buried deep, and without benefit of clergy, by a party of rejoicing yokels.

The dwarf, whose name was Joseph, ran forth and back between manor house and camp, whistling in high spirits. He was a lively little man of uncertain age, flickering eyes, and a sly smile. He fetched wine and cakes, with the Lady Clara's compliments and thanks, and took back King Torrice's poetical expressions of devotion. He fetched jellies and sweetmeats, and a pretty message from the lady to the import that she had made them with her own hands of the very last of her store of honey and other such ingredients: whereupon the King sent back to her, by the two squires in their best suits of velvet and Turkic leather, his last crock of brandied peaches, a cup of silver gilt, and a necklace of French workmanship.

The squires went side by side, with Joseph strutting importantly before. Master Peter carried the crock, which was considered by King Torrice as the senior gift, and Master Gervis carried the cup and necklace. Peter did not like the mission.

"Much more of this tomfoolery, and by Sir Michael and Sir George, I cast my new gentility like a snake his old skin and go back to my currycombs!" he muttered to his companion, as they marched along the most direct path to the great house.

Gervis laughed at him. Gervis had been born and bred to this sort of thing, and liked it.

"Then the more fool you, my Peterkin!" replied Gervis. "There would be no gentility but for the thing this mission of ours is a token of. Without it, chivalry would be naught but dust and sweat and spilled blood and broken teeth; and if bruises and empty bellies and foundered horses were the only rewards for questing, how long would knights-errant continue to ride? Our royal old Torrice prates of the Soul of Beauty, but it's the soft eyes and red lips which beset his ways that have withheld him all these years from the softest armchair in the biggest castle of Har. And for young Lorn—do you think he rides only for love of weary marches and hard knocks? Nay, nay, my Peterkin! He seeks that which he can neither remember nor forget. The Soul of Beauty? Not so! The eyes and lips and hands and tender breast of a damosel he knew are his quest: and that she happened to be a heartless witch as well as an enchanting companion is his sad misfortune."

"I've had neither time nor opportunity for such plays, and no more acquaintance with elegant damosels than with luring witches," said Peter gruffly.

"But you have bussed goose girls behind haycocks," said Gervis, and as Peter ignored this, he added: "Goose girl or damosel or Queen Mab herself, the only difference between them are rosewater and moonshine. They all ply the same arts: otherwise, there would be no more chivalry in the courts of Camelot and Carleon than in forests of red swine."

"A pox on it!" muttered Peter.

People of all ages and several conditions gathered about their path from every direction. There were wobbly gaffers and gammers, and able-bodied men and women, and youths and wenches, and toddlers and babes in arms. Only a few wore the bronze collars of serfs, but all appeared to be of the humblest sorts of peasantry—plowmen and herds-men and ditchers, without a yeoman or steward among them, nor even a smith. All stared curiously and hopefully, yet fearfully, at the two squires, though they bore gifts in their hands and had only short ornamental daggers at their belts.

"Bah!" exclaimed Peter; whereat the nearer members of the crowd cringed backward as if from a whip.

"Are they sheep?" he continued, but less emphatically. "The tyrants were but six—and right here I see enough brawn to overcome a dozen such."

Joseph turned his head and replied, with a rueful grimace:

"You say truth, fair sir: but lacking a master, muscly brawn has no more fight in it than clods of earth. Sir Gayling and his squire were long past their physical prime;

nor had they ever been notable cavaliers, but bookmen and
stargazers and alchemists. They were murdered in my
lady's rose garden by the base knight Drecker—spitted like
larks, and as easily; and the high steward and Tom
Bowman the head forester—old gentlemen both—were
waylaid and done to death in the North Wood; and the
miller, a masterful man, was slain trickily in his mill by
the other dastard knight; and their six knaves set upon
Ned Smith working late at his anvil, and slew him; and
after that, the four that had come alive out of the smithy,
murdered three farmers and a master cheesewright in
their beds."

"Weren't there any men about the house—butlers and
the like?" asked Peter. "Scullions? Grooms and gardeners?"

"All too old," said Joseph. "Boyhood companions of
poor Sir Gayling, most of them."

"A dozen old men hobbling on sticks, or old women
even, would have served to chase off Drecker and his
rogues," said Gervis. "Better still, a mixed force. I can see it
in my mind's eye: the old lady herself, up on her palfrey,
leading a host armed with crutches and distaffs against the
invaders. That would have confounded them, and saved us
the trouble of killing them."

He chuckled at the conceit, then sighed. Being young
and romantic, he had hoped for something more amusing
than the relict and household of a doddering old philosopher. The dwarf's only answer was a slow, peculiar smile.
And so they passed through the wide gate and were met in
the courtyard by an ancient major-domo and two old
lackeys. After having names and style and mission shouted
into his left ear by Joseph, the major-domo, leaning on his
staff of office, led the squires into the great hall.

Chapter Four
DAME CLARA ENTERTAINS HER CHAMPIONS

The squires were gone a long time on that errand: fully
two hours, by King Torrice's impatient reckoning.

"So here you are at last!" the King exclaimed with a
poor effort at severity. "I began to fear that Merlin had waylaid you in the guise of a distressed damosel. Now what of
your visit, lads? Were my poor gifts well received? And

what is your opinion of the poor lady, and of the situation generally? The late Sir Gayling, I gather, devoted his time to stargazing and kindred impractical pursuits, with the result that his affairs were in a sad way even before his foul murder. The manikin has hinted as much, at least, in his own elusive manner. But even so, we have no time to administer the estate of every distressed person who receives our chivalrous services. We are knights-errant, not lawyers or magistrates. Have I neglected my own earthly interests all my life—the one score baronies and five score manors of my Kingdom of Har—to concern myself, at this late day, with a stranger's petty problems of lost rents and ravished cheeselofts? Not so, by my halidom!

"I am sorry for the poor old dame, of course; but we have already done our knightly duty by her. If she will accept a few hundred crowns, she is welcome to them. But we must be on our way again by noon tomorrow, without fail. Now tell me your opinion of this Lady Clara, my lads. Her messages have been prettily worded—but her manikin Joseph is a clever fellow, I suspect."

Gervis slanted a glance at Peter, but the senior squire continued to look straight to his front.

"Yes, sir," said Gervis. "Very clever. I mean very pretty. That's to say, the lady was very polite. And she sent another message to Your Highness—and Sir Lorn—and it includes Peter and me too. It is an invitation to supper this evening."

Torrice sighed.

"Supper with a mourning widow," he muttered. "Do you know, dear lads," he went on in a better voice, "I fear I took a strain in the spitting of that rogue Barl. It looked easy—but the fact is, I'm a shade past my physical prime. A wrench when the full weight of man and horse was arrested by my point, you understand. A wrench of the back, which has already extended upward to the neck—a thing not to be disregarded, especially at my age. I have seen young knights incapacitated for days by just such wrenches. I shall stop here and rub my neck with tallow. See—I can hardly turn my head. And I am sure that my company would be of no more comfort to the bereaved chatelaine than her tears and moans would be to me. With a grandson and two squires to represent me at the supper table, I shall rest here on my cot with an easy conscience, no matter how uneasy a neck."

Again Gervis slanted a glance at Peter; and this time it was returned.

"Then we may go, sir?" cried Gervis, joyously.

Torrice regarded him with raised brows.

"It is the wine, sir," said Peter. "Gervis enjoys his cup. Dame Clara is very hospitable. We have tasted her wine already, sir. Wines, I should say—various but all rare. The despoilers did not get into the cellar. Old Sir Gayling's father was a collector of vintages from many lands, but Sir Gayling drank only milk and whey, it seems. And the lady said that she would produce even rarer vintages at supper than those already tasted by Gervis and me. And the butler told me there will be a lark-and-pigeon pie for supper."

"And strawberries and a syllabub," said Gervis.

"Say you so?" murmured the King; and he bent his brows and stroked his whiskers consideringly. "Poor lady! She might take it to heart, as an affront—my refusal of her hospitality. I don't want to hurt her feelings, but neither do I want her or any woman to think me discourteous, which she might if I excused myself on the plea of a crick in the neck. So, on second thoughts and for our common credit in the poor dame's eyes, I shall go—and grin and bear it."

Sir Lorn, who had lain flat and motionless and silent on a cot throughout the conversation, now swung his feet to the ground and sat up and spoke in a dull voice.

"I'll stay here. The poor lady owes me nothing at all—neither supper nor thanks."

"Nonsense!" his grandfather protested. "You pulled down the biggest of them all—and you afoot! No champion in Arthur Pendragon's train could have done it better, my dear boy."

"And to what end, sir?" Lorn muttered. "I pulled down the biggest rogue from the biggest horse—and they are gone unscathed, man and horse! But your rogue, and all the rest of them, are buried deep, and their good horses are ours. Peter and Gervis bloodied their swords, and the grooms their knives. Only I failed in duty. I'll stop right here, sir, by your leave."

But after half an hour of argument—in which Gervis was almost as voluble as the King, and even Peter grumbled

and swore in support of the majority argument—Sir Lorn
gave in.

Joseph reappeared at the pavilion to escort the guests
to the manor house. The dwarf was still in green, but now
of silk and velvet instead of wool. The knights and squires
were sumptuously garbed. Having arrayed himself as if for
a royal feast at Westminster or the court of Camelot, the
King had insisted that Lorn and the squires should help
themselves to what remained of his extensive wardrobe. Sir
Lorn and Peter had accepted no more of this additional
finery than could be politely avoided, but young Gervis had
taken full advantage of the opportunity. They made the
short passage from pavilion to great house on foot, with
Joseph strutting before. People came running.

"Mark His Kingship's mortal great whiskers with more
hair in them than three horses' tails!" cackled a toothless
gaffer.

"I vow they be all kings an' princes," shrilled a woman.

A young man cried: "It was him—the old gentleman—
as run a spear through Sir Barl—through shield an' mail
an' breastbone—like skewer through duckling."

Another cried: "And I see the big young Prince there
pull Sir Drecker to earth like a sack of corn an' set dagger
to gullet—an' Sir Drecker get up an' run an' ride away with
his head half cut off."

"Not so!" cried the first. "I see that too, but not like that,
Dickon Cowherd. I was up in the pollard willow. I see the
Prince spare his gullet, an' kick his ribs, an'—"

"Mind your manners, you louts!" screamed the dwarf,
with a baleful glare around and a hand at his belt.

It was still daylight without, but the torches flared and
smoked in the great hall. The tottering major-domo met
King Torrice and his companions at the threshold and led
them within. Joseph ran ahead and disappeared. The
guests advanced slowly on the heels of the house steward.
The King looked about him alertly, narrowing his eyes
against the wavering reds and blacks of flames and shadows. He observed trophies of arms and the chase on the
wall—weapons of chivalry and venery of an earlier time;
and moth-eaten boars' heads with upthrust tusks; and
pale skulls and horns of stags and wild bulls, and one even

of a unicorn; and toothy masks of wolves, badgers, wild-cats, otters, and a dragon; but though he gave the green fangs and leathery forked tongue of the dragon a second glance—an inferior specimen, in his opinion, obviously—his concern was for the weapons.

He stepped twice from his place in the slow procession to jiggle antique swords in their sheaths, and nodded at finding that they would come clear easily, despite the dust of idle years. He glanced and smiled meaningly at his grandson and over a shoulder at the squires. Peter and Gervis grinned and nodded back at him. Good old Torrice! Always the gentleman! He would as lief and as likely be seen consorting with murderers as wearing arms and armor—little begemmed daggers are but table-gear—when supping with ladies; but to ascertain the whereabouts of the nearest weapons, just in case of accident, was no breach of etiquette.

The major-domo drew aside a curtain of arras and stood aside with it, bowing low. The King and Sir Lorn halted and blinked, and the squires halted at their heels and blinked past their shoulders. For a moment, all their eyes were dazed by the shimmer and shine of tapers. For a moment it seemed to them that the place was full of slender, pointed yellow flames, and gleams and sparkles of fire from metal and crystal.

"Welcome, King Torrice," said a lilting voice. "Welcome, Sir Lorn. Welcome again, friends Peter and Gervis."

And now they saw her, but vaguely and glimmeringly at first, like a face and form materializing from the sheen and soft radiance about her, but more clearly as she approached, and definitely when she stood within a small step of the King and extended a hand.

"This—forgive me, my dear! Your Ladyship must try to excuse me—forgive me—my confusion—surprise," he stammered.

"You are forgiven," she murmured, and laughed softly.

He sank on one knee, took the proffered hand lightly and pressed his lips gallantly to the bejeweled fingers, while his twirling wits cried a warning between his ears:

This isn't real—nor right! More devilment of Merlin's, this—or worse! Have a care, old fool!

But he was smiling blandly when he straightened his

knees and released her hand, though he staggered slightly and blinked again.

Now the lady gazed at Lorn, and he stared back at her. She smiled a little with her bright, soft mouth; and her eyes, whatever their color in honest sunlight—were black and warm and limpid. But his eyes were clouded strangely, and his lips unsmiling. She put out her hand shyly and uttered a tender whisper of soft laughter. Then he knelt lightly, took and kissed her fingers, and rose lightly to his feet again—but to sway and stagger for a moment, and steady himself with a fumbling hand on the King's shoulder. Squire Peter saluted the lady's hand without kneeling to it, but his face and the back of his leathery neck were red as fire. Squire Gervis put even the King's courtly gesture to shame, and kept his lips on the jeweled and scented fingers so long that he might well have been testing the pearls in the rings.

The guests found themselves at table: but how this came about, not one of the four could have told you. It was a round table, and not large. It was spread with damask as white and bright as snow, and illuminated by scores of beeswax tapers in tall, branched sticks of silver; and there were other clusters of tapers in sconces on the walls. Stemmed cups of foreign crystal as fragile as bubbles to the eye, and vessels of gold and silver, some of them studded with gems, glowed and glinted like flowers and stars. Behind one chair stood the major-domo in his robes of office, with the manikin beside him, and behind each of the others stood an ancient footman in a livery of murrey and pea-green laced with tarnished silver. There were only five chairs. There was but the one lady present. The King and Peter were on her right, and Sir Lorn on her left—but thanks to the smallness and shape of the table, none was far removed from her. In fact, the squires could gaze at their ease, whereas their masters had to turn their heads slightly to look at her.

"My companion, the Damosel Mary, is indisposed, but hopes to join us later, with her harp," the lady informed them all, but with her gaze and smile on the King.

Torrice acknowledged the information with a feeble smirk. He was still mazed. He had braced himself to meet the lachrymose gratitude of a bereaved dame of advanced

age, and heartbreaking pleas for further relief. And what
had he met? Could this be the widow of a doddering old
stargazer? He had seen, and had to do with, beauties in
every court in Christendom, and dames and damosels of
devastating charms in many sylvan bowers and remote
castles, and—or was this but vain thinking?—ladies whose
enchantments were more than human, without losing his
freedom for long at a time. And to lose it now! His very soul,
at last! Nay, it could not be! Not his free and questing soul!
He would not believe it. He glanced past her, at his grandson. Lorn was staring fixedly to his front, with a pale face.
Torrice glanced farther, at young Gervis, who was regarding their hostess with bright-eyed, pink-faced, and raptur-
ous ardor. He looked at Peter, hoping that his practical,
unvisionary, tough ex-groom at least would be unaffected
by this thing which had already enmeshed his gentler companions. But not so! That matter-of-fact young man was
gaping even more ardently than Gervis.

Yellow wine was poured. It made giant topazes of the
cups of crystal. The lark-and-pigeon pie was served. The
King had set out with a fine appetite, but where was it
now? He had only a thirst now. He drained his cup. It was
refilled, and so he emptied it again. The squires also had
lost their appetites and retained their thirsts. But the
young knight, it seemed had lost both. Of the five, only the
lady comported herself without sign of mental or emotional
disturbance. She sipped the yellow wine occasionally and
composedly, but not—so Torrice observed excitedly—from
a bubble of rare glass, but from the little silver-gilt cup of
his giving.

And when he saw, at that incomparable white throat,
the modest necklace which he had sent to her, a confusion of shame and exultation all but suffocated him. Why
had he not sent his finest remaining string of emeralds,
or of diamonds or rubies, or brought it in his pouch? Why
had he ever distributed such things—priceless treasures
from the secret and immemorial treasure chest of Har—to
the right and the left up and down the world and over the
years? He moaned at the thought of the wasted expenditures of his lifelong quest. No exception could be taken to
the quest itself, as he had proved on the bodies of hundreds with spear and sword: but it graveled him now to

recall, however mistily in most instances, the innumerable necks and bosoms of beauties—ay, and the wrists and fingers—adorned by him on his long and crooked road to Beauty herself.

For he could not doubt he had found her—Beauty herself, soul and body in one—though this astounding realization was tinged with a fearful reluctance and a sense of weariness that was almost of despair. His crystal cup was shining like a topaz again. He drained it once more and sighed profoundly. So this was the end of the high quest! And the achievement was as dust and ashes in his heart and mouth—in the heart and mouth of an old man. For Merlin had destroyed his dream of immortal manhood. Now he mourned the fact that his quest had not lasted out his mortal life. Now he knew that, however far he might ride in the months or years remaining to him, the marvel he had sought would lie behind him, found by him, but not for him to grasp.

His crystal cup glowed again, but now redly like a great ruby. He drained it. He turned his head and met her questioning gaze. Or was it questioning? Or telling? Whichever—whatever—it held his own gaze fast.

"Who are you?" he asked; and his voice sounded strange to him, and from far away.

She whispered, leaning a little to him and smiling: "I am the lady of the manor."

He said: "You are very young, and Sir Gayling was old—but not so old as I."

She veiled her eyes and unveiled them instantly, even brighter, and deeper, and kinder than before.

"You are not old like poor Gayling. He was so old that only the stars were old enough for him to love. But I know about you, King Torrice of Har, who have kept a young heart without the help of sorcery, on a high quest. Oh, a mad quest—of pleasure and excitement and change: but you called it noble, and by a noble name—the Quest of the Soul of Beauty."

"It is noble," he protested, but weakly. He tried to avoid her gaze, but in vain.

"I am a poet too, not only a knight-at-arms, not only a lord of lands," he went on confusedly. "Beauty! I have sought her at peril of limb and life, at cost of blood and treasure. The Soul of Beauty. I have made songs to her: the best in all Christendom. They have been stolen and sung by generations of jinking troubadours. But I am not the Lord God, nor Archangel Michael, nor even a sneaking wizard, to know soul from body at a glance. There was Lorn's grandmother. There was nothing of beauty there deeper than her skin. And the Princess of Castile, with—but what matter now? It was long ago."

"And now you have given up," she sighed, and withdrew her gaze.

He saw that the cup of crystal had become a glowing ruby again; and again he turned it back to a bubble of air.

"No, I have found you," he muttered. "Beauty! Soul and body in one. And mortal. And I am mortal—but old—as old as Merlin; but not ageless, like that warlock. There is nothing now—the quest ended—only the hope for a quick end left—and God's mercy!"

She looked at him. His head drooped, and he stared down at his trencher with unseeing, desolated eyes. She glanced to her left. The young knight, staring fixedly at a candle flame, paid no heed. She smiled at the squires, both of whom were regarding her ardently. She turned back to the old King.

"I know all about you and your quest, and the Irish grandson and the trick Merlin played you, long ago, in the guise of a hag in a red cloak," she said.

"The old palmer told you," he muttered. "He was Merlin."

She laughed softly.

"Yes, he was that warlock, that poor palmer. Do you think I did not know? Or that I did not know about you without any help from him? Look at me."

He looked at her. She smiled and touched his nearer wrist with light fingertips.

"Do you see that for which you have quested and bled, and kissed and ridden away from, all your long, mad life?"

He nodded and moaned.

"Nay, do not grieve, dear Torrice. You are old, 'tis true—but the beauty you quested for is old too. And I am old too."

"Are you? What are you?" he gasped.

"Are you afraid of me—even if I am a sorceress?" she sighed.

Chapter Five
WAS IT SORCERY OR INSPIRATION?

It was late when the Lady Clara's guests returned to the pavilion beside the river and the willows. Joseph, who had guided them with a lanthorn, stopped only long enough to light a few tapers for them. King Torrice sat down heavily on the first couch he chanced to stumble against, and held his head with both hands. Peter and Gervis did likewise. Only Sir Lorn appeared to have the complete mastery of his legs.

"It was the wines—yellow and red and green," moaned the King.

"And pink," moaned Gervis.

"Pink? Nay, I saw no pink. What did you see, Lorn? Did you see a pink wine?"

"No, sir, only yellow—and I drank but two cups," mumbled the young knight, who stood steadily enough, but with a hand to his brow and his eyes burning in his pallid face.

"There were wines of every color," said Peter thickly, "and I drank them all—like one bewitched."

"And you're drunk!" Torrice cried fretfully. "You too, Gervis! Me too! But you, dear lad? You must be sober—on two cups."

"I don't know," muttered Lorn.

"You can't be otherwise, dear lad. Two cups. Tell me what you saw. Tell me of this Dame Clara. She looked very young to me. How did she look to you?"

"Yes, sir. Very young."

"And—ah!—comely?"

"Beautiful!" cried Gervis, springing to his feet, only to reseat himself as suddenly and clasp his head again.

Lorn nodded.

"And *you* found her beautiful, dear lad?"

Lorn nodded again. Squire Peter uttered a short, harsh note of despairing laughter.

"Why don't you say it?" he cried. "Drunk or sober, you could see she's beautiful! I could see she's beautiful, and I'm not afraid to say so—tell the world!—mauger my head! Me, stable-born! That lady's beautiful, I say! Rose of the world! Who says she isn't?"

"You are drunk, good Peter," said the King. "Calm yourself. My poor brains are jangled enough without your unmannerly howls. Nobody says she's not beautiful. I asked for a sober man's opinion, that's all."

Peter muttered an apology and hung his head.

"Sir, I'm not sober, but I want to say that I think as you do, Your Highness—Your Majesty," said young Gervis, speaking with care and a look of profound deliberation. "I think—my studied opinion, sir—she is everything you named her in your wonderful song."

"What's that?" cried King Torrice. "What song?"

"Your latest, sir—and most wonderful, in my humble opinion. The one you sang tonight."

"You're mad! I did not sing tonight. But hold! Or did I? Now that you mention it, I seem to—but no, I'd remember it—unless I was bewitched!"

"Gervis speaks truth," said Sir Lorn, gravely and sadly. "You sang tonight, sir; and it was a song I had never heard before, and the best I have ever heard. It was after the Damosel Mary played her harp and sang a few ditties."

The King protested that he knew nothing of it.

"Then you were bewitched in very truth," said his grandson. "For she made a great to-do with the biggest harp I ever saw."

"And a voice to match it," said Peter.

Torrice protested ignorance again, but uncertainly.

"And yet you left your seat and went to her and took the harp from her," said Gervis. "You must remember that, sir! Your eyes were wide open. And Lady Clara said to the damosel, who tried to push you away—and she was old enough to be Lady Clara's grandmother: 'Let him have it, Mary.' So she let Your Majesty have it, but with a scowl on her face. Then you made a song to Lady Clara. You sang like a flute, sir, and now and again like a trumpet, but mostly like a flute; all the while the harp sobbed and sighed and hummed like little breezes in a forest of pines. You called her Beauty and Desire, sunshine and moonlight and starshine, saint and enchantress, Love and Life and Immortality, goddess and witch, a rose and a dewdrop and a star, and by some heathenish names I had not heard before. And Lady Clara wept but did not hide her face, and smiled through her tears. And the ancient damosel covered her face with her hands, and so did Sir Lorn, and even Peter had to wipe his eyes."

The King turned a troubled, inquiring face to his grandson.

"It is the truth," said Sir Lorn grimly.

The King looked at Peter.

"It is Christ's truth," honest Peter told him, gruffly. "Nay, Satan's, more likely! You were bewitched and bedeviled, sir. No mortal man—not the best poet in the world—could make such a song else—nor any drink from this side heaven or hell!"

"Inspiration!" cried Torrice fretfully. "Must you bawl witchcraft and deviltry just because I make a good song? I'm a poet. Pure inspiration. But as I cannot recall it—song nor incident—not clearly . . . the wine may have something to do with it. But enough of this! Let me sleep now. We all need sleep."

"May I suggest, sir, that Duke Merlin bedeviled the wine?" ventured Gervis.

"Hah—that old trickster!" the King exclaimed. "What more likely—since he brought us here on his bedeviled horseshoes? He doesn't love me, that warlock! He first tricked me long ago, in the matter of an elixir. And today he stayed Lorn's dagger from Drecker's throat. And tonight those wines! We must be on our guard every moment, at every step. But now let me sleep!"

After a little while of grumbling and uneasy tossing, the dark pavilion was silent save for the old King's fitful and uneven snores, and the occasional sighs and moans of his companions. Every one of them suffered strange dreams. Torrice fought with a knight in black armor, both of them afoot in dry sand, until arms and legs ached with weariness; and his sword broke on the black helmet, but that same stroke brought the sable knight groveling in the sand; and when Torrice tore away the helmet—behold, the thing disclosed was a fleshless, eyeless skull! He had done battle with a dead man.

And Sir Lorn wandered about the margins of autumnal tarns and in desolate mountain gorges with red sunsets flaring at their far ends. And the squires pursued damosels who turned into hags in red cloaks, and creatures of mist and moonshine, and hedge goblins and young dragons, between their hands. All were dreams of ill omen, according to the best authorities; so it was fortunate that only illusive and elusive fragments remained with the dreamers when they woke. . . .

It was another fine summer morning. Sir Lorn, who had taken only two cups of the Lady Clara's yellow wine, was the first of the four cavaliers to wake. He went out from the pavilion softly and into a new world of level sunshine and dew-washed greenery. His eyes were clear, but his mind and heart were darkened by dream-shadows. As he looked about him, the shadows withdrew. He saw Goggin and Billikin busy among the horses; and he heard them too, for the lively fellows were whistling to match the birds in the willows and orchards. Observing the increase of the herd by the five big black chargers, yesterday flashed on his mind like pictures:

Five strange horses? Five instead of six! He alone had failed to contribute a good beast to the herd and a dead rogue to the common grave! Again he saw Drecker galloping off unscathed; and he blushed with shame. To blame the warlock Merlin did not occur to his honest mind. He blamed his own faint heart. To slay a man horsed and spear in hand, or afoot and sword in hand on even terms, had never distressed him greatly, for he had never—unless in that time of which he had no clear memory?—engaged to the death with any save tyrants and murderers and false knights of sorts; but to kill one beaten and disarmed and squealing for mercy, he lacked the required hardihood. He knew this, and felt guilt and shame. And then he thought of that old questing king-errant, his grandfather, asleep there in the pavilion behind him. He had seen that champion in six mortal combats, but never had he seen him put a disarmed and beaten foe to death.

So he thought less shamefully now of having spared that false knight.

Young Gervis issued from the pavilion and greeted his master with a merry face. Sir Lorn regarded him with surprise, having expected to see pallid cheeks and bleary eyes.

"It was fairy wine of a certainty, sir, for even if I had drunk as little last night as you did, I swear I'd feel no brighter than I do," babbled the squire. "And I pray the same for the King and Peter. I have suffered some horrid dreams—but they have fled already, glory be to the holy saints! And now to bathe and shave, sir."

"Shave what?" Lorn asked gravely.

"I have numerous sprouts, sir," Gervis informed him proudly: "and 'tis a full sennight since I last laid steel to them. And may I venture to suggest that a touch of the razor might become you as well, sir; for I seem to remember having noticed something last night—and that by the dazzle of tapers. We may meet her again—the lady of the manor, that is to say!—at any moment; and in broad daylight, I hope. That's to say, I hope the King doesn't intend to ride away without seeing her again."

Lorn fingered his chin and cheeks thoughtfully, and puckered his brow, before he replied:

"I hope not. He can't do that. She—these defenseless people—are still in peril. It is my fault, for letting Drecker escape. So it is my duty to remain till all danger from Drecker is past. He will see that, at a word from me—my grandfather will. And I think you are right about my face. But my razor is duller than a hedger's hook."

"You may use mine. It is of Damascus steel and honed to a whisper. Come down to the river, sir, and we'll both use it."

So they went down to a screened pool in the river and bathed and shaved. They were joined there by Peter, who raised his eyebrows for a moment in acknowledgment of their smooth faces, but reported matter-of-factly that he had inspected the horse-lines and found all correct.

"The shoes?" murmured Lorn.

"Every shoe still firm in its place," Peter assured him.

"Is the King awake yet?" asked Lorn.

"He was combing essence of lavender into his beard when I saw him last," said Peter.

Gervis laughed and said: "A dash of the same, and a touch of the razor, would not be amiss with you, my Peterkin."

Peter nodded, stepped close to his fellow squire, took the razor of Damascus from unresisting fingers, and a little vial of crystal from Gervis' wallet with his other hand, and knelt and stooped to the mirror of the pool—all without a word or a smile. Merry young Gervis laughed again.

"But that's not lavender, my Peterkin! 'Tis essence of laylock.

"Anything will serve but essence of horse," muttered Peter.

Gervis winked at Sir Lorn.

"There's sorcery in it, by my halidom!" he cried, and laughed again. "And sorcery more potent than any of old Duke Merlin's hocus-pocus. When did our Peterkin ever before prefer lavender or laylock to honest horse?"

"I don't agree with you," Lorn said gravely. "I think all this babbling of witchcraft is childish—in this case. It is all quite human and natural—especially for Peter to become more particular about his toilet, no matter how suddenly. As for your fairy wine—it was good wine, pure and old, that's all. There's no sorcery here."

"I but joked, sir," Gervis replied. "But you cannot deny enchantment. There was enchantment last night of more than the juice of earthy grapes, else how did the King come to make that song, and sing it like an angel, without knowing anything about it?"

"Inspiration—as he told us himself," said the knight; but his tone was more troubled than assured. "He is, in truth, a great poet. I admit that the wine he drank made him forget the performance when we told him of it last night—but I think we shall find that he can recall it now, and even the words and air of the song."

They returned to the pavilion, leaving Peter still splashing and scraping.

"Look there!" gasped Gervis, gripping his master's arm.

They stood and looked. The curtains of the pavilion's doorway were drawn back to right and left, and King Torrice sat smiling out at them across a table bright with napery and silver dishes and polished horns and flagons. Behind him stood the manikin Joseph and one of the ancient footmen.

"Fried trout and hot scones!" he cried. "Strawberries and clotted cream. Brown ale and dandelion wine. Lady Clara sent it over. Come and eat, dear lads. No time to spare. Where's Peter?"

"No time to spare?" Lorn echoed. "What d'ye mean, sir? You cannot possibly intend to take the road today, dear sir— and that parlous rogue I spared, foul Drecker, still at large?"

"Certainly not!" retorted the King, fretfully, with a quick change of countenance for the worse. "We recognize our responsibilities, I hope. I said nothing of taking to the road again." His merry smile flashed again. "We are to attend Lady Clara on a tour of inspection of her demesne, to see what damage it has suffered. She sent word of it with our breakfasts. Half-armor and swords. All six of us mounted."

Both Sir Lorn and Gervis looked their relief. They took their places at the table and ate and drank as if for a wager. Peter arrived, smelling like a spring garden, and with his face shining like a summer apple; and upon hearing the King's news, he sat down and fairly gobbled and guzzled.

They paraded in the forecourt of the great house within the hour. Sir Lorn was up on his white stallion, but the King rode the black charger from which he had so recently hurled the late Sir Barl. The squires were on black warhorses too, and the grooms Goggin and Billikin forked the squires' lively hackneys. All six wore breastplates and long swords, but there was not a helmet among them. The King's, Lorn's, Peter's, and Gervis' caps were of crimson velvet, and the grooms' were of leather. The gentlemen sported long feathers in theirs, the knights' fastened with gold brooches and the squires' with silver. The Lady Clara appeared from the gloom within and paused under the arch of the doorway, with the Damosel Mary, seemingly old enough to be her grandmother, blinking over her shoulder. The King and Sir Lorn and the squires came to earth and louted low, caps in hand, like one man. The lady blushed like a rose and curtseyed like a blowing daffodil. She was encased in samite of white and gold, and from the white wimple which framed her face soared a pointed hat like a steeple with veils of golden gauze floating about it like morning clouds.

"Our jennets were stabled beyond the wall—and carried off to the forest, saddles and all; so Mary and I must go afoot," she cried in pretty distress.

"Nay, our horses are at your service," the King told her. "Choose any two that take your fancy, my dear."

"Gramercy!" she laughed. "But the saddles?"

"Hah!" Torrice exclaimed; and he regarded the great war saddles with baffled looks.

Then Gervis spoke up, in dulcet tones.

"If I may venture a suggestion, Your Majesty and Your Ladyship, I suggest pillions. And may I add that this newly acquired steed of mine is as gentle and easy-gaited as a jennet for all his size and strength, and is therefore peculiarly suited to the task of carrying double."

Torrice eyed him dubiously, then turned a glance of doting inquiry upon Dame Clara.

"The very thing!" she cried, with a swift widening and half-veiling of her multicolored eyes; and she turned her head and called for two pillions.

(Lorn thought: I can't make out their color, even by daylight; and they are not always black by candlelight. Something with a sharp, hot edge stirred in his brain. Memory? A thin splinter of it from that lost time by which he was haunted night and day, and yet of which nothing remained to him save the sense of loss? He tried, fearfully yet hopefully, to remember. He racked brain and heart cruelly but in vain. He sighed.)

Two of the ancient footmen brought two pillions and followed their mistress and the Damosel Mary down the steps. Dame Clara, moving very slowly because of the attentions of King Torrice and the squires, inspected and seemed to consider each of the four chargers, and spared gentle glances even for the hackneys upon which Goggin and Billikin sat like seasoned men-at-arms.

"May I sit behind you?" she asked the King.

His eyes shone, and his lavender-scented whiskers rippled. He strapped a pillion to the back of his saddle with his own hands, mounted with but little apparent effort, leaned, and held down his right hand. A hand touched his, a foot touched his stirruped foot, and she came up to the pillion like a white bird. From that soft perch she pointed at Sir Lorn's saddle with her left hand, while holding fast to the King's belt with her right. And so it was that Damosel Mary had a higher seat than the lady of the manor, by half a hand. Lorn's face wore a polite smile which was entirely muscular. His eyes were blank. Gervis look dismally dashed, and Peter grinned derisively. As the little cavalcade moved off, the manikin Joseph leaped up behind Peter.

"What else would happen to me?" Peter grumbled.

"Worse might have happened to you, my friend," said the dwarf. "Would you liefer it was the big damosel gripping you about the middle, as she even now grips the young knight? You might do far worse than ride double with poor Joseph."

"I am glad to hear it, since I seem to have no choice in the matter," said the squire. "But will you be so kind as to tell me why?" he added.

"There are many reasons why," the dwarf replied. "One is, I was born with seven wits, whereas you and your grand friends have only five—and those somewhat deranged in the cases of your old king and your young knight. But I was born with seven, but at a sad cost to flesh and bone. If I had your stature, King Arthur Pendragon would be taking his orders from me."

"I believe it," said Peter, with mock solemnity. "I feel your power and see it in your eye, but I don't quite understand it. I never before met a person possessed with seven wits. Is it the power of knowledge or wisdom or cunning?"

"Of all three," the dwarf answered, complacently. "I know everything; I understand everything; and I can think as quick and crooked as any witch or wizard."

"In that case, you would know Duke Merlin if you saw him."

"Yes, it was that old warlock brought you here, though he pretended to be a holy palmer. But he didn't fool me. He drank two quarts of wine and took the road to Camelot. He said he was going to Tintagel, but I knew better."

"You are wonderful, Master Joseph. Now tell me why you and Merlin brought us to this place?"

"To rid the lady of her oppressors."

"So they are friends—your mistress and Merlin?"

After a moment's hesitation, Joseph said: "No, it was old Sir Gayling, the stargazer, who was Merlin's friend."

"And yet Sir Gayling was stabbed to death in a rose garden, while his friend the powerful magician played his hocus-pocus elsewhere," sneered Peter.

"As to that, my friend, I could enlighten you if I would, but I know without trying that it would be too much for your five poor wits," the dwarf replied, in a voice so insufferably supercilious that Peter was hard put to control an impulse to reach a hand behind him and brush the little man to the ground. "However," Joseph resumed, "I shall satisfy your curiosity concerning the Dame Clara."

But, at that very moment, King Torrice drew rein at a word from his passenger; whereupon Sir Lorn drew rein, and Peter drew rein, and the dwarf slid to the ground, and every rider drew rein. Peter and Gervis fairly flung themselves from their saddles in desperate competition for the honor of dismounting Dame Clara from the King's pillion. Gervis won. The lady descended to earth like a feather, and the King followed her down smartly.

All were down now save Sir Lorn and his passenger from the back of the mighty Bahram. The knight could not dismount in the orthodox manner while Damosel Mary remained up behind him; and he was not in the mood to sacrifice his own dignity, not to mention proud Bahram's, by quitting the saddle with a forward, instead of a backward, swing of the right leg. His grandfather and the squires were too intent upon Lady Clara to perceive his difficulty; and it was not until the dwarf had pinched both the squires, and Peter had come—however ungraciously—to his rescue, that he dismounted.

Afoot, they inspected a farmstead in which the farmer had been murdered and from which five beeves had been driven into the forest by the Drecker gang and there handed over to confederate but less daring outlaws, and a bag of silver pieces taken and pouched by that rogue knight himself. Next, they inspected a second farm from which a dairymaid and cheeses and barrels of ale had been carried off after the murder of a stubborn cowherd; and a third in which the master had been tickled with knives— he was still in bandages—until he had handed over all his life's hoardings of ducats and crowns. And all this was no more than a representative fraction of the villanies perpetrated by the scoundrel Drecker.

"I don't understand this," said King Torrice, who had suffered more footwork and more emotional strain than he could endure with manly resignation. "Are your people mice? Nay, for mice will fight. Then why didn't the rogues make a job of it, instead of only killing and thieving a little every here and there? Why didn't he put your own house and household to the torch and sword? Hah!—now I recall what the manikin told me—that the foul Drecker aspired to your hand!"

He leaned against his horse and clapped a hand to his

brow. The lady hung her head and touched a very small handkerchief to her eyes. Sir Lorn moved close to her; and if he thought, it was subconsciously. Without a word, and with a dazed, faraway look in his eyes, he laid a hand on her nearer arm and propelled and guided her, gently but firmly, a few paces aside to where his great white stallion stood watching them. King Torrice lowered his hand from his fretful brow and blinked after them, but before he could utter a word of inquiry or protest, his squire Peter spoke at his shoulder.

"Sir, I've but now heard it all from her dwarf. Let us mount and ride into the fields, and I'll tell you the whole story."

There was no argument. The King mounted with alacrity, though a trifle stiffly. He was eager to hear what trusty Peter had heard from the lady's dwarf, and even more eager to get his weight off his poor feet.

Chapter Six
The Dwarf Told Peter and Peter Told the King

The Dame Clara (so Peter told King Torrice) was one of four daughters of a gentleman of remote kinship with the late rich and star-struck old philosopher of Joyous Vale. The father, when young and single, had cut a dash in the train of old King Uther Pendragon for a few years, but had been cheated out of all his patrimony by certain fashionable companions; and too hot of head to retire from court gracefully, he had brawled with, and mortally wounded, one of the cheaters in the King's own hall; and so he had fled for his very life and not stayed his flight save to sleep, and to eat when he could find food, until he was across the Marches of Wales.

A Welsh chieftain of the lesser and wilder sort—not one of the nine princes—had befriended and practically adopted him; and so, in due course, he had married a beautiful daughter of the chieftain. Married, as single, they had continued to live with her family in her parental home, which was a confusion of stone and timber towers and halls, and bowers and byres, overlooking a glen of crofts and huts, and itself overhung by a great forest of oaks. Strange to say, the life had suited him better than it had his mountain-bred wife. This had not been so in the first year, but with the arrival of the first daughter, and increasingly so with the arrival of each of the following three, the mother had bemoaned the lack of social opportunities for young ladies in those parts. But the exiled courtier had laughed at her—for he preferred his present to his past and looked to the future with gusto. In hunting wolves and bears and wild boars, in occasional armed clashes with encroaching neighbors or invading savages, and in less frequent but even more exciting raids into the Marches under the banneret of his father-in-law and the banner of Prince Powys, he had found life very much to his taste and nothing to worry about. But he died in the course of one of those battles of the disputed Marches, leaving hundreds of mourners, chief of whom were his widow and four daughters.

Now for a jump of time and space to Sir Gayling of Joyous Vale. Hearing from a wandering soothsayer that the most knowledgeable of all living stargazers, and the one possessed of the finest astrolabe and cross-staff in the world, inhabited a high tower atop the highest mountain of Wales, Sir Gayling had set out to find him, accompanied by his squire and lifelong friend Master John of Yarrow (who was as old and almost as stargazy as himself) and a few servants. It was a most otherworldly and untraveled company, for the gentlemen had never before been farther afield than Salisbury, where both of them, as youths, had studied astrology and kindred sciences under the famous Friar Gamish; and the servants had never been out of the Vale.

But they went unmolested, day and night, league after league. Some took them for holy men, others for mental cases (and so equally under divine protection), and yet others for magicians or worse. Their innocence was their armor. Jinking thieves and all manner of roving, masterless knaves, shared the best of their stolen meats and drinks with them, and honest farmers and lords of castles alike entertained them honorably. They came into Wales in due course, unscathed and in good health, and Sir Gayling and Master John still keen in their pursuit of knowledge.

There they asked the way to the highest mountain in the world of everyone they met, and at every door, but the answers were mostly conflicting. One point which all their informants agreed upon, however, was that it was somewhere in Wales. In most cases, the person questioned simply pointed to the highest summit within his range of vision. Up and down, up and down and around, toiled the questers after stellar wisdom. They found the people hospitable but inconveniently scattered. They were glad when they came at last, after weeks of fruitless mountaineering, upon a narrow valley full of crofts. The crofters regaled them with strange and potent liquors and collops of venison, but it was not long before a little man in green came to them and requested them to follow him to his master.

It was the manikin Joseph himself; and his master was the father of the widow with four beautiful daughters. The chieftain was an old man by then, and the widowed daughter had silver in her black hair, and only one of the beautiful girls remained unmarried and at home. She was the youngest and most beautiful—and, as you may have guessed, her name was Clara. The travelers were so well treated that they almost lost sight of their reason for being so far from home; and when the mountain lord himself had assured them, after mental searchings, that he had never heard of an outstanding Welsh stargazer in all his life, nor of an astrolabe, whatever that might be, but could name the world's twenty greatest bards and harpers and ten greatest warriors, and all of them Welshmen, Sir Gayling decided to let the matter rest—and himself with it—for a few days. The cushion of the chair he sat in was softer than his saddle, and the bearskins underfoot did not cut and bruise like rocky mountain tracks.

Lapped in comfort, he drowsed while the widow told her romantic story, which was always in her heart and never far from her tongue. She began by telling him that her husband had been an English fugitive like himself, only larger and much younger. He protested sleepily that he was not a fugitive. She continued with a glowing description of her lamented partner, and a dramatic account of his career at King Uther's court, his justifiable slaying of a false friend in the royal presence, and his subsequent flight. Sir Gayling, who had heard rumors of an affair of the kind a long time ago, bestirred himself sufficiently to inquire as to the gentleman's name and style.

"Roland of Fenchurch, the Earl of Fenland's third son," the lady informed him proudly.

"I heard something of it at the time," he replied; and he went on, though reluctantly, for he was still drowsy, to say that the Fenland family was distantly related to him on the spindle side.

As the lady accepted this information in silence (a very busy silence, but he didn't know that), he thought no more of it till the following morning, when Master John told him that the widow had questioned him, John, exhaustively concerning Sir Gayling's life, condition, affairs, and establishment; and he confessed that he had answered her fully, though against his better judgment. The old squire was suspicious and uneasy, but the old knight laughed at him, saying that the lady's curiosity was perfectly natural. Even when his anxious friend suggested that she was contemplating a second English marriage, he refused to be alarmed. Days and nights passed, and ran into weeks— days of ease and good cheer, and nights in feather beds— so peacefully that Master John forgot his suspicions of the dame's intentions and both old stargazers forgot their mission. Nothing in the place was too good for them, and their servants and horses grew fat and frisky with idleness and high living.

But this idyllic time came to an end. One morning the widowed daughter of the chieftain and mother of the beautiful damosel requested an astonishing service of the knight. Addressing him as Cousin Gayling, and with a hand on his shoulder and a compelling gleam in her eyes, she advised him to set out for home within the week, so as to establish Clara comfortably before the first hard frosts. The stargazer could only gape at that: but when she added that Clara would prove to be the ideal wife for him, he cried out in agonized protest. She laughed at him kindly, even affectionately, and made known her plans to him patiently and with the utmost good humor, as if to a dull but beloved child. His continued protests became feebler and feebler, though no less agonized. The damosel herself was of no help to him. When he protested to her that she could not possibly want him for a husband, she contradicted him, politely but firmly.

Well, they were married by the domestic chaplain of

Prince Powys before many witnesses. The bride and her mother were radiant, the company was merry; but Sir Gayling and Master John were dazed beyond words. They set out for home with a formidable escort, to which the Prince and neighboring chiefs had contributed generously to assure them a safe passage of the Marches. Twenty leagues south of the border, the bulk of the escort turned about and withdrew. Only the bride and her grandfather, her mother, her harpist ex-governess the Damosel Mary, the family counselor Joseph, and a score of clansmen on mountain ponies remained in addition to the original English party. Forty leagues farther on, every Welsh heart save Dame Clara's, Damosel Mary's, and Joseph's was seized by irresistible and unreasoning nostalgia for the mountains and airs of home; and in a fit of mob panic, the old chief and the widow and their highland cavalry wheeled about and headed back on the long road to Wales.

The ladies were somewhat dashed by that, but Sir Gayling, who had feared that his mother-in-law intended to make of Joyous Vale her permanent abode, congratulated himself and Master John. . . . Two days later, they were joined by two cavaliers who introduced themselves as Sir Drecker and Sir Barl, knights-errant from King Arthur's court. Their manners were excellent, and they made themselves very entertaining; especially Sir Drecker, and he very particularly to Sir Gayling and Master John, to whom he declared a keen interest in astrology—and a lamentable ignorance of it.

From then onward all the way to Joyous Vale, the two old stargazers belabored their pupil's ears with stellar truths and mysteries. But the dwarf noted the furtive rovings and oblique glances of Drecker's small but lively eyes. Trust Joseph—by his own telling! He warned his mistress against the stranger, and received in return an enigmatic smile. His warning to Sir Gayling won a promise of consideration upon the proper drawing up and study of Sir Drecker's horoscope, which would require at least ten days. But Joseph continued to watch and suspect, wore a shirt of chain mail under his tunic, and added a short sword to his armament of daggers.

They reached Joyous Vale in safety, however, and found all as the astrologers had left it five months before,

save for a few natural deaths and those mostly of old age.
Dame Clara established herself and her ex-governess in
the best bedroom, and Sir Gayling and Master John
returned thankfully to their old quarters and neglected
telescope at the top of the tower and set to work on Sir
Drecker's horoscope. What might have happened if that
task had been completed is anybody's guess, for upon the
departure of the self-styled knights-errant within the week,
the astrologers laid it aside and forgot it in the pursuit of
more abstruse stellar secrets.

Winter came and passed uneventfully. Sir Gayling and
Master John were happy with their books and arguments,
and since philosophically accepting the rumored Welsh
astrologer and his peerless instrument as mere myths,
with their telescope too. Also, they became aware of
improvements in food and service, and the whole economy
and atmosphere of the place; and each confessed to
himself, though neither to the other, that the adventure
into Wales had been nothing worse than a loss of time.
April brought back Sir Drecker and Sir Barl. Sir Drecker's
original intention was (by Joseph's reckoning) to carry off
Lady Clara and the old knight's treasure chests, but he
changed it for the more ambitious plan of marrying the
lady and settling down as a lord of lands. The first step
toward his goal—the transforming of a wife to a widow—
was mere child's play for him, but then difficulties developed. The gates of the great house were closed and barred
against him. Accepting that as a purely provocative gesture
on the lady's part, he subdued the tenantry, murdering
and robbing and despoiling just enough to show her who
was master, and bided his time.

That is the story, as told (rather more than less) by the
Welsh manikin Joseph to the squire Peter and by said
Peter to King Torrice.

"It's a queer tale, but I've heard queerer," said the King.
"How old did you say she is?"

"I didn't say, but Joseph told me she will be eighteen
very soon," Peter answered.

"Eighteen or eight hundred," the King muttered. "If but
eighteen, how can she be what I believe her to be—the
achievement and the end of my quest?" He looked at Peter

keenly and added: "If that is the whole story, why has Merlin dragged us into the affair? He is not one to take all the trouble of conjuring up a forge and shoeing our horses just to save a distressed lady from a tyrant. But whatever and whoever she is, and whatever that old fox's game may be, we are committed to her protection."

He looked back at the farmyard from which he and his squire had come away and saw it empty. He turned the other way then, and looking widely over meadows and cornlands and orchards, saw the little cavalcade enter the outer court of the great house; and he sighed. Peter, who looked too and also saw that Lady Clara rode pillion with Sir Lorn, chuckled to see that Damosel Mary rode pillion with Gervis.

"This is no laughing matter," the King reproved mildly; and he added: "Have you forgotten that the rogue Drecker is at large?"

Peter replied that he had not forgotten Drecker's escape.

"Has it occurred to you that he will return some day, any day now, with all the cutthroats and robbers from forty leagues around at his heels?" demanded Torrice.

"It has, sir; but, knowing that you would bring the subject up in plenty of time for us to do something about it, I haven't worried over it, sir," replied Peter.

The King looked embarrassed and muttered: "I hope you are right, but I must confess that I had quite forgotten the peril we are in—not the rogue, but the menace of him—until now, God forgive me!"

Chapter Seven
The Lady Rides with a Hand on Sir Lorn's Sword-belt

The Lady Clara rode home on Sir Lorn's pillion, up on the great white stallion Bahram.

"King Torrice told me of your quest," she murmured.

He neither spoke in reply nor did he turn his head to glance at her. She murmured again, leaning a little closer to his apparently unresponsive back.

"But how can it be one and the same quest, if he searches for that which he has never known, and you for something you have known and lost?"

Lorn continued to gaze straight to his front in silence. The great warhorse's advance was very slow, despite much showy action. He tossed his head and plumed his silver tail; but high though he lifted each massive hoof in turn, it was only to set it down softly on practically the same spot of ground.

"You heard his song?" she murmured. "The things he called me? Poor old man!—it must have been the wine he drank. If I am a wicked old witch, how can I be the end of his quest? And yet he truly believes me to be both, it seems—poor me!—and he is unhappy and afraid now for his quest's end."

"Not afraid," he said. "Whatever he may believe, he is not afraid of it. He has never feared anything—neither its end nor its beginning."

"Do you too take me for a witch?"

He let that pass.

She sighed: "You do not take me for the end of your quest, that is sure."

Her right hand, which grasped his sword-belt, transmitted a slight quiver to her heart.

"He is mad, I fear, for how could he think me beautiful? And now he is unhappy because of me, in his new madness, and you are still unhappy in your old madness. So your unhappiness is my fault too, for if I were actually as your dear grandfather sees me in his madness, you might forget your loss or mistake me for the lost one. But I am not, and you do not; and so two brave knights are unhappy because of me—one in the foolish belief that his quest is ended, and the other because he knows that he has not found what he seeks."

Again her hand transmitted a quiver from his sword-belt to her heart. He spoke a word; but it was to Bahram, who instantly stopped his shilly-shallying and went forward at a purposeful walk. But not for long.

"I fear I'll be shaken right off, at this pace," the lady whispered.

At another word from Lorn, Bahram resumed his dilatory posturings.

"If I were a witch," she said, "I would make myself appear to the King as you see me, and to you as he sees me."

Though the only response she received was by way of the telltale belt, she smiled quite contentedly at the knowledge that, no matter how he might pretend to ignore her, she could make him tremble like a leaf. . . .

Later, Dame Clara told one of the ancient servitors to find Joseph and send him to her. It took four of the old men the better part of an hour to carry out the order.

"Take my compliments to King Torrice, and remind him that I am expecting him and Sir Lorn and their gentlemen to supper," she instructed the manikin. "And don't take all night about it," she admonished gently.

"They won't come," he said, consequentially. "Too busy. Even Sir Lorn is busy. And why shouldn't he be busy now—that moonstruck quester!—since 'tis all the fault of his fuddling?"

Before Dame Clara could speak, for astonishment and indignation, Damosel Mary spoke.

"How now, little man? If you have forgotten my teachings of ten years ago, I shall have to take your education in hand again."

Joseph had not forgotten. Sadly deflated, he recalled to mind the matter and the occasions referred to by the gray-haired damosel. That stalwart and learned governess had not confined her instructions to little Clara, but had given the household dwarf and mascot a course in manners that, being much needed and long overdue, had proved extremely painful to the recipient. Now he ducked and turned to slip out by the way he had swaggered in; but Lady Clara was upon him like a falcon on a partridge.

"No, you don't!" she cried. "Oh, you saucy knave, how dare you speak so? For a pin, I'd send you back where you came from! Fuddling? What d'ye mean by that, you jackanapes? How dare you speak so of that—of your betters? For a pin—at one more word—I'll shake you out of your boots, you wicked Joseph!"

She had him in both hands. Her face was pink; her eyes shot fire and her lofty headdress was askew. She shook him like a clout.

"And quite rightly too," said the old ex-governess judicially. "The silly rascal has outgrown his boots anyhow. But stay your hand, my dear, I beg you, so that he may tell us more of this business that's afoot—unless he invented it to puff up his own importance—before he loses the power of speech, which might happen if he bit off his tongue."

Clara complied instantly, but kept a grip on Joseph with one hand while straightening her headdress with the other.

"Now then, out with it!" she demanded, but in a softer and reasonable tone of voice. "Tell us what it is they are all so busy about."

He hung limp and gasping in the grip of that small white hand and rolled his eyes piteously. Never before had he been treated with violence, or angry words even, by his beautiful young mistress.

"He needs wine, poor fellow!" she cried.

The damosel thought so too, and brought it quickly. He drained the cup and recovered his breath and something of his assurance.

"It's the rogue Drecker," he said.

"Drecker? But he's gone," the ladies protested.

"That's it," he said. "He's gone, whole and horsed. Would they fear him now if he were dead and buried with the others? They'd not give him a thought. But now they must guard against his return."

"But he dare not come back!" Clara cried.

The dwarf shot an oblique glance at Mary; and as she was not watching him, but gazing thoughtfully at nothing, he risked a sneer.

"Dare not?" he questioned, with curling lips. But he kept the curl out of his voice. "With all the outlaws of the forest at his heels? And this time it will be with fire and sword. This time he will take what he wants—and that will be what brought him here the first time, and everything else he can carry off—and hot torches and cold iron for the rest."

"But our defenders?" she whispered. "They'll not desert us?"

"Six," Joseph said contemptuously. "They were enough against six—enough to slay five, anyway. But against sixty or eighty or a hundred? That will be another story."

"Not so fast, little man," the governess interrupted. "Why not a thousand, while you are about it? But tell me first, does Drecker's army grow on trees?"

"You can say that," the dwarf answered, with more than a hint of his old impudence. "On the ground under the trees, anyhow. Runaway serfs and all manner of masterless knaves and gypsies and thieving packmen and renegade warders and archers, and first of all, the band that has been receiving and marketing our beeves and cheeses all the while."

"And just what have our defenders become so suddenly so busy about?" asked Damosel Mary.

"Bringing the people closer in, with their livestock and goods and gear, and setting them to work on walls and ditches, and making men-at-arms of clodhoppers," Joseph told her, civilly enough.

"We must get busy too!" Clara cried. "We're both good bowmen, Mary. We'll teach the old men to shoot. My grandfather Cadwallader made me a little bow when I was only four years old; and when I was six, I could pick his cap clean off his head without waking him up, at ten paces. I hit him only once, and that was only a scratch; but after that he always retired to his chamber for his naps. There must be scores of old bows and arrows somewhere around here. We'll look high and low; and we'll have new ones made, if need be. I know that one of the cooks used to be a bowyer. We'll start now. Where has Joseph gone?"

"You let go of him, my dear," said the damosel resignedly.

"Good riddance to him!" the dame cried. "He would only tell us where to look and then what to do and how. He will be much happier advising the King and Sir Lorn. Now to work!"

Chapter Eight
WHEN TWO MEN LOOK OUT OF ONE MAN'S EYES

There was little rest in Joyous Vale that night, either within or without the manor house. Lady Clara permitted only the oldest and shakiest members of the household to retire to their couches at the customary hour. As for the old ex-bowyer Tomkyn, it was long past midnight when he was allowed to creep off to bed; and as for the dame and the damosel, they heard the false dawn saluted by sleepy roosters. And so it was without, abroad over the whole manor to the edges of the forest on every side. By sunrise, every farmstead and croft had been warned and set astir by one or another of the King's party, or by Joseph up on one of the King's ponies: and when the chatelaine, wakened from a short sleep by the hubbub without, looked out from her high window, she rubbed her eyes and looked again. For the inner court was gay with the colored pavilions which Drecker and his rogues had pitched, and left perforce, under the willows beside the river. The chivalry had moved in. The outer courtyard was not so gay, but it was far livelier. Here were tents of hide, makeshift shelters of spars and thatch, heaps of country provisions and household gear, pens of swine and poultry, excited women jabbering and gesticulating, gaffers seated on bundles of bedding, and barking dogs and shouting children dashing around.

The home orchard and paddocks had also undergone a startling change. The latter were alive with horned cattle and sheep, all in confusion and many in violent disagreement, and herds and woolly sheep-dogs trying to restore order and keep the peace with sticks and teeth. Through the orchard greenery appeared the tops of hastily constructed stacks of last year's hay and straw, and arose the bellows, moos, and bleats of more displaced livestock. Beyond all this moved wains and wheel-less drags, horse-drawn and ox-drawn, the loaded approaching and the empty departing; and groups of rustics coming and going; and here and there a cavalier in half-armor riding this way or that.

Dame and damosel were back at their self-appointed tasks when King Torrice presented himself. He had been in the saddle sixteen hours, with two changes of horses, and yet looked fresh as a daisy. It was only leg and footwork, or sitting on chairs, that fatigued him.

"Lady, I crave your indulgence for the liberties I have taken with your people and property, and shall continue to take, for your own and their good—but all with due respect to your title and lordship, madam," he pronounced.

Lady Clara dropped what she was about and jumped up and toward him, and extended both hands to him. Still regarding her gravely, he received her hands in his own, then blinked and started slightly and looked down curiously at the little hands in his big ones, at the right and at the left, then turned the right palm-upward and fairly stared at it, then the left and stared at it.

"Blisters!" he exclaimed.

"We have been making arrows, Mary and I," she answered gently and shyly. "And splicing old bows. And twisting and waxing bowstrings."

He looked her in the eyes, then stooped over her hands again and touched his lips lightly to each of the blistered palms in turn, muttered "Gramercy, my dear!" and straightened and backed out by the way he had come in.

Clara returned to her work, but fumblingly. She blinked to clear her vision, and tears sparkled on her cheeks.

Mary eyed her thoughtfully.

"A grand old man," said Mary. "Well, a grand old knight-at-arms, however—and as good a poet as any in Wales, even. But as simple and innocent as a baby, or poor Sir Gayling even, for all his questing and gallivanting; and I'd liefer have him for a battling champion, in the ding-dong of rescue and defence, than for a husband or father."

"Is that so?" cried Clara. "I don't believe it! We don't know anything of him as a father, but we can see that he is a good grandfather to poor Lorn; and I have my own opinion as to what your answer would be if he asked you to marry him."

"Fiddlesticks, my dear! And if you contemplate becoming the Queen of Har yourself—and a crook of your finger is all that's needed—I advise you to be quick about it."

Clara stared at her ex-governess and asked tremulously: "Why do you say that—and look so strange?"

"Because you have no time to lose; and if I look strange, who wouldn't, after glimpsing a dead man in a living man's eyes?"

"What d'ye mean by that? Speak out, or I'll shake you!"

"Calm yourself, child. I mean what I say. I saw him dead—that poor old king—just as surely as I foresaw your own grandmother dead while she was still walking and laughing, and just as surely as my grandsire True Thomas foresaw and foretold the death of King David at his marriage feast and was whipped for the telling. It is when you see two pairs of eyes glimmering in the eyeholes of the one head—and one pair of those eyes are cold and blind."

Lady Clara cried out, "To the devil with your soothsaying!" and clapped her hands to her face; and her tears burned and stung the abraded palms. Mary sighed, brushed a furtive hand over her own still face, and took up her work again.

At noon, Lady Clara told the major-domo to send Joseph to her. That important person received the command in silence, and with a weary shake of the head. He was thinking of the easy and peaceful years before poor dear Sir Gayling's mad expedition into Wales. Those had been the times. There had been no big Welsh damosel then to drive honest men around every day with besoms and mops, in pursuit of honest dirt and dust and cobwebs; and no giddy young dame to demand gleaming crystal and shining plate, and tarts and jellies and custards for every meal till the cooks and scullions were fit to tear out their beards. And now it was worse. Now it was the very devil. Sweeping and scrubbing, and polishing and burnishing and cooking, had been hard enough on the poor fellows, but ferreting out ancient war-gear and repairing it, grinding edges onto rusty swords and axes, splicing old bows and whittling new bows and arrows, and being driven and drilled by Tomkyn the ex-bowyer, was harder.

"The whole world be turned upside-down," grumbled the major-domo; and instead of going on the lady's errand, he went in search of some hole or corner in which he might evade Tomkyn's officious attentions for a little while. Imagine a major-domo hiding from a cook! Such a thing could never have been in the days of Sir Gayling. And so, quite naturally, the dwarf failed to answer his mistress' summons; but Squire Gervis presented himself some three hours later, and quite of his own volition. He was dusty, but in high spirits. When he took Dame Clara's proffered hand, he turned it over tenderly, gazed at it adoringly and said that he had heard about it from the King.

"How fares the dear King?" she asked softly.

"That old wonder-boy is as lively as a grig," he replied enthusiastically. "And as merry too. And even Sir Lorn is companionable. That's the way it always is with those two. The prospect of a fight, and never mind the odds against them, acts like mothers' milk—if you'll forgive the expression—on those mad questers."

"Mad?" she whispered; and Damosel Mary looked up from her work with glue and feathers on a clothyard shaft and said, in the voice of a governess: "It's a very wise man, or a fool, who dares cry 'Mad!' at his fellows."

Unabashed, Gervis replied with unabated good humor:

"A fool, then! And in my folly I repeat that our noble friends are mad. Who but a madman would spend a hundred years and more—some say two hundred—in pursuit of the very thing from which he turns and flees whenever he catches up with it?"

"What thing is that?" murmured Clara.

"He calls it Beauty," he laughed.

"Nay, he calls it the Soul of Beauty," she murmured.

He shrugged a shoulder delicately and winked politely.

"And what have you to say of Sir Lorn's madness?" she asked gently.

"I'll say that is different," he answered, with a touch of gravity. "Who wouldn't be mad, after a year in Fairyland with the Maid of Tintagel, or Helen of Troy, or maybe it was Queen Mab herself? But he is mad, our poor Lorn; and it's struck deep, else he would forget her now, whoever she was."

He gazed adoringly into her eyes, and she smiled back very kindly, and a little sadly and with just a flicker of pity.

"It is sometimes difficult to distinguish madness from foolishness," said Damosel Mary.

He turned to her and shook a playful finger, then turned back to Clara.

"I'll tear myself away now, back to my duty, before one of those mad questers appears and drags me away ingloriously by the scruff of the neck—for my folly."

And he was gone as lightly as he had come.

Chapter Nine
THE INVADING HORDE

Dame Clara told the dwarf Joseph to take post on the tower and keep watch on the edges of the forest from dawn till dark: but he excused himself on the plea that he could not be spared from his duties as galloping aide-de-camp to King Torrice. This was on the night of the second day after the King's and Gervis' visits. For two days and a night now the lady had been neglected by her champions, save for the verbal message from Torrice, by Joseph, to the effect that she had nothing graver to worry about now than the blisters on her pretty hands, and that he would compose another song to her as soon as the dastard Drecker reappeared and was finally disposed of.

"He sounds very sure," she said to the messenger.

"And with reason," he replied condescendingly. "We are ready and waiting for Master Drecker and his riffraff. Every stratagem of defense and attack is planned; and we have made more than a score of men-at-arms, all horsed and harnessed and armed, out of your clodhoppers of yesterday."

So Joseph escaped back to his active military duties; and at the first pale gleam of the next dawn, Lady Clara herself took post on the watchtower, leaving the command and business of the household archery to Damosel Mary and the bowyer Tomkyn.

She peered down at a shadowy world, but not a sleeping one. A few dark figures moved to and fro about the inner court, and more in the outer court, and yet more in the paddocks beyond and about the edges of the home orchard; and her heart swelled with gentle pride and sweet gratitude and perhaps with even tenderer emotions at the thought that she was the inspiration and cause of this vigilance and devotion. She wept a little in happy sadness, but soon dried her eyes on the silken lining of one of the hanging sleeves of her green gown. As the clear light increased, rising and flooding, she saw more and more, and farther and farther. Thin feathers of smoke uncurled above the leafy roof of the orchard, the busy human figures increased in number and formless bulks of darkness took shape. Now she saw the abatis of new-felled forest trees which enforced and topped the old wall of tumbled field-stone around the home farm, and four massy clumps of leafy timber far out toward the four nearest screens of the surrounding forest, and at a point where nothing taller than hay had grown previously.

By now she could see to the forest walls all around, beyond the farthest meadows and cornlands and deserted steadings. The forested edges to the westward, struck full by the level rays, showed leafy boughs and brown boles like a picture on tapestry, but to the eastward they were still gloomed with their own shadows. . . . It was from the shadows that the first running figure appeared. It was of a tall man in leather, with a strung bow in his left hand. He checked for a backward look, then ran again. A horn brayed in the shadows and was answered from the right, and then from the left, as if by echoes. A second man in leather appeared, and three more a moment later, all running like partridges from the shadow of a stooping hawk. A leather cap lifted and fell to earth, leaving the shaggy hair of that runner streaming in the wind of his flight. The watcher on the tower could make nothing of that: but after another had stumbled and run on with bowed head and hunched shoulders and in zigzagging jumps, and yet another had fallen flat and then crawled like a snake, she made out little glints and gleams in the sunshine, and knew them for flying arrows.

Again a horn brayed, but louder and nearer this time. Now a horseman appeared as if from nowhere, galloping toward the screen of shadow from which the men in leather were fleeing, gesticulating, and screaming. Four of the runners turned and set arrows to their bowstrings and shot, hard and fast, into the green gloom.

The rider drove through them, wheeled, dismounted, and laid hold of the crawler with both hands. The wounded man rose to his knees, to his feet, and sagged across the horse. It was a small horse, but hardy; and so the rescue was made, with the pony running like a dog, the wounded forester draped across like a half-filled sack and the rescuer running beside and holding him in place. He was a small rescuer. Boys of nine years have been taller.

"Joseph!" cried the lady on the tower. "'Tis none other, by my halidom! Run, Joseph, run!"

All the visible actors in that flurry of action disappeared among the hedges and walls, and under the thatched roofs, of a steading. Now, for a long minute, nothing moved in Lady Clara's wide field of vision—though she looked in every direction—save a few feathers of smoke and wings of birds and ever-trembling leaves of tall poplars. No more arrows leaped from shadow to shine. Nothing moved on the ground. The horns were silent now, but cocks crowed in the home orchard. She gazed abroad and down in growing and fearful wonder, peering for some sign of awareness of danger, listening for a sudden commotion and shouting of armed men; but the great house below her, and the bright landscape all about her, were as still and quiet as if they lay under a spell. Was some wicked magic at work here, to her undoing? What of her champions?

But no, she had already seen little Joseph and five scouts in action; and she refused to believe that any spell save death itself could withhold the hands of that old king and the squires from her defense. Of Lorn she was not so sure. Even though she had made him tremble with a touch of her hand on his sword-belt, she did not blink the fact of his old bewitchment and sojourn in Fairyland. What were her frail enchantments, though exercised with all her heart, against those of ageless sorcery? For that dear knight—for succor from those dear hands—she could but hope and pray.

Now from the lightening rim of gloom from which the five vanished foresters had emerged stirred again, and the base of that green obscurity was alive suddenly with a score of men in leather and wool, with strung bows in their hands. They did not dash forward, but extended to right and left and advanced cautiously, setting arrows to strings. As many more invaders now emerged and formed a second line. A few of these were bowmen too, but most of them carried boar-spears, short axes, or halberds. Close behind these came a fellow with a burning torch and two with a black kettle slung from a pole between them. The torch smoked blackly and flamed palely in the sunshine, and a thin haze of heat quivered above the kettle.

"The rogues! They mean to set us afire!" cried Clara.

Again she looked all around, and again in vain for any sign of a defender. The skirmishers continued to advance, and with more assurance. A big knight in full armor, on a black horse to match, came into view in rear of the two score skirmishers, riding at a foot-pace. He signaled with a hand—its mail flashed in the sunlight—and shouted a command, whereupon the fellows in front drew together on the run and headed straight for the steading into which Joseph and the five foresters had disappeared. The knight followed them, but neither fast nor far, and soon drew rein and sat with uneasy shiftings and turnings, as if he too (like the watcher on the tower) was puzzled by the stillness. The two score raiders halted and sent a flight of arrows into the farmstead, and then a second flight, and three fire-arrows flaming like comets: but no shaft came from hedge or wall in retaliation. They loosed a dozen fire-arrows, one of which struck a thatched roof, stuck there, and blossomed like a great poppy. And still the spell was unbroken.

Clara, up on her tower, was as spellbound as the menaced steading and the field spreading stilly all around from the silent house under her to the still walls of the forest. She wanted to scream, but her throat refused. It seemed to her that the forest watched and waited expectantly, and that everything within its sinister circuit, seen and unseen, would start and cry out in protest but for the same fatal hand that gripped and silenced herself. . . . Once more she tried to scream—and for cause, God wot—but with no more success than before. That same span of leafy gloom stirred to life again and spewed forth running men; but this time it was a multitude. It flooded into the sunshine like a dark tide flecked with glinting spear-points and upflung blades and spotted with garments of tattered finery among the jerkins of drab leather and wool. An awesome sound rose from it like the hum and growl of sea surf. It flooded to and around the mounted knight, and bore him with it toward the smoking farmstead into which the vanguard continued to shoot fire. It did not check, but in its weight of hundreds, carried the first two score forward with it against the still hedges and silent walls. And then the spell broke.

A hundred arrows darted from hedges and walls and gables; shouts and the braying of horns shook the smoke and were answered by shouts and horns from the right and the left; and more arrows darted forth and struck and stood quivering. From the ambushes of felled trees on either hand came armored men on large horses, shouting and with leveled spears, breaking from the trot to the gallop—a dozen from the right and a dozen from the left. Lorn led one party, up on the mighty Bahram, and in front of the other charged King Torrice under his plume of black-and-white ostrich feathers. The invading flood recoiled; and its front—what remained alive of it—turned upon the pressure from behind, screaming and striking for a way of escape. Now it was every knave for himself, of those murderous hundreds.

They were spitted like partridges. Lorn was among them. He threw his spear aside and hewed with his sword. They were split like fish. The white stallion tore them with his teeth and crushed them under his terrible hooves. Torrice was among them, not charging now but reining his black horse this way and that and using his great spear as a lesser craftsman might use a light sword, prodding here and there. Though a master of every chivalrous combat tool, he held that the spear was the knight's first weapon. Peter and Gervis were among them. Like Lorn, they too had discarded spears for swords for such infighting as this. Goggin and Billikin were among them, plying their long blades like gentlemen born. Twenty armored rustics on plowhorses were among them, hacking with axes and bashing with spiked maces. And even the big knight who had brought them here with promises of easy rich rapine now took part in the slaughtering of them, cutting them down and riding them down in his frantic efforts to win clear and away. Screaming like trapped beasts, the remnants of the horde broke in every direction—but not all of them to safety, for the dwarf Joseph and the hundred archers from the burning farmstead were on their heels.

The lady on the tower shut her eyes. She cried out, but in the din of triumphant shouts and horns from the house and courts below, her voice was no more than a whisper in her own ears. After a little while, she looked again, avoiding the motionless shapes on the ground. Footmen still ran in groups and pairs, pursued and pursuing, to the flashes of knives and axes. Some of the horsemen still galloped and struck, but most of them moved more slowly and with an air of aimlessness now.

But King Torrice and all his five men, and Joseph on his running pony, were still in play. And Drecker, clear of the rabble at last, was riding like a madman for the nearest edge of the forest. His spear was gone. His great shield was cast off. He dropped his sword and cast off mace and battle-axe from his saddlebow. Anything for speed with which to escape a red doom: for that old king and that young knight were after him, converging on him from right and left. But he hadn't a chance. At the very edge of the forest—But the watcher on the tower had closed her eyes again.

Chapter Ten
QUEST'S END

King Torrice of Har was dead. The exertions of that last mêlée and the final stroke on Drecker's neck had stilled that long questing forever. He had lived to be carried in by Lorn, and to smile and murmur a few words at the touch of Clara's tears on his face. Now he lay on a couch of silks and furs in the great hall, in full armor, with tall candles at his head and feet. His hands were crossed on his breast, on the cross of the long sword that lay there unsheathed. His helmet, with its proud plume, was at his left elbow. Clara and Lorn knelt on the right of the couch and the squires on the left. At the head of it, a wandering friar read from a great missal, now muttering and now chanting. All the surrounding gloom was full of kneeling people, and over all rang and sighed and sobbed a dirge from the Damosel Mary's harp.

Clara turned her face to Lorn.

"He told me he was happy—in his quest's end," she sighed.

The young knight gazed at her with clear eyes.

She sighed again.

"But what of *your* quest?"

He moved his right hand a little toward her; he found her left hand and clasped it.

"I have forgotten what it was," he answered.

CASTLE CAVANAUGH

Chapter One

THE SPELL IS BROKEN

A young local gentleman named Michael, but generally called Rufus for the color of his hair, offered his services as squire to Sir Dennys ap Rhys. The young knight was flattered, but embarrassed too.

"What would I do with a squire?" he asked. "Not once have I couched spear or swung sword, except against dummies, since King Malachi made a knight of me last winter; and now it is April."

"Nor nobody else," said Rufus. "A poor place for adventurous, chivalrous spirits, this Cavanaugh country, divil a doubt of it! But they say it was second only to Dublin in Malachi's father's day, an' his grandfather's too. Malachi himself was always more of a schemer nor a knight-at-arms—nothing like your old King of Har! And he would sooner cheat a neighbor out of a mountain or a bog than take it from him in a decent fight. But what with rheumatics and a beautiful young wife, maybe he's more deserving of pity than blame. However, the fact remains that you'll never win to knightly fame around here, so you'll be riding away back to the great world one of these fine spring days, if you're half the hero I take you for; and the sooner the better; and I'll tell you frankly that what I want is a respectable excuse to be riding away too—from the apron-strings of a watchful widowed mother an' two doting spinster aunts."

"But I am a poor man," Dennys protested. "All my fortune is the mountainy men and horses I fetched from my distant home beyond the waves, and the old warhorse and harness and arms and shield of King Torrice's bounty, and the gold spurs King Malachi bestowed upon me so graciously."

"Don't give it a thought," Rufus told him cheerfully. "I'll not come afoot nor empty-handed—don't worry. I'll make no demands on your pouch till it's full an' spilling over, divil a fear! Man, Denny, you wouldn't find my match for the job if you ransacked all Ireland. I've got the gentility for it, Michael MacMurraugh being the name; an' better still, I've got the congeniality. Ah, Denny boy, my mouth waters at the thought of the jinking company we'll keep, an' the grand brawls we'll get into up an' down the civilized world!"

"Not so fast!" Dennys protested. "I am still in two minds about leaving. If it wasn't for my duty to my dear parents, and all—to show them I'm alive—I'd stop right here, or hereabouts, indefinitely."

"And you'd be wrong!" Rufus retorted, still smiling with his lips, but with a grave look in his eyes. "You'd be doing yerself a disservice, and maybe the world too. Now I'm talking to you as a friend an' man to man, Denny boy. Oh, I know what's on your mind, don't try fooling yerself I don't. Now listen to me! You've done your duty by that little maid a hundred times over. Who took her away from those tormenting vagabonds, single-handed an' at the risk of his life? It wasn't Sir Lorn, who had ridden off in search of her five years ago and met the Queen of Egypt or some other witch an' forgot all about her. No, it was Dennys ap Rhys. I've heard all about it from Little Brigie herself, and that great wench Eliza too. And all you get for your trouble is goldy spurs from her father and a kiss from her mother— and him a king, an' her a queen! They could have made it a barony of land. But never mind that now. The little maid is safe anyhow, secure in the strongest castle this side Dublin; and in nine years' time, or maybe less, there'll be more bog-trotting kings' sons after her than a tinker's dog has fleas. She has no more need of you, Denny boy. So now you can give all your conscience an' effort to your sacred duty to your poor sorrowing parents, who are doubtless mourning you for dead at this very moment."

"You may be right," sighed Dennys.

"Sure I'm right!" cried Rufus. "And the sooner we get started—for it's a long road, by your own telling—the better for the grieving hearts of your parents, and for your own soul too."

That is how Master Michael MacMurraugh became Sir Dennys ap Rhys' squire. The doting mother and aunts offered no objections, for they believed the young knight to be a fixture at King Malachi's court and had no suspicions of their darling's adventurous designs upon the wide and wicked world. They may even have hoped that his squirish duties would divert his mind from the blooming milkmaids and giggling goose girls of the home farm.

Here we must pause before describing the very lively events to come, in order to briefly recall the stirring happenings that brought this grand and great young knight Dennys to Ireland:

Young Dennys ap Rhys, the son of a northern chieftain, found a strange young knight who had lost his memory as well as his orientation, wandering in the wilderness. All that the stranger could recall of his name was *Lorn*, to which Dennys and the family added *Le Perdu*. That he was a knight was proved, despite his youth, by his golden spurs, superior arms and armor, and his noble white charger.

Months later, the two friends left the mountain barony, in search of chivalrous adventure, with Dennys acting as the knight's self-appointed squire. In the royal town of Carleon they met and were befriended by King Torrice of Har, an ancient knight-errant and absentee monarch who ever since his remote youth had been riding ardently, if sometimes confusedly, in quest of the Soul of Beauty.

In a questionable quarter of Carleon, Dennys rescued a little girl from a man and a woman who were in the act of trying to deface a birthmark just below the child's left shoulder blade with a red-hot awl. The mark (so he learned later) resembled the rosy imprint of a tiny hand. While winning to safety with her, he had to kill several ruffians. The only name she knew for herself was one the gypsies had given her when she had been kidnaped in her infancy. It was Cynara. A stalwart peasant woman of King Torrice's following, Eliza by name, took the little maid to her heart.

Dennys, who had received hard knocks in the course of that rescue, was out of acting for days, during which time the restless old King and young Sir Lorn le Perdu—both quite irresponsible—became boon companions and finally rode off together on the King's endless and hopeless quest, leaving Dennys, the little girl, Nurse Eliza, and several old retainers in mortal danger. Having sworn to protect Cynara while he had life, Dennys got the little company clear of the perilous inn and town between midnight and dawn, leaving corpses of rogues behind him. His intention was to battle through to his distant mountain home, where his little maid would be protected from her enemies by the strong arms of his kinsmen and the jealous ghosts of his ancestors. But Fate ordained otherwise.

Dennys and his charges had not gone far before they were set upon by a mob of forest outlaws; and in the middle of that unequal conflict—and in the nick of time—the questers, King Torrice and Sir Lorn le Perdu, happened along and made mincemeat of the outlaws. Then the bemused young knight chanced to get his first glimpse of the birthmark on the little maid Cynara; and in a partial recovery of his memory, he knew it for the mark of the Fairy Hand, and the child for an Irish princess. He told them about it. Brigid, the infant and only child of King Malachi Cavanaugh and Queen Brigid, had been kidnaped; and six young knights, of whom he was the youngest, had set out in six directions to recover her, mauger their heads. He, Lorn, had searched through all Ireland for three summers and three winters; and then something queer had happened to him in the mountains of Killarney—a thing so queer that he could remember nothing between it and his meeting with Dennys ap Rhys in the northern wilderness. Of crossing the sea and wandering in a strange land he knew nothing.

So instead of taking his little maid Cynara to his mountain home, Dennys joined in escorting Princess Brigid Cavanaugh back to where she had been stolen from. . . . They were welcomed joyously at Castle Cavanaugh. Queen Brigid and King Malachi could hardly believe their eyes, for it was five years since the Queen's young cousin Lorn—Lorn Geraldine, to give him his true name—had ridden away in search of their lost darling. Dennys was knighted; for both King Torrice and Sir Lorn gave him all the credit for the rescue. And the ancient questing King was filled with joy at the discovery that Lorn was his grandson, and with confusion at meeting Lorn's grandmother and being claimed by her as her first husband. But—

"This is no life for us, my dear lad—all cooped up in a castle with domestic responsibilities," said the questing grandsire to the questing grandson.

And so there was another flitting of those two—and more adventures until they rescued the lovely Lady Clara from the recreant knight Drecker and his varlets. King Torrice died happy after that last grand battle; and Sir Lorn found the end of his quest in the company of Lady Clara.

Rufus proved himself a devoted squire from the first. On his fourth day of service, he took Dennys to their stable and introduced him to something new there. It was a big red roan six-year-old gelding. He stood sixteen and a half hands and was proportionately long and broad.

"It's Hercules!" Dennys exclaimed. "The King's best charger! What's he doing in here?"

"He's yours," Rufus said. "A free gift! Malachi's a cousin of mine of some sort—my own father and he had the same great-great-granddaddy—so I talked him into it without much trouble. He started an argument; but once he grasped the idea that all that was keeping you at Castle Cavanaugh was the lack of a second charger, he changed his tune an' threw in the saddle an' bridle to boot."

"D'ye mean King Malachi wants me to leave?" Dennys asked, startled.

"Well, you can take that for the meaning, Denny boy, if I be any judge of implication," said Rufus cheerfully.

"But—but why?" Dennys demanded. "What has he against me?"

"You can never tell for sure with Malachi," Rufus replied, with a considering air. "It might be that he begrudges you bed an' board an' corkage; for there's a mean, thrifty streak in him he got from his mother, who was a—but never mind that now. Or it might be the kiss Queen Brigie gave you for fetching home Little Brigie—with him wondering if maybe that wasn't the only one—for there's no denying a low, suspicious streak in him. Or it might be the little maid's partiality for you: for I wouldn't put it past him to plan to marry her some day to the highest prince in all Christendom. Thrift, suspicion, ambition; it may be any one of them, but more likely it's all three of them."

Dennys went red, and he went white, and he went red again. He gripped Rufus by a shoulder. He opened his mouth, but it wasn't till the third gasp that he found his voice.

"A pox to him! I'll throw the gold spurs back in his face, by the Holy Bones! And the horse too—mauger my head!"

"Easy does it, Denny boy—an' leave me good right arm in its socket, if you love me," protested Rufus. "Listen to reason, now, an' don't go hacking your own nose off now to spite Malachi's face. God knows you earned all he's given you—not to mention the half of his kingdom he didn't give you. So ride off with what you've got, an' thank your guardian angels the spell is broken."

"The spell? What spell is that?"

"The spell of enchantment that's been blinding an' binding you."

"And what enchantment might that be?"

"If you don't know, then I'll tell you, Denny boy, in the way of my duty as a true squire and a true friend. It's the bewitchment that's made you forget your mother an' father an' the hills of your distant home, an' kept you mooning here in Castle Cavanaugh. Do I have to put a name on the witch?"

"No—but any man but yourself who calls her a witch pays with her life. She's no witch. Princess Brigid, or Little Brigie, she's Cynara to me. That's the name she called herself by—the gypsies had given it to her—when I found her. She needed me then, and I was at hand; and if she ever needs me again, I'll know it and come to her again—or you'll know the foxes or the worms are at my bones."

Then he smiled, to Rufus' relief.

"So forget about spells and witches, and warn our fellows for an early start tomorrow," Dennys added.

Chapter Two
VISITORS FROM THE COURT OF DUBLIN

They did not make a start on the morrow, either early or late, for Fate intervened that same evening in the shapes of four knights-errant and their attendants from Dublin. One of the four was a nephew of King Anguish of Dublin himself, and all the other three were cavaliers of distinction, and even the squires were gentlemen of the highest Dublin fashion. Word of it set castle and town in a hubbub, and flew over the country. A grand feast of welcome was held that very night, to which the local nobles and knights came galloping from every direction without waiting to be invited, with their dames and damosels clinging behind them on bouncing pillions. King Malachi wore his finest robes, and Queen Brigid matched her diamonds with the stars in her eyes, and her coraline gown with the bloom of her lips and cheeks.

Dennys and Rufus were at the feast, but Dennys went away to his chamber in a remote tower long before the finish. Now that he knew he had overstayed his welcome with the King, and had made up his mind to leave, he had no heart for that sort of thing. It was hours later when Rufus came stumbling in—and there was Sir Dennys still sitting on the edge of his couch with his head in his hands.

"MacMurraugh forever!" cried Rufus, staggering about and flourishing his arms.

But not for long. When he struck his shins on his couch, he fell across it and lay there. Dennys roused himself from his sad thoughts and went to his squire's assistance. He lifted him, swung him, and laid him straight, with a pillow under his head. Then he returned to his own couch and lay down; and when he heard Rufus snoring softly, he blew out the candle and tried to follow that good example.

He lay flat on his back, with his legs straight and at full length, and relaxed all his muscles. But his mind refused to relax. No matter how tight he shut his eyes, his thoughts continued to jig and race across them, as bright as pictures on a new arras, and as lively as conjurers at a fair. There was no justice in it, for surely he had the right to an easy conscience now that he knew the little maid had no more need of him, and he was determined to rejoice the anxious hearts of his parents at the earliest possible moment. What more could a man do to deserve an easy conscience and a quiet mind that would allow him honest sleep?

But no, the pictures kept jigging and flashing between his twitching brain and his shut eyelids: the devil take them! He sat up and opened his eyes at the surrounding dark. He left his bed and groped around until he found the leather bottle he knew about, tilted it to his mouth, and swigged the strong ale till he was out of breath. He thought that would soothe him to sleep; but on his way back to bed, to put it to the proof, he fell over Rufus. The squire yelled, "MacMurraugh forever!" and grabbed him by the throat; and they were battling on the floor for dear life when Rufus came to his senses.

"Would you murder me?" gasped Dennys.

"So it's yerself!" muttered Rufus. "I mistook you for a Dubliner. What goes on anyhow? Who threw me out of bed? Leave me at him, an' I'll heave him clear back to Dublin Castle!"

"You drank too much," Dennys told him, still gasping.

"Too much? Man, I'm dry as tinder this minute! Me gullet's full of ashes."

Dennys went groping once more, found the leather bottle and took it to Rufus, who was back on his couch but still muttering belligerently. Then he returned to his own bed and tried again to compose himself to slumber. He heard the gurgling of the bottle and found it a soothing sound. He closed his eyes. He was on the verge of sleep; he was even adrift in that sweet tide, when a squashy thud brought him back to reality, and he knew that his companion had finished the ale and dropped the empty leather bottle on the floor.

"That laid the dust—but I could do with its mate," the squire announced in a strong voice.

"Go to sleep," said the knight.

"Bring on that Dubliner now, an' we'll see who hits the floor first this time!" Rufus demanded, his voice yet stronger. "Or bring 'em all on, all at once, squires an' knights all together—an' we'll make 'em rue the day they ever left Dublin, Denny boy—you an' me together, an' never mind the odds!"

"Compose yourself and go to sleep now," begged Dennys.

"We have a busy day ahead of us, Rufe. We'll need all our strength."

After a brief silence, Rufus uttered a hoot of laughter and followed it with wild words.

"A busy day, is it? Ah, me dear Sir Dennys, day ain't the word for it. Call it a week, anyhow."

"Call it six months, and you'll be nearer the mark, if you are talking about the whole time we'll be on the road," said Dennys. "But go to sleep now, and never mind looking so far ahead."

Again Dennys closed his eyes, but only to open them at another outburst of laughter and wild words from his squire.

"Home, is it? Sure, Denny boy—an' all in good time. But now we got some previous engagements on our hands. Didn't I tell you? Eight Dubliners on our hands. One thing at a time, Denny boy. First the Dubliners, an' next the wide world."

"What are you saying?" Dennys demanded, sitting up now with both feet on the floor. "What are they to us— these visitors from Dublin?"

"I told you," Rufus answered, in a thick but reasonable tone of voice. "An' if I didn't, I'll tell you now. I don't like 'em. Nor their airs an' graces, nor their winks an' sneers, nor their brag. Dublin this, an' Dublin that, till you'd think it was the only place in the world. And their smelling salts! The way they kep' sniffing at their little vials of smelling salts. But I bided my time an' dealt with 'em one by one, without violence or commotion, in a most gentlemanly manner. First, one at a time an' without a hubbub, I challenged the four squires to mortal combat—each in turn— in my own name; an' I didn't lay a finger on 'em nor even speak louder than a whisper. Man, Denny boy, ye'd been proud of me, the way I kep' my temper an' minded me manners. Then, one by one an' in the most elegant style, I challenged the four knights to mortal combat."

"You couldn't do that," Dennys protested. "A squire can't challenge a knight. And if you think I'm going to hang around here after all the distress of making up my mind to leave, while you brawl with four squires, you think wrong. I start for home tomorrow—to return, please God, when my little maid needs me again."

"Not so fast, Denny boy," said Rufus. "I didn't challenge

the knights in my own name, divil a fear! I know the rules an' regulations an' all. I challenged them in your name."

"In my name? You couldn't do that, even drunk!"

"I did it, anyhow."

"But I have no quarrel with those knights!"

"You would have if you'd stopped longer. They as good as said they've seen prettier queens than Brigid."

"They didn't say it to me, or in my hearing; and I am not her champion, anyway. I'll explain it to them."

"Would you make a liar of me for a little thing like that—an' me your true squire! But not so fast, now! D'ye mind when Little Brigie was fetched down for a minute to bid them welcome?"

"I'd mind it if I'd seen it. That must have been after I had left and come up here. But what about it?"

"So you didn't see the look on their faces when Malachi held her up in his arms an' sang out: 'Gentlemen, this is our daughter the princess.'"

"What look was that?"

"Well, it's hard to describe: there was amusement in it, but that wasn't all. There was more than amusement in their half-shut eyes, and in the curl of their lips too. It was what you could call a contemptuous look."

Dennys stood up. Rufus could not see him, but he could hear his hard breathing. Then Dennys fell to pacing around between the two couches, still breathing hard and high. He went six times around without a word, then stopped and spoke in a voice Rufus had never heard out of him before.

"Did you say *contemptuous*?"

"That's what I said," Rufus answered.

Without another word, Dennys returned to his bed and lay down. But he did not lie still. The cocks were crowing in full force, and the little birds were piping and twittering in the trees all around, before he stopped twitching and turning.

Chapter Three
King Malachi Was No Ornament to Chivalry

First thing in the morning, King Malachi proclaimed a whole sennight of celebrations for the entertainment of his noble and genteel guests from the court of King Anguish of

Dublin, and without the loss of a minute set about ordering the same, and dispatching messengers in all directions. There would be jousts and tournaments and feasts
for the chivalry and quality, and sports and games and
merry-go-round and free ale for the commonalty, and all
manner of junketing for one and all. For Anguish of Dublin
was generally reputed to be the most powerful of all the
thirteen kings of Ireland; and Malachi was eager to do him
honor.

This King Malachi was no ornament to chivalry—as
you may have gathered from the words of his third cousin
once removed, Squire Rufus. The nature he had been born
with, and rheumatism and a late marriage and other circumstances and conditions of his life, had made a queer
character of him. He was more a schemer than a man of
action, but he loved excitement: the excitement however,
had to come *to* him to do him any good. He was not one to
go out after it, or make it for himself; and yet extraordinary
occurrences and surprises were the only things that could
get him out of bed in a good humor. For weeks after the
recovery of little Princess Brigid, he had been as lively as a
cricket; but the novelty of his relief and joy had soon worn
off, and he had started complaining, and kept it up, of his
pains, and the wind from the wrong quarter, and life in
general: but now, with the important Dubliners to entertain, he was the last in bed at night and the first out in the
morning, and all smiles all day long.

King Malachi and Dennys met by chance in the outer
court of the castle early on the first morning after the night
of the first feast.

"Good morning to ye, Sir Dennys!" cried the King, with
a grand smile.

Dennys doffed his cap and louted low, but he kept a
stiff face.

"How d'ye like your grand new horse?" Malachi asked.

"A noble horse, sir, and I thank Your Majesty most
humbly for your generosity and all former kindnesses to a
stranger in a strange land," Dennys answered, with his lips
still as straight as his gaze.

"Not a word, me lad!" the King exclaimed heartily—but
his eyes flickered to the right and the left. "Nothing's too

good for Sir Dennys ap Rhys, wherever he came from—or would I've made a knight of ye with my own sword? Well do I know what I owe ye, me lad. And speaking of knights, I've a request to make ye, Sir Dennys. From some words of your squire I gathered ye're thinking of depriving us of your company one of these days, which act would distress me greatly at any time, but particularly so just now when I've got these gentlemen of King Anguish's court on me hands; and I'm asking ye to postpone your departure for a sennight or so, and help me to amuse our guests."

"I was about to offer my services for that very duty," Dennys told him gravely; "and Your Majesty may be sure that I'll do the utmost in my humble power to amuse the gentlemen from the court of Dublin."

Malachi returned thanks warmly; and then each went about his own immediate business.

Word of the prospective high jinks spread like a fire in the heather. All sorts and conditions and shapes of humanity came crowding into Cavantown, and the pick of the quality into the big castle itself. Knightly armor and gear were hunted out of dark corners and overhauled by smiths and tinkers, and heralds shook the camphor out of their best tabards and dusted off their books of rules. A grandstand was erected at an edge of a large meadow handy to the castle; and the booths of fortune-tellers and dealers in elixirs and miraculous salves, and the hovels of makers and purveyors of pies and pancakes and frumenty, sprang up all around overnight like toadstools.

Dennys and Rufus looked well to their arms and gear and horses. Rufus wanted Dennys to invest in a new shield, but Dennys said no, and argued that a proven shield like the one King Torrice had given him almost a year ago—and it was a battered old piece even then!—possessed virtues of experience which a young knight would be foolish to ignore.

"You could say the same for the old warhorse he gave you at the same time," Rufus protested.

"So I could, and so I do," said Dennys.

But he consented to have the old shield repainted by a young limner of the town. Over the dented and dimmed device of King Torrice of Har—gules, a rampant unicorn argent, armed or—was laid a field of white, and on this were depicted two tawny brown wolves walking each with one forepaw off the ground. The walking wolves was the emblem of ownership which generations of Dennys' ancestors had embroidered on their banners and carved over their doors. The painter, who was also something of an authority on the science of heraldry, admired his handiwork vastly.

"Truly, what action!" he exclaimed. "What color! Your Honor couldn't find brushwork to match it anywhere else in all Ireland. Note the divilish menace of the red eyes. And of the fangs! 'Twas no simple matter to show up the ferocity of the fangs on a white ground; but by using a touch of ochre an' accentuating the red gums, I've mastered the problem as ye can see for yer self. And in addition to its obvious merits as a work of art, it is a grand an' striking shield of arms; and here is how it reads in the high parlance of heraldry, in case anyone asks ye: *argent, wolves passant, proper.*"

Dennys was delighted with it, and Rufus was favorably impressed. Dennys handed over three silver crowns in payment, which sum was not only more than he could afford, but more than the young artist had ever before received for one of his creations.

The first event of the first day was a tournament in which sixteen local champions would contend with blunted spears, in the spirit of cooperation rather than a competition, to afford onlookers—high and low, foreign and local— a lively and harmless spectacle of the trappings and attitudes of chivalry and of such spearmanship and horsemanship as could be reasonably expected at such short notice. Swords and daggers were proscribed, in case an unhorsed contender might forget, in a flare of temper, the rule demanding his instant retirement from the field. After the first tilt, those remaining in their saddles would be faced by replacements, and again after the second; and after three courses had been run, the survivor or survivors of the most clashes would be named and acclaimed.

The sixteen volunteers for the first tilt were placed in opposing lines, eight to a side, by officious heralds and marshals of the field, who performed the task according to a mysterious law or formula of selection known only to themselves. Dennys, who was there on his elderly gray charger Harhar and with his old shield covered with cowhide to protect the new paint, found himself opposite the only other covered shield in sight. Dennys had glanced apprehensively at the high central seats in the grandstand: but no, King Anguish's nephew Sir Cassidy and two of his companions were there, lolling in silks and velvets to right and left of the King and Queen and little Princess; and he had heard from Rufus that the fourth Dublin knight was in bed with a headache, for which he blamed his host's barbarous usquebaugh. He was relieved; for if it came to being unhorsed with a blunted spear, he would rather suffer the indignity from anybody else than any one of the Dublin knights. His account with them could be settled only with sharp spears, or better still, afoot with swords. Now, though he would do his best to maintain his seat, he would accept a tumble philosophically, if need be.

But I'll do my best even in this bit of mummery, to please the little maid, he thought. And that's as like as not to be good enough; for if the gentleman over there is more experienced than me, and a local knight, the chances are he's been settled down these ten or maybe twenty years since his last joust; and if not that, the chances are he's less experienced than myself.

Rufus was still beside him, giving final tweaks and pulls at the latches and tags of his harness, and behaving generally like a fussy dame with her daughter about to appear at her first formal ball.

"You'll do now," said Rufus. "If anything comes off, including yerself, don't blame me. There's nothing to worry about anyhow, with the Dublin knights all accounted for. But keep an eye on that feller opposite all the same, for I can't make him out. It's a country horse he's up on, all right, and it's local armor he's wearing; but himself's no Cavanaugh or Kelly or Geraldine or Bryan or Ryan, I can tell by his shape an' style, unless he's one of the wild ones from over the Mountain. Keep an eye and a point on him, anyhow, and hold on tight and trust in God, Denny boy!"

"*All squires outside!*" bawled a herald.

Sixteen squires retired to the sidelines, running or sauntering or strutting, each according to his individual humor or his opinion of his own or his principal's importance. King

Malachi stood up in his place and waved a hand; whereupon two heralds blew simultaneous blasts on their trumpets quicker than echoes, and the sixteen cavaliers set
their chargers in motion at a variety of gaits and speeds,
and a spatter of handclaps rose from the grandstand, and
wild whoops from the ranks of crowding commonalty from
the edges of the field. Old Harhar started with a sedate
hop, reduced it to a smooth trot, and almost immediately
broke the trot into an easy hand-gallop, all without urge or
hint from Dennys, who simply sat tight and concentrated
on his spear and shield and onrushing opponent.

And that knight was surely a rusher! Or was it the
horse? The big beast had its head down and was charging
like a bull; but Dennys could see that the rider was pulling
to lift that head for all he was worth, short of using both
hands. The oncoming spear wavered, and the big knob of
oak on the tip of it wobbled up and down and around. But
if he hits us anywhere at that pace, Harhar and I'll both be
grassed, thought Dennys. But he continued to give all his
mind to his own spear and shield and leave the rest to his
wise old charger.

Dennys felt a quick twist under him, and then a shock
that tingled his muscles at wrist and shoulder, and then a
pressure that bent both his spear and his back. But not for
long! The ashen shaft of the great spear broke like a dry
twig, and the pressure was gone with the crack of it; and
there he sat straight and secure on a sedately walking
horse. He saw his recent opponent's charger still charging,
but clear of the course and the fringing crowd, and homeward bound at full gallop, with streaming tail and upflung
head. And he saw the knight he had unhorsed rise slowly
to his feet and walk away, leaving an unbroken spear and
dented shield on the ground behind him. Dennys felt
pleased and proud—but his pride was more for Harhar
than himself, for he knew it had been more a trial of horses
than of cavaliers. Now the wise old charger wheeled about
and ambled back to the exact spot from which he had
started. Dennys dismounted and embraced his high neck.
Rufus came running with congratulations and a new
spear.

"I'm proud of you, Denny boy!" Rufus exclaimed. "But
I must say, for the ease of my soul, if you'd been up on a

wild uncivilized colt too, like that feller you grassed, the divil himself would be hard put to it to know the answer. And what d'ye say now to giving Harhar a rest now an' riding Hercules this tilt? And I'll tell you why. That feller I can't make out—but there's something about him I don't like—is out of it for a spell, anyhow. But I wouldn't put it past him to get back into the third an' last tilt, in another disguise and on a better horse—for if he wasn't disguised this time, I'm the Queen of Spain!"

"But the rules!" Dennys objected. "And why all this talk of disguise?"

"Never mind that now, bless yer innocence!" Rufus said. "Just do as I say, Denny boy, and I'll enlighten you when it's all over. Ride Hercules this run; and stick on; and I'll tell you wot next when I see it."

So Denny mounted the big red roan gelding and took his place again, with Rufus at his nigh stirrup.

"Four survivors only," said Rufus. "But that don't mean twelve were grassed. That couldn't be. Most of them were run away with—clear off the field of glory, an' maybe all the way home—poor fellers! And the knight confronting you this time is one I know about, an' nothing to worry about. Sir Shane is the name. They say he was a champion jouster before he came home an' settled down to family life, which was so long ago my mother could have married his eldest son instead of my father if she'd had a mind to. So she says, anyhow. But I doubt that you'll have to give the old gentleman so much as a poke, for I'll eat my helmet if that wild colt he's up on don't bolt for home at the blast of the trumpets. So all you've got to do this time is ride straight an' easy, an' watch out you don't get run away with yerself."

"*Squires outside!*" bawled a herald.

"Don't let him get the bit in his teeth, an' there's nothing to it, God bless ye!" said Rufus.

King Malachi stood up under the royal canopy and waved a hand. The trumpets sounded, and Hercules responded with a crooked leap. But Dennys held on. He held onto everything, with everything—onto spear, rein, saddle, and hide with hands, knees, and heels. He caught a fleeting glimpse of Sir Shane flying, spearless, from the field, pulling hard with both hands. But he could not spare that old knight a thought or a second glance, for he had all he could do to keep himself on top of Hercules, and Hercules on the field. It was a notable exhibition, anyway, of human and equine determination and deviltry and gymnastics; and when the trumpets sounded "*Cease action!*" man and horse were still there and still together, and spear and shield were pointed and dressed in approximately the right direction.

Three remained of the second tilt, of whom Dennys and one other were survivors from the first.

"You did grand, Denny—but the worst is yet to come," said Rufus.

"How so?" Dennys asked, who by now felt himself a match for anyone short of King Arthur Pendragon's fellowship.

"Never mind the questions now, but get back onto old Harhar, and pray to every saint you know the name of," Rufus answered.

"I am riding this big red fool again, mauger my head!" Dennys asserted. "I've got the mastery of him now. And another thing: if I'm to be grassed this time—which I doubt, mark you!—it will be King Malachi's gift that shares the humiliation with me, and not the grand old charger King Torrice gave me."

The squire sighed and said that he admired the knight's sentiment, anyway. So Dennys limbered the kinks out of his elbows and knees and climbed back into the same saddle. He returned to his place, with Rufus at his near stirrup.

"Now d'ye see who's in front of you again?" Rufus said.

"Again? Why he's a stranger to me."

"He's changed his armor and his horse, that's all—or my eyesight's failing. And he's got a red cover to his shield this time instead of plain cowhide. He's the same gentleman you grassed the first tilt, Denny boy, or you can send me home to me mother an' aunts. And it's no local colt he's up on this time."

"But you can't see what it is, the way it's draped in fine cloths to the knees and hocks."

"True for ye, Denny boy—an' God spare yer innocence!"

"Don't talk to me like an uncle!" Dennys exclaimed.

"You may be nineteen—but don't forget I was in seven stark fights on my way to this place with King Torrice and Sir Lorn, not to mention the skirmish I was in at Carleon when I slew three rogues single-handed for my little maid there. And what were you doing at that time, friend Michael—besides chasing milkmaids?"

"Hah!" Rufus barked, blinking hard and fast for half a minute, and his face as red as his head.

Then he smiled, and then he laughed.

"Well said, Sir Dennys!" he exclaimed. "That's the spirit, Denny boy—but keep it for yer enemies, an' spare yer true friend; and here's me hand on it."

They shook hands.

"*Squires outside!*" bawled a herald.

Then the trumpets brayed.

Hercules went straight, but in bumpy bounces, fighting to get his head down between his knees and grab a tooth-hold on the bit. The opposing charger came straight too, but swiftly and smoothly; and Dennys' spear was plowing the sod at the moment of contact with his opponent's level weapon. Hit fair in midshield, and bounced by bucking Hercules in the same instant, he was lifted from his saddle and flung to the ground.

"Just as I thought, it was Sir Keel, the Dubliner who pretended to be sick abed," Rufus informed him. "I sent Maggon back to the castle to spy on him—and sure enough, he wasn't there."

"But why all that trouble to give me a spill?" Dennys asked.

"It was Malachi's idea, depend upon it, the scut!"

"But why?"

"To bring ye down a peg in the esteem of Little Brigie, I wouldn't put it past him."

"But why?—damn him!"

"Because he's jealous an' ambitious an' crooked, like I told you, the dirty scut!"

"And how did he like it?"

"Grand, by the way he laughed."

"And the little maid?"

"Little Brigie? I didn't notice her."

"Look me in the eye and say that again."

But Rufus did not look Dennys in the eye. His glance

slipped and slid and darted, like shallow and fast water over pebbles.

"Young Kelly was grassed that time too—once out of three tilts, the same as yerself," he said, talking fast. "So the two of you tied for the prize; so the heralds will be looking for you in a minute, to parade you to receive yer share of it."

"You heard me ask a question," said Dennys. "How did the little Princess take it?"

"She's young," Rufus said, flickering his glance everywhere but into Dennys' eyes. "Only six and a mite over. And maybe I was mistaken, what with catching that fool Hercules an' everything."

"Did she laugh at my tumble? I'm asking you, Rufe—man to man."

"And if she did, who cares? For she's only a baby—and how would she know if she laughed or cried, in all that excitement?"

But he hung his head while he spoke. Dennys blinked at him, nodded and stepped up into old Harhar's high saddle.

"I'm off," Dennys said in a queer voice. "Follow if you want to, or send my fellows and horses and gear after me, and go home to the apron strings."

"And wot about the Dubliners ye've still got to fight with sharp spears, including that fox Keel?" Rufus asked him, with a look straight in the eyes at last.

"They'll keep, and I'll keep," Dennys answered, twisting a bitter grin. "I'll bide my time—but not in this accursed hole."

"Ride along, then," Rufus said. "South, an' take yer time; an' I'll be after you with our fellows an' horses an' gear as quick as I can get them together, Denny boy."

When the heralds bawled for Sir Dennys ap Rhys to come forward and receive his share of the prize for winning two jousts out of three, they got no response; nor could they find hair or hide of him, or of Master Michael MacMurraugh either. So the young Kelly got the entire prize. King Malachi expressed deep concern about Dennys' disappearance, but smiled slyly behind his scraggly mustaches for all that. He was rid of that young foreign nobody—Welshman or Cornishman or whatever he was—

cheaper than he had hoped for; and to have detained him for just long enough to be humiliated right under Little Brigie's eyes had been a clever trick. But he did not like the way his daughter kept on sobbing and sniffling, nor the queer looks the Queen gave him and Sir Keel. But never mind a few sulks and queer looks for a day or two! It was the duty of a second-rate and ambitious king in doubtful health to look ahead.

Chapter Four
THE KEEPERS OF THE BRIDGE

Dennys was a changed man now from the one whose employment Rufus had talked himself into. He had been a boy, for all his hardiness of both body and spirit—and a cheerful boy, at that; but now he was a man, and a cheerless one into the bargain. His temper, which had been as warm and friendly as high and proud, was now grim and bitter and hard; and Rufus had all he could do at times to keep himself cheery and chummy. One morning, six days out of Cavantown, Rufus spoke right out, but with a smile and a bantering tongue.

"God send us some bloodthirsty knight-errants or dragons before we start bashing each other, Denny boy!"

Dennys gave him a quick look.

"You too, Rufe?" Dennys said in a bitter voice.

Rufus had not expected that reply. It made him feel at fault and ashamed, and angry with himself, and therefore angry with Dennys.

"Wot d'ye mean, me too?" he cried. "If you think I've played you false, put a name to it here an' now! Is it me who sulks an' glowers all day long, with never a smile or a civil word? Just because I serve you freely, do I have to take snarls an' grunts for wages? And when I crack a joke, it's 'You too, Rufe?' like as if ye'd caught me trying to slit yer gullet! God's wounds!"

For answer, Dennys drew rein and sat and stared straight ahead between the ears of his big red horse, as still and silent as a knight of stone; whereupon Rufus drew rein too, and sat staring to his front without sound or motion. What the knight was thinking, and what the squire was thinking, and what might have come of their thoughts if a diversion had not come before either of them spoke, or moved, will never be told. . . . The groom Oggle, who had been scouting a hundred yards in advance, came back upon them, his small mountainy horse running like a frightened dog.

"Ho-ho!" he cried, pulling and yanking to a rough stop. "A pair of great champions keeping a bridge, with their spears in their hands an' their shields dressed!"

Dennys turned his head and looked at Rufus, and Rufus turned his and looked at Dennys; and the squire grinned, and the knight smiled. Then they went forward at a jog, stirrup to stirrup, with the grooms and spare horses and beasts of burden crowding after.

"Two of them," Rufus said. "That's easy for me, Denny boy."

"Easy now," Dennys warned him. "We haven't seen them yet, nor heard them."

A few seconds later a turn in the track brought the bridge and its keepers into their view. Before them a narrow meadow, split by a yet narrower stream which brimmed its greening banks, ran to right and left through greening woodland, and at the near end of a short bridge, two knights full harnessed and armed, and mounted on tall horses, awaited them. The track went across the young grass to the bridge, and from the other end of the bridge across the farther strip of meadow and into the forest beyond. Dennys and Rufus continued to advance, though at a walk instead of a jog-trot; but when one of the knights raised and flourished an arm and shouted "Stand and parley!" they stood.

"Leave this part of it to me, Denny boy, for I do believe I've heard rumors of these gentlemen," Rufus said.

Dennys nodded.

Then Rufus sang out: "Wot d'ye want to say?"

"Only this," the stranger answered, coming nearer to save his voice. "If ye're earls or better, 'twill cost ye two silver crowns apiece to cross this bridge; but the charge for knights and simple squires is only one crown a head."

"An' wot if we haven't got any crowns?" Rufus asked.

"Then ye can pay the toll in provisions."

"Wot if we cross the bridge anyhow?"

"Ye can't do that, young sir! It's ag'in' the rules!"

Rufus laughed indulgently.

"I've heard tell of Yer Honors, but that was when I was a child listening to tales at my granddaddy's knee," he said. "The mighty Keepers of the Bridge! One or t'other of you once poked that same brave ancestor of mine into the river here. But that was a long time ago. So will Yer Honors kindly listen to me now: I am but a squire, and maybe a simple one, but this knight is Sir Dennys ap Rhys, with gold spurs three inches long on his heels. But silver crowns are something else. Not that we couldn't spare a few if we had to, but the truth is that our hearts are not so much set on crossing yer bridge just now as on getting into a fight— a ding-dong combat against equal or even superior forces. But I have a suggestion and an offer to make Yer Honors, in Sir Dennys' name an' me own both."

"What the devil's all this about?" Dennys asked. "I'll not pay a crown, or a groat, but will fight the two single-handed, if need be."

"Easy now," cautioned Rufus. "I've a suspicion these poor old champions haven't fought anybody, nor been paid a crown by anybody, in the last fifteen years an' maybe more. Too old, poor souls! But have patience, Denny boy; and if I don't raise a few brawls for us, call me a Saracen!"

Now the knights of the bridge were stirrup to stirrup and with their helmeted heads together. Now the one who had spoken before, spoke again.

"We will listen to yer suggestion, young sir."

"Gramercy," Rufus acknowledged. "This is it, sir: let Sir Dennys and me take yer places here, as Keepers of the Bridge, till the spring water subsides. And we will keep it at both ends."

"And yer offer?" asked the other.

"Half of all the crowns we take, on the words of a Tudor and a MacMurraugh!" Rufus said.

The knights of the bridge put their helmets together again for another minute.

"Did ye say MacMurraugh?" the spokesman asked.

"Ay, but not a black one," Rufus answered.

His vizor was open. He hooked a finger inside his helmet and brought a red curl to view.

"A grandson of Red Dunstan himself," he added.

The two let their spears fall to the ground, pushed their

shields aside to their left shoulders and dismounted. They advanced then, on foot, peering through the bars of their closed vizors. All their movements were slow and yet jerky. They stood at the squire's near stirrup; and one, and then the other, jerked the mailed gauntlet from his right hand.

"Shake on it, MacMurraugh," said the spokesman.

Rufus ungloved and grasped the thin, veiny, bony hands in turn.

An hour later Dennys and Rufus had the little bridge to themselves. Their spears leaned against one of the stone parapets. They were not mounted, but the knight had an arm through Hercules' bridle, and the squire one through old Harhar's.

"The poor old souls!" said Rufus. "They were glad enough to hand over to us. It was Malachi's father gave them this bridge, for pulling him out of the river one night he fell into it full of usquebaugh, when they were all young. And they made a good thing of it so long as they were able to collect the toll. It was pay or fight in those days; and if the traveler who chose to fight instead of fork over won the passage, that's all he got for his trouble; but if he lost, he had to pay ten times the toll, or his horse an' harness. And there were few better jousters in these parts than Sir Gorrill an' his brother Sir Craig. But it was easy come, easy go. And look at the poor old gentlemen now, with all the roofs leaking, an' only rusty hams an' black bread in the larders. It's no wonder their eyes an' mouths watered when they saw our pack-ponies."

"It is your idea," Dennys said. "And I'm telling you now, if it doesn't produce action by this time tomorrow, I'll be off."

"Here it comes!" Rufus cried; and he stepped up into Harhar's saddle, closed his vizor, grabbed up his spear, and left the bridge by its farther end at a sedate trot.

After a quick look, Dennys followed his example and then rode after him.

"Stand an' parley!" cried Rufus, in a cracked voice.

Dennys came up on his squire's right and drew rein there just as the two leaders of the approaching cavalcade pulled up in front of them. The strangers wore velvet caps with gold brooches in them, but were in full armor otherwise. One was larger, older, and more abundantly bewhiskered than the other, but not much more important-looking. Both had poddy eyes, thick noses, and fat lips.

"Don't be silly, old men," said the elder, and he threw a copper penny on the ground. "Make way now, ye old loon—and the saints be with ye!"

But Rufus did not stir, nor toss his leveled spear; so Dennys kept himself and his spear in place too, and his mouth shut. Since his arrival in Ireland, he had learned to leave the talking to the Irish—especially the first word.

"For lords an' better, two silver crowns apiece," Rufus squawked, his voice like a sick crow's. "And for knights and simple squires, one silver crown apiece. 'Tis the rule of the bridge and the law of the King."

The other cried: "There's been no tolls paid here in fifteen years, ye old galoot—not since the day a green squire defied an' grassed the two of ye single-handed. It's doles, not tolls, for the bold Keepers of the Bridge now."

He threw down another copper penny and wheeled his charger forward. His companion did the same. But both were stopped in a horse's-length by the points of Rufus' and Dennys' spears at their throats. They reined backward, cursing, drew their swords, and slashed at the spears. The squire's spear-point of tempered steel fell to the ground, cut clean away from the ashen shaft; but Dennys lowered his in the nick of time, then swung it upward and inward and struck his man a buffet across the ribs that shook both rider and horse. Both travelers retreated, wheeling their horses and bawling for helmets and spears. Two attendants ran to them, each with a lance and a plumed casque. Dennys and Rufus kept their ground. Rufus tried to make a joke of the pointless condition of his spear, but his face was red behind his vizor.

"It's lighter an' easier to handle now," he said.

"The big fellow is mine," Dennys said.

Rufus cursed and cried: "I'll go on where I left off!"

"Then you'll use my spear on him."

"The divil with that!"

"You heard me, Master Michael. If you must go on with the bigger and better man, you will use the better spear. Or keep the spear you have and take on the second-best cavalier. Make up your mind now, for here they come—and the biggest one straight at you!"

"Give it here, then."

They exchanged spears.

"Leave the footwork to Harhar," Dennys charged. "And the headwork too. Keep a straight spear now—and away we go!"

Dennys, on Hercules, went full pelt at the younger of the strangers. The big roan knew his master well enough by this time to run straight and hard. The stranger's point struck Dennys' shield a hand's-span off center and glanced aside, but the pointless shaft of tough timber caught the opposing shield fair in the middle and held there. Both big horses were set back by the shock, but unequally, and both riders were pressed against the high backs of their saddles, but unequally also, for Hercules was the stronger horse and Dennys the stronger man. For a long moment, the headless spear bent in an arc: then, as the stranger was lifted clear of his high crupper, it sprang straight and flung him away.

But Rufus was less fortunate, despite his undamaged spear and Harhar's craftiness. For all his practice tilts at wooden dummies, he missed his opponent's shield and person entirely, whereas the other's point, driven straightly and furiously, pierced his shield, and would have entered his breastplate had not the war-wise old steed given back instantly and with a sidewise fling of his hindquarters to relieve the pressure. So Rufus rolled on the ground, but with undamaged breastplate and breastbone.

Dennys dismounted in haste and ran to him, and would have stooped to lift him, but for a cry of warning from Rufus himself, who was up on one elbow. Dennys turned, sword in hand, and sprang to meet the onset. He slashed, twisted aside, sprang in again, thrusting and hacking with his sword and shouldering like a charging boar. The spear broke. The horse, struck on a flank by Dennys' shield and full weight and an upthrust iron knee, grunted and flinched and lost both pace and direction. The rider loosed the butt of his useless spear and drew his sword, only to have it hacked from his hand.

The horse, pressed by a hard shield and belly-kicked repeatedly by Dennys' mailed knee, staggered aside, crossed its forelegs, and stumbled to its knees. Dennys struck his starkest stroke then, and his enemy's helmet clanged like an anvil. The maddened horse staggered up, made a plunging wheel and bolted; and the rider (his left foot now firmly in the grasp of Dennys' two hands), came sidewise from the saddle and hit the ground like four hundredweight of iron and rocks. Dennys let the foot and leg fall with a secondary thud and turned to Rufus, who was sitting up and staring at him.

"Are you hurt?" he asked.

Rufus, still staring, got to his feet slowly and shook his head. Then Dennys surveyed the immediate and surrounding scene. His last opponent still lay motionless and silent. The first, who had fallen to a pointless spear, was standing now. His vizor was raised, and he was looking at Dennys. And all the others of that party, men and horses alike, were looking at Dennys. And Dennys' and Rufus' own four fellows, who must have got wind of the brawl back in the bridge-keepers' house in the woods, were staring at Dennys too as they came running with boar-spears and short swords in their hands.

Dennys looked at his squire again.

"It's your idea—this keeping the bridge. What do we do next?"

The squire looked about him on all sides before answering. He spoke vaguely, with a curiously diffident air.

"I don't know, sir. Ye kept the bridge, divil a doubt of it! Do we take four crowns now, or their steeds an' horses? And if that one's as dead as he looks—well, I don't know wot we do next."

"You could open his vizor and see if he's breathing," Dennys said.

Rufus went to the fallen cavalier and knelt and pushed the vizor up from the face.

"He's puffing like a grampus, but his eyes are shut and he's bleeding at the nose," he reported.

At that moment the other stranger approached and confronted Dennys, blinking his popping eyes and showing his teeth.

"Four silver crowns," he snarled, and threw the coins on the ground.

"Pick them up and hand them to me," said Dennys.

"Not so fast!" Rufus cried, scrambling to his feet and stepping in between Dennys and the stranger, with his face to the stranger. "Ye owe me for a good spear too. And by the rules of this bridge, and of chivalry too, the horses an' arms an' gear of the both of you are forfeit to Sir Dennys ap Rhys here."

"Hah! So that's it!" the other snarled. "Usurpers an' tricksters! Ye murdered the poor old lawful keepers, that's it, ye thieving, ditch-whelped foreigners! And now ye'd rob an' cheat in their names. But it won't be for long."

"We didn't lay a finger on them," Rufus retorted. "The poor old gentlemen sit at home this very minute, eating an' drinking their fill for the first time in years. Ye can go see for yerself if you doubt the word of a MacMurraugh, me barnyard chantecler!"

"A MacMurraugh, d'ye say? Ye'll not be the first of that breed to hang by the neck. And yer friend too, whatever name you give him—the two of ye'll dance on the air for this day's work, or I am no MacGorfey!"

"MacGorfey?" Rufus echoed after him, in a changed voice.

"So ye've heard it!" the other jeered; and his savage grin widened, full of teeth pointed like a wolf's fangs.

Just then the big cavalier on the ground sat up and blew blood from his nose and spat it from his mouth. The grinning knight jeered again within six inches of Rufus' face.

"King Gorfey! Maybe ye've heard of him too?"

Rufus was silent for long enough to count ten. Then he spoke in a subdued and uncertain voice:

"It was only the bash of his own weight when he hit the sod. The loss of a mite of blood will do him more good nor harm. See, he's up on his feet now! And they've caught your horses. On your way now—an' no hard feelings over a bit of sport, I trust, Sir MacGorfey?"

"Prince is me style an' title," was the jeering reply. "And if we go now, the sooner we'll be back—and with a score instead of five in our train, including the sherrif's hangman."

"Not so fast," said Dennys, elbowing his squire to one side. "Lend a hand to King what's-his-name, Rufe. As for you, prince or whatever you are, get out of your harness.

I'm keeping your horse too; and the knave-knight's horse and armor and arms. King or whatever he is, I'll teach him not to ride at a knight on the ground."

Then King Gorfey spoke up in a grim voice. He was standing now, supported by one of his five varlets. His nose had stopped bleeding, but his beard and mustaches were ruddy and clotted.

"Do as the rogue says."

Fifteen minutes later, on spare horses, those two headed back the way they had come, with their train at their heels, leaving their war-gear in piles on the ground, and their chargers in the hands of Oggle and Maggon. One of the other grooms picked up the four silver crowns and held them out to the squire; but Rufus was regarding Dennys so wildly yet fixedly that he gave no heed; so the fellow extended them toward Dennys.

"Keep them, lad; there's one for each of you," said Dennys.

He smiled at the squire then, and asked: "Why d'ye eye me so wildly, Rufe? Haven't we done what we set ourselves to do?"

"It was King Gorfey," Rufus said, in a desperate cracked whisper.

"I've never heard of him," Dennys replied, still smiling, but with just a hint of asperity in his voice. "How many kings have you got in Ireland, anyway? But what of it? How much glory and gear would a knight-errant win if he didn't stand his ground against all comers? And a foul knight is foul if he fights foully, no matter what title he goes by. You don't want to take curses and threats of hanging seriously in this game, so long as you spare the weak, help the help-less, and keep the laws of chivalry."

For answer, Rufus told the worst of all he knew and had ever heard of the kings and tribe of Gorfey. The first Gorfey, according to the chroniclers, had been out of a wood nymph and sired by a bog devil. And ever since, most of the women had been nymphs and the most of the men devils, no mat-ter what decent people they bred to; and the only humanity about any MacGorfey, to this day, was the physical appear-ance. And starting within a league of the bridge, ten leagues of Gorfey territory lay across the way to Dublin, with Gorfeytown itself astraddle the track somewhere.

"We are dead men if we stop here," he said.

"It was your own idea," Dennys reminded him.

Rufus grasped his head with both hands and cursed himself for a fool.

"Is this the only way to Dublin?" Dennys asked.

"I was never there," the squire confessed miserably. "Nor more than five leagues from home before. The only way out of this I know is back the way we came."

"Take that road, and you'll be a knightless squire," Dennys warned.

Rufus grasped his head again and moaned.

They mounted and went back to the old bridge-keepers' house in the fringe of the forest, followed by their grooms and the chargers and war-gear of the terrible Gorfeys. When Sir Gorrill and Sir Craig heard what had happened, terror paralyzed them for long minutes from scalps to soles, wits and muscles alike. The use of their legs returned first, and they started for the nearest door with surprising agility, and would have been out and off into the forest if Dennys had not collared them.

"Calm down, honored sirs, and aid us with your counsel," the young knight begged, shaking them gently the while.

Chapter Five
THE MACCORMICKS

They left that place at the crack of dawn, by a secret path, led by the old knights' only remaining servant, who had been born in that forest and was as fearful of the deadly displeasure of the Gorfeys as were his masters. Nothing living was left behind in the tumble-down steading, but the mice and squirrels in the thatched roofs, and the owls in the lofts.

Knights, squire, grooms, chargers, spare horses, pack-beasts, and three lurchers followed the guide like a long, frayed rope dragged by him uphill, down dale, and around swamps and quagmires.

Sir Gorrill carried a cat and nursing kittens in a basket on his saddlebow, and was hung about with bags and more baskets. Sir Craig, likewise festooned with personal and household gear, had a tame crow on his right shoulder.

In addition to their ex-masters' forfeited war-gear, the forfeited Gorfey chargers wore baskets and bags too, and a pannier containing quacking ducks and another full of clucking hens.

Even Dennys and Rufus, up on Hercules and the squire's own half-trained brown stallion, bore more than their personal arms. Each, in his softness of heart, had permitted himself to be cluttered up with useless knick-knacks and heirlooms. Only Harhar was unburdened, save for his war-saddle and a spare shield and spare lance. Dennys had foiled, kindly but firmly, all the old bridge-keepers' attempts to make a pack-horse of that wise and noble steed.

It was a slow and vulnerable company: but such was the guide's knowledge of that wilderness, they did not meet with a human being of any sort in the first sennight of travel. The days passed in safe and steady progress— and easy, save for the passages of four full streams—and the nights in rest and slumber in grassy glades. Only the provisions of food and drink suffered. Supper on the seventh evening disposed of the last of the ducks.

On the eighth day they met and were joined by three masterless men in tatters and undressed wolf-skins who, by their own telling, had been sentenced to death by King Gorfey more than fifteen months before, on the charge of preying on His Kingship's wild pigs; and though they had escaped to the wilderness with their lives, they had left their ears behind with one of the Gorfey forest wardens. Likely as the story was, one or another of the grooms kept an eye on them from dark till daylight. By that time, they were well clear of the boundaries of Gorfeyland and within the domain of the decent race of Cormicks, to their guide's best knowledge and belief. He turned the cavalcade onto a well-beaten track next morning, and to a town of farm-steads, and a mill and manor house of squared timbers before noon.

One of the three crop-eared fellows ran to Sir Gorrill's stirrup and shouted up at him:

"The lord here be Sir Finn MacCormick himself, sir, and he'll make Yer Honors welcome."

"Ye don't say so!" the ex-bridge-keeper cried joyfully. "Finn MacCormick! God bless all, I know him well! But maybe it wouldn't be the same one? For that was a long time ago, come to think of it."

"Here be himself coming to welcome ye, anyhow," said the fellow.

The lord of that barony proved to be the same Finn MacCormick whom Sir Gorrill had known thirty or more years before; but he was much younger, though well past the peak of physical agility, than either of the brothers of the bridge. He was a large, hearty lord in a long fur-trimmed gown and slippers to match. He made the travelers welcome with both hands; and so did his lady, who was much of his own proportions and manner. He took the knights and squire into his own house, and he sent a steward away to the home farm with the others, to introduce them, men and horses, to the best of everything in house and barn.

When Sir Finn heard the whole story of the brawl at the bridge, with what led up to it and what came after, and had it all sorted out in his mind, he was all but overcome with conflicting emotions. (This was at dinner, with the Lady MacCormick and the two youngest and unmarried daughters at the table.) He shouted with delight and reached across and patted Dennys on a wrist. He cursed furiously and banged the oaken board till the trenchers hopped, and the cups and horns slopped over. Then he laughed. Then he spoke, with what breath was left to him.

"Well, ye're safe here. Ye've no call to go any farther, any of ye. Not in me saintly sire's day, nor in me own, has any of that breed of divils got as far as this—not in this direction, anyhow—save only as a corpse an' a curiosity. D'ye mind those three poor rogues with cropped ears who joined ye at the deserted hermitage? Well, they be our security, or a small fraction of it, anyhow. There be over ten score such and their women an' brats, along an' round-about the way ye came; not all of them earless, but every-one of them scarred or marred somehow by a Gorfey. They live on MacCormick deer an' wild swine, an' free bread an' cheese an' ale when they choose to come an' fetch it away; and in return for me bounty, they make the woods impass-able to our common enemy. So, friends old an' new, ye be safer from King Gorfey right here than ye'd be in Dublin itself, an' we'd be glad to have ye stop out yer natural lives with us."

The dame said it would be wonderful, but the damosels said nothing and kept their eyes on their trenchers. Dennys and Rufus were silent too, though the former blushed slightly and the latter fidgeted. But Old Gorrill spoke up in a hurry, eagerly and anxiously.

"D'ye mean that, Sir Finn?"

"Sure I mean it, old friend!" cried MacCormick. "Wasn't I the first who ever unhorsed ye at your bridge—an' me just turned twenty? An' then Craig, here, gave me a tumble. An' then the three of us made a night of it in your grand house in the wood there; and I've never drunk as good liquor since. Sure I mean it!"

"And Craig too?" quavered Sir Gorrill.

"Sure, an' Craig too! An' these young gentlemen too. The more the merrier!"

The poor old ex-keepers of the bridge fairly wept with relief and gratitude. Dennys thanked Sir Finn warmly, and explained the necessity of his return to his distant home.

"That goes for me too, sir—unless Sir Dennys has had enough of me," the squire said, in a contrite voice and with a look at match it.

The four MacCormicks looked at him curiously, and then as curiously at Dennys. The old brothers of the bridge were too busy and blind with their tears of relief to notice anything.

"Not yet," said Dennys, but loud enough for all to hear.

Then he leaned to Rufus and murmured: "If the spill Gorfey gave you is on your mind, forget it."

"That's not all," Rufus muttered.

The ale and usquebaugh were getting the better of the squire's discretion now; and Dennys, whose own head was a mite harder, recognized the symptoms.

"Forget the rest of it too then, and eat yer pudding!" Dennys ordered; but there was affection as well as authority in his whisper. "And if I ever have cause for complaint, Rufe, I'll tell you, never fear!" he added.

The squire cheered up instantly.

"Gramercy, Denny boy!" he exclaimed, with a grin in his best manner; and he disposed of his pudding with gusto. . . .

Two days later, Dennys and Rufus took the road to Dublin and the world beyond again, leaving the horse and arms of the younger Gorfey with the brothers Sir Gorrill and Sir Craig, in settlement of their business at the bridge.

Chapter Six
WITH THE BIG LEAGUE

Sir Dennys and Master MacMurraugh reached the coast without mishap and found a ship of sorts; and after an argument on the subject of passage money with the half-score greedy shipmen, they embarked with their four trusty grooms, their seven horses, and three of the crew, leaving the remainder of the disputants licking their wounds, back among the rocks. They reached a wild spot on the opposite shore without loss of life or limb.

Three days later they encountered a knight-errant. He did not look very formidable, and his manner and voice were pleasant. He told them that he had taken a vow not to change his shirt until he had unhorsed twenty cavaliers, that the tally now stood at eighteen, and that he was beginning to itch. So Dennys obliged him, and was pushed—no more than pushed—over Hercules' tail. Then Rufus volunteered, and was tossed into a holly bush. The victor stripped, bathed in a convenient spring, and donned a clean shirt. He was in high spirits, and deeply grateful to Dennys and Rufus for having afforded the means of fulfilling his vow; and to show his gratitude, he joined the younger cavaliers and remained with them on all the long road to Camelot.

He had been knighted three years before by Sir Uwaine, a renowned champion, and his name and style were Sir Errol of Highwood. On the way to the royal town of Camelot—and it was long and crooked—he gave Dennys and Rufus much practical advice on the subject of unhorsing one's antagonist while remaining in one's own saddle, and often illustrated his words with a dummy spear. They proved themselves apt pupils. Arrived at Camelot, where King Arthur and his court were in residence, Sir Errol presented his new friends to half a dozen representative knights and two earls, and then left them and went about his own affairs, which were probably of an amorous nature. . . .

For a time Sir Dennys and his squire and their modest retinue were hard put to it to maintain a genteel appearance. But for a prize of five crowns won by Maggon in a wrestling match, and the successes of an Irish gamecock that had been fetched all the way from Cavantown by one of Rufus' fellows, they would have gone hungry more than once. For weeks Sir Dennys took nothing but tumbles in the lists. But his bones were tough; and he set his jaw and hardened his heart. And then came the day when, in a grand passage of arms, he vanquished a mighty earl.

More good came of that success than the lawfully forfeited horse and armor; for His Lordship had been so favorably impressed by the young knight's courteous treatment when he had him at his mercy on the ground, that he repurchased the lost property at twice its value, and invited Dennys to supper. And that was but the beginning. Fame and fortune were Dennys ap Rhys' for the taking after that; but for a secret bitter whim, he refrained from taking in full measure. Over and over again he turned his back on Opportunity and rode aimlessly in the wilderness, bidding his squire come if he wanted to, or stop behind with one-half of their money and goods if he would; and Rufus always went along, though not happily.

In the course of years, Sir Dennys went so high (despite his frequent retirements) that he suffered the honor of a tumble from the spear of Sir Launcelot du Lake—and even higher than that, when the greatest knight in Christendom smilingly declined his respectful invitation to engage afoot with swords and daggers.

"It pains me to refuse you, my dear Denny, but I suspect that it would pain me more to humor you," the peerless champion said, with all of his famous charm; and then he took both Dennys and Rufus to dine with King Arthur and Queen Gwynever, Queen Isoud, Sir Tristram, the Queen of Orkney, and Sir Dinadan.

Michael MacMurraugh also advanced in those years; and yet he did not seem to be much happier than Dennys was, though he caroused oftener and laughed louder. He too appeared at times to nurse a secret wound or regret. But he prospered in goods and gear and made a reputation as a ladies' man and a wit as well as a man of his hands. He was in no hurry to be knighted, and vowed that he would not accept the accolade from any hand but that of King Arthur or one of the five highest knights in the land. He lost his heart frequently and found it just as often. He learned tricks of repartee and rhyming from Sir Dinadan, and of horsemanship and swordsmanship from the greatest living masters of those skills, only to receive the worst beating of his career at the hands of obscure riffraff in a remote wilderness.

Chapter Seven
NEWS OF A PRINCESS

The moment Dennys heard that voice asking the shortest way to the buttery-hatch, he left his chair beside the couch upon which Rufus was dozing uneasily, and went out to greet its owner. The beribboned lute slung to the left shoulder, and a certain artificial airiness of dress and manner told Dennys the stranger's occupation as surely as the voice had told him his nationality.

"Welcome to this poor retreat, Master Minstrel," said Dennys, with a slightly more successful attempt at cordiality than he usually achieved in addressing strangers or even mere acquaintances. "Come in with me, and the best we have of food an' drink, such as it is, shall be brought to your table."

The troubadour doffed his cap and bowed, but with a hint of suspicion in his glance.

"I have a hurt friend here who will be better for your native songs and talk, I think—if you are what I take you for," Dennys said.

"An' wot might that be?" the other asked, still with only the corners of his eyes on the knight.

"An Irelander," said Dennys.

"I be that, however ye guessed it!" the troubadour cried enthusiastically, with both his eyes full upon Dennys' now. "And as straight from Dublin as any man could come by twisty ship an' twisty tracks; an' the divil only knows why I made the trip! But here I be, with regret in me heart an' nought in me belly—but at yer service, sir, for all that. Larry the Rhymer! Maybe ye've heard tell of me?"

"It's my friend who's the Irelander," Dennys apologized hurriedly. "But come this way now, Master Rhymer, for bite and sup before I take you in to him."

In a few minutes the minstrel was busy with a jack of strong ale and a cold roast fowl, and Dennys was back beside Rufus' couch.

"Now that your bones are mended," said Dennys, "all you need is a bit of cheering up; and then we'll return to Camelot for the pair of gold spurs Sir Dinadan has ready for you."

The squire's only reply was a wan smile.

"I have a hungry Irish minstrel out in the hall," Dennys went on. "I'll fetch him as soon as he's emptied his jack and cleared his trencher. He's a Dubliner, but that's better than nothing. His songs and tales will amuse you, lad."

"Ye've a kind heart, Denny boy," Rufus said, with another wan smile; and then he closed his eyes.

Dennys waited long enough, then fetched the minstrel, who entered still licking his fingers and his lips. Dennys made him known to Rufus, and Rufus to him, with grave formality.

"MacMurraugh, d'ye say?" the minstrel exclaimed heartily. "And a very good name too. I've heard it highly spoke of many a time. And I've got a good name meself, which is Toole, me own dad bein' a near cousin to the O'Toole himself, him of the barony an' castle of Bally Tooley. But bein' a tenth son meself, I took to music an' poetry, an' not to the discredit of them difficult arts neither, by the name an' style of Larry the Rhymer. Maybe ye've heard tell of me?"

"Who hasn't?" Rufus murmured, in a tired but polite voice; and he closed his eyes languidly.

"Give him a song to cheer him up," Dennys whispered to the minstrel. "His flesh is healed and his ribs are mended, but he's low in mind an' heart. He's been a long time a long way from his native home; and that's his trouble, in my opinion, though he doesn't say so."

"Why doesn't he go home, then?" asked the minstrel.

"He wants his gold spurs from one of King Arthur's best knights first. That's one reason."

"Man, Sir Dennys, if the poor feller be homesick, I can make him a song that'll knock all the gold spurs this side

Jerusalem clear out of his mind! Just tell me the name an'
whereabouts of his own particular home spot on the darlin'
old sod, and I'll show ye."

"But I'm only asking you to cheer him up, Master
Rhymer."

"Sure! Sure! But give it a name now, an' leave me show
ye wot a real poet can do when he sets his janius to it."

"D'ye know anything about the Cavanaugh country?
Castle Cavanaugh and Cavantown? That's his native
home."

"The Cavanaugh country! D'ye tell me so? Man, ye've
put yer finger on it! No one with two ears could help
himself from hearin' about the goin's-on in that country
when I was fool enough to come away from Dublin. And if
I had to leave Dublin, why didn't I go to Cavantown? But
never mind that now. Them goin's-on inspired me to song,
anyhow. Hark ye to this now!"

Larry the Rhymer pulled his lute around to his front
and went to it like one bewitched as well as inspired.

"There dwells a queen in Cavantown,
Full beautiful to see;
An' there a princess dwells also,
More beautiful than she.
So spur ye unto Cavantown,
If ye would be in style,
An' see a nation's chivalry
Competing for a smile.

"The King sent out his singing men
To sing his daughter's charms:
And every son of Ireland now
Would have her in his arms.
That king sent out more singing men
To tell, throughout the land,
Only the greatest might aspire
To win his daughter's hand."

Rufus opened his eyes and sat up and gave Dennys a
queer look: but Dennys did not look at him, but white-
faced at the minstrel, so he lay flat again. The minstrel
caught a few deep breaths, rolled his eyes at the rafters,
and went on with the song.

"Nine kings be there at Cavantown,
And princes by the score,
And earls with num'rous kegs of gold,
An' dukes with maybe more.
So if yer wealth bes that of Ind,
An' ye would be in style,
Go try yer luck at Cavantown
An' maybe—"

"Stop!" shouted Dennys, so fiercely and with a gesture so furious that the singer stopped with his mouth still open and Rufus sat up again.

They both stared at Dennys, but with very different expressions on their faces. Dennys stared at neither of them, but into space seemingly. His lips, as bloodless as his cheeks, squirmed without sound a few times before he spoke again. Now his utterance was faint and broken.

"This princess? Who is she? Give her a name!"

The troubadour stammered, "Yes, sir—I was comin' to it—to her name, sir—which is Brigid, the same as that of the Queen."

Dennys croaked: "She's nought but a child—the little maid. Little Brigie. Cynara to me."

"She's fifteen," Rufus said quietly. "It was nine years ago we came away."

He turned to the minstrel and said: "Ye could go to the hall now an' wet yer vocal cords after yer grand performance, me talented friend. Just shout for wotever ye want, and if we have it ye'll get it. See ye later, Larry lad."

The bewildered minstrel was glad to get out of that room—and not only because he was thirsty. He suspected both the knight and squire of madness.

"I have something to tell you," Rufus said.

Dennys gave him a vague look and did not speak.

"If ye think me trouble is I'm homesick, ye're mistaken," Rufus went on, in a flat voice. "Harky now, and I'll tell ye—if I die for it. An' good riddance too."

But Dennys said nothing to that, nor so much as nodded, but sat with his elbows on his knees and both hands to his head.

"Will ye listen?" the squire cried bitterly. "To me confession. To as mean an' knavish a confession as ever a MacMurraugh had to make, God help me!"

Dennys looked at him then, but still vaguely, and spoke vaguely.

"It's the fever, Rufe. Don't excite yourself now."

"To hell with the fever!" cried Rufus. "It's a confession, d'ye hear! D'ye mind the time the tricky Dubliner gave you the spill, back at Castle Cavanaugh?"

Dennys, who was now regarding the sick man curiously, nodded assent.

"Sir Keel was the name," continued Rufus. "He grassed ye hard an' clean, for all to see. And King Malachi laughed even harder than the Dubliners did. D'ye mind that now?"

"You told me about it," Dennys said, in a low voice. "I couldn't see for myself, for a few minutes."

"And it was the truth. But listen to this! Ye asked me if Little Brigie laughed. And I told ye yes she did. D'ye mind that?"

"I've never forgot it—nor ever will," Dennys whispered.

"Then ye can forget it now," Rufus whispered; and he lay back on the pillow and clapped trembling hands to his face. "Forget it now—for it was a lie! She didn't laugh. She went white as her wimple."

Dennys spoke first after that, after minutes of silence.

"Why did you do it?"

"So's to get ye safe away—then an' there," Rufus moaned. "Safe away from Malachi—an' the deadly mischief I'd talked ye into with the Dublin knights. I was afeared for yer life."

He paused; but as Dennys did not speak, he moaned on again, still with his hands to his face:

"Ye were no match for that bog-adder Malachi. And ye were overyoung for those champions. Ye'd be dead a long time now—by treachery or a sharp spear—if I hadn't fetched ye away. But the spell had to be broke first. An' only a lie could break it. So I lied."

"So that was it!" Dennys said, and stood up. "So that is the truth of it—at last?" He walked to the window and gazed out at the horses in the paddock, but he didn't see them. Instead, he saw a hoof-scarred field, and a grandstand gay with banners, and a little maid with a face as white as her wimple. "She didn't laugh," he said. He walked around the room and then to the side of the squire's couch. "It was a vile lie," he said. "Ay, a villainous lie—but it didn't break any spell. And if it brought me out of there alive, it was a good lie too. For I'm not overyoung now. Horsed or afoot, I'm old enough now for any Dublin knight, or the biggest champion in all Ireland. So I forgive you the lie, Rufe—and I thank you for it."

Withdrawing his hands from his face, Rufus sat up. But he did not speak, for he hadn't the words for what he wanted to say. But Dennys went on like one talking to himself.

"I'll start tomorrow. If I keep on, and avoid all combats, I'll make the seashore in a sennight. If I have luck finding a ship, I'll be in Ireland in—"

He was startled out of his soliloquy by Rufus. The sick squire was up on his feet and bawling for his boots.

"Easy now!" Dennys cried, jumping and taking a gentle hold on the other. "Ye're a sick man, Rufe. Lay down now. It's the fever. I'll send for the chirurgeon to draw off some more of the poisoned blood."

"Not so!" Rufus shouted. "There's nought wrong with me blood—wot's left of it—now that poisonous lie is out of me heart. A sick man, d'ye say? Man, Denny, me strength right now is the strength of ten!"

With a wild laugh, he grabbed Dennys by the shoulders and shook with all his might. But it was himself, not Dennys, who was shaken; for the knight stood as steady as a house founded upon rock. So he ceased that violent demonstration of vigor as suddenly as he had commenced it.

"'Twould take the strength of twenty to unbalance Sir Dennys ap Rhys," Rufus cried; and with another shout of laughter, he flung both his arms around Dennys' neck.

"Did ye think to go without me?" he chuckled. "Man, Denny boy, for all yer prowess, not to mention me own, wot would you do without me back at Cavantown now, an' all the liars in Ireland collected there?"

"Easy now, Rufe lad!" begged Dennys. "I'll not go without you, perish the thought! If you can fork a horse tomorrow morning, well an' good. If not, we'll jounce you along in a litter. But leave my neck for some of those kings an' princes to try to break, I beg you!"

Rufus released him and ran, somewhat unsteadily, to grab his boots from the fellow who had answered his shouts. The troubadour appeared in the doorway at the same moment, with a horn of ale in his hand, attracted by the hubbub; and while he stood gawking on the threshold, a small man in a fur-trimmed gown, holding a barber's basin in one hand and a lancet in the other, darted past him from behind. But not far; for Rufus, though but half booted and hopping on one foot, was upon him like a pouncing hawk.

"So it's yerself, Doctor!" cried Rufus. "Ye'll have no more blood of mine, ye doddering vampire!"

He gave the little man a spin and grabbed the mazed minstrel by the front of his jerkin.

"And for yerself, me grand balladmonger—if it's high jinks in dear old Ireland you want to sing about, turn right round an' come to Cavantown with Sir Dennys an' me," he shouted fiercely, but grinning all the while; and he gave big Larry the Rhymer a spin, then pulled on his second boot, draped a long cloak about him and strode wobblingly away to inspect the horses. . . .

They left that place next day, in the coolness of the early spring morning. Trusty Oggle and Maggon rode in front, right squirely armed and mounted. Dennys and Rufus rode next, in half-armor; the knight on a great impatient black warhorse that had been the property and pride of a first-rate champion of King Arthur's court less than a year before. Chester was its name. The squire rode easy-gaited Hercules, whose red roan coat was now frosted with white hairs, but who was still a charger in a thousand, save in the matter of wind, despite his fifteen years and a few scars which ached in wet weather. Dr. Goffkyn was on a mule; and the troubadour, who had arrived on his own feet, bestrode a good horse. Spare chargers, beasts of burden, and armed and mounted grooms completed the imposing cavalcade.

Chapter Eight
THE ROYAL FAMILY OF CAVANAUGH

It was April again, and again King Malachi was on the receiving end of more royal and noble and generally high company than he had pictured in even his most ambitious dreams of over a year before. It had been fourteen months before, to be exact, that he had sent out the first five minstrels to tell the world of the beautiful princess who would some day wear the crown of Cavan Land as liege lady of all the tribes and clans of the innumerable mountains, bogs, forests, and fat farms of a one-twentieth part of the surface of Ireland, in the commendable hope of getting himself the richest and most powerful king or prince in the Emerald Isle for a son-in-law.

With such an ally, he would achieve great things. What with trickery here and force there, by manor and barony and now and then an earldom, he would expand his borders till his power and possessions were second only to those of Anguish of Dublin. But he would have to continue to be careful of his health; so all hand-to-hand physical encounters would be the business of his son-in-law. It was a grand ambition. So, in March, he had sent out more minstrels; and the minstrels' efforts had commenced to bear fruit in April. And now it was April again.

King Malachi lay on his bed and clawed his beard and the thin hair of his scalp, and Queen Brigid sat in a chair by the window and gazed at what she could see of the landscape between narrowed lids, and with a queer smile on her pretty face.

"Did ye say four already?" asked the King.

"Six now," the Queen murmured.

"Can't ye speak out?" he barked.

"I said six now," the Queen cried; and then she added, in even louder and more derisive tones: "But I should have said seven, at least, for here's another party just topping the hill."

Malachi cursed and groaned.

"If they keep on coming like last summer, I'm ruined!" he wailed. "Ate us out of house an' home! An' for wot?"

"It was yer own idea," she reminded him.

"The idee was all right," he yowled. "Did I invite every hungry an' thirsty bum in Ireland to come an' live on me? Not so, by Judas! All I told them rhymesters was to let the world know about the beautiful young princess who's me only child an' heiress to the crown of Cavan Land, an' that the best prince in all the world will be lucky to get her. An' wot happened?"

"Ye overdid it, ye poor man," the Queen replied, with mock commiseration in her voice and face. "Or was it all the fault of the minstrels? However that might be, every man claiming royal descent—an' that means every bog-trotting spalpeen in Ireland—an' with a beast of any description to carry him this far, came to take a look at, an' maybe make a play for, one of the seven wonders of the world."

"Never mind that trash!" Malachi fumed. "I soon gave them to understand they could pay their own way or go home. But the big shots—the genuine widower kings an' certified bachelor princes—wot of them? They filled this castle and me three best mansions in the town without so much as by-yer-leave; an' emptied the cellars an' larders without so much as a thanky; an' destroyed the sod of me best meadows with their infernal joustings an' tournaments—an' all for nothing! Did any one of them take so much as a second look at Little Brigie? Divil a fear!"

"The poor child didn't encourage them," said the Queen. "She didn't try to look her best for any of them. In fact, she pulled faces at them."

Malachi sat up and gave his beautiful consort a searching, suspicious glimmer from his round eyes, which were as opaque as polished pebbles. (You could still call her beautiful, for all she was the mother of a fifteen-year-old daughter.)

"But they stayed on!" he cried. "Some of them till the first snow. And I wouldn't wonder but some of 'em—that old cheat King Farrell, an' young Flaherty, an' I could name more—would be here yet if the victuals an' drink hadn't given out!"

She gave him an amused and faintly contemptuous glance and asked gently: "Would ye have had me pull faces at them too?"

"Tell me wot's bringing 'em back!" he squealed.

"If it's to see if the future Queen of Cavan Land is improving in appearance, they're not hoping to find a growing resemblance to her father, that's a sure thing," she answered lightly; and her voice was as thin as her smile.

The King flung his fists in the air, emitted an inarticulate, gasping curse, and fell back on his pillow; at that moment a gentleman of the household coughed outside the curtained doorway and then intruded his head.

"Visitors," he said.

"Name them," snapped Malachi, without changing his position.

"There's King Farrell of Armath again."

"Not at home! I be a sick man, tell him!"

"And Prince Flaherty an' the O'Connor an'—"

"Give 'em the gate!"

"The gate, d'ye say? Man, they be all this side the inner door itself already!"

Malachi came up again like a released jack-in-the-box, and with his mouth open for a blast; but no blast came forth.

"Where's herself?" he whispered, sliding his pebbly eyes.

"She went out," the gentleman of the household replied in an indifferent voice, but with a faint leer.

"Fetch her back, then! Tell her me poor heart's give out ag'in. Tell her I be on the stroke of death."

The other withdrew instantly; and though he spoke no word of comment, the leer widened on his face. He was some sort of cousin to the King, and even older, and had served him a long time and with constantly decreasing respect and no affection whatever.

Malachi swung his legs over the edge of the bed and sat hunched up there with his bowed head gripped desperately in both hands, twitching and muttering in an ague of jealousy. It was a two-fold fit of the distressful passion: jealousy of his queen combined with fear and concern for the contents of his recently replenished cellars and storerooms. That is the kind of man he was, God help him! When he heard sounds of slippered feet and trailing skirts, he fetched up a groan from the very depths of his vital organs, but did not look. He strained his ears for a response, but in vain. He groaned again, and even more terribly. Still no response. So he raised his head and looked to see who was there. It was his daughter, Little Brigie.

She stood just within the chamber, regarding him with enigmatic eyes. More than that might be said about those eyes by someone with the requisite vocabulary and a poetic license; but to say they were indescribable is the easiest way to describe them. The expression of her mouth was enigmatic too. She was tall for her fifteen winters and thin for any age. Thin like a birch sapling. Slim, that is the word; for her face was still childishly rounded.

"So it's yerself," said the King, blinking at her.

She said nothing to that, and looked nothing.

"Me poor heart's leppin' like a horse—an' maybe the nex' jump will be the end of me!" he gasped.

Having heard that before, and more times than she had fingers and toes to keep count on, she let it pass without comment. He sighed profoundly and changed his tune.

"Harky to me now, me own darling little daughter," he whispered. "Ye wouldn't want to be the death of yer poor loving old dad now, would ye? I've always been a kind, doting, protecting father to ye, an' whoever says different is a liar, an' now all I'm asking of ye in return is practically nothing at all. Can't ye be polite to me royal friends now an' give some of them a pretty smile now an' then, instead of sneering an' sulking an' pulling ugly faces at them the way ye did last summer? I bain't asking any favors for that old baboon King Farrell; but take young Flaherty, now. Prince Flaherty! Handsome, and his father's heir. An' here at Castle Cavanaugh again, at the first blooming of the pretty flowers, asking for a kind look from ye. Can't ye do that little thing now to oblige yer poor old dad?"

Then the Princess smiled, though very faintly.

"Why?" she asked.

"Why not?" he yelped back at her.

After a brief struggle to get another strangle-hold on his temper, he found his wheedling voice and manner again.

"All for yer own happiness an' glory, me own darling child," he continued. "And I'll tell ye the truth, now, even if it chokes me. A year back, me grand idee for your happiness was to find ye the mightiest man in Ireland for a husband, an' never mind his looks an' wotnot. But I see now it wasn't the right idee. It was all wrong. Riches an' power bain't everything, I can see that now. Love's the great thing—dances an' merry-go-rounds an' all—just like the poets tell it.

"So now ye can take yer pick of all the world for a husband, an' me blessing along with him—within reason. He's got to be a prince. And ye'll admit that be only reasonable, all things considered. An' a prince with a good chance at his father's crown an' all. Take young Flaherty, now. Or the O'Connor's eldest son. Or Sir Cassidy of Dublin; for even if two or three do stand closer than him to the crown of his

Uncle Anguish right now, I wouldn't be surprised if he was the only one left to put it on by the time King Anguish has to take it off."

"I don't want a husband," she said quietly. "Not now, and maybe never. I be in no hurry, anyhow."

"Have a heart, me own precious child!" Malachi wailed. "Haste be the principal thing in this case, can't ye see that! Pick one anyhow, even if ye don't marry him right off—or we'll be suffering all the diviltries an' monkeyshines an' wicked, useless expenditures of last summer all over again!"

"Whatever happens, ye'll have only yerself to blame for it," she said; and she turned and went out.

For a while after that rebuff from his only child, King Malachi Cavanaugh was a crushed man there on the edge of his grand bed with his face in his hands. He was crushed too flat even for groans and moans; and the only sound he made was a weak, piteous, whimpering sort of whisper, thin and wordless. Feeling sorry for himself was an old story; but now he plumbed the uttermost depths of self-pity. And shame—an emotion quite foreign to his nature—was mixed up in it; and as if that was not enough, remorse thrust its freezing, twisting fingers into the very valves and sinews of his being. He saw all the crimes and cruelties, great and small, of which he had been guilty since childhood; and all his treacheries and knaveries and meannesses of act and thought. They glowed red on the black of his shut eyes like figures on a tapestry woven and embroidered in hell. And they moved, wavering like flames, and passed and vanished and were replaced. And all the sobs, and cries for mercy, and curses on his soul that he had ever heard or imagined sounded a thin and damning accompaniment in his ears.

But not for long. Malachi rose to his feet and cursed his weakness. He snarled and sneered at it. He laughed at it; and the look of fear and horror went out of his eyes, and the glimmer of sly cunning and greed came into them again. He went to the door and thrust out his head and listened. Twangs of a harp and lilts of song and laughter came up the curved stone tunnel of the stairs to him. He changed his dressing gown for a grand robe of velvet and fur, and his slippers for boots of red Spanish leather, and combed his

beard and went down to the great hall, fixing his face into
a false, smiling mask on the way. He wasn't beaten yet, by
Judas!

Chapter Nine
MID-JUNE IN CAVANTOWN

By midday, Castle Cavanaugh was full again of visitors
too important to be refused hospitality with impunity; and
by the middle of the month, additional dozens of equally
puissant personages had arrived and spilled over into the
best houses in the town. With these and scores of lesser
nobility and gentry and their entourages of attendants and
vagabond hangers-on, castle and town and the adjacent
countryside buzzed and rang and shook and clanged day
and night. The congestion and hubbub of the same date in
the previous year had been child's play in comparison. The
fame of Cavantown as a pleasure resort had grown and
spread during the winter, evidently, for scores of new cavaliers were added to the returned participants in last summer's junketings. There were even a few additional royalties.

King Malachi's cellars and larders were escaping lightly
this year, however, thanks to the fact that King Farrell, and
others who had shared in the exhaustion of Malachi's
stores and hospitality a year before, had come this time well
provided with victuals and drink, and some of them even
with gifts. All this put a better complexion on the whole
business, in King Malachi's opinion, though he would have
been yet more pleased if the gifts to himself had been of
greater value, or those to his consort of less, in certain
particular cases. Even so, he would have resigned himself
to enjoy the general excitement, to scheme for further possible profits and to try to forget the wear and tear on property, but for the behavior of his daughter. Of the Queen's
behavior, his grounds or excuses for complaint were neither
more nor less than they had been last summer; but of Little
Brigie's the same could not be said. He cornered his
daughter and expostulated with her.

"All I asked of ye was a mite of ladylike civility toward
a few of them and special smiles for whichever of the handsome young princes ye might fancy the most, so's to narrow things down an' ease the situation generally. An' wot

happened? In the place of pulling ugly faces at the richest an' highest, an' ignoring the rest, like last summer, now ye give the glad eye to one an' all! There bein't any sense in it—nor kindness to great or small—but only ruination for yer poor parents an' yerself too, the way I see it. D'ye want to have every knave an' loon an' swashbuckler in all Ireland, an' maybe in Christendom, brawling an' bashing here? It'll get worse an' worse, if ye don't put a stop to it! It'll get to be more than flesh an' blood can stand, or even stone an' timber. A few more years like this, only worse, an' the very walls an' roofs of me town, an' this castle itself, will be sprung an' cracked an' burst all abroad with the conflicts an' confusion of it. An' all I ask of ye now is the lift an' crook of a finger: an' then we'll have a grand wedding instead of ruination for one an' all!"

"Last summer I made liars of yerself and yer wandering minstrels, and ye didn't like that," the Princess replied, in a reasonable low voice and with a demure smile. "Not that it made any difference; for they stopped all the same, even if not a single one of them did give *me* a second look. And now that I'm trying to look the part the mistrels gave me, still ye're not satisfied. Ye be a difficult man to please, Malachi Cavanaugh!"

"Not so!" cried the King. "There bain't a more reasonable an' soft father in all Ireland than meself. Any other father would pick a suitable husband for ye, an' that would be the end of it. Take yer own granddaddy the O'Kelly, now, an' the way he married off his prettiest daughter without so much as—ah, well, never mind that now! But it was a grand, suitable match for the girl, anyhow. An' all I ask for *my* daughter is the beckon of a finger to her own free choice of any one of these squawling, bashing springals—so long's he be royal—an' leave the rest of them go home."

"Maybe they wouldn't go home," she countered.

"They wouldn't come back nex' year anyhow, an' you a married woman an' all."

"Maybe they would, just for the fun of it."

"But not here! You could go live with yer husband; an' that could be in Dublin Castle itself, for no more trouble than a nod of yer head at Prince Cassidy."

She seemed to study on that. She stood silent for a full minute anyway, with downcast eyes.

"To tell ye the truth, five or six of them are so wonderful that I can't make a choice among them," she murmured. "There's Cassidy and Red Flaherty and Gerry O'Connor and maybe two or three more. Five or six, maybe. And more arriving every day. It's hard choosing, especially for a young girl."

"Well, I'll not deny that," said Malachi, with a sigh of relief, for her attitude was more cooperative than he had expected. "I'm giving ye the flower of all Ireland to pick from, an' that's a fact. Take yer own time, me dear—but make it as short as possible, or ye'll have nought only cripples or worse to bestow yer pretty hand on, the rate they're bashing an' slashing every day in me best meadow."

That was that; and Malachi hoped for the best, and kept on hoping, though he looked in vain, day after day, for signs of improvement in the behavior of Little Brigie's suitors particularly, and of the visitors generally. By the end of May the place was like two or three armed camps with two or three country fairs stirred into them. As for the Princess's own behavior, he could not see any change for the better: but every time he questioned her, she replied in a dutiful voice that she was doing her best to find herself the ideal husband.

"I bain't asking for a miracle!" he grumbled.

To Queen Brigid he said over and over, with a queer mixture of distress and brag in his voice, he would wager five crowns that Dublin itself had never seen a match for Cavantown right now.

There was a tournament—a grand free-for-all—every fine morning, and more personal affairs, or sports for the commonalty, every afternoon, if it did not rain; and there was dancing and such every night at the castle, never mind the weather.

On the morning of the middle day of June, two strangers appeared on the scene while Prince Cassidy and young O'Connor were choosing sides for the main event. Cassidy had a full side of twenty, and O'Connor had only eighteen, when the newcomers appeared at the edge of the field. A herald came running, and asked them their names and styles.

"Never mind that now, but tell us wot's the argument all about," said one of them.

"Only Cassidy an' O'Connor at it ag'in," said the herald. "Just now it's O'Connor wanting to take a man from the other side, so's to make it nineteen each, an' Prince Cassidy refusing to agree."

The newcomers exchanged glances through the bars of their vizors, and the one with two walking wolves on his shield nodded his head. At that, they both got into motion and advanced slowly but purposefully upon the point of dispute, and when within a horse's length of it they came to a standstill simultaneously, stirrup to stirrup. The disputing princes looked at them, and the old chief herald himself came hobbling from the sideline. And the stranger who had spoken once before, spoke again.

"At yer service, O'Connor. An' that goes for me friend here too."

"Gramercy!" cried young O'Connor. "Follow me, an' we be all ready to go!"

"Not so fast!" exclaimed Cassidy: and then he went on, in a superior drawl: "There be rules to observe in such matters, me dear Gerry, even if no Connor has ever heard of them in his remote ancestral bog. And one of them says ye can't fill up yer side for a passage of arms with just any two rogues in knights' harness who happen along."

The talkative of the two strangers leaned forward in his saddle and snarled: "Go take a sniff at yer smelling salts!"

"Easy now, for the love of God!" protested the old chief herald, panting and shaking. "Leave this to me now, me lord princes an' gentlemen all! There bes nothing to it. 'Tis a mere formality. I've only to put a few questions to this cavalier. Honorable sir, wot's the name of yer honorable companion behind the shield that reads—leave me to take a closer look now—ah, argent, two wolves passant, proper? Just answer me that now, like between friends, an' no bones broke."

"Sir High Herald Connell, yer question discloses ignorance unpardonable in a gentleman of yer position an' repute," was the answer.

"Never mind it, then. Two walking wolves, hey? But let it pass. Only tell me now wot device ye've got under the cover on yer own shield."

"I could whisper it in yer ear, but I'll not risk it. If it was overheard, some of these carpet-knights would flee the field, an' as for this elegant Dubliner, it would take more than a sniff at his smelling bottle to keep him on his horse."

At that, Prince Cassidy urged his charger forward till it stood head to tail with the talkative stranger's charger, and the right kneecaps of the riders struck and ground together.

"Liar!" he rasped. "Buffoon! Insolent varlet! Ye'll die for that!"

"Back up an' pull over," said the other, sneering in a soft voice. "Me horse don't like to be crowded."

Speechless with rage—and vastly to the high herald's surprise and relief—Cassidy complied, and wheeled and rode back furiously to his waiting twenty. Then young O'Connor returned to his party at a reflective walk, with a stranger at either stirrup. He glanced to his right at the stranger who had not yet uttered a word.

"Wot ails yer tongue, noble sir?" he asked.

He was answered by the other stranger.

"There's nothing ails it, only it bain't Irish."

"D'ye mean he's a furriner?"

"Man, to hear him talk, he might be anything. Anybody! Did ye ever get as far from home as across the salt water to any of King Arthur Pendragon's courts?"

"No."

"Leave me tell ye, now. If me friend was to give tongue, everybody within hearing, including that scut Cassidy, would twig he wasn't an Irishman. An' wot then? They get to figuring out who he is. They think of all the champions they've heard the troubadours sing of in the last ten years or so: Launcelot du Lake, Tristram de Liones, Lamorak de Galis, Sir Gareth, Sir Gawaine, Sir Ector de Maris, who is King Arthur's half-brother, and maybe of that terrible king himself—an' then wot chance has me friend of finding a fight in this place. All these ferocious spear-busters an' village fire-eaters would be effacing themselves under the surrounding haystacks in no time at all."

"D'ye tell me he's one of them grand champions?"

"I tell ye nothing, only mum's the word."

O'Connor asked: "D'ye reckon he will oblige me by deigning to give Prince Cassidy a tumble?"

"Sure! But wot does that leave for me to lay on the sod?"

"Be ye good enough for even a bigger man than Cassidy?"

"Leave me tell ye about that. Even if I bain't one of the renowned champions I named over just now, that's the company I've been keeping the last nine years, on an' off; and ye can see for yerself I be on ag'in right now. Only show him to me, an' then forget him."

"The one with the shield checkered black and white. Strong an' tricky! He'd leifer break rules than fight fair, an' rather break backs than rules even. If there was any law an' order here—but nobody minds old Malachi an' the heralds now—he would have been despurred an' drummed out of the country before this. He be too rank for Cassidy's stomach, even: but they be always on the same side, because Cassidy's afeared of him—and maybe he's afeared of Cassidy. The name be Gorfey."

At that, the talkative stranger twitched from head to foot inside the plates and chain mail of his damascened armor; but it did not show on the outside; and his voice was steady enough when he spoke.

"Gorfey, hey? I've heard the name. Would this be the King or the Prince?"

"He calls himself Prince."

"Does he, now! Well, ye can call him mud now, an' forget him!"

They took their places. The stranger with the wolves on his shield faced Prince Cassidy, and the chatty one faced Prince Gorfey. The high herald and half a dozen of his assistants were bawling along the opposing ranks, repeating the rules over and over.

"Obey the orders of the King—and heed the prayers of the Queen and the Princess—and the laws of high chivalry. Let no sharp spear oppose a blocked spear. And let no mounted knight ride down or strike at any unhorsed knight."

The grandstand was crowded, but the royal box in the middle of it was empty. The talkative stranger asked a question of his right-hand neighbor.

"Where's the royal family?"

"Malachi stops at home now, for shame of the way his orders an' commands are ignored an' broken: but the ladies will be here—one or both of them—to cry for fair play an' mercy; an' they might as well stop at home with the old man," was the reply in a bitter voice.

"Here they come now."

"Ay, Little Brigie and Nurse Eliza."

"Little Brigie? But look at the height of her!"

"Take my advice, Sir Stranger, an' save yer attention for the murdering boar ye've been fool enough to get yerself opposite to."

Just then the trumpets sounded the onset. Sods flew from urgent hoofs. Sparks and splinters flew, as forty knights banged together with a variety of results. Prince Cassidy went over his horse's tail for the first time in years. The surprise shook him and shocked him as profoundly as did the initial bang and the thump when he hit the ground combined. What with all three together, he lay like a log until helped to his feet and off the field by two squires. Prince Gorfey also was the recipient of surprises. The first was to find himself half out of his saddle and with only the butt of a splintered spear left in his grasp, and to see his antagonist still firm in seat and stirrups, and swinging half a spear at him like a flail. The second was when that five-foot spar of ash descended upon his crest. He was unharnessed and lying in his own bed when he recovered from that surprise.

The victory lay with young O'Connor's party, and with plenty to spare. The falls of Cassidy and Gorfey had heartened the weaker side, and weakened the Cassidy contingent more than proportionately, what with astonishment and dismay. The judges gave their decision, and the heralds proclaimed it, and at least three-quarters of the spectators applauded it. Then the Princess summoned Prince O'Connor to her.

"That was a joyful surprise to me, Gerry," she said.

"No more so to you than to me," he replied.

"When I saw that cruel Cassidy hit the sod, me heart sang; and when I saw that wild boar Gorfey follow suit, I nigh burst with joy!" she cried.

"Then ye saw how little I had to do with it," he said. "It was the two strangers. But for them, 'twould be the same old story over again—and a few more cripples, liker than not."

"Where are they?"

"Gone. They just took a look at Cassidy an' Gorfey on the ground, an' then rode off together in the excitement."

"Where to?"

"I don't know that. And I don't know their names nor where they came from. The one who did the talking refused to tell, an' t'other never uttered a word."

"Will they be back tomorrow morning?"

"They didn't say."

"Well, it was a grand victory anyhow, Gerry, and I'll hope an' pray for yer side again tomorrow."

Then Princess Brigid returned to the castle, with the great Nurse Eliza on one side of her, as big as a man-at-arms, and an old dog as tall as a wolf walking stiff-legged beside Nurse Eliza. Two little pages—a Kelly and a Ryan—romped behind her, pretending to carry the train of her robe, but stepping on it most of the day. But they did not find that game as much fun as usual, for not once did she turn and make a slap at them. She seemed to be in a mood of abstraction. Word of the extraordinary outcome of the tournament had flown home ahead of her, and caused such excitement of conjecture and general satisfaction (but the King's satisfaction was spoiled by vague apprehensions) that she gained her own chamber without attracting the attention of either of her parents. And there Nurse Eliza left her, and went to see to the bandages of poor Prince Flaherty, who had been sorely wounded by the mighty Dublin Prince three days before. But Eliza was back in no time at all, to say that Dauber Driscoll requested a few words with the Princess.

"I won't let him try to paint my picture again, so he might as well go right away," said the Princess.

"It's not that," said the nurse. "It's something he says he thinks you might like to know; an' since he wouldn't tell me, the jackanapes, and I'd like to hear it, I'll tell him to come in."

Which she did, and with no more protest from her royal young mistress than a resigned and affectionate sigh.

Dauber Driscoll made his best leg and his best bow. The Princess extended a hand to him, which he kissed with all the grace of a confirmed courtier.

"Now wot is it ye think I'd like to know?" she asked, kindly but indifferently; and then she added, in a changed voice: "But if it be anything ye think about that horrid picture ye painted of me last year, I don't want to hear it!"

"No, no, Princess Brigie!" he exclaimed, with a red face but a cheerful smile all the same. "Me thoughts of that presumptuous attempt to capture Yer Highness's looks with earthy pigments be the same as yer own. Unspeakable! I want to tell ye about a different kind of picture entirely. Me poor skill bain't a match for transcendent human beauty, I admit; but it has its uses, for all that. Take beasts an' birds, now—dragons an' eagles an' lions an' wolves an' the like. Where be the artist in all Ireland can limn ye a more ferocious an' realistic wolf than meself?"

Princess Brigid's only answer was to sit forward with a start and widen her eyes. Nurse Eliza looked interested too.

"Nowhere!" the painter answered himself. "And the best wolves I ever painted were on a knight's shield—and still are, or I don't know me own handiwork when I see it. That was years ago—but it came back to me this morning like yesterday. Argent, two wolves passant, proper. But you were maybe too young then to remember, Princess Brigie? Or maybe not?"

"I never saw that shield before," she said, in the ghost of a whisper.

"It was covered, that's why—to save the fresh paint, I guess," said the artist. "But it's been touched up many's the time since then, I could see that."

A hand as big and strong as a pikeman's fell upon his shoulder.

"Tell it, Master Driscoll, or I'll shake it out!" Eliza growled.

"Whose shield was it?" the Princess whispered.

"Didn't I tell ye? It was that young furriner's—Sir Dennys'—the night before the day he cleared out."

The nurse released his shoulder, and Princess Brigid stood up and took his right hand in both her hands and cried in a thin voice: "Was that him?"

"It was his shield, anyhow," he said.

"Where is he now?" she asked.

"I don't know that. The two of them rode off when I wasn't looking."

"Will he come back?"

"If he don't—an' that tomorry morning—he bain't the man I take him for."

"D'ye think he came back to see me?"

"Wot else would he come here for?"

"But I was only a child then!"

"Ay, but his squire as good as told me then that ye'd bewitched him."

"If he isn't here again in the morning, will ye go an' find him for me?"

He looked uncertain and then murmured: "Maybe I could try."

Then she kissed him. He blinked. He rocked on his heels.

"Find him?" he gasped. "Sure I'll find 'im—an' fetch 'im!" He gestured wildly. "Ay, by the ears, if need be—mauger me head! Ay, if he was twice as big! Alive or dead!"

He turned and staggered from the room, waving his arms. The Princess blushed and laughed softly.

"I'd kiss the Dragon of Watley for less than that!" she cried; and she laughed again and kissed Nurse Eliza.

Chapter Ten
Pax Vobiscum

It was a more orderly junket than usual at the castle that night, but the spirit of it was far happier, even merrier. With both Cassidy and Gorfey absent, the bullying and swashbuckling element was curiously unassertive. Even Cassidy's boon companion and fellow-townsman Sir Keel sat glumly through the feast. His fear was—and it was Prince Cassidy's too—that word of the goings-on at Cavantown had reached the court of King Arthur Pendragon, and that the morning's setback might prove to be only the first of a series of defeats and humiliations for himself and his kind. It was grand fun to knock boys like Flaherty and O'Connor around, and doddering old fools like King Farrell, and village champions generally; but if you ran the risk of a prod from one of Arthur's professionals every time you wanted a bit of sport, where was the fun of it? And he wished himself safe back where he belonged.

Princess Brigid was in high spirits. The Queen felt gay too, for she both disliked and feared Cassidy and Gorfey.

So they danced gayly with whoever asked them. It was not long before Dauber Driscoll came up to the Princess, where she was laughing at King Farrell's old jokes and compliments, and requested the honor of the next. The poor artist was so gorgeously attired that she had to look at him twice before she knew him; and old Farrell blinked at him a dozen times, and even then did not know him.

"'Tis borrowed plumage," he whispered; and he laid a hand on her little waist and whirled her away with the music.

"Did ye find him?" Princess Brigid whispered.

"I did that—an' sure enough, it was himself, just like I said it would be. A real artist knows his own brushstrokes even after nine or ten years. And he knew me like a shot, an' so did Rufe MacMurraugh, an' if I had been a long-lost brother, they couldn't have treated me better; and when I give him yer message, I could have had his best horse an' best suit of armor, but all I took was his best suit of clothes."

"What message was that?"

"I said to him: 'Denny,' I said, 'I give her me word I'd fetch ye to her, alive or dead.'"

"Ye've been drinking, Dauber."

"I was thirsty, sure enough."

"Did ye fetch him?"

"Well, now, that bain't for me to say. D'ye see that dark corner over there?"

"Which one d'ye mean by 'over there'—with us twirling like a whirligig?"

"The one with the holy friar in it, that's the one. His Reverence has the answer. I'll know 'im when I see 'im ag'in. But you keep yer own beautiful eyes open too, like a good girl—Princess, I mean—for me own feel kind of blinky with fatigue an' all."

"A friar? D'ye tell me Denny's gone and turned holy?"

"I tell ye nothing. Only keep yer eyes open."

"But he couldn't do that! Not my Denny!"

"Don't go putting words into my mouth now. I be doing me best for ye, God knows!—an' me poor head going around even faster than me feet, God help me! But this looks like the place. Ay, this be the corner—an' His Reverence himself in it, just like I said."

He released her and leaned heavily against the nearest

wall. She found herself confronting, and at no more than a pace's distance, a tall figure robed and hooded in black.

"*Pax vobiscum,*" said a muffled voice from the shadow of the hood.

"What have ye to say to me?" she asked unsteadily.

"I have to question you, lady, on behalf of the knight Dennys ap Rhys," was the muffled answer.

"Question me, then—and speak up!" she cried in a cracked voice.

"Tell me then, lady: do you need this knight?"

"Yes, I need him."

"What for?"

"Who be ye to ask me that? But tell him he would know the answer if he had kept his vows instead of running away when I was a mere baby."

At that, the friar started and trembled. But he spoke quietly again, in the same muffled voice:

"I know about that. He was told that you laughed when you saw him unhorsed by that Dubliner, so he rode away. He didn't run away."

"He was an unkind fool to believe it!"

"I'll not deny that. But when he heard it was a lie—that you had gone as white as your wimple—he came back to you as fast as he could!"

"Why did he do that?"

"You could call it witchery—or you could call it love— or you could call it both. For I love you, my little maid! I'd battle my way through hell for you, my little Cynara!"

"*Denny!* Take me in yer arms now—friar or wotever!"

The painter snapped away from the wall and slipped between them.

"Hist!" he hissed. "Not now! Get along now, Sir Dennys, an' leave this to me. The windmill—inside an hour. Beat it! Here comes snoopy old Farrell! Get out! Leave it to me!"

The tall friar strode from that corner, pushed his way through revelers to the outer door and disappeared. Dauber Driscoll laid hold of the trembling Princess by the left wrist.

"That was himself," he whispered. "D'ye still want him?"

"Yes," she whispered.

"Enough to ride to Camelot with him?"

"Yes. Where did he go to? Leave me go after him!"

"Easy, now. Go change yer dress, now, an' meet me at the garden postern. An Big Eliza. An' the old dog too, if ye want."

She snatched her wrist out of his fingers and went darting and skimming away. And here in her place was King Farrell, peering and blinking.

"I thought I saw Princess Brigie here," said King Farrell.

"Ye did that, sir. She was right here just now. She went to look for the Queen, sir."

"Did she that? I was looking for the Queen meself. Have ye seen Her Majesty lately?"

The artist was on the point of saying, "I see her now," but he changed his mind, for a reason as queer as it was sudden, and said he had not. So he was instantly left to himself, to act upon that queer, impulsive change of mind. He made his way quickly to Queen Brigid, where she had escaped momentarily from her admirers to a patch of wavering darkness in the opposite corner.

"I beg the honor of a few words with ye, madam," he murmured.

She looked at his gorgeous clothes (which were a mite too big for him in every direction), and did not know him.

"Alexander Driscoll, ma'am," he prompted her.

She gave him a pretty smile.

"So it's yerself, Master Dauber! A dozen words, if ye say so, me friend—only don't ask me to sit for me picture again!"

"It's about the Princess, ma'am."

"Little Brigie? What about her?"

"D'ye mind a young knight ye once befriended named Dennys ap Rhys O'Tudor?—the same wot fetched Little Brigie home to ye nine or ten years ago?"

"Why wouldn't I mind him, poor boy—and with shame every day of me life for the way Malachi treated him! What about him?"

"It was Sir Dennys grassed Cassidy this very morning, and it was Rufus MacMurraugh grassed Gorfey."

"Glory be! So he's still alive an' hearty, thank God! What be his plans?"

"Easy now, and I'll tell ye. He plans to take Princess Brigie away, clear out of Ireland, mauger his head."

"He can't do that!"

"Why can't he—if she don't object?"

"He can't take her away from her own mother! Not even from all this wicked clashing an' clawing, an' a greed-crazed, twisty father! Not away from me!"

"Easy now, Queen Brigie. I was thinking the very same thing meself. Why would he? Sure he wouldn't! Not him— nor any other right-minded gentleman. With Little Brigie gone, it's yerself would be carried off by Cassidy or Gorfey or some other crazy ruffian. For who would stop them, once they'd finished off young O'Connor an' old Farrell an' all the decent kind? Not King Malachi, that's sure! The most he'd do would be send the sherriff after them with a bill for damages. But ye've got to stir yer sticks now, lady! *Tempus fugit!*"

"Wot d'ye mean?"

"I mean, go change yer dress now, an' meet us at the garden postern in no time at all. Quick now! Here comes that scut Sir Keel. Now or never, ma'am."

He gave her a pinch and a little push. She gasped—and was gone.

"I saw the Queen here," said Sir Keel.

"Ye'll be seeing stars when Sir Launcelot du Lake takes a bang at ye tomorry morning," sneered Dauber Driscoll.

And then he was gone.

Sir Keel stole away too. His fear was confirmed. He went to Prince Cassidy's room. Cassidy was sitting up to the table, with a cup in his hand and a flagon in front of him.

"We'd better be packing!" gasped Keel. "The jig's up! One of them's Sir Launcelot. T'other may be Arthur Pendragon himself."

The Prince hiccuped and sneered.

"How would either of them know about the smellin' salts?" he jeered. "Ye're a fool! I'll name the two springals for ye. The young Welshman ye played the trick on when we were here nine years ago, and the local plowboy who went away with him."

"Which was it laid yerself cold on the sod?"

"A mere accident! I wasn't expecting a straight spear. It was the furriner."

"The one I grassed, long ago?"

"Ay, the same, only bigger. And ye can grass him ag'in tomorrow—for keeps—with help, if need be. I'll see to it. And our wild pig Gorfey will fix the local boy for keeps too, for he be murderin' mad. So don't ye worry about Launcelot du Lake. Have a drink."

"How d'ye know it was those two?"

"A friend of mine was listening at a door when Driscoll the limner was telling Little Brigie."

"Hah!" exclaimed Sir Keel; and he helped himself to a drink.

"And with them gone, an' O'Connor an' his like all laid up with broken backs, then we'll see wot happens to Gorfey an' his pack, by night an' by day," Cassidy continued. "Little by little, ye understand! I got it all planned in me mind. And then—well, it's Little Brigie for me, an' Big Brigie for you."

"She don't seem to like me."

"Wot of it? Little Brigie don't seem to like me, neither. Wot of it? The Queen will find ye a pleasant change from Malachi. Drink up."

Sir Keel sat down to his second cup, and relaxed.

Chapter Eleven
THE ROAD TO CAMELOT

Dauber Driscoll waited impatiently in the blackness of the porch of the garden postern. Now he wore a cloak over his borrowed finery, and beneath it he fairly bristled with daggers. He had done well so far, but this waiting in the dark was beginning to get on his nerves. Ay, he had handled the Princess with firmness and tact; and if he had maybe exceeded his duty in the matter of the Queen—well, he had a heart, hadn't he? Sure he had a heart—and a head too, praise the saints, even if he did let his cardiac impulses push it around sometimes, as in this matter of the Queen.

But that was not worrying him. He had handled her as tactfully and firmly as he had handled her daughter—and all on the spur of the moment too! And they would thank him for it on their bended knees when they came to think of it. It was this waiting that fretted him. What the devil was keeping them now? He loosed two of his daggers in their sheaths. He stepped out of the little porch into the dim starshine of the garden as noiseless as a cat, and back again as quick as a weasel. He had left the inner door ajar, that he might listen at the crack of it. Now he listened again. Now he opened it softly.

"Yerself?" he whispered.

"Meself," whispered Little Brigie.

They almost filled the porch, but without a sound. He touched a hand to a shoulder on the level of his own and felt iron under cloth. That would be Nurse Eliza: for it was common talk that she was always armored and armed beneath whatever garments she wore. He felt the tall old dog against his knee. He closed the door behind them all but a crack, and stood close to it, with an ear at the crack.

"Why d'ye wait?" the Princess whispered.

"One more to come," he whispered back. "An' here she be."

He opened the door wide enough to let a slender cloaked and hooded figure slip through, then shut it tight behind her. He put his arms and folds of his own cloak about her, and shielded her through between the Princess and the big nurse, and out of the porch, like something both sacred and breakable. Then he took her gently by an arm.

"Folly me now—quiet as mice," he whispered over his shoulder.

"Sly Dauber!" exclaimed the Princess, in a giggling, hysterical whisper.

"Mind yerself!" he hissed like an adder.

They passed from the garden into an orchard. All was dim starshine and hulking gloom. They came to a wayside ditch and crossed it.

"Who goes?" demanded a rough voice.

It was a truculent voice too, and there was malt liquor in it.

"Stop here an' keep quiet!" Dauber whispered.

He loosed his hold on his companion and went forward a few paces.

"Who wants to know?" he asked.

A big but fumbling hand seized him by the throat. There was a grunt, and right after it a queer thumping sound on the hard road, like the flopping of a great new-landed fish. Then silence.

"This way now," he whispered, but with a catch in his voice. "A step to yer left now, if ye please."

He didn't want them stumbling over a corpse—even that of a wild MacGorfey—and getting all panicky. He took the nearest to him by an arm again. But at that moment the Princess, just behind him, cried out in a piteous, sobbing voice:

"Me mother! I clean forgot her! I can't leave her—all by herself there!"

At this, the Queen snatched herself away from Master Driscoll and turned and grabbed the girl in her arms. And there they stood embraced, sobbing and crying endearments in the middle of the track, for any night-hawking knave to hear. Poor Dauber! He reached into the confusion and laid a hand on Nurse Eliza.

"To the mill with ye now!" he besought her. "Tell Sir Dennys I got them both—this far—an' to come lend a hand before they wake up the whole town! Run, now!"

And without a word of question, Eliza ran. And she was back, with Dennys and Rufus, and spare horses, in no time at all.

Eight hours passed before King Malachi missed his wife and daughter. Another hour was spent in searching through the castle and around about. Then an old gentleman of the household said that in his opinion the ladies had flown the coop, and small blame to them. Malachi called him a knave and a fool, and said there was not a better husband and father in all Christendom than himself; and he grew so wild at the endangering of his ambitious plans that he lost all sense of discretion and accused Prince Cassidy of having had them carried off and hidden somewhere.

Cassidy gave him the lie. But it was an idea. So the Dublin Prince straightaway accused Prince Gorfey of it, right there in front of their host. Gorfey gave Cassidy the lie, and a tweak of the nose along with it; whereupon they both drew daggers and went to it, without the manners to go outside or into the next room, even. And they stabbed and slashed till the wild boar was dead and the elegant Dubliner drained to the last pint of his blood. The excitement and confusion were such, what with one thing and another, that it was past noon when young O'Connor thought of the two strange champions who had won the prize for his side the day before. Then he mounted the first saddled horse he came to, and took the shortest road to the sea. . . .

Two days later, and on another horse (which he had bought with a diamond ring), he came to a wayside chapel and questioned the priest in charge.

"Sure I saw them," said the priest, with a satisfied look. "It was at this same time yesterday. It was me first sight of the Princess, but I'd seen Queen Brigie before, bless her sweet face! And I married them meself—the girl to Sir Dennys O'Ray or something like it—and a truly liberal young knight. An' the Queen giving her away instead of the King, himself being indisposed as usual, or playing at it anyhow, the old fox!"

A few hours later, and after dinner, young O'Connor mounted and headed back the way he had come, riding at a snail's pace. The road to Camelot was not for him, poor prince—without a princess and on a spavined horse.

LEGEND'S
END

REVOLT IN THE FOREST

Chapter One
THE PENDRAGON

It was a golden morning of September, with the smoke-blue of Michaelmas daisies like wisps of mist under hanging wood and brambly hedge. Sir Osbert placed a hand on my shoulder and addressed me in honeyed tones, but loudly enough to be heard by others.

"Dear son, I hope you feel inclined for the chase this glorious morn, for the larder is sore in need of a fat young buck, or even two, by Saint Hubert's favor."

I bowed and mumbled my readiness for the chase with such grace as my lack of inclination, and my native honesty, permitted. My hazy but lively intention had been to rove the forest alone and unarmed, in romantic and inoffensive search of a hamadryad, or a naiad beside the river, or the White Damosel of Copel, or even of something less illusive in the vicinity of Ralph Forester's rustic dwelling.

But I made no protest. I was not Sir Osbert's son. He was a Norman: but in my father there had only been a one-fourth part of that upstart blood, and in my mother no more of it. They had been English; but in their veins had run a yet older strain than that of Angle and Saxon and Dane—a hot, high pulse of the blood of British heroes and princes. All these forests and farms around me were of my ancestral domain of Dragonland; and my name was Patrick Pendragon, as my brave father's had been; and yet I bowed and murmured acquiescence to my stepfather's smiling suggestion. An accomplished and untiring smiler was this Sir Osbert de Montfoi.

"But for his sprained leg, your brother would hunt too," he added, still smiling.

I looked at Roger de Montfoi, who lolled on a bench. He did not meet my glance; nor did he smile, but continued to stare sullenly at the floor. He was no brother of mine, nor yet half-brother, but Sir Osbert's son by an earlier marriage of the smiling Norman's than that to my widowed mother— by Sir Osbert's telling, at least. He was five years my senior; and I had been ignorant of his very existence until his sudden appearance at Dragon Castle six months after my mother's death. Now I went to the table and broke my fast with a wheaten scone, half a cold roasted capon, and a horn of ale.

"'Ware the crossbowmen," old Nick Pottle breathed at my ear, without moving his lips, as he set the trencher before me.

I did not look at him; and he was gone in a moment, and I did not turn my head and look after him. But I glanced up at Sir Osbert, who stood some five paces off and still smiled with his face toward me; but whether the smile was for me or for his own thoughts, only the Norman and the devil knew.

"You will take our three best crossbows, Martin, Noel, and Jacques, dear lad; and Ralph Forester will be on the watch for you, with his hounds," he told me.

I bowed dutifully and said nothing. But I thought something. Why those three black-visaged foreigners? They were newcomers to Dragonland, and neither woodsmen nor huntsmen, fowlers nor hawkers, but captainless soldiers, or worse, by their looks at the time of their hiring by Sir Osbert. There were a dozen better suited for the purpose in the household and garrison, and scores on the surrounding farms and crofts. Why these three strangers for the chase? Though the question was put to myself only, and silently, I lowered my glance to the trencher while asking it, so that he might not see the shadow of it in my eyes.

"Keep them in front of you," Nick Pottle breathed at my ear, setting the horn of ale before me.

I looked straight into the old butler's eyes this time and read the desperate warning there.

"Gramercy!" I exclaimed.

He withdrew instantly, bowing and backing, and was gone.

"For the long horn," I added; and I grasped it and lifted it in my right hand, smiled straight and innocently at my watchfully smiling stepfather, and took a deep draught.

It was in truth a long horn, and rimmed, banded, and stepped with silver; ancient and revered as an heirloom come down from the mighty Arthur himself, who had (according to Thomas the Rhymer) mastered the monstrous wild bull that had grown it, with his bare hands.

When I lowered it, Sir Osbert nodded approvingly, and his smile was even more benevolent than usual.

"Drink well, dear son, but do not tarry needlessly, for your horse and the knaves await you at the eastward postern," he charged me, in an unctuous voice; and in the act of turning away, he added, "Good hunting, Patrick"; and then, without a backward glance, he glided from the hall.

I made short work of what was left of the capon and the bread, wiped my knife and sheathed it, drained the horn, and got to my feet.

"Come here, young fellow," said a low and toneless voice.

I was startled, for I had forgotten Roger de Montfoi. He still lolled on the bench, but now stared at me instead of at the floor. He lifted a hand and beckoned. I went to him.

"You have a good horse," he said. "And you can ride. Ride, then—before you get a quarrel in your vitals."

I gaped at him, speechless.

"Keep those rogues in front of you till the covert is thick, then spur into it and ride for your life," he continued impatiently, scowling up at me. "And take this." He passed a little deerskin purse from his hand to mine. "A few crowns, and a few of your mother's rings. Pouch it, you fool—and get out! And ride hard and far! Wake up, dolt—an' God assoil you!"

Then I understood.

"Would he murder me—on me own land?" I gasped.

He grimaced savagely and hissed: "Save yourself, fool!"

This was it. I was to go hunting and die of a mishap. Old Nick Pottle's warnings had not convinced me of the starkness of my peril, though they had disturbed me. For years now I had suspected, known even, that my stepfather would trick me out of my heritage in his own good time, with Norman "justice" on his side and that untiring smile still on his face, leaving me in the situation of a favored poor relation or privileged retainer; and I had begun to consider the prospect philosophically: better the heel of the loaf than no bread. I was not ambitious.

But that my life was in danger was a possibility that had never occurred to me till now. The ancient butler's whispers had no more than disturbed my peace of mind, but Roger's words and looks convinced me of the worst. I was to die of a crossbow quarrel in my front, or in my back, while chasing a fat buck in my ancestral forest, unless my wits and my horse could save me. Dazed with terror and self-pity, I left the hall.

The narrow postern stood open. I halted in the inner gloom and looked forth. There in the soft sunshine stood my big colt Star Boy with a groom at his head, and the three foreign hirelings stood a few paces farther out, each with his crossbow in his hands and a short sword at his belt. I wondered, stupidly, which of the three was my murderer. Or would they share the deed evenly, as they would doubtless share the reward? My throat was dry, and my joints felt like water. Sagging weakly at the knees, I prayed desperately for strength to mount, to gain a vantage-point of thick covert with the men of blood still in front of me, then to ride for my life. My knees were stiffened, but my heart was all but stopped, by a touch on my shoulder. It was Sir Osbert. He stood close beside me, with a hand on my shoulder; and he was smiling, though not at me, but straight before him and with the look of seeing nothing in particular.

"Come, my son," he murmured.

We moved together, side by side, from dark to light. And suddenly I hated the golden sunshine with the blind hatred of fear. All eyes turned to us; and the three foreign hirelings stiffened their backs. Now I saw Nick Pottle and two more old servitors grouped a little to the right, motionless and watchful. Did I start, or was it the Norman's hand on my shoulder? Was he too surprised at the presence of these old men? But it would be madness to hope for help from them, poor helpless souls!

And now my despairing glance was caught and held by the weapons of the three foreigners. The short bows were fully bent, the stout cords winched back full stretch. They had naught to do now but lay each his bolt in the groove, take aim and twitch a finger—and my blood would spatter and drench the ferns and smoke-blue flowers like any stricken buck's. I must have moaned, for my stepfather gave me a quick glance, then followed the line of my horrified stare as quickly.

"What's this?" he cried. "What do I see? Bent bows? God's wounds! Release them, fools!"

He left me and moved swiftly to within a few paces of the three crossbowmen.

"Knaves, fools, rogues!" he berated, for all to hear. "What would you, dogs—shoot a farmer's cow, or one of our peacocks, or some poor crofter, even, twixt here and forest's edge? Such things have happened—and knaves like you have hanged for them! Harky to me, fools! 'Twill be time enough to crank your bows when the forester joins you with his hounds, and time enough to lay your bolts when the hounds give tongue."

I heard all this and did not believe a word of it. My wits were steadying, and the horror and despair that had all but stopped my heart were burned out suddenly by anger—anger and hate, pulsing now hot and now cold. I mounted Star Boy and wheeled him, and sent him prancing straight at the three ruffians, who had to scatter to save their toes.

"Lead on!" I cried at them, with curses.

I did not look at the Norman in passing him; nor did I give him a backward glance later, but herded the bowmen out of the yard and across the bridge that spanned the moat and off over the fields toward the nearest point of wood. It was not the way to Ralph the Forester's lodge, for I knew now that all my stepfather's talk of joining that honest huntsman and his hounds was a lie. Now, with curses and menacing gestures, I hunted the rogues before me. They too cursed while they ran; and they gesticulated with their useless weapons, the sprung bows of which I gave them no time to winch taut.

I dragged a pole of oak from the mill's woodstack in passing, and with this projected now like a spear and now swung like a quarterstaff, I kept my intended slayers from slackening their pace or scattering. And so Star Boy and I

harried them into the greenwood and plunged in close on
their heels.

There they scattered like running partridges, but we
went straight on, through thick and thin. I flung the
miller's pole away and crouched low. I gave Star Boy his
head. He knew as much about this sport of woods-running
as I did, for it was one of our favorite pastimes. I had
taught him the elements of it as a yearling; and now when
he was a four-year-old, I had only myself to think of—to
guard my head and keep my saddle. He ran fast, but not
wildly. He leaped mightily, but never blindly. Despite his
tireless action, he kept his wits about him, and always legs
enough under him for a quick swerve to right or left, from
heavy timber, or a quick jump to clear suddenly disclosed
boulder or prostrate tree trunk.

Star Boy came to an easy stop in a narrow glade and
heaved a gusty breath. I dismounted and eased the girths,
then ran eyes and hands over him from face to tail, from
knees to hocks, to find that he had suffered nothing worse
than a few minor scratches from hollies, thorns, and
brambles. Then I listened for sounds of pursuit, but heard
nothing more than our own breathings and the natural
sounds of the forest. If crossbow quarrels had been loosed
after us, as doubtless they had been, I had heard nothing
of them in the leafy tumult of our flight. But in truth I felt
no fear of those three knaves now, but only a harsh contempt for them. I had mastered and bedeviled them all the
way between castle and forest, for all who looked to see,
and then outwitted them; and I knew that if I had only
them to worry about, my horse and I might remain where
we were indefinitely, in perfect safety.

But I was not so dull as to believe that I had won to
safety, even for a few hours, by escaping from those three
foreigners. Sir Osbert had a few more of the same sort in
his pay; and of the household and chief tenantry a full
score were Normans now. Only such ancients as Nick
Pottle indoors, and hinds, herdsmen, and woodwards of
field and forest, were of the old bloods and loyalty. There
might be a general pursuit under way at this moment; for
surely my behavior in the open fields had convinced Sir
Osbert of the uselessness of his crafty scheming. If I were
to die of bolt or blade now, there could be no pretending an

accident of the chase, for I had unmasked him to friend and foe alike in my violent flight.

All this was clear enough to me, but Roger's part in it puzzled me, and I could only suppose that his conscience was more tender than his father's. Doubtless he would sit easier in my place, and sleep easier within my ancestral walls, as a result of his warnings. Whatever my fate, and whether known or unknown to him, he would consider himself clean of blood-guilt. He had charged me to keep the three rogues in front of me, to break away from them in the wood and then ride hard and far; and I had done just that—and here I was, and still alive. I had to admit to myself that his warnings, even more than old Nick Pottle's, had convinced me of the imminence of my peril and so saved me from the crossbow quarrels which his smiling father had planned for me.

"Gramercy, dear Roger," I said, and laughed uncertainly. "You have washed your hands of my blood, whatever may befall me later. You told me how to outwit the murderers, and then to ride hard and far; and here I am, scatheless. And now I will ride far and farther, with God's permission and help—clear out of Dragonland, if I live so long—homeless and disinherited. But if there be any mercy and justice left under heaven, I shall some day ride home again."

I looked around me. No woodward or poaching gypsy knew this wilderness of hill and dale, mere and river and massy forest, as I knew it. I made a quick decision to go into the Har Hills, which formed the eastward boundary of Dragonland. Their eastward slopes and the lands beyond lay in the vast lordship of Devereaux, of which I knew nothing save by hearsay. But in ancient times, before the first Norman and the first Devereaux, the crowns and both slopes of those mighty hills and leagues of country beyond had been Pendragon land.

I moved off, bidding Star Boy follow me. Upon coming to a small stream which flowed from the hills, I mounted and rode into it. The water broke about Star Boy's knees as he plodded against the current. He stood and drank, straddling his forelegs a little, then plodded on. As we advanced, the water gradually ran swifter and the boulders in its bed grew larger. After an hour or so of this, Star Boy turned to the right and scrambled ashore of his own accord. We kept to the course of the stream, and within sound of its broken but ever-strengthening song, until the sun marked high noon. Then I got down again, loosed the girths wholly this time, and pulled the saddle off and set it on the ground.

The colt shook himself like a dog. I unbridled him, and he straightway rolled in the fern with a mighty flourish of formidable legs and hooves. I glanced down at the saddle, and for the first time, noticed the fat wallet strapped to one side of its high peak and the leather bottle hung on the other side. I knelt and investigated. The wallet contained three wheaten scones, slices and drumsticks of roasted fowl secured in a linen napkin, and half a dozen plum tartlets similarly wrapped and somewhat crushed. This was Nick Pottle's doing, I knew, for he had been acquainted with my taste for plum tartlets ever since my infancy. The leather bottle was full of our rarest old mead.

"Gramercy, good Nick!" I cried, and made two bites of a tartlet.

I drank sparingly from the bottle, ate half a scone, gnawed two drumsticks to the bone and disposed of another tartlet, then went to the stream and drank my fill. Star Boy cropped white mountain clover. I repacked the wallet. And suddenly and sharply, as if a voice had spoken in my ear, I remembered the purse which Roger de Montfoi had given me. I took it from the pouch at my belt and untied it and shook the contents into the palm of my left hand. Five silver coins, and the six bejeweled rings that I had so often, in my childhood, admired on my mother's slender fingers! Roger had spoken the truth.

More puzzled than before, I returned coins and rings to the purse and it to my pouch. A little later I called Star Boy in from his grazing and saddled and bitted him; and we resumed our way into the Hills of Har, by climbing glens between hanging woods, through coppices of tough young thorn and holly and over heathery knolls. Red deer sprang away from us. Grouse puffed up and whirred to right and left from under our very feet. We came upon a great red boar at his truffle-hunting under an oak. I was on my feet, with Star Boy at my heels, when we came upon him. He wheeled and faced us, and I recoiled against the colt. The boar stood, and Star Boy stood, and I scrambled to the saddle. The beast's yellow tushes curved up a full span and more from the hinges of his earthy snout, and his little red eyes burned out at us from behind and between them. And here I was with no other weapon about me than the little knife which I had employed at breakfast!

I felt Star Boy quiver under me, and knew that all his muscles were ready for quick and violent action; but whether in flight or fight I could not guess, but in flight I hoped. The boar made the decision. He wheeled and plunged into the underbrush and went crashing away; and it was neither flight nor fight for us, glory be to the saints! I think that Star Boy felt the same about it, by the way he expelled his breath and relaxed his muscles. After that, I kept a sharper outlook to our front and both flanks, for there were white bulls as well as red boars in these wild ancient hills. According to the bards, it was somewhere hereabouts that the greatest of all great Pendragons had achieved the trophy from which I had quaffed my ale at breakfast.

We were in strange country now, the wildest I had ever known. These were mountains, not hills. Grim crags gloomed over us, and eagles screamed and soared from the crags. Star Boy kept close to me when I was on foot, which was most of the time now. Well before sunset, I chose a place for the night and eased Star Boy of saddle and bridle, to crop wild clover among clumps of fern and knuckles of rock at his pleasure. I cut me a cudgel and a stout eight-foot staff of thorn from a coppice nearby, and gathered dry fern and heather for my bed. I made the bed in a place with rocks on three sides of it—rocks high and steep enough to keep off any attack save of eagle or wildcat. I supped on bread, fowl, a tartlet, a long draught of water, and a short draught from the leather bottle. Star Boy came nuzzling up and coaxed a scone and a tartlet out of me, against my better judgment.

It was a chilly night, and I retired early, with fern and heather over me as well as under me, and cudgel and staff handy. I gazed straight up at the stars; and soon they began to dance and drift, and I slept and dreamed of smiling Sir Osbert, scowling Roger, trembling Nick Pottle, and the red eyes and tushes of that wild boar, all mixed up. I woke with a start and sat up, cudgel in hand. God assoil me, what was this pressing against my side? . . . It was only Star Boy, with all his twelve hundredweight of affectionate brawn and bone disposed peacefully and confidingly beside me. Thanking my guardian angels that he had done it without stepping on me, I closed my eyes again. . . .

We were up and on our way again at dawn, and on the height-of-land by sunrise, and well down the far slope and deep in Devereaux country before noon. Now I felt fairly safe from pursuit; but fears of what lay before me began to breed and take shape. There was starvation, for one menace. The wallet would soon be empty—and what then? How long would I last on a diet of bramble berries and haws, if I failed to find a human habitation before long? And what if I happened upon murderers and thieves? This was not Dragonland. The woodwards and charcoal-burners, even the poaching outlaws, might be Normans or worse in this strange wilderness.

I reflected dismally that I had been wiser, maybe, to have remained on my own side of the mountains, where the poor and the outlawed at least were my friends. There, befriended and abetted by the poor and furtive, and roving gypsies—the riffraff of the world, in Norman eyes—I might elude Sir Osbert till he thought me dead, or fled forever, and so forgot me. But it was too late now, with the Hills of Har behind me, for idle lamentation. If I had fled too fast and far and thoughtlessly from the peril I knew, nevertheless the unknown perils before me must be discovered, and faced and suffered, or avoided, as Fate would have it.

Chapter Two
THE DAMOSEL BLANCHE

I ate sparingly at midday, but even so there was little left in the wallet—a few scraps of meat, two tartlets, and half a scone. I climbed a tall fir and looked abroad in every direction but that from which I had come, and saw only the rolling roofs and jagged spires of the forest: no thin feather of smoke to suggest fire beneath a pot, nor any little patch to suggest a man-made clearing.

These slopes were less rugged than those we had ascended; and the little stream we followed now was, after its first rocky spurts and tumbles, a gentle thing as compared with the brawler we had left on the other side of the height-of-land. It soon looped, with no more than an occasional riffle and splash, between low banks of hazel and willow and fern. So I kept to the saddle, when once mounted after dinner, for a league or more. I let Star Boy do the work. He had dined more fully than I had, and would surely sup fuller; and when I thought of tomorrow's breakfasts, I envied him.

"You'll have no more than skin and bones to carry on your fat back yet, lad, unless I'm fed or murdered within the next few days," I told him.

And so we went a league or more, following the ever more softly flowing brook among thickets of willow and hazel, and clumps of sweet fern and smoke-blue drifts of Michaelmas daisies. Star Boy picked his way discreetly and yet maintained a good pace, while I sagged loosely in the high saddle, my thoughts gloomy and bitter and confused.

Star Boy came to a sudden stop, that jerked me out of my unhappy reverie. He tossed his head high, turned it to the right and pricked his ears sharply forward. I looked and harkened in the same direction, which was toward the stream a few yards off. I heard a faint sound that might be— but I knew was not—the sobbing murmur of the stream. My first thought, quick as a flash, was of a naiad. (Such creatures—nymphs of water and wood and heath—were ever at the back or front of my mind.) I dismounted quickly and, noiselessly as a falling leaf, stole to the colt's head and charged him, in a ghost of a whisper, to stand still and silent. Then I moved stealthily toward the sound, though the thumping of my heart now deafened my ears to it.

I parted the last pliant screen. My heart jumped and stood still and my breath failed in my nostrils. . . . Naiads, so I had been told, were clothed only in spray or mist, if anything, and dryads in leaves or gossamer, when clothed at all; but this one wore a garment of white samite. She crouched with her back to the stream and her hands to her face, and russet tresses lay loose about her quaking shoulders. How long she would have remained so, and I stock-still and staring, if Star Boy had not come forward, thrust forth his head and snorted in astonishment, I do not know. She straightened up on her knees, lowered her hands and stared at me, then at the colt, and at me again.

"Have my prayers been answered?" she whispered.

Naiads don't pray, I thought, crazily. Or to devils, if they do. Nor speak with human tongues; but this one lisped in Norman French. Then I bestirred my stiff wits and muscles, but not to much effect. I croaked like a raven and doffed my leather cap.

"I prayed to Saint Anthony—for I am lost," she whispered, still staring incredulously.

This must be a damosel, I thought. But I had as little personal knowledge of damosels as of nymphs or dryads. Of wenches and simple maids I was not entirely ignorant, but all I knew of damosels was from books and hearsay. I advanced a pace from the bushes, halted again, and bowed. Star Boy advanced with me, passed me by half his length and lowered his outthrust head to the damosel. Still kneeling, she took his muzzle between her hands.

"A noble horse!" she cried softly. "A cavalier's great charger!" and she pressed a cheek to his nose.

At that, I advanced all the way and found my tongue.

"He is my colt—and the best in the land."

Smiling at me, she got lightly to her feet; and I saw that the skirt of her gown was muddied and bedraggled.

"You are a cavalier?" she queried, lowering her glance shyly.

Did she mistake me for a churl? Me, Patrick Pendragon! My outraged pride filled my eyes with tears.

"And what are you?" I cried.

She looked at me again, and quickly away again.

"But I knew it—a cavalier in very truth! I did not doubt it. You are the answer to my prayer. Do not be—angry. But you are so young. And to find you in this dreadful wilderness!"

She fairly gabbled in her embarrassed haste. But I was not pacified. So young, she said. God's wounds! Hunted from my castle and lands I might be, but I was still a gentleman, and eighteen and large for my age, by my halidom! I brushed the moisture of offended dignity from my eyes.

"And what are you?" I asked again, bitterly. "Naiad or dryad or human maid—how do I know what you are— alone and weeping and bedraggled here?"

"I am human," she whispered. "I outrode my companions—and while I rested, my jennet ran away and left me. My name is Blanche."

Mollified, I told her that I would see her safely home, and that she might ride Star Boy all the way. She thanked me gently, and still with her eyes downcast. I wanted to see those eyes again, for I was wondering about their color. I had thought them green at the first look, and blue at the next, and just now green again. I had heard, or read, that though human eyes may rightly change from blue to green and back again, and even to gray and the mixed hues of moss agates, only unhuman eyes, and those of witches and warlocks who had given their souls to Satan, could turn from blue or green to red. She called herself human—but did not every soulless witch do the like, in the bewitching of unwary mortals? Or might not a water sprite or dryad appear, to mortal eye, to be garbed in white samite instead of in mist or gossamer? She had called herself Blanche. What more likely then that she was the White Damosel of Copel, who was known in some lands, and in some ancient songs, by the name of *La Belle Dame sans Merci*?

"Permit me to help you onto the saddle," I said; and I placed a hand on the right and on the left side of her round waist, in readiness to lift her and to gaze searchingly into her eyes, for a glimmer of red, while about it: but at the touch, and the realization that my thumbs all but met in front and my fingertips behind, my wits and muscles alike ceased to function.

"Wait—I am hungry," she sighed, without looking at me.

Hungry! God help us! All my doubts as to her mortality fled at that word, but it did nothing to relieve my distress of spirit. In truth, I felt worse than I had before it was spoken; for it would seem that such a threat to one's soul as I had but now feared for mine, may be easier for a young man to face than a reminder of an empty stomach.

"We set out at sunrise—and I have fasted since then," she whispered, and sighed again.

I pictured the broken scone, the scraps of fowl, and the two remaining tartlets, and sighed also. Then, calling up all my power of will, I withdrew my hands and turned from her to the wallet hanging limp from the horn of the saddle.

"It is not much," I mumbled, handing her the broken loaf.

I did not look at her, but I heard the crunch of teeth on crust; and that innocent and homely sound disturbed me strangely. I felt anger first—against poor old Nick Pottle for not having packed a great sack instead of a mere wallet, against her for having ridden so far and losing her jennet at the last; and then angry shame for myself. What a poor knave was I—what a disgrace to my blood and name that I should have suffered myself to be chased and frightened into a situation in which I had nothing but broken bread and meat and two squashed tartlets to offer a hungry damosel. Or naiad or dryad or fatal enchantress—what matter which, so long as she was lost and alone and in need of food!

I did not watch her eat, but when I guessed that the half scone was finished, I gave her the napkin containing a wing and a few scraps of fowl. She made short work of them. Then, and still without looking at her, so sharp was my humiliation, I gave her the tartlets.

"That is all," I mumbled.

A minute later I ventured to look at her. She was regarding me shyly, from beneath dropped lids, and at the same time licking plum jam from her fingers; and at that sight—but the blessed saints only know why!—my heart leaped and my spirit soared and I laughed right out. She opened her eyes wide, and as blue as the sky; and her face bloomed pink as eglantine; and she laughed too, but like a high, tossing chime of little bells. She fell silent, and veiled her eyes again, and again I glanced aside.

"Now I must take you home," I said; and once more I placed my hands on her waist to lift her to the saddle, but stood blinking at them and it instead, in mazy wonder that they all but spanned it.

She did not move, but she whispered: "I do not want to go home."

"Why not?" I asked, still staring in wonder at my brown thumbs on the white samite.

"Philip de Courtville," she whispered, and paused; but as I had nothing to say to that, she whispered on:

"I outrode and eluded him this morning. I have escaped. I'll not return to him."

"Is he your father?" I asked, and looked at her averted face. "Or your guardian?" I added.

She shook her head.

"Your husband?"

"Not yet," she whispered faintly.

Then we stood silent for minutes, while Star Boy fidgeted and swung his great head inquiringly.

"You will starve else," I said.

At that, she gave me a startled look, grasped the front of my jerkin with frantic fingers, and cried: "Was that all you had?"

"Ay, to the last crust," I admitted, in desperate voice. "Fool that I am, not to have more! But I too am in flight—chased from my home and pursued and hunted through my own forests by a murderous usurper."

She cried out even more lamentably than before, set her face hard against the front of my jerkin, between her gripping hands, and burst into tears. And so we stood for a long time. I tried to think, but my poor wits staggered around and around like drunkards in a tavern. In a mazed way I almost wished that I had found the fatal enchantress the White Damosel of Copel instead of this Damosel Blanche; for a nymph or sorceress would not demand victuals of me, whatever else. But it was not in my dazed heart to wish it quite. I moved my hands up from her quivering waist to her quaking shoulders. Soon she quieted a little.

"What would you have of me?" I asked.

"Hide me," she whispered against my breast.

I had nothing to say to that. Next moment, suddenly, she withdrew and lifted her face—wide eyes and tear-wet cheeks and parted lips.

"Hark!" she whispered, turning her head a little. "Be still! Hark!"

I heard nothing but her voice and the commotion of my agitated heart.

"A horn!" she cried, releasing her grip on the breast of my jerkin and breaking backward and aside a pace from my light hold on her shoulders. "There again," she cried, and pointed. "Philip's horn! He is leading the search for me himself!"

I heard it then: a tootling Norman horn. I glanced at Star Boy and saw that he heard it too. It was not far off, of a certainty.

"You must mount now, to escape him," I told her.

She looked at me blankly, but only for a moment.

"Shout!" she cried. "Shout, you dolt!"

But I did not shout. Then she screamed, long and high; and the Norman horn tootled higher in acknowledgment. I mounted, without a word. She glanced at me and cried breathlessly, "Wait, and he will reward you!"

"I am no stranger to Norman rewards," I replied bitterly. "My name is Patrick Pendragon."

I mounted and wheeled Star Boy and moved off through brake and brush. I heard her uncertain cry for me to return, but soon lost it in the leafy commotion of our passage.

"God send me a soulless nymph next!" I muttered. "Or Satan's own daughter! Anything but a Norman damosel!"

I left both course and pace to Star Boy.

"A narrow escape," I muttered; and looking at my hands, I thought of the waist they had held and all but spanned. "But she liked my tartlets," I sneered: and I laughed so strangely that Star Boy stopped and swung his head to look at me.

Chapter Three
BEN TINKER'S CAVE

Star Boy went on, but now at a snail's pace; and I did nothing to mend his pace or shape his course, but sat limply and tried as limply to put that damosel out of mind.

"Faugh! She's not worth a thought," I muttered. "Clinging to me one moment and screaming for her Philip the next! I know goose girls and foresters' wenches with better manners."

But I looked at my hands again, and even held them up before me and spanned a circle of empty air, or more truly described it, for I left the tips of my thumbs about two inches apart and did not quite join the tips of my middle fingers. Even so, and despite the knowledge that the size of my hands would do credit to a smith, I gazed at them in wonder, and marveled at the thought of the waist that had so recently filled their circumscribed bounds.

"More like a swan's neck," I murmured. "Nay, more like a lily's stem." And I might have ventured upon yet more poetical flights of fancy had not a chance downward glance encountered the flat, empty wallet on the saddlebow.

Now a different vision possessed my mind's eye.

"But she ate like a plowman!" I gasped; and at this incongruous thought I uttered a yelp of mirthless and derisive laughter.

Star Boy checked, and tossed and swung his head to bring one inquiring eye to bear on me.

"No heart!" I told him bitterly. "Clutching hands and greedy stomach. A true Norman! She made a fool of you too—but she didn't devour your last crust. There's grass and clover everywhere. So move on, brother."

He moved on. I paid no attention to the course, but became vaguely aware that we were in fairly rough country again. Well, what of it? With Sir Osbert and his hirelings hunting for me through my ancestral forests, and this Devereaux country all in Norman hands too, might not this rugged border-land, these Hills of Har, prove the safest place for a deposed, forsaken, friendless, and unarmed Pendragon? Would not death by starvation be even less painful here than within chance sniffing-distance of hostile cooking fires?

Had I been armed, I would have felt, thought, and behaved very differently. Had my weapons been spear and long sword, I would have asserted myself before now, and spilled blood as well as lost it—a quart of new blue blood for every spurt of old red blood, by my halidom! But with only churlish staff and cudgel to fight with, what more could even the last Pendragon do than fade away and finally expire of hunger far from sight and knowledge of the mocking eyes and false hearts of his enemies? This spiritless gloom and resignation was not true to my nature. This was certainly not the mood in which I had chivied and bedeviled the three crossbowmen. In truth, my meeting with the Damosel Blanche had done me no good.

"A merry meeting, my Lord Pendragon," said a voice from the thicket of holly and thorn half Star Boy's length in front of his nose.

The colt stopped, and I sat up straight. It was a twangy voice, and somehow familiar.

"Gramercy," I said, tightening my grip on the staff.

The thicket parted, and a tall and startling figure stepped into view. Or rather, it was the head that was startling. Eyes as black and bright as jet glittered beneath black and bushy brows; gold of earrings shone through tangled black locks; and the long and swarthy face was all but split across by a gleaming array of white teeth. In one hand he held a long wooden spoon.

"Ben Tinker!" I cried, dropping the staff and leaping down from the saddle.

He dropped the spoon and embraced me; and though I had never done such a thing before, nor ever felt the remotest impulse to do so, I embraced him in return; and though his scent was of ill-cured hides and other and probably worse things—as unlike that of the damosel as the fragrance of a rose differs from the smell of burnt grease—I held on as long as he did. Then we unclasped and each took a short step backward.

"A merry meeting, in truth!" I exclaimed.

His smile widened, if possible, but he closed one eye with a quizzical air.

"I did not expect to see Your Nobility in this wild place," he said. "And so meanly furnished for foreign travel," he added.

I told him my story, from Nick Pottle's first warning whisper to the crossing of the hills, in the fewest possible words, and without any mention of the damosel. He was angry and relieved, but not surprised.

"The old fox made his play sooner than I expected," he said; and then he cursed for minutes in Romany, Welsh, English, Norman French, and even hedge-Latin, for he was a much-traveled tinker.

"Nick Pottle did what he could, but it was Roger de Montfoi who told me how to outwit the rogues—and I can't think why he did it," I said.

"The human conscience is a strange thing," he replied, with a knowing wag of his head.

He picked up the wooden spoon.

"But the human stomach has claims to consideration too," he said. "This way to supper, my good lord."

He turned and rounded the thicket from which he had emerged. I followed him closely, and Star Boy followed me. Beyond that tangle of holly and thorn we made a crooked passage of a jumble of boulders and bushes. He stopped and turned.

"Welcome to Tinker's Castle," he said, louting low.

I saw a sharp elevation of rock and vine and hanging wood before me, and a confusion of brush and wood and tumbled boulders all around, but nothing of a castle; and what was more to the point, nothing of supper—not so much as the smoke of it, even. The gypsy flashed all his teeth at me, then stepped back past me to Star Boy and quickly had the saddle off and on the ferny ground, the bridle atop it. The colt shook himself and moved away in search of tender grass. Ben Tinker stooped again, detached the big bottle from the saddle, shook it, unstoppered it, and sniffed at the orifice.

"Hah!" he exclaimed. "This is all that was lacking in a feast fit for Pendragon of Dragonland. This way, my noble and doubly welcome guest."

He entered a clump of hazel and twisted pear, with his wooden spoon and my leather bottle still in his hands, and me close on his heels.

"Mind your head!" he warned.

I stooped low, made a few more stumbling steps and found myself in a cave. For seconds I could detect nothing in the gloom save a low red glow far back in it; but as my eyes became used to it, I made out the rocky walls and roof, vague shapes as of household utensils and a tinker's pack, a pallet of fern and hides, and—best of all—an iron pot squatted low above the red embers. But my eager nose served me better than my eyes. It led me straight to the pot, from which Ben had already lifted the wooden lid and into which he had sunk the wooden spoon.

It was a stew of venison and wheaten dumplings, the flavor sharpened with sage and other herbs. And this was not all. A roast bustard, which had been kept hot in a clay oven, followed. The bird was stuffed with beechmast and truffles. Large though it was, it was tender: and largely though I had eaten of the stew, I did more than justice to the second dish.

"Gramercy!" I said at last, and licked my fingers.

He passed the bottle of old mead to me; in a little while I passed it back to him; and so it passed back and forth till its weight was vastly reduced.

"Your Lordship's arrival was indeed timely," said my host. "And pray do not think I refer solely to this rare old liquor, my rare young lord. In truth, I was about to set out for Dragon Castle within the sennight at latest, to fetch you away. But Sir Osbert was too quick for me, and you were too quick for him, and so here you are, without any effort on my part. I see the hand of Destiny in it. The gods are propitious."

His diction, sententious even when employed in his trade of soldering pots and pans, was now exaggerated by his intercourse with the leather bottle. It sounded pleasantly on my ear, but its import stuck somewhere short of my brain.

"Fetch me away?" I mumbled. "The gods are propitious? What are you talking about, good Ben?"

He leaned toward me, made a long arm, and pressed a hard forefinger on my ribs.

"My good young lord has slept soundly, lulled to a false sense of security by that old fox's smirks and smiles. But others were awake. Others—and this gypsy tinker not the least of them—kept watch and ward. But tell me, my dear lord—my innocent and ignorant dear lord—what is Your Nobility's estimate of the numerical strength of your trusty following at this moment?"

My trusty following? I thought of old Nick Pottle and a few more ancient retainers, and half a dozen plowmen and herds of my acquaintance, and Ralph the Forester and some charcoal-burners, and a few woodwards and outlawed poachers, and some friendly cotters' and farmers' wives and wenches. I smiled bitterly; the fellow was drunk, I thought, scornfully, oblivious to my own condition.

"You are drunk, my good tinker," I said.

He laughed heartily and gave my ribs another jab.

"Three score and a dozen," he cried. "Awake, my lord! That is the strength of your trusty following within your own boundaries, not counting women and totterers and toddlers. And all good bowmen."

I said nothing, but thought him mad as well as drunk. Now I remembered his reputation for whimsy among the scullions and grooms of the castle, for whose amusement he had often played the part of a merry-andrew, and that he had even been summoned to the great hall on several occasions to play the fool before Sir Osbert.

"Every man of them shoots a straight shaft," he went on. "Some straighter than others, true enough, but the least straight is less crooked than the flight of a bolt from a Norman crossbow."

"Every longbow in Dragonland, save those of foresters and roving outlaws, was broken and burned when I was a little boy, and again five years ago," I said.

"Oh, my dear innocent lord!" he protested, with a hoot of laughter. "Have you never heard of a longbow hid in the thatch? But even if bows and shafts are broke and burned, think you that yew trees and ash trees break and wither throughout the copses and forests of England? And think you Ralph Forester and Sam Bowyer, to say nothing of Wat, Hob, Tom Woodman, Luke ap John, and poor Ben Tinker, sleep the sunny years away while my lord seeks dryads in sylvan glades, and wakes rhymes and poetical phrases in his head?" He leaned yet nearer—we squatted facing one the other on low stools—and laid hold of my belt and shook me. "Would you have a bow and shafts, Pendragon? So be it! And a sword? A long and strong and sharp sword—your father's sword? Good! So be it!"

He released me, left his seat, and moved away into the farther gloom. I continued to sit motionless, dumbfounded. What was this talk of my father's sword? The gypsy had sounded even madder and no longer merry when he spoke of it. He was back in a minute. He stooped beside me and laid something across my knees. It was a long, broad, and straight sword in a scabbard of bull's-hide bound with silver and copper. Its double-handed hilt was bound with deerskin, and the straight guards were set with green and yellow gems.

"It is the sword Dragon-killer, as old as time and sung by ancient bards," I said, wonderstruck. "And it was lost longer ago than I can remember."

"Nay, naught but the hilt is old as time," said the gypsy, speaking quietly and naturally at last. "The blade was forged for your father's father by the greatest smith in England, and set into the ancient hilt."

"But it was lost, long ago—hilt and blade and all!" I protested.

"Nay, not lost, but taken away so that no Montfoi might ever wield it in battle against its own lord. It was brought away from the armory in the tower, that it might strike the usurper down on the destined day. And now that day is in sight. Draw it and heft it."

I drew forth the great blade. It gleamed as clean and dark as new ice on a mountain tarn.

"Is it too heavy for you?" the gypsy asked softly.

I stood up, gripping the hilt in my right hand, and extended the mighty weapon to the extent of my arm and held it at that.

"See," I said. "Is it too heavy for me?"

I recovered and tossed it to my left hand and extended my left arm. I tossed it back and gave it a short whirl on a level with my shoulders. Ben Tinker retreated a few paces. I laid hold with both hands and slashed harder and wider, until Ben cried upon me to desist.

Chapter Four
THE MAN IN LEATHER

I heard strange and inspiring talk that night, much of which taxed my credulity, though I would fain believe it all. By Ben Tinker's telling, every true heart in England, and in the whole island of Britain, was hot and sore to bursting in rage of hate against the Norman oppressor; and as for the native folk of Dragonland, they had been praying and scheming for Montfoi's downfall ever since my mother's death; and the case and state of the poor and oppressed of the vast domain of Devereaux were even more desperate, for they had suffered three generations of Norman lords and tyranny.

"But I never heard so much as a whisper of it," I protested. "Neither indoors nor out. Why wasn't I told?"

"For your own good," the gypsy replied complacently. "In ignorance lay your safety. By this poor tinker's orders, dear lord—else the eels and carp of your ancestral moat would have disposed of your remains before now. A wise precaution, for here sits Your Nobility with all your limbs and faculties, in good health and good appetite, and strong enough to wield the Dragon-killer with one hand."

He took up the leather bottle and shook it. It was empty. He dropped it, offered me his couch of dusty fern and smelly skins with an expansive gesture, then sank to earth and rolled over once and slept. I stole forth and bedded down in the open; and thanks to a full stomach, and despite Ben Tinker's momentous information, soon fell asleep. I slept till sunrise, when Star Boy awoke me with inquiring nips and nuzzles. After bathing in a nearby ice-cold stream, I returned to the cave and found my host replenishing the fire beneath and about the pot. He sprang forward and cried out at the sight of me.

"I feared it was but a dream!" He gripped my shoulders. "Nay, 'twas no dream! My young lord, safe and sound!"

I pointed to the big leather bottle and asked if he had thought it too a dream.

"Hah, the bottle!" he cried. "But it is empty! Now it all comes to mind. That was good liquor. The three rogues! Their backs have been flayed before this for letting you escape, mark my words. And the great sword. I wondered to see it lying there. That was rare old mead. But it all comes back to me now. And here you are, and big and powerful enough to wield Dragon-killer. Here you are, Pendragon—and our enemies as good as dead already!" He unhanded me and turned back to the fire, where the pot was beginning to steam. "But to breakfast now—and naught but ale to wash it down with," he concluded.

He went away after breakfast, with a bow and a quiver of arrows at his back, a short sword and a long poniard at one side of his belt, and at the other side, to balance them, a large wallet crammed with smoke-dried venison and scorched barley scones. I had offered to go with him, and he had refused to consider it, politely but firmly. I was to remain in the cave, or inconspicuously near it, to show no smoke and to keep Star Boy within discreet though vague bounds, until his return in five days' or a sennight's or perhaps even a fortnight's time.

"And if you are not back by fourteen days from now, what then?" I had asked; and he had refused to take the question seriously.

I found a dozen yew-wood bows in the cave, and as many staves of the same wood not yet shaped, and a score of beeswaxed hempen bowstrings in a crock, and bundles of clothyard shafts, most of them barbed and fletched, but some not yet completed with steel and feathers. I strung a bow and went out and shot at a mark. Later, I found a sharp knife and whittled at an unfinished bow. Star Boy and I passed the long afternoon together, wandering idly around and about. Again I supped on the stew in the pot, but with diminished relish.

I slept outside again, but not as peacefully as on the first night, for I was beset and harassed by dreams and nightmares from the moment of closing my eyes until Star Boy woke me at dawn by snorting in my face. . . . I ran through the great hall and up a winding stairs in Dragon Castle, with Sir Osbert in swift but silent pursuit. I turned my head and looked back and down at him, and he looked up at me, and I saw his red lips smiling in his curly black beard, and the glinting of his eyes which were half shut as if in silent laughter, and I knew without seeing the weapons that he held a dagger in either hand.

I rode Star Boy through thick and thin, over brake and boulder, while unseen pursuers shook the thickets behind us. And I knew suddenly that I did not ride alone. Slender arms encircled and held me tight, and slender fingers clasped my sword-belt at either side of the massy buckle, and I felt a disturbing pressure between my shoulder blades as of a soft breast; and I knew, without looking farther, that the Norman damosel rode a-pillion. . . . I was afoot and with the great sword Dragon-killer in my hands, and before me a large man armed with a long sword and a long shield stood on ever-shifting feet like a dancer, but menacingly. Blood trickled down my left arm. I leaped and struck—and awoke to the colt's anxious snorting in my face.

Unable to stomach another breakfast of that stew, and equally unable to find any trace of the roast bustard, which had doubtless been carried off by a fox, I helped myself to a bow and arrows and went in search of a fresh breakfast. Star Boy followed on my heels. I searched for hours, flushing grouse which flew too unexpectedly and hard, and starting hares which ran too fast, without glimpsing so much as the tail of a bustard; and by noon I was back at the cave, thinking better of the contents of the iron pot. I was about to enter the screening thicket of hazel and wild pear, when a sudden snort and thump and thudding of hooves behind me checked and turned me. I saw Star Boy charging to the right, and a human figure in leather bounding before him. Next moment the fellow went up the inclined trunk of a half-uprooted oak like a squirrel. He held a boar-spear in one hand. I set arrow to string.

"Drop that spear!" I yelled. "Quick—or I'll spit you like a partridge!"

He looked my way, saw the bending bow, and dropped the spear to the ground. The colt wheeled and came back to me. I advanced slowly upon the intruder.

"What brings you here?" I asked.

He glared down at me like a wildcat, but made no answer. And he may spring like one, I thought; and I let the bow fall and drew one of Ben Tinker's knives from my belt.

"Who are you, fellow?" I asked.

"Stark," he snarled. "A poor herd. A serf."

"A serf? Where is your iron collar?"

He glowered in silence.

"Filed through and torn away, is that it, fellow?" I went on. "An outlaw, then. And you flee your Norman master. But what brings you here? Do you seek the gypsy?"

He started, but did not speak.

"You know Ben Tinker," I continued. "Well, so do I. He is my friend; and his friends are my friends and his foes my foes."

"You are a lord," he muttered, sliding his suspicious glance from the brooch in my cap own to my buskins of Spanish leather, and aside to my noble Star Boy and back to the brooch.

I cried: "A lord in truth, fellow, but not in fact, for I am fled my lordship—chivied by Normans like any crop-eared poacher!" I laughed bitterly. "Down on your knees, rogue, to mighty Lord Patrick, the last of the princely Pendragons!" And I struck a wild attitude, and laughed again and yet more bitterly.

The outlaw dropped from his perch to the ground, and crouched huddled there with his elbows and knees under him and his forehead on the moss. I waved Star Boy away from him.

"What now?" I asked, in wonder.

He shuffled and hitched himself forward and pressed his forehead on my right foot, then on my left, and hunched motionless again. Seconds passed before I was enough recovered from surprise and embarrassment to stoop and lift him and stand him upright.

"Gramercy!" I muttered.

I took him to the cave and made him free of the stew. I told him of my long acquaintance with Ben Tinker, of my recent lucky meeting with him, of my flight into the greenwood and the cause of it, and of Ben's departure on a secret mission. He harkened attentively, and with an air of abject humility even while gobbling soggy dumplings and gobbets of venison. He was a better listener than a talker; but after I had fetched him a second cannikin of ale from a little cask at the far back of the cave, I received almost more information than I could grasp.

By Stark's telling—and in few and uncouth words, at that—he was but one of the hundreds of poor, desperate men in the forests and waste places of this Devereaux country who thought of little else than revenge upon their lord and the meaner tyrants who served him. And so it had been as long as he could remember, and before he was born. His father had been flogged to death for slaying a deer. A mad cellarer who had cursed this lord to his face for hanging his son for the sticking of a wild pig, had been starved to death in an iron cage. But now the tyrants' days were numbered—here and beyond the Hills of Har and yet farther. Ben Tinker said so. He was their prophet. Now they but awaited their destined champion to lead them—even Pendragon, the last lord of the old bloods. The gypsy had for years wrought and planned for it; and Stark believed it.

All this I knew, or at least had been told by the gypsy himself. But Stark had more to tell. Ben Tinker was not their only captain, nor I their only champion. There was Sir Philip too, captain and champion in one. My ears pricked at that name.

"A mighty lord from the great world," the fellow continued. "Norman sired, but English dammed. His heart bleeds for us poor downtrodden folk. He will give every man a cot and craft when he is our lord."

I asked if he spoke of Philip de Courtville, and he said he did. I was puzzled; and I asked if he knew anything of a damosel named Blanche. He uttered an uncouth hoot of laughter, which offended me out of reason.

"Not so loud!" I warned him. "I don't begrudge you a full belly, good Stark—but another blast of insolence in my face, and I'll dent that cannikin on your empty head!"

He fairly groveled at that. I had to speak coaxingly, and give him more of the tinker's musty ale, and even pat him on the back, before his assurance was sufficiently recovered to permit him further speech. By Stark's telling, the damosel was Blanche Devereaux, the hated lord's only daughter and youngest child. The tyrant had two sons by a former marriage, the older of whom was the damosel's senior by more than twenty years. Guy was his name; and little was known of him by the vassals and churls of Devereaux, for he had left home when a mere lad, to serve as a page at the King's court. There were rumors that he passed much of his time in knight-errantry and the rest in extravagant carousings in the highest court circles. The younger, Simon, was at home, and a match for his father at grinding the faces of the poor.

"If your wicked lord has two male heirs, how will your soft-hearted Sir Philip ever get possession of Devereaux by wedding the damosel?" I interrupted.

The fellow started to hoot again, and uttered the first villainous *ho-hah* before stopped by my menacing gesture.

"Have a care, my good loon," I said softly. "Answer my questions, if you can, but spare me your impudent emotions."

Again he abased himself, and again I reassured him of my good will, calling him a true English churl and more fool than rogue at bottom. He soon recovered enough of his assurance and poor wits to answer my question.

This champion of the poor and downtrodden, this Sir Philip de Courtville, was not (by Stark's telling) a suitor for the damosel's hand in wedlock, whatever she and her sire and her half-brother Simon might believe to the contrary. He was not that kind of Norman lord. His love was not for other lords and Normans, but for the poor folk upon whose birthrights they lived and fattened. And as for the Damosel Blanche, she was but an excuse for his frequent appearances in the country, while he spread his promises of deliverance to crofter and cotter and hunted outlaw, and for his sojourns at the castle while he spied out the weaknesses of its walls and garrison. She, little fool, was but noble Philip's instrument for the destruction of her kind. He would take her or leave her, at his own good time and pleasure.

"Not so loud, rogue!" I muttered.

I controlled an unreasonable impulse to cuff him. The devil take this Philip, I thought. The poor man's friend, is he? Ben Tinker did not so much as name him to me; and I did not like the tootle of his horn; and try as I might, none of Stark's praise of him pleased me. Who is he to set true Britons free, I asked myself. Courtville! Who is he to take or leave that damosel at his own good time and pleasure? I looked at my hands and thought of the waist they had all but spanned. I laughed bitterly.

"Courtville or Devereaux, it's nothing to me," I cried; and still restraining the impulse to cuff the poor churl's ear, I left the cave and sought Star Boy's more congenial company.

That night I left the cave to Stark and made my bed outside again: but instead of sleeping in it, I took up a position close to the cave's mouth and remained wide awake. I suspected the lout within, by his prating of the virtues of Philip de Courtville, to be far too simple to be quite trustworthy. And he soon proved my suspicion right. He came tiptoeing forth with a bulky and long bundle on his back and a knife in his hand. I dealt him an open-handed blow that sent him reeling and the iron spinning. I took him by the scruff of the neck and shook him till his burden of goods and gear fell and scattered on the ground. Then I saw, by the light of the stars, the great sword of my fathers, noble Dragon-killer, lying there; then my indignation flared to high anger; and I drew the bull-hide scabbard from the sacred blade and beat him with it. He twisted and squirmed and bellowed, and rolled on the ground and groveled at my feet, still bellowing.

"Have mercy, lord! Spare your slave! It was for Sir Philip—at his command—by Christ His wounds! He would have the old sword—that every Englishman might know him for the true champion—as it is sung by old bards!"

I sheathed Dragon-killer and stirred the rogue with a foot, gently enough.

"This touches my honor," I said. "This hilt is not for your base hands—nay, nor for your master's neither—for my gorge rises at the very name of him—Philip! And I would trust that skulking mongrel no farther than yourself, cur!"

I raised him then and felt him over. Finding no broken

bones, I thrust him back into the cave and told him to stay there, promising that if he ventured forth he would be either cut in two pieces by the offended sword or trampled to a pulp by Star Boy's hoofs. But to make trebly sure of him, I barred the cave with great boulders.

Upon removing the rocky barricade and entering the cave in the morning, I found my prisoner deep in drunken sleep beside the empty cask. I made a flambeau, lighted it at the embers under the empty pot, and searched the cave from front to back and side to side. It was an armory, in very truth. Here were short swords and daggers and boar-spears by the dozen; and a jumble of armor of various periods and designs. The collection suggested numerous thieveries, and many pieces showed signs of smith-work and tinkering. I found a coat of fine Spanish chain that fitted me, and pieces of plate enough to make up a fair and serviceable suit of knightly harness, though somewhat tarnished, and even a helmet that fitted, though the hinges of the vizor needed oiling and the plume was broken.

Then I went to work on the fellow in leather, for whom I now felt less of charity and pity because of his sufferings from Norman hands than of animosity and distrust. I shook him. I might as well have shaken a corpse. I dragged him forth by the heels and rolled him in dew-wet fern, and got no more than a grunt for my efforts. Then I carried him to the stream and threw him in, but gently withal. He came out spluttering, and wide awake. I drove him back to the cave, but in the softness of my heart I grilled some smoke-dried venison from the gypsy's store with my own hands. He had no appetite for it, but I broke my fast, though it was in truth strong meat. Next I filled my wallet from the same store, then saddled Star Boy and harnessed myself, and armed with Dragon-killer and a short sword, a dagger, a bow, and a quiver of clothyard arrows. Then I made a leash of bowstrings, made one end of it fast about Stark's middle and mounted with the other end in my hand.

"Lead on," I told him. "Lead me to your noble Philip, that champion of the poor and oppressed."

He did not move.

"Bestir yourself," I continued. "Would you fail in duty to the generous master who has promised cots and crofts and full bellies to all poor native sons and daughters of these lands—and the castle too, no doubt, unless he occupied it himself? Bestir yourself, good Stark. He sent you for this sword. Here it is. Here is the sword of Pendragon, and here is the Pendragon with it. Lead on, rogue!"

"Spare me!" he bawled, flinging himself to the ground.

"Stand up," I said. "Or must Star Boy raise you with his teeth?"

He scrambled to his feet.

"Lead on, and straight, or the foxes will gnaw your bones," I said. "Bring me to your generous champion, and I promise you he shall receive the sword he sent you to thieve from Ben Tinker's cave—receive it unsheathed, and by point and edge, and to his death or mine, by my halidom!"

Our progress was slow, for the poor loon halted often to beg me to go my way and cast him free to go his. He even tried to frighten me from my intention of confronting Sir Philip, with talk of his size and knightly prowess and fierce temper.

"He will slay you on sight, lord!" he whined.

"In that case, he will have my sword and my horse too, and your reward will be doubled," I replied.

We rested at noon. Star Boy, unsaddled and unbridled, found good grazing nearby. I ate of the smoke-cured meat, but sparingly. Stark did not touch it. I gathered bramble berries from the nearest thicket and gave him a handful of them; and he ate them with such signs of relish and gratitude that I let him pick more for himself, then took him to a nearby stream, where we both drank. We traveled again, and with fewer delays. We halted at sunset.

"How far now?" I asked.

"No more than a league, lord," he muttered.

"Then I shall find him in the morning, bright and early," I said.

He was silent.

"Have you lost your tongue?" I asked.

Without looking at me, he whispered: "He will kill you, lord."

"I doubt it," I said. "But if I die, it shall not be alone, or this is not Dragon-killer and I am no Pendragon."

He went down on his knees to me.

"Nay, spare me the blood-guilt, lord! He has strangers with him now—in half armor, with crossbows. Not poor

English forest fugitives. A dozen such, before and behind him and at both elbows—ready to loose a bolt at the cock of an eye. Let me go now, and you await me here, and I will bring you a dozen true men by sunrise. Heed me, lord! True forest men with English hearts and bows. Then I will take you to him. I swear it, lord, by Christ's wounds! Hold the great sword to me, and I will swear on the cross of the holy hilt."

"I would not trust you, poor rogue, if you swore a hundred oaths and kissed a hundred crosses," I said. "You made to rob me of Dragon-killer last night, and would have slit my throat too, I think. Come to this tree now, and I will secure you for the night."

"*You* are my lord now!" he cried.

"A quick change of fealty," I sneered.

He was silent a moment, kneeling there with bowed head. Then he raised his head and looked at me.

"I did not strike you while we plucked berries in the thicket, lord," he said slowly. "Nor when we knelt together and drank at the stream. Nor when you turned your back upon me to mount your horse. Look to your belt, lord."

I looked down at my belt.

"To the right side, lord. To the silver-hafted dagger."

I looked. The sheath was empty.

"Your dagger, lord," he murmured, and laid the thin blade at my feet, and bowed his head again.

I stared down at it stupidly. He had taken it while we picked bramble berries. He could have stabbed me a dozen times since then. Or he could have cut his leash and escaped into the underbrush. Or he could have waited and freed himself at night; and if I had suddenly become aware of my loss at any time, he could have sprung upon me quicker than I could have sensed my peril. I turned and moved away a pace and stood so a long minute. When I turned again, the fellow still knelt at the same spot, but with his head up again, and the dagger still lay where he had placed it. I stooped and took up the weapon, and stepped close to him. He did not move, save for his twitching eyelids. I cut the bowstring at his middle, then sheathed the keen blade. His eyelids ceased their twitching. Then I drew the weapon, sheath and all, from my belt, and extended it to him, with the silver hilt advanced.

I slept but little that night. At one moment, thinking of the incident of the dagger, I trusted the fellow utterly, and at the next I feared the worst for my simplicity.

As well trust a wolf or a wildcat, I told myself. And yet he had me at his mercy and spared me. But he is a simpleton as well as a savage, at best. Even if he truly means no harm to me, the best I can expect from him is never to see him again.

I made a second and more secret couch of dry fern and heather, and lay on it with Dragon-killer unsheathed at my right hand and a knife in my left fist. But in a little while I sat up and called Star Boy closer. I dozed off, only to start up at the cry of a night-bird. I dozed again, only to be brought to my feet by the piping of a cricket. I was startled out of a mad dream by the barking of a fox. I slept again. I opened my eyes and wondered what had wakened me. The sky beyond the forest boughs above me was gray with dawn. I heard Star Boy grazing nearby. Then I heard a thin ghost of a whisper:

"Ten true men, lord."

I hesitated before speaking, to conceal my surprise and relief.

"I did not look for your return so soon. Well done, Stark!"

He appeared then, crawling from the dewy brake, and knelt beside me.

"I made haste, lord. And every one with bow and spear and knife; and Tom Shaw with new bread and a roasted goose, and Larkin boiled bacon, and Griffith a bottle of usquebaugh. Every man seized his gear at the word."

"What word?"

"Pendragon, lord. And Dragon-killer."

At a low call from Stark, they came from the shadows and gathered about us; and Star Boy moved among them, interested but undisturbed. Some were tall and others short, some broad and others narrow, some in wool and others in leather and yet others in both, but all raggedy. Every one had a bow and quiver at his back, a short spear in his hand, and a black knife in his belt.

"Tell them your name, lord," Stark prompted me.

"My name is Patrick Pendragon," I told them.

They louted low. I raised the great sword high, first by

the hilt, then by the blade, and cried out its name; and at that they all louted low again. I gave it to Stark and told him to let every man view it close and handle it if he would. So the sword sung by bards since ancient times, and named by them the destined slayer of all tyrants, passed among the ten. Every poor fellow sank to his knees when it came into his hands. Some kissed the hilt and some the blade.

When Stark gave it back to me, he cried: "But no man can strike the tyrants to earth with it save only its true lord."

So I swung Dragon-killer at the length of my right arm, around and around, till it hissed in the still air, then tossed it to my left hand and swung it as wide and fast, then wielded it with both arms till it sang like a harp-string.

Chapter Five
DRAGON-KILLER BITES DEEP

Stark and others scouted before me and the rest followed on Star Boy's heels. The sun was halfway up the sky, when Stark came back to me, finger on lip. Sir Philip and his fellows were close at hand, in a grassy glade. Stark and I whispered together. I dismounted, and all my fellows save Stark strung their bows. Then Stark led me forward, and Star Boy followed me close. We stood and peered out through the screening thicket. I saw a knight, fully harnessed and helmeted, seated on a log with his back to us. A fellow in bedraggled finery of velvet and lace and a steel cap stood nearby at the head of a tall red horse, with a long spear upright against one shoulder and a long shield against the other. The little glade was thick with men, some lolling in the fern, but most of them on their feet, standing or stirring. A dozen of them, at least, wore steel caps and breast- and backplates, and carried crossbows and wore short swords; and I knew them for Normans, or worse. The rest, numbering eight or ten, were in wool or leather, carried longbows, and stood apart from the others.

Stark left the thicket, cap in hand. The squire said a word, and the knight got to his feet and turned. His vizor was open, and I saw the shine of his pale eyes.

"You, rogue?" he cried. "And empty-handed! Where's the sword, fool?"

Stark shouted: "Dragon-killer is here, and Pendragon too!"

Every face turned to him. I mounted, drew the great sword and advanced from cover. Now all eyes were upon me. Star Boy stood, tossing his head high; and I brandished Dragon-killer. The knight shouted and ran to the red horse. A crossbow whanged, and I felt a sting on my left arm. A bowstring twanged beside me, and the Norman with the spent crossbow spun and fell with a clothyard shaft through his middle. And now Philip was up, with his lance leveled and his shield dressed. I had neither spear nor shield. The red horse wheeled, galloped, wheeled again, and came hurtling at us.

Star Boy jolted into motion. He went forward and this way and that, skipping more like a man on two feet than a great horse on four; and I leaned wide and slashed wide—and the Norman knight drove past with but half a spear in his hand. My great colt flung about and in savage pursuit, roaring like a lion, and he struck a red rump with an iron-gray shoulder; and I struck too, but a glancing blow in my haste. But between us, the Norman was knocked to the ground and his horse sent staggering.

He drew his sword and dressed his shield. I dismounted and faced him. He was tall and broad, and his sword was as long as Dragon-killer, but narrower, and he shifted his feet like a dancer, and covered himself well with the long shield. Then I knew him for the man in the dream. I ran at him, leaping crookedly and swinging the old sword with both hands. He drove his point and missed. My blade struck an edge of the shield and cut halfway through—and halfway through the armor and the man behind it. Blood spurted to the hilt and over my hands. I wrenched it clear and staggered backward; and Philip de Courtville sagged to the red grass, and rolled once and lay still.

I had never killed before. All my fighting had been done with wooden swords and blunt spears, in play with boys and old soldiers. I felt a steadying arm, and looked and saw it was the fellow Stark. He held a stone bottle to my lips. I spluttered, but swallowed enough of the fiery stuff to save my credit.

"Well struck, lord!" he whispered. "Now they know the true champion."

There was shouting and confusion all around us. The fellows in leather and wool yelled, "A dragon, a dragon!" and hunted the strangers in breastplates and backplates like hares. I saw the knave in tarnished finery leap to the saddle of the big red horse.

"Save me the red horse!" I cried.

Looking again, I saw that the saddle was empty and the red horse held from flight by many hands. Then Stark took me to a little river, and Star Boy followed us. I washed myself clean of Philip de Courtville's blood; and Stark bound the nick in my left arm with my handkerchief and then cleaned the great sword. I felt better.

They carried the dead back to a rocky knoll and left them for the wolves and foxes and ravens to bury. There were but two corpses in native leather and wool. Of the strangers, only one had escaped, by Stark's reckoning.

"One is enough to bring Devereaux about our ears," I said. "So we must move to a safer place, easier of defense, and send out runners to find Ben Tinker and rally him to us there."

We moved half a league to a smaller glade on higher and rougher ground, and from there sent out six active woodlanders, to scour the country for the gypsy in six directions. We dared not make fire, so did not hunt fresh meat, but dined on what we had, which was not much. I refused to accept more than one leg of the goose.

"A Norman lord would take the whole bird to himself," said an old man in a bearskin tunic.

It was not a case of share and share alike in the late Sir Philip's horse and war-gear, however. I named the red horse, the sword and secondary arms, and a spare lance and shield, and (after trying it on) the plumed helmet, for my very own.

The sun was no more than halfway down in the West, when Ben Tinker appeared suddenly, flashing his teeth, and came running to me and embraced me; and the bowmen cheered.

"I didn't wait for you at the cave, good Ben," I mumbled, embarrassed by his sudden appearance as well as the embrace.

"So I see, my good young lord," he replied, cocking an eyebrow.

"Stark came asking for you," I went on, talking fast but thinking faster. "To tell you this Philip—that Philip, he's dead now—was mustering the people. He called himself their champion. And he needed the old sword Dragon-killer to prove it—to prove himself their destined savior. Stark came to warn you. And he told me all about the champion. So I found armor in the cave and came away to see this champion, with Stark to guide me—and with Dragon-killer. And with ten of Stark's good friends. And he led me to him and his following of foreign rogues in half-armor, with crossbows. And I slew the false champion with Dragon-killer—and his ruffians are all dead too, save one who got away."

"It was well done, good lord," cried the gypsy. "And as for you, friend Stark—well, you are a better man than I thought you. To say true, good Stark, I have always—but let it pass!"

Stark, standing near us, with bowed head, mumbled, "Gramercy! Gramercy, Captain!" but did not raise his head.

The gypsy stepped back and blew three blasts on his fingers; and instantly the surrounding bushy edges of the greenwood became agitated and spawned forth a swarm of rustic figures with bows across their backs and spears in their hands.

"Two score and seven, and more on their way, my dear lord," the tinker informed me, in a complacent voice and with a fine show of teeth.

Turning, he bawled: "I have long promised you a true English champion—and here he is: the Lord Pendragon from over the western mountain. An English lord—ay, and of the ancient blood of British Arthur! No upstart turncoat Norman hedge-runner, this! And he has Dragon-killer in his hand—that ancient sacred sword—just as I promised you. And it has already drunk the blood of that knave I never trusted, Philip de Courtville. Now you know which of us was right, my simple friends—you or this gypsy. My true lord of Dragonland here—and many's the pot and pan he has watched me mend in the kitchen of the castle of his fathers, from which a Norman usurper has hunted him into the forest—cut the artful impostor in two this very day. Your noble Sir Philip—faugh! He went down before your true champion and the old sword like a basket of wind—just as I promised you!"

Some sank to their knees, and many went down on all-fours, and cries of, "Lead on, Dragon-killer! Lead on, lord! Lead on, Norman-killer!" filled the glade and echoed to and fro between wood and rock.

Ben Tinker moved away and mingled with them, with friendly but authoritative words and gestures; and then Stark raised his head and looked me in the eyes.

"Gramercy, lord!" he whispered. "Had you told him the truth—how I had come to steal the sword for the Norman Philip—he would have flayed me alive—that gypsy!"

"I guessed as much," I said. "A proven friend's hide is worth a lie."

He knelt at my feet. I raised him and told him to look well to the horses and gear. The gypsy came back to me and advised me to send out more scouts to bring in more rebels and to watch the Normans.

"Doubtless you've already done so, good Ben," I said. "If so, good! If not, do it. You are the captain. And I give you that knave Courtville's red horse and long sword too, and whatever of his gear I am not using myself."

At first blink of dawn we moved out of there, with a dozen bowmen fanned out in front. Ben Tinker, harnessed and armed, rode at my left hand on the tall red horse, and cut a commanding figure. Stark was at my right stirrup; and I saw that he now sported a steel cap and breastplate and some tags of velvet. When we issued upon the open farms, the morning light was wide and clear. Trumpets sounded from the battlements of the hulking gray castle of the mighty Devereaux. We heard the clank and clang of the descending drawbridge. We halted.

"Let them show themselves, my dear lord," said the gypsy. "Let them come to us—or as near as suits Your Nobility's purpose."

He flashed all his teeth at me, till they seemed to fill his open vizor. He was in high feather. A big knight on a big black horse appeared beneath the raised portcullis. His plume and shield were black and white. He rode onto the bridge at a slow, thumping walk.

"The Lord Simon," said Ben. "A strong knight, but

ponderous. Could you match him, if need be, my good Lord Patrick?"

"I could do what I can," I said; but my mouth was dry.

After Simon Devereaux rode five couples of large men-at-arms on horses to match. The narrow bridge swayed with their weight. After the horsemen came footmen with crossbows and pikes, a score of them at least, and all in short surcoats of black and white, like magpies. Clear of the shuddering bridge, the knight shook his charger to a trot, and from that to a galumphing gallop; and the men-at-arms did the same, forming in line on his right and left as they came up with him; and the footmen ran in among the horses; and so they all came thundering toward us, and shouting "Devereaux! Devereaux!" like one man.

Then the gypsy looked behind us for a moment, cried out a few words, and looked to our front again. A bow twanged; and then a multitudinous twanging of waxed strings and humming of sharp feathers filled the air, and points and feathers glinted high and low in the level rays of the new-risen sun. Long shafts struck and quivered in the sod and stubble before and behind the charging Norman line. A riderless horse came charging to the fore, wheeled, and charged back through the line.

Horses stumbled, staggered up, and plunged this way and that; and two stumbled again and lay kicking. Another saddle showed empty as the horse wheeled and galloped for home. The footmen lagged behind and loosed their crossbows, but the short bolts went wild and wide. And still the English arrows flew in swarms. The shouting of the war-cry grew ragged, and ceased altogether save for the bellowing of Lord Simon. The charging line became bent and ragged, and slow and slower, till only the knight and the black horse, both untouched, came on full tilt.

"Spare him," I said to the gypsy, but with a dry mouth.

Again he cried back over a shoulder; and instantly the song of hemp and feather fell to a whisper and then to silence. Then I closed my vizor, laid the long spear, dressed the long shield, and stirred Star Boy forward.

"Traitor!" roared the big knight.

Later, I wondered how he had learned of the revolt without hearing of Courtville's death too, but at the moment I could only pray. He came hurtling on, cursing

me for a false knight and traitor, and bulking larger, and
with his curses clanging louder in my ears, with every thud
of my dismayed heart. We met before Star Boy had gathered
full headway. I went backward clear out of the saddle, and
came to earth on the flat of my shoulders.

The surprise and violence of that contact knocked dismay from my heart and confusion from my head. I came to
my feet with Dragon-killer in my right hand. Star Boy came
galloping to me, and I waved him away. The Norman
plowed to a stop, heaved around, and came thundering
back at me, man and horse both roaring. I threw the long
shield at him and sprang aside. The black horse swerved,
then plunged, reared upright and turned, staggering, on
his hind legs; and I saw that Star Boy had attacked him on
the other side, with hooves and teeth, and that the knight
was toppling backward from the saddle. I ran in and pulled
him to the ground, spear and shield and all, smote him on
the helmet with the pommel of the old sword to quiet him,
then knelt on his breast and rattled a dagger on the bars
of his vizor.

"Strike, traitor cur—and be done with it!" he gasped.

"Fool, I'm not that double-traitor!" I told him. "I cut that
scurvy knave in two yesterday. My name is Pendragon."

I opened my vizor. Now the woodlanders were running
to me and gathering around; and I saw the Normans in full
flight for the drawbridge, every man and horse of them who
could stir a leg, with the lord's riderless black leading them;
and I saw Star Boy galloping back to me, strong and triumphant. I stood astride the prostrate Devereaux, with
Dragon-killer in my right hand and a long dagger in my left.

"This knight is my prisoner!" I cried.

The bowmen checked; and now Ben Tinker came
among them on the red horse, berating them for fools and
pointing castleward till they bent their bows again. The
drawbridge was packed tight with frantic men and horses,
and swaying with their struggles, when the long shafts
began to fall upon it, thinly, then thick and thicker and
faster like snowflakes in a growing storm; and soon there
were more men and horses in the moat than on the quaking
planks.

The gypsy dismounted and came to me and helped me
to stand the Lord Simon Devereaux upright on his feet.

"Look you, if any man harm this prisoner of mine, I will serve him as I served Philip de Courtville," I told him.

"And I will flay him into the bargain, my noble lord and champion," Ben cried heartily.

"I know that voice!" cried my captive. "The gypsy, mauger my head! The saucy tinker!"

"You say truth, my large lord," Ben acknowledged, flashing all his teeth. "The saucy gypsy tinker, mauger your head. And a right honest tinker have I always been to you, though not so honestly paid for my skill. So if I sometimes carried off a stray knife or scrap of armor, can you blame me? And it seems now, Your Mightiness, that I have stopped more than pots and pans for the noble race of Devereaux—even their castle, it seems."

"God's wounds!" muttered the knight.

I gave my captive into Stark's keeping, after the gypsy had called all the English together and told them that the person of the Lord Simon Devereaux, along with his arms and harness, was the private property of their champion and liberator the Lord Pendragon of Dragonland, and to be treated as such, or larger fruit than acorns would burden the nearest big oak.

Chapter Six
THE DAMOSEL AGAIN

When the people of the farms and crofts of that great valley saw our strength, they showed themselves in couples and groups, with gestures of submission and welcome. We advanced, spreading to right and left, and hemmed in moat and castle. Bolts and long arrows flew from battlements and keep, but in vain, for all our people took shelter under thatched roofs, and in orchards and hedges. Whatever warning the Normans had received, it had come too late for the peasants and herds to drive the cattle behind moat and wall and take refuge there themselves; so, having witnessed the defeat of the garrison and the ignominious fall of their great Lord Simon, and finding acquaintances and kinsmen even, and their friend the tinker, among the invaders, they considered themselves fortunate to be without, instead of within, the walls of Castle Devereaux.

Fat capons and even fatter ducks, that had been intended for the high table of the castle, lost their heads and feathers and were spitted and broiled to a turn and devoured by the victors. There was cider too. But all was not feasting and drinking. Captain Tinker picked master-bowmen and sergeants and told them their duties, and demonstrated the maintenance of discipline by cuffing the ears of a big swineherd who had said that now that he was free of the Norman yoke he was as good as any man and would take orders from no man.

We decided to starve out the family and garrison of the castle, for they had only their stores and what horses had survived our arrows, while we had the beef and mutton and venison of field and forest, and pork both wild and tame, and the granary and mill, to draw upon. More bow-men joined us. After dark, a watch was posted all around the moat and at its very edge.

The gypsy and I were resting by the hearth of a farm kitchen, when Stark came to us, breathing fast.

"Lord, I caught a rogue beside the moat," he whispered. "There were three, but two got away. The old lord and the damosel got away. They were in a little boat. He was a strong and stubborn rogue."

"Take your time, my friend Stark, or our noble Lord Patrick will be as confused as yourself, not to mention this poor tinker," said the gypsy.

Stark retold the story. He was at the edge of the moat, and was struck on his new breastplate by the haft of a dagger, the blade breaking short off. He grappled with the fellow and soon had him down and by the throat; and then the rascal begged for mercy, and promised him a great reward to be let go, for he had brought the old lord and the damosel across in a boat and must take them over the mountains to the protection of Sir Osbert de Montfoi; the old lord had a green wound in one leg, taken by mishap in the chase a few days ago and could not go fast or far without help, and so would make a rich man of him upon his, Rudolph's, advice.

And while Stark reflected, the tricky knave got him by the throat, but soon lost that advantage. And when Stark went down to the water he found a little boat, empty. And he discovered two sets of footprints beside Rudolph's in the mud, and one was of very small feet. So he had made haste to tell his lord of this thing.

"And what of Rudolph?" asked Captain Tinker, flashing his teeth and his earrings.

"The stubborn knave!" muttered Stark. "By the time I got his fingers off my windpipe, he was dead."

The gypsy nodded, then eyed me reflectively.

"With mighty Simon trussed in the cow-shed here, and the old tyrant and the damosel lost in the wilderness, where they will perish of starvation, if nothing worse, the hateful race and rule of the bloody Devereaux perish and pass," he declaimed sententiously.

"I have been told of another son," I said, for lack of anything else to say.

"The gay Lord Guy," he sneered. "When he comes home—if he ever thinks of it and can find the road—it will be to discover his castle under your dragon banner and Ben Tinker its high seneschal."

"I want no castle but my own," I said.

"And you shall have your own too, my dear lord," he said. "Tomorrow, or the day after, these knaves will surrender. Then we will march westward and over the hills, join with Ralph the Forester, and lay siege to that old fox your stepfather with five score English bows."

"Gramercy," I said.

"But for that vagabond rogue Philip and the gullibility of good Stark here and his kind, we would have dealt with Sir Osbert first," he added.

He got to his feet, said that he must make the rounds and see Tom Miller on a matter of wheaten meal and the brewer on the subject of strong ale, and left the kitchen. But Stark remained.

"Are you a skillful tracker, good Stark?" I asked.

"I have tracked a doe on dry moss, lord," he answered.

"In the dark?"

"I have eyes like a cat, lord."

"I am thinking of that Norman—and his daughter—footloose behind us. The gypsy may be wrong about them. They may win all the way through to Dragon Castle in their desperation, and then Sir Osbert will send to right and left for help—even to Beaufort and the St. Clairs—against our arrival. They must be stopped. We must stop them."

Stark muttered: "Alive or dead!"

I sprang up and gripped his neck with my right hand.

"Harm so much as a hair of her head, rogue, and you will curse the day you were born!"

He sagged to the clay floor and groveled at my feet. I raised him by the neck and shook him.

"Lead on now! Nay, fetch all the good wife's cooked meats and loaves in a poke first."

I released him, staggering. I girded on my belt then, with Dragon-killer and two daggers, and strode to where the woman and Stark were in violent dispute over a boiled ham. I flashed silver crowns and pennies in my palm, at sight of which she relinquished the ham and Stark thrust it into a bag. I gave her the coins and charged her grimly with a message for Ben Tinker.

"Tell the gypsy captain to join me at Ralph Forester's, and to look well to my horse Star Boy and bring him to me there."

We stole away, each with a bow and quiver and a full poke on his back. It was a night of misted stars and no moon. Stark soon found the tracks of the large and small Norman boots at the edge of the moat, and from there we followed them into a ditch and along the ditch to a coppice. From there, with Stark down on all fours at times, we won to a spur of the forest. He lost the tracks, but found them again in a sedgy hollow, only to lose them again and find them again. But he gave up at last, in a grove of pines floored with dry needles. There we lay down and waited for morning. After sunrise, we went forward at a fair pace and with few checks, and were on the first rising slopes of the Hills of Har well before noon. A little later, at the top of a bank above a fast stream, Stark checked and pointed and whispered.

"Look! The wet stones! We are close upon them!"

I looked and saw wet footmarks on three flat stones in midstream.

He brought his bow to his front and strung it, and reached for an arrow. I seized the reaching hand.

"Did I save you from the tinker to have to break your neck myself, fool?"

He whined a warning of crossbows, but I was in no mood to hear or heed. Mind and heart were strangely disturbed, and my mouth was even dryer than it had been at the onset of Lord Simon. I pushed him aside and sprang past him and down the bank.

"Stand!" screamed a desperate high voice.

I was in midstream then, with one foot on a rock and the other leg knee-deep in the swift water—but I stood. And I looked, and stared agape at what I saw. There, not ten paces away, was a lad with a crossbow in his hands. Nay, it was a mere boy—but boy or lad, he was not what I had looked to see. He was in stained leather and wool, like a scullion or stableboy. I gaped at the weapon, the short bow of which was bent to the full. But though it had been aimed at me when first glimpsed by me, it was lowered now and wavering.

"You?" he cried.

I drew up my wet leg and stood with both feet on the rock. I had nothing to say, but felt a profound disappointment. Stark came splashing, and mounted beside me; whereupon, for want of words, I grasped him by the nape and shook him hard.

The scullion on the banks said: "I saw Philip on your horse and thought he had killed you."

"Who are you?" I cried, then laid hold of Stark again and cried: "Do you know this saucy boy, fool?"

"The damosel!" he gasped. "Mercy, lord! I thought you wanted her."

"You lie!" I cried, and released him with a fling.

He staggered, splashing, righted himself halfway between me and the lad with the crossbow, and stood with his back to me.

"Lady, he is my master," he wailed. "Pendragon, the English lord. He cut Sir Philip in two pieces—that false knight—at one stroke. And he bade me track you down and bring him to you. And now he is gone mad."

"Let be, rogue!" exclaimed the lad. "You did well. Go tend your natural lord now. He lies helpless in the brake back here, sore spent."

"No lord of mine now, that old Norman!" protested Stark.

"Peace, fellow!" I cried. "Do as you are bid. You have a stone bottle in your poke. Give the Norman drink. Do as you would be done by."

He looked back at me, then waded ashore and up the bank and into the bushes. I left my rock and waded ashore too.

"You are not that damosel," I said.

"They cropped my head and stained my face and clothed me as you see," she whispered, not looking at me. "That my father and I might escape to Sir Osbert. Why have you hunted us down?"

I had no answer for that. I took the crossbow from her hands and tossed it aside.

"Help us now and my father will give you half his lands," she sighed.

"Half his lands!" I sneered. "I have lands of my own, and a castle too—and there will be no Osbert Montfoi nor any other Norman in Dragon Castle by the time you reach it."

"You do not like me now," she sighed.

"If that was you, I never liked you. Why should I like you, then or now? And since then I have slain your lover and taken your brother captive."

"He was not my lover."

"So you say, damosel. And I think he would not be if he could see you now. But he is dead, and of my hands, and sees nothing."

She put her hands to her face and wept. Stark reappeared at that moment.

"Lord, his wound is open and bleeding again," he told me. "If we but leave him lay, he will be dead in no time, and his soul before God with all his crimes upon it, and no need for us to lift a hand against him."

I went to the Norman with him, and it was as he said. I pulled off my jerkin, and my shirt of fine linen after it. I cut a sleeve from the shirt and tied it tight around Hugo Devereaux's bleeding leg, below the knee and above the wound. That pitiless harsh lord winced and cried out, and opened his eyes.

"Peace, Norman—and thank God it is not a bowstring round your neck!" I snarled at him.

He moaned and closed his eyes. I donned my jerkin, then tore the shirt to strips and took them down to the stream. The damosel still had her hands to her face. I gave her no heed, but washed the strips of linen in the spring-cold water, then took them back to the moaning Norman and bound his wound with them. Stark looked on idly, with a puckered smile that was at once stupid and sly. In rising and turning, I bumped against the damosel, who must have followed me up from the stream. Now her face was all smirched, where tears had washed the dark stain away in streaks.

"He was not my lover!" she cried, sobbing. "Rouse my father and ask him. I feared him—and my father too—and Simon. And I hated him."

She pushed past me, stooped over the unconscious lord and laid both hands on his shoulders.

"Let be!" I said harshly. "Would you kill him—your own father—to shake a last lie from him?"

I pulled her up and back, roughly. I turned and eyed Stark with a look that unpuckered his sly smile.

"What now, lord?" he whined, cringing.

"To the tinker's cave. And by the shortest way. Do you know it?"

"Yes, lord. It is not far."

"I will see to the sick Norman, and you will carry everything else."

Stark went in front, with both our bows and quivers and heavy bags of provender on his back, and I followed with the stricken Devereaux in my arms; and the damosel, all unheeded, came last. I had to lay my burden down often, to rest both myself and him. We reached the gypsy's cave well before sunset, and found it as we had left it; and the Norman lord was still alive.

Stark and I ate heartily, but the damosel would not touch the good food. As for her father, he parted his lips whenever the mouth of the stone bottle was held to them, but not once did he open his eyes. There was still light in the sky when I sent Stark away with word for Ben Tinker to look for me at his cave on his road to Dragonland. The fellow went willingly. I made beds of dry fern within the cave for the damosel and her father, and carried him in and laid him down. She helped me pull the fern, but I gave her no heed, and she did not speak. I made my own bed between the mouth of the cave and the screening thicket, and lay there with Dragon-killer bare at my right hand. For a long time I turned restlessly, but I slept at last.

I awoke as if at a voice in my ear, but I was alone. The sun was new-risen, and fern and sere leaf and bark and twig all gleamed white with frost, and the air was still and silent. For a minute I did not know where I was or how I had come here. Then I entered the cave. The new beds were near the front of it.

"Are you awake?" I asked; and got no answer.

I fumbled forward; stooped low and discovered the damosel crouched over her father. I touched her lightly on a shoulder, whereat she raised her head.

"He is sped," she whispered, and sank her head again.

"Christ assoil him!" I whispered.

I extended a hand again, and then the other hand, and laid hold of her middle lightly and raised her gently to her feet: and now I could only think of how my thumbs and fingertips all but met around her. She turned in my hands, and I tightened them. Her face was naught but a pale blur in the gloom.

I croaked: "You loved Philip de Courtville. And I killed him. And if he rose from the dead, I would slay him again. If you did not love him, why did you cry out to him?"

She moaned: "I don't know—but not for love. Then I cried out to you—cried louder after you—not to leave me—to wait for me. But you heeded not—as if you did not hear—and rode away."

"I heard," I croaked. "I heard your cries: 'Philip! Philip!' D'ye think me deaf—and a fool to boot?"

I loosed my hands from her and turned and stumbled forth from gloom to level sunlight.

Chapter Seven
TREACHERY

I wandered restlessly for hours, but to and fro and around and about, never beyond bowshot of the cave and yet always out of sight of it in screening underbrush. Once the damosel called to me, but I remained silent and hidden. She cried my name, "Patrick, Patrick," in a plaintive voice—but she soon gave over. I returned to the cave before noon and found her outside it. She must have washed her face, for all the dark stains were gone, but there were tears still on her cheeks. I gave her but a quick look, and she did not so much as glance at me. But she spoke, in a mere whisper.

"I feared that you had left me."

"If I left you, you might well fear," I said, harshly.

She bowed her head and twisted her hands together. They were clean now and looked strangely small and white at the ends of the scullion sleeves.

"We must—a grave must be—made," she whispered.

"Stark will soon be back," I said, kindly enough.

I brought one of the bags of meat and bread to her, and we sat on the ground on either side of it. She only nibbled the heel of a loaf, and I did but little better. I thought of reminding her of her appetite at the time of our first meeting, when she had emptied my wallet of its last scrap and crumb, but changed my mind. Or was it my heart that checked me? She was small and helpless; her father lay dead, her brother was my captive, and her home was beleaguered by her enemies, who were my friends; and now she, not I, was the hunted one. And she looked so poor and forsaken and piteous, nibbling at that crust, that my heart twisted. The crust was softened by her tears—a bitter sauce. And so, though I thought of Philip de Courtville and so of cruel truths to be said to her, I got to my feet and left her.

Slow hours passed, and the churl Stark did not appear. The sun sank, and yet he did not come. I made a little arbor for the damosel within two paces of the cave's mouth, and charged her to dart back into safety at any threat of danger. We both ate again, but still in a sad silence; after which I made my own bed on the farther side of the thicket. But it was long before I lay down, and after that it was long before I slept, for I was worried at Stark's absence and even more fretted of heart and mind by something I could not, or would not, give a name to. But I slept at last; and though my dreams were wild and confused, my sleep must have been sound indeed, for I required a rude awaking.

I was jerked to my feet by strong hands. I tried to strike out even before I opened my eyes, but only to find that my wrists were bound together in front of me. I tried to kick then, but only to learn that my feet were hobbled, and by so short a cord that my own violence threw me down upon my face. I twisted onto the flat of my shoulders and struck upward with both feet close together. I felt them hit, and heard a savage grunt of surprise and discomfort.

My eyes were wide open by now, God knows, but as the light was only vague starshine, I saw but vaguely. A large shape rolled in the fern, and I flung myself upon it. . . . I put up a fight, but it was a losing one from the start. With bound wrists and hobbled feet, and outnumbered too, what else could I expect? Overcome at last, I lay still. Battered and bruised I was, but I believed all my bones to be intact; and I knew, and was as puzzled at as grateful for the fact, that no deadlier weapon than a cudgel had been used upon me.

"Up with you, fool!" snarled a voice I had heard before; again I was jerked roughly to my hobbled feet.

And now I saw his face. He was Simon Devereaux, my captive. And now I became aware, for the first time, of something in the grip of my bound hands. I raised it and stared at it, for seconds in bewilderment and disbelief, then in sickening and scorching anger and hate. It was a leather jerkin; and though it was ripped from top to bottom, I knew it: Stark's jerkin! I dropped it to the ground and set my feet on it.

"Dog eats dog," jeered the Norman. "Saxon eats Saxon. Dogs will be dogs."

"His dirty leather shirt came away in my hands," I said, in a splinter of voice. "It will be his dirty hide next. But not in *my* hands. The gypsy will attend to him. I am neither gypsy nor Norman. As for you, Simon Devereaux, why not slay me—with my sword, since I took yours in fair fight— now that my hands are tied?" I sneered. "With Stark holding me from behind, you might hack me to death—butcher me somehow—fumbler though you be."

After a long pause, the Norman chuckled wickedly.

"I'm not to be tempted. You are for Sir Osbert to dispose of; and I mean to get you to him on your own feet. He should consider you fair payment for a brief period of harborage and hospitality. I'm quite sure that you will wish yourself dead of my hands, by sharp steel, before he has done with you."

I said nothing to that. We were still a long way from Dragon Castle; so I decided to save my breath and strength as far as possible for any distance short of Sir Osbert's grasp.

We were soon on the march, stumbling in the confusion of misty starshine and forest gloom. Stark led the way, limping, and bare to the waist, save for the longbow and poke on his back. The Norman floundered close on his heels, with a short sword in his right hand and an end of a fathom of rope in his left. He wore my ancestral sword Dragon-killer on his back, hung from his neck. I came next, with the other end of the rope which he held in his left hand knotted to the front of my belt. I was being led like an ox to the slaughter. The damosel came last.

The heavier of the two pokes of provender was on my back. When Simon stumbled, which was frequently, I was jerked forward, or to the right or left, at the end of that short rope. At times I was brought down on all fours, but managed to scramble up always and stagger on. I was so sore from crown to heel that I moved in continuous pain and with a confused and clouded mind. I thought dully that it would be a long time before we reached Dragon Castle, at this rate, and that the longer the time on the way, the better for me: so I fell again, but this time of my own accord, and remained down on my elbows and knees in defiance of the Norman's savage curses and jerks on the rope.

We shall never get there, at this rate, I congratulated myself.

But it was not as well thought of as my dazed brain had imagined, for the Norman turned back and kicked me in the ribs till I stumbled to my feet again.

Sometime later—sometime before the first crack of dawn—I was dully conscious of a fumbling and plucking at the poke on my back; and though spent almost to the verge of insensibility, I reasoned that it could be none other than the damosel there, as the traitor and Devereaux were both in front of me, may their souls squirm in hellfire! And I wondered stupidly, for the moment, what she was about. But another fall and a few more kicks gave me other food for stupid and painful reflection.

At the first gray lift of dawn, I fell yet again; and now I was past caring for kicks. I waited in a stupor of indifference. But the kicks did not come. Instead of feeling the toes of Simon's boots on my ribs, I heard his voice calling and cursing. It reached my exhausted consciousness as if from a long way off or through a thick fog. He was calling a name—"Blanche! Blanche!" He shouted it next, with threats and curses. I heard treacherous Stark's whining voice.

"Have a care, lord! Not so loud! They are roving far and wide, lord, with strung bows."

"Go back for her, rogue!" the Norman ordered him.

I thought: If I had my fingers on his fat neck now, he would be dead before their return.

But it was only a mad thought, for I lacked even the energy to try to raise myself from the ground, or my dizzy head on my aching neck even, that I might look at him. Soon he began calling again, but not in full voice, and for both churl and damosel; and next I heard that traitor-cur's whine again, telling that the damosel had turned aside some way back and asking if he should track her down. He was answered with curses, and cuffs too, by the sound. I was not molested. I heard Simon breaking his fast—the champing of his big teeth on meat and bread and the gurgles of a bottle. Only the gurgles interested me—they stirred a craving in my poor stomach.

"Feed him, rogue," said the Norman. "Keep up his strength for the march home to his stepfather. Or do you want to carry him on your back, dog?"

I heard Stark's approach. It sounded cautious and reluctant. I heard him set something on the ground, close to my head. Then I came alive with hate and hurled myself like an adder from its coils or a wildcat from its crouch. I struck Stark with my tied hands clasped before me and all my flying weight behind them; and he went over backward, and over again into the nearest thicket. I swerved to my right, jumping with hobbled feet close together. There sat Simon Devereaux, stone bottle in hand, gaping and staring, his stout legs spread wide and flat on the moss. I saw crumbs of bread and trickles of liquor in his curly round beard. Then, with a wild shout, I was upon him.

Now my hands were unclasped—and behold, the bottle was between them! Now it was at my lips. Gulping fast, I made one more jump, then stood so and continued to swig the strong liquor till my craving was satisfied. I lowered the bottle and looked at the Norman. He sat as I had last seen him, still gaping in astonishment, but now with something added that might well be discomfort, for I had kicked his paunch in my assault upon the bottle.

There was a dagger in his belt and a short sword lay unsheathed beside him, but both his hands were empty.

Now! I thought, my pain and weariness gone. Now is my time! He is at my mercy again, the fumbling fool! Hurl the bottle in his face, then leap in again, and the sword is mine! And then—then I remembered Stark. He was not in sight, but I pictured him standing behind screening hollies with strung bow and notched arrow, watching and waiting for a signal from his new lord. And when my gaze returned to Simon, the sword was in his right hand, and the long dagger bare in his left.

"Set the bottle down," he ordered.

"If my hands were free, and if we were alone, I'd match my empty fingers against your steel and send your red soul yelping to hell," I said.

"Right heady liquor," he jeered. "You will need a cask of it when Sir Osbert gets to work on you."

Then he cried out for Stark: "Show yourself, rogue! The noble Pendragon has refreshed himself and is ready to march."

Seconds passed, and a minute, without sound or sight of Stark. The Norman called him again, and louder and with curses, but still without result. He got to his feet, grunting and cursing, and set about kicking at the surrounding thickets and beating them with the flat of his sword. I was as mystified as he was, but felt less perturbed than he did by the churl's failure to show himself.

"He has gone in search of yet another lord, to sell both of us," I said in bitter jest.

He turned and glared at me.

"But not together," I continued, developing the thought. "Nor in the same market. He will sell you first, to the English rebels. The foresters will not be as considerate of your Norman carcass as I was. But he will gain little by that sale, save popularity. So, if he can contrive it, he will keep me hidden from them and take me secretly to Sir Osbert, thus cheating you doubly, first of your life—for the woodlanders will hang you by the neck without argument—and secondly of Sir Osbert's reward."

He continued to glare at me, but now with fear as well as savagery in his eyes. I uttered a hoot of bitter derision.

"Or more likely he lies senseless in the thicket here, stunned by the blow I dealt him with these bound hands," I added.

This I did not believe, though I liked the idea; and if I had thought that, by some miracle, I had broken the false rogue's neck, I would have rejoiced. But the Norman did believe it, evidently, for he thrust his way impetuously into the thicket, with renewed cursing. I could hardly believe my eyes. Now or never! I set the bottle down then, and with my hobbled feet placed close together, I jumped after him. He is a fool, I thought. The blessed saints are on my side. For in there among the hollies and thorns my chances against him will be doubled. But I tripped in my second jump and came down on my knees at the very edge of the tangled wildwood; and before I could rise, I heard a cry of dismay from the heart of the thicket.

Instead of rising to my feet, I sank forward onto my hands and crept into the tangle. I advanced cautiously, close to the ground, worming my way along with no more sound or stir than a stalking fox. Soon I saw his boots close before my eyes. They were motionless, and their heels were toward me. I rose to my knees, then slowly to my feet, without stirring a leaf or twig. Here he was, and with his back to me. He was breathing thickly. I held my own breath, raised my clasped hands high, made a silent prayer, and struck down on the base of his neck with all my strength. He yelped and staggered forward. I hurled myself upon him, striking again and yet again while he lunged and fell, and then till he lay still on his face. Working with desperate haste, I freed my wrists on an edge of the short sword, and then my ankles. A minute later, his wrists were bound, but behind instead of before him, and his feet hobbled, but with even shorter play than mine had known. I stood astride him and laughed exultantly. But not for long. When I saw what he had seen and cried out at, I stopped laughing.

For it was the false rogue Stark. He lay face down, a knife sunk between his naked shoulders. It was sunk to the haft. My stricken wits stirred as slowly as the chilled blood in my veins—almost as slowly as the congealing blood on Stark's back. The damosel! And now this rogue! And next—would it be Devereaux or me? Was the slayer foe or friend? I turned and burst out of that fateful thicket, and well clear of it, and turned again to face it. All was still and silent there for minutes. Then I heard, and soon saw, a commotion there; and the Norman hobbled into view and fell. He heaved up onto his knees and gaped at me.

"Did you knife him?" I asked.

He shook his head stupidly.

"And the damosel?" I asked.

"The little fool," he croaked. "She gave us the slip. She isn't—back there. Only Stark."

After a pause in which I fumbled for another thought, I asked: "Had he his bow and shafts?"

He only gaped at that.

"On his back?" I continued. "Bow and quiver and poke—when you last saw him—alive?"

He nodded stupidly.

"Not now," I said. "They're gone."

His wits were even slower than mine, for I had given him a sorry pounding. Seconds passed before he got my meaning. Then he uttered a thin scream of terror, heaved up from his knees, started to run on his hobbled feet and crashed to earth. Again he lay senseless—but this time of his own doing. I turned him over on his back and sat him upright, but he thumped flat again. I fetched the bottle and forced liquor into him, waiting all the while for the twang of a bowstring and the sudden agony of iron in my vitals. He opened his eyes.

"Why don't I cut your throat and be rid of you?" I cried.

He moaned, and shut his eyes.

"Get up!" I cried, and cursed him.

He sat up, but kept his eyes shut tight.

"On your feet!" I snarled; and I laid hold of him and yanked him upright.

He stood swaying, but now with his eyes open and rolling fearfully. I took the great sword Dragon-killer from him and hung it at my own back. I picked up the bottle, found it empty, and flung it down. Now my wits were desperately clear and active. I stepped well away from the swaying Norman. Making a slow and complete turn, I challenged the surrounding coverts.

"Here I am, Patrick Pendragon, if it's me you want—whoever you are. And there's Simon Devereaux, my enemy. Whoever you are—friend or foe—loose your shaft and have done with it."

Nothing stirred. No one answered. It was broad day by now, and bright and still. I stepped back to my captive and told him that we would return to where the damosel had lost touch with us and cast about for her tracks. He muttered that he was hobbled too short for walking.

"Then you'll have to hop," I told him.

I hopped him along before me, with an occasional gentle prod of the short sword, till he fell exhausted. I left him flat and gasping, and went on alone. I soon found the spot where she had turned aside. The imprints of her heels were still sharp on moist ground, but only for a little way. Then they were gone utterly, though the ground was still moist; and then I knew that she had removed her boots; and so, thinking of the fumbling and plucking that I had felt at the poke on my back hours before, I knew that she had not parted company with us by accident. I pulled the bag around to my front and looked into it. Its contents were less than I remembered them, for a certainty. But what was this? I plucked it forth and stared at it incredulously.

"A knife!" I cried. "A knife?" I repeated, in a lower voice. "But why? That damosel? To cut myself free? But she could have cut me free. But no, for my hands were tied in front of me—and I was roped to her brother. He would have caught her at it. But why?"

I put the knife in my belt and went back to my captive like a sleepwalker. He was where I had left him, but now sitting up and looking wildly around.

"Ease my arms—or strike me dead!" he screamed.

"So you are not easy?" I said, trying to fix my thoughts on him. "In torment, even? But what was the torment you promised me at Montfoi's hands?"

He cursed—and I laughed. He prayed. I jeered at him for a blubbering, soft, shameless knave.

"Your poor arms!" I jeered. "And what would have happened to my arms—arms and legs and eyes and skin—had you got me to Sir Osbert?"

He begged for mercy—of me, and of the blessed saints, and at last of the holy Mother of God. I cried out in shame at that—in shame for him!—and stepped behind him and severed the cords that bound his wrists. His big arms fell to his sides like lead. I stooped before him then and slapped his mouth.

"Gramercy!" he mumbled.

I turned away in disgust.

What next? I asked myself, trying to think. To Ralph Forester's now. Stark did not give my message to Ben Tinker. The gypsy will look for me at Ralph's. Stark sold me to this Norman. And now he is dead. . . . The damosel gave me a knife. She took food from my poke and left a knife in its stead. And she took her boots off so as to leave no tracks. She could have killed me—sunk the knife between my shoulders. I killed her Philip.

The Norman startled me out of that maze with a yelp of laughter. I turned upon him savagely and would have struck him on the mouth again but for the look of him. He was mad. It was in his eyes and on his lips.

"You didn't find her!" he hooted. "But she'll find us!" Then he sank his voice to a flabby-lipped, blubbering babble. "She slew Courtville and the churl. Dead as mutton. And took his bow an' quiver. And me next. She's a fiend from hell."

"So are you—and a fool to boot! How could she slay the churl? It was a strong man's stroke."

"She's a witch. So was her mother. Out of Wales."

By now he was the complete idiot, rolling his head and slobbering.

"But what have you to fear from her?" I asked. "Even if she killed Stark—and only a madman would think it—why would she kill you?"

He gave me a sly look.

"She hates me," he whispered. "I forced the marriage. And she tried to kill him, that night—but he fled an' turned traitor—but she got him at last. Let him fry in hell, that traitor! But she killed him in stark hate. And she hates me too. A she-devil! And she'll kill me too."

I shook with disgust and senseless anger. I dropped the short sword on the moss beside him and stepped back one pace and drew a dagger.

"Stand up!" I cried. "There's your sword. Arm yourself an' stand—and God's wounds! I'll kill you like a toad!"

He rolled his head, and his eyes in his head. He was a driveling idiot. Cursing, I stooped and recovered the sword. But why waste curses on him? He was already accursed.

"I slew Courtville!" I cried in his foolish face. "Do you hear me? He was always a traitor, and worse, rot him! Slashed him in two. And I would to God I'd served you the same way, while you still wore the semblance of a man."

He rolled his eyes and his head, and his flabby mouth hung open and awry.

Chapter Eight
A Fight in the Dark

I had a rendezvous with Ben Tinker at Ralph the Forester's hut; and if I succeeded in keeping it, I would send out a strong party of my own people, led by my trusty friend Ralph himself, to find the lost damosel and bring her safely to me. For she deserved my good opinion after all, it seemed, and so my help and protection: for had she not hated Philip de Courtville and tried to kill him? Or was Simon a liar even in his madness? And she had thought to befriend me.

I knew this for true, by the knife in my poke. And by then I would be in my ancestral castle again, and the biggest oaks of the home park would hang as thick with Sir Osbert and his hirelings as an orchard with apples. And there, in Dragon Castle, she would be safe, though every other Norman in England perished. To the fate of Simon Devereaux, or of Roger de Montfoi, I did not give a thought, so hot was my eagerness to make amends to that pitiful desolated homeless wench in scullion attire for my unjust harshness. My heart ached with remorse, and with pity as if for a wounded fawn, or a hurt and homeless dog, or any cotter's brat lost and affrighted and uncomforted.

Great was my haste. When weeping Simon fell and cried for mercy before we had gone a rod, I paused only long enough to cut the hobbling bowstring at his ankles, then stepped over him. He might follow, or lie and die right there of starvation or by the hand of the mysterious killer, for all I cared. I went fast, then not so fast, and very slowly after a few miles. I was still sore and weak from the Norman's handling and footing, and the way was rough; and now the knife in Stark's back, and the disappearance of his bow and quiver and bag of food, were at the front of my mind again.

I cast fearful glances before me and around, and strained my ears and tried to steady my heart for the twang of a bow and the buzz of an arrow, as I staggered onward. When I stumbled and fell, I lay and gasped for breath; but when Simon came stumbling, and fell beside me and lay whimpering, I scrambled to my feet and ran again. Now detestation for the mad Norman put the threat of the hidden slayer from my mind. Now I ran better than before, watching the ground to save my feet, and skirting obstructions instead of bursting through them or floundering over them; and when I fell, I continued to advance on all fours until able to rise and run again. When I splashed into a cold brook, I rested a little and cooled my throbbing head, and drank sparingly. And so—running, creeping, resting, and running again—I continued upon my westward course.

I rested and ate at noon, listening all the while for sounds of the mad Norman's approach. I heard a deer start and bound away in the underbrush, but nothing of Simon. I wondered—without emotion of any kind—if the mysterious killer had made an end of him, or if he had stopped to drink, guzzled too much cold water, and tumbled in and drowned. Or had he simply lost all track of me, in his terror-ridden madness? I did not care what happened to him. I wondered idly what he would do when he felt the pangs of hunger—if he lived so long; for he was without food. But I did not care.

By midafternoon, I was on the height-of-land, and I was over it when the sun sank before me, beyond the sloping, spreading forests of my own Dragonland. I ate again, made a couch of dry heather, lay down with the great sword Dragon-killer unsheathed at my side and was soon asleep. . . .

Sometime later a great bird beat at my face with its wings. I put up a hand, but found nothing. A dream. But it came back and beat again, and harder. I made to hit it away, but there was nothing. I sat up then and stared about me. There was no light. There was no sound.

But I was wide awake. My right hand closed on the hilt of the old sword. I lifted it noiselessly and got to my feet as noiselessly. Seeing nothing, hearing nothing, yet I felt deadly peril like a cold hand on my heart. I stood with Dragon-killer bare on my right shoulder and both hands on the long hilt, and strained every sense to detect the threat. There! A small, dry rustle of twigs. Silence again. I held my breath. There again—the stir of a fumbling, cautious foot on moss this time, dull and heavy, but fainter than a whisper. And yet again!

I moved backward one slow move, and another as slow, without lifting my feet; but the naked steel lifted a little from my shoulder as if of its own accord. And yet again—a labored breathing now, but not mine; and then a swish in the sightless air, in my very face—then a stroke on the ground at my very feet—on the dry heather of my bed—and a gusty grunt.

Then Dragon-killer struck—struck and found flesh and struck again. . . . I staggered back, with all the strength of fear and rage gone as suddenly as it had possessed me. I slumped to my knees. All was still and silent again. The heavy, struggling, inarticulate commotion on the ground had ceased. Releasing my hold on the great sword, I slumped lower, even onto my hands. I had killed something. Something lay dead there. It had come to kill me in my sleep, but I had killed it. Thanks to the beating wings that had wakened me, or to the dream of them, I was still alive. I turned and crawled away, dragging the old sword with me—but not far. I slumped flat to earth; and there I lay in a daze, too spent to move, till dawn.

When the silver wash of a new day reached me, I roused and stood and turned. I looked at Dragon-killer. The great blade was dim and brownly stained. I cleaned it on the nearest clump of fern, sheathed it, and hung it at my back again. Then, with a sharp effort of will, I forced my way, through coppice and underbrush, toward the place of the blind kill. I went slowly, reluctant yet eager, urged by a fearful curiosity. What had I slashed and hewn to death in the dark? What—who—had struck at me in the dark? I reached the spot. . . . He lay face down, sprawled, cleft from shoulder to waist, slashed halfway through—a sodden red mass. I knew him by his boots and sword. I had left that long sword somewhere and forgotten it; and he had remembered it, recovered it, and followed me—only to slash it down across a bed of dry heather. I turned and fled.

Chapter Nine
THE RENDEZVOUS

The sun was high before I paused to drink at the nearest stream and break my fast. Then westward again, until hunger and weariness stopped me again for a little while. At the fall of dark I crawled into the heart of a thicket, where I lay in dreamless sleep till sunrise. Now I was in familiar country, deep in Dragon Forest; so I traveled with renewed vigor, though every weary muscle and sore bone protested. I was midway the length of a grassy glade, staggering slightly but at a good pace, when a clothyard shaft appeared upright suddenly in the sod before me. I came to a staggering stop, and cried out, as suddenly.

"Pendragon!" I cried.

A figure appeared from the forest gloom in front of me, a quarter bowshot off, and stood. His bow was unbent before him, but a second arrow was notched on the slack string.

"Sam Bowyer!" I cried. "Don't you know me, Sam? Your true lord?"

Then I laughed, and toppled and fell, and scrambled to my knees and remained so, still laughing. The bowman jumped and came running. He dropped his bow, stooped and laid hold of my shaking sides with mighty hands, and lifted me. He pressed me to his leathery breast, then held me off at arm's-length and stared.

"Young Pat!" he cried. "Lord Patrick! And we mourned you for dead. God's wounds! Alive an' laughing!"

"I'm not dead—of a certainty," I gasped.

"But they are," he shouted, in gusty mirth. "All three of them: Jacques an' Noel an' Martin. One by one. I got Jacques that very day—through the neck. A pretty shot at a hundred paces. And Watkin caught Noel that night, behind Dick Miller's woodstack. And only yesterday Martin's corpse was fished from the moat. That would be old Nick Pottle's doing, liker'n not. So perish all your foes!"

He took me to Ralph Forester, carrying Dragon-killer and the poke for me. Several more bowmen, attracted by Sam's loud talk and laughter, joined us on the way. Hob and outlawed Luke ap John were among them. Each in his turn knelt to me, then sprang up straight and embraced me manfully.

Ralph was there, with a score of fellows loosing their shafts at marks in his forest clearing. He leaped to me with a shout of joy and embraced me like a father; and all the fellows within sight and hearing—born Dragonlanders to a man—tossed their bows and caps in the air and bawled my name. I leaned on Ralph and asked him what news of Ben Tinker.

"A messenger came in last night, with good news," he said. "They have the Devereaux holed up and just about smoked out, an' they'll be on their way any minute now to help us smoke out our own precious Normans. All's well, my young lord! Pendragon an' England for ever!"

"I could have told you that myself," I said, leaning yet more heavily upon him and pressing a hand to my head. "And more! Old Devereaux slipped out and now lies dead and deserted in the gypsy's cave. But Ben doesn't know—unless he's found him since. And Simon Devereaux is dead too—I killed him myself, with Dragon-killer. But hold! The damosel is astray in the forest—somewhere this side of the mountain! The Damosel Blanche. She's garbed like a scullion boy. She befriended me. Gave me a knife. I'll go find her."

Whirling blue spots and golden sparks flew alternately across my vision, and I sagged in the big forester's arms. He eased me gently to the ground. Someone raised my head and pressed a horn of mead to my lips. I grasped it, drained it, let it fall, and scrambled to my knees and then to my feet.

"I'll find her," I cried, staggering around. "Make way! Follow me! A score of you—of the best—follow me!"

Then I lay down again on the comfortable ground and floated away on soft clouds. . . .

I was in a hut when I recovered consciousness, supine on a narrow cot. By the wavering shine of a smoky hearth-fire and the feeble gleam of a tallow dip, I saw that I was not alone. An old man with a long white beard sat huddled on a stool within reach of an arm.

"Who are you?" I asked.

He raised his head with a jerk that lifted the tail of his beard from the floor, and straightened his back with another jerk and turned his face to me.

"Hah!" he exclaimed. "Alive, huh? I mean awake."

"Who are you?" I repeated. "And where am I?"

"Calm yourself, young man," he said. "Your Lordship, I am your preserver, Doctor Matson. Don't you remember me?"

"Yes, you once pulled out a tooth of mine."

"Quite so. But I've done you a greater service since. Your Lordship was on the point of death when I arrived and let the fever out. I drained it from your brain and heart in the nick of time."

"Gramercy! But where is Ralph Forester?"

"Gone—and all the people with him. Gone to the castle, to play a tune on Sir Osbert's ribs."

"Gone there without Ben Tinker? He was to wait for Ben! And for me. I'm lord here!"

"Nay, the gypsy came, with two score bows. And they all went together—six score of them."

"Did he bring my horse Star Boy?"

"There's a great horse tied in the shed. Don't you hear him kicking?"

I sat up.

"Lie down!" cried the doctor. "Calm yourself!"

But I lowered my feet to the clay floor and stood up.

"My boots! Hah, here they are!"

But when I stooped to put them on, my head spun and I all but fell. So I requested the doctor to help me. He refused. Then I saw the great sword Dragon-killer upright in a corner, with the gems of hilt and scabbard burning red and green; and I stepped to it and drew out the long blade like a leaping flame. The ancient chirurgeon changed his tune at that sight, and helped me into my boots, and then into my jerkin and tunic, most obligingly. He opened the door for me, snatched a brand from the fire, and followed me from the hut into the night—all eagerness now to be rid of me and Dragon-killer. The night was still and blind and chill.

"To my horse!" I ordered.

The doctor waved the smoldering brand to enliven the

flame, then held it high; and just when its lurid shine disclosed a structure of planks and poles, the nearest wall bulged and quaked and the air shook in our ears to a mighty blow.

"There he is," said the doctor.

"Star Boy!" I shouted. "I'm with you, lad! Stand still now. Here I come."

Then Star Boy trumpeted. I found the door in a few wobbly jumps and opened it; and even as I made to enter, he came thrusting forth. I steadied myself against his massive chest, with both my arms in a fond embrace of his massive neck. Now we were in darkness, for the doctor had fled back to the hut, torch and all. Star Boy was without saddle or bridle, but I scrambled onto his back.

"Home, lad," I said. "You know the way. But take it easy."

And so I set out on the last stage of my return to my ancestral castle, with the same horse under me and a feeling in my still confused consciousness that the acquisition of the mighty sword on my shoulder more than made up for my shortage of saddlery.

Chapter Ten
Saint George for England!

Star Boy went along as if he could see in the dark, with many short divergings, but few and only momentary checks. Not once did he stumble. Now and then he swung his head and breathed a warning of scraping boughs. I sat him with assurance, depending on my legs only to keep my seat, and gripped Dragon-killer's hilt with both hands so as to keep the great blade flat and steady on my shoulder. I was conscious of the strength of my legs and arms, but at the same time, dimly aware of a lack of corresponding vigor above and between my ears. In fact, my head felt as light as a blown-up pig's bladder for children and fools to play with.

"That old doctor drew off too much of my blood," I complained. "My brain feels like feathers. He drew off the fever, so he says, but he should have left enough blood in my head to keep my wits from blowing away."

I babbled of this and that; and though I heard myself,

and without approval, I babbled on. Star Boy acknowledged my ramblings with occasional gusty snorts which sounded sympathetic.

"That rogue we caught in a tree—Stark—played me false. But he is dead now. Sold me to Simon Devereaux. That fat fool kicked me grievously. But where is he now, that blubbery Norman? Ask Dragon-killer. He carved him like Sir Philip. You know what we did to Philip. You were there, lad. Cut him in two pieces. But the damosel gave me a knife and ran away."

Later the blackness around us turned to woolly gray; and I told Star Boy of it. And when the gray brightened to silver, I told him to that. A little stir in the chilly air brought a tang of burning; and now I saw that all the wood before us was blue with smoke rising from little fallen fires, and mingling and drifting with the frosty mist.

My heart leaped and swelled.

"Up, lad!" I shouted. "I'm home again! Up, sluggards! Saint George for England!"

The smoldering fires took to sparks and flame, and men in wool and leather and shaggy fur came crashing through brush and brake, bending and stringing their bows. Star Boy pranced majestically and trumpeted loud and long; and I flourished Dragon-killer high and wide, sweeping and turning the great blade till it shone and flashed like a living flame in the waxing light.

"Patrick—our true lord!" the men shouted. "A Pendragon! A Pendragon!"

"And the old sword!" I cried, whirling it yet higher and wider. "Dragon-killer, the Avenger! Dragon-killer and Norman-killer!"

They crowded around, clamoring; and though Star Boy showed nothing of either hostility or alarm, he took this moment to indulge in a mighty shake from muzzle to tail, like a wet dog, and so unwittingly twitched me from his back—Dragon-killer and all—and into the arms of half a dozen of my people. . . . Supported by a dozen hands, I was drinking from a long horn when Ben Tinker thrust his way through to me and grabbed me to his armored breast, and splashed the good ale over both of us in doing so.

"How's this?" he cried. "Alive, by my halidom—by my

pots and pans! I left you at death's door, lord. Old Matson let a raving fever out of your brains—and I feared he had let your dear life out with it. But I dared not tarry, lest the churls lose heart and scatter back to the coverts before the usurpers were hanged from your battlements. Praise be to God for your miraculous recovery, my dear young lord. My heart rejoices."

"Gramercy, good Ben. I'm well enough in my legs and arms, but I'm not so sure of my wits. There's a thought in my head—or should be—I can't put a finger on. What have I forgot? Did you say you hanged Sir Osbert? And did he stop smiling?"

"Nay, sweet lord, not yet. But all in good time. We've not got in at him yet. But the knaves are coming out to us, like rats from a doomed ship. Five swam the moat last night and gave themselves up most politely. Hah!"

"Our trusty old servants?"

"Nay, those dear innocents be too old to risk cold water. Five of his hired bullies, lord. Normans, or some such mongrels. And more of them will swim it tonight, mark my words."

"Did you hang the rogues high?"

"Nay, my dear young lord—fie upon you!—neither high nor low. We treated them with the nicest consideration. They passed without a yelp. I'll venture to suggest, Lord Pat, they didn't know they were quit of this wicked world till they found themselves heels over head in hell. Hah! And even now five true Dragonlanders in Norman jerkins, and with bottles and horns in their hands, are displaying themselves to the envious watchers in the castle. There be less painful ways of entering a stronghold than breaching its walls."

Because of the sensation of lightness and fuddled effort in my head, I was not as vastly impressed by the gypsy's cunning as I should have been. I complimented him, however; and when food was put before me, I ate hungrily, the while Star Boy disposed of a measure of clean barley. By that time, the tinker captain had returned to his task of inspecting and alerting the six score beleaguering bowmen, and to hearten them with the news that their true lord and the old avenging sword had rejoined them. A bed of fern and wolf-skins was spread for me beside a sheltered fire;

and there I lay down and slept, with the sword Dragon-killer beside me, and Star Boy not far off.

My sleep was sound and dreamless and long—all day long, for the sun was down again when I opened my eyes and sat up. The fire beside me had sunk and broken to coals and the coals had filmed with gray ash. I fed it a handful of dry fern and a few dry sticks that lay within my reach, and it blazed up. By that wavering shine I saw Star Boy, who came to me instantly, but no other living thing. All had gone to join the gypsy's tightening grip on Dragon Castle.

"Hist! Patrick!"

I lifted the old sword and sprang to my feet, and Star Boy wheeled.

"It's me—Roger."

The horse relaxed. Something came crawling into the firelight. It was Roger de Montfoi, foul with mud and slime. He crawled to my feet and clasped me about the knees.

"Save me, good Pat—as I saved you!"

"So you did. Why did you do it?"

"My mother was English. Help me now—a horse now—and you'll see no more of me!"

"Not so fast! What of Sir Osbert?"

"Dead—of a clothyard shaft. And the old men and the scullions are turned upon the soldiery with spits and burning grease."

He freed my knees and sprang up and ran to Star Boy and made to mount him, but Star Boy swung around and bared his teeth. Even as I cried out a warning, Ben Tinker's horse—the tall roan I had taken and given to him—crashed into the firelight and stood staring. He was saddled and bitted, but the reins dragged, and he had one foot through them. Had the gypsy come to grief? I moved forward to see if there was blood on the saddle, but Roger moved faster. He cleared the reins, sprang to the saddle, wheeled, and went crashing away.

"Mad," I said to Star Boy. "Crazed with terror. He'll break his neck, poor fool! Couldn't he trust to my protection? I am lord here, God wot!"

I harkened to the swiftly diminishing sounds of Roger's flight till distance swallowed them, then threw more dry stuff on the fire and got myself and the great sword up and onto Star Boy.

"We'll join the fight," I said.

Before he could lift a hoof, a man in leather dashed into the light and stumbled against my left leg, grasping and sobbing. I bent down and gripped him by a shoulder with my left hand.

"What now, fellow?"

"A horse! A great red horse! He came this way!"

"Be still, fellow! What of it?"

"The gypsy's horse. He broke away from me—and I'll be flayed alive. Leave me go—for Christ's sake!"

I tightened my grip on him.

"Don't you know me, rogue? Your true lord—and the old sword Dragon-killer? Harky to me now! How goes the fight for my castle?"

"Spent, lord. Over an' done. The drawbridge came down, an' now it's full of Englishmen bawling 'Pendragon!' an' every Norman's dead. But the captain's horse, lord! Leave me go!"

"He went that way," I lied, and released him; and he plunged into the thicket.

"Home, now," I said.

But Star Boy had moved only a few paces into the dark beyond the fireshine when I checked him with a word.

"The damosel! I must seek her. She befriended me. She gave me a knife."

"I am here," said a small voice in the dark; and then: "I've never been far away," it added.

"Is it you?" I asked. "Can you get up?"

I felt a pulling on my jerkin, a quick weight on my left foot, a soft pressure against my shoulders and slender arms about my middle. Then Star Boy moved again. He went slowly, cautious step by step.

"I thank you for the knife—but I didn't have to use it," I said.

She made no answer. After a short silence, I spoke again.

"I was unmannerly to you, at the cave. I regret it. . . . Why did you give me the knife?"

"In case you might need it," she murmured. "In kindness."

"Gramercy," I muttered.

She murmured on: "For the same reason I killed Stark."

"*You!*" I cried. "God's wounds! It was sunk to the haft."

"And for the same reason that I woke you to defend yourself from Simon," she murmured.

"Gramercy," I muttered. "I thought it was a bird."

My head was in a daze. Soon a confused sound as of wild voices pulsed on the still black air, waxing and waning and waxing again; and now Star Boy quickened his pace.

"Hold fast!" I cautioned.

The slender arms tightened around me. A minute later we issued from the forest onto a field of stubble, and beheld the red and yellow of scores of torches tossing against the night and flinging sparks like stars. They flamed again in the black water of the moat, and tossed from end to end of the drawbridge. They tossed around the battlements.

Star Boy neighed and broke into a trot.

"Hold fast!" I cried; and the slender arms closed yet tighter.

Now my head and heart felt as strong as my legs and arms.

"A Pendragon!" I shouted. "A Pendragon! Saint George for England!"

The great horse galloped. My companion held to me with arms and breast and her face pressed hard to my left shoulder. I waved the great sword high in one hand. Torches came tossing to us. I saw men shouting up at me, with wide mouths and the torch-shine red in their eyes— "A Pendragon! A Pendragon!"

They thickened about us. Star Boy galloped through them, holding straight for the drawbridge. Cheering Dragonlanders sprang away to right and left before him. Planks drummed; beams creaked; great links of iron twanged like harp-strings—the whole bridge boomed and swayed to the fury of our passage. We gained the court-yard in a spurt of sparks struck by iron-shod hooves on stone.

The courtyard flamed, smoked, rang with welcoming torches and shouts: "A Pendragon! A Pendragon!" I saw Ben Tinker and Ralph Forester, bawling and pressing through to us. "Home again, my dear young lord!" "Welcome home, Lord Pat!" I saw old Nick Pottle clawing a passage to me through the archers. But I paid them no heed. I twisted about and took Blanche Devereaux in my arms—and the old sword flamed over us like a tongue of fire.

"I would hold you safe here till life's end."

"In pity."

"Nay, in love. In love and worship, till life's end—by God's wounds!"

More PENDRAGON™ Books from
GREEN KNIGHT PUBLISHING

AVAILABLE NOW

The Pagan King
by Edison Marshall

The mysterious Song of Camlon tells of a mighty warrior who will win the crown of Cambria. This is
Arthur's great destiny—or so prophesies Merdin the seer.

To claim his birthright, the simple Welsh rustic
must overcome the tyrant Vortigern, his brilliant son
Modred, and the other formidable foes arrayed against
him. Is Fate the architect of Arthur's success, or is his
rise to power determined by the strength of his sword
arm and the shrewdness of his advisors? The naive
young warrior must learn much about his enemies, and
the prophecies that so rule his life before he can step
from the pages of dark history into glorious legend.

Long out of print, *The Pagan King* is one of the first
modern novels to rediscover the Arthurian legend's
Welsh roots. In Edison Marshall's splendid retelling,
readers will share the agonizing losses and thrilling victories of one of the world's greatest heroes.

PRAISE FOR *THE PAGAN KING*:

"TRUE FANS OF ARTHURIAN LEGEND AND OF HISTORY
WILL REVEL IN THIS RE-TELLING."
—*Realms of Fantasy*

"A VERY FINE HISTORICAL NOVEL."
—*Science Fiction Chronicle*

GK6209. ISBN 1-928999-17-4. 336 pages.
$14.95 US; $21.95 CAN; £10.99 UK

More **PENDRAGON**™ Books from
GREEN KNIGHT PUBLISHING

<u>AVAILABLE NOW</u>

Exiled from Camelot
by Cherith Baldry

The court of Camelot is unsettled by the arrival of Loholt, King Arthur's illegitimate son. Driven by the need for an heir, the king embraces the stranger, though not everyone in Camelot so readily accepts the mysterious young man. Arthur's seneschal and foster brother, the redoubtable Sir Kay, is especially wary of Loholt's motives. And when Loholt is killed, Kay finds himself under suspicion of murder.

Stripped of his knighthood, Kay forges an unwilling alliance with the renegade Briant and his lover, the enchantress Brisane, who seek to bring down the men closest to the king. If Sir Kay cannot redirect their plot or win back the court's trust, nothing will save Camelot from the twin threats of war and evil sorcery.

PRAISE FOR *EXILED FROM CAMELOT*:

"AN ORIGINAL NOVEL OF CONSIDERABLE MERIT."
—Science Fiction Chronicle

"A REMARKABLE STORY."
—Realms of Fantasy

"ONE OF THE HALF-DOZEN BEST ARTHURIAN NOVELS I HAVE YET READ."
—Phyllis Ann Karr,
author of *The Arthurian Companion*

GK6207. ISBN 1-928999-16-6. 320 pages.
$14.95 US; $21.95 CAN; £10.99 UK

More PENDRAGON™ Books from
GREEN KNIGHT PUBLISHING

IN BOOKSTORES NOVEMBER 2001

Legends of the Pendragon
edited by James Lowder

Green Knight Publishing's second original anthology is a collection of stories exploring the earliest days of Arthur's realm. What made Britain ready for the coming of Camelot? How were the Round Table's victories and failures foreshadowed in the tragedy of Vortigern, the tyrant who welcomed the treacherous Saxons as trusted allies; the prophecies and magical acts of the ever-mysterious Merlin; the deeds of Uther Pendragon, father to the future king; or the training and earliest adventures of the young Arthur himself?

Legends of the Pendragon presents all-new Arthurian short fiction with a wide range of tones and styles, including works from such notable and best-selling authors as Phyllis Ann Karr, Cherith Baldry, Nancy Varian Berberick, Darrell Schweitzer, and Keith Taylor.

PRAISE FOR GREEN KNIGHT'S FIRST ORIGINAL ANTHOLOGY, *THE DOOM OF CAMELOT*:

"A TRULY SUCCESSFUL COLLECTION OF ARTHURIAN TALES, NOTABLE FOR ITS VARIETY OF PERSPECTIVES AND ITS POIGNANT HOMAGE TO A DREAM'S DEMISE."
—*Ceridwen's Cauldron*

"A DISTINGUISHED ADDITION TO MODERN ARTHURIAN FICTION."
—*Tipworld.com*

GK6211. ISBN 1-928999-19-0. 320 pages.
$16.95 US; $26.95 CAN; £12.99 UK

More PENDRAGON™ Books from
GREEN KNIGHT PUBLISHING

IN BOOKSTORES NOVEMBER 2001

The Follies of Sir Harald
by Phyllis Ann Karr

It isn't easy to be a villain in King Arthur's Britain, particularly when the opposition is so formidable and even the furniture in your castle is dead set against you. After six long years of struggle, the Quillerstone Couch still turns into a ravening lion whenever Sir Harald tries to sit on it. And that's the least of Harald's problems. To Sir Kay he owes both horse and armor, yet the mysterious knight who owes him the same has vanished.

The field of romance is no less perilous for Sir Harald, populated as it is by: the Aloof Fair One, for whom he turns renegade; brave Deborah, for whom he could wish himself a Jew; Maid Procne, who has, alas, already recorded the story of Harald's shame; and the puckish Joiselette, who somehow becomes his guardian elf. . . .

From Phyllis Ann Karr, author of the classics *Idylls of the Queen* and *The Arthurian Companion*, *The Follies of Sir Harald* is a wonderfully whimsical tale of love and adventure set against the colorful backdrop of Camelot.

GK6212. ISBN 1-928999-21-2. 256 pages.
$15.95 US; $25.95 CAN; £11.99 UK

All Green Knight titles are available through your favorite local bookstore, on-line bookstore, or by mail from Wizard's Attic, 900 Murmansk Street, Suite 7, Oakland, CA 94607. You can also see Wizard's Attic on the World Wide Web at www.wizards-attic.com.